Jack and Ruth Bohnett
October, 1948

The Running of the Tide

The Running

OF THE *Tide*

~~~~~~

by ESTHER
FORBES

~~~~~~

HOUGHTON MIFFLIN COMPANY BOSTON
THE RIVERSIDE PRESS CAMBRIDGE *1948*

PRINTED IN THE UNITED STATES OF AMERICA BY
KINGSPORT PRESS, INC., KINGSPORT, TENNESSEE

To
Ferris Greenslet

Chapter One

Hewn logs spliced and bolted formed a spine which rested upon bed-blocks. In turn this rested upon the gray gravel of her mother, Salem. Upon the keel, the keelson. At the bows, the stem. At the stern, the stern post. Ribs of oak sprang up and out. The unborn thing had a skeleton. Anyone could see this was to be a ship.

As the embryo grew, so also grew the gigantic womb that formed it. Guy ropes, like delicate membranes held it to land. A multiplicity of ladders bound her to her mother. Like all unborn things, she was parasitic and fed from all about her. The locust for her trunnels came from no farther than Salem Neck. Her white oak from over Danvers way. Yellow pine for her inner skin from round Ipswich. The hackmatack for her mighty knees from along North River. So she sucked the forest into herself.

At three months she had decks, steerage, forecastle, poop, quarterdeck bulwarks, cabins. Then the shipwrights' work was done.

Iron workers followed the caulkers. They set chains and pumps.

Joiners and carvers followed. There was gingerbread upon her stern, bright quick-work upon her bows, delicate paneling in her cabins. Before she was even born, she had certain pretty perfections — as a child may have eyebrows, lashes, fingernails.

Painters began when the joiners left. Lemon-yellow waist against blue-black topsides. Pale blue inside the bulwarks.

One day an ox cart lurched down bustling Derby Street. On it was enthroned a goddess — the figurehead of the new ship 'Tirey Becket was building for Old Ma'am Inman.

The red ox moved with the slow majesty of its kind. Merchants stepped out of counting-houses to see her; clerks stared with invoices in their hands. Wharfingers and seamen, porters, riggers, sailmakers — with their thimbles strapped to their palms; women and fancy girls, urchins yelled and ran after her. She was beautiful to see — the bold wooden woman, blocked and chained to the cart. She was poised to fly forever forward, without one backward glance. Her white and gilt draperies blew behind her as though she already fought the storms. She had a lifted head, thrust up and out in the manner of figureheads, and a passion-swollen neck. Her nostrils were disdainful; her bitter lips parted. The wild, beautiful staring eyes were fixed on something that never was and never would be. Not one downward glance did she have for the merely human Salem which ran to cheer her. In fact, she had such a lofty crook in her neck, she would never be able to look down at the green wooden wreath she held before her in stiff hands.

As the cart lurched over the littered cobbled street, it tilted the flying figure. Sometimes she seemed about to give her wreath to her admirers upon her left hand. Sometimes to those upon her right. Nevertheless, she held it fast.

It was the day the figurehead arrived at Becket's Yard that the ship received a soul, and one might say she quickened. This was her fourth month.

At last her time was completed. Now she must break from the gigantic womb, leave the matrix of her New England town. She trembled as the blocks were knocked from beneath her but would not start. It was a winter day, cold and lowering. There was broken ice in the harbor. She was still a thing of land, forest, and workshop, and seemed loath to move from the safety of snug town for lonely sea.

The audience assembled for her launching grew cold and bored. Some went home. Her midwives tried one trick of their trade after another. She would not move. They whispered together, scratched their heads. Then, suddenly, as if she had made up her mind to risk it, she took the ways with a rush, and the owner's youngest grandchild hurled a bottle after her careering prow.

"Ship! In the name of God I call thee *Victrix*."

It was her stern hit the water first. A wave rose as she flashed out into the icy harbor. It rushed up over the beaches, rose and sucked at wharves. It set moored dories a-bobbing, and great East Indiamen, decked all over with flags and bunting for this day, rose and fell in grand obeisance to her — the youngest daughter of the Salem fleet. But the *Victrix* looked ready to turn beam ends. She shot out so far into the ship channel, she barely missed the *Belisarius*. As her tidal wave subsided, she came about, acknowledged her audience with a bow so deep her prow plunged into the sea. Slowly, calmly, it rose again. The woman with the wreath had for the first time tasted bitter salt.

She was still a helpless thing. Her first gesture to her new environment was a timid one. Her anchors feebly grasped the shallow muddy bottom.

Although launched and baptized, she still had no masts and no rigging, no sails, no guns; but she was already an entity and she was in the sea where she belonged.

❧ 2 ❧

THE YOUNG *Victrix* lay off Inman Wharf. Every mast was set. Her rigging tight and black with tar. Her deck holystoned to white. Now she was complete and laden, her people signed, her papers cleared. All she needed was a breeze.

Some at their anchorage, some tied up at wharves, were eleven other great ships waiting for a wind. Twelve Salem ships heading out beyond the ends of the world and now becalmed, not to mention assorted small craft, sloops, coasters, heeltappers.

The old ships, like the good *Belisarius* at Crowninshield's Wharf with their *Minerva* beside her, the *Amazon* and the *Brutus* at Derby's, the *Hazard* and the *Ulysses* at anchor — all these eleven other ships seemed philosophical about their imprisonment, but the young *Victrix* was fretty at her anchorage — at least, so it seemed to Dash Inman. He stood at the far end of his grandmother's wharf and watched her soberly. Now she is reconciled to a sea life, he thought, remembering her launching. Now she wants to go. He, as much as Becket, had designed her. Every piece of wood that had gone into her he had passed on. He had watched the sailmakers at their sewing. McIntire had carved her figurehead to suit his fancy.

On either side of Inman Wharf were others stretching like fingers out into Salem Harbor, each striving to reach deeper water than its rival. Orne's, Crowinshield's, Derby's, Union, Forrester's, and White's. At some of the wharves returned ships were hove down for cleaning. At Becket's Yard a new ship was rising. At the Inman's was the *Mermaid* fresh back from St. Petersburg. Standing about on these wharves sober-eyed men stared at the becalmed vessels, studied upon the weather. Dash knew the talk going round — when the calm broke, the wind would come up nor'east, so it was said. You couldn't move a ship out of Salem Harbor when the wind was in that quarter. And nor'easters are apt to last three days.

Yet he had a feeling — nothing but a feeling — this was not to be so. He fell to pacing the wharf, back and forth. Unconsciously the amount of space he allowed himself was the exact length of the average quarterdeck, for he had been a mate at sixteen and a captain five years now — ever since he was nineteen. He had a smart, quick step — no landlubber's careless loungings. Even on the stout cob wharf he seemed determined that no sudden pitch was going to land him on his beam ends. He was a strongly built young fellow of little more than average height. The set of head, shoulders, and chin suggested authority. Men do not get that particular carriage from taking other men's orders all their lives, nor had he. He had an impressive face, bold and blunt-featured, with fine hazel eyes and a curiously muscular mouth. That mouth had been formed by all the yelling he had done from quarterdecks — and even more by the times he hadn't yelled but said nothing. By the times he had gritted his teeth and spoken quietly when God knew he wanted to swear. The times he had kept his hands in his pockets — so afraid he might bash in some fool's head. It was a strong, almost hard, very disciplined face. But the discipline had come from himself— not from any superior here or in Heaven. It was years since he had been out of sight of land without complete say-so over everybody in reach of his voice.

But the obviously young face looked white and worn. A girl might think it romantic — here at last was one of those passionate souls that can die for love or honor, such as one found more often in novels than in life. To a clergyman it might suggest cards, wine, and women. To a medical man a tropical disease with which seamen sometimes returned home but to die. But the overtightening of the face, the wearing away of flesh showed the fine structure underneath of the cheekbones and emphasized the brave set of the mouth — a broad mouth, the upper lip thinner than the lower, which had a way of thrusting itself out upon occasions. Now, as he walked, it was thrust out at the weather. Such mouths were known locally as "Inman mouths." Again he stopped at the end of the wharf, brooding and thinking of nothing. Slowly he licked his fingers and held up his hand. There was not a sign of a breeze. He studied the shore along Marblehead. Fishermen are smart to guess weather. As far as he could see, they were as becalmed over there, with their little high-haunched heeltappers, as Salem merchants were in their great full-riggers. No sudden darkening of the harbor suggested as much as a cat'spaw moving. The flag to his left hung limp on Fort Pickering's staff. The sounds of the waterfront came to him clearly through the soft sunny May air. The creak of a moored dory, the suck of tides about slimy piers, porters rolling casks, a winch unloading and men he-hawing as the cargo came out of a hole. The caterwauling of gulls and the music of shipwrights' adzes and hammers.

His dark head lifted, the nostrils stiffened. He could not feel it, nor see it, nor hear it. But he knew a wind was coming up. And it was coming fresh and perfect — from the west. It was the uncanny sixth sense of the good seaman that had told him — his very blood and bones; for he carried within himself finer navigating instruments than any he could buy.

The broad mouth relaxed into a smile. He wanted to yell out, "Hurrah! We are off!" to all the waiting ships. But on general principles he "didn't say much." He was a somewhat taciturn young man, and for better or worse took and kept his own counsel. There was little of the jolly tar in his somewhat complicated nature.

Over the bulwarks of the *Victrix* a lank gray-bearded face had been watching him. It was old Jemmy, the shipwatcher.

"How's that, Captain Dash?" he yelled.

"I didn't say nothing," Dash called back.

"How's that again?" The old fellow was pretty deaf.

Dash had no idea of telling all Salem what nobody but himself had had the wit to guess.

He cupped his mouth with his hands.

"Look like three-day nor'easter to you, Jemmy?"

His voice rang out marvelously, every syllable pitched exactly right to cross the hundred feet of water and penetrate the half-sealed ears on the anchored ship. The old man looked delighted. Perhaps he had been hounding Captain Dash so he would have to yell loud enough to make him hear.

"Yep, it does, Captain. Yep, it does."

Dash turned and walked confidently back to the head of the wharf and his grandmother's counting-house. It was a comical building. The lower story was left open so a dray could drive under it. Outside stairs led to the offices above. Within, he knew his widowed grandmother sat at her desk in the inner office and his youngest brother Peter and old Fessenden, the clerk, in the outer office. He knew what he should do. Tell Ma'am time had come. Ask her permission to consult with the captain (for the captain chose the exact moment for casting off), ask first her and then Captain Magee if it wasn't time to summon the ship's people aboard and put on last things. He stood and fingered the limp house flag that hung before the counting-house. It was navy blue cut by a broad white diagonal. How could you tell an owner that you had an idea time had come? Yon can't talk about such secret knowledge to a woman — especially to one who also happened to be your employer and your grandmother. He might have told young Peter — but Ma'am? No.

Under the stilted-up counting-house were three crates of live chickens. He had bought them — for every detail of the *Victrix* voyage he had taken upon himself. He had been feeding the smelly things for a week. Over against the big brick warehouse — a bit empty and he knew it — was a pen holding Bouncing Bet — a sow who had been twice to India and back. By the looks of her, the people of the *Victrix* would be eating piglets before they got to Good Hope. He'd have to remind Magee to hunt up a proper mate for her in, say, Batavia, so the supply of piglets would be good for the voyage home. Also there were a few sheep shut up in a warehouse. That warehouse had just been sold to Billy Gray. The whole wharf was mortgaged. He gritted his teeth, for it was his fault.

Only the living things, men and live eating animals, remained to go aboard. Well — while he was figuring what to do next he'd get these chickens aboard. He picked up a crate and took it down a ladder to a moored dory. Went back for the other two crates and looked at the sow. She and the sheep were too tarnation noisy. He didn't want Ma'am sticking out her cute little head — asking him as she always did, all day long, whatever he was about. Standing in the dory he sculled the little way to the *Victrix*.

The old shipwatcher was there at a gun port taking in the crates as he handed them up. The *Victrix* had eight real guns and four "quaker" or wooden ones. England and France were going at each other hammer and tongs. They didn't leave much space between them for a "peaceful" neutral trader. You had to fight for what you got in this world — and Congress had said armed French ships could be attacked on sight.

"Captain Dash, it ain't fitting for you to carry chickens aboard yourself, sir."

"It's fitting for Clerk Dash," he yelled back. "Put 'em in the longboat, Jemmy, for now."

"You moving livestock aboard now, sir? You fixing on getting out of here — no matter the wind? You going to kedge out — use sweeps?"

"Oh, hell — I'm tired of feeding these things. You can mind them now. Grain's in the galley."

He swung himself on deck and the shipwatcher, a hermit by nature, scuttled forward with his cud of tobacco. Dash looked suspiciously at the decks. No, he had been spitting downwind and straight as a seaman should.

He went up the gangway ladder to the poop deck. From here he got a pretty view of her — the varnished masts, the black lace of shrouds against the delicate girlish sky of May. She was 99 feet long, 28 wide, and 336 tons burthen. This was as large a ship as shallow Salem Harbor accommodated with ease or was expedient in the uncharted waters of the Pacific. It was ships of this size that were by 1800 making Salem the wealthiest city in the world.

Here by her wheel, facing the binnacle before him, her captain would stand, watching the helmsman at the steering wheel and the stars, keeping the sails set every moment to best advantage, listening for the singing chant of men with the sounding lead, the cry of the lookout, the half-heard dangerous roar of surf. He could almost feel the ship surging beneath him. His stance broadened.

His feet seemed to grip the planks as a hawk grips a bough, and he was swaying slightly, thus unconsciously his body produced for his delight the ancient rhythms of his calling.

But — no more of this brooding. He wasn't her captain. He wasn't good enough — even yet. He did not deserve her. He had done wrong, and deep in him was the old New England belief that the man who had done wrong had better suffer for it. This was apart from any law of God's or man's. Long accustomed to his own say-so, he was perfectly ready to be his own judge and his own culprit. Not for him any running to a priest — "Forgive me, Father, for I have sinned." He was proud as Lucifer and looked to neither God nor man to tell him what he ought to do. His pride took him full circle and came out in manners so modest as sometimes to seem diffident.

But he longed for the *Victrix*. Tomorrow at dawn — that's when she was going to sail. In his pocket (not on his grand-mother's desk where it belonged) was her portledge bill, giving the names of her men, the advances most of them had drawn, the ventures allowed to each. There were nineteen names in all. His grandmother had picked Captain Magee, and the rest were men Dash wanted. His younger brother Eleazar, or "Liz," would be first mate. Dan Obrian, a rough, capable fellow he had taken from a Derby ship where he had been a foremast hand and put in as the *Victrix* second. Handled right, he believed Dan would make a clever officer. Handled wrong, a big-mouthed bully. He left the wharf and stepped off down Derby Street. First thing he'd tell Magee, then the mates, and send someone to call out his crew. Maybe Mr. Africanus would show up. He was a knowing old fellow and had a way of presenting himself exactly when Dash wanted a messenger, thus earning a few pennies. The *Victrix* must catch next morning's high tide — due at four-thirty. At low tide she was actually sitting on mud. He wasn't going to wait for afternoon tide — see the whole boiling of them stepping out ahead of her. No. He walked quickly, wrapped in concentration. He always walked like a man who knew exactly where he was going — never looking back, never looking to see if anyone followed him. But ever since boyhood people had followed, for he was born to walk first and a little alone. Even now admiring eyes and a whisper followed him, but he did not know it.

MA'AM INMAN sat in her inner office with a letter in her hand. She had a good view of the *Mermaid* graving in the yard, but none of her wharf and the *Victrix*.

Mercy Inman, Esquire
Salem, U.S.A.
Dear Sir,

The old lady took off the spectacles one grandson had brought her from France and tried a pair another grandson had brought her from London. She had a darning-basket full of them on her desk before her. She sat tidy and little on her high stool, her feet neat as a young girl's in heelless slippers curled about the stool legs.

"Me, as Senator of Orloff and Marbury," she read. Of course he meant representative. Those poor "Rooshuns" didn't know much about representative government —— She put the letter down. You couldn't fix your mind on anything today — not with twelve great ships waiting for a wind: a wind that would not come. And when it did — "O dear Father in Heaven — it will be a year, two years, before I know how she's fared. O Heavenly Father, give your poor impatient servant the strength to wait." Her head (mostly covered by a large cambric cap) was bowed. How would she prove — that *Victrix*? Would the new ship be the salvation of the old House of Inman — or the last nail in the coffin? She herself was well over seventy, and she had at last been such a zany as to put all her eggs in one basket. Dash — that crazy Dash! Eight months ago, when he had lost her her *Antelope,* she had been so angry with him she had told him he'd not have another ship of hers to throw away for a year at least — if ever. She had told him he was to sit right here in the counting-house and clerk it. She was going to get more ballast into him to counteract all the sail he had always carried. It was time he learned what failure looked like — for there had been little but success before in his life, but usually on other men's ships. When she died, she wanted her grandsons trained as good sensible careful captains and merchants. Dash was oldest of the four — and she admired him most and trusted him least of all. He'd make or wreck anything — a ship or a woman or a country. He was born to make or wreck.

Seemingly he had sat on his stool and clerked it as modestly as his youngest brother, Peter. He hadn't complained — any. He had just grown whiter and more worn-looking — as though he was injured and bleeding inside. He had bought and sold cargoes, seen to the upkeep and lading of the ships, seen to crews — and the building of the *Victrix*. And utterly corrupted her. For it was he who had made her want the new ship more than anything on God's earth. Made a gambler of her, the most cautious merchant in Salem. She might as well face it. He had become the merchant — and she the clerk. And for the life of her she could not see how he had done it. He had not pushed her aside — made her feel old and useless the way Liz did. He had made her feel his own age, young and eager. Crazy as himself. No, he had not gone against her, but swept her along with him. And that's magic for you, she thought. They used to hang people in Salem who weren't half the witch that fellow is.

Ah, well . . . Perhaps he was right. Her cautious management of the House had not been too successful. If things had been going real well, they could have absorbed the loss of the *Antelope*. Folk said she did wrong to stick so to Baltic trading. The money was in the Far East. Folk said she did wrong to hire her captains so often among the older men — let her grandsons command Derby and Crowninshield ships or go so often as mates on her ships. She wasn't quite ready to trust them. But the first time she had given Dash an East Injunman to command, he had lost her. He had never lost a ship before, and he had commanded the Crownin-shields' *Belisarius* at nineteen.

"Peter," she called.

From the outer office a boy of seventeen or so, with a quill pen stuck in the black curls over his ear, sauntered in. He was still a little gangling. Although his long arms and legs did not look well composed, his face was, for his expression was strikingly clear and serene. It was an expression more often found upon an elderly face which can look back upon a long well-spent life and look down a little upon young folk still struggling against the inevitable sorrows and frustrations of life. He smiled at his grandmother with benignity. His three older brothers — famous Dash, doggy Liz, and capable Tom — were primarily her employees. Peter was really a grandson and the very apple of her eye. They called her Ma'am. He usually Grandma.

"Peter, what's Dash up to?" She had a lively young voice.

"*Dash?*" Peter looked as puzzled as though he had never heard his brother's famous nickname. He was working for a split second in which to decide how much of what he had seen Dash doing these last few minutes was fitting to tell. He'd seen him scull out with the chickens. And he guessed he was now out summoning the ship's people. As long as he hadn't chosen to tell the owner, Peter was not going to.

"Why, I think I saw him a few minutes back, sort of fiddling about the wharf. Then he sort of roamed around a bit, and finally just now he was heading west on Derby."

"You shouldn't waste so much time hanging out the window, Peter."

At this reproof Peter smiled kindly from ear to ear. He had the "Inman mouth." It sat better upon a man than a woman. Anyone could guess he was Dash's young brother, but he was an attenuated version. Nobody had ever said Peter was handsome.

"I want him to be sure Captain Magee understands a few changes some of our neighbors have made in their ventures. That Susan Pickman! Never saw an old party change her mind so often. She's entrusting to us another cask of ginseng. And fifteen boxes of spermaceti candles, not five as first she said. Mr. Knapp has added to his venture. He wants Indy shawls. I've told them the *Victrix* may never go out farther than Isle de France — but I trust Captain Magee's discretion completely." She was studying the slate she used for memoranda.

"Dash has added all those changes. Captain Magee will get them all right."

"What about the ship's boy — Billy Bates?"

"Dash took him to Doctor West. He cut open that felon. He's fine."

She herself could think of nothing more she might tell Clerk Dash, but it irked her that she never knew "what he was up to."

She tapped her teeth with her slate pencil.

"Where's Liz?" It was Liz who had just brought the *Mermaid*, laden with Russian hemp canvas and Swedish iron, back from the

Baltic. It had been his first command of any ship of hers. Now he was to go as mate to the Far East.

"Liz?" Peter repeated calmly, looking thoughtfully at the ceiling, taking all the time he needed to decide whether there was any covering-up he had better do for Liz. "He's out in the carriage with Mother — making his farewells."

"Farewells? Why, those ships are going to be stuck where they are for five days more."

"Mother's taking him over to Derby farm and round Danvers way."

"Oh, Liz and his mother!" the old woman said impatiently; "sometimes I pity Liz."

"You needn't, Grandma. He doesn't mind being a mother's monkey ashore — just so he can get him a good command at sea."

"Well, I never see him anywhere except ashore. And those pantaloons of his — tighter than a frog's skin. And waistcoats — three deep. He never looks like a serious seaman to me."

She knew Liz had been disappointed, when he came home with the *Mermaid* (and a good decent voyage he had made), to hear his grandmother had already signed Captain Magee to command the *Victrix* — and all he was to be was mate. He had already gone as mate on the Crowninshields' *Astrea* to India. He was twenty-one, and he thought his grandmother might trust him as master of the new ship. He had still been in his sea clothes when he had suggested this. She had almost relented. And next day she had seen him in those pantaloons of his — the beau of Salem.

"If Liz only looked more serious, I might have entrusted the *Victrix* to him. I know he is a very sharp young man. And I do hate — once more to see captains' shares going outside the family."

Peter gazed at her soberly. He had none of his oldest brother's intensity, and his eyes were much darker without any of those hazel flashes in them which could set a lady's heart rocking or a lazy foremast hand trembling. But like Dash he had an expressive face. Now the dark eyes reproached his grandmother because she had not said, "I might have given the command to Dash."

She went on: "Tom is very competent. All the merchants tell me how competent Tom is. But Cousin Crowninshield does not expect his *Nautilus* back from India for four or five months yet. I wanted Tom to have that chance to serve as mate under Captain

Jake. Yet I think if Tom had been to hand, I *think* I might have trusted him. He wasn't. And I can't feel Liz is real serious. I hadn't any choice but pitch on Captain Magee — once more."

Peter said nothing, but thought of Dash, white and broody, these last eight months — ever since he had got his "shore leave" for losing the *Antelope*.

His grandmother, feeling the reproach in his eyes, said: "Captain Magee would just as soon not go — I'm afraid. Not at his time of life. It's a boy's world — sailing our ships — and he's a man turned forty. He hasn't the heart for adventuring that the younger men have."

"Isn't that why you like him?"

"Well, at least he's sensible. Steady. I've been employing him for years — waiting for my own young captains to grow up. But sometimes I do wish I had kept Tom closer to hand. Or could forget what Liz looks like ashore."

But Dash? Peter's eyes reproved her.

She said abruptly: "Dash Inman lost the *Antelope* and stove in our fortunes. He's going to have a year to think that over. And when I say a year, I don't mean any eight months either. If he don't like this decision of mine, he can get him a command from some other house. And don't you go throwing it up against me that I won't give him the *Victrix*. He's a-going to have twelve months in which to cool his heels."

"Grandma, I haven't even mentioned Dash."

"Oh, go away, Peter! I can read you like a book."

~ 4 ~

AT THE CHARITY HOUSE on Pickering Hill, overlooking the harbor and close to the graveyard, a group of inmates sat about enjoying the sun. It is hard enough in the best of weather to be poor, but fair misery in winter. The suns of May lay like warm shawls on their shoulders. Here were a few old seamen, too decrepit to finish their lives as clamdiggers or shipwatchers; a silly fellow soft-headed from birth. Old women whose wits had dulled by time and rum. A young slattern with an odd assortment of children. A few black folk.

The most impressive in the group was a large Negro. All were dressed decently enough for that low station in life to which it had pleased God to call them, but this black man was elegant. On his head was a tall beaver hat, threadbare but well-brushed. He wore a bright green broadcloth coat with brass buttons. His linen was clean. He sat with huge hands resting on the head of the malacca cane King Derby had given him fifteen years before, as silent, inscrutable, all-knowing as an idol.

There was nothing ridiculous about Mr. Africanus's stylish dressing. White children did not throw snowballs at his high hat as they did at those of other black folk who longed above their station.

"Seems like those ships will be setting there till Doomsday," said a woman.

There was no one in Salem so rich or so poor they could ignore the coming and going of the ships. All the town depended upon the ships. The Charity House inmates had time to study them.

"No," said an old foremast hand, "not Doomsday. Three days — at least in this latitude. When the wind sets in to come, it's coming nor'east. But I mind me a time at Surinam . . . me and George Crowninshield . . ."

"Old George or young George?"

"Old George."

"Was that the time you got the elephant?"

"No, ma'am. That was me and *Jake* Crowninshield. Bombay."

"Who were you with when you tried to get the tiger?"

"That was the *Good Fortune,* Captain Inman. Dash and Tom and Liz's father."

The slattern began to swear at her little brood. The silly fellow went on with a soliloquy that only sleep ever stopped. But Mr. Africanus said never a word. He lifted his head, and his nose, broad and noble as a lion's, stiffened. Apple blossoms! He could smell apple blossoms! The chances were these were from about the Pickering house — southwest from here. If it really was apple blossoms . . . Sometimes street girls had a little scent left on them when the Judge put them here. He had been fooled by them before. One thing was certain. He had not smelled kelp, eel grass, tar, coffee, spice, and sandalwood from the waterfront all the afternoon.

Suddenly — Smash! Bang! He could smell fish frying. Now, if this came from the Pickering house, it might mean little enough. His nose screwed slightly. The fish did not smell real fresh. The fat was not of the quality you'd expect from the gentility. Suppose that fish was being fried at the Widow Mullet's. That was quite a step southwest from here. Then he'd know.

"Captain Hawks, sir." His great voice boomed, interrupting the old seaman's yarns of strange beasts carried to Salem. Hawks had never been aught but a foremast hand, but time had given him the honorary title of captain.

"Yes, sir — Mr. Africanus."

"Would you favor me a bit?"

"Always glad to oblige."

"Will you step over to Squire Pickering's and see what they are cooking? And if it's fish, don't you bother to go farther. If it ain't fish, step along until you locate it. It is, I'd say, a third-day cod. Not good clean lard. Mutton tallow. Poor man's cooking."

No one else had smelled a thing. All conversation but the silly fellow's monologue stopped in wonder.

Captain Hawks, a cheerful boozy little old liar, got himself to bandy legs and hobbled off. The silence was intense. They all knew the chances were he now would send out someone else. The Negro was frowning with concentration.

"Dorothy Belinda Gould." This was a skinny, pale child with flat, expressionless, colorless eyes. A few months ago she had been taken up for "lewd and lascivious conduct."

"Yes, sir," she piped eagerly, leaping to her bare feet.

"Miss Dorothy, I've heard you boast how sharp your sight is. I want you to go to Graveyard Hill yonder. At the top you'll find a flat oval tombstone. There's a skull cut in one end of it. Now, if you will stand on that, you can see the ships and wharves good. I'll tell you *what for* you are to look at."

"Oh, yes, yes!" she cried, springing lightly up and down.

"We've got six really big wharves here. Can you tell them apart?"

"Of course I can," and she named them. She had a cockney sing-song.

"Very good, miss. You are a good bright little girl."

The girl wriggled with pleasure as if she had a tail to wag.

"You all know I gets my pocket money from remembering people's birthdays and going round and wishing them happy returns, and from remembering lists of folks and going about and telling them they are wanted at parties and funerals. But most of all I ever get is summoning up a crew of a ship — just about taking its departure . . . Now, if I can figure out anybody who's planning to move out his ship and get to the counting-house in time, I'll get hired. There are twelve great ships waiting to go. If I can find out which is going first, I may get the job. Miss Dorothy, do you know all the house flags?"

"Well, now! Yes, I do." She squealed with pleasure. The girl was so shy she would hardly answer anyone except only Mr. Africanus.

"Derby's?"

"All white."

"Crowninshield's?"

"Blue, red crown."

"Inman's?"

"Navy, cut sidewise, with white."

"I don't suppose you know the ships?"

"Oh yes, I do. Captain Hawks taught me. The *Brutus* and the *Amazon* and the *Belisarius* and the *Active,* and the pretty one, the new one — that's the *Victrix* — anchored off Inman Wharf." And she named the seven others.

"Now, you go where I told you. And you study those ships. If you see any supplies going on — powder or kegs of drinking water, live eating animals —— "

"I'll watch 'em."

She slipped delicately away, light as a fawn, over the graveyard fence. Over her the sky was blue, all about her the earth blossomed. Mr. Africanus turned his head, seemingly watching her slight figure, running uphill among the gravestones. He could not see her, for he was blind.

Captain Hawks came back first.

"The Pickerings are having chicken. It was the Widow Mullet's fish."

"I want to thank you, Captain."

All sat waiting the return of the second dove he had sent out of his ark. Dorothy Belinda Gould came dancing back, her plain face pink with excitement.

"Mr. Africanus, oh, Mr. Africanus — there wasn't a thing stirring one end of Derby's Wharf to the other. The Crowninshields' either. Nor Forrester's, nor Gray's, nor Orne's. But at Inman's! ... Mr. Africanus. I saw a man carrying crates of what looked like chickens to me. He went out to the *Victrix* and he put 'em aboard. I know it was Inman Wharf — because they've got that long-legged counting-house. And I guess it was an Inman, for he had such dark hair."

"A hat?"

"No hat."

"Then it wasn't Liz. I think it was Dash Inman — himself."

He rose gravely to his large flat feet.

"It would be Captain Dash. For he's the only man 'cept me in Salem smart enough to know just when a wind's coming . . . Now I'm going down to see if he doesn't need my help. If one of you ladies will be so good as to examine there's no lint on my coat and my shoes don't look dusty, I'll be about my business."

Although rich Salem wives often gave him the families' largest cast-off clothing, not one man in Salem had such enormous feet as Mr. Africanus. His clumsy shoes, made by a one-armed cobbler here at the Charity House, alone betrayed his domicile.

⚬ 5 ⚬

Feeling ahead of him with his malacca cane, Mr. Africanus slowly made his way into Essex Street. It would have been shorter to have followed the waterfront, but this route was too beset with dangers for a blind man. On Derby Street there were drays, ox wagons, casks, bales, chests, swearing porters (smelling of the rum in their bellies and the coffee and sandalwood in their arms). Tipsy home-come seamen with monkeys and parrots on their shoulders, queer shivering Lascars, waiting a return trip to India. Some of these might be strangers and not know Africanus's high position in Salem society. They might plague him or jeer at him. Also on Derby Street was a clutter from shipyards. A bowsprit half-blocking the way. Riggers at work, leaving hoists and spars for him to trip over. He preferred the genteel, almost parallel Essex Street.

His cane went ahead of him like a supersensitive foot. Tap, tap, tap. His big feet in shambling nail-studded shoes followed thoughtfully. The heavy, brooding face had none of the thin, smiling often seen on blind faces. It was knotted with concentration, lined with years. No one knew how old he was, but he was probably nearer sixty than the eighty or ninety he claimed.

Before crossing North Street he paused. The rumble of heavy wheels. Although courteous to everyone, he had a special respect for the gentry. He waited ready to lift his hat. He smelt cheese, dandelion greens, ham. A countryman bringing produce to market.

Again he stopped. This time before crossing Court Street. To his left he guessed some poor wretch was sitting in the stocks. A group of idle boys were pestering him. Such boys never smelt the same as good apprentices, doing their work dutifully, minding their masters. They smelt cruel. He sighed and passed on.

Although along Essex was a sprinkling of fine mansions, it was the shops he liked best. One after another he smelt the shops. A stationer's, good paper, bindings, printer's ink. This was Mrs. Pretty's. Next was a husband and wife who made black fruitcake. He lingered here. Once, when they burned a batch, they had given him some. He recognized the cake shop where Salem bought hearts-and-rounds and diet bread as they called spongecake. And cookies. He went by a cent shop and smelt liquorice and cinnamon drops, heard the aged proprietress's voice wishing him good day, and smelt a smell of cheap yellow soap from this poor decayed gentlewoman. He always walked very slowly past food shops. Although he had none of the beggar's mannerisms, he was often given things to eat. A bell tinkled. Somebody was going in. Another bell. Somebody was going out. And all about him was a lot of come and go and bustle. He heard his own name over and over. He smelt new Russian leather, and then, before an East Indy shop, he paused to enjoy the curry powder and sandalwood, tea, coffee, and spice. Next was a wine merchant. But if he was too slow, Dash Inman might have hired just anybody.

A carriage was standing by the curb. A woman called to him, "Mr. Africanus!" His hat was off. The sweetness of the groomed horses, the oily fragrance of fine harnesses, and the quality of the lady's voice made him bow low. He smelt attar of rose. That was the young Mrs. Derby everybody said was so beautiful.

"I think you are about the size of my coachman — isn't he, Patrick? Mr. Africanus, if you need an overcoat for next winter, stop by at my house. It's too worn for my coachman — but will do well enough for you."

"Thank you, Mrs. Derby, ma'am." He did not hold much with all these young Derbys — although people said they married beautiful women. Purse-proud and swollen they seemed to him — and good old King Derby only a few months in his grave. Folk said it would not take the sons and their beautiful wives long to finish off the greatest mercantile fortune ever amassed in America. He did not think Mrs. Derby had very good manners. Her offer of an overcoat had not been politely made. He was at once critical and pitying of bad manners.

A little girl came up to him and walked a block, holding his hand. She said nothing, but he remembered how a year ago her whole family had been at Charity House after her father, a rigger, had fallen and broken his leg. Her pa and ma never spoke to him. They preferred to forget their humiliation, but little Totty often joined him, walked a block holding his hand like this, then her quick little legs would tire of his shuffling and off she ran hippety-hippety-hoppety-hop. Most of the money Mr. Africanus made by his errands, he spent on rock candy for the children at Charity House.

Two, three — or was it four girls pushed past him, loud and laughing girls, eating cookies on the street. Not ladies. A whistling baker's boy had a basket of new hot rolls on his head. From somewhere a pig was squealing. He heard a robin calling and a gull. Coming up from the custom house were merchants — blasting the daylights out of Mr. Jefferson — if ever he got to be President it would be the end of civilization. He stopped, not quite sure which side street he would now take down to Derby Street and Inman Wharf. Yet he believed that Dash would wait for him. Certain merchants usually brushed him aside. Would not employ him. But the Inmans always favored him. Especially Dash.

As he stood pondering his course, he heard a quick, smart step — one of those short steps that takes a man safely all over a ship in rough weather, and a voice clear, low, say his name.

"Mr. Africanus."

"Captain Dash, sir." Dorothy Belinda Gould had been right

about what was in those crates she had seen him put aboard. For besides soap and leather, tobacco, there was a slight taint of chickens. "Captain Dash . . . I was out looking for you."

"You guessed it?"

"I know it."

"Mind now." Dash took the portledge bill from his pocket and pulled the old Negro into the doorway of a shop. The owner had died that morning. The shop was closed and hung with black. "I want you to get my people down on the wharf eleven o'clock tonight. Mate Obrian will be there to put them aboard. I'll read you the names of my people. I myself will tell the officers."

He read slowly and did not move on to the next name and address until Mr. Africanus had nodded his head. "You've got them? You won't forget?"

"Not I."

"Shall I read them again?"

"Captain Dash — don't you go insulting me."

"Look ye. My *Victrix* is going to be out of this harbor come dawn tomorrow. We'll show those Crowninshields and Derbys and Grays and everybody a clean pair of heels. Why, we'll be hull down beyond Baker's about the time they are waking up and wondering if that's a wind shaking their bed curtains."

"That's sure right, Captain."

"You tell my people privately. I don't care to have all Salem know what only you and I have the wit to understand."

"Your ship's going to be first."

Whether or not the *Victrix* was the first or last vessel to leave made no difference in a voyage of such length. An older man than Dash would not have cared nor a wiser one than Mr. Africanus. Both cared passionately.

"It's her first voyage. I'm going to have her first to start."

"Captain, is it that you are going yourself to command her?"

Instantly he regretted his question. Possibly a young man in humiliation smells unlike a happy young man.

"No," said Dash cheerfully. "You've heard tell I lost the *Antelope*. Magee will command the *Victrix*. I stay here."

The old Negro's heart went out to the young man whose face he had never seen. Everybody else in Salem might know the color of his hair and eyes, the shape of face and shoulder. In his darkness he knew more important things. He felt the people about him almost as disembodied spirits. Such a woman was bad — although so well spoken of. This man mean. The next timid. Dash always came and went through his darkness like a fine sailing breeze — something that struck and carried you.

"Captain," he murmured in embarrassment, "you are the finest captain ever was even in Salem. Everyone says so."

"No. Not everyone." He laughed, and laid his hand, warm and strong, an affectionate hand, on the old man's sleeve. His hand said, Don't you go feeling bad because you think you humiliated me — made me say "I lost the *Antelope*." Out loud he said, "Mr. Africanus, if you will give me one of your shoes, I'll take it to my bootmaker in Boston and have him make you good boots. Just a memento of all the crews we have summoned together — and nary a one called wrong. It's something your pay doesn't quite cover."

The old man was so touched he could not speak. To think the gentleman was not too proud to carry the gigantic shoe from a pauper's foot to Boston with him! And the money! He had heard the Inmans — in spite of the great house they were building — were just a mite hard up.

"Captain Dash, you've put it so pretty a man can't refuse. Seems like I long for nice boots more than anything this side of God's mercy."

"Well, leave me one shoe — one's all I'll need. And a piece of twine to show the size of the calf — ten inches up the leg."

"You mean I'm to have genuine *high* boots?"

"Yes."

"You don't suppose they might be Hessian boots — with tassels on them? Captain George Crowninshield let me feel of his once."

"That's what you're going to have." Suddenly his mood and voice shifted and hardened. "Now you get forward with your duty. Sure you don't want to repeat that list back to me?"

"No, sir," he said humbly.

"Stop tomorrow at the counting-house for your wages."

"Yes, sir."

Africanus heard the bright step leaving him, heading for Brown Street where Captain Magee lived. "That gentleman sure knows where he's going. And, let me see," thought the old Negro, "I'll call Billy Bates first. Although he's farthest out — right on the Neck. He's just a little boy first time ever to sea. I'll give him extra time with his ma. Lemuel Ovington and Rickie Locker were boarding at Mrs. Murphy's down along Daniel's Lane. At Fisher's House he'd find Parker and Narbonne — boys from inland farms. All the rest were living with parents. Only Doctor Zack, the Negro cook ("doctor" was what they called cooks), was old enough to have a wife and establishment of his own. H'd call him last because Doctor would ask him in and give him plum-duff or some other deep-sea dainty. Like many another Salem ship, if you included the three officers and omitted the cook, the average age was about twenty. So having worked out an itinerary for himself, his elegant cane feeling before him as delicately as the antenna of an insect, Mr. Africanus "got forward with his duty."

～6～

CAPTAIN MAGEE had said No, sir . . . the wind wasn't a-coming up. Dash had said Yes, sir . . . so it was.

So they had argued. At last the "old man" of forty had given in, making once more the same vulgar joke. "Dash, I guess your mother was full of wind those nine months she carried you. You're smarter about such things than there's any sense to. But suppose you're right, what's all the hurry? It don't make no difference whether you're last or first out of the harbor. Matter of fact, I'd like last best. Least danger of fouling other folks' cables. Getting that *Victrix* out from where she is, setting so close to the *Elizabeth* and the *Herald* will be like a game of jackstraws. I'd prefer afternoon high and the channel to myself."

"Yes. All to yourself. Like the last horse in a race."

"This isn't any sporting event. This is plain business. You young fellers are always in such a tranation hurry! Hurry to Batavia — so's you can be the first Yankee this year to die of fever. Hurry to Sumatra and the pepper trees. Get to Mocha first. Get to Canton, teas are coming in from the mountains . . . hurry, hurry, hurry! Get to Manila — and enough hemp to hang yourselves. Be first man eaten by the cannibals on the Cannibal Islands. No sense." But he agreed.

"So you're so heart-set on it, Dash, I give my consent to calling out the people. You've my permission to proceed." Dash had already "proceeded," so he said nothing, but his face had a guileless serenity that made him look like Peter.

Well . . . thank God, he'd kedged and talked that old scow around. Next he'd go home and see if Liz, first mate, was home from his junketing. Then he'd go down Wapping Way and order out Dan Obrian. And one thing more. There had been arguments about the size of the *Victrix's* right bower anchor. All the experts — even Dash himself — had agreed that the present one was sufficient. Now, without having given the matter one conscious thought, Dash had decided it was not sufficient. The *Victrix* wasn't going to be real steady. He had a picture of her . . . anchors dragging, heading for palmy atolls and coral reefs, and the terrific silvery drive of a tropical storm. He often did this — saw the picture, felt the fear, and then his quick mind went back and justified his intuition. He knew an anchorsmith who would furnish him with the size he wanted. Thaddeus Croft. Only yesterday he had seen Mr. Croft finishing the anchor. It had been ordered for the Derbys' *Herald*. But, of course, the Derbys could wait . . . he'd get that anchor. Why he would get it and the Derbys would wait he never stopped to analyze. But it had something to do with a little boy — no more than seven or eight — with extremely expressive hazel eyes who years ago had hung, lost in silent admiration, about Mr. Croft's chain and anchor smithy — while young Derbys of a similar age, dressed in muslin pantaloons, were playing battledore and shuttlecock with their mamas.

He came down Brown Street and the Common was before him. It was mucky enough, with five pools of stagnant water. At the east end of it were vast ropewalks, running downhill to Collins Cove — and there carried out on piles over the mud flats. Tanners too. People had thought his mother foolish to build her new house facing the Common. But it was there the old house had stood. She already owned a large parcel of land on the corner of the Common and Brown, and she confidently believed that in time it would be a choice residential section of Salem. It wasn't yet. But his mother had a way of guessing which way the winds of fashion set.

It was an imposing white house, gazing disdainfully across the muddy acres of the Common at ropewalks and tanneries. Four years ago things had looked so good his mother had pulled down the little old house all her children had been born in and started McIntire off on this new one. It was still unfinished. Some scaffolding had been left about the roof where a cupola was to go. Mrs. Inman had thought that if the scaffolding was left up, anyone could see this was a house a-building, but two winters had turned it gray. Anyone could guess that for some reason the money had given out. McIntire had designed a good many expensive gimcracks for it. A carved and paneled door under a Doric-columned portico. Fan lights and a palladium above it. There was nothing but the plainest of pine doors as yet. There were to be gates and a white fence, and on the top of every post a carved Grecian urn. There were neither fence nor gates. The gardens had not been re-done anywhere except on paper. They were still an unfashionable tangle of roses and mints, hollyhocks, Seckel pear trees and sheets of violets and daffodils run wild, and only on paper were the new stables. The old barn was still there, hanging on to the new house, looking like a cow out walking with a lady of quality. The sight of the house pleased Dash because it was as clean in line, as effortless as the finest ship, as beautiful as the most beautiful woman. It hurt him because it was the *Antelope* which should have furnished the money to complete it.

The front door (such as it was) was open, for the May day was enchantingly soft and warm. To his right, behind closed doors, were the double parlors. Unfinished and unfurnished, without a mantelpiece or a cornice. They were waiting an upswing in the family fortunes.

The hall itself was complete and magnificent. The stairway rose slowly to a broad and sunny landing, paused there for some time and continued its stately progress. It was carved and exquisite as a seashell. The hall had French landscape papers in gray and white. Nobody entering would realize that Lucy Inman had bought, for almost nothing, little scraps of this and that, so long as the coloring was all right. You had to look sharp to see the patterns did not make sense. Naples and Corinth were hopelessly mixed. Ben Franklin (in the dark of the lower hall) was not ascending the Hall of Fame the French paper-maker had designed for him, but was sneaking off into a grotto full of naked nymphs.

And old Ben looked as though he were relishing the proposition Mrs. Inman had put up to him.

Seemingly there was no one at home.

Dash stood with one blunt hand on the newel.

"Liz — ahoy, Liz?"

From a room on his left a dark and ruddy young fellow sauntered out to meet him, saying nothing but grinning (like a true Inman) from ear to ear. He wore the bright blue coat and big silver buttons of a ship's officer.

"Tom! Why, Tom, what's up? Didn't the *Nautilus* get to Batavia? Nobody expected you back for four or five months."

"Dash!" Tom's eyes went to his older brother's face. An equally devoted but more emotional man would have shown how shocked he was. The Inmans were a black-haired, white-skinned folk, tanning darkly, easily, smoothly. He had never seen Dash's face so naked before. The loss of his sea tan was like losing a protective veil behind which he had formerly lived and worked. Something terrible had happened to Dash. But Tom wouldn't speak of it.

"When we made Isle of France, Captain Jake decided it wasn't safe to try for Batavia."

"Why ever not?"

"Of course it's Dutch. And since France overran Holland and a lot of traitors there joined up with France, that makes England at war with Holland — even out there."

"Yeh . . . I know, and we're not to go trading with her enemies. But she can't have enough fleet out there to do any serious blockading."

"And then, of course, we are fighting this undeclared war with France — and her allies. Captain Jake thought, even if we got there, we might get condemned."

"Oh," said Dash, "we can get condemned and lose a ship just going to the West Indies. If we stayed home because we might get condemned, we'd never get farther off than Baker's Island. I'm disappointed Jake Crowninshield hasn't more guts. Was a fine smart captain — once."

"No. He did right. That *Nautilus* of his isn't any *America,* and it isn't the good old *Belisarius*. It's damned slow. And you've got to be quick — like a flash — to chance things around the East Indies these days."

"What did Jake do?"

"Jake bought a condemned prize — British. At Isle of France. The ships are piling up there, Dash — looking for buyers. This thing is a ship — the *Raven*. He left me to put her in sea-shape and he shopped along the Coromandel coast to Bombay. Came back with a cargo of goods for me. Cleared then. Himself for Mocha — and coffee. You don't have to be fast for the Red Sea — just armed well. Sent me home with the *Raven*."

"How'd she sail?"

"Leaked by the bowsprit. Men at the pumps night and day mostly. Pumps never sucked mor'n six times all the way home. I couldn't fix her."

"I take it you were master — Tom?"

Tom did not blush. Or if he did he was too high-colored to show. He had waited six months for this moment. More even than to Miranda Fields, Tom had longed to tell Dash he had now commanded a vessel east of Good Hope — was an "East Injun captain." Tom was twenty-three.

"Aye."

"Gosh," said Dash, looking at him with affection and understanding. His face was so expressive, no words could have said more to the younger boy. When Dash said "Gosh" like that and looked at you, it meant more than any word from anybody else. Tom and Liz had both served under him. It was he who had taught them navigation and trading. And how to behave like men and hold themselves like officers. As long as they walked the quarterdeck, it would be a little in his stride.

"Let's have a drink."

"I was having a drink."

They walked through their mother's sitting room — a pretty, feminine room of pale blue and amethyst, and went into the dining room. It was here the boys often sat and discussed their problems, studied their charts, leaving the sitting room to their mother and the girls — and sometimes to Liz.

"You didn't take the *Raven* to Salem?"

"No, Boston."

"Why not Salem?"

"Captain Jake told me to sell her. Nobody here is such a fool as to buy such a tub. Then, too, lots of folk like Boston better. No matter what tides, you can get in and tie up. It would have taken a day to get the *Raven* in here. She's too big for our harbor — four hundred tons."

"Hell," said Dash, cutting a lemon and squeezing half in his own and half in his brother's glass, measuring out the sugar and rum. "I like Salem."

"Then I took Manning's stage up. My gear's following. Everybody's all right round here?" And once again he glanced curiously at Dash's driven face.

"Of course."

"Of course I went first thing to Pa Crowninshield to report. He told me you all were all right. And Nanny married to Jack West?"

"Four months ago."

"Aye," Tom said. "Pa Crowninshield" (behind his back they all called the senior George Pa to separate him from his son) "told me we have built us a new ship."

"We had to have another ship — or retire from the sea. Tom, you know the French seized our *Harlequin* — Captain Ruck. He hadn't got a crew list to suit them. At Gibraltar a year ago we lost the *Dorcas,* Captain Magee, to the British. Stopped on her way home from India to trade French West Indies. That was six months ago. Now, those were good rich ships. We couldn't afford to lose them. We did. And in betweentimes I did, just as I wrote you, wreck the *Antelope* — very rich, back from Dutch and English India. All we have left is the *Mermaid* (Liz came in on her from the Baltic two weeks ago — she's graving) and that damned silly little old brig *Fox Fire* — that's so slow I can't tell which way she's going. A hundred tons only."

"Yet she was the first American vessel to sail to Kronstadt — first time Russians ever saw our flag it was flying from *Fox Fire.*"

"Oh, aye, aye, I've heard tell. 1784. Dad did that. She'll do a while longer on the Baltic run. Too slow for Far East. Ma'am is right about one thing. We — as a House — have always made on Baltic trading and always lost on Far East. The *Harlequin,* the *Antelope,* and the *Dorcas* were all East Injunmen. We lost every one."

"But the new ship — is she Baltic bound?"

"No. Cleared for Isle of France and — Far East."

"How'd you persuade Ma'am?"

"I kedged her. And that ship — well, she's quite a ship. 'Tirey Becket built her. He builds the best and fastest ships in the world. I don't care if he does go crazy — sometimes — and run around on tippy-toes. He's a genius. And the ship's a beauty. She's anchored off our wharf, laden and cleared. We've got the usual cargo — thirty-two thousand pounds of New England butter, seventy barrels of salmon, codfish, of course, and rum. Spermaceti candles from Nantucket, one hundred tons bar-iron Liz brought back on the *Mermaid* from the Baltic, snuff from Newburyport. And she's going to pick up wines at Madeira on her way out. And Tom — one more thing she's got, ten thousand dollars in hard cash. Her crew's already called. She goes out at dawn tomorrow."

"How'd you pay for her — and wherever did you get the specie?"

"Come down to the counting-house and I'll show you the ledgers. Oh, we've sold a warehouse to Billy Gray. We've rented space to sailmakers in the old wooden warehouse. We sold some safe-seeming shares we had on the *Herald* and the *Mount Vernon* and mortgaged the wharf. You can guess, losing three ships and all their cargoes in one year, we had some pretty bad debts. Well — we've got a lot more. Mortgaged this house too."

"Mortgaged before it's really finished . . ."

"Why not? If only the Devil had appeared to me, I'd have mortgaged my soul."

"But however did you get Ma'am to do it?"

"Why, she wanted to — much as I. You and Liz don't understand her." Dash made another drink. After a moment he asked: "Tom, you got my letter at Good Hope? Explaining things? That was after the *Harlequin* and the *Antelope* were gone geese — but before we lost the *Dorcas*."

There was a long silence while Tom offered his deepest sympathy that Dash had lost the *Antelope*. Her cargo might well have brought one hundred thousand dollars. For Dash had done his "shopping" in India and at Batavia magnificently. His original cargo had been turned over at least four times and always with profit. And then one night of rain and gale and she had gone to pieces on the Peaked Hill Bar off Cape Cod. Those long octopus tentacles of sand stretching far out into deep water. She had gone through every danger on the other sides of the earth to meet destruction on her own doorstep. This had been true many times of New England ships.

"You got off all your people?"

"Everyone — even old Bouncing Bet."

"Cargo?"

"I was floored with sugar. That can't stand much wet. I had spices and fifteen hundred chests of tea, and silks and nankeens."

"Dash — you didn't say in your letter. How did it happen?"

" I said enough when I said I lost her."

Tom dropped his eyes to study the sugar crystallizing at the bottom of his glass. Dash certainly had taken it hard.

"But the new ship?"

"She's a beauty. *Victrix* we call her. Tom . . . it didn't quite come out on her trials how fast she is. She's tricky, and she wasn't handled quite right. Masury, her rigger, is already talking of cutting down her sail a bit. I think in *her own way* she can carry more than they've given her. Magee'll never dare even unreef her. She may be a little crank and finicky. I don't know. But Becket's boasting she'll prove the fastest sailer and will sail closest to the wind of any ship he ever built. If that's right, you might go so far as to say she's the fastest vessel in the world today. I mean if Magee's got the stomach to give her head and let her rip."

"Holy mackerel!" Tom's eyes widened in wonder. "But you don't mean Magee's going to command her?"

"Yes. But I think perhaps if Ma'am had known you'd be back in time, she'd have entrusted her to you."

"Magee! . . . Oh, my God, Magee!"

"Ma'am thinks he's safe."

"Safe? He let the British walk off with the *Dorcas* — why the hell did he stop when they fired across his bows? He always stops. Remember when you had little old *Fox Fire* in the Mediterranean, took her right through the Battle of the Nile — I was your second. Everybody told you to stop — but you didn't. Wasn't any time to stop. You remember we did real well moving in fresh food for Lord Nelson. But what pleased me as far as we were able, you and me — and little *Fox Fire* — helped Nelson stop that rat — that damned rat of a Napoleon."

"Ma'am was pleased, too, for then at last she trusted me with an East Injunman. But I lost that ship. So it's right I can't command again. For a little."

"It couldn't have been your fault."

"It was. I took on a pilot to take me through the Vineyard. The weather was working up for something. Since I had left home, there were a lot of new lighthouses Federal Government had set up. I trusted him to understand them, for I did not. Well . . . the wind blew out the lighthouses and the blamed idiot never guessed. That's all."

"Can't you get some money from the Government — those were their lighthouses."

"The Government? Have we a government? No. It won't protect our sea lanes. It's only recently it's said we can arm and fight the god-damned French. Not a nickel out of them. They'd say their lights were on. But governments always lie like hell."

"And our government hasn't got a nickel. After all, we Salem merchants had to build a frigate to protect us."

"*Essex* — she's sent out to Batavia to convoy home sacred merchantmen."

"I bespoke her — just south of Good Hope. First American frigate ever went that far from home. That shows you, Dash, how bad things are about Java way."

"Tom . . . if I had the *Victrix* — I'd chance it."

"A very fast ship, a smart Yankee captain and crew like mustard, could make a fortune."

"She's fast."

The young men looked at each other thoughtfully.

"Dash, you haven't been sitting here clerking it for eight months?"

"That I have."

"Just because your grandmother told you you couldn't have a ship of hers for a year! Didn't you get other offers?"

"Of course I did. Four or five others. Derbys' *Herald* . . . Crowninshields' *America* — good offers like that."

"But you preferred to sit and repent."

"Aye."

"With nothing to repent of. You wanted to stew in your own juice."

"Aye, I've stewed aplenty."

"You look it."

"No, I don't."

At that moment Tom felt he loved Dash more than any other

human being — more even than his Miranda Fields. There had been times when in his own way he had envied him. He knew himself to be "competent." Dash was something far beyond mere competency. Ship's people loved and obeyed Dash — and only obeyed him. That was better than Liz. The people obeyed him too — but often hated him. Dash had something Tom couldn't find a word for. He loved him for it and sometimes in his generous way resented it.

"Dash," he said, hoping to move the conversation out of shoal water, "I'm driving over to Newburyport tomorrow, of course, to see Miranda Fields. Why don't you and Polly Mompesson come along? The Fields would be proud to welcome her."

"You forget Polly Mompesson." Dash stood up as though ready to leave. His white face marked, naked, a little driven.

"I'm sorry. It looked clear sailing when I left."

Evidently he had hit a reef. He had never seen two people so in love. Here again he felt a humble realization of his own inadequacy. He and Miranda, couldn't love that way, even if they had wanted to. And he wasn't sure they did. There was something rather rattle-brained, childish, unsteady, not "competent," in being literally swept off your feet the way Dash and Polly had been. Of course Dash's bad luck would make marriage impossible until he had mended his fortunes. Squire Mompesson would never let his girl marry a man with his fortune yet to make. Could it be Polly had gone off with someone else? She was such a fly little flirt. Nothing a man could really anchor to — like Miranda.

"Come down to the wharf and see my ship," said Dash.

But they heard a swish of wheels on the gravel. A carriage was stopping at the side entrance. Lucy Inman and Eleazar were back from their junketing.

"Tom, tell Liz to be aboard the *Victrix* by eleven tonight. That's orders" . . . forgetting he was only a clerk, poor fellow, and clerks never gave orders to anybody. "I'm off now — to see Crofts about a bigger bower."

Chapter Two

⌁⌁⌁⌁⌁⌁⌁⌁⌁⌁⌁⌁⌁⌁⌁⌁⌁⌁⌁⌁⌁⌁⌁⌁⌁

P ETER STOOD in the bedchamber he shared with Liz — such times as Liz was home. The room was full of things Liz had brought home the week before from the Baltic.

Although the *Mermaid's* cargo had been such solid goods as hemp and bar-iron, steel, canvas bagging, Liz's own venture was more esoteric. Amber, for instance. The man who could buy it in the Baltic and sell it to the Chinese would make a tidy profit. The Chinese were crazy about amber. Russian furs. Americans were so ignorant they hardly knew the difference between sables and squirrels. Not so the Chinese. Furs and amber had already been baled up, not to go in the hold, but under the first mate's bunk in the cabin of the *Victrix*. Clocks, too. The French Revolution had done away with the old twelve-hour-a-day system in whatever country it had reached in Europe. Nothing would suit but the decimal system. A smart man (like Liz Inman) could pick up the old clocks for little. The Americans loved them — they were so pretty and foppish — and the Americans were old-fashioned people with twelve hours in every day. Liz had a dozen clocks — gilt and enamel, crystal and silver, porcelain, and a wooden curiosity from Nuremberg — ticking and striking all over his and Peter's room. Each one (Peter noticed) was calling its brother a liar. Liz had ordered Peter to mind and wind these clocks and keep them set. He wasn't quite sure yet where he would sell them. Liz had a passion for clocks. Dash loathed them. And Dash didn't like the nasty little fauns pulling off the last garments of the gilt nymphs; the silly shepherds that stuck out their little fingers as they held their crooks. Liz did. But he had an idea they'd be more appreciated in the southern than the sensible northern states.

Then he also had fur-lined Russia-leather boots for himself and the six or eight ermine skins he was going to give to whichever six or eight Salem girls he happened to like best when the time came. Liz was pretty bad about the girls.

The Russia-leather, the furs, gave off a pleasant scent.

At the foot of the bed Peter and Liz shared was a gray-green sea chest. Nobody had told Peter that now had come the time when Liz's things should be packed in this chest. But Peter had guessed by watching Dash. Where Dash was concerned, he was getting to be like a dog who knows what his master is going to do sometimes before the master. He wondered if Liz himself knew. He was still downstairs with his mother and Tom. There was to be a little supper party tonight, with a butler hired in to help Mrs. Cady. And good (but not the best) Madeira. Probably Tom was sitting in a corner reading back newspapers, trying to get caught up on what had happened during the year and three months he had been gone. He'd leave the planning of the party, suddenly got up in his honor, to his mother and Liz.

The older and nautical brothers all looked upon Peter as their valet, and humbly Peter accepted the rôle. He packed and unpacked for them. He ran their errands and carried their love-letters. He protected their private lives from the scrutiny of the older generations. He listened when they wanted to talk. Now he began on Liz's chest. He did not want Dash fretted up over the mate's dallyings. When a porter came up from the wharf for the chest and gear, it was going to be ready. First he laid out on the bed such things as Liz would wear tonight. Creamy pantaloons, a bright blue silver-buttoned coat, white shirt, high beaver hat so pale it was almost white. A gold-headed cane some woman had given him once. In the chest he put full-checked shirts, square jackets, loose duck and fustian trousers. And beside the chest a canvas sack of sea boots and tarpaulins. Such things a mate would wear upon a quarterdeck. In the varnished sea hat he stowed woolen socks and mittens. Many a cold watch would be stood before at last the *Victrix* came out on tropic seas. By closing his eyes, Peter could see the strange world. He never had, and chances were he never would, but they existed for him — always just behind his closed lids.

A bamboo chest had been carried down from the attic. Here were the seersuckers and pongees suitable for officer's wear at Bombay, Calcutta, Batavia, Canton. And Peter knew what also was inside, and held his breath, for as he opened the chest came a spicy fragrance — a mere ghost of a smell; you would hardly say whether it was cinnamon or camphor, sandalwood or incense — yet it was the aroma of the Far East. Peter had delayed opening this chest until the last moment. Like a wiser Pandora he had not wished to turn this soft fragrance loose through the upper hall. He had not wished to make Dash more miserable than he was.

The boy's flexible hands went confidently about the accustomed work, but he was dreaming of that magic land beyond Good Hope.

He heard Tom and Liz come up the stairs together. As usual, it was Liz who was doing all the talking. Tom went to his room, Liz joined Peter.

"That's the trick, boy," Liz said. Evidently someone had told him he was to go this night. "Don't go putting tropical stuff on top of things I'm going to need for the North Atlantic."

"I haven't."

Peter almost stopped his work. When Liz, because he was four years older and healthy, ordered him about like that, he wasn't so keen to oblige.

Liz stripped of his shirt, was leaning over the washhand stand splashing water on his face. He was a beautifully made man. Peter, watching him, was conscious of the fact that when he himself leaned over washhand stands, it was not so much the long rhythmic muscles that stood out, but the vertebrae and the two flat dishes of his shoulder blades. The face that Liz buried in a towel was as handsome as any you might find on a Salem quarterdeck — and Salem was famous for its beautiful women and handsome men. Peter was as conscious of Liz's fine looks as was his mother. But you had to give Liz credit for one thing. He didn't think much about it himself.

"Don't go jamming that tarpaulin hat full of socks — idiot boy. And go to Dash's room and fetch me his sextant. He keeps it in his commode."

Peter settled back on his heels. "Did Dash say you might take his sextant?" he demanded sternly.

"No. But he isn't using it. Anyway, it belongs to the House — not to him. It always goes to the best command. That's me — just now. I'm chief of the *Victrix,* and Dash is as landlocked as an old hen." But obviously Liz was a little scared of Dash. He had not asked him for the prized sextant, and now — the last moment — he was trying to get Peter to sneak in and get it.

"Get it yourself. I won't."

"Idiot boy," Liz said pleasantly. Liz rarely lost his temper. It was one of the most provoking things about him. But he had a gift of making other people lose theirs — even the philosophical Peter, easy-going Tom, the disciplined Dash, his adoring mother, and his skeptical grandmother, fellow-officers, seamen, and girls.

"So the idiot boy won't do as told?"

"No. Get it yourself."

"Maybe."

He wasn't going to get it. In spite of his brilliant, somewhat hard exterior, he did not quite want to push Dash aside. "I'm not sure but I like mine better," he said. He was a better man than he liked to pretend. The beautiful Dutch sextant stood for something vaguely understood and accepted by the three brothers.

"Long 'fore you get back, Liz, Dash is going to be at sea again. And he'll be master of any ship he puts foot on. For he's an East Injun captain. All you've ever done is command the old *Mermaid* to the Baltic and back — and now what are you? Nothing but a no-account mate."

"If anything happens to Magee, I'm master. Might push him overboard. And now," he said, as his face began to emerge through the neck of his frilly shirt, "stand by." He tipped back his head and with three sharp short downward thrusts of his chin settled the intricate linen expertly about his throat . . . "Now you might hand me my coat and see if you can get it on without mussing *anything.*"

Peter jumped to obey. Watching Liz dress never lost its fascination for him. Liz's hair was so dark it had purple lights in it. It was not rough and curly like most of the family's. Seemingly in half a second, with a wet comb and no mirror, he had every hair lying just as it should. Beau Brummel could have done no better with valet and hairdresser to attend him. Liz settled the broadcloth coat on his handsome shoulders, buttoned it about his slim waist. The pale pantaloons did indeed fit him like a frog's skin. The sheer white linen popped out under his chin at the most devastating of angles. He shook his head, freeing one dark lock across his forehead. This Napoleonic touch of negligence was the last word.

Grandma thought he prinked for hours. He did not. He was born stylish like a black tomcat with white paws and waistcoat. And born handsome and provoking and grinning and tough. But he hadn't been tough enough to ask Dash for his sextant. His own toilet complete, he looked skeptically at Peter.

"You haven't dressed yet?"

"Yes, I have. I'm cleaner than you are. I washed farther down."

"Well, take off your coat and have another try at your hair. You and Dash go around looking like a couple of orphaned poodle dogs."

"I'd rather be Dash's litter than your spawn — or whatever it is *frogs* have."

Liz laughed pleasantly. You couldn't insult him. "Now mind, Peter, supper is six sharp." He glanced at his array of little imported clocks, all ticking their hearts out, their little pendulums going. Some displayed their tiny bowels. One of them struck three. "Gosh damn it, Peter, mind I told you to keep those clocks *set* and wound, and while I'm gone you are to take care of my clocks, see?" And miraculously the old-fashioned Nuremberg clock opened a little door and out came twelve apostles in a row and that clock struck twelve. "Peter, you'd better give up — go live at the Charity House and let the town support you as Salem's village idiot. Can't even be trusted to take care of clocks. No gumption. No nothing. That's my little brother Petey."

Peter had learned from the gifted Liz how to pass through life uninsultable. Who's coming tonight?" he asked, promising nothing:

"About what you'd expect. Mostly family. Ma'am, of course — and 'Sephus Hobey, because he boards with her. And a couple of pretties for Tom and me. Jack West and Nanny, of course." He paused, laughed, arched his dark eyebrows. "And guess what for Dash? Polly Mompesson! Why, I've only been home a week, but I've seen enough to know that is a thing of the past. It makes me laugh to think Mother is inviting Polly to give Dash a good time."

"Some things," Peter said, "are not as funny as they seem to little minds."

Liz looked pleased at this compliment. "One thing I like about Mother is that she's always mixed up on our *affaires d'amour*. Can you believe it? She wanted to dig up Josie Orne for me? Josie won't speak to me."

"Why?"

"I forget just why. I think I tried to seduce her a couple of years back and didn't try hard enough. That hurt her feelings."

"Oh, Liz . . . you can't talk that way about a lady. She's no Kanaka."

"Can't I? But I only mentioned that to show you how little Mother knows. Everybody else in Salem has guessed that Josie can't abide me." He was setting a gray pearl pin in his neck ruffles.

"Polly won't come," Peter admitted slowly. "Mother has asked her before. She says she will, and last moment writes a little note and says she won't."

"Dash has been tactless. First thing he did after he lost a ship was to ask Mr. Mompesson for her hand."

"Did he tell you?"

"No. I guessed it. And Mr. Mompesson sent him packing — of course. And Dash was too proud to hang around where he wasn't wanted. And so gosh-damn stubborn he wouldn't get to sea again and mend his fortunes. And so on."

"How did you know?"

"Guessed it." Liz's smartness did not endear him to his youngest brother. He preferred his mother's mistakes. "All I had to do was put two and two together. That was easy. But . . ." He was not satisfied with the gray pearl pin, took it out and handed it to Peter, who obediently got out a velvet box and put it away. "Pearls don't do a thing for a man," Liz said. "The less the better." And Peter knew this was the secret of Liz's doggy dressing — to own gray pearls and know enough not to wear them. "And Dash has — after that — been neglecting Polly. Maybe he's got a new girl?"

"Not Dash. No. There won't ever be anyone else for Dash."

"Simple. That's simple of Dash."

"What do you mean?"

"Nothing." A clock struck six. "God blast those clocks! But at least that one's *almost* right." He looked at his own watch. "Peter, we're trying Marcy at the table with the grownups tonight. She's our sister and has to learn manners sometime. You're to sit next to her. Don't let her eat like a puppy. Or get to talking too much. Don't let her play tick-tack-toe on the tablecloth. I don't think they teach her anything at Mrs. Rogers's. Kick her if she squirms . . . Peter, I want my malacca cane in the chest. The gold-headed one will look too heavy in the tropics . . . where's Dash?"

"*Victrix,* of course."

"Well, he'll be late again." Liz left him.

◆2◆

ALREADY some of Liz's clocks were twirping, chattering, and saying six. Peter stood at the head of the stairs and looked at the great clock on the landing. It was five of. He could hear Lamb, the hired-in butler ushering in guests. He heard his new brother-in-law, Doctor Jack West, calling Tom's name. Little shrieks and giggles doubtless from the two unnamed "pretties." He heard Polly Mompesson's laugh — pretty, touching, unreal as a music-box tinkle. A nostalgic laugh, as though already recalling past pleasures more than enjoying the present. Oh Polly . . . Polly. Why hadn't she sent that second note?

The great clock on the landing cleared its throat and very slowly struck six. Dash had not come.

Perhaps he was already in his own room. Peter went there and sat disconsolately on his bed. This had been Nanny's room until she had married Jack three months before. Dash had never asked his mother's permission. He had simply moved in his own things from the room he had shared with Tom. Peter knew it was because from here he could get a view of the sea and the ships, and here he could feel himself alone. The room was designed in the dainty pink and silver Mrs. Inman thought appropriate for a young girl. Silver cupids held back the canopies of the maidenly pink bed. The commode — where Dash kept his sextant and certain sacred nautical instruments — had come from France and had assorted little loves on its door. This room had never suited his sister Nanny's somewhat practical personality — only her mother's conception of a young girl. It suited the disgraced and sorrowing young captain even less. But Dash had never even noticed.

Lamb, a shivering skinny yellow Jamaica boy, was knocking on the jamb of the open door. "Mrs. Inman's compliments, sir, and her most respectful request that you and Captain Dash come right down — straight away. Now."

"We'll be right down."

Lamb's eyes rolled and bulged at the sight of Dash's treasures. He had a collection of curios — too odd or too ugly for downstairs display. Paddles carved by South Sea islanders and their squat gods of wood and mud. A thatched village. On his mantel a mummified monkey. He had strange shells and carved ivory and growths of coral and the queer black horn spoons of cannibals, and books everywhere. But Lamb could not see another young gentleman anywhere about. "Thank you, sir," he said doubtfully. "The guests are all come, she says, and you are making cook fidget."

"I told you we'd be right down."

Peter might have gone down himself. Let Dash be tardy alone. His passionate loyalty to his oldest brother made him want to share even this slight disgrace with him.

The fall before, Peter had expected to enter Harvard. He had been a good student at Exeter. It was doubtful if he would ever be rugged enough to go to sea. As a mean second choice he would go on with his education. Then the financial shock of the lost *Antelope*. He had said he would not think of adding expense to the family. He'd clerk it down at the counting-house. No, he did not want to go to Harvard — yet at the time he had longed for it. To chum with his best friend Blainey Phipps — go on to something else — he hardly knew what — but something where a physique frailer than his steely-built, all-enduring older brothers' would not be so bitter a handicap. There was only one real reason why he had not gone. He could not bear to leave Dash now marooned on land. Blainey had written him every week exactly what books they were studying. Peter had kept up with his theoretical class at Harvard. About this he had plenty of gumption. Once let Dash be a captain at sea once more, and he would go to Harvard.

He had never known Dash well until these last eight months of his "shore leave." Peter had only been seven when Dash had run away from Exeter and shipped as a foremast hand of fourteen. From then on, he'd seen him only coming and going again, and all the merriment and the parties and the cakes that attended his departure, and in what triumph he always seemed to return — the world and its seas truly an oyster held in his square brown hand. His face so tanned the teeth and eyes looked amazing white. And that look of confidence bold and modest. Undefeated — undefeatable. Dash always brought his little brother little presents — and dropped kind words with them. But he was like a prince on horseback, doling out his largesses — and always passing proudly on. Then Dash came home — and had not gone again. Then Peter came to know him.

Peter's benignity, that lack of gumption that so worried his elders, came as a solace to the young captain. Peter did not seem to pity Dash. He had already accepted the world as a place which contains much disappointment, humiliation, and injustice. In his world people were always losing the things they set their hearts upon. His calm, easy pessimism gave strength and healing to the somewhat showy, usually successful Dash.

And in return Dash gave parts and parcels of his secret self. Long hours after midnight they had sat and Dash had talked. Peter, who had never been farther in a boat than Portland, nor farther from home than New York, could (as Dash talked) smell and feel the teeming life of India about him. "And Bombay," Dash would say, "is a very pleasant island. You trade with the Parsees — the most intelligent people I have ever met." Or, "Mountain tea is the best — the coolies run hundreds of miles from the inland mountains . . ." and he would see the red earth of China and hear the coolies' sing-song. He had smelt the fragrance of the Spice Islands drifting miles out to sea through soft black velvet tropic nights. He had heard the patter of the sandalwood ponies in Java. The bark of seals upon Ascencion, and the shipworm at work at Port North-West — Isle of France. He sailed under the dark shadow of Java Head and saw the phosphorescent lights upon the fins of sharks. He had played upon the beaches in the great roaring surfs of the Pacific with brown Kanaka girls — when Dash talked.

Ships, too! They were not mere contrivances to Dash. Nor was his sea life merely an extremely dangerous and uncomfortable method of making his living. He was a true adventurer — and like all adventurers had something of the child and the poet in him. But never had he talked thus freely to anyone before.

Dash must have slipped up the back stairs, for he had suddenly materialized on the threshold. For some reason he looked tired — sick and tired to death. There was dust on the sleeve of his corduroy jacket and a smooch on his face . . . He looked at Peter. The fine eyes softened. Like many another born leader of men, he combined with an obvious virility certain other qualities — more oblique, less tangible, and usually associated with women — something softer, more mysterious, more dreamy and aware. It was partly these qualities that made men so loyal to him. His face, with its muscular mouth, square chin, and often thrusting lower lip, looked hard enough. Then it would relax and smile. The effect was often devastating. It explained why, although ladies might give Eleazar gold-headed canes, they were often overready to give Dash more. For every girl he smiled at was confident that he had never looked at any other girl like that before. So his eyes lingered on his willing slave, and with that softening glance paid for anything Peter might do for him, even for the lost Harvard.

"You've changed — haven't you?"

"Yes."

"I don't see any need . . . just family."

Why should he seem so tired? — he who at sea could stand forty-eight-hour watches — never tire.

"There's going to be girls besides family."

Peter wanted to warn him that "girls" might include Polly. "Dash, Mother's mad at you already. If you take time to change, she'll be madder, but if you don't, she'll be furious."

"Well, if I'm late, the *Victrix* won't be. Peter — last moment I got us a monstrous heavy anchor from Croft. Right bower. Trouble getting it on, but it's on now — just right."

"Ship's people called?"

"Oh, aye!" He laughed. "Mr. Africanus — gosh, I like that man! Knowing as a weathervane — that man." He was taking off his clothes, evidently determined to make his mother madder rather than furious. "A smarter crew never left Salem. I picked them every last one . . . Peter, go down and tell Mother I'm on your heels." He yawned, and looked rather touchingly young with his tousled hair and pale, dirty face.

He was thicker-set than Liz. His muscular structure was surprisingly heavy and round. You'd never guess to see him in his coat how powerfully he was built. He sat and like a dirty schoolboy began polishing his boots with his discarded shirt. He spat on his boots and polished harder. This was against all the rules of the house. Next washday Mrs. Cady would be holding up the shirt to Mrs. Inman and complaining one of her boys had polished his boots with a shirt — again. Peter wanted to protect him — against Mrs. Cady, and his mother — against all the world, and against himself.

"Tell her I'm hurrying."

He wasn't hurrying. There wasn't a thing he could do right about a house — nor a thing he could neglect about a ship. He and his mother were often at loggerheads, and mostly it was Dash's fault.

"I've got Liz packed," Peter said.

"Good. Porter will be up with a handcart at eleven sharp."

"Dash, you really know . . . how can you be so sure a wind's coming?"

"Maybe I've guessed wrong. I'm not *sure* at all."

"Dash —— " Peter burst out. "You'll be at sea now soon. Why, there are only four months left . . ."

"Maybe." He was brushing his heavy rough hair — cut short in the modern manner. "But it was the *Victrix* I wanted. I've watched every trunnel Becket set. I want her the way a man wants one particular woman — and all the others are harlots and trash to him — and no good. It is as if the *Victrix* grew out of my heart."

He could say these things — grandiloquent things. Peter always responded to Dash's eloquence. It was partly the voice — so clear, low, and a little precise. There was an unconscious rhythm and a banked fire to it that made Peter go gooseskin — and girls who had lost him remember and cry.

"Dash — would you rather I went down?"

"I don't care."

Up the stairway, floating into the bedchamber, came the bright nostalgic tinkle of Polly Mompesson's laugh. Dash was pulling on his boots with boot hooks. He lifted and turned his head. Said nothing and went on pulling.

"There," he said, getting to his feet. "I'm done."

Once again Lamb was knocking on the jamb, his protuberant eyes rolling in his yellow face.

"You young gentlemen, if you please. Young gentlemen, Mrs. Inman says . . ."

"All right, all right — but you're not paid fifteen cents an hour to go snapping at my heels."

"Oh no, sir. Never. Thank you, sir."

Curiously, Dash's spirits began to rise. His face lightened. Lamb was British-taught. He thanked for everything. Every order, every insult, and everything you took from him. This un-Yankee quality fascinated the young Inmans. They had been teasing him about it for years.

"It is I who should thank you."

"Yes, sir, thank you, sir — I mean, no, sir — thank you, sir."

"No, no, Lamb. Thank you, thank you. Let me have the last and final thanks."

And he ran down the stairs as though he had not a care in the world, not a worry, not a disappointment.

Peter, who lovingly followed Dash's moods, could not always keep up with him. He still looked a little harassed and torn when the two of them entered their mother's sitting room together.

～ 3 ～

THERE WERE LILACS on the tables, on the white mantel. The May day, not yet ended, had been warm, and through open windows the fragrance of more lilacs and apple blossoms filled the pretty sitting room. And there were the fetching light dresses of the women, the creamy pantaloons and dark bright broadcloth of the men. Under every masculine chin were formidable masses of snowy linen.

"Ralph Inman," said his mother, swimming toward Dash through her guests, "I *declare* you are always *late*."

It was only she who ever called him Ralph, and then only when irritated with him. She said she had heard of boats named for men, but never before a man named for a boat. The *Dash* had been a tiny boat and he but a little shaver. People along the wharves would pick up spyglasses and search through darkening storm and pounding seas and see one tiny sail — "That's the *Dash*." Homecoming proper ships a mile or two out beyond Baker's had read the name *The Dash, Salem,* and cheered her. When Mrs. Inman refused to use his nickname, she was unconsciously trying to put him in his place — for his nickname was part of his fame. She had never controlled the independent little thing as a boy. Nobody had. She had no say in him now he was a man. So she pricked him and sometimes picked on him, never letting him forget that no matter how highfalutin' he might be at sea, in her own home she was boss. This had not made the last eight months easier for him.

So now she came at him and called him "Ralph." She paid no attention to Peter (just as tardy as Dash). He was such a mouse she never enjoyed scolding him. She was a handsome woman, with thick close-cropped gray curls bound with silver gauze. Her long elegant figure, stiffly middle-aged and well-stayed, was displayed in a skimpy French "goddess" gown. Its peach-color blended with and exaggerated her naturally bright complexion.

"Ralph," she went on, blundering in where not even Liz would have dared to tread, "Polly says it's weeks since you have been to see her." It had been months.

Polly Mompesson curtsied with fluent grace. You could guess she had gone wholehog on these new French fashions. Not much more underneath the white silk dress than an actual nymph would wear. Lucy Inman was as carefully busked and stayed as in the days of her girlhood — days of great hoops and pompadours; for it is hard for women to escape the underclothes of their youth. Polly looked as silken and boneless as one of those eastern shawls women boasted they could pull through a wedding ring. Her slim body rose and sank. In her determination to show no chagrin over Dash's neglect of her, her pretty smile showed nothing — only the stereotyped smile of the belle. She could smile at every man at a ball just like that. Dash knew.

She was an enchanting little creature — delicate in coloring, features, figure. Perhaps only a little thing to paint upon a fan. Close the fan and forget. Or really a nymph with no soul to entangle a mortal — only the delicacy of her flesh. Or a doll to dance with, flirt with, and forget. But the eyes in the midst of the bright mask of her face protested. They were disturbing and beautiful eyes, with a sensitive downward turn to them at the outer corners. Her eyes flashed a protest. No! No . . . ! I'm not really a nymph — a doll. I'm not a figure painted on a fan. Do not forget me . . . do not forget.

So she glanced at Dash.

The glittering "Grecian curls," the bright lips, the piquant nose all coquetry, but the truthful eyes darkened and lingered in his.

"Polly . . ." contrary to etiquette he put out his hand to her. She grasped it. Her fingers tightened convulsively. He was leaning toward her. I love you, his eyes said, and I will never forget. Hers widened and a flash of white showed under the clean blue iris. But why . . .why . . . Oh, Dash, what has happened to us?

She quickly got herself under control. Her fashionable training had taught her never to show even with a glance a true emotion. Four years before, her coquetry had worked — Dash, the twenty-year-old captain of the Crowninshields' *Belisarius*, she at eighteen the belle of Salem. But, for some reason she could not understand, the same methods had not worked these last eight months.

If now she could only have left her hand in his a moment longer, said the right thing or have said nothing, a tiny bridge might have been thrown across the chasm between them. If she had been younger or even older, once during the eight months of his disgrace she would have gone to him, put her arms about him, said the right thing — or nothing.

Some instinct of self-destruction even now was making her do the wrong thing.

"Why, Ralph," she said, imitating his mother, for the girl was a pretty mimic, "you dreadful boy . . . always late — oh, tush, Dash — no, I mean *Ralph*."

The love and reproach had left her eyes. They were only mischievous. It was good fashion for young ladies to be mischievous.

Lamb was opening the door into the dining room.

"No, Ralph, do not bother to offer me your arm. While you were upstairs *primping*" — her eyebrows rose and became Mrs. Inman's eyebrows, reproaching him that his hair never lay on his head like Liz's — "I was thinking how well I'd known you and Tom and Liz for years, but how little I knew Peter. Yet he's now a grown gentleman. I thought I'd ask Peter to take me out . . . Peter?"

Peter, a born observer of other men's successes and failures, had been humbly watching the by-play. He was glad when Dash had simply taken her hand (when he should not have) and he had interpreted correctly that first exchange of glances. Then something had gone wrong. Why was it these two seemed unable to do anything except frustrate and hurt each other? He was young enough to think if they were only married, all would be well.

Then he heard her say his name and understood his orders. He came out of his reverie and jumped toward Polly, his left arm crooked to receive her white hand. But is it your left arm you offer? No, you offer your right. Oh, why had he been so stupid in dancing school? Why wasn't he more observant? His palms grew wet. A fatuous smile upset the usual benignity of his expression. Now both arms were out like a brooding hen. He tripped over a footstool. Thought it was Little Joe, the house dog, and muttered an imprecation. Then he heard, through the blood drumming in his ears, old Monsieur de Herriot's voice saying to his dancing class, "If you by mistake offer a young lady your left arm, you can excuse yourself by saying, 'Eet eez clozer to zee heart.'"

Closer to the heart . . . Polly. Closer to the heart.

Dash already had his little grandmother, so pretty in her best gray silk and finest lace cap, on his arm. There was nothing Grecian about her costume. Mrs. Inman was leading the way to the dining room on the arm of the Reverend Doctor Josephus Hobey. Liz's smooth, treacherous frog's legs had slid him closer to Polly. And she, the jilt, had taken his arm. Idiot boy — Liz's black eyes mocked him, and Polly's sidewise blue glance repeated these words more softly, not too loudly, for, although Peter might be small fry, she had never yet thrown back a fish because it was too little.

Nature had not designed Peter to carry off the belles, but to comfort the wallflowers. So, as Polly slipped away from him with that provocative sidewise glance, he was left with the obvious wallflower of this small occasion — his youngest sister, Marcy. Marcy was a stout, rambunctious child of ten. She had been watching and understanding Peter's flounderings.

Dash, as eldest, had the head of the table. Opposite him, across a long spread of damask, silver, crystal, and more apple blossoms, was the Reverend Doctor Hobey. He had a rococo face, curved and dimpled. Everything about him — eyes, chin, and mouth — was round and soft where the Inman pattern tended toward the square and blunt. Only a year older than Dash, who still had much of the charm of boyhood about him, he seemed a settled man. It was almost as though he had been born middle-aged. And born to be a scholarly bachelor, and live forever with elderly women like Madam Inman, who would always adore him. Yet the gray eyes were sharp and sure. There was much strength packed behind his many curves. Although Liz was always teasing his grandmother over her infatuation with 'Sephus Hobey, he and all the Inmans liked and admired him. He was not an outstanding clergyman, but he was an outstanding scholar. Only he, in all America, could translate the state papers dealing with the North African pirates and write back in their own language. Many a time express riders from Washington had come to Salem bellowing his name. Arabic was but one of the fifteen languages he had mostly taught himself. The captains liked his intelligent interest in the strange lands they knew, brought him back the proper books and information. They liked his goodness, and a purity as touching to them as the purity of a young girl. His favorite relaxation was local nature study.

Three afternoons a week, Marcy went to her grandmother's quaint old black house at the head of Inman Wharf for lessons with him: natural philosophy, the classics, mathematics, things she did not learn at the fashionable Mrs. Rogers's. He had also done much to help Peter with his solitary studies, and lent as well as borrowed books from Dash and Liz. Mrs. Inman did not care what 'Sephus taught Marcy — just so long as he kept her out of her usual scrapes. She had only lifted those expressive eyebrows of hers that day Doctor Hobey had come running to her, breathless, to tell her the child had a brilliant mind and it must be developed.

"I don't worry about developing her *mind*, Doctor Hobey," she had said, "just so she sometime develops a *shape*."

The little girl was built like a woodchuck. This remark had hurt the kind, scholarly young clergyman, and made him feel tenderly toward Marcy. What was wrong with a world where even a mother cared more for a girl's shape than her mind?

Doctor Hobey in neat black, standing, blessed the meat. There was a scraping of chairs as six men attempted to seat seven ladies.

Then exclamations. There were thirteen at the table! But all were saying they did not care — except Polly. Polly made much of her superstitions, as walking under ladders, knocking on wood, black cats across her path. And always some superior masculine mind was ready to pooh-pooh her fears, protect her from these filaments of her imagination. Polly saw to it that men did not get out of the habit of protecting her — even from her own foolishness.

Lucy Inman was frankly bored. She was afraid the roast would be ruined — first Dash's dawdlings and now Dash's girl's absurdities. A house this size and only one servant made her care more for Mrs. Cady's feelings than Polly's. She made up a face and sighed. But 'Sephus Hobey was quoting a Chinese proverb (in the original Chinese) to her, and Tom was saying that lots of people nowadays thought thirteen a lucky number. Doctor Jack West began on the medical angle of the dilemma. People's minds did influence their bodies. The luck you got was often what you expected — and so on. Nanny Inman West cast down her eyes and waited. Madam Inman, the only person seated, calmly unfolded her napkin, picked up a spoon, and looked as though nothing had happened. The two pretties hadn't a word to say. It was not the protection and wisdom of her own sex Polly wanted, and every woman knew it.

At last Mrs. Inman said, impatiently, "Marcy, you may as well eat in the kitchen with Mrs. Cady and Lamb. We can't wait all night."

But Marcy took nothing quietly. If Miss Polly was scared, let her go eat in the kitchen with Mrs. Cady and Lamb. She wasn't scared and wouldn't leave.

Polly, the pretty center of all this romantic confusion, glanced at Dash's face. He had not said a word. He was gazing off into space. So she gave in to Tom. Yes she had heard that people nowadays were finding thirteen a lucky number. Evidently she was as willing to accept the latest mode in superstitions as in bonnets. Marcy was still muttering rudely, but at last the diners were ready to be seated.

Peter found himself between the pestiferous Marcy and Polly. Beyond Polly was Liz. It was Liz's duty and honor to seat the belle. But he and Liz pulled out Polly's chair together. Marcy, with sisterly good will, pulled out Peter's chair. He barely missed sitting on the floor.

Peter had been in his present state over Polly only during these last months that Dash had been neglecting her. It was half for himself and half for Dash he worshiped at this popular shrine. His wet palms, his paralyzed brain, beating heart — in fact, what might be called his "love," was something of a stop-gap for his elder brother. That he could be in love with anyone so beautiful, so courted, and five years older than himself, had not occurred to him. Then, too, she was Dash's girl. The No Trespass sign was large and clear to read. It had hurt him that Dash had not laughed and loved her the more because she was so nice and silly about thirteen at the table.

"Miss Polly —— " Peter began, determined to get ahead of Liz. He could not make his voice sound natural — far less like Dash's precise low speech. "I saw you yesterday at the launching at Briggs's."

In a whisper Marcy repeated these innocent words . . . "I saw you at the launching at Briggs's."

Polly knew exactly the state of the young gentleman's palms, brains, heart. She turned her long-lashed eyes upon him with an expression of incredulity. It was a becoming expression, but (if Peter had happened to think of it) odd that anyone could be so surprised at meeting anyone else in a town of only ten thousand inhabitants.

"Really?" she exclaimed. Peter licked his lips. To help him she added, "It was yesterday you saw me?"

"Yes. At the launching at Briggs's."

Her eyes had never been so close to his before. They were not actually blue as he had thought — really more gray. But blue lights in them. She fastened these eyes expectantly upon his face. How sweet and yet how sad was that downward turn at the cheeks. He was at a poetic age. How could one ever describe those eyes?

"Briggs's?"

"That's right. You guessed it. It was at the launching at Briggs's. Very good launch, yes. Very good launch. Ship got off in fine style."

But it was not to hear about a launch, but herself, that Miss Polly let her eyes linger in his. And now he saw actually — not gray at all — clear brilliant blue. "You were there." Everything he said to his left was being whispered back to him from his right. He took a moment from his enchantress to scowl at his tormentor. "You had on . . ." but how describe that shade between gray, lavender, and blue?

"But what did I have on, Peter? You're not going to leave me there forever, are you, without anything on?"

The girl had a provocative nature. She was not the one to let the gentlemen do their own dreaming of her beauty. She often helped their imagination with a hint. But he was too gallant to leave her forever with nothing on at a public launching.

"A dress — I guess you'd call it a French dress. Just the color of your eyes," he said soberly. "And you stood on a rock just by the surf and looked like Venus rising from the waves."

"Venus did not rise in a French dress! You must have been quite close to see the color of my eyes."

"I wasn't then. Just now" — and to Marcy he managed an aside, "Eat your soup and shut up."

"Why, Peter," said Polly. "I was planning to eat my soup. But I won't shut up. Marcy, dear" — she leaned across Peter as she spoke, her glittering Grecian curls almost in his mouth — "how do you like your lessons?"

"I hate Mrs. Rogers. I love Doctor Hobey."

He smelt her faint perfume, and, from the point of vantage he enjoyed, saw more of her enchanting bosom than was usually possible. Then he guessed it. Dash sat beyond Marcy at the head of the table. It was toward him her fragrance, her smiles, curls, bosom, and creamy voice were all directed. And Dash was turned away talking with his grandmother.

Liz broke in. Polly shrugged, and made a *moue* at him. Ever since dame school, children's parties, dancing school, Polly had "hated" Liz Inman. This is a very provocative attitude for a pretty girl to take toward a handsome, self-confident young man. It was an old game between them, beloved by both. But why didn't Dash — even look at her?

Doubtless he and his grandmother were still discussing the *Victrix*. Polly hated the *Victrix*. Not once since they had come into the dining room had Dash looked at her. A lump rose in her throat. When Mrs. Inman's note had come that afternoon, she should have declined. But she had felt she would die if she did not see Dash — and was almost equally sure she would die if she did. Polly often threatened herself and the world about her that, if this happened or that did not, "she would die." Now she wished she were home again. She glanced secretly at Dash's profile, then flung herself shamelessly into her old hate-love flirtation with Liz.

"Polly," he was saying, "if you will admit you were a horrid little girl, I'll admit I did use to pull mittens and bonnets off horrid (and pretty) little girls. It was not the act of a gentleman, but you were so enchantingly horrid and so wickedly pretty, I couldn't help it."

"You used to throw my bonnet into treetops and leave me screaming."

"I did."

"You stepped on my feet on purpose at dancing school. You stood on them."

"I know it. But a nice polite little boy never does such things to a nice polite little girl. Admit you were a stuck-up little moppet. Admit you were horrid."

Suddenly her face looked honest and sad.

"You are right, Liz. I was horrid. I still am."

The seriousness and docility with which she had taken his teasing, and a sudden curious darkening and widening of the eyes, touched Liz as her coquetry had not.

"No, no, Polly. I'll admit the truth — at last. I was — well, I was crazy about you. That's why I couldn't let you alone. Do you remember my red sled?"

"Of course. You never asked me to ride on it."

"Polly, I used to lug it to school longing and hoping . . . I can't explain. When you're young enough, you don't know how to show a girl you think about her all the time. But you do want to do something to make yourself stand out. So, well — because all the other boys begged you to ride on their sleds, I'd say, 'No, you can't.'"

"You certainly succeeded in 'standing out.' In a perfectly nasty way. You were my nightmare."

"I lay awake nights thinking, 'I'm going to put a bent pin in Polly's seat. I'm going to put a dead mouse in Polly Mompesson's pocket' — and dreaming of you — and me — always coasting down Pickering Hill on my little red sled."

She was laughing, but not paying much attention to him.

Lamb had removed the soup and carried in a juicy brown roast. This he set on the sideboard. Dash rose to carve, as he always did when home. The butler put warm plates beside him. Dash stood and glanced about the table. It was a high-chinned, masterful glance, possibly inappropriate for this small, domestic occasion — as calm and imperious as though he stood upon a quarterdeck. Polly's fingers clenched. He's trying to remember who likes their beef rare — who well done — and she bitterly resented the judicial remoteness of his gaze. Oh, why did people go on so about Liz, she wondered. All handsome men look more or less like Liz, she thought — and act like him — pah! — there's nobody in the world like Dash. And I don't know — why he acts the way he does — I don't know why . . . I don't know . . .

Dash had the carving knife in one hand and the steel in the other. He struck them together — swish, swish, swish. Polly shuddered and gritted her teeth. She never should have come to this party. Her papa had been right. She was much too nervous, the sound of the knife against the steel sent a shudder through her. She could feel one little prop after another giving way inside her. Dash's eyes met hers thoughtfully. He's thinking, Polly likes just a little of the outside, no fat, and Yorkshire pudding. That's all he's thinking about. A wave of emotion throbbed through the delicate traceries of veins, nerves, stopped the pumping of the blood in one place, held it suspended in another, closed and dried her throat. She was not sure whether she wanted to laugh or cry. But she longed to go home. Oh, Papa, Papa — I wish I hadn't come! She knew Liz was leaning over her, whispering. Was he going on about always having loved her? She neither knew nor cared. She hated Liz Inman — and wanted him to know it. Horrid, conceited beast! I love you, Dash . . . if you don't love me I shall die. She felt he must hear the words only her heart formed. But he went on with his serving. Now he was filling his own plate. His back was turned to her.

She did a dreadful thing. Her left hand disappeared under the fall of the tablecloth, and there was Liz's hand waiting for hers. The guests were so closely placed no one could notice. But even this maneuver did not take her mind off Dash. Her right hand raised a wineglass to her lips. Her left lay in Liz's muscular fingers. Her eyes were fastened desperately on Dash's back. She felt dizzy and had an illusion that he was walking away from them all — that he would not once ever turn his head and even glance back at any of them. He was walking through sideboard and roast and silver, and through wallpaper and wall. And never looked back. Not once.

"Polly," Liz was murmuring, "you've got two Inmans in love with you already. How'd you like a third?"

"Tom?" she questioned, her eyes widening with incredulity. It was much the same expression she had used earlier on Peter and with much the same effect upon the far tougher Liz.

"Why, ha, yes . . . Tom. Tom, of course."

"If you tell me Tom admires me, I'm flattered, of course."

"But not surprised. Aren't ladies always supposed to say they never guessed such a thing?" Inadvertently he had gone back to his old bantering. "You forward minx. You expect everybody to be in love with you, don't you?"

"No," her bright lips smiled, but her eyes looked almost despairing. "Only you Inmans." She was surprised to see that Liz was actually a little excited. This flattered as well as surprised her. He had none of Tom's ruddy color, but under his tan she noticed an uncomfortable flush. Locked and double-locked in the midst of all her pretty fripperies and exquisite sensibilities was an unfashionable amount of sensuality. She, too, flushed.

The "pretty" who had been invited by his mother to amuse Liz (while Polly amused Dash) sat neglected to his left. This young Derby, gossip said, was romantically attached to Liz Inman — and a great thing it would be for the Inmans to unite their debts to old King Derby's fortune. Liz had addressed her a few times, then he had quickly turned away to go on with his old fight with Polly Mompesson. Triumphantly Polly realized she had completely cut out Miss Derby. In the pursuit of her chosen career, she was as ruthless as any Yankee captain trading with an ignorant Fiji Islander. She felt no pity for the less beautiful, less experienced younger girl, forced by unkind circumstances, and Polly Mompesson, to listen to Doctor Hobey's dissertation on the sea-anemone (no, in spite of its name it was not a plant), instead of holding Liz Inman's muscular hand under the tablecloth. Polly felt no remorse. In fact, she thought it served Miss Derby right, because she had too large a bust and her nose was a trifle pudgy. In her world people were always punished for things like that. She saw no injustice.

Liz was bending close to her. As her hand had been withdrawn, he had boldly let his grasp her above the knee.

"What?" she asked him. She had not been listening because Dash had turned from his grandmother and was laughing over something Marcy had said. Marcy was insisting that the *Victrix* ship cat was to be "Robin"—just turned three months, and ready and anxious to leave the Inman kitchen and see the world.

Liz was saying that he wanted to show her those unfinished, unfurnished double parlors across the hall. He said (very blandly) that even McIntire had never got his proportions more perfect. "You can understand his artistic genius better," he said solemnly, "before a room has been cluttered up with furniture and hangings and people." But Liz's hard, bright eyes told her it was not for any architectural enjoyment he wished to show her these dark and empty rooms—after supper and alone.

She pressed her napkin to her currant-smooth lips.

"I'm sure Miss Derby will also be interested, Liz." For now she was taking the next step. First, she had made him neglect the poor loving girl. Now she would force him to repudiate her. He did so quickly.

"No. No Miss Derbys," he whispered into a shell-pink ear. "Just you."

"Oh," she said. "Thank you for having my *architectural* education so to heart. And of course, as you have said, one can understand the architect's genius much better if a room isn't too cluttered with people."

Then she had an ugly thought. The first time Dash had kissed her—four years ago and the house just built. He had used exactly this trick to get her alone. Nobody, nobody else in the world (and the little flirt knew more of such things than was proper), could kiss like Dash Inman. After him, other men's kisses seemed to be something they had read about in books. Other men "made" love as they "made" their manners, "made" conversation—but it was as if love made Dash. That first kiss of his—it was as if no woman ever in the world had been kissed before. It had meant everything to her—and now she felt certain he had told his younger brothers. Probably first Tom—and he had lured that stupid Miranda Fields into the dark and empty rooms and smacked her — most completely. And Tom had told Liz and . . . oh, by now even *Peter* knew this trick. That kiss had meant everything to her. Had it meant nothing to Dash? — except a smart maneuver?

"Yes," she went on desperately, "I'm a-dying to see those lovely rooms which I've only seen about thirty times before! But of course you'll be too busy tonight — for you'll be going straight from the table to the *Victrix*. Peter . . ."

"Yes, ma'am?"

"Peter, I'd adore to see the double parlors Mr. McIntire designed for your mother. 'Tis said he never got finer proportions. Perhaps, as soon as we've pushed Liz off to his ship . . ."

"Oh, Miss Polly, yes, Miss Polly. But you can't see much by candlelight." And he made what seemed to him a much bolder proposal. "Tomorrow morning I'll call for you in a chaise. Bring you over to see them."

Liz laughed, and Polly began to giggle. She giggled and could not stop. She went from one fit to another. Stopped to sip wine and went on again. Slowly, even the last conversation stopped (Doctor Hobey was now off on the sea-horse). All eyes were fastened in consternation on the aristocratic Miss Mompesson behaving worse than any green country girl.

The two pretties looked smugly genteel. Marcy wanted to be told the joke. Doctor Hobey's eyes were round with astonishment. Nanny West (theoretically a great friend of Polly's) was telling her doctor husband to do something. Madam Inman directed Lamb to fan her. Mrs. Inman was irritated and thinking about a pitcher of cold water over her head.

"My dear *girl*," she said, overaccenting her words as she always did when displeased, "you *must* stop. Nothing in the world is as funny as that."

The hysterical girl buried her face in her napkin. It wasn't really funny that Peter — a big boy of seventeen and ever so tall — did not know why men like to show pretty girls dark and empty rooms. She knew — but she hoped nobody else knew — that her laughter was close to tears. Dash knew. He had seen her this way before, but never in company.

If only they were alone, he would put his arms about her and hold her tight to him. He remembered the time eight months ago when Mr. Mompesson had told him he'd never consent to his daughter's marrying a man of "broken fortune." All he had said back was, Yes, sir, and he'd mend them. Polly had eavesdropped. Afterward she had berated him because he had not pointed out that her fortune was enough for the two of them, and her berating had gone off into hysterics. You couldn't argue with her when she was like that, but you could hold her tight and at last she would stop. Soon afterward, unbeknownst to her father, he had taken her to Baker's Island. He'd built a fire and night had come. With the growing of the dark, darkness had grown in them. He had almost forgotten that there are things gentlemen do not do — and one is to seduce a young lady who has entrusted herself to your care — on a lonely sea-girt island — behind her father's back. He had quite another code for, say, Pacific islands and brown girls. But this pulsing, living, wild body he held in his arms was really Polly Mompesson. And the island was Baker's. The spot was Salem Harbor. It was he who had had the sense to call a halt. He knew then it was not merely from himself he must protect her, but from her own weak, willful, passionate nature. This knowledge made him feel tenderly, almost maternally, toward her. Then he told her flat out. They could never meet again thus secretly and alone. It was dishonorable and a torment to them both. Then she had had hysterics. She had lain moaning on the sand twisting and biting her forearms. By the little light of the bonfire, he had seen the red parenthesis marks, the flash of white under the iris and the white flash of teeth. And yet, as he had held her very tightly in his arms, told her over and over to stop it, she finally had. Now if only he could put his arms about her, her head upon his shoulder, she'd soon give a little shudder and come up out of it, looking as though she did not know where she had been, and cling to him. Now, as for the first time since they had sat down, he dared look at her (for he loved her so he could scarce bear the sight of her), her face was buried in her napkin. He longed to hold her in his arms.

He knew the exact moment when her laughter began to turn to tears. He leaned toward her. "Polly!" he said sharply, commanding her to stop. Her shoulders stopped shaking. "Polly!" She put the napkin down from before her face and looked about her in bewilderment. It was as if she had forgotten where she was, was not sure who it was had commanded her in that sharp, soft voice.

Then their eyes met. Her eyes widened and stared. As if hypno-tized and still obeying him, she rose unsteadily to her feet.

All six gentlemen rose and Lamb stood stiffly at attention. The silence was appalling.

"I haven't felt well all day — a little fever, perhaps — Madam Inman . . . Mrs. Inman. I'm afraid I caught cold at the launching yesterday."

Doctor West, as a physician, had already gone to her, was stand-ing behind her chair.

"I don't see why all you young ladies don't catch cold," he put in genially. "You don't wear enough to keep out a draught — much less a hearty spring day."

"You'd better go home now, Polly," Dash said.

"I think I should. I'm nothing fit for society . . . Doctor West . . ."

Young Doctor West had a homely, horse face. And red hair as upstanding as his own character. He was an honest man, too hon-est not to let his face express the fact that he was "tickled silly" (as his young wife noticed) at Polly's suggestion that he drive her home.

"My chaise is right outside. No. don't stop to say good night. I'll have you home and in bed where you belong in three shakes of a lamb's tail."

Dash stopped abruptly. He had supposed he would take her home. But so perverse was she, so seemingly bent on her own destruction, it was another man's name that she had said. She could push other people into disaster — Liz or Peter, Dash himself. Little Miss Derby, Jack West (and that would include her great friend, Nanny Inman West), but herself she could not save.

～4～

BY THE TIME Jack West had returned from his pleasing errand — for even your most happily married man and a doctor to boot would consider taking home so much dependent loveliness a pleas-ure — Tom, for whom this little party was supposedly given, had come into his own. At last, encouraged by Dash, he was explaining the difficulties and successes that he had had. The two pretties were oh-ing and ah-ing like self-conscious little Desdemonas. Doctor Jack took his place. Opposite him Polly's had been removed.

"What was the matter with her, Jack?"

"Nerves. Oversensibilities. All those fashionable things. I blame the novels. When young Salem females read nothing but the Bible, their hysteria took a different form."

"Witches," said Madam Inman.

As a child she had heard the old folks tell of those terrible days, now a hundred years and more away. "Then the afflicted children did cry out." The trials. "I am a Bible woman." But nothing had saved the witches from hysteria. Young girls had been the worst. And wooden carts creaking down Essex Street on their way to grim Gallows Hill.

"Yes," said Marcy, who remembered every story told her. "And they hanged Tabby Inman," she went on dreamily. "They hanged her on Gallows Hill. And her face turned black and her tongue stuck out. They hanged her by the neck until she was dead . . . dead . . . dead."

"What of it, Marcy? She'd be dead by now, anyway. And she was only one of eighteen."

"They hung them all on Gallows Hill — with their tongues sticking out. And the Mompessons drove by in their coach and laughed at Tabby Inman."

"Heavens, Marcy! No. How you exaggerate! In the first place, no one ever got a coach up Gallows Hill, but —— " and Madam Inman turned to Jack: "I know what you mean. If you read in your Bible, 'Thou shalt not suffer a witch to live,' hysterics takes one form in our young girls (after all, it was hysterical young girls who accused our witches)" — "Like Sukey Mompesson" — "Hush, Marcy, I'm talking to Jack — And if you read *Pamela* and *The Coquette,* it takes another."

"Mother," said Marcy, "what are hysterics and when will I be old enough to have them?" There was seemingly nothing — good or bad — this girl did not long for.

"*Never,* Marcy. Don't think of such a thing."

"I'm too young yet."

"And I," said Madam Inman, kindly, "am too old."

What 'Sephus Hobey told her about her youngest grandchild

interested her — interested her more than did the little girl herself. She was an extremely exhausting child. So unlike dear Peter, who from babyhood had been such a comfort — such a solace. And yet (because "he had no gumption") sometimes an irritant as well.

Nanny said, "Were her papa and aunts surprised to see Polly?"

"No, no. Not at all. Squire Mompesson had asked her to return early and she was completely herself by the time we reached Federal Street. I did slip her a sleeping tablet — in case she needed it tonight. Ah! Pigeons!" And he began quickly to catch up on the course he had missed with the hearty absorption of his profession.

"Jack," Peter interrupted, "why did she?"

"I don't know," he said bluntly. "It's outside a doctor's orbit. Perhaps she has not enough to do. She's over twenty. Twenty-two, isn't she? Perhaps it is contrary to Nature for a grown woman to be unmarried and childless." And he beamed at his Nanny, four months married and pregnant already.

Nanny, when surrounded by her own family, seemed a little colorless. The broad Inman mouth was a handicap to her. The dark hair, fine white skin, an asset. She was a good unimaginative young girl that had never made anybody any trouble and never would, but when surrounded by her family seemed like a changeling. It was great good fortune for her early to escape a family nest where she never had belonged. Her one fault was abysmal curiosity. This had irritated her own family, but rather attracted Jack West. As a physician he always held the best cards. Her childish curiosity amused him. Never did a girl get a better husband for a bad fault than Nanny Inman.

As Jack West made this suggestion, that Polly's hysteria might be cured by marriage, Peter glanced surreptitiously at Dash, but Dash was trying to get more information out of Tom about the state of affairs east of Isle of France. Perhaps he had not even heard.

Then Lucy Inman corrected Marcy for playing tick-tack-toe on the beautiful damask with a fruit knife, and dessert was brought in. It was a molded masterpiece made by Mrs. Cady and supervised by Marcy. The shaking cream, delicately flavored with rum and lemon, was surmounted by a tiny wooden ship. The Inmans' house flag was on her foremast. "Victrix" was painted on her stern. Marcy was exclaiming in wonder and admiration of her own work. She had persuaded Doctor Hobey to do the printing for her. She had got the ship out of a bottle and made the house flag herself. The toothpicky little ship seemed unappetizing as well as tactless. Very little had been said of the sailing of the *Victrix* because you could not mention her without emphasizing Dash's disgrace.

Dash picked the little ship off the molded cream and smiled at Marcy. She had been expecting, fearing, reproof, for she had gone to his room and smashed his bottle and stolen from him this little ship. This smile, when she had been dreading a scolding, acted like magic upon her. Liz would have been sarcastic, Tom would have told her the truth — she was a thief. Peter, of course, wouldn't have fussed any. But Dash — you couldn't be sure what he would do. He might have crumpled her with one glance. Instead, he had raised her to Heaven with a smile. No one ever quite knew what he was going to do.

There was a ring at the front door. Lamb quivered like a bird dog, not sure whether Mrs. Cady was to leave the kitchen or he his serving.

"Please go, Lamb," said Mrs. Inman.

He came back and addressed Madam Inman in a shocked whisper.

"There's a servant come to the *front* door, Madam, with a letter for you from Captain Magee."

"Captain Magee? Fetch him in."

"Thank you, Madam. The letter or the servant?"

"Both."

"Thank you, Madam."

A big bald fellow came rolling in. Far too old to go to sea, at least in a Salem ship, he still clung to the belling canvas trousers, checked shirt, and beribboned varnished hat of his erstwhile calling.

"Why, Oscar Grafton!" Strange to call him a servant. "What's amiss?"

"Ma'am Inman . . . Captain Magee and I were both moving barrels around his cellar this evening. Fixing everything convenient for his old lady while he was gone. Then a cider press fell on him and busted him up — a little."

"Busted up Captain Magee, Oscar?"

"Fair stove in one foot. Your pa's with him, Doctor Jack. I

fetched him first thing right off. Then he wrote this letter and told me to find you."

Madam Inman held the letter at arm's length, twisting her head to get the best possible focus. She said:

"Broken ankle and probably some foot bones. Jack, how long will that take to mend?"

"Over a month for a guess, Ma'am. Two, maybe."

"She'll miss the trades." It was Liz who had spoken. She saw by his face how heart-set he was on this voyage, although he always pretended to her (and she guessed to other women) that nothing made much difference to him.

Tom said: "Sometime we are due for a big run in with the British as well as the French — out there. I'd advise no delay, Ma'am."

Marcy, with her usual tactlessness, burst out, "Grandma — Granny — you've got to pick a new captain and right away quick, haven't you?"

"Yes," said the old lady.

She stood up. Small as she was, and a little bent with years, she dominated the room. All the gentlemen rose, too, and towered above her. But she was the owner of the wharf, head of the old House of Inman. What ships were left were her ships.

"Lucy," she said to her daughter-in-law, "excuse me, please. You understand this is an emergency. And your sons. I wish to consult with them. In the gun room."

"Of course, Mother Inman."

The boys stood frozen behind their chairs. Peter was not quite sure whether he was included. She realized that. "You, too, Peter."

She led the way out of the room. The young men bowed their apologies to their mother and stalked after her. Their flexible young backs were rigid, and they moved slowly — so anxious were they not to appear overanxious. At such short notice she'd have no choice but pick one of them. Good captains didn't grow on every bush in Salem — either they'd be already to sea or waiting on orders. One of them was going to command the *Victrix*.

THE LITTLE GUN ROOM had not, like the sitting and dining rooms, been opened all day to the suns of May. It seemed still wintry here and already darkening. Here, in the old-fashioned manner, the woodwork was painted greenish blue and the floor ox-blood. The rest of the house was as glittering white as a wedding cake. Madam Inman thought this a blinding, ugly style. Over the fireplace was the very musket the boys' father had carried to Bunker Hill, and the ancient rusting matchlock a very early Ralph Inman had died beside, stuck full of Indian arrows at Bloody Brook. There were pistols such as ship officers carried, a stack of good modern rifles, boarding pikes, cutlasses, and queer weapons one or another of this seafaring, curious-minded family had picked up all over the world. One might read the history of the family in the weapons in the gun room.

"A fire, Ma'am?"

"If you please, Liz."

Liz struck a steel. The tinder and the dry wood caught. Madam Inman knew she was trapped. She couldn't get out of this room without saying to one of these three young captains, It is you who shall command the *Victrix*. Which one it would be, she had not, could not, decide. There's no hurry, she thought. Her mind was not so much upon the *Victrix* at the moment as on the family and the old House of Inman — which this one voyage might make or break. It had been started by her husband in 1750 — actually fifty years ago! What little ships — little trade! West Indies mostly.

"Please be seated, gentlemen," she said.

Lamb came in with a tray of glasses, decanters of port, brandy, whiskey, rum, Madeira, water, lemons, sugar.

"Thank you, Lamb. Put your tray here. Tom, you know your brothers' tastes. Pour drinks for yourself and them. I'll have Madeira, of course."

Self-conscious as they were, they tried to appear nonchalant. The socially gifted Liz attempted a small joke about their grandmother's fine nose for Madeira — but his bright, hard eyes slightly mocked her — We've got you cornered, Ma'am. You've no choice but pitch on one of us. You're still thinking we're too young, but you've got to do it.

"When I was a girl," she said, stalling for time, "no gentleman ever drank a drop that did not come from the grape. Wines and brandy, yes. But rum, gin, and whiskey were thought fit only for porters, foremast hands, and sluts."

She never had liked and never would that these boys drank so much rum and water, flavored with lemon, and, to make it more vulgar, they poured in sugar as well. Such slops cultivated no palate.

The small ferociously armed room danced with firelight. The orange glow flowed over the faces of the four young men, exaggerating the family resemblance.

"I wonder," she said, "did any of you happen to think that this is the first time you have all been at home for, let me see — eight — no, nearer nine years? I have longed to see you all together, not children any more, but grown men. Dash, you were sixteen and just home on the Derbys' *Sabrina* — first mate — and you'd set out naught but foremast hand. I had pitied Captain Derby when he signed you — you were such a naughty bad boy, and then you came home a full-fledged, responsible man — and an officer. Tom was going out next day — ship's boy. *Fox Fire,* Magee master. Liz — let me see, you were thirteen — still at Exeter. Peter —— " She stopped.

She'd never forget that day. Old Doctor West had come to her privately in her counting-house to say he did not want to worry Peter's mother, but someone in the family should know Peter was going to be hard to raise. He did not like the way his colds held on. Of course, nothing to worry about — and Madam Inman had been worrying ever since. She looked from one grandson to the other, and pitied them as the old often pity the young. She had seen many other equally handsome lads grown white, bent, old. The unself-conscious, radiant — well, yes, *beauty* of young manhood is something no man ever sees in another man. No young woman can ever realize how brief it is. Perhaps, she thought, only old women understand. There they sat — that dangerous, wicked younger generation, who preferred "slops" to Madeira and pantaloons to breeches, who had cut off their pigtails, and yet into whose hands, for better or worse, her generation must pass on the responsibilities of the House of Inman — and the world. The thought of eight years ago carried her to earlier memories.

"Now you are together, I'd like to say something to you about the history of the House. Fifty years ago your grandfather started out as a West Indy trader — real good, cautious man. Tom's most like him. And he did real well. But the war with England broke that trade, and he went into privateering with various partners I won't stop to mention; and at the end of the Revolution every ship was lost — except the brig *Fox Fire*. She was building. By then your father was a grown man — you were twelve when he died, Dash — you remember him? It was his lungs got him. Died and buried in Surinam. Well, you know how he took *Fox Fire* on a venture to the Baltic. Went out in stone ballast. We hadn't a staple to ship. Those were very desperate days with American merchantmen. But we — we Inmans — did get a little corner on the Baltic trade and other men found the way to trade to India and China. Of course, we ventured there — but didn't do real well. Luck against us — the *Antelope*, the *Harlequin,* and the *Dorcas* — every one an East Injunman and every one lost within the last two years. But we've done a good trade buying up other folks' Indy goods and toting them to Russia. We're mighty well known at Petersburg, Hamburg, Lübeck. Yet I know bigger fortunes, greater gambles, come from the Far East. I didn't quite cotton to the idea of risking so much — in fact, making a last throw on another East Injunman. But I've done it."

She paused and sipped her Madeira.

"You were naught but a parcel of children," she said, "when first your father died and, two months later, your grandfather. Then I saw I had to step in. I've never tried to do more than hold things together 'gainst the time you were grown men. King Derby and Father Crowninshield, as *you* call him, both advised me to sell out everything — wharf, vessels, warehouses. But I held on. And one thing I have now I had not ten years ago — and that is, three young gentlemen — everyone a captain, and folk tell me every one good and able. If the *Antelope* had but cleared Cape Cod, we as a House would be back on our feet now. But she didn't. It's no time to go putting all our eggs in one basket — but that I have. I picked the most careful man I could think of — Captain Ephraim Magee — and he's fallen from under me. I know you resent it that I've so often let captain's share go outside the family — and was so doing once more with the new ship. Tom — he's twenty-three, and might be considered old enough. But no one thought to see him for six months more. Liz — he'd never commanded ship of mine until this last voyage of the *Mermaid* — and right smartly he traded, too." She did not mention Dash.

Tom thought: If I'd have been here, I'd have got her. I guess she's giving her to me. It's lucky I remind her of Grandfer. But it's going to be hard on Dash. She's his ship. But even if Ma'am said, "Dash, you go," would Dash do it? Or was he too sot on setting and stewing the whole twelve months in his own juice? No matter how well you knew him, like a cat you couldn't say which way he'd jump.

Liz knew he would get her. If anything had happened to Magee after sailing, Liz as first mate would automatically take over command. And he had proved his worth as captain — even to his skeptical grandmother. He knew he was good — even if he did like fancy waistcoats. But there was a hard factualness about him. He knew he wasn't, and never would be, as good as Dash. It sickened him to face the truth. And he felt ashamed that he had been holding Polly's hand under the tablecloth. His loyalty to Dash surged through him and shamed him.

Peter was the only one who made no pretense at nonchalance. He was sitting next to Dash, holding his thumbs until the knuckles whitened. "O God," he prayed, "make her say it. O God, give Dash the *Victrix* . . . Keep me locked in Salem all my life — but let Dash go."

It was Peter's sharp and agonized face Madam Inman looked at as she next spoke. Dash was leaning so far back in his chair and out of the firelight, she couldn't see him.

"I've never gone back on my word," she said; "the whole business has been built upon that fact. I said the captain who lost the *Antelope* was to have no ship of mine to waste for a whole year. Of course, if he wanted somebody else's, he could take it. Gentlemen, tonight I go back on my word. Dash, please to consider yourself master of the *Victrix*."

She could hear the air go out of Peter as he collapsed with relief. But would Dash go? Had he punished himself enough to satisfy whatever god or demon lived with him? Even Madam Inman, who approved of such atonement, feared he would refuse.

Dash moved, and Madam Inman saw his face. Sometimes she

forgot how young twenty-four is. He was the eldest. She had had to count on him for so much so early. He had not had much care-free boyhood — responsibility had come over-young to him. But still he was a child to her.

He said quietly: "Ma'am, I thank you for your confidence in me — once more. I will do with the *Victrix* to the best of my ability."

There was no look of disappointment on the other brothers' faces. Peter had tears of joy in his eyes.

"Dash, I need give you no orders. You know more of her cargo and route than I do. I'll send Lamb to Magee to get her papers."

"I've got them, in my pocket."

"You have? You always were the fellow to get ahead of yourself. But mind ye this, Captain Dash. The *Victrix* is not insured beyond Batavia. You'll be right cautious?"

"Aye — that I will."

"Remember Bible reading every Lord's Day. Some folks say there's no Sabbath off soundings. That's not true of my ships. Now, I guess you boys will be pretty busy fitting up Dash to go. I'll make your apologies in the sitting room and tell 'em what's what. Now — one word more before you go. I've been proud of you often before — but never prouder than tonight when I read in your faces every one of you wanted Dash to go — to be set above yourself. So long as you brothers hold fast and together like that, there's no danger can come to the House of Inman."

~6~

THE BOYS STOOD, tall, dark, self-controlled, and bowed their grand-mother out of the room with the grand old-fashioned bows she liked. Then the three oldest shot up the stairs, running for the attic and Dash's chest. Peter came more slowly. He wasn't a cap-tain, and he never would be. But now, with Dash let loose and happy, he could do next best — go to Harvard. He had saved up the money. It was nothing but his inability to let Dash sulk alone that had kept him home. Instinctively, he knew that he must break free of his family tradition — make a place and a name for himself, utterly shut of what the name Inman stood for. Here he would never be anything but the boy not good enough to go to sea — but at Harvard . . .

In the dark of the hall he felt himself grasped by something short, compact, powerful. Marcy had hidden under the stairs.

"Peter, Peter! Dash got her?"

"You've guessed it."

"I knew it — I knew it!" She still had not recovered from that moment when she had expected to be snubbed for breaking his bottle, stealing his ship, and had received a smile.

"Dash! Dash!" she screamed, running up the stairs. "You've got her! You've got her!"

"Aye, Marcy," his voice floated down from above; "that I did." His voice hung in the air a warm and living thing.

Peter knew a voice like that would get more results from a crew than Tom's loudest oaths or Liz's bitterest invective. Why couldn't Ma'am ship Peter as clerk? He wanted to cling to Dash and never leave him. He was filling out a little. He had hardly coughed all winter. Harvard (and he knew it) would never be but a second choice for him. He longed for the Far East — and the swarming, gold-roofed cities. Tigers burning in the night. The white elephants bearing the kings of Siam. The jewels on the women's ankles. The palmy coral atolls. Black volcanic islands rising mysteriously from the Pacific floor — the burning blue and the loneliness of the great scarce-known Pacific. Pirate junks — with bats' wings. Wives wrapped in dead men's arms singing as the flames leaped. Bearers running down from the mountains with the tea. This was the world beyond this world, of which he dreamed — a world beyond good and evil, death and time. Sometime he would see it. But even as he thought of it (and how little he had coughed), he began to cough. It was a hacking, dry cough.

He stood undecided in the lower hall. He was loath to join the females (and Doctors Hobey and West) in the sitting room. And loath to intrude himself upon his older brothers. He could hear them getting Dash's chest down. He heard Liz call the "sing-out," a "Yo-ho heave-ho . . . roll and go." They were getting a little rackety. Mrs. Inman had seen to it that her sons did not bring loud-voices, big oaths, uncouth walks, forecastle manners, home with them from the sea. They'd be getting a reprimand for all this noise.

"Yo-ho heave, ho . . . roll and go!"

Sure enough, the sitting-room door opened and out shot Lamb, and he was frightened because, Peter guessed, his mother had told him to reprove the young gentlemen for their sea-yowlings, and never in all his life had he reproved three Yankee captains at once before. It was a lot to expect at fifteen cents an hour.

Marcy came down the stairs. Around her neck were the jawbones of a shark — one of Dash's souvenirs. Evidently he had bribed her to keep out of the way.

"If you fall down," said Peter, "you'll get guillotined."

"Better people than I have been guillotined," she said airily. The Inmans were Federalists, and did not hold with France.

"Well, you go sit with Mother. Do. And don't go bothering us men any more."

"If I bother, Dash might give me his mummified monkey."

"No. Stay down here and gossip and sew like a good girl — and try not to talk all the time."

She gave him a pretty look out of her bright greenish eyes. "Nobody in there except 'Sephus wants me."

"Don't go calling him 'Sephus, just because we men sometimes do. Marcy, I'll tell you what you can do. You go to the kitchen and get a basket and catch the kitten to sail as the ship's cat."

"Oh, yes, yes! It's Robin is going to go, and I'll carry her down myself and put her on — just as the *Victrix* sails."

Lamb came slinking down the stairs, looking more frightened than when he went up.

~7~

IT WAS LONG after midnight. Peter lay half-asleep on Dash's maidenly pink and silver bed. He knew his brother was not really doing anything — just fiddling with his duds. Everyone else in the house was asleep. Liz, as the mate, already was aboard with the ships' people. And so was Dan Obrian, the second. The captain went on last and traditionally with some style and fanfare. There'd not be much style to this almost secret sailing. His own family, of course, would go down to see the ship sail. That's why they were wisely sleeping now while they could. If the ship sailed. Not a whiff of a breeze had yet come.

"Get up, Pete," Dash ordered. "I've got to move the bed."

Set in the baseboard and behind the bed, Dash had recently contrived himself a secret "glory hole." Peter squatted beside him with the candle and watched him take out the ten thousand dollars in gold secreted there. Two hundred dollars of it represented Peter's venture upon the *Victrix*. All the family had, according to their financial capacity, ventured on her. It had been painfully accumulated. Now Dash seemed ready to repack his whole chest to make place for it. Obviously, he was stalling for some reason. Perhaps he himself had begun to doubt his own prognostication of the weather. Here also Peter kept the money for Harvard.

"Pete?"

"Aye?"

"Do you want to sew on a button for me?"

"Aye — of course."

He moved the candle closer and took up the ditty-bag. The pale nankeen jacket (such as a gentleman might wear in, say, Bombay) had lain packed away so long, it still had a little of the heady scent of the Far East. Peter's efforts to thread the needle and tighten the horn button woke him up entirely. The great clock on the landing cleared its throat and struck two. Then, like a pack of puppies after it, Liz's French clocks from across the hall began to chirp. Last thing Liz had done was to set his clocks himself and select a few as a venture on the *Victrix*. And the idiot boy was to look sharp, keep these left behind wound and set until he returned. Peter yawned contentedly. Those little clocks weren't going to be wound until a year, two years from now, or whenever the *Victrix's* returning sails were sighted. He listened to his little charges and more intently he listened for the wind. Dash was a bit fretted, he noticed. Perhaps he, too, had begun to doubt it.

"Pete?"

"Aye."

"When are you going to Harvard?"

"I've been thinking. Well, yes, I'm going — next term. It doesn't take much money. I've saved all my clerk's wages. And I figure I've enough to start on."

"Pete, you've got to go! You know that? You've *got* to go."

"Yes, I know it."

So Dash knew as well as Peter that he must not bide about Salem, the one unsuccessful member of his family. He must break out from the pattern. Go his own way in a different world.

Dash had given up his fiddling. He sat squarely on his shut chest. He'd made up his mind to something. "Perhaps sometime, if happens you are in Marblehead, you might look up a girl for me . . . over there."

"Gosh, Dash . . . aye, aye . . . of course."

"You tell her how I came to sail so suddenly."

"I'll tell her."

Dash went to the pretty painted commode, took out the Dutch sextant Liz had longed for. His hands caressed it as he turned its screws.

"You tell her I won't be back for some time . . . and say good-bye. No, put it a bit stronger than that. You know — more loving."

"You're the captain."

Peter thought of Polly off into the vapors because Dash couldn't bear even to look at her.

"No. I guess I'd better write her a letter — flat out."

He went to his chest, took out an ink horn and a quill pen. Very slowly he sharpened the pen with the little knife on his watch chain. Not finding notepaper to hand, he took up a ledger and tore out a back page. Deliberately he moved the candle closer to him. So this was why he had been stalling around the last half-hour. This was what he had been so slow to make up his mind about."

"She doesn't read easily," he said. "I'll have to almost print it for her." Peter watched him carefully forming each letter, saw him reach in his chest again, take out red sealing wax, fold the brief letter, and seal it.

"Now that's settled. Give her the letter."

"Aye. I suppose so."

"Now I want a hand with my chest. I'll get a handcart from the barn."

He had a brace of pistols on the bed. Peter took one up.

"I'll go along and help guard."

"Good."

"But Dash . . ."

He couldn't let him go like this, without one word for Polly. Dash had been in his shirt-sleeves. Now he stood up and slapped his gray beaver hat on his head. He pulled his blue coat about his well-set strong shoulders and buttoned the silver buttons. As he assumed these symbols of his masterhood, unaccountably Peter's heart sank. That hat, coat, and the very expression on his face changed. He was no longer Peter's Dash. He was no more the moody, somewhat romantic figure he had been during the eight months of his self-imposed punishment. Once again the world was his ovster and the seven seas lay at his feet.

"Well?" Dash demanded.

Peter had nothing to say to this magnificent stranger. He hasn't told me that girl's name, he thought. I've a mind not to ask him. But he did.

"You haven't said who she is."

"I haven't? Well, it's on the outside of the letter." He saw a flick in the expressive dark eyes that reminded him unpleasantly of Liz's idiot boy.

"Of course, I'll do as you say, Dash. But . . . oh, my God, why ever did you . . . "

"Belay!" Dash commanded. This meant you go no farther in your complaints.

You'll break Polly's heart, Peter thought wildly. She loves you so. What the hell, Dash . . . what the hell? He studied the address on the letter in his hands.

"Dulcey Delaney?" He looked at Dash reproachfully. "You were over in Marblehead quite a lot this spring. Buying salt fish for ships and so on?"

"Yes. Quite a lot. Now you help me with this chest. And keep an eye on that girl. Help her all she needs. I'm much beholden to her."

"I'll go over later today."

"There's no hurry. Just sometime."

Dash stood waiting, mysterious and remote. Peter tried to think of exactly the right thing to say about Polly. He couldn't bear to let him go slipping off out of things like this. Gone for a year at least, perhaps two years. Or longer.

"Dash . . . "

The Captain lifted a hand commanding silence. He was listening and grinning. His eyes glittered in the candlelight. Then Peter heard it, too. Through the soft, still-damp leaves of May came the merest lisp of a wind.

"Wait," Dash whispered. The curtains at the open window quivered and blew inward. "South." It came scented and warm as south winds often come, heavy with lilacs. Then stopped, rested a moment, and made a fresh bold start. Right up Essex Street it blew, slipping about the house, rustling the trees on the Common — fresh, taut, and full of conversation.

"South South by west."

Dash lightly tossed the sextant and caught it. His hat was pushed far back on his head. His square mouth had broadened and showed a line of white lower teeth. There was not a thing Peter could say to him. You might as well talk to the wind itself. He was "the hind set free" in the Bible.

For him there was no longer a Polly, nor a Dulcey person. No mother to nag him, or grandmother to pry at him. No Peter either to go to Harvard or clerk his little life away on a little stool. Really there was no Salem, no firm land. Nothing but heavens above him and the sea below and a breeze to carry him.

As they listened, a blind blew shut.

Peter could not put out hand nor word to stop him.

"Roll and go!" said Dash.

But he was really gone already.

Chapter Three

~~~~~~~~~~~~~~~~~~~~~~~~~~~~~~~~~~~~

PETER GLANCED at his brother's empty stool. He himself felt as empty, and his head as cluttered as his brother's desk. Dash had never come back to redd it up. It was, as a sailor would say, a hurrah's nest, "everything on top and nothing to hand." He'd put it shipshape. Dash often left confusion behind him on shore, but he guessed all was in good sea order aboard his ship. The *Victrix* had been gone six hours.

By closing his eyes he could see once more the silent, opalescent dawn — so dewy and wet, so pearly-soft, so dappled. Birds chirping from bushes, gulls half-awake, floating in over the wharves. And the cries of the *Victrix* seamen — "Yo-ho *yeoh*!" and up came the anchor. "Oh, masthead, here ahoy!" The sails had been loosened. She leaned gently upon the breeze. And there upon the quarter-deck he had seen Dash diminish and disappear.

The sails of a young ship were not white, but a soft dun color. The sailmakers did not bleach their canvas. They left that to sun, sea, and time. So a young ship was always a tawny thing — as a young gull. That secretive, soft color, Peter thought, is indeed the color of youth. Only with maturity are ships, gulls, horses, white.

By now decks are cleaned and anchors stowed. And Liz, as chief mate, might have written already that first line in the log — a line which so often began Salem logs.

Pigeon Hill, bore N.N.W. Distance 7 leagues. From which I take my departure.

73

Already the people had been divided into larboard and starboard watch. And Dash had stood at the break of the poop and made one of those speeches masters always make first day out, promising to be decent and careful of his people, and demanding in return complete, instantaneous obedience to himself and Mr. Inman and Mr. Obrian. Because it was Dash, the sailors would toss caps and cheer him. And cheer him again. It had been almost unseemly when Peter and Dash had arrived together around two this morning and the men had realized it was Captain Dash himself who would command them, not staid Captain Magee. They'd yelled their heads off. And Dash had had to silence them.

By now those two boys who had never been to sea before would be pretty well rid of all their longshore wash and wish they were back on their farms once more. The scuttle butts were filled with fresh water. The black cook, Doctor Zack, was singing in his galley — you could smell coffee and scouse cooking. A mate was crying, "Tumble up here and make sail," and the *Victrix,* leaning over in the wind, was off on her first long tack, throwing back the water, the woman at her prow staring fixedly at nothing, dangling her green wreath above the heads of fishes, waves, and drowned men.

Yes. In six hours the routine of the ship would be well established — a routine nothing but disaster or landfall ever broke.

Madam Inman came in from her office, a gigantic old-fashioned spyglass under her arm. She had little view from her window, and was no longer pretending this could be considered a working day.

"It's a fair sight," she said — "eleven great ships all at once struggling to be free of wharves and anchorage and beating out to sea." Together they leaned out of Peter's window.

"And the twelfth is well off and away."

"Ah . . . ah . . . The *Brutus* is afoul of the *Belisarius.* It would be a Derby ship afoul a Crowninshield, wouldn't it?"

"Look," said Peter. "The *Herald's* only taking on her powder *now.* We had ours on a week ago."

"We shouldn't have. We might have blown the wharf right out of the harbor. But Dash would rather blow up a wharf and his grandmother and half of Salem than keep that ship waiting. He never consulted *me.*"

They could hear the ancient, unearthly sing-out of the seamen as anchors came up and heavy foresails were sheeted home. The sails filled like the sudden opening of gigantic sea flowers as wind and sun caught them.

At every foremast flew the house flag of the owner. The dark blue and scarlet crown of the Crowninshields. The Derbys' white square — "that pillowslip," Madam Inman called it contemptuously. Yet this flag had brought home the greatest wealth America had ever known. There was the Hodges' red and white checkerboard. Forrester's white, edged with navy. All displayed the flag of their young country. But, judging from the variations in these flags, no one seemed quite sure just what it was.

"The *Dawn*," she said. "Twenty-four guns. She's trying for the Mediterranean. Captain White said on 'Change yesterday a man can afford to lose four out of five ships on the Mediterranean route and make a handsome profit. But he wasn't thinking of the men. Some people care more for profit than human beings. I couldn't bear sending a ship to the Mediterranean just now. Peter, take this glass. See if you can make out how many of those guns are quaker."

Peter obediently studied the *Dawn*. "Ten of them for a guess."

"I'm not sure but our quaker guns have served us as well as our metal ones. Your father once saved his life, in a wreck, riding on a quaker gun."

"We're at war with France in all but name, and there are always the Algerian pirates. Quaker guns don't help against them."

"Peter." She was relishing the sight of a heavy brig trying to clear Union Wharf. They had their sweeps out. "I'm declaring a holiday. Long as I have lived I've never seen such a sight before. Mr. Fessenden's already over to Beverly getting a new hoist for the *Mermaid*. And Tom hasn't even shown up yet."

"Tom's sleeping."

"He didn't even get up to see the *Victrix* sail."

"No. Tom always sleeps when he first gets home. And then he drives over to Newburyport to see that Miranda Fields of his."

"Well, I'm locking up the counting-house. Then I'm going up on my roof and pure enjoy myself."

She could not say, "Come with me, Peter." The young can say, "Come with me," to the young. The old must say, "I am doing so-and-so — come with me if you wish." She paused, hoping he would say, "I will come too." But he was thinking of Marblehead and did not. He gave his grandmother a steadying hand down the ladder-like outside stairs leading to the wharf. It was only since the *Antelope* had been lost that she ever needed a hand. She was thinking, When I get too stiff to navigate the stairs, then I'll retire. Fact is, if anything goes wrong with the *Victrix,* I'll have to retire anyway — there won't be a thing left.

Her house stood at the head of the wharf. It was black with time, steep-pitched, crabbed. The second story overhung the first. Lilacs reached to the eaves. About the enormous central chimney was one modern convenience — a captain's walk. Nobody knew how old this house was — "the witch house," children called it. For it was here Tabitha Inman had been taken up for witchcraft — at this very hearth she had made her poppets. Here before this door the horse of a certain Cecil Mompesson had fallen down dead. And it was his little daughter who had said she had seen Goody Inman making an evil sign. This had been the first accusation against the old woman. But not the last.

Strange, Madam Inman thought, even a hundred years and more ago, Inmans and Mompessons hadn't mixed, and had becharmed each other. And seemly Mompesson girls had always been hysterical little things.

She herself had come here a bride over fifty years ago. And the wharf had been naught more than a few boxes of cob — and those out of line. But year by year the bigger trade and the wharves stretching out and out, desperately reaching for deeper water — and the lawsuits!

Now such fortunes were being made, you could not believe your eyes, nor the figures you saw on the custom-house books. Neither her son nor her husband had lived quite long enough actually to see this flamboyant success. Seemingly the wealth of the world was funneling to Salem. Springing up out of it came the great houses, silk gowns, pianos, French perfumes and French hair-dressing. Gardens, carriages, imported carriage horses. Servants (not old-fashioned "help"), silver, gold, diamonds. And ladies could afford to have the vapors, and gentlemen gout, valets mistresses. She could not see that anyone was better off. She thought the East India trade had been a corrupting influence upon the virtuous old towns of the Puritans. She did not like the modern taste in houses — ugly square boxes, she thought them. Nor the white woodwork inside, nor the spindly French furniture. Nor the skimpy, costly, half-naked way women dressed. She did not like the new fashion of naming girls Pamela, Lucinda, Clarabelle, Clarissa, Roxanna. She thought the stagecoaches went too fast these days — it did no one any harm to get stuck in a slough now and then: it gave them time to think. That was the trouble with the world today. People went so fast they had no time to think where they were going. She did not like the formality of the gardens, nor the informality of manners.

Peter interrupted her thoughts. "Grandmother . . ."

"What, Peter?"

"How much water does Salem Harbor draw?"

"Why, you know — 'tis a wretched poor harbor."

"About ten feet or so?"

"At low tide, yes."

"If our ships get as much bigger in the next twenty years as in the last, they'll not be able to go in and out the harbor. Then I wonder what will happen to Salem."

She stood stock-still and stared at him. "Why, Peter Inman, there's no point in a ship being more'n four hundred tons. Of course, the British and the Dutch have been building over one thousand tons for years. But they can't go where we can go — not in uncharted waters. That's why we've grown so rich — going where nobody else has ever traded. Going where nothing's charted properly."

Peter said slowly, "Sometime every port in the world will be charted and the channels plainly marked."

"Nonsense!" she said briskly. It sounded almost like blasphemy to her, and she thought of God's words to Job, "Where wast thou when I laid the foundations of the earth? Declare, if thou hast understanding, who determined the measures thereof, if thou knowest."

She had a sudden vision of Salem deserted without one white topsail in sight. It couldn't be. Yes . . . it could be. Thank God, she would not live to see it.

Peter did not offer to go with her. At her own gate he handed her the spyglass. "You'll have company up there," he said, and gestured at the captain's walk.

Standing close to the old stacked chimney was a solitary black figure, Doctor Hobey. He had his spyglass to one eye. As he stood there, the wind flapped him a little and he looked absurdly like a weathervane. Only a little down the street, Father Crowninshield, as the Inmans called this distant relative, had a weathervane just like him atop his house — a merchant with glass eyes, a brass spyglass.

Thus it was, all over Salem. Men, women, and children, sailors and fancy girls, clergymen, merchants, riggers, ropemakers, sailmakers, hostlers, school teachers (and their little scholars), gentlemen, ladies and scullery maids, black folk and fish peddlers, paupers, nurses with babes in arms — all had deserted the workaday world below them and taken to hilltop and housetop, captains' walks, cupolas, trees, ridgepoles. They clung to the upper branches of Salem like roosting birds.

So Salem watched as one great ship after another made sail and followed, the one behind the other, like a flock of sheep passing through a gate of water between the Miseries and Baker's Island.

Doctor Hobey thought it a beautiful sight. The May sky so blue and softly flecked with clouds — the wind so fair, the ships stately as goddesses inevitably making their departure. Ships under sail! What a calm, commanding, celestial air they had! And God bless you, he thought, for with them, as he well knew, went the hearts of Salem.

❧ 2 ❧

THE OLD BARN harmonized but ill with the glittering glory of the new house. Peter sat inside on a short bin. Davy Jones, the Newfoundland yard dog, pressed against him. The bear-like head, the good little eyes, yearned up at him as Peter absent-mindedly fondled his ears. Davy Jones's tail thumped the splintered floor in ecstasy.

Mr. Mullins was harnessing Bacchus and Ariadne to the carriage. Until he finished, Peter had no chance to get out Dolly and the old chaise and start for Marblehead.

The coachman was a Yankee, bony, leathery, lantern-jawed. He had suspicious gimlet eyes, hidden under gray-thatched eyebrows. Mrs. Inman considered him perfect — especially when he would go month after month with no pay. She could not quite afford to keep a carriage, but did so on a shoestring. It was almost impossible to get a Yankee man into livery, upon a box. Most of her friends had black men or coachmen imported by their husbands from England or Ireland. But she had said she must think of her small boys. Boys will hang about barns. She did not want them to hear "things" from a coarse African or ignorant Irishman. She was lucky to have an old Yankee with all the old Yankee virtues. Mullins had fought at Bunker Hill, Cowpens, Yorktown — that was proof he was a high-minded man. He was smart enough to realize that he could (when paid) earn a better living on a box in Salem than hoeing his ancestral, hard-scrabble acres over in Tewksbury. She had thought for more than ten years that he was perfect. But she knew him only formally — on his box. Not in his moments of relaxation. In a barn, his conversation was extremely barny. Mr. Mullins had been, in some ways, a liberal education for young gentlemen with their way to make at sea.

Even as Mr. Mullins harnessed the bay pair (old horses, but as carefully preserved as ancient belles), he was rumbling with oaths, obscenity, profanity. It was as though he had a witches' cauldron in his little round belly and had only to open his mouth and out came smoke, nauseous gases. It was not at the provoking animals this turgid stream was directed (Ariadne would not back straight), but at his employer. Behind her back, with true old Yankee democracy that would have amazed Mrs. Inman, he called her "Lu-lu."

Peter should have been on his feet striking that long goat face. Men were not supposed to take insults to ladies (especially to their mothers) sitting down. But familiarity with Mr. Mullins's vocabulary had not so much bred contempt as an indifference so complete it was almost deafness. He thought of Marblehead and went on pulling Davy's ears.

Mr. Mullins and the four Inman boys had had years of warfare. They, being young and high-spirited, would catch his verbal missiles and throw them back at him. But they never had blabbed on him, and time had developed between them something less than friendship but complete confidence. All this had been behind Lucy Inman's back. It had been understood from the beginning that men stuck together.

Grumbling, the coachman put on his high rosetted hat and his mulberry livery coat. He swore at both, accusing them of a curious assortment of sexual perversions. He settled a greasy black stock around his stringly old neck. And what did Lu-lu mean, keeping his horses waiting! He did not like to leave the barn until he actually saw Mrs. Inman standing at the side entry. Now he began dadblasting her for her tardiness.

Little Joe, the shivering Italian greyhound, sat outside the necessary, which was well concealed with lattices and trumpet vines, and waited. Although Davy was the most decent of creatures — honest, noble, dignified — Little Joe was a cheat, a liar, and notoriously low-minded. For instance, nobody could modestly "slip out back" without danger of his attendance. By his indecent guard duty he advertised just where they were. If he got bored, he scratched. When the door opened, he barked. The yard dog had only an old strap about his enormous neck. Little Joe's collar was yellow kid studded with silver gilt. But clothes do not make the gentleman. Nor weight the fighter. Davy, big as a man, never quarreled. Little Joe (behind Davy's back) sneered at every dog in Salem. Davy was humble. He would have made a better watchdog if he had had more self-confidence. Little Joe liked to show off. He'd run down Essex Street, with one leg held up, merely to show how well he could do it. He was always getting above himself, jumping on damask chairs and snarling at anyone who dared try to dislodge him. He bit people, going up behind to do his nipping, and without warning — thus proving himself less honorable than a rattlesnake. Davy was a good clean fellow. There was no offal so old, or dung so fresh, that Little Joe would not roll in it.

Lucy Inman was proud of him as a fashionable accessory, but she didn't like him. Her boys teased the nervous little thing. Marcy, who had more affection in her than she had objects on which to dispose it, tried to pet him. Of all the world, he despised Marcy most. But he kept smartly out of Mrs. Cady's way and Mr. Mullins's. Both, by the nature of their callings, often carried brooms. He respected the cats — and there were never less than four or five of them about. When he saw a cat, he ran first.

Little Joe barked. Mr. Mullins peered at the lattices and trumpet vines about the necessary, and, with so scatological a remark it was well Peter was not listening, mounted the box.

"You tripe," said Peter. "Maybe this time you'll fall off your monkey seat and break that piece of brass pipe with a whistle in it you call your neck . . ."

"Peterkins, you can . . ."

"Sure I can," said Peter, not realizing he had agreed to deeds luckily beyond the power of any man.

The polished hooves, the harness, the bay coats of the horses flashed, the bright wheels glittered, and with a flourish the carriage drew up to the side entry where Mrs. Inman waited. Mr. Mullins respectfully touched his rosette. Little Joe, with a sneer, sprang into the carriage, scratching at the dove-gray broadcloth to make a comfortable spot for his grasshopper body. Mrs. Inman, tastefully dressed in puce with a little shawl to match the one scarlet feather in her hat (à la banditti), sat beside him, but not closely enough to get scolded.

"Where's Peter?" she asked. "I saw him five minutes ago."

"*Master* Peter" — his inflection corrected her careless informality — "is in the barn, Madam."

She thought of calling to Peter to go with her out to some headland where they could watch the departure of the ships. But yesterday she had had Liz beside her. Ever since he had been in his petticoats, Liz had been her favorite companion for carriage exercise. Peter somehow always spoiled it. Only last week he had assumed the most exaggerated air, bowing left and right at the "canaille" in the street, telling Mullins to keep right on and he'd come to the guillotine. She had not been able to help laughing at him. But it was nothing to laugh at. People were saying if Mr. Jefferson was elected there really would be a guillotine right here in Salem. Luckily, dear General Washington had died a few months before. His would have been the first head to roll. No . . . she did not quite want Peter. She could have pulled Tom out of bed, but he would merely have gone to sleep again. Only Liz, Mr. Mullins, and Little Joe really understood the almost ritualistic importance of a lady abroad in her own carriage. Then she thought of Cousin Frances.

At heart, unknown to herself, Lucy Inman did not like men. They were too prone to want their own way. Often they drank and got noisy and boastful. You just got a new dress fitted and found you were with child. They did not care what they did with their pipes and their feet and newspapers. The money they made on their ventures they wanted to put into more ships — not more wallpaper. But she disliked them as much for their virtues as for their faults — their bigger turn of mind, more spacious attitudes toward life, she found boring. She was at her best with other women — who adored her as they often will a woman who seems to have everything to make her desirable to the gentlemen and yet prefers her own sex. She was a little lioness at ladies' tea parties, witty, pretty, fashionable. As a young girl her skepticism of the male had not shown, or had seemed like girlish coquetry. But in middle age it was more apparent. Like many women of her type, she had married well. In her way she had loved her husband, but had enjoyed him most when he was at sea and she could brag about him to the girls. Of all her friends, Frances Cunningham was dearest.

"Mullins."

"Please, Madam?"

"Mullins, do turn the corner into Essex and stop for Mrs. Cunningham."

"Yes, Madam."

Since her husband's death, Frances Cunningham had rented the lower floor of her house to the Misses Stackpool. Their modest sign proclaimed "Ladies' Goods." On either side of the front door the windows of the old living rooms showed glimpses of gloves, slippers, gauzes from India, artificial flowers from France. Poor Frances! How dreadful to be forced to rent most of your own house for a shop — have only the back door, back stairs, and the upper chambers for oneself. Captain Cunningham and Captain Inman had been men of the same age, so Lucy thought of Frances as her own contemporary. She was really nearer to her son's ages, but Frances called them by their first names and their mother had taught them to call her "Cousin Frances." There was no blood relationship. She herself referred to Frances as "my young friend."

Lucy was glad she had thought of her. Being kind to this poor young friend of hers took her mind a little off her loss of Liz.

The carriage swayed to a halt. Gingerly Mrs. Inman prodded Little Joe. He was as bright as a silver dollar and long ago she had taught him to get out at this house, run to the back door, bark and scratch until Frances appeared. Little Joe wrinkled a supercilious lip as though he felt it beneath his dignity to fetch anyone out of such a common house. But he jumped from the carriage and, unfortunately, looked behind.

Davy Jones had never ridden in the carriage, but he yearned toward it. Today he had followed it at a respectful distance. When Little Joe saw what this great black hulk of a dog had dared to do, he flew into a paroxysm. His eyes popped and glazed with hate. The hair stood up on his skinny back. He screamed and bared teeth and gums. The big dog obediently started for home. Little Joe snapped at him, but Davy did not turn his head. He kept on going.

Before Mrs. Inman could get herself out, Mrs. Cunningham appeared. She was plump, and trim as a bird. Her hair was the russet of a brown thrasher — heavy, coarse hair, such as in ill health tends to look like a wig. Her eyes were very quick, pretty, dark and beady as a bird's. And like a bird she was continually cocking her head, her eyes. She twittered, and hopped about.

It was "darling Frances" and "dearest Lucy" as the ladies, who had not seen each other for three days, embraced. No, no. No need to change . . . just fetch a bonnet and a shawl. And the day's so warm you may want your parasol. Both agreed they would not miss that last sight of the ships for anything.

The ladies settled themselves and gave up whistling for Little Joe. They were still discussing where they would go. Mrs. Inman noticed a man, standing with his back to the street, reaching inside one of the windows in which the Stackpools showed their modest wares. A robbery in broad daylight? No, he was very artfully arranging the display inside. He had a silver fan in one hand, pink silk stockings over his arm. In the other hand was a fashion doll. He arranged his goods, then stepped back on the sidewalk to study the artistic effect.

"Oh, Frances, who is that?"

"Hush, dear, wait till we've started." Mrs. Inman called "Nahant" to her coachman. The carriage rolled forward. She craned her neck to watch the stranger.

"My dear Lucy . . . I've been longing to tell you." Cousin Frances was all of a twitter. "The Stackpools employ him. He's vastly clever. French."

"I suppose one more of those poor aristocratic refugees? Like Monsieur de Herriot, the dancing master?"

"Oh, no . . . he's a Jacobin. He came over with Genet."

"Genet! That monster!"

"But something happened — he daren't go back. He's too revolutionary. You know Napoleon doesn't want them too revolutionary these days."

"France is like a disease."

"I only hope it doesn't spread to this country. If Jefferson is elected . . ."

"They say he will make America a part of France, with Napoleon king of the world."

Thus the ladies discussed politics. Then went back to Flanneau — Jacques Flanneau was his name. He had been a ladies' dressmaker before the Revolution. The poor old Stackpool girls got him for a song, my dear. One thing Frances mustn't tell — but then she would, and Lucy mustn't tell, and she went into peals of laughter. Mullins, sensing something good, let the horses drop to a walk.

"A little faster, Mullins, please," Lucy Inman ordered.

"They're real old horses, Madam," he countered. "Can't keep 'em trotting up all the hills."

The ladies drew together, with a parasol between them and Mr. Mullins's large ears.

"Don't tell anyone," Frances whispered. "He had no more than got here — four days ago — and he asked Miss Unity to *marry* him. He had the brazen effrontery . . . Fancy, a quite young Frenchman marrying a woman of her age!"

"Miss Unity!"

"Yes. And when she wouldn't he asked Miss Clara in almost the same words. And she's even *older*."

"My dear, this is a French farce — not life."

"Well, anyway, it did perk up the poor old things."

"Of course they'll have to discharge him."

"They can't. Why, the first day he was here he put a fashion doll in the window and in came Mrs. John Derby. She's never stepped into the shop before. He waited on her and she bought yards of things. Next day we had two Crowninshields. He's a gold mine. And he can make dresses. He is a sempster. They can't discharge him, but they thought they should tell me . . . about his amorous disposition — seeing he and I sleep alone in that house."

"Where does he sleep?"

"In the old kitchen. He sleeps and cooks there and dresses dolls. And sews all night. He's a wonderful workman."

"Well, I suppose you have a good lock on your door. And one advantage of getting older is we needn't be so afraid of outrages as young women."

Frances said nothing, but tilted her head in her birdlike way. Lucy Inman was forty-nine, Frances only thirty.

"But promise me, dear, if he ever so much as looks at you, you'll move right over with me? You know there will always be a room for you."

Mrs. Inman had long been determined that this useful and loving woman should become part of her own ménage. But there was some secret kernel of independence left in Frances. She would not. She would come over and sew curtains for hours. She was utterly dependent upon Lucy for whatever gaiety she had in life. She looked like a lady companion and was one in all respects except the fact that she was not paid and would not "move over."

The comfortable springs of the carriage, the sweet suns of May, lulled them. Lucy poured out her heart to Frances . . . oh, how she would miss Liz! And didn't she think him the handsomest, most amusing, cleverest man she had ever known? Frances Cunningham cocked her head at the most sympathetic angles and chirped the most understanding monosyllables. She generously forgot all her own worries (and amorous Frenchmen) and beat her little wings in honest distress over Lucy's loss of Liz.

~ 3 ~

DAVY JONES disappeared among the currant bushes and there dug a large damp hole into which he could flatten himself and bury his humiliation. Peter suggested to him that he drive over to Marblehead with himself and Dolly. Seemingly it was not for the old chaise he longed, but the elegant carriage. He would not look up.

At last, stubborn Dolly, with the chaise at her heels, poked down the driveway and turned to her left, although Peter had thought to leave Salem by Essex Street. This parallel route via Brown and Federal would do as well. Suppose on Federal Street, under Squire Mompesson's elms, he saw a doctor's rig waiting. Then he would know that Polly was really sick. It had shocked him, seeing her go to pieces before their eyes the night before. Dash had told him to keep an eye on that Dulcey person, but not a message had he sent to Polly. He wondered if she yet knew he had gone. He broke off a piece of rock candy and ate it.

Certainly someone from his household should inquire for Polly. If his mother was different, she would have thought of it. For the first time he thought his mother lacking in decent manners. Marcy was old enough to take social responsibilities. No, she wasn't. Tom . . . as soon as he woke up, he'd be heading for Newburyport and that dull Miranda Fields of his. How could anyone who had ever seen Polly Mompesson prefer such bread and butter! And it pleased Peter to think he had got Dolly ahead of Tom, and Tom would have to go to Manning's stable and hire. Tom certainly would never think of stopping to inquire for Polly's health. Probably he didn't care.

Federal Street lay ahead of him, broad and quiet under its elms. Lined up on either side, like ladies and gentlemen standing up to dance, were the stately houses. Before him he caught sight of Squire Mompesson's. As though stalking a timid prey, Peter drew the willing Dolly to a stop. The Mompesson house did not jump back into North River. It held its own, square, white, majestic. He looked at the balustraded rooftop. It was empty. There was no doctor's rig tied to the hitching-post. Neither old Doctor West nor young Doctor West was in attendance.

Of course, he would not ask to see Miss Polly herself. But he would inquire. Leave the name of Inman at the door. He chirruped to Dolly and sluggishly approached the door. He could look down the driveway. The coach-house door was open. The carriage gone. Doubtless the ailing girl, her papa and aunts, were all off to a headland and the last sight of the ships. Peter tied the old pony to the hitching-post carefully. She had a way of undoing hitching-straps and waddling off home, leaving young Inmans to walk.

He settled his hat, unconsciously imitating Dash's rakish angle, ran up the stairs, and pulled the brass bell knob. Then he realized he had no gloves, and was ready to dash back to the chaise. How could he speak to a servant of Polly Mompesson without gloves? Far away, a bell had rung. He heard a dog bark. An enchanting pert maid in a pink dress was opening the door and curtsying to him.

"Good morning," said Peter.

"Good morning, Mr. Inman."

Peter had never before been to this house which his older brothers and Nanny knew so well. The fact that the maid called him by name seemed to give her an unfair advantage. He felt trapped, and could not think of what to say next.

"Do step in, please."

"Oh *no,* thank you, *no.*" No fly was ever warier of the spider's web. "I have only come to inquire . . . my family would like to know . . . we heard Miss Polly is poorly. In fact, how is Miss Polly?"

The pink calico minx was enjoying herself. She was as great a belle in her walk of life as was her mistress in her large one. My, she thought, what a nice young man — so sweet and shy and in love. Because she liked him, she was ready to tease him a little — and also help him. Polly had said she would see no one this morning, but the maid was not going to send this charming young sufferer away.

She looked at him in mock bewilderment.

"Miss Polly . . . why, *our* Miss Polly isn't poorly. She got up ever so early to work on her flowers. Sir, perhaps you have the wrong house? We've got three Miss Pollys right here on Federal Street. Do you mean Miss Polly Mompesson?"

"Why, of course I do." What other Miss Polly on Federal Street, in Salem, or in the world, was worth inquiring for?

"If you'll step in, you can ask her yourself."

"Please. I'd rather not disturb her." And he thought guiltily of the letter he was carrying to Marblehead. It was in his pocket.

"Give me your hat and gloves."

She knew he hadn't any gloves — and should have had. She sucked in one pink cheek to keep from laughing. But she maneuvered him inside the house.

"Mr. Inman, you step the length of this hall and go out that door. Keep going straight between the counting-house and the coach-house and down the stairs. So you'll get to the garden. She's there, and you ask her yourself how she feels." She was willing to go against her mistress's orders to help the dear, scared "little man." Peter was over six feet.

So, by some mental superiority, she got him out the rear door and across the flagged court and down the stairs. He was in the great back garden which sloped before him to the banks of the North River. The bulbs and flowering currants were in blossom. Apple trees and pears foamed above. He smelled the pungent masses of box bush and, as always in Salem in May, he smelled lilacs.

Close to the rustic garden house he saw Polly herself. Evidently she had been kneeling too long, for now she straightened herself, was stretching and yawning. She heard feet on the gravel path and looked up.

He had never seen her before except fastidiously decked to drive out, call on his mother, shop, stop for tea, or to dance or dine. She looked much simpler and nearer his own age this morning. Something of his embarrassment left him. She drew off the old gloves she wore to protect her hands. He took the hand she frankly offered him, and looked down at her with that expression of serenity and kindness his grandmother thought habitual. Polly did not seem so breathlessly beautiful today, but actually even prettier. He could not but notice she had a faint sprinkle of freckles over her tilted nose. Her white cotton stockings and old slippers were soiled with garden loam. Her faded blue calico was not half so fresh as the pink one her maid wore. There was a streak of skepticism in Peter's nature. Perhaps he always before thought her beauty more dependent upon artifice than it was. Now he saw her — just as she was — and could hardly believe his eyes.

"I wanted to ask you if you felt all right today," he began easily. "You gave us quite a scare last night. My mother wished to hear . . ."

She put a finger to her bright little lips and shook her disarrayed blond curls. "I haven't told anybody. Not Papa, nor the aunts. I simply said the party was dull and I wanted to come home. They don't know how badly I behaved. Peter" — her voice was quick and eager — "I've been trying to think how to send my apologies to your mother."

"Oh, please . . . please, don't."

"Will you tell her for me?"

"Don't think any more of it."

"Then here are my apologies, sir. You may do with them as you see fit."

"But you really feel all right now? Did you sleep well?"

"No," she said; "I haven't slept well for months. But I don't want *them*" — she gestured toward the house — "to know."

Peter was touched by this confidence.

"Let's sit down, Peter."

Close to the summer house were bamboo chairs, a table, and a lounge, brought from India. She flung herself on the lounge, her hands clasped behind her neck. Her glance was skyward.

"Miss Polly, shouldn't you do something about not sleeping?" Why, this might bring on a decline.

"There's nothing you can do — except not talk about it."

"Have you asked my brother-in-law?"

"Papa prefers his father. But they all say the same thing. I must calm myself, and get more fresh air — gardening, walking. But not overexert. That's why I'm out here today. I didn't want to plant seeds. I didn't want to do anything. But sometimes you have to do something." She was still gazing at the sky. Peter wondered if anyone had told her that Dash had gone.

"Miss Polly . . ."

"Why do you call me 'Miss'? Your brothers never do. I went to dame school with Liz. You make me feel like Methuselah — or whoever the oldest woman in the Bible may be."

"I'd like to call you . . . that." But he could not say "Polly." As long as he was Peter and she Miss Polly there was a barrier between them.

"Say it," she demanded.

"Polly."

"I told Flip — that's my little maid — not to admit anyone today. Then I heard feet and thought it was Nanny."

"Nanny?"

"Oh, she's so curious. She'll be here before long. And Flip won't be able to stop her. She'll die if she doesn't know exactly what it was so upset me last night. Peter, don't you ever tell her." So she took it for granted that Peter, the almost stranger, knew secrets her "best friend" did not. "Yes," she went on dreamily, "I couldn't sleep, and then, in the middle of the night, I heard a shutter clap to.

At first light I got up and went to the attic and pushed up the trapdoor. Oh, I forgot to say, first I got Papa's spyglass from the library. Dawn was like the inside of an abalone shell. Wonderful!" She flung out her bare round arms. "I felt a breeze on me. And there *she* was — sails squared away, dropping off through all that pinkness and yellow shine. I watched her till I could see her top-sails no more and the sun had risen and it was full day."

Peter was sure she knew, but he had to ask. "You know Dash did get to command her?"

"I didn't know for certain until Flip brought up my morning chocolate and said the milk boy had told her. But before that, I really knew Dash was on that quarterdeck, going away and away, so far away. Oh, I felt it last night when he stood up to carve. It was in the strangest way — I could feel him leaving then, growing smaller and smaller. And he wouldn't look back."

"Then what did you do? I mean when you came off the roof?"

"Cried, of course," she said simply. "Then I put on my clothes."

Peter knew his next question was hardly delicate, but he couldn't help asking.

"Didn't you have on . . . er . . . any clothes when you were up on the roof?"

"Oh, no," said the coquette. "Nothing to speak of." Not explaining the dressing-gown, the heavy shawl, letting him paint what pictures of delight as might occur to his still youthful imagination.

Peter's palms grew moist. Actually he saw the most divine form in Salem, standing in a gossamer nightgown on the roof of the Mompesson house. It was dawn; the wind blowing — and she dressed in practically nothing but her papa's spyglass. Polly let him ponder this thought.

"Do you do that — often? Aren't you afraid of catching cold?"

"I never did before."

Neither spoke for a moment, then she said casually, "Happens Dash sent you to me with a farewell?"

"Dash . . ." What was he to say? The letter in his pocket weighed him down. "Yes . . . naturally, of course. Dash wouldn't think of leaving without a message for you. Of course." And he almost hated Dash that he had left no word for Polly and actually a letter for someone else. I might tear it up, he thought angrily.

"*Of course.* Do tell."

Peter, although accustomed to being a little evasive about his brothers' goings-on, was not an experienced liar. But she was once more flung back, on the couch, gazing skyward. It is easier for your amateur to lie to a profile than to a full face.

"He wanted me to tell you . . . that is, he said tell Polly . . ."

"Yes?" she whispered, seemingly in a dream of love.

"It was so very late when it was decided — he felt he could not come to you at such an hour — it might have upset you."

"Peter . . ." His eyes followed the tilt of her beguiling nose, a tilt which was repeated in the line of the upper lip. Her face was turned away in maiden modesty. "Peter, did he say tell Polly I love her?"

"Why . . . that was the upshot. Yes. You've hit on the general idea."

She whipped up her little body and was on her feet, facing him — her eyes blazing, wide open and angry.

"You tarnation gosling! Why do you say such things? You liar —everybody lies to me," she stormed, "and I'll lie back to them, if I want to. Papa, Aunt Birdseye, Aunt Brattle, you, Dash. Dash most of all. Dash never sent me a word."

"Polly . . . please, Polly." He was afraid she would go off in another hysterical fit.

"Dash has been trying to forget me — but he can't. And if he could, I wouldn't let him." Her hands made tiny fists. "And yet he went . . . he's gone."

"Polly," Peter begged, "remember he can't do anything about you. I mean, your father hasn't encouraged him even to hang about until he has mended his fortunes. He had to go, didn't he? And the *Victrix* is a fine command."

"I hate the *Victrix*. I hope she sinks." Suddenly Peter saw the flash of white under the iris as she realized what she had said. "Oh, God!" she whispered, "dear God, no. I take that back." A look of guilt filled her beautiful eyes. With an effort she got control of herself as she realized she had cursed the *Victrix*. She went on quickly, "And one more lie I might point out to you. Dash lies when he acts as though I meant nothing to him — now."

"I know that, Polly." Peter spoke confidently. There was a lot he did not know about Dash, but he knew he loved Polly

Mompesson. "But I was afraid perhaps you didn't. I know he wasn't forbidden the house, or anything so old-fashioned and drastic. And yet he didn't come. It was as if he was so unhappy about having lost that *Antelope,* he wanted to punish himself. Didn't feel worthy of you — because he loved you so much and had naught to offer. He had to go on hurting himself more and more. I can't explain. But he does love you, and when he comes back next time . . ."

"God grant he comes again." She was still a little dazed because she had hoped his ship would sink, and she was very superstitious. She went on thoughtfully: "If he never came, I'd die. I couldn't live without him. If he ever left me, it would kill me. You know that?"

Peter did know it. What a fragile creature she was, and yet packed into her frailty such strength of feeling — enough to shake her to pieces. It was not hard to imagine her dying of a broken heart.

"I think, I *know,* he will always love you, Polly. And never anybody else. He couldn't."

"Peter, you will come to me often? And every time you come, say 'Dash loves you.' I might lose heart."

"I will come and come."

"Peter, I don't know. But perhaps nobody should love anyone as much as I love him. You love him too?"

"Yes," he said simply, "more than anything or anybody alive or dead — more'n God and right and wrong, or anything anybody can think of."

"You shouldn't, either."

"No, I shouldn't."

"So we can suffer together — if we have to?"

"Yes."

Polly was such an artificial little creature her moments of complete honesty enchanted. But she was rarely honest to an equal. Only to her inferiors, like Flip, or Peter. She had never been so truthful to Dash himself.

The pink maid was tripping down the path. "Mrs. Jack West, Miss Polly." And there on her heels came eager Nanny.

"Darling, when Flip said you were not receiving, I knew you did not mean me. Why, *Peter Inman,* what are you doing here? Polly, what's Peter here for? Does he often come?"

"I just stopped by to inquire for Miss Polly's health. Miss Polly, I'm leaving you now. Your servant, ma'am." He wasn't going to call her "Polly" in front of that confounded Nanny.

But he lingered a few moments longer.

"I don't need to ask about your health," his sister was saying. "Actually you look more like a flower than flowers themselves."

"It was sweet of you, Nanny, to stop."

"That slight pallor," Nanny went on, a little slyly, "does so become you. Of course, Peter has told you our wonderful news? Dash is commanding the *Victrix*."

"Oh, yes. Peter came to deliver his farewells — as well as ask for my health." She gave Peter a quick, comical, secret glance.

Nanny had taken off her floppy straw hat and was fanning herself with it. She was a nice-looking girl, not pretty, but rather handsome. She had never been a belle, for she lacked both the imagination, flair, even the ruthlessness necessary for such a position. Although a year younger than Polly, she now had taken a step ahead of her. While Polly had been toying with a dozen men, and even had, it was said, the much-touted Dash Inman in her pocket, Nanny had married a very desirable young man. She had had only one offer, but that had been a good one. It is often the way. And now Nanny was "Mrs." and a matron, and could look down ever so little from this superior height at the mere Miss Mompesson.

Polly, who had been so bluntly honest, the moment before, with Peter — almost a stranger — was now neatly mending her fences and setting up new ones against Nanny's curiosity. As Polly foxed and deceived her friend, Peter thought how clever she was, but Nanny, equally smart at this game, disgusted him. So they chatted about a new "indispensable," as they called their pocketbooks, Mrs. Derby had brought back from New York with her, and hoped the old Mr. So-and-So would not marry his dead wife's companion. Had Polly seen the French dressmaker at the Stackpools'? Vastly clever, Nanny vowed. And both agreed they were thankful for him and wished Salem had a man who could really dress heads with taste. So they edged about each other.

Peter at last made his manners and left.

∼4∼

SQUIRE MOMPESSON sat alone in his stately dining room, staring at, but not eating, his second breakfast. On rising, he had a dish of tea. Then he took a constitutional. This might include a stop on 'Change, underwriting other men's ships, or a glance at his extensive waterfront real estate. Alone among wealthy Salem men, he had never been to sea himself. If he looked down upon the working captains, he was the only person in Salem who did. More obviously, the young captains looked down upon him, although they often were dependent upon him for financial backing. He had never staked life, and health, in far lands and upon distant seas. All he had ever risked was money. He was something of a parasite upon them, reaping where he had not sown, rarely proving kind or encouraging when things went wrong. Because he knew the captains looked down upon him, he was always suggesting that as long as they were going to sea they were little better than laborers. Not until they retired, as many did in their twenties, and were in a position to hire other men to sail their ships, did he consider them exactly gentlemen.

As if in contrast to the reckless expenditure of energy among the seafaring men, he lived by hygienic principles. Tea and a long, brisk walk in the good, wholesome fresh air. Then, at noon, this second breakfast of his, eggs and gruel, toast, fruit, boiled milk. Dinner was at the fashionable hour of three. And then there was time for genealogy, reading, or rest, or a carriage drive with the aunts if Polly was too concerned with her beaux. He did not believe in straining muscles, mind, or sensibilities.

His hygienic principles had preserved him well, and yet they made him seem more a man of characteristics than of character. There was something wrong in a man of sixty-odd with so unlined a face. Under the great frizzled wig, it was almost as clear a pink porcelain as his daughter's. He appeared neither young nor old, but a little like a potter's conception of an elegant elderly gentleman of the old school. The fact that he clung to satin smallclothes, knee buckles and silk stockings, velvet, gold-laced coats, wigs, and the fripperies of the pre-Revolutionary great gentleman increased the impression that he was a figurine from Meissen. So did his size.

He was a little man, not only of barely middle height, but exquisitely small-featured and small-footed. He had dainty, unmanly hands, always bright with costly rings. It was only by looking at the shrewd, bright eyes, the tight mouth, that one realized he not only could hold on to a fortune but make one.

Now the ringed hands tapped the mahogany before him. According to his schedule, Polly came to him during second breakfast and toasted toast for him. Today she did not come.

Something had gone wrong the night before at the Inmans'. Of course she had been correct not to explain before his sister, Mrs. Brattle, or his first wife's aunt, Mrs. Birdseye. But now was the time she should come to him with her heart secrets. He relished all her conquests, and the two of them had often laughed as she recounted the amusements of the night before, ridiculing her admirers. She always implied that no man in the world was quite up to her own papa. She would strut and mimic Mr. Pickering with his quizzing glass as he had ogled her. The clumsiness of General Paddock as he caught his spur in her train. The callow calfishness of some young captain's love. He might be a great man on quarterdeck, she would suggest, but quite unfit for the niceties of the ballroom. Every compliment she received, he was confident she shared with him. She never received a note or poem without asking his advice before answering it — so he thought. He realized such complete confidence between a father and daughter was rare and precious. It was almost as if he and she were defending the fort of her maidenhood against the onslaughts of the world. He and she together.

I begged her not to go to the Inmans', he thought. They, all of them, even that Nanny, seem to tire her. She went against my expressed advice. I could have told her she would find it dull. Yet Polly had not looked bored as she had made her sensationally early return on Jack West's arm. She had looked a little febrile. She had refused the wholesome, quieting tamarind water he had urged on her. She had said good night and gone to bed, and he had noticed on her face an expression almost of stolidity, something secretive and, to him, frightening. He had come to associate this slightly forbidding expression with Dash Inman. He told himself she had no interest in him. Men who interested her she talked the most about, asking him if So-and-So was not the handsomest man he'd ever seen. Didn't he think Mr. This-One's poem melting? If she should fall in love with Mr. Blank, would he approve? About Dash she had never had much of anything to say. Yes, she had danced three voluntaries with Dash. Yes, he had been one of the water party the night before. And he had called for her and returned her. But what he had said evidently interested her so little she never repeated it.

He had the pleasure of telling Dash that time, eight months ago, when he had the poor taste to ask him for her hand, that not only was he financially in no position to be thinking about a wife, but that he must have misunderstood his daughter's playfulness. She had not evinced the least interest in him, and "I have her complete confidence, Captain Inman." The fellow had not gainsaid him, but had given him a queer, knowing, scornful look, as though to say he knew more about the state of Polly's heart than her own father. Well, at least he was off — at last. *He'd* not be upsetting Polly for some time now. Mr. Mompesson was one of the *Victrix's* principal underwriters. As he sat and wondered what had gone wrong the night before, he had a moment of blind hatred against her captain so intense he would gladly have lost all the money he had risked on the *Victrix* if only he could hear that she had gone down — all hands. It was in vain he told himself, "He doesn't interest her in the slightest. She has never talked about him. Obviously, eight months ago, when she realized I considered him an undesirable suitor for her, she sent him packing, for he had abruptly ceased his attentions." But underneath this logical interpretation of events was a more emotional knowledge.

He had told Flip no guests were to be admitted this morning — so anxious was he to have Polly all to himself at this very hour. Yet, as he was returning from his constitutional, he had seen Miss Nanny — no, it was Mrs. Nanny these days — sneaking across the courtyard heading for the back garden. Surely Polly would not let a mere Nanny delay her habitual attendance upon her father? He asked so little of her, he thought.

He heard feet in the hall. Ah, now Polly was coming to toast toast and confide in him. Of course, he would not ask her flat out, but she would be anxious to tell him all. In his mind he saw her thrust out a lower lip, mimic Dash, and as soon as she did, it would be once more he and she against the world.

"Polly, my dear" — his voice was a full round bass, beautifully modulated, surprisingly powerful from such a little body — "Polly, aren't you going to toast my bread for me?"

"It's me, sir." And the youngest of the Inmans — he could not remember his name — was standing at the threshold and bowing to him. He did not like his looks. Peter was something of a diluted version of his oldest brother.

"Well, sit, sir," he said, imagining that possibly he might learn something from him of last night's occurrences. "Long's you're here." And he called Flip to bring coffee. "I never touch the stuff myself. It's rank poison. Nor does Polly. One cup of tea in the morning for each of us. And that's all the tea. But coffee only for guests. Certain ports set well on my stomach, others do not, and I discard them. Distilled liquors, never. Very little meat." But even as he boasted of his simple, wholesome diet, he took snuff from a silver snuffbox and sneezed.

"If you will excuse me . . . I've eaten breakfast hours ago."

"Sit. Sit, please." Peter sat. The coffee appeared instantly. Evidently it was already a-brewing in the kitchen.

"It is always a pleasure," the elderly man went on, his foppish manner at variance with the depth and richness of his voice, "to welcome an Inman to my house. Our families — certainly two of the oldest in Salem — have long been entwined, so to speak."

"Oh?"

"When the first Mompesson arrived in Salem — that was Cecil the First, Gentleman — in 1645, he came into Cat Cove on his own vessel, The *Adder*. Among his entourage — indentured servants and such — was "one" Inman. First name unknown. Must have been a stout fellow, for he carried his master to shore through the surf, piggy-back. I've often thanked God the fellow was surefooted and strong-backed. It was thus the Inmans and the Mompessons arrived in Salem together."

Peter began to wish that "one" Inman had stumbled.

"So I always feel when I meet an Inman I should express my thanks . . ."

"Don't mention it," Peter said blandly.

"Genealogy is one of my little hobbies. Very instructive. Very. Now, that Cecil the First set up with some state — state for those primitive days. In fact, kept a carriage. Some fifteen years later, there was a litigation in Salem. Seems a Goodman Inman, first name unknown — possibly the same fellow as that 'one' Inman, but now freed of service — was obstructing the king's highway just about where your family have their wharf today. And Cecil — the second of that name, I'm the fifth — was unable to move his carriage, and so struck the fellow."

Peter's eyes looked like Liz's. "Did the Inman fellow strike back?"

"He was set in the stocks for daring to strike his betters. Cecil the Second was a magistrate of the Great and General Court — and so on. But slowly the Inmans were crawling up. This country has given great opportunity for the lowly to rise — but if Jefferson is elected, we'll have nothing but the lowly on top, sir. By 1700, the Inmans must have been catching, drying, and peddling fish. The town records accuse them — in the quaint language of the day — of a 'pestiferous noisesome nuscince from ye stages of ye fish'. . . I forget just how they put it. The upshot was their fish stages stank. You've been taught your family history? Decent, plain people — until fairly recently."

"I know we started as fishermen. And the land about Ma'am's wharf has been in the family forever. And," he added, "in 1692, when the witches were abroad, a Squire Mompesson brought charges against Tabby Inman. Poppets, or something. Something about a dead horse. I've heard Grandma tell."

"No, no. It was not the Squire, Cecil the third, but his daughter Sukey who was bewitched. She did not live to be sixteen. Shocking occurrence."

"Shocking, indeed, sir."

"More coffee?"

"No, thank you, sir."

Peter could feel the dislike in the man's staring blue eyes, in his calm, belittling words. He felt it in the eyes of the ancestral portraits upon the wall, in the dragon snout of the coffee pot. But why? Why on earth did Squire Mompesson hate him? Then he knew. He was so jealous of Dash, so afraid of him, hated him so much he had plenty left over for the entire family.

"That daughter, Sukey, vomited fur. Needles were drawn through her flesh," Mr. Mompesson went on. "Of course, her father was distracted. Medical science was in its infancy. I've never blamed him."

"And Goody Inman had mumbled . . . or something?"

"She was found by our courts to be a 'rampant hag,' and hung. I don't see what else they could have done."

Peter studied him curiously. Was he actually talking with a supposedly intelligent, educated man who believed such things? Of course, servants and children often did.

"Thank you for your hospitality, sir," he said, standing up, "but my horse will tire of waiting for me."

"A good, high-spirited horse that hates to wait is as much the mark of a gentleman as a fine leg and immaculate linen." But he was curious to know why Peter had come. It was a convention that the day after a dance gentlemen called on all their partners — "I hardly thought Polly stayed long enough last night to stand up to dance," he said.

"No, we didn't dance. I just stopped by. I hoped she wasn't too tired — or anything."

"She's happy this morning," he said, not too truthfully, but determined that no one should find her depressed the day of Dash's departure; "happy as a little wren, delving among her flowers. Yet it takes but little to upset her, I'll admit. We are a very old family. Perhaps the blood does begin to run a little thinly in our veins. Now, I think I must go out in the garden and warn Miss Nanny — no, I should say *Mrs.* Nanny — that perhaps she has made a long enough visit. I have noticed that Polly, if you will pardon me, sometimes finds Inmans a trifle exhausting." With this insult ringing in his ears, Peter left.

With some difficulty he roused his high-spirited mare and got her moving. Once he glanced back at the Mompesson house. The white balustrades stood out against the dark blue noonday sky. He could almost see a white figure crowning all. It was not exactly Polly — in her little bed-gown and her papa's spyglass. It was almost the figurehead of the *Victrix* — that more massive woman, also in white. The fierce eyes were wide open to the dangers or glory that lay before her, her green wreath clasped in her hands, not given to any man.

The *Victrix!* Already the sea surged up, washing her breast. Salt already had formed on her bitter lips.

IT HAD BEEN PART of Dash's recent queerness that he had done but little sailing. Once, if he had had to go to Marblehead or Gloucester, Lynn, Newburyport, or even Boston, he went by sailboat. He said stages smelled, and horses made him sneeze. These last eight months he had hardly once taken the *Red Herring,* which was kept moored off Inman Wharf for, as Madam Inman said, "churning around the harbor." In the old days Peter was always hearing about the turtles, picnics, and water parties gotten up whenever Dash or Tom or Liz happened to be home. Two or three small sailing boats, full of young people, would go out to Baker's or Eagle Island, or as far as Nahant. They would catch fish and go wading, lie about in the sun. Then dark came, and they would build fires, fry their fish, and make coffee. The girls would unpack hampers of hearts-and-rounds, seed cakes, jellies, fresh bread — the men would produce wine for all, and rum for themselves. It was good courting on a water party, Liz had often told Peter. Thus it was Dash had courted Polly, Peter knew — far away from her father's watchful eye.

So home by moonlight. Peter could hear the singing coming closer and closer as he stood on the wharf, ready with a boat hook and to give a hand unloading girls. As the boat came closer, he would hear the soft, throaty laughter of love and the rattle as the sail came down.

Many times these last months Dash had headed Dolly for Marblehead — buying fish, of course. In his disgrace, he preferred dawdling Dolly to the bright, pleasurable *Red Herring,* although unlike many deep-sea men he was monstrous smart with small craft.

It occurred to Peter that Dolly would remember whereabouts in Marblehead Dash had been leaving her. Somewhere near that Dulcey person. If ever Polly knew, Peter believed it would kill her. Girls were supposed to die from disappointed love — and surely no girl could have greater aptitude for such a fate than Polly. And Mr. Mompesson! Peter knew now he hated Dash. How he would gloat and preen himself over anything he could hold against him. Whatever that Dulcey and Dash had been about, Peter would send her packing. And he'd keep her mouth shut.

Marblehead struck Peter, as it did most Salem men, as a squalid, fishy place, rocky and cluttered, uncivilized — in spite of the sprinkle of gentlemen's houses. A loathly place where no decent person would choose to live. Folk here were savages and spoke a dialect only they could understand. It was said they lured wealthy, homing Salem ships upon their rocks, and picked the bones. This was called "mooncursing." Peter did not know whether this was true or not. He did know that no people on the New England coast were quicker to row out to wrecks and save the shipwrecked men than these same Marbleheaders. They and their dories could get through surfs the deep-sea men of Salem could not. But they never expected to die in bed. If the fishes ate them, why, they said, they had been eating fishes all their lives. Fair turn about — they said.

When Dash had been signing the *Victrix* people, he had three times refused Marblehead fishermen. He said he'd rather have lads off inland farms who had never smelled salt water. Marbleheaders had no discipline. Each man fished "on his own hook," and one man was as good as the next on their little heeltappers. No East Injun mate could teach them otherwise. Their ships were so small no one ever had to go aloft. If you told a Marblehead fisherman to lay aloft, he'd spit and tell you to do it yourself. He was no monkey to go climbing ropes. The Marbleheaders had boys of ten or twelve to do their cooking for them — not older, respectable Negro men like Salem. By and large, they were Republicans, and Salem folk were Federalists. There was hardly a thing the two towns had in common except that both got their living from the sea.

Dolly was rounding the corner of one of those slab-sided gray houses which projected, in the individual manner of Marblehead, out into the narrow street. Evidently she knew where she was going. She made a few more turns and stopped before a small grogshop. The sign before it said this was the Sea Urchin. Peter got out and hitched her to a rusty anchor lying about. Everything lay about in Marblehead. It was not shipshape.

He entered a dark and dwarfish room, ordered ale and alewives, bread and cheese. The broad, barelegged woman looked at him as if she half-knew him. Of course, she had seen Dash many times. He wasn't going to ask her questions. He knew she had a dirty, suspicious mind.

Even as he paid for his meal and told her he was leaving his horse, he caught sight of a spare, black back. A clergyman. Certainly a clergyman would have no low thoughts over a simple question.

"Sir," he said, when he had caught up with him, "I'm a stranger and I'm seeking directions."

The young clergyman stopped. He had a studious look as though he had been a great Latinist at Harvard not long ago.

"I've lived in Marblehead a year, sir," he answered, "but I'm still a stranger myself. One might say the physical geography of Marblehead I know very well. But not the spiritual. What street do you wish, sir?"

"Not a street, a family."

"What family?"

"Do you know any Delaneys?"

"Delaney? Yes. Corruption of the French de la Nayes. I've interested myself in the history of this remarkable town. Many families came from French-speaking Channel Isles. Very long ago."

"Can you tell me . . ."

"If you wish to learn of them as they were, a hundred years ago, I can tell you. Of their present status — ask the selectmen or the overseers of the poor."

"Slipped, have they?"

"Slipped, and the name all but gone. What's left I'm sure the selectmen will give you for the mere carting away. Perhaps I'm hardly fair to them. Some have become dependent, through drink or old age. All have been godless folk. But there have been many stout fishermen of that name."

"Could you direct me to their houses?"

"Oh, they are vastly scattered — here and there. Which Delaney do you wish?"

"I don't know her real name. She's called Dulcey."

"I know the young person. Dulcey — corrupt French again — is her real name. I doubt if she was ever baptized."

"Would you head me in her general direction?"

The wooden young face stiffened. "Why?"

"Why not?"

"I must beg your pardon, but it is hard enough for our fisher girls to keep their virtue when confronted with only local temptations. I'm not going to direct any young blade from Boston or Salem to their doors."

Peter laughed, embarrassed and flattered. No one around Salem considered him either a temptation or a blade.

He looked at the clergyman kindly. "I mean no harm." Then he looked down and murmured, "It's my brother who sent me."

"Oh, your *mother*." Doctor Fisher had not quite heard the word. "Well, in that case . . . Most of the Delaneys used to live about Peaches Point. There are none there now. Dulcey's sister Anna married Bob Swift in what we call Outer Village. While he was off fishing, Dulcey moved in to bear her sister company. But Anna died in childbirth awhile ago. And Bob drowned at sea. So Dulcey lives alone in her dead brother-in-law's shack — hovel. I hardly know how to describe these fishermen's houses."

"Oh."

"The selectmen do not like young girls to live alone. Unfitting for a destitute female — of some bodily charm. We — I am a select-man, sir — are planning to bound her out in domestic service."

"Does she want to go for a servant?"

"She's under age, and a destitute orphan. We are her natural guardians. Now, if your *mother* is looking for a likely serving girl, Mr. . . . Mr.?"

"Inman, sir."

"Mr. Inman. Thank you. Salem, I see. I'm the Reverend Elias Fisher — I think Dulcey might work out very well. Smart girl. Never have heard a word of scandal against her. But all these fisher girls are lax. Lax. I could tell you things that would flabbergast you. Well . . . now, how to get to Outer Village."

He explained the route, the fish stages to be passed, the rocks to go over, and then down to the sea again. "You'll recognize her . . . hovel. It has a pair of whale's jaws set up as a gateway. Very Gothic. They look big as the jaws of hell."

"Thank you, Doctor Fisher."

Peter walked the path around the rocks and scrambled up ledges. The smell of fish, split and drying, grew stronger and then less. He came out on a headland and saw what he had almost forgotten — the last of the Salem ships, like butterflies on the quivering blue horizon.

Here ahead of him was a scattering of "hovels." One stood apart and above the others. It had a Gothic entrance made of a whale's jaw. So he knew this was hers. About the forlorn spot was a fence of broken oars, ribs of whales, things like that.

The door of Dulcey's house hung weakly open. Inside, it was

neat as a pin, the black hearth swept. He realized one reason for this neatness was abysmal poverty. Not even a slattern could have got so little out of order. Apparently Dash had not been showering her with expensive gifts.

He walked to the top of the granite headland, against which, to leeward, the house snuggled, and looked down upon a little beach. Women were sitting about, mending nets, and now he could hear their voices. Against the unending blue of sea and sky, with the sun beating down upon them, they made a handsome picture. The women looked generous, statuesque, in the bright clear light. They gestured largely, flinging out their arms from their shoulders, unlike the mincing of ladies. Their laughter was coarse and came from their bellies, unhampered by stays or gentility. Rough as the scene was, it was somehow familiar. Just so his mother, Cousin Frances, and other women brought their sewing, worked and gossiped. This was the same thing on a vastly more impressive scale.

"Where's Dulcey?" he called, well hidden behind the rocks. "Dulcey." Immediately one of them stood up and started toward him. The other women laughed. And one of them, the most monstrous big woman he had ever seen, got to her feet, shading her eyes with an enormous forearm, and stared at him. She looked magnificent, poised like this, but more like a sea monster than mortal woman. He backed out of sight. He was afraid of them, a little.

He had know she would be blond. Dash fancied fair girls. But blondness in Salem implied whiteness. Only the white of the eye and bright coarse teeth were white in Dulcey. She was sunburnt, sunbaked, and almost beautiful. Beautiful as bread is beautiful, not, he thought, in any other way. Probably not good as ladies are good — but as bread is good. Good to eat when you are hungry. His heart constricted and sank. It might be harder than he had expected to protect Polly from her. Polly was a darling frosted cake, so lightly, skillfully made, so sweet and delicate. But here, coming up out of the sea, was bread itself. And bread is the staff of life.

He saw the eagerness in her eyes change to suspicion. She stood stock-still below him and looked up. Her broad brown feet clung to the rocks like limpets, her faded heavy hair was pulled back into a great knot on her neck. Stray locks about her face were white as wool against a face tanned and weathered to ruddy brown. Her deep-set gray eyes gazed at him. She wore a striped skirt kilted up before so that the wear of her toil would come on her petticoat. A lady would have put on an apron. The tight bodice and the full skirt set off her erect, plump, short figure admirably. Napoleon's wife might decree sheer muslins and waistlines up to one's armpits, and no hips, but Fashion did not penetrate very far down in the social scale. Dulcey was dressed much as laboring women had been dressing for hundreds of years. She stood square and amazed and looked up at Peter.

He approached and offered his hand to help her up over the rocks. You might as well offer your hand to a coney.

"I'm Dash's brother. I'm Peter Inman."

She smiled readily, a fine warm smile without suspicion or guile. "Then you're his youngest brother."

"Yes."

"He's told me of you. You do look like, and you call out like him. I thought 'twas he."

But she did not talk like a Christian. She spoke broad and quick. It was a little hard for Peter always to follow her as it was for most Salem folk to understand the "Maulheaders" as they called themselves. When they reached her hut, she gestured, with that widely flung gesture he had noticed among the women on the beach, to an overturned rotting dory, and said they would set and "jaw awhile," but what it sounded like to him was "Jor of ile."

He and she sat. She had a certain dignity. For a moment, neither spoke.

"Dash asked me to come over and see you. And to tell you he has gone to sea."

"To sea?"

"You are his friend. You'll be glad to hear that, last moment, he got command of the *Victrix*."

"I didn't know he ever wanted to go to sea no more. I thought he was sick of seafaring."

"Not quite." Already Peter was half-pitying her. Dash had obviously not told his small but burly charmer much, and that little had not been true.

She was digging a hole in the sand with one great toe and filling it with the other. Toes as useful as an ape's. The face she turned toward him was trustful, the cheekbones high and heavy. The mouth was very handsome, and deeply indented at the corners. He admired the glass-like purity of the gray eyes. He doubted if she was as old as himself.

"Is he coming back soon, Mr. Peter?"

"No, the *Victrix* is a big, long-legged ship, heading out beyond Good Hope. Why, she might go around the world."

"Three months, maybe?" This was about as long as the Banks fishermen stayed out.

"No," he said gently, "the world's a deal larger than that."

"What did you say his ship is called?"

"The *Victrix.*" He was relieved because Dash had told her nothing of this ship which had grown out of his heart. "When the *Victrix* starts out, she goes to the ends of the earth." But "round the world," "ends of the earth," meant nothing to Dulcey. I'll bet she thinks the world is flat. Such pristine ignorance fascinated him.

"Did you ever see a map of the world — or a globe?"

"No, I never did."

"I'll bring a map over sometime and show you. I'll bring a globe, if you like."

"Thank you," she said, without enthusiasm.

He could feel her sitting there beside him, puzzled. He guessed she did not have much machinery to think with. She wasn't thinking of the size of the world — she was thinking of Dash. After a time, she seemed to have come to some conclusion.

"So he didn't meant it when he said he couldn't bear to go away ever . . . any more." Thank heavens she did not add "and leave me."

"No. He was clean daft to get to sea. He had to go. It's in him and he has to go." He waited for her to take that in. It did her no harm to realize that the things that meant most to Dash he had not shared with her. Poor Dulcey, he thought. Still, he owed it to Polly — and Dash, too — to put her in her place. But you couldn't put a person in her place who was staying there. This was part of her dignity, an animal dignity that made him think of Davy Jones.

He had seen brawling fishwives at Salem market — big, loose-mouthed women. If she would act like that, he could deal with her. She sat in silence, seemingly completely at home in her own world. A tiny world, and doubtless flat, that contained nothing in it farther away than the Grand Banks of Newfoundland.

"Dash," he went on, "isn't the sort that talks much about the things that mean most to him. I don't mean he isn't honest. And very honorable. Anything . . . any obligation he has, he stands back of."

"He's gone now," Dulcey cut in philosophically. "But I guess he'll come back."

Never to you, Peter said to himself, never to you, my fine Dulcey. He went on aloud: "He wants you to feel, while he's away, that you've got a friend in me. We Inmans will stand back of you. He told me he was much beholden to you."

For the first time, she spoke roughly. "What do you mean by that?" It was as though he had insulted her.

"Nothing much." Now all he had to do was leave the letter and go. He thought he had made Dash's farewells "loving" enough. Now for the letter. Dash had said there was no hurry, but he might as well get it out and give it to her.

"Dulcey, get this through your head. It will be a year at least — maybe two. Or maybe . . ."

"Never. And let me tell you something. You say Dash don't tell all his feeling to everybody. Not the things he feels most about."

"No, he doesn't. Not Dash."

"When did he tell you about me?"

"Well . . . just this morning. 'Fore he sailed."

"If there is one person a man doesn't tell anything it's his little brother — see? And if a man loved a woman very truly, he isn't likely to go talking, is he?"

She was standing before him a little threateningly. If she thought Dash really had loved her, he wasn't going to give her any letter from him. Not yet awhile.

"What of it? Suppose things went a little wrong with him. Did he ever say *Antelope* to you?"

"No, he never did."

"When he comes back next time, he's going to be different."

"And feel differently about people?"

"Toward some people, yes."

"I guess you are trying to tell me he's through with me." She looked at him with her candid gray eyes, and slowly shook her head. "He isn't through with me."

She was exasperatingly stubborn, and yet he found something touching, almost lovable, in her belief in Dash.

"Dulcey," he said, "how old are you?"

"Sixteen."

He put out a hand to her with sudden affection. Hers was rough, muscular — such as a man might cling to in adversity. He thought of Dash's hands — sure and slow in motion, square, and very strong. As his hand went into hers, he had a vague emotion, a mere reflection of what Dash had really felt. Not feelings of his own.

"I'll come again." He got to his feet. "I'll show you a globe. I'll take you rowing."

She laughed. "Mr. Peter, I'll take *you* rowing. You're a pretty boy" (she said "pratty bye") "and no mistake, although tall as a beanpole. I'll bet I've got more muscle on my arms than you have in those spindle shanks." She flexed a bare brown forearm at him. It was as brawny as a man's, and yet not in the least like a man's, and coated with white fuzz. "See?" He saw and shuddered. "Now that Dash," she went on, "he's solid muscle. He can pick me up and hold me so I can't wriggle. He's mighty powerful, although not so tall as you. When did you say he was coming back?"

"That's what I've got to tell you. It doesn't make any difference to you when he does come back. But I'll be here — right over in Salem. All the time."

"You're good, Mr. Peter. You're the sweetest little man I ever met. Now I'm telling you — because I see you're wondering, and you're too polite to ask. Dash does love me."

Peter had nothing to say, for now the *Victrix* was to sea, standing off the New England coast. And the trades would carry her on and on. Beyond the Equator, and on and on. Lost at last in a golden dream beyond the ends of the earth. Doctor Hobey had told him of certain sea animals that go ashore to have their young — turtles, seals. Then go back to the sea really to live. Dash was that sort of animal.

She pressed close to him. She did smell a little of fish-nets, tar and sweat, but also sweetly of her life in the sun. There was a pleasant intoxication to her.

"I think maybe he did love you," he admitted, against his will, but thus close to her he could feel the shadow of what Dash had felt.

"Does," she demanded.

"No" — he looked at her soberly — "did."

She grabbed him above both elbows with a strength that would have started a seine from the bottom of the sea.

"*Does,* my sweet little man."

"No. I'm not arguing. I know."

She shook him. It made him snicker to be held in such a grip. She was unfeminine, and yet so very female. She pressed heavy and warm against him, her broad and ruddy face broken with laughter. "I said *does,* and now you say it."

"Did."

"Why, your arms are like kindling wood, Mr. Peter. You've got a waist like a fine lady." She grabbed him about the waist and flung him off the dory, then sat on him.

"Say it, or I'll put sand in your mouth." They rolled over and over, but the same gallantry that keeps the tom from using his strength against the she-cat kept him from seriously resisting her. What the argument was about, both seemed to have forgotten. At last, all he could do was lie on his back, laugh, and look up at her straddle across him, her petticoats halfway up her thighs. Head and shoulders were against the sky, the fair hair had loosened and hung about her. Although honey-white where the sun had been at it, underneath it was as warm a brown as pulled molasses.

"I'll say it," he agreed, "if you'll get up off my stomach."

"Say it."

"Dash does love you."

Once on his feet and the dory between them, he added: "But he won't a year from now. Two years. I'll say 'did' and I'll say 'does,' but I won't say 'will.' "

He leaped over the rocks and away, confident that his long legs would save him.

Once more at the Sea Urchin, he sat and ordered grog. She had been amazingly good-tempered. He shouldn't have pitied Dash quite so much these last few months. Sometime soon he'd have to go over again and give her that letter. But he wanted her to get used to the idea that Dash was gone, and never coming back to her, first. Then even a loving letter would do no harm. As soon as he had spoken of Dash's obligations to her, she had looked insulted — "What-der-yar-mean-by-that?" — rough and sharp. It was almost as if he had said, "If you find you are going to have a baby, we Inmans will help you." My God! Could *that* have been what

Dash had meant? "I'm much beholden to her," he had said. Exactly what does being "beholden" to a girl mean? Dash couldn't have been so wicked as to seduce a girl — a little, poor, unprotected, orphan girl. Maybe Marblehead girls were lax, as Doctor Fisher had told him. But he had also said there was nothing, nothing at all against this girl's reputation. But, of course, Dash never could marry her. His mother would die of shame, having to introduce anything like that as a daughter-in-law. But Ma'am was an old-fashioned woman. She'd say it was Dash's duty and no good comes to a man that escapes his duty. And suppose he did marry her? According to Squire Mompesson, it wasn't so many generations ago Inman women had been about like that, kirtle-skirted, fishy, sitting in the sun mending their men's nets. Peter had liked that broad, sunny scene upon the beach. He had read enough Rousseau to have a sentimental feeling about the beauties of the natural life. But that was all in books. Transfer it to fact and he could not imagine it — not in fashionable Salem. Not in his mother's double parlors. And he thought of Polly, and the very taste of the grog sickened him. Never, never in the world could she understand how even as Dash's soul clung to her soul his miserable body had been over in Marblehead rolling around in the sand with dirty fisher girls. Polly loved him with a passion a girl like Dulcey could not even imagine. And Dash loved Polly. Peter knew this. Whatever he had given to Dulcey, it was nothing but the ashes falling from the pure, flaming torch of his love for Polly Mompesson.

That damned letter! He took it from his pocket, turned and turned it, wishing he had the dishonesty to break the seal. It was nothing but a little love note. A farewell. Yet it might be Dash had promised to marry her. You couldn't ever tell what Dash would do. You never got to know him so well you could say what he would do or say in any given situation. No matter how much you loved him, you could never encompass him.

Dolly had made good time, for she was heading for home. Peter had one comforting conviction. If Dulcey really was in a "delicate condition," she'd never have gone bouncing about, pulling him off a dory, sitting on his stomach. Women "in the family way" sat at home and sewed little garments and thought high thoughts so it would be a high-minded baby. They leaned on arms and fainted.

Fortunately for his peace of mind, he did not remember the bitch

Trinity. She had been so pregnant she could hardly waddle. Dash had put her in the cool cellar, she was suffering so from the heat and her condition. There she had found a rat, had broken twenty bottles of wine, killed her rat, and never thought twice about the matter.

As he left Marblehead and took the long sandy road home, he felt assured that the worst possible was not to be. Really . . . Dash, the finest, bravest, most admirable, wonderful man he had ever known, didn't do things like that. And yet he felt depressed as he realized he did not really know Dash at all, as a whole. Only those fascinating scraps and corners of himself that he had, during the last eight months, doled out to him. Why, the second Dash had put that high beaver hat on his head, buttoned his captain's coat about him, he had become a stranger. Peter did not know Dash at all, and he loved him the more because he was strange and mysterious to him. And, ever so slightly, he was afraid of him as people always fear the loved and mysterious, be they gods or mortals.

～6～

MAY WORE AWAY and spring with it. June and July. Tom was off with *Fox Fire* on the well-tried Baltic route. Captain Magee had taken the *Mermaid* to Surinam for cotton. So Peter and old Fessenden and Ma'am ran the counting-house. They had little to do, except, best they were able, juggle one creditor against the next and keep up the interest on the money they had borrowed to build the *Victrix* and send her out with ten thousand dollars in her pocket. Word had come from her. She had called at Madeira to buy wines, had been chased by strange craft, presumably French corsairs from the West Indies. "She is flighty," Dash had written, "and she's no pack horse. But she can outsail anything in sight. And sails closer to the wind than any vessel I have ever been on. Please inform Mr. Becket, Ma'am, of this fact."

In August, Peter would go to Harvard. Although his boyhood friend, Blainey Phipps, was now two years ahead of him, they would chum together. He had been to Cambridge, carrying one load of books. He had seen the black little rooms he and Blainey would share in old Massachusetts. Doctor Hobey had written such a letter of recommendation for him that the President himself had welcomed him. Made much of him. And here there would never come to him the heady smell of the sea he was not strong enough to follow. In these learned attics were no sea chests, inadvertently holding within them the fragrance of the Far East. Here was only the smell of books and generations of choice and goodly young men. Even if he climbed to Massachusetts's roof, he would never see the tall white ships coming home.

That trip to Cambridge convinced him it was here and nowhere else he belonged. Little encouragement did he get from his own family. Except that Dash had always known he must not linger on, clerking it at Salem. But Doctor Hobey backed him.

Peter kept his promise to Polly. Often as might be, he went to her. He put up, not only with her father and her aunts, but also with three or four flirtations in which she was engaged. Peter noticed that her father enjoyed them as much as she did. He preened himself over her conquests.

The most rampant among her suitors was, at the moment, a Mr. Fred Briscoe from Baltimore. She had met him at Balston Springs the year before. Mr. Mompesson often took her there, or to other fashionable watering places, not so much to take the waters as to give her genius greater scope. Mr. Briscoe was a landscape architect and had arrived in Salem this summer to do over certain old-fashioned back yards. Obviously, Mr. Mompesson approved of him, for he had invited this distinguished, wealthy, but not very virile young man to be his guest for as long as he pleased. Nobody was talking about Polly and Dash any more. All the talk was of Polly and Fred.

But as often as Peter and Polly had a moment together, he would tell her Dash loved her. Then her enchanted eyes would soften and linger in his as though this was the first declaration of love she had ever heard. At eighteen, Peter was eligible to grown-up parties. With so many of Salem's young men always to sea, the girls had to accept partners older than they might have preferred. Or younger. He now knew at first-hand the pleasures of water parties, picnics, balls, little dancing parties. He never presumed to offer to escort Polly himself. Fred Briscoe did that. Peter watched and admired and loathed her carryings-on. He had moments of acute jealousy, not for himself — consciously, at least, — but for Dash.

But his promise to Dulcey he did not keep. He did not take her rowing. He showed her no globes. He had not delivered Dash's letter. It was easier to try to forget her, and as for that letter, had not Dash particularly told him "there was no hurry"?

It was Friday afternoon and he was in the back yard, a magnificent tangle of all sorts of old-fashioned things. Thank heavens his mother could not afford to hire Mr. Briscoe to do it over in his modern, classical taste. Peter was only trying to keep cool and float his soul on the Horace in his hands. Like most other scholarly young men with poetic leanings, he had tried his hand at translating Horace into English verse. It was the President of Harvard himself who had suggested he experiment with putting it into Greek. This morning, for the first time, he had found he could do this without once stopping to use English as an intermediary between the two classic languages. Besides the sea captains and fishermen in his blood, there was also a sprinkling of clergymen. Perhaps it was these dead scholars who somewhat formed the tastes of the young Inmans. Although his mother and Nanny read nothing, and Tom little but newspapers, Marcy was an avid, ferocious reader, and Dash and Liz always whiled away the long voyages by reading books that would have been beyond the comprehension of the average college graduate. They were always bringing back with them strange and often old books in Dutch, French, Latin, Spanish books of travel, books by Jesuit priests. Books with maps of Java or Sumatra, with even strange stories of the forbidden, unknown, only half-believed Kingdom of Japan. Give either Dash or Liz a long voyage and a dictionary and they could read anything. Peter's tastes were far more literary.

A little way from him, Marcy and some friends had set up a dolls' school about the old Seckel pear tree. At this time of year, all the little girls had a passionate need for dolls of a certain size. They must have dolls who could wear flower-clothes. Their heads must be big enough for campanula caps, and foxglove buds made mittens for them. Hollyhock ruffles were the skirts and hollyhock gonners a proper-sized cheese for them. They got the naked, wooden things at a certain cent shop whose mistress, remembering her own childhood, was always well stocked with this size in July.

Why had the dolls been so bad as to bring their cheeses to school with them? They had been talked to and talked to. They had been stood in corners. Peter heard the little girls' excited chatter. From the page before him, Horace spoke.

"Summer treads
On heels of spring."

He heard Davy Jones's massive barking, and from within the house Little Joe scratched and yapped. A wharf-rat boy was approaching with a live lobster in his hand. Davy was cautiously standing a long way off, but his booming was magnificent.

"Ask the cook," said Peter. "She might buy."

"You Mr. Inman?"

"One of them. I'm Peter Inman."

"I've a letter for you. This lobster's my wages."

The paper was dirty and the letter unsealed. Crudely printed was a single line.

See me now Swifts stand. Dulcey.

The Marblehead girls often came over twice a week for fish-market day to sell what their men had caught.

"You coming, sir?"

"Of course I'm coming."

Not once had the little girls lifted their heads from their intense secret play. But those dolls who had brought cheeses to school with them were being punished by having their nonexistent ears pulled. Marcy had volunteered to do the pulling and the bawling for all of them. Bibby Gibault was crying in pity for them. Emmy Crown-inshield had hidden her favorite in her pocket.

The warmth of the day, the soothing velvet of Horace, the make-believe of the girls, and the passing of time had lulled Peter. He'd like to see Dulcey again.

The fish market was almost sold out, for it was close on closing time. Now there were more market men and women than buyers. They were carrying dripping baskets to the boats moored at the foot of the street, and pushing and pulling handcarts. Old fish were being thrown to cats. He heard one woman call another a terrible name.

Then he saw Dulcey. She had the real fishwife stance, so broad, so honestly connected with the soiled and fishy earth beneath her.

She looked as though she could give as good as she got — and the fishwives were famous for their ready wit.

She recognized him. "Lobsters . . . see and buy," she chanted in the manner of her kind. "Who'll buy? Who'll buy? Lobsters . . . see and buy." Then, in a lower voice, "It's a long time since I've seen you, my little gentleman."

"I've been thinking of that."

"I never did get to see . . . a globe, was it?"

"No. And I never got my rowboat ride."

She looked down at her bare feet.

"Do you come over often to sell lobsters?"

"I'm sort of related — by marriage — to the Swifts. They have a lobster stall over here on fish-market days. Tuesdays and Fridays. I come now and then. I was over here last Tuesday."

"You were?"

"I looked to see you," she admitted. "I went to the Common. I looked at the house folk said you lived in. It was so big I couldn't imagine knocking. I went to the wharf and saw what they said was the Inman counting-house. I hadn't any idea Dash was so rich. He didn't act rich. You didn't act rich, Mr. Peter. I didn't know what to do. Today I thought to send a message to you."

"You can write?"

"And read a little. My brother-in-law taught me. Then he died and Annie died. But the Swifts have been good to me. Annie was my sister."

Her eyes slowly filled with tears as though the memory of her dead sister had suddenly overcome her. Her eyes looked beautiful and crystalline, gray as glass, with heavy fringes. Her face was thinner and less rosy. The deeply indented, curly mouth had uncurled the way a pig's tail uncurls, Peter thought, when it's unhappy.

"Something has gone wrong?"

She did not answer, but her tears fell. His heart began to pound.

"Dulcey, what's gone wrong?"

"Mr. Peter, I'm three months along."

Ever since he could remember, ladies were putting their hands to their mouths, whispering, "She's three months along, four months . . . six . . ." And at last, at nine, came delivery and the clergyman — lately Josephus Hobey — standing up in the pulpit and giving thanks that So-and-So had been safely delivered. Blatting out to the whole world something which, for nine months, had been an uncouth secret.

"Did you know before Dash left?"

"No." She was staring at him with that look of animal dignity he had noticed before. "I don't think it would have made any difference. I couldn't have borne to have told him. When I was with him there wasn't anything but only him. I didn't care what happened to me. Oh, I didn't care for anything but only him . . ."

Peter sat down weakly.

"Not there, Mr. Peter. It's all over fish scales. Sit on this stool." He did not move, and the thin hands he put up to his face came away wet. He thought of the tales he had heard — not in his mother's sitting room, but in Mr. Mullins's barn.

"Dulcey, are you sure it is my brother's child?" He was sorry he had said it. Her face looked stricken.

"I'm sure."

The things he had learned from Mr. Mullins weren't going to help him any more than the things he had learned from his mother's friends. The heat, the smell of the fish, this knowledge, sickened him. The bustle and raucous confusion of the departing market folk was ill-suited to the serious course of events.

"We can't talk here, Dulcey."

"No."

"When will you be over again?"

"I can on Tuesday. That's next fish-market day."

"By then I'll have thought something out." He spoke confidently, and she looked at him trustingly, but he felt helpless, too young for such responsibility. He came, however, from a long line of men used to command others. Even the least of the Inmans spoke masterfully, when cornered.

Now he realized that a group of women, doubtless the ones she had sailed over with that morning, were calling to her to hurry. He saw again the biggest woman he had ever seen. She was guffawing, and he felt she was talking about him to her friends.

"In a moment, Mammy Swift," Dulcey called to the sea monster.

"Does she know?"

"Nobody knows."

"You haven't told anybody?"

"No. I don't carry my heart upon my sleeve no more'n Dash."

"You're not to say a single word to anybody. You hear me?"

Now the contingent from Outer Village was putting up sail, calling to Dulcey.

"I've got to go now," she whispered to Peter, and called to the impatient women, "Wait a moment, gossips," using the quaint old-fashioned word.

"If I ain't here at the fish stall next Tuesday, walk along toward Marblehead real late and I'll start walking to meet you."

"By then, I'll know what to do."

She smiled, almost happy now that she had someone with whom she might share her worries.

"Mr. Peter, you're a real good boy. I've got six or eight lobsters I was too low-hearted to try to sell. I'll give them to you. Hold out your arms. Don't be scared — they've wedges in their claw joints."

"O God! I don't want lobsters."

"You don't?" She ran away laughing, jumped into the dory. "You've got 'em anyway." She cupped her hands as she called. And he saw the other women laughing. The sea monster stood, shaded her eyes with a gigantic, bent forearm, and stared at him. She would certainly know him if she saw him again.

Worse yet, as he turned into Essex Street, he met Polly Mompesson, driving out with a cream-colored pony and a basket cart. Fred Briscoe sat beside her. He knew they were laughing at him. He did make a spectacle, a young gentleman with six lobsters clasped to his unwilling bosom. The animals were fingering his face with their beady feelers. A high-spirited Southerner would have tossed the lobsters into the gutter. A smart New Yorker would have thought to hire a boy to carry them. Peter was a born Yankee. You didn't throw anything away. You didn't expect much personal service around Salem, no matter how rich a town it was.

⌒ 7 ⌒

To go to Polly with the taint of Dulcey upon him, her lobsters and her sweetness, her sorrows and her sunshine, vulgarity and tragedy — and yet somewhere in this mixture, Dash's child was growing —

seemed impossible. Then, too, Polly and Fred Briscoe had laughed at him. He waited for three days before he called. Next day would be Tuesday and then once more he would be face to face with Dulcey. Before this time he felt a need again to worship at Polly's shrine, swear his fealty to Polly — not exactly his, but Dash's.

He found her out in the garden. This last month she had received only within doors, for everybody knew Mr. Briscoe was doing great things in the Mompesson garden. Since last Peter had been there, the old rustic garden house had gone. Miraculously a tiny round Greek temple had arisen. It was white and slender as a nymph, and columned all about. From somewhere Mr. Briscoe (like Moses) had produced water. A microscopic stream plunged twice in artful cataracts, broadened into a pool, marble-edged, before the temple. And over it leaned the merest child of a weeping willow. Gardens, lawns, trees, had been torn up. The new grass was but a green fuzz, touching as the first hair on a baby's head. By its youthfulness, it created spring once more in midsummer. New trees, still guyed with ropes and assiduously watered by gardeners, had replaced ancient ones that once spotted the place with their shade. Peter could not but admit that Mr. Briscoe had created a miracle. This was no longer Salem. It was an enchanted land, allegorical and Grecian. Such a land as he had dreamed of, reading Horace, could almost see in landscape wallpaper such as his mother had in the hall.

Polly, sitting on her bamboo couch, pouring out tea, looked as allegorical as the little world about her. As was proper, she had votaries around her. Surely Fred Briscoe was a handsome fellow — in his negligent, tired, romantic way. Captain Jake Crowninshield was here — and what was a happily married man doing, worshiping at the shrine of love? There were two Derbys, and Old Doctor West. The aunts sat with embroidery hoops and downcast eyes. Beside Aunt Birdseye slept an ancient moldy poodle.

Everyone knew that Derbys and Mompessons were Federalists, and the Crowninshields Republicans. Sometimes they wouldn't speak to each other, but here all political differences were forgotten. And, taking his ease, not far from the goddess, was the high priest of the cult himself. Mr. Cecil Mompesson the Fifth sat so near the pool he could poke at the sea horse, from whose mouth the water trickled, with his gold-headed cane. Surely these waters of Lethe, his hygienic principles, or mere good luck had wonderfully preserved him. Doctor West, of equal age, looked years older.

Peter joined the group, and Polly asked him to go to the "fane," as she called her new summerhouse, and fetch her boiling water. She would make fresh tea. Wonderingly, he entered the little temple. It was flagged with stone. In the middle was a stone table and on it an alcohol lamp with a copper pot, singing. It was before this domestic but seemingly allegorical flame Peter prayed. "Dear God, I've got to push one woman aside to save the other one. I can't save both. Dear God, give me wisdom to do right, and strength to do it."

The bright pot sang. He heard Jake Crowninshield laugh, the sea horse gargle, as Mr. Mompesson poked his cane at it. He heard Polly's voice ring out as eager and as heedless as a romping child's. He had no idea of the turn the conversation might have taken. And what did words matter in the ritual of a cult? Such cults, he thought, probably antedated man's power of speech. He found a pot-holder and carried the boiling water to the table.

All that was being discussed was whether or not the bamboo garden furniture should be painted white and "made to do," or discarded. Then Fred Briscoe would design new furniture. Polly was opposing Mr. Briscoe. She was determined to keep the old set, which her father had bought some years before. It was the Crowninshields' *Belisarius* had brought these things from India. "And your brother, Peter, was her captain, wasn't he, Jake?"

Captain Crowninshield nodded. "Dash, yes. Good ship, *Belisarius*. Good captain. That was the richest voyage she ever made." And all Dash ever got from it was captain's share.

Peter drank his tea. The conversation omitted him, but he did not feel neglected. Polly had practically said, Dash picked out this furniture in Bombay, therefore, I'll never part with it. He sat beside the high priest and hoped he would be allowed to drink his tea and look at Polly — enchanting in a pale green flowered muslin with a gilt fillet in her hair — renew his vows of loyalty and soon leave.

Squire Mompesson was addressing him. "I'm glad to see that at least one of our young gentlemen has the taste and sense to cling to the smallclothes and long stockings of a gentleman." Peter was, as often before, wearing out Liz's cast-offs. "This fashion" — and he gestured, with long hands, delicate as porcelain and frilled with lace, at the pale pantaloons of the assembled gentlemen. "Pantaloons! Trousers! We called them 'tongs' when I was a lad. Workmen and servants wore them. But no gentleman ever put them on. It is bad enough when the lower classes ape the dress and manners of their betters, but that a *gentleman* should copy the fashions of the lowly! Such a thing has never before happened in the history of the world."

"I guess not, sir."

"A gentleman is always known by his fine leg, and always will be. That French Revolution — this upstart Napoleon — got our young people by the ear."

Peter glanced nervously at Jake Crowninshield, who held fast to these Frenchmen. Squire Mompesson took snuff, sneezed and warmed to his subject. As he talked, Peter watched Polly. Mr. Mompesson was tapping his silver shoe buckles with his cane. The slight noise drew Peter's attention from Polly. The old man's little legs were marvelous, springing up so handsomely from small ankles, swelling out so nobly at the calf, turning in rather sharply to form the small kneecap. "We, at least," he was saying to Peter, "have sense enough to think a good leg is nothing to be ashamed of." So he was back where he started from. Peter drew his spindle shanks under his chair. He saw Polly was following the conversation and ever so little laughing at him.

"Truth is, Mr. Mompesson, I'm always wearing whatever it is my next older brother, Eleazar, cast off the year or so before. I'm not proud of my legs and I don't mind workingman fashions."

"Let the ladies, from now," said Captain Jake, who had been drinking his tea half brandy, "have the legs."

"The ladies?" Polly's eye flicked over him. "Why, Jake, didn't you know ladies have only feet pinned on the bottom of their skirts? I learned that years ago."

Captain Jake's handsome lips parted, his bold eyes caressed the long delicate line from hip to ankle. The new dresses were very revealing. It was not an appropriate expression for a happily married man.

"Then may I say, Polly, I hope you are no lady. Couldn't bear to think those pretty little feet are all there is to the . . . to the situation."

Squire Mompesson roared with laughter and an ugly flash came in his eyes. He's always like that, thought Peter. The more flirtation . . . well, yes, the bolder she is, the better he likes it. She was a naughty girl to set them all thinking about legs. Take Peter. He had only been thinking of Squire Mompesson's legs, but now he was thinking of Polly's. The high priest, at the same time, egged on the worshipers and guarded the sacred image. He wanted troops and troops of men, old and young, married and single, bad or good, to come and worship and kneel — and not ever *touch*. And Peter knew that was why he hated Dash. Dash had doubtless dared to touch, and Mr. Mompesson had guessed it. He had walked in and kicked the high priest aside, just like the canaille going into Notre Dame.

And what did this all mean to Polly? He saw her as a bright fly caught in an evil web. Struggling to free herself. Peter could not free her. Dash could.

Peter, well taught at home to put things away, returned the copper pot to the fane. "Miss Polly," he called from between the twinkling white columns, "shall I douse the fire?"

"Oh yes, do. Thank you, Peter."

He doused the fire.

Already the day seemed ending. The evening breeze came in, cool and dank from off the North River. Smelling of eel grass and salt marsh and death and decay. It was as if the door of a tomb had opened.

When he came out to make his adieux — and he did not come quickly — Mr. Mompesson was wrapping his daughter in a white woolen shawl Flip had brought. It seemed to Peter he was watching the high priest put away the sacred image until next festival day.

"There, my dear," he said, "snug as a bug in a rug."

Captain Jake was bowing and leaving. Peter made his manners and turned to go with him.

She called after him. "Peter . . . Peter." He looked back. Her little face was strained, her neck long and stretched out as if struggling to escape the white cocoon of wool that smothered her.

"Ma'am?"

Her eyes were wide open, and she had an almost desperate look. "Nothing. Only . . . Peter, you've hardly talked to me at all."

"May I come soon?"

"Yes! Yes! Come again soon, Peter."

～8～

NEXT DAY, Peter told Mrs. Cady that those lobsters he had bought last fish-market day had tasted so good he was going to buy more today. Mrs. Cady looked at him suspiciously through rectangular spectacles. She had often sent him marketing, but never before last Friday had he taken the initiative.

"My, Peter, you've got such a passion for lobsters that if you was a young wife, I'd say you was in the family way."

Peter smiled bleakly. It was not a subject he could joke about.

Dulcey was not at the Swift stand. He bought his lobsters of Mammy Swift. Her face was so fat and shiny, her eyes so little and twinkling, he thought she was winking at him. Evidently Dulcey had decided to walk halfway from Marblehead and meet him on the road.

Mrs. Cady told him he had been overcharged. "You're not much of a shopper, Peter. But I guess you've brains enough for Harvard."

Then he heard the church bells, cling-clang. Now the market was closing. He went upstairs and got the letter, for the seriousness of events made him feel he could no longer postpone delivering it. He went to the barn, endured Mr. Mullins's barrage, and harnessed Dolly. The mare, with the chaise dangling at her heels, crossed the Mill Dam and through the shipyards of South Salem, wandered down a sandy cartpath leading to Marblehead. On either hand were salt marshes and rough sheep pasture. He saw the surf ruffling white about Tinker's Island and Pig Rocks. Breaking the dreary expanse of sand marsh and poor pasturage was an immense hairy group of old willows. Dolly stopped. Seeemingly she had seen Dulcey before he did, or remembered where it was her previous driver had often stopped.

Dulcey stepped out on the road, smiling and confident, and ready to be admired. And why not? She wore her best clothes. The red calico was unfaded. She even had a fresh white cap and kerchief. She's done this before, Peter thought. She didn't like Dash always to see her, smell her, in the clothes she tends market in or mends fish nets.

It was a lovely trysting place, and amazingly private. She told him to lead Dolly off the road. The mare and chaise were almost hidden behind willows and a dune. And under the trees were boulders to sit on, and sparse, drying grass to lie upon. The long day was drawing to a close, and all about them, from far away, came the tiny tinkle of sheep bells.

Her wide gray eyes fastened trustingly upon his face. Hadn't he promised, by today, to have thought something out? The fact was, he had thought of nothing.

"Dulcey," he said at last, when they had settled in the nest, "what was it you said? Three months?"

"That's how I figure it."

"How soon . . . well . . . how soon does it show?"

She laughed. "Mr. Peter, look at these petticoats. It hardly shows ever, on us. Now, fashionable ladies in skin-tight skirts — that's a cat of a different color. I've been told it shows next morning on them."

He did not admire her humor, but appreciated her good spirits. He began counting on his fingers.

"I've done that already. It's January."

"A lot can happen before January."

"Dash might come back."

"No. Not likely. Don't count on Dash — any. But he did leave a letter with me . . . for you."

"He did? You've got it?"

"Yes." She did not criticize him that he had waited three months to deliver it. She was either too kind, or too stupid.

"He knew I could read," she said complacently.

But not very well, thought Peter. She mouthed every word and kept her finger under it a considerable time before moving on to the next. He was aching to know what Dash had written. Was he . . . well, so like his grandmother that he had promised to marry her? Peter had a handful of dried grass in his hand. He braided it, shaped it into a little mat, threw it away. The suspense was more than he could endure.

"Let me read that letter to you."

She shook her head. "I can read real good. And he's written it so nice."

124

"Oh, for Heaven's sake, give up trying." And, at last, he took it from her. "Shall I?"

"Yes, you might. I've understood pretty well up to the time he says something about two ladies."

"Well, this is it."

Dear Dulcey:

I have one regret on leaving. That is that I must go without a word to you. You have been a dear . . .

Peter stopped short, he felt he could not read this word to her.

"Wife," she prompted him.

. . . a dear wife to me, not in the sight of man, not in the sight of the God of New England, but in the knowledge of earlier, happier, more heedless gods. Dulcey, I leave this letter as an instruction to you.

"I wasn't sure of that word."

"An instruction . . . he means you are to do what he says next."

"Yes."

If, in our worship of Aphrodite, we have inadvertently worshiped Ilithyia as well . . .

"That's those two ladies I didn't quite get."

He explained to her the difference between worshiping the goddess of love and that of children and childbirth, and went on:

. . . and you find yourself with child . . .

"It was nice of him to think of that. Some men don't."

Peter's eyes had leaped ahead. What next he must read sickened him.

. . . you are to go to the Selectmen of Marblehead, tell your story and show them this letter, for I do admit that, of any child born of you, Dulcey Delaney, before February 1801, I, Ralph Inman, am the father. The Selectmen will tell you how to bring bastardy charges against me.

"What are those?"

"Oh . . . I don't know exactly. But you go to court. And they grab the man. Or, if he's away, they attach enough of his property to support you and the child. Well . . ."

Needless to say, I hope I have not put so shameful a burden upon you. But do not fear to name my name. Trust Peter in all things.

My dear love, farewell,

DASH

Peter could see the paragraph in the Salem *Gazette*. The editor would tuck it modestly between the sailing of a Crowninshield ship and the fact that the *Astrea* had been bespoken or the *Mermaid* was sailing. But it would be there. Dulcey Delaney, of Marblehead, had, in the Quarterly Court, now sitting at Salem, brought bastardy charges against Captain Ralph Inman. She had his written admission in her hand. Oh, it might be in such small type all the old people would have to put on spectacles to read it. The roar that went up from the news would shake every teacup in Salem, every ledger in every counting-house. And Ma'am would be very white and silent about it. Of course, Dash would have to do "his duty" to this girl when once he was home again. His mother would talk of buying her off, and sob — but in the end it would slide off her. Everything bad did, eventually, slide off his mother. Mullins — how Mullins would gloat and spit! Squire Mompesson would preen and gloat. At last he'd have reason enough to forbid Dash, ever, to pay his addresses to his daughter.

Peter closed his eyes. And there, waiting for him behind the lids, was Polly's bewitching, tip-tilted profile. He saw the long, delicate, clean line of her neck. This would kill her as surely as if you put your hands about her throat and strangled her. She loved Dash so much, was so absolutely sure of his love, it would kill her.

"Shall I, Mr. Peter?" Dulcey sounded doubtful.

"Dulcey, you're not ever to go to the selectmen with your story and that letter."

"Oh? But if not that, then what?"

Peter leaned back, his hands clasped behind his neck, gazing at the sky through the umbrella of willow leaves. The air was filled with the tawny pinks of the long afterglow. Soon it would be dark.

"I'm thinking."

"It would mean he'd marry me when he got back?"

"No. Not necessarily," he said sharply.

"Sometimes men don't," she admitted, with the sad knowledge of her poverty. "But the law can make them?"

"No. All the law can do is get money."

"I don't see how I ever could go to the selectmen. They are terrible cross men. Cuffey Kane — she was a friend of my sister Annie's. They got her. The selectmen did. And they locked her up in jail and the ministers came and preached sermons at her. And if she hadn't run away to Salem, she'd of been bound out to a strict matron and . . ."

"What happened to her?"

"Oh, now she's a . . . a you know what. We call them whores over here, but I guess you've got a nicer word for it. Mr. Peter, I couldn't bear the selectmen to know."

Peter himself thought that if the Inmans stepped forward and took charge of Dulcey, kept her in Salem, the selectmen wouldn't do a thing to her. Nowadays, selectmen cared a lot more for the taxpayer's money than they did for morals. He'd heard his grandmother say so. They'd be pleased to be rid of the expense of locking her up and preaching at her.

"You wouldn't get a husband by going to them, and they'd be terribly mad with you." It did no harm to frighten her a little. *"Terribly* mad. All you'd get would be shame and scorn — and maybe a little money."

"But if I had the money, I could go away and say I was a married woman. Somewhere in the country. I could hide until Dash came back to me."

Peter seized upon this idea. "I have some money. Some — not much."

"To spend on *me?"*

It was for Dash he might spend it. And, for Polly, give up Harvard.

"Yes," he said, and then burst out angrily, "Oh, why was Dash such a fool!"

"He wasn't a fool, Mr. Peter," she said gently.

Perhaps not. Perhaps it was Dulcey, with her generosity and vulgarity, her animal stupidities — and wisdom — that had saved Dash. Polly couldn't — she'd been sheer torment to him. Yes, she could have, if she had not been so groomed and civilized. Imprisoned by her father and her environment until she was more an image than a real woman. And he thought with loathing of the high priest of her cult.

"If I boarded somewhere, Dash could marry me when he came back."

"No, he won't. I told you to forget him."

She was silent. He sat up and slowly re-read the letter. It hardly looked like Dash's handwriting at all, being almost printed. It was an honest, blunt admission of seduction. There was not a word in it, though, about marriage. It was easy enough for Peter to say, "No, he won't ever marry you," but he really did not know which way Dash might jump. He might say, "I did it, didn't I? I don't sneak out. Of course, I don't love her and she isn't the wife I'd choose — but she's what I've got. And she's all I deserve." As selfishly as that, Dash might do "what's right" without thinking about it from Polly's point of view. He'd be heroic and give up Polly. But why must she be so cruelly punished to satisfy Dash's remorse and honor?

I might tell Dulcey I'll keep this letter for her. And tear it up. A smart girl could run quite a blackmail with it, after, say, Dash is married to Polly. He felt she would give it to him if he asked her. She was too ignorant to use it — rather than too honest.

Then he heard her sniffling. She was crying.

"Dulcey . . ."

"I don't want a baby! I don't! I wish it was dead."

"Dulcey, don't. Every girl wants a baby sometime."

"I don't. Ever. I hate them."

"Dulcey," he said tenderly, "be a good girl and stop your noise."

He gave her his handkerchief. She cried a little longer and he felt so sorry for her his own eyes began to smart.

"Peter," she whispered, "are you crying, too?"

"Not quite. Almost." They both gulped, and laughed together.

"Come, now. I'll drive you home. It's almost dark."

Before them was the rocky knob of Marblehead, on either hand the long, flat stretches of the quiet sea.

"And tomorrow morning, Dulcey, meet me here by these willows. Say eight o'clock. I'll get away from the counting-house *somehow*. Dulcey, we'll drive out into the country — Lynn way or Beverly. We'll find a farmer's wife who'll take you in, for pay."

"I can say I'm married, and my man to sea."

"Or I can say I am your brother-in-law and you are a widow. Or your brother, perhaps."

"You're so good to me." And at the thought of his goodness, her nose began to run again. Peter had the handkerchief. She wiped her nose on her forearm with hound-like snufflings. Peter's fastidious blood congealed.

"Mr. Peter, this is far enough. Dash never went closer. He said it did a poor girl's reputation no good to be seen out with gentlemen. Put me out here." Dolly came to a willing stop. "Mr. Peter, would you like to kiss me?"

He did not want to, but he did. He did not like the quality of her skin, bright and hard as an apple. Nor the smell even of her Sunday clothes. He was glad she offered only a cheek, not the gorgeous curly mouth which rarely concealed the white, slightly crooked teeth within. Yet it was vaguely disturbing to be leaning out of a chaise, kissing a girl in the half-dark.

In some ways Peter was as backward about such matters as certain of his brothers had been forward. He got more emotional release writing a sonnet to Miss Mompesson's footprint on the sands of time than kissing Dulcey Delaney.

9

THERE WAS A READINESS about Dulcey that was, to Peter, one of her most attractive qualities. It was the readiness of a puppy. You whistle and it comes wagging. You slap your knee and it bounces. Throw a stick and it runs. You say "bad dog" and it rolls over in despair. He couldn't say "bad girl" to Dulcey. He did not feel it. The badness was her absent master's. Not hers. Peter had a fastidious nature, not given to the sins of the flesh, nor could he easily understand a "fallen girl," except in Horace. He liked pure, unattainable girls, more fastidious, even, than himself. Now he began to understand something of another sort — a little dirty, fishy, earthbound, and completely fallen.

Day after day, during August, they drove, in one direction and then another, into the countryside. It would have been fairly easy to have hidden her in such a port town as Salem, somewhere along the waterfront. But like many another naïve and sinful couple, they believed in the anomaly of the country — the country, where any news is so rare a very young gentleman in a chaise, trying to hide an even younger girl, probably pregnant, was seized upon as the most interesting thing that had happened since Farmer Whittle had been gored by his bull.

Dolly waddled down one lane and then another. The joe pyeweed, goldenrod, asters, and swamp maples were beginning to show the colors of summer's end. When a pleasant, solitary, neat farm was seen, Peter would stop and inquire. The farmer's wife would listen suspiciously to his story, which he unwisely varied. Sometimes, indeed, Dulcey was his sister, again his sister-in-law. Sometimes a married woman with a husband at sea, sometimes a widow. But no matter what rôle he cast her in, she always looked exactly what she was — a young girl in trouble. The farm woman would look from the pretty, anxious face under the leather hood of the chaise to the distraught young man, obviously from the upper class. For the first time, people looked into Peter's calm, clean eyes, and read evil and lechery in them. Neither avarice nor pity touched the farm wives' hearts. Peter's obvious youthfulness was even held against him. It showed a precocious depravity.

Peter did not dare absent himself too often from the counting-house. He was almost sick with grief and worry. Yet Dulcey did not sicken. It was as if she knew that pregnancy is the natural state of a young female and marriage but an afterthought. Yet she, too, now that August was ending, was begging him to hurry. Wisely or not, she had asked about among her Marblehead friends and found what might be done.

One day, when they were returning, more discouraged than usual, she told him that in Puddle Alley lived a woman. "She's got five or six — you know, whores — and a girl caught like I'm caught can go to her and get a midwife and everything free and no questions asked. And then the girl works for her until it's all paid back. I'd not have to, of course, for you've got money."

"What happens to the baby?"

"Oh, those poor little love-children," she answered, callously, "as you nice people call 'em. We call 'em just plain bastards. They are apt to do poorly, and then they are buried in the sea, with rocks tied to them. And no questions asked."

Dash's child born in a brothel, rotting at the bottom of Salem Harbor! Never!

"That won't do — ever, Dulcey."

"Then you think of something," she answered, almost angrily, "and something pretty quick. If not, I won't have any choice. I'll have to go to the selectmen. And tell them."

"Dulcey . . . what if . . . well, suppose you didn't show the letter, but just told them . . . that it was me."

"No one would believe it."

"All those farmers' wives do."

"But it isn't true."

"I don't care any more what's true and what isn't."

"I don't think Dash would like it. And he did tell me what to do — you know."

"Oh, to Hell with Dash! He walked off, didn't he? He doesn't care. He doesn't care . . . *that!*" — and he snapped his fingers. It was not true, but the situation was wearing him down, and the new term had begun at Harvard and he wasn't there. "Oh, now, stop it, Dulcey." She had burst into tears. "I didn't mean to make you cry. I never saw a girl that could cry and laugh as fast as you can."

"I guess I've got to do as Dash told me," she sobbed. "I'm scared of the selectmen, but it would be worse if they found out and I couldn't say who . . ."

Peter stopped Dolly. "No. Now listen." He put an arm about her shaking shoulders. "If worse comes to worst, I'll marry you myself."

"But then Dash couldn't, when he comes back."

Peter withdrew his arm. Ready as she was to run any direction he suggested, she was stubborn about some things. He could not get the idea out of her head that Dash was going to marry her.

"You've got to get this straight. He isn't going to ever marry you."

"I wish I could drown the baby. I wish it was dead."

He heard her out, but at arm's length. They had, this last month, gone through the same scene over and over. He could understand how she might attract other men. But, to him, she was slightly repellent. What she had to give was not what he wanted from women. She was too much the animal, and her pregnancy emphasized the fact. And yet he was fond of her. He felt protective toward her.

"Peter, couldn't we *say* you and I are married? Would anyone bother to find out?"

"You bet they would. My family would." Still, this was an idea. "Dulcey, we might find a man badly in want of a little ready cash who'd say you were his wife. Just long enough for the baby to be born."

"And until Dash came back."

"Yes. Until Dash came back." He was tired of telling and telling her that would make no difference. He felt so tired, and, unlike almost any summer he could remember, he'd coughed a lot.

"It would be a shameless man that would do that," she went on, thoughtfully.

"Lots of men do worse things for five hundred dollars. Murder people, for instance. And it would be kind of him. You know there are lots of men in this world who are both hard up and kind."

Dulcey immediately brightened as soon as he had tossed her this new stick to chase, but neither she nor Peter had the least idea where to lay hands upon such a man.

Peter, hands in pockets, walked Salem's waterfront, presumably doing the routine work of his little job. As he passed disreputable men, he'd ask himself, What would you do for five hundred dollars? Those who looked wicked enough to do anything did not look kind. And time was slipping through his fingers. At last — and it was already September — Dulcey quietly told him she had made up her mind. There was nothing to do but go to the selectmen. To this he felt forced to agree. But he made her promise to wait until October. He was an opportunist by nature. He was confident that there was a way out and somehow he'd stumble on it.

The youngest and physically frailest of four brothers, Peter had long been forced to go at his problems a little obliquely, as youngest children often are. He had never been able to protect his own personality by frontal attack. This was impossible against Dash, Liz, Tom, even his grandmother and mother. It was through the interstices of the family Peter moved, going his own way, saying little, never complaining or showing, or even feeling, resentment. He was a free man. His graceful submission to his elders was a façade only. Behind the façade, he was a touch slippery, and could get out of anything he really did not want to do, like an eel slipping out of a creel. Outwardly he seemed ingenuous, open almost to naïveté. And very young, even for eighteen. Never had he been able to plot his own course, or say, as the older boys could and did, "I'll do this, or this. I will not do so-and-so." Peter was in the habit of lying low, watching for an opportunity. This he was now doing.

Chapter Four

J ACK WEST came to look at Peter, his homely horse-face perturbed.

"Peter, you promised me not to have another cold. I'm going to
lock you up — at least until your fever's down. People with weak
chests have to take their colds seriously. Whyever, wherever, did
you get it?" And then, because his diagnoses often went beyond
accepted medical practice, he asked suddenly, "Peter, is anything
worrying you?" Jack theoretically never listened to Nanny's gossip, but when she heard from her apple woman, who had it from
her neighbor over in Beverly, Mrs. Henshaw, that one of the Inman brothers — but she wasn't sure which — had been trying to
hide some sort of a doxy among the decent women of Beverly, he
had felt obliged to listen. There was only one Inman it could be.
The others were all at sea.

"Why, no . . . Except I am already over a month late in getting
to Harvard. Blainey won't be able to hold his half of the room
for me forever. And now I'll be still later."

Jack felt he could not question him and left.

Peter was kept to his bed for three days. No matter how far away
Liz might be, this room was always his room. Six foolish little
clocks gestured to him. Idiot boy, they were thinking. Now they
had stopped ticking and striking, and after five months were a
touch dusty. His mother was better at arranging flowers than dust-
ing, Mrs. Cady overworked. "What's idiot boy going to do next?"
the clocks' static, staring faces demanded.

He said, out loud, "Idiot boy is going to Harvard."

It had been a hard decision to make. The first of October was not far away, and he had agreed that, if nothing before then turned up, Dulcey was to show her letter. Then let the heavens fall. And Polly die of a broken heart. There hadn't seemed to be one thing else to do. And yet something still might turn up.

Now the time had come to pack books, boots, pantaloons, breeches. An old leather trunk had been brought down from the attic and stood half-full at the foot of his bed. It was such an old-fashioned thing, he might, as his mother suggested, get laughed at for a yokel. Of course, she wouldn't understand why he preferred it to one of the wooden sea chests. Even college porters would know a sea chest meant that the young gentleman came of seafaring folk. "Your great-grandfather, the Reverend Peter Morton, carried that old trunk to Harvard with him," his mother had said. "I declare, no one has been to college since. Or anywhere, except to sea. Of course, the ladies have." True, she had hatboxes and feminine luggage aplenty, but he preferred the shabby little old leather trunk. He thought tenderly of Great-Grandfather Morton leaving Salem for Harvard those many years ago. It was in his footsteps Peter would follow — not the bold, broad way to sea.

The spacious landing where the great clock stood was a favorite place for Mrs. Inman to sit and sew, especially on days too warm for a fire, yet cool enough to make one appreciate the sun streaming in through the high palladium window. As Peter came back from Dash's room, where he had gone for his money hidden in Dash's secret glory hole, he saw that his mother was sitting there with her "young friend," his Cousin Frances. About them were waves of tossing white muslin, curtains for bedchambers. And as usual his mother was idling and chatting, and Frances Cunningham was working like a bitch-beaver. Even back in his own room, going on with his packing, Peter was still conscious of how close they were.

"Frances," Lucy was saying, "I believe we" — she meant "you" — "have made this pair shorter than the others. Where's my tape measure? O dear, yes."

"They can be lengthened." Lucy was always sending poor Frances back to do her work over again.

Peter dumped stockings in his chest and spread them to protect the hat Liz had given him before he left and which Peter still considered almost too swell to wear. Every pair of stockings had been darned by Cousin Frances.

"Frances, don't bite threads, dear. You'll chip your teeth."

"I've been biting threads all my life and I haven't a chip."

"But teeth get more brittle as we get older."

A pause. The ladies sewed.

It's funny, Peter thought, Mother is always telling Frances not to bite threads and she always answers the same way. She doesn't do everything Mother tells her to.

He was putting apples in his trunk, and sat on the edge of his bed to eat one. He was still weak from his recent fever. His teeth crunched into the firm skin, the fine juice foamed up over his lips. He had a daydream of himself and Blainey chumming in old Massachusetts together, eating apples. Blainey was going to be a lawyer. Peter suddenly made up his mind. If they'd have him, if he made good, he was going to stay on there forever. He'd be a scholar. A true scholar. And perhaps a halfway poet, on the side.

"No, I don't know why he wants to go," Lucy was saying, "but there, it's not my business. He has saved every cent himself out of his clerk's pay. You know the doctors say he's not hardy enough for a sea life. Mother Inman doesn't think he shows much gumption as a clerk, even. I don't think he really cares much about going to college. He has put it off, and put it off so. For no reason. Poor Peter. I guess he just doesn't want much in this life — and that's all he'll get."

Not want college? It was freedom itself. He had to go. It was lucky he hadn't had to spend his hoarded money on Dulcey. Now he was going tomorrow, or the next day. He was going. And dreaming of Harvard, he no longer heard the voices of the women on the landing.

"They told him he could buy a partnership for five hundred dollars. But he hasn't a cent. I don't think any sensible person will lend it to him. He's so queer."

"But, Frances, if they don't lend it, he might kill someone. These French refugees are so desperate."

"Oh, pooh, Lucy. Not Flanneau. He'll marry money. Frenchmen are amorous. He'll find some lonely old party. You know I told you he had no more than arrived than he asked Miss Unity

Stackpool, and then Miss Clara. Or he'll find some girl in trouble whose father has five hundred."

"Tell me . . . has he approached you yet, Frances?"

"Well, yes . . . he has."

"Oh, how droll! What did he say?"

Cousin Frances giggled like a schoolgirl. It was a nice, silly sound, coming from her.

"He got very excited and mixed up. Usually he speaks quite good English. Of course, he was impressed when he found out that I own the house and that the Stackpools pay me rent. I had to lie. I told him that, by the terms of my deceased husband's will, I lost what little property I had if I remarried. Lucy . . . I wonder who'll be next? You don't know anybody who'd like a quite nice, kind, queer husband? He isn't so very old — somewhere in his thirties. He has the most marvelous taste. As you know, all the ladies who can afford it are dying to have him design dresses for them. And he's talking of branching out. Buying imported goods here, and selling them for profit elsewhere. He's going to make a lot of money, sometime. And anybody can have him for five hundred dollars. Why . . . if he had only gone at *me* differently . . ."

"Oh, *Frances!*"

"Well, there now! He's so obliging, and not bad-looking. Perhaps we Americans are sentimental. We can't imagine marrying except for love. The French are so practical. Flanneau just calls it a 'dot,' and that makes it sound respectable. I don't think he really wants a wife — just some money so he can buy a partnership."

Peter was standing, unseen, upon his threshold. He saw a way out. Not a good or honorable way — but a way out. The opportunity, the thing that "would turn up," had materialized. Frances had said before he had really begun to listen — a "girl in trouble."

What was going to Harvard, compared to saving Dash? He, Peter Inman, who had never amounted to much, could do that. And how grateful Dash would be! Never again could he put on his high hat and button that blue coat about him and become a stranger. Part of him, always, from now on, would belong to Peter, because he had saved him. He, Peter, would hold the unattainable in his hands.

He rushed to Dash's room, so quiet, so empty a room. His mother always packed up and put in the attic Dash's ugly curios. This room held no memory of him. It had blandly returned to what his mother had designed — a young girl's bower, or, now Nanny was gone, a neat, nice, spare guest room. Liz haunted and still possessed the room he and Peter shared. But Dash seemingly had left no memory.

Peter flung himself down upon the bed, buried his face in the pillow, where, night after long night, Dash's head had rested. Sick as he had been, still weak as he was, he began to cry. He cried and cried. He had given up something very dear to him, but for a person even dearer. The joy of such self-sacrifice uplifted and intoxicated him. The long months of waiting and waiting and not knowing how he could help Dash were over.

Polly, too. He wanted to run to her and say, Polly, I've done it. Now you can marry Dash — and never know. I've saved you, too, Polly.

Dash's voice echoed in his ears. "You've done real well, Peter. Thank you. Thank you."

Frances was gone. Mrs. Inman, on her way to her own room, saw Dash's door open. It shouldn't be open. Rooms that were not being used stayed clean better if closed. There was Peter sprawled across the bed, the nicely laundered pink spread rumpled and creased. She would like to have slapped him. How could he be so careless? She saw the dark, ruffled head pressed deep in the pillow, the lank, lithe body, the desperately clenched fist. It had always bothered, rather than worried, her (she did not worry much) that all her younger sons so looked up to Dash. But Tom and Liz, she guessed, were already shaking themselves free from such schoolboy adoration. Peter hadn't. Why, Peter is so lonely, so homesick for Dash, he's in here crying. I think Peter has been crying. It would not have disturbed her that a grown man of eighteen was crying like a girl. She had no respect for male pride, and little conception of manhood. Men did cry sometimes — what of it?

"Peter . . ." she went to him and put a hand on his averted shoulder.

"Yes, Mother." He sat up.

No, not crying. His face was flushed and his eyes literally like stars. But she had never seen a happier face, fiercely, exuberantly happy. Could he have been drinking? Her handsome nostrils felt for any aroma from him. There was none.

"Mother," he burst out passionately, "I'm not a-going to Harvard. Mother, Mother, I'm not a-going to go."

"Oh, child, don't take it so hard." Probably he had got word from Blainey that for some reason they had decided not to take him.

"But I'm not taking it hard," he went on, curiously excited.

He seemed so unlike his usual calm self she feared something had gone wrong with his weak chest. Could it be the symptoms which precede spitting blood? She always had hated unpleasant physical manifestations.

"Peter, dear, do quiet yourself. There!" She had a moment of compassion, of understanding of him. "And you wanted to tell Dash. That's why you came here? There isn't anybody else, is there, you might want to tell?" For I am here, her eyes said. And I am your mother, the gentle hand on his shoulder insisted.

"No. No, thanks. But I'd like to tell Polly that I'm not going."

She shrugged slightly and withdrew the softness of her eyes and the hand on his shoulder.

"I hardly think Polly will be so *wildly* excited, Peter."

"Oh, no. Of course not. No. She won't understand. But I want to tell her and I'm going over now."

First, he went to his own room, took out, from among his papers, one brief manuscript. It was called "Miss Mompesson's Footprints on the Sands of Time." Although he had, again and again, written poems to her, he had never shown her one. This time he would.

⏤2⏤

FLIP TOLD HIM Miss Polly was in the dining room, for it was twelve o'clock and Mr. Mompesson sat to second breakfast. Peter should have known enough not to have chosen this hour for a call. Polly would be toasting toast, and confiding in her papa. The pretty minx of a maid knew that she should send him away to please the master, but announce him to please her mistress. Often faced with similar dilemmas, she always made the same decision. Peter was seated in the little sitting room which was looked upon as Polly's own.

His exhilaration had already dropped from him. Down to earth once more, flat down to earth. First, he had not talked with Flanneau. Nor to Dulcey. Second, he intended to arrange a fake marriage, not a real one. If Dash felt obligated to marry Dulcey on his return — he never could get the idea out of Dulcey's head, not even with a crowbar — he still would be free to do so. Now, he could hardly recall that delirium of tears and joy and renunciation and martyrdom he had felt but half an hour before. He saw that it was the curious coincidence that Flanneau needed five hundred dollars for a partnership that had brought about his decision, for this was exactly to the penny the amount Peter had to hand. If it had been only two hundred and fifty dollars Flanneau wanted, or five hundred and twenty-five, he would not have been so sure that all was now settled.

Polly came in almost immediately. The September day was bright, clear, cold. She had on a green shawl over her usual muslins.

"Oh, but it is cold," she said. "Do light the fire, Peter. I've promised Papa I'll wear this shawl all day and sit near fires. Where have you been? I haven't seen you for days and days."

Ever since he had decided that there was nothing more he could do but let Dulcey go ahead, tell the selectmen, and bring her charges, he had dreaded to see Polly. He felt that inadvertently he was betraying her.

"Busy," he said, smiling. "You know I've been getting ready to go to college."

"Flip, Flip," she called. "Coffee, please, for Mr. Inman."

In no time, Flip appeared, twinkling with pertness and starch, carrying the heavy silver service. Peter saw that there were two cups on the tray. Squire Mompesson had told him three times — he was a repetitious man — that coffee was poison, that neither he nor his daughter ever touched it. He watched with interest as Polly poured a cup for herself as well as for him and began nonchalantly to sip it. So . . . by no means did she always do exactly as her father ordered.

"Now, if Papa comes in," she confided, with conspiratorial intimacy, "I slip my cup under this lounge and let my shawl fall so — see?"

"You do drink coffee?"

"Of course. But no one except my dearest, most intimate friends know. Flip always has it ready. Papa thinks it's for visitors and servants. It is not. Flip makes it for me. I drink gallons. Every day. But don't tell." He realized Polly had had so much do-this don't-do-that in her life she was a little tricky and defiant underneath. This was a quality he could understand. "Oh, Peter, the funniest thing happened this morning. Flip told me . . . I couldn't tell Papa because he is so against our help having followers. But I have to tell someone. Did you know that Flip is quite a belle in her own circle? I declare I'm glad she does not move in *mine*. I'm afraid she'd cut me out. And I do help her. Why, I couldn't have a pretty maid in the house without a follower. Father can't understand why our maids always marry off so fast. Once I married a grim old cook to a quite nice young poultryman. But there . . . as I was saying. This morning when Flip brought up my breakfast, she told me she was going to marry one of the *Victrix* people — soon as ever he comes home again. It is such a bond between us. She told me she was reported again, only yesterday. The Forresters' *Enchantress* bespoke her. I've forgotten just where — and of course it was months ago. Flip was so happy and I was so happy, we kissed each other. 'Darling,' she said, 'I'll run down and make you coffee. Your papa is out walking.' And, 'My dearest Flip,' said I, 'bring two cups.'"

"Which man is it?"

"Danny Obrian, second mate. Oh, I knew he was interested in her. But I didn't know it was all settled — way back last May before the *Victrix* sailed. I've peeked into the kitchen to see him. A monstrous handsome man. My dear, such shoulders! Hands like hams. Blond as an angel. Lah, Peter, as we talked, I wondered if I'd get the best of it. Merely the captain."

"Dan's a good man. If he wasn't, Dash never would have signed him as an officer."

"He was naught but a Derby foremast hand before Dash got interested in him. And your grandmother, too. Flip tells me your grandmother has long had an eye on him."

She stirred and drank her coffee contentedly. "He'll soon be a captain. And, of course, he'll make his fortune. All our captains do, sooner or later. And marry Flip. Then he and she will move to the top of Salem society. I'll have the fun of entertaining my own maid in my own house, say, five or ten years hence. Oh, it's happened before this in Salem. Flip will know how to behave — and that's more than I'll say for Mrs. Dick Crowninshield. You know she was a chambermaid in New York. I never see her but I feel like telling her to fetch me clean linen. But Flip says she is never going to let her maids be so saucy to her as she is to me."

Polly's pleasure in her maid's romance, her nonchalant acceptance of an actual democracy — so different from her father's standards — the sight of her drinking coffee behind her father's back warmed Peter.

"But I've told my story," she said. "Tell me yours. When do you start for Harvard? I will miss you terribly, Peter."

"I'm not going, after all." As he said the words, he felt again the excitement, the magnificent knowledge of all he was giving up — for Dash, and for her. "Polly, I wanted to tell you right off. I've decided not to go." In his own ears, his voice sounded shrill and high-pitched.

His mother was right. The news did not excite Polly.

"I'm so glad. Then you will be here. I've never understood why you or anybody else wants to go to that place. You know, Papa's Cousin Frick has the chair (I think they call it a chair) of mathematics. Papa and I visit him often in Cambridge. You can't believe what frumps the women are. And the men — the very best Cambridge has to offer aren't at all like Boston and Salem good society. When I'm in Cambridge" — and she yawned slightly — "I do nothing but get caught up on my sleep. There's nothing else to do."

"If I went, I wouldn't sleep."

"I feel so sorry for my little cousin, Georgiana Frick. She's only fifteen — so clever and odd. Very odd. I've a mind, sometime, to take her to Salem under my wing. Peter, if I decide to give Georgiana a chance to meet really attractive men, will you promise to be nice to her?"

"Of course, I will."

"And she's quite literary. She writes poems."

"Polly, I wrote you a poem. Recently. I want you to have it." And he added, because she would not know unless he told her, "It's a pretty good poem. The best I've ever done."

He gave it to her and watched her face as she read. He saw a dimple come and go. At least it somewhat amused her. Nothing more. Perhaps she did not like the obvious lightness of his approach. For the point was that not even Miss Mompesson's Footprints left much mark upon the Sands of Time.

"It is a little too Herrick," he admitted modestly.

"I think it is lovely. May I keep it for my album? Who is Herrick?"

"One of the old boys." But he felt sad that he had to tell her. "And of course I want you to keep it. It's the only copy I have, and I want you to have it," he said, not quite admitting even to himself that the entire brief, pretty thing was so well written in his memory he could go home and put it down again, word for word.

"Fred writes lovely poems, too," she added, as if determined to squelch him completely, "but his are more . . . more serious."

That was what she hadn't liked about Peter's poem. It was not an "effusion." It was really more about how brief is feminine beauty — not even the loveliest footprint may outlast the next tide — than it was about her. She didn't care whether or not it was a good poem. She didn't care, either, about Fred Briscoe's broken heart. But Peter had always known that Fred had never been anything but a stylish fan Polly had held up between her heart and the world's gaze. No one but Dash meant anything to her.

Polly put the poem idly down. If it blew into the fire, she'd never even notice.

"I pray every night," she admitted, "God keep the *Victrix*. I didn't mean it when I said I hoped she'd sink. Peter, are you laughing at me?"

"I'm not."

But it frightened him a little that she could believe such nonsense. You expected the Dulceys to believe in Old Diamond and the Screeching Women of Marblehead. Even Mrs. Cady thought, come Halloween, all the ghosts of Salem got abroad. Half the foremast hands believed in witches and weather breeders and phantom barks.

"Polly, you romanticize everything. You're bored, sitting around, and make up things to keep you excited. Old Doctor West says you shouldn't. Yet you do. And you shouldn't."

"Is that it?"

"That's it. You ought to get to work on something." Work: the old New England cure-all. "Why don't you make wax flowers, or paint on glass, or study botany, or *dust?* Don't you ever dust?"

"Why, I never do anything about the house. The aunts run things. We have three maids. Papa won't have a houseman. He thinks they are dangerous."

"You shouldn't dance and flirt all night, and mope all day. No wonder you get morbid."

"You sound just like Dash," she said, relaxing and closing her eyes in utter content. "Morbid? Well, yes, maybe. But" — and she was imitating her father's rich, booming tones — "we are a very old family, Mr. Inman. Perhaps the blood begins to run a trifle thin."

"Stuff and nonsense."

"Just like Dash! Peter, darling, let me sit like this and shut my eyes and you go on scolding me. I love it so."

She lay back and the green shawl fell about her. It was a marvelous shawl, embroidered all over with microscopic flowers. It made a flowry sward for her.

He did not scold her. After a long time, he whispered: "Do not forget me" — he had caught the exact inflection of Dash's voice — "I love you. Polly, I'd give anything in the world to make you happy."

Her long lashes fluttered and lifted. "You'd give up going to sea for me?"

"Well . . . at least I'd give up going to Harvard. I don't know much about the sea."

They both laughed and she settled herself again.

"If I don't open my eyes, I can think it is he."

He whispered, "I love you." Always before he had made such declarations in Dash's name.

"I know," she said trustingly.

He saw that she was lost in her own dreams. She was silent a long time, then shivered slightly. I'll bet she is still wondering if her cursing the *Victrix* did it harm. How can she be so ignorant? But she might be chilly. He got up and very quietly mended the fire.

Her eyes were wide open now, staring unseeingly out of the window behind and beyond him. She's thinking — perhaps the *Victrix* is already lost.

Perhaps she would never return. In time she'd become one more of those lost ships — first, upon the owners' and underwriters' books, and then in sea ballads and the stories old servant women told children. Oh, give her time and she'd be beating forever homeward for the already haunted New England shore, speeding up against the wind, the crew fixed and staring like men of stone — the phantom bark, the spectral crew. There was already God's plenty of such ships. There would be nothing left of her or her captain but the old stories. Dash would grow into one of those demon masters. Soon everyone who had actually seen his face would be gone. Naught left of him but the legend, and a wooden portrait on his mother's stairway. Perhaps the *Victrix* was already lost — and now nothing remained of Dash except the child Dulcey so unwillingly carried.

Suppose this terrible thing had happened, not to Dulcey, but to Polly. It was only a little slip in Dulcey's low social order. It would be cataclysmic, utter destruction, in Polly's walk of life. He thought of the consternation of the old aunts. Squire Mompesson would drop dead. Polly would have fit after fit. The scandal, the women's avid eyes. Mr. Mullins's coarse jokes. Yet through it all he believed that Polly would have borne the child proudly, lovingly, knowing that that was all that was left in the world of Dash Inman.

This "moppet," as Liz called her; "little bird," as her father thought her; flirt, as Salem, not without reason, judged her — this overbred, overcivilized little creature had more primitive drive in her than the crass Dulcey.

He couldn't interrupt her reverie by saying, Polly, suppose the *Victrix* is lost and you know you are going to have Dash's child next January — what would you do? He knew the answer to the question he could not put. Polly had something Dulcey had not — great love. She loved Dash more than Dulcey could ever love anyone. Law, society, church, might all say Dash's duty was to the girl he had betrayed. Peter confidently, at that moment, decided otherwise. Dash's duty was to the girl who loved him so much she could not live without him.

He leaned toward her and laid a hand on her shoulders, softly, gently. She came out of her reverie, or trance. Her hand went up and caressed his hand.

"Thank you, Peter," she said.

"Why did you thank me?" he asked, in wonder.

She shivered, and drew her green shawl about her. "I felt something queer. Did you, when you were a child, think angels watched over you as you slept?"

"No."

"I did. Just now I was almost asleep." Yet her eyes had been wide open and fixed. "I haven't slept well for days. I felt an angel taking care of me. It was a warm, lovely, safe feeling. And I came to and I wanted to thank someone. So I thanked you."

"You should have thanked God," he said, seriously. He tucked the shawl about her. "Sleep now. Go to sleep. Everything's all right. It's settled. I'm going now."

Flip was at the front door letting in his sister, Nanny.

"Why, Peter Inman! Why did you come in the morning? Do you often come in the morning? Why aren't you at the counting-house?"

Before he could get away, Flip told him Squire Mompesson wished to see him in the dining room.

It was only, of course, because he was angry that Polly had left him. He looked at Peter contemptuously.

"A cigar? Never smoke them myself."

"No, thank you, sir."

"How did Polly seem to you this morning?"

"Why, very well."

Her father sighed, shook his great wig, and pronounced his sentence. "Poorly. She's doing poorly, I'm afraid. Such a change in temperature always upsets her. I *asked* her to remain in bed . . . but I hope you did not tire her?"

"No, sir." He noticed that Squire Mompesson had his gold watch set against his goblet.

"Your visit was exactly half an hour. Mrs. Nanny I will give ten minutes. I've noticed, by and large — and no insult intended — Inmans seem to exhaust her. Perhaps I should use more paternal authority . . . very delicate nervous system . . . thin blood. She should spend more time lying down. I must . . . I shall insist."

Peter felt ghastly, ghostly screws delicately turning, screwing down the lid of a glass coffin. In the coffin lay Polly Mompesson. It was like an old wives' tale. A princess under an evil spell, asleep in a glass coffin, waiting for the prince to come, smash the coffin, and get her alive once more. He felt the danger, and, with almost horror, looked at the weirdly unlined face of the old man. A vampire. He half-feared him, and his gorge rose.

From across the hall, within Polly's sitting room, came to him the clear chiming of the Iphigenia clock. Peter had come to love this clock, but until this moment he had never thought who Iphigenia was. She was the girl sacrificed by her own father on the altar of his gods. Agamemnon had killed her with his own hand. He glanced at Mr. Mompesson. So that sort of thing had been going on for two thousand years — and more.

Squire Mompesson was holding the watch in the flat of his hand now, counting off the minutes until he would cross the hall and send Nanny packing. Peter bowed stiffly, and made his departure.

Out on the street, he bent his head and silently swore that with God's help he would set Polly free. The coffee drunk behind her father's back, her encouragement of the followers of her pretty maids, her intimacy with Flip — these were all such little revolts, little tappings on the heavy crystal lid of her coffin. She hadn't the force to break the lid herself. It would take a sledgehammer. Nor was Peter a wielder of sledgehammers. He knew that.

❧ 3 ❧

To THE REAR of the house, two lights were burning. The one upstairs was Cousin Frances's. The one below, Flanneau's. Peter knew that he slept and cooked his own meals in the old kitchen.

He did not dare knock at the back door. He was afraid Cousin Frances might recognize his voice. He rang the front doorbell. Before it had stopped jangling, he saw, through the side panes, a candle approaching. Bolts slid back. The Frenchman stood before him, peering and blinking, unable to see well.

"You are come," he sighed, "for Mrs. Derby's gown? But I sent word this afternoon it cannot be completed until tomorrow morning."

He had mistaken Peter for a servant.

"No, Monsieur Flanneau. I came merely . . . well . . . It is not for Mrs. Derby's gown. No."

"Ah, step in." The shop at the front of the house was closed. "Step far back to my workroom. Yes, yes."

He had observed Peter's guilty confusion and thought he understood it. The gentlemen of Salem were beginning to trust him to select gifts for their ladies. But if it were a gift for a married lady, they came to him slyly and looked guilty. He had learned much about Americans in the seven years since he had come over with Genet.

The old-fashioned kitchen was well kept and swept. The man was a neat housekeeper. The blue trucklebed was immaculate. There was a pot of marjoram and another of thyme. Flanneau seated himself by his whale-oil lamp, and, sighing sadly, picked up his embroidery hoop.

"Your pardon, sir, but I must stitch, stitch, stitch, all night. I stitch and you talk. Yes?"

It was a fawn-colored velvet he was working on. About the low neck he was embroidering gold leaves, sewing on pearl beads for grapes.

"Monsieur Flanneau, I have come to talk money." Now, for the first time, he looked up. He had a quaint face, sallow and thin, with groping, red-rimmed eyes. It was the saddest face Peter had ever seen. Lank, drab hair framed it. It hung down a little longer and a little sadder than any other hair in Salem. Something about this melancholy face attracted Peter.

"Money," said Flanneau, at last, picking up his hoop again and smiling slightly, "as you say over here, talks."

"You want to buy a partnership with the Stackpools, don't you?"

"I do. It is not fitting that I should be only a journeyman, sewing under two old ladies. I have ideas. I must have authority. I was not born to work for others. You feel for me?"

"How much money do you need for a partnership?"

"One thousand dollars. And the sign goes up, 'Flanneau and Stackpool,' over the door."

"Oh!" This was utter defeat. "I heard talk of five hundred."

"But five hundred — that is quarter interest only. Then the sign would read, 'Stackpool and Flanneau.' But possibly, possibly five hundred would suffice it."

Peter was silent for a moment. Flanneau threaded his needle and sewed. He looked what he was — a fine craftsman. It did not seem strange to him that his craft happened' to be the making of ladies' gowns.

"Monsieur Flanneau . . ."

"Monsieur Inman . . . correct me if I have the name wrong."

"Inman is right. I have heard, and you correct *me* if I am wrong, that you would take the money in the form of a 'dot.'"

"This is the custom, the wise custom of my own country. A dot goes with a wife."

Peter was breathing hard. "I can give you the dot, but not exactly a wife."

"Ah?" He let his sewing drop and looked at Peter curiously, with pale, leaden eyes.

"Monsieur Flanneau, I'll put my cards on the table. There is a young lady. She must have the protection of some man's name. And soon. And she's not exactly a lady."

"A peasant."

"You might call her that."

"The peasant," cried the erstwhile revolutionary, "is the flesh, muscle, bone, of any country. What are ladies? Pah!" And he shook Mrs. Derby's ball gown. "But what is your interest in this young person?"

The men looked straight into each other's eyes.

"You can guess."

Flanneau nodded. "I have guessed."

He took off the hoop and reset it. "I have four more hours before I may sleep," he murmured, and bravely plunged his needle into a box of pearl beads. Obviously he was very tired, and Peter realized that a man may show his mettle with a needle as well as with a sword.

"Well?" Peter prodded him.

"It is this that I understand. Correct me if I mistake myself, for what you suggest to me is unique . . . I use the word correctly?"

"Yes, it's unique, all right."

"You give me the dot — not that I marry the young person — only that she may *say* she is married to me?"

"You've got it. That's the gist, sir."

"She must have — and right soon — the protection of a man's name?"

"Yes."

"And not" — he smiled suddenly, teasingly — "the so honorable name of Inman?"

"Perhaps she may have it sometime. I don't know. Not now."

"Your family would disapprove such a marriage, would cut you off with the shilling?"

"No. It's much more complicated than that, Monsieur. It is very complicated."

"Perhaps you are a minor? When you reach the . . . I do not know how to say it . . . then you will marry her?"

"I'm not studying on the future. But — well, yes, perhaps in a year or two she might really marry an Inman. I propose a stop-gap only."

"Is it not what one calls over here 'skulduggery'? I use the word correctly?"

"Absolutely correctly. Your English is very good."

"Will the young person consent? She might prefer to raise the scandal against you."

"She'll do as I tell her. She's no one to lean on but me."

"You have proven a not very strong prop for her virtue."

He sewed so long and silently that Peter wondered if he had dismissed his proposition entirely. But Flanneau was thinking.

"You pay me five hundred dollars. I permit the young person to live with me here? Share my home and my name? That for one year. But there are complications."

"Like what?"

"Love."

"What about love?"

"I understand that if a gentleman loves and is loved, he will not surrender a young person to marriage except in name only. I permit. I acknowledge your prior claim to her. I do not interfere. No. I say I *permit* that you may continue to see the young person, and for this privilege and for the support of the child, I believe five hundred dollars a year is not unreasonable? Correct me if you think I am unreasonable."

"I think," Peter managed, "that it is not unreasonable."

At least, he would not be absolutely cut off from Dulcey. He could not bear, now that he thought of it, not to go on seeing her. And the child. Perhaps this was all in the world left of Dash.

"Yes. But understand I am not as yet agreeing. I am merely thinking how such a proposition might work itself out." He snipped a thread. "But tell me a little of her. You understand I cannot even *lend* my name, I cannot live under the roof with a disagreeable or evil person. I am a sad man. I cannot endure jangling — scenes."

"She is very young. Only sixteen."

"Ah, ah, an age to be shaped yet. She will obey me? Cook, wash, mind the shop for me? I lose too much time as now doing women's work."

"I think so."

"Of personable appearance?"

"Very."

"Under the circumstances, how can I ask of her moralities?"

"One slip only, and I swear it."

"Although — if I came in with you on this matter — I will permit a quiet, decent relationship with you, I will not tolerate other men. I will not give succor, share my life with . . . should I say a trollop?"

"Trollop is a good word. She's not a trollop."

"Under my roof, she may have one respectable lover. And that is all. Not Harry, Richard, and Thomas."

"I see your point."

"Her disposition is happy? Alas, I am sad, melancholy, heartbroken enough for two."

."Very happy."

"She will sing as she works." He dreamed aloud. "Happy, so happy she is safe. She and her little one. She shall cook and mind shop — and mind me. She will sing lullabies to her baby." He rocked back and forth, Mrs. Derby's gown cradled in his arms.

"You think . . . we can arrange things?"

"Perhaps, yes. Of course, I must see her first for myself." He was studying Peter's face curiously. "You trust me much, sir, that I will keep my end, implied of our bargain. Do you not fear I may forget she is not in reality my wife?"

Peter looked confused. He had not thought of this obvious possibility. He felt not only as young as he was, but years younger.

"To assure you," Flanneau went on, "I shall confess, confide the truth, and you shall tell the young person. But I am . . . ah, the word! The word! I am . . ." he reached for a French-English dictionary on his mantel. "Imp . . . imp . . . I cannot say it."

Peter looked where he pointed. "Impotent? How'd it happen?"

"Ah, sir, once I would have said it was the will of the Bon Dieu. Then Revolution. So there was only the Goddess of Reason to blame. Robespierre decreed God again. Then — His fault. But now . . . how do I know? I do not know what Napoleon may decree. Still . . . each man has his own sorrows. Yes. I have tried and tried. It is not my fault. I have drunk certain elixirs, taken potent baths. But they are not for me. You feel for me? Once I was married, and my wife, Annette, she killed herself in her despairs. If" — and he looked at Peter pointedly — "my Annette had had a lover and children, she might not have. So you see how it is I do not regret that the young person is enceinte. I am not disturbed that another man" — again he looked at Peter — "a very young man, has done for me what I am unable to do for myself. I have longed, for years, for the comradeship of a happy, singing wife, singing over her baby. Annette, she had nothing to sing about. Mr. Inman, if we close this skulduggery of ours, your child shall rest in loving hands." He stretched them out. Craftsman's hands, yet, as he said, loving. A strange place to consign Dash's child.

"And now, please, you shall tell me how I am to see the young person. I do not ask to speak to her, but I must see. I can judge fine velvet by a glance. Is a young person harder to judge?"

Peter explained to him about the fish market and the Swifts' lobster stall. He knew she would be over again next Tuesday.

Although nothing had been settled, he was confident all was going well.

~4~

"HE IS A SEMPSTER," Peter said.

"A what is he?"

"Sempster. A woman who sews is a sempstress. And a man who sews is a sempster."

"A sailmaker?"

"No. He makes ladies' gowns."

"He does?"

He and Dulcey sat on the overturned dory in her sandy garden, the Gothic arch of the whale's jaws behind them — facing out to sea. Dulcey had not been quite so ready to follow this new suggestion of his. She had made up her mind there was nothing to do but go to the selectmen. She was afraid of them and hated the thought of the scandal, but she had decided, weeks before, that that was the only thing she could do. And also, it was what Dash himself had bidden her. When Peter had told her he had found the ideal man to protect her until Dash came home, she had struggled a little against his decision, but he had overridden her. Something in his blood and background came to help him, for men of his name had long sent other men to death in icy shrouds, and said good-bye to loving ladies in distant ports. But he did not want merely her obedience, but a little enthusiasm.

"Dulcey, do you ever walk up Essex Street and look in shop windows?"

"Yes."

"Have you noticed the Stackpools' 'Ladies' Goods' shop?"

"Yes."

"He's working there, at the Stackpools'. He's going to be a partner from now on. And branch out."

"Would he make me a dress?" she asked, listlessly.

"I think any man who could would love to make you a dress."

"Will he let me look at things?"

"Of course."

"And finger them?"

"Maybe. It's his shop."

"I've longed, sometimes, to step inside."

"But Dulcey, you'll be living there."

Then her face brightened. "I'd love to live with all those pretty things. Peter, last winter I saw the nicest red woolen muff, sewed all over with white kittens' tails. And every tail had been dipped in black ink."

"That's ermine. We Inmans often bring in ermine from Russia."

"Well, I could hardly believe there were that many white kittens even in Salem. It had a bonnet to match. In some ways I'd rather live there than in your house. Your house is frightfully big and white. Begging your pardon. And it is real close, isn't it?"

"Our back yards adjoin, although we face the Common and the Stackpools face on Essex."

"So you won't forget me . . . you'll come to see me real often? Peter, I feel a little . . . well . . . I guess I feel a little scared."

"But not as scared as of the selectmen?"

"Just about the same, I guess." Her beautiful, curly mouth was drooping. She did look scared.

He had no idea of telling her of Flanneau's generous offer. He blushed to think of it. "Dulcey, if you'll go ahead and do as I say, I promise you I'll be there a lot. I'll not forget you. I'll take you driving with Dolly. Not every day, but pretty often. Dulcey, we'll be together, you and me and the baby. I promise it. If you do what I want. But if you don't — I mean if you dare show that letter — I'll never speak to you again. Then, too," he went on, desperately, "I know you want to marry Dash when he comes back. If you lived in a place like Flanneau's, you'd learn a lot of manners."

"How to be a lady?"

"At least, you'd be meeting ladies all the time. You could learn to act and talk like them. And if you went to the selectmen, they might shut you up in jail, Dulcey, and you'd have lice and learn to swear, and become sort of a jail-bird. Dash would despise you."

"The Stackpools are ladies, aren't they?"

"Yes. Real genteel old parties. Come down in the world a bit."

"Well, if they came down to a shop, I guess I can come up from it."

Now, at last, he knew he had struck the right chord. She was going to consent and, at last, with some enthusiasm. "All you have to do is go live with him, and, of course, do what he says. And act as though the baby was his baby."

"He isn't mad about the baby?"

"No. He can't have a child of his own. He's glad you are going to have a baby. I wanted to explain to you about his not having children. So you needn't ever feel scared of him."

"He can't?"

Peter tried to explain to her. Dulcey's ignorance forced him to use Mr. Mullins's vocabulary. Words he had taken for granted no woman understood. She understood no others.

Her face coarsened and she laughed heartily. He supposed it was a thing the vulgar would laugh about.

Her mind went back to the clothes. "I don't want anything until after January. These old things are good enough for having babies in. Then I'm going to have a white muslin, with a cherry sash, and black gloves up to *here*. Mr. Peter, there's a young lady in Salem who has a cream-colored pony and a basket car. Do you think he'd get me one?"

"Emphatically I don't think. You're not his wife. He's not rich."

She went back to Flanneau. She thought it was a funny man who could not do "that."

"He's not a funny man. He's melancholy and honest and hard-working."

"Well, I still think he's funny if he can't do 'that.'" But she subsided with a sigh. She was thinking of how fine a lady she would be by the time Dash got home. She in her muslins and cherry sashes, and her nice talk. She said, a little mawkishly, "Well, what's the matter with him is terribly refined. I think I might learn how to act from such a refined man."

◄ 5 ►

COUSIN FRANCES was one of those useful, indigent, unattached women who fasten themselves to more positive, and usually older, richer women. Frances made the boys' shirts, hemmed sheets, hung curtains, darned. She was more interested in Lucy's domestic problems than her own. More interested in her wardrobe than in the drab half-mourning she affected. She would listen, day after day, to Lucy's conversation, which was much more amusing than anything poor Frances would have been apt to pick up. Her patroness rewarded her shadow with old dresses, carriage rides, caddies of tea, and genuine affection, although she bossed and bullied her. She said she couldn't live without dear Frances, and, to Frances, life would have seemed empty without Lucy. Frances clung to the Inmans. She would have been a forlorn enough widow woman without them. Then, too, she loved Lucy and knew Lucy loved her. Nobody else loved Frances Cunningham.

Although still young, and with her bright, dark, birdlike eyes and pretty, plump figure, not unattractive, Frances considered herself, and was considered by everyone else, to be too plain, dowdy, and old for gentlemen's society. She was kept by Mrs. Inman for the more intimate, private, feminine hours of the day. Of course, this did not exclude her sons — she was like an aunt to them. When Frances ate a meal at this house, it was not by invitation written on a little card. The invitation was always delivered at the last moment because "nobody was going to be there."

This night, for instance, Lucy had asked her to stay because "there's no one here but Peter and me. I'm afraid it will just be those baked beans left over from Saturday, but I know you don't mind." Frances, who never expected anything more or anything better, chirped and twittered with pleasure.

The somewhat grim, frankly economical meal having been eaten, and the three seated once more in the living room, Frances did not dawdle a moment about getting on with her darning. It had been so lovely of Lucy to ask her — Lucy, who was so beautiful and gay and had such lovely clothes and knew such stylish people and was so witty and had such an exciting family. Lucy had been telling her about that marvelous evening party the Derbys had given, and the marvelous food they had eaten, and the marvelous clothes the ladies had worn. Frances had no envy that she herself had not been there. In fact, she would much rather have stayed home, got her stays and her shoes off early, and eaten her usual corn-meal gruel for supper. But she loved to hear about it. Mrs. Inman, who had been a little bored by it all — it was a very stiff, formal affair — got more pleasure in describing the party to Frances than she had had in attending it.

"And little Mrs. Derby wore again that *marvelous* dress Flanneau made her. I hope the day is coming *soon* when I can afford to have him make me a dress, but in the meantime . . ." she shrugged and picked up her embroidery hoop. She much preferred to embroider than to darn. Tonight she was putting pearl beads and gold leaves about the neck of her old purple velvet. Half the ladies in Salem had been similarly employed since Mrs. Derby had first worn that gown.

"By the way," said Frances, "speaking of Flanneau, I forgot to tell you . . . but the oddest thing has happened."

"What, dear?"

"Flanneau has just told the Stackpools and me that he has been married all the time."

"*Married!*"

"Yes. He decided not to have his wife join him until he was sure the situation here suited him." She gnawed at the soft darning cotton, but got her teeth through it. "But now he's a partner, he has gone to fetch her."

"I saw the sign going up today."

"He says it is her relatives who lent him the money to buy that partnership. I must say he seems very happy, for him."

"I hope Salem doesn't lose him. I hope he stays on, now that he is moving his family."

"They'll be back in a few days." Frances gnawed through another thread. This always put Mrs. Inman's teeth on edge. "And, Lucy, you know I have always kept the entire second floor for myself, although I never use anything but those two back rooms. Flanneau wishes to rent my two best front rooms for himself and his lady."

"I wouldn't, Frances. You don't know anything about them."

"Well . . . I've said yes. He's so excited and happy, for him. He's painting them himself, and I've lent a little furniture. He was so grateful he kissed my hand."

"Pooh! I wouldn't let him. Amorous *monkeys*. All of them. Peter, won't you go to the kitchen and fetch our evening tea? You know, Frances, it is almost impossible to run a house this size with only Mrs. Cady. If you had any sense at all, you'd rent *all* of your house to that Frenchman and come over and live with us."

Frances merely tilted her head and said nothing. She was not going to let Lucy swallow her completely.

Peter came back with the tray. Frances was saying, "You know, I'm pleased that she is having a baby. Next February, he says. I'd love to have a baby in the house."

"Mercy! I've had six — no, seven, if you count poor little Effie between Peter and Marcy. And I couldn't stand a baby around at my age. But you are so much more phlegmatic than I." She did not say, "But you are almost twenty years younger."

Lucy put down her embroidery hoop. "Why, Frances Cunningham! You told me months ago that he proposed to both Miss Unity and Miss Clara. Let me see . . . " and she counted up on her fingers like an expert. "If that child is born in February, he must have been married all that time."

Frances flushed. "I think . . . you see he talks so oddly when ex-cited . . . I think they misunderstood him. All he was really talk-ing about was a partnership. But he made such protestations of undying devotion and sharing their lives, they misunderstood him."

"But *you*, Frances?"

She laughed, shamefaced but good-natured. "Oh, I was hoping you'd forgotten that. I thought he was proposing honorable mar-riage. But if he was married at that time . . . he was not."

"He made improper advances?"

"Oh, you know these Frenchmen. He was lonely, and because I was a widow . . . men always think widows are approachable."

"No fools like old fools. You must have given him some encour-agement and you were all of a flutter when you told me. Why, you said if he'd only talked love instead of money, you might have . . . But what about that five hundred dollars — didn't he want it for a dot?"

Frances turned an ugly, mottled pink which combined shock-ingly with her red hair. "I think . . . Isn't it funny . . . " (they had both forgotten Peter behind his paper) "I think he was offering me five hundred dollars."

"My *dear!* Five hundred! You flatter yourself. *Cleopatra* would never have had the conceit to ask five hundred dollars!"

"I haven't any idea what women like that do charge." She was obviously a little hurt.

"I think a dollar when a woman's young — as they get to be *our* age, fifty cents."

"Frankly, Lucy, Captain Cunningham was so much older than I when we married, he did not tell me as much as Captain Inman told you."

"Frances, please don't bite threads. Your teeth are going to look like bucksaws. There, take these scissors, do."

Frances obediently thanked her for the scissors.

~6~

AMONG HIS DUTIES to his society, Josephus Hobey loved best the instruction of children. Little groups of little boys, little groups of little girls, always came so many times a week to his study on the second floor of Madam Inman's old black witch house. Here he gave them religious instruction. Sometimes he tried to combine his own passion for natural history with the shorter catechism and took a troop out walking. Then nature won out over religion. And yet, he thought, how better can you love and understand God than by loving and understanding the world He has made?

A tiny beach, bounded on three sides by granite and on the fourth by the sea. Here was a spot sun-warmed and windless — a coign in which summer still lingered, even into October. His eight chattering little girls skipped over the rocks like kids, their flimsy, heelless slippers, wet from the salt marshes, through which he had dragged them, clinging to granite better than his stout boots. He looked at his bedraggled crew of little revelers and decided he had better dry them out before he returned them to their mamas. Not only were their feet wet, but their ankles and their long, impeding skirts. Now he would sit them in the sun in a proper row, and teach them at least a parable. Nothing but the difference between gulls and terns had he taught them today, and how to tell rock from swamp maple.

The goat-footed girls were dashing ahead of him and racing on the hard gray sand. The tide was out.

"Children, children," he commanded, cupping his hands about his mouth, "I want you to sit. *Sit,* children, and wait for me. Sit and dry your clothes."

It was, of course, Marcy Inman who was leading the revolt. She was flying down the beach, her wet slippers, sodden stockings, discarded. This large and heavy child ran like a boy, but like a girl she screamed as she ran. She was much the biggest in his flock. What superhuman — or subhuman — energy the child had! What would maturity do with a girl like this? Seemingly there was no place for her. Yet he felt her abundant virtues. It was as if she had too much of every good thing. Too much height and weight, too much affection, too much generosity, too much intellectual curiosity. And surely too much animal spirits. If there was one thing for which the world had no use, it was an adult Marcy. It was the fashion for ladies to droop. Lively as a colt — but possibly of a draft breed — she pranced and ran upon the beach.

Now the children were playing tag. Of course Marcy tagged Bibby Gibault so hard she had knocked her down, and "Cry-Baby Bibby" was bawling. Emmy Crowninshield, only eight, had her skirts tucked up too high, and that Valpey girl, who was supposed to keep an eye on Emmy, had already cut her foot or sprained her ankle, and with a martyred air was limping off to sit by herself. That Veronica Valpey was always getting hurt, or pretending she was hurt. Off into a corner she would go, sniffing and looking disgustingly brave. Josephus had to remind himself to be very kind to Veronica. She had been "taken in" by one of the Crowninshields, for her dead father had been a friend of theirs. Already she was earning her keep by "keeping an eye" on Emmy. Half-servant, half-adopted daughter. He felt sorry for Veronica. Love her he could not.

He called to the children again. If it had not been for Marcy, they would have obeyed him. She careened and she galloped, and there she was flying down into the sea, although he had told them today was far too cold to go wading. Yet, perhaps a splashing in the tonic sea might stave off any colds they had caught in the salt swamps. Now they were all leaving stockings and slippers on the beach and following Marcy into the sea. Bibby had stopped crying. That Valpey girl had forgotten which ankle she had sprained. They were reveling in the cold, sparkling sea water. Were they not, every one of them, daughters of deep-sea men?

Now he descended to the level of the beach. Too late to save his dignity, he called, "Girls, I think it is warm enough to wade, but only ten minutes by my watch."

Marcy came charging down upon him. He could see why smaller children got out of her way — he felt a little scared himself.

"Come on, Doctor Hobey, come on!" she chanted as she galloped past him and came up on another tack. "Come on, come on!"

"No. No, Marcy."

"Come on!" She had him by the wrist.

"Well . . . maybe I will. Just while my shoes and stockings dry in the sun."

"Come on."

With his pantaloons neatly rolled about his small white knees, he descended the beach and walked demurely into the life-giving sea. At only twenty-six he had the air of a cautious man of twice that age. All the girls had their ankle-length dresses up about their waists. But it was tiny Emmy Crowninshield who was making a spectacle of herself. He hated to tell her that by civilized standards she was immodest. Veronica Valpey came up to him and slid a snake-cold hand into his.

"Doctor Hobey, *look* at Emmy!"

"Yes, yes, I know."

"Doctor Hobey, *she hasn't any drawers!*"

But wasn't Veronica being brought up in that beautiful house almost as a daughter because she was also Emmy's nursemaid? He wanted to tell her that Emmy's drawers, or lack of them, was her business, not his. He couldn't bear to remind this proud, unlovable child of her dependent position.

"I think," he admitted lamely, "they began to fall off over an hour ago." Sometimes his bachelor state was a handicap to him. And why, why was Emmy always losing her drawers?

"But Doctor Hobey . . . *there is a man!*"

He looked where she pointed. Sitting side by side on a rock, so close to the sea they were almost in it, were a man and a woman.

"Oh, but that's only Mr. Africanus."

"He's a *man.*"

"But he can't see."

"Doctor Hobey, if Emmy hasn't any drawers on, I think you should go and tell him to go away. He's nothing but a Charity-House man." How loathly, ugly, is the snobbishness of the poor and dependent! "That woman might tell him and that would be the same as though he really saw."

"No, no, Veronica. You look out for your own self. I don't care if Emmy hadn't a stitch on — neither does Mr. Africanus. Let the child play, and the old man sun himself in peace."

Veronica dropped his hand in disapproval. "I think I have stepped on a piece of coral," she said, and limped haughtily to sit alone once more.

Coral! It amazed him how little these children knew of their own coast. Coral brought from Ohayee, the Sandwich Islands,

God knew where, was more real to them than their own horse-shoe crabs and barnacles.

He thought to sit a moment with the inmates of the Charity House and enjoy the pretty picture the girls made, strung out along the beach.

"Good morning, Mr. Africanus," he said cheerfully. "How's business?"

"Poorly, sir, poorly, Doctor Hobey."

The old Negro's face, always tense and locked, seemed blacker both in mood and color than he had ever seen it before.

"Doctor Hobey, if you haven't met this young person, her name is Dorothy Belinda Gould. Stand up and bow to the gentleman."

The child — she could not have been more than fifteen — delicately balanced her body on the rocks and curtsied. She was meager, plain, thin, and didn't dare lift her flat, expressionless face to look at him. But as graceful as a fawn.

"Dorothy Belinda Gould?" he questioned. "Why, yes, I've heard the name. I don't think we have met before."

"No, sir."

"Dorothy Belinda," Mr. Africanus explained, "was taken up six months, eight months ago by our constable for lewd and lascivious conduct."

'Sephus Hobey almost laughed. How could such a skinny, sexless little thing be guilty of "lewd and lascivious conduct"? She had nothing to be lewd with. You could as well accuse a clam.

"The rest of the party," Mr. Africanus went on, "were ordered out of town, but Dorothy Belinda was so young they put her in the Charity House just to hold her."

Doctor Hobey did remember a troup of folk, English or Irish, that had appeared in Salem early in the year. They had a little show. A trick donkey, or dogs. A man who played the fiddle and a woman who danced. They went to low taverns, sailors' boarding houses, brothels, mean streets. And, oh yes. The woman danced at night with a lighted candle on her head.

"Dorothy Belinda, did you dance with a lighted candle on your head?"

She looked at Mr. Africanus. "Tell him, yes, I did," she whispered.

"So she did, sir," Africanus boomed.

The girl must have a kind heart. It was evidently she who had led the blind man to these rocks to take the sun and soak his feet in sea water. Africanus liked her. Doctor Hobey had never once disagreed with the Negro's opinion of anyone.

"I don't think she should still be at Charity House," Doctor Hobey said. "I'm afraid some way she has been forgotten. I'll take the matter up with the overseers of the poor. What did the judge say, Dorothy Belinda?"

She pressed her pathetically thin little body close to the old Negro. "Tell him he said it wasn't decent for me to go traipsing about with Mr. and Mrs. Harp." She had a cockney accent.

"Were the Harps good to you?"

"Tell him . . ."

"No, no, speak straight out to me."

"Why, Doctor Hobey won't hurt you nor scare you, child. You just speak out loud and pretty to Doctor Hobey. Be a brave girl."

She swallowed and stared, opened her pale lips, then blurted out, "Yes, sir. They bought me five years ago from my grandma in London."

"Bought you?"

"They paid fifteen shillings for her, sir," Africanus amended, smiling. "If she weren't so shy, she'd tell you — like she has told me — she thinks our Salem constable stole when he took her from the Harps and never paid a cent."

"Well," she piped, "if I was worth fifteen shillings five years ago, I'm worth a lot more since the Harps taught me to dance and carry on."

"Carry on?" asked Doctor Hobey.

"Sit in sailors' laps, sir."

"Oh, I see." He did not care to go into that — and what difference could it make to this plain, odd, and, he believed, fundamentally decent little girl? "Didn't you have a trick donkey?"

She smiled for the first time. "A darling donkey. You could make it kick people. The sailors loved that."

"So you had a good time?"

"Yes, sir."

"But they have been good to you here at the Charity House."

"But my clothes — you tell him, Mr. Africanus."

"First she did miss her red skirts with bells sewed on, but she's coming to like what she has on better, aren't you, Dorothy Belinda? She's coming to like to be respectable."

"Yes. Nobody ever beats me here."

"Doctor Hobey, what I want to get for Dorothy Belinda is dismissment from the Charity House, and a kind woman who'll go bond for her good conduct. One that won't scare her. She scares mighty, mighty, easy. And she should be taught to be a neat serving girl. She's a real good girl and won't bother anybody, nor ever again go dancing down the dark streets with a lighted candle on her head."

"But if my new mistress wants me to, I can. But if she don't, I won't."

'Sephus Hobey was thinking of Mrs. Inman. She was always saying that her Mrs. Cady was overworked. For a year, whoever signed the bond would get the girl's services free. After a year of good behavior, she might stay on, on wages, or find a new mistress. The bedraggled young thing touched him. He saw that the appalling life other people had led for her had not embittered or cheapened her. There was even a naïve purity about her.

"Would you like to be bound out as a servant?"

"I don't want to leave Mr. Africanus, ever."

"But it would be right here in Salem. He would come to see you."

"I'll do whatever Mr. Africanus says is best."

"She's getting less frightened all the time, Doctor Hobey. She'll go."

'Sephus Hobey thought of the Inman house — a happy house, full of laughter and the come and go of the young captains, sun and sea breezes in summertime. The glow of firelight and candles in the winter. Dancing feet and someone playing the piano, and someone else trying to play the old fiddle. He thought of Mrs. Inman herself. He did not approve of her because she had a good head and was not in the least intellectual. But he had to give her credit for making a happy home.

As he turned to leave — for the ten minutes he had promised his charges was long up — his eyes fell on the Negro's feet, dangling in a salt-water pool. He had never seen feet so large, so sooty black, nor so rather charmingly lined with dusky rose. But what was he doing here? Why was he soaking his feet in salt water instead of proudly walking the streets of Salem, earning a penny by remembering a birthday, or carrying messages?

"You said your business was poorly, Mr. Africanus?"

"Poorly, poorly." His face snapped shut and 'Sephus questioned Dorothy Belinda with his eyes.

The girl, too shy to speak up much for herself, answered him eagerly.

"He can't do his work no more. He lost his shoes."

"But can't he get another pair?"

"No, sir," Dorothy Belinda went on. She had a squeaky little voice. "There's not a gentleman in Salem wears his size. The keeper says soon as snow flies he'll give him new ones. But now he has to go without. He says his feet will harden up and he'll get used to it. He says bare feet never hurt nobody — till winter comes."

"But it does hurt you, Mr. Africanus?"

"It's like I can't make out without shoes, Doctor Hobey. I step on rusty nails and broken glass. My feet don't ever harden up. I guess I'm too old." He lifted a rosy sole to show an injury gray and gaping from the soaking.

The girl went on "A sailor, Captain Hanks, he told us if he soaked his feet in sea water they'd harden up. So of late we've been coming over here to see how it works."

"Does it work?"

"No, sir. Nothing will work for me but shoe leather."

"How did you lose your shoes?"

"I lost only one. I was told if I'd leave one shoe for a sample at a certain gentleman's door, he'd take it to Boston and have a fine pair of boots made me. Hessian boots with red leather tassels. Something more suitable to my general style of dress than clodhoppers."

"But if the gentleman changed his mind, surely he would have returned the shoe to you. Have you asked?"

"He's done and gone, sir."

"Have you asked at his house?"

"I've tried to. But the coachman curses at me. They've a little dog that bites my heels, and a big one that stands off and roars like a lion."

Of course. The Inmans.

"I left my shoe modestly at the kitchen door. But the coachman picked it up next morning for trash and threw it into the sea. But I guess I'll get more shoes soon now. Charity-House shoes."

Doctor Hobey could sympathize with the keeper. Poor people were supposed to go shoeless, except in winter. But what was right for one person was cruelty for the next.

"Who was the gentleman?"

"I won't say — ever. He never meant to do me such harm. He's the finest young gentleman in Salem. I'm still grateful to him for just thinking of anything so handsome. Boots! Hessian boots, running right up your calf! Just like Captain George Crowninshield Junior. But, fact is, soon I'll get something sufficient to my station in life. And I can be out and about my work once more."

"I wish you had come directly to me. Always come directly to me."

"I couldn't have walked it," he muttered gloomily. From the Charity House to Madam Inman's was not so far as to these rocks, but he would have run considerable risk of nails and broken glass.

Doctor Hobey looked at his watch. He must hurry his girls. And actually today he had given them no religious instruction.

They had been quiet for a long time, and when he joined them he saw why. Polly Mompesson was sitting on a boulder, surrounded by them. She wore a dark silk cloak with ruffled shoulders. Her bonnet was fresh and bright as though just out of the milliner's hands. She had an "indispensable" of emerald-green velvet, with long gold ribbons on it.

His dirty, disheveled children were crowded about her, looking as forlorn as wet kittens. In every eye, even in Marcy Inman's eye, he read adoration. Now, for the moment, every one of them wanted to be just like Miss Mompesson. Nothing seemed to Doctor Hobey less appropriate to the scene than Polly, with her exquisite, finicky daintiness, and that ridiculous "indispensable." The seaside, the granite rocks, and the bedraggled children all belonged together. Polly did not. Then he saw what she was doing. One after another of the children she was restoring to proper order, combing out their snarled hair, pinning it, tying it on top of their heads. Doing other little things he could hardly understand.

He resented this. Why could not his little girls be left alone —for once? Why could not they, like their brothers, grow up unself-consciously in this, their natural heritage of sun and sea? Polly had given Cry-Baby Bibby a new hair-do. She had pulled all her hair to the top of her head and pinned it there. Now the others were all giving little mouse-like squeaks — very correct little squeaks — because they all wanted their hair done "a la Virginie." Even Marcy. Marcy more than anybody. Seemingly she, who, half an hour before, had been as unconscious of her mop of dark curls as a gull is of its feathers, was ready to tear it out by the roots — if only Miss Polly would dress it for her "à la Virginie."

Unnoticed, he went to his neat pile of stockings and shoes. He was sad and perhaps resented it that the children, who had started out on this ramble clinging to him, longing to be told the difference between gulls and terns, now thought of nothing but the last ridiculous fashion in hairdressing.

Unconscious of his disapproval, Polly looked up and smiled at his approach.

"How do you like my labors?" she asked. "At least they will go back to their mothers looking like little gentlewomen."

"See, see, Doctor Hobey," Bibby was demanding, "don't I look grown-up?"

"Indeed you do, Bibby."

"I'm going to be a belle when I grow up," Veronica announced, "just like Miss Polly." Poor child — she already had her Grandmother Corwin's great nose.

"Of course. But now we must hurry." He did not want to tell Polly "how he liked her labors." He abominated them.

And now she was ordering the little girls, "Two by two, young ladies. Little ones first, big ones last. Make a crocodile, dears — just as Mrs. Rogers has taught you."

There, on the lonely beach, they made a crocodile — with the sea flinging itself at their feet, hissing and retreating again, singing its old song that man comes, man goes, but it goes on forever. And fashions come ond go even more quickly than man.

The crocodile set forth toward the highway. The little heads were bowed, and how touchingly vulnerable the young white napes looked! They weren't even speaking to each other and they carefully avoided keeping step. Keeping step was too manly. Surely Miss Polly had them all in marvelous good order. Their white stockings might be soiled, but were trim and tight. Everything that should button was buttoned. Nobody would guess that Emmy had, as usual, lost her drawers. Doctor Hobey secretly lamented their decent gentility. They had forgotten him. All they wished now was to show Polly Mompesson what perfect little donkeys they were.

Polly, who had laughed for them, was now silent as she walked beside Doctor Hobey. He knew she was depressed. It was strange, meeting her, of all people, so far out from town on this lonely beach. Why had she walked, not driven with her pretty pony, and Fred Briscoe beside her? But of course, over a month ago Fred Briscoe had been sent back to Baltimore with a final "no." There had been considerable talk. If Polly had not intended to marry him, why had she kept him dangling so? Could it be she was still thinking about Dash Inman? Yes, he thought. And she came to this lonely spot to mourn and look seaward and think long, sad thoughts of Dash.

"Miss Polly," he said at last, confident that his thoughts would chime in with hers, "I was talking to Mr. Africanus."

"I saw you," she said, without interest. And yet, even her absent-mindedness had a prospective intimacy about it. Doctor Hobey was young. He was a man. Such rarely escaped her net.

"I discovered a really sad thing."

"Yes?"

"The old fellow has had no shoes, not since the sailing of the *Victrix*."

"The *Victrix*?" Her voice quickened.

"The finest young gentleman in Salem — so Africanus put it — promised to have boots made for him if he would leave one shoe as a sample at his door. He promised Hessian boots, with red tassels on them. Made in Boston. But he went away — 'done and gone,' as Mr. Africanus says. The coachman threw away the shoe. Africanus cannot walk barefoot. Being blind he hurts his feet."

"Oh," she said sharply, "that was Dash!"

"I think so. Boots like that cost a great deal of money. Come winter the Charity House will give him new shoes, suitable, useful, but that was not what the young gentleman promised."

"Doctor Hobey, I know it was Dash!"

"So do I. Africanus is too loyal to say his name."

"At the end he went so fast he forgot everything. I can see how he forgot about the boots."

He guessed that, in her mind, the old blind Negro and she were together. Both had suffered from the same carelessness.

Of course, it was a ridiculous charity — paying such a sum for boots for a pauper. Dash shouldn't have put such an idea in the old man's head. This was merely intellectual disapproval, however, and he was tempting Polly to fulfill Dash's obligation. She needed something to take up her mind, loitering about like this in the morning. Probably she had not even known where she was going when she started out. And dressing — overdressing — the hair of the little girls. Knocking out of their heads the difference between swamp and rock maple, gulls and terns. This extravagant charity to Mr. Africanus seemed more appropriate to her temperament than making aprons and mittens for the poor. He glanced at her profile. Her color had risen.

"Don't tell Papa. Papa would think it a waste of money. I'll send my own cobbler over to measure his feet this afternoon. Red tassels, did you say? Hessian boots? I hope they cost a lot. He shall have them. But don't tell anyone. Don't tell Papa, but especially don't tell the aunts."

"I won't tell a soul, Miss Mompesson."

"Let it be a secret. I want to do it for him."

"Him" did not refer to Mr. Africanus.

❧ 7 ❧

EARLY IN NOVEMBER, the first snows fell. They had not waited until the one-armed cobbler at the Charity House had cut and sewed Mr. Africanus's new shoes. Nor until the Boston bootmaker had completed Miss Mompesson's order. December blew in off the gray and restless sea, bringing more snow with it. Broken ice piled up, and pushed wharves out of plumb. Boatmen worked all day to keep a ship channel open. Down every hill, children slid on sleds. In counting-houses, ink froze in bottles. In bedchambers, citizens chattered with the cold as they broke the ice on the pitchers upon their washhand stands. The weather-wise said it would be a hard winter. Still the days shortened, and everybody knew that it was not until "the days begin to lengthen that the cold begins to strengthen." Farmers carted manure and sold it for people to bank against their houses. Some very elegant mansions wore these rustic garlands of warmth.

Now when Doctor Hobey took a nature ramble, Marcy Inman was the only child hardy enough to go with him. On certain blue, still days, he hired a sleigh and jingled out into the spotless white countryside. Sometimes he took Marcy, sometimes Madam Inman. He never combined his two favorite females in one sleigh. Marcy exhausted the old lady.

He hoped the gossip about Peter had not come to either of them. Marcy was too young to be told, Madam Inman too old. There is always someone who feels it her duty to tell the mother. There were plenty who felt a clergyman must know. He had heard the story over and over. But the grandmother is considered too old. Luckily. It would almost kill her if she knew what people were saying about her dear Peter. Seemingly, everybody knew that last summer Peter had driven a young woman all over the neighboring countryside, asking people to board her. Sometimes he said she was his sister, and her husband at sea. Sometimes she was a widow and he her brother-in-law. Then Flanneau had suddenly married Peter's girl. And had money for a partnership. The Flanneau baby, when born, would be Peter Inman's.

'Sephus felt sure this was not true. The very people who said it was so, he knew did not quite believe it. He had noticed before that there are two types of gossip. The sort everybody repeats, but nobody really believes. This may be ugly while it lasts, but is apt to be short-lived. The other gossip, although it may have little to rest on, yet everyone believes. Often in the end it proves to be true. It is as if the mass mind has some ancient wisdom in it. Doctor Hobey believed that, if only Peter himself stopped feeding the flames, the gossip about him and the Flanneaus would die down. He felt it was his duty, both as friend and spiritual advisor, to "talk" to Peter. Peter was hard to catch.

Then it was Christmas Day, unobserved in Doctor Hobey's society, but festive with greens and carols at the Episcopal Saint Peter's. This "popery" did not bother Doctor Hobey. It did Ma'am Inman.

Marcy had finished her Latin lesson with him. She was down-stairs with her grandmother. It was teatime and the old lady hated to have him tardy. Yet he decided to wait. This time he would catch Peter alone. Peter had told him he was coming over to borrow some of his French books. Of course, it would be poetry that he craved — Ronsard, Villon. But Doctor Hobey realized that he would not come until he thought he would be downstairs drinking tea. He did not want to meet him alone. He knew what Doctor Hobey wished to say to him. Ma'am will be disturbed by my dawdling, 'Sephus thought, but I'm going to catch Peter.

There was a rap on his study door.

"Come in."

Peter had a suspiciously guileless look upon his face. He had left on his heavy great cloak, muffler, and gloves, as if to prove that he only expected to borrow books and run. Butter couldn't melt in his mouth, Doctor Hobey thought, a little angrily, and, for the first time, wondered suddenly. Could the gossip possibly be true?

"Won't you sit a moment, please?"

"No, thanks, and Grandmother is already waiting tea for you. She told me to tell you to hurry."

"Peter. Sit. Do."

This was not an invitation but a command.

"Thanks. But I'll take my books and be gone." He had already found the two volumes on the shelves.

"Flanneau tells me you are an apt pupil."

"Well . . . I've never studied French before. It wasn't taught at Exeter. Nor is it at Harvard. The last year or so I've been plugging mostly at things that would help me at Harvard."

Doctor Hobey had been bitterly disappointed, after all the help he had given him, that Peter had, at the end, merely said he "guessed he'd rather not." What was the matter with the fellow? You couldn't call him lazy. He had one of those quick, retentive, Inman minds, like Dash, Liz, Marcy. Why was Peter such a fool as not to go ahead and use it? He did not use it at the counting-house. Ma'am said he was bright as a button — and yet a fiddling clerk.

"Peter, I'm sorry to tell you, but I must. I must ask you, for a while at least, to discontinue your French lessons with Flanneau."

Peter turned from the bookshelves and almost dropped Villon.

"I haven't much to do. I've enjoyed learning French. I think Flanneau has enjoyed giving me lessons."

"Yes. Certain Salem gossips have enjoyed making much of the fact."

"Oh?"

"Yes, 'oh,' Peter. You are not a child, and you're not stupid, about most things. I think you are a little too trusting. You wish the world well, and take it for granted the world wishes you well. *Sit down*."

He sat. Doctor Hobey could not help notice the odd, evasive look in the handsome eyes.

"Now, look here. I'll beat about no bushes. I'll be brief. *In primo*. People are saying that Flanneau's child's keel was laid — to use sailor talk — before Flanneau arrived in Salem. I don't know whether that could be proved."

"He came in May. As I figure it — Mrs. Dulcey expects in February — he must have married her by June."

"Oh, nonsense. Nonsense, Peter. But I won't argue. That cock-and-bull story he told everybody, including myself — about having been married all the time — and not sending for his wife until October is worse than nothing. Even to try to launch such a story is an admission of some sort of guilt. And it was absurd for him to say his wife's people gave him the money for a partnership. Dulcey Delaney hasn't any people. If she had, they would not have had five hundred dollars. *Secundo*. It is believed that the real father gave Flanneau the money for his partnership — if he would marry the girl. *Tertio* is something like this. The human race — being what it is, and, I'm afraid, not half so attractive as you think — loves to find hidden things. Children hunt the slipper. Adults like nothing better than 'hunt the father,' Peter." His eyes begged him to explain everything. "Peter, I can't believe you're involved in such an unsavory mess. But you are about Flanneau's house all the time. And it is not Frances Cunningham you go to see. Now I'm *sure*" — but he was not — "it is because you are so crazy to learn French. But there are not three people in Salem who would believe that. There are only two things, so it is believed, a man is crazy about. The first is money and the other is love. Obviously, you are not getting any money by your hanging about. So it must be love. Guilty love. Of course, somebody seduced that Dulcey. And somebody paid Flanneau to marry her — that's as plain as the nose on your face. I don't care who. But I do care that you, a perfectly innocent bystander, should behave in such a way as to let himself be the scapegoat."

Peter was not looking at him. He was fingering the binding of Ronsard. He wasn't denying anything.

"Peter" — said Doctor Hobey, a little angrily — "under the circumstances I believe you should stay away from the Flanneaus. It is folly for you to take those French lessons. *I'll* give you French lessons if you wish. It is folly for you to be always running over there with curios and globes and things to show Mrs. Flanneau. It is folly for you to drive her out with Dolly. Oh yes. I've had to listen to a lot of gossip going around. Now, man, you must do your part. I don't, myself, think that scandal has anything to rest on. No roots. Nothing to feed on, except what you so foolishly give it. It can't strike down into the earth. It would wither away and be forgotten if, to continue my botanical symbol, you'd stop fertilizing and watering that wretched little weed."

"I'll think things over. But, Doctor Hobey, I can't help but feel sorry for Mrs. Flanneau. Suppose everything you say is true. Shouldn't people — her neighbors — help her a little? Show what you call, in the pulpit, Christian charity?"

"No!" Doctor Hobey thundered, irritated because Peter had forced him out onto a theological limb. He was a great one to preach Christian charity on Lord's Days. "Show charity to your mother, grandmother. And yourself. Mrs. Flanneau has told me the child is to be named Peter if it's a boy, and *Petra* — of all unlikely names — if it's a girl. You've got to forbid that. And she is not to call you 'Peter,' ever, but 'Mr. Inman.' But the crux of the matter is simpler than that. Don't go to see them. Drop the whole thing. And the whole thing will drop you."

"Thank you for talking to me flat out, Doctor Hobey. I'll think about it."

Gone like that — running off down the stairs, slamming the front door, and away into the snow. Nothing promised. Nothing denied. Nor confessed.

For the first time, Peter had seemed to Doctor Hobey something of a lonely fellow. A little forlorn. No wonder the warmth and coziness of the Flanneau kitchen attracted him. It had attracted Doctor Hobey, who, also, twice a week, had been taking lessons in French pronunciation. Yet, in spite of what he had said, he did not really believe a love of French was the reason for Peter's continual hanging about.

Well, at least he had warned him. Peter would certainly take his good advice. But, would he? He had always thought of Peter as a sensitive, poetic, romantic sort of fellow. Now he wondered if he had even got under his skin. Seemingly he had a hide on him like the Bull of Bashan.

❧ 8 ❧

MADAM INMAN heard steps come down from Doctor Hobey's and heard the front door close softly. So he wasn't going to stop. She was beginning to worry again about the *Victrix*, and nobody in the world, not even the good man of God she kept on her second floor, was such a comfort to have about, if you were worried, as Peter Inman.

She sat close to her great black hearth, the bricks worn by the come and go of generations of Inman feet. With Tabby the witch among them. A betty lamp lighted her as she supposedly read again the last letter she had from her ship. Apparently they were basing themselves on the Isle of France, and it was jammed with American ships. Liz wrote that at the present moment Isle of France was the greatest trading post he'd ever seen. Goa and Bombay were good trading. China possible. But Java and Sumatra and all the Dutch islands were almost cut off. When Holland had been overrun by Napoleon, certain traitors among the Dutch had joined with him. This had, automatically, at the other end of the earth, made England at war with the Dutch islands. It was pretty hard for a neutral trading ship to get in, for England was blockading as well as she could. So while Napoleon was talking about invading England in Europe the British were talking of seizing all Holland's colonies in Asia. They might be able to. The French fleet was reduced to a nest of pirates in the West Indies. England had beaten the French at sea. But it looked as if she were going to lose her own island. So the fact was, going to the Dutch islands for coffee and spices was pretty chancy. She sighed, and tried to put her mind on the *Gazette*. From nowhere else in the world could spices be obtained. And most of the world's coffee supply.

Dash had done about what she would expect him to do. Shot up the Red Sea, got a whole cargo of coffee from those terrible Mohammedans, had had a little fighting, not much — because his ship was so fast — gone back to Isle of France and sold it at vast profit to the more timid masters. Why hadn't he had the sense merely to take it home himself? That would have been a handsome profit. Liz wrote they might go for Mocha again. No, neither of her young men was content with well enough.

The Red Sea was the most dangerous in the world. Not because of its waters, but because of its men. Of course, Dash had gone with boarding nets up, had picked up twenty extra men so double watches might be stood day and night. But oh, she hoped he would not try it again. It was a pirates' nest. And it was wicked of him to trust a ship as he did the *Victrix*. He ought to put his trust in God.

Why, even now the *Victrix* might have been seized by those Arabs. It was four months ago — last September — that Liz had written that letter. By now the ship might be sunk, her men killed. Madam Inman moved restlessly. The waiting and not knowing she felt was draining her.

Yet, could he be so foolish as to try for Batavia? Everybody on 'Change was saying that that was too great risk for a sensible captain to take, just now. As soon as England could summon one more ounce of strength, of course, they could seize the islands as they already had taken Ceylon. Then it might be safe. Not now. Now the most important thing for a ship to do was keep out of Batavia.

"Marcy."

The girl did not even look up. Her power of concentration irritated her grandmother.

"Marcy, when I speak to you, close your book and answer me."

"Yes, Grandmother. Yes, of course. Did you say anything?"

"No. Not yet."

Her eyes were going sidewise to her book, to Ovid and his lovely gods and playful goddesses.

"It is past six. But we'll wait a little longer."

Marcy's lips were moving because the Latin words sounded so round and full and beautiful in her mouth. She was long past the stage where she needed to translate, even in her mind, into English.

"Oh yes," she said vaguely, "do let's wait."

"Then you're not hungry, for once."

"No. Not more than usual."

"Well, I'll wait. Just a little longer."

She took off her spectacles and bowed her white dotted cap. She folded her hands. And waited. What a large part of a merchant's life was waiting! You sent out the ships that would make or break you, and the young men upon the ships were often your own flesh and blood and the ship's people your neighbors' boys. Then you waited and waited. Sometimes it was two years before you knew how you had fared, and what had befallen the young men. She had heard of three-year waits. How could Dash be so foolish as once again to try for Mocha? He'd got in there once without being murdered. Why try again? And the Dutch East Indies. Why, if they went there, they'd be walking straight into a trap. The English would sink them for trying to run her blockade. The Dutch would seize the ship, jail the ship's people — and no one lived long in a Batavian jail — if they got through the blockade. America was at war with France, and Holland and France now were one.

She wished sensible Captain Magee had been in command. He'd have known enough to have bought coffee in Arabia and taken it back here with him. No, he'd never have had the hardihood to try. Captain Magee would have bought the coffee at Isle of France some other younger captain had had the courage to fetch from Mocha. She had not an idea where the *Victrix* might be by now. All she might do was wait.

She sighed, took off her spectacles and folded the newspaper she had only pretended to read.

"Marcy, tell Rose we will wait no longer for Doctor Hobey." 'Sephus Hobey wasn't going to ruin her disposition with his dawdling — even if the *Victrix* did.

'Sephus entered the sitting room, murmuring apologies, just as Rose came in with the tray. Rose was a dwarf, barely four feet high and almost equally broad, and seemingly thicker through than tall. She had a very white, sensitive, intelligent face, sunk in her misshapen shoulder, and she always wore the highest, biggest mob-cap in Salem. Madam Inman had never had the heart to tell her that great caps made her look even shorter. Rose thought they made her look tall. She had the voice of a man.

Marcy followed her gleefully, carrying a plate of little cakes. The contrast between the too-big, too-healthy little girl and the deformed older woman was shocking.

"Ah, 'Sephus. Draw up to the fire. Marcy, wait until tea is passed before you begin on cakes." No wonder the child was too fat. She ate with the same absorption she went at her Latin books. "Then pass them to Doctor Hobey and me. 'Sephus, I've been sitting here wondering. I do wish I knew where the *Victrix* is to-night. I wish I could see her. I can't help fretting myself about her . . . out in those wicked, heathen lands."

"No matter how heathen the lands may be, Ma'am, God is with her. She is in God's hands."

"Doctor Hobey," Marcy put in, "I can't imagine our God, the one and true God," she added rapidly, "out there with all those other gods, can you? I mean, I think of our God hanging about in white wooden churches with steeples and church bells. I can't see Him out there, fighting it out with those other gods."

"The God of the New England meeting-house," Doctor Hobey said, smiling, "is the God of the whole world."

"And Dash and Liz . . ." Madam Inman went on. "They are really very young, when you come to think of it, to" — she had almost said "to die" — "to have such responsibility."

"May God keep His hand over them as well."

"Amen. Amen to that. But I wish I knew — really knew. I wish I could see them, now this moment — the day before Christmas. Know what Dash is up to. Doctor Hobey, as soon as you have finished your tea, might I ask you to lead us in a few words of prayer?"

❧ 9 ❧

CHRISTMAS DAY, half a world away, the *Victrix* was going, largely before the wind, rolling upon her course. The vertical sun poured melted gold upon her. The sea was like opal below her. Over everything was a layer of mist, thin as a counterpane. The islands about her, the tall white ship herself, seemed to float in air, a disembodied spirit. Thwart-the-Ways, Cap-and-Bells, a hundred islands, floated around her, behind her, before her. Over the pearly waters, outrigger canoes skated on the mist like black water bugs. The beautiful, double-breasted Javanese proas dipped like gulls. The *Victrix* was the only "proper" ship for miles. She was going grandly, her figurehead leaning out before her, showing the way. The dark shadow of Java Head, the dangers and terrors of Sunda Strait, were well behind her, but Batavia lay before.

It was, as the captain had written the owner, "just a mite difficult." But with a fast, smart ship, a pilot who knew shallow, secret channels, it seemed worth the risk. Dash knew that Java and her capital of Batavia were famished for European goods. He guessed her own coffee and spices were stagnating in her go-downs. The Dutch might welcome him as something of a savior or they might condemn him, seize his ship — stick him and his people in jail. Batavia was the most fever-ridden, deadly city in the world. But one of the difficulties of being a neutral trader was that you never could tell before you got to the next port what treatment you might expect.

Because of the dangers of this uncharted, reef-ridden channel, and the danger of being attacked by native pirates, the captain had ordered double watch stood. Although the day, Christmas Day, was ending in Salem, here it was just beginning. The three officers, burned black by tropical sun, their lips split, and their eyes red-rimmed — for none of them had had their clothes off for four days — stood on the quarterdeck. Doctor Zack, the Negro cook, was handing them coffee, and in a soft, low monotone cooing at them. About his loins he wore a calico apron. That and his soft words gave the little black man a maternal quality, for he was something of a mother to the entire crew. Because he was so much older, no seaman, and of a different race, he could presume to tell even the officers that "there warn't no sense at all" in their losing their sleep. "Jest you go lie down, Captain." None of the three paid any attention to him. Liz was winding his watch. Obrian, a huge, formidable blond hulk of a man, opened his mouth to roar at the helmsman — it was his watch — remembered his captain cared neither for fists nor roars, and stepped over quietly to bespeak the fellow.

Dash said, "God willing, we'll anchor in Batavia Roads tonight."

Chapter Five

~~~~~~

T HERE IS NOTHING in the world, thought Peter, wakes faster than an old woman who does not believe in banks and does believe in burglars.

Standing on a great drift, he reached an unlocked larder window, pushed it up, and dropped inside. He almost landed on a dozen mince pies, made early and kept frozen to be used all winter. Now he was in the kitchen, and now tiptoeing up the back stairs. He fingered along the upper hall, guessed this was Doctor Hobey's study door, went in, feeling his way through the confusion of books and stacks of papers. In the bedroom beyond, a shaft of moonlight struck through the half-closed shutter, pointed out the square box of the canopied bed. The bed curtains were closed tight against the cold. As he opened them, the moonlight fell upon a mound of blankets and the top of a warm nightcap.

"Doctor Hobey." He touched him.

"Yes? Who is it?"

"Me, Peter. Hush, don't wake Grandma."

"What's happened?"

"The baby was born this afternoon. Dulcey thinks it's going to die. Please come and baptize it first. She cares terribly about its dying a Christian."

This business of unbaptized babies going to Hell! The clergyman groaned as he pulled his reluctant, plump body out of its warm nest, felt for his clothes. How evil was the old belief that Hell is paved with such! Yet this idea did linger on into the enlightened nineteenth century. How could anyone love and worship so cruel a God? This primitive superstition — as he thought it — had got him out of bed many a night before this. Although an advanced thinker, he had no missionary zeal. He never came out and fought for his own conception of a purer, more loving God.

There was no need for a lantern, the moon lay so bright on the still, white, snowy town. Peter walked rapidly, with bent head, leading the way. Along Derby to Neptune Street, Elm into Essex. Stackpool and Flanneau was the first house they had seen with candles lit.

"We called a midwife yesterday and things went on and on. So I got Old Doctor West. Jack's out of town. The old doctor said everything was good enough and went home. You know he thinks midwifery is beneath his dignity. Lots of old doctors do."

"The baby came early?"

"No. Just between you and me, no, it didn't. It came right on time. They lied a little at first. You can understand why."

"I see."

Upstairs they found that little group so often assembled in these circumstances. The good old midwife — this time it was Cora Colbey — with the baby, silent and still, in her arms. And of course a neighbor woman, tonight Frances Cunningham. She was holding the young and almost delirious mother's hand, mopping her forehead with a handkerchief dipped in rosewater. The distracted father. All that was missing, Doctor Hobey felt, to complete this ancient tableau, was a medicine man, a witch doctor, a priest. Some maker of mumbo-jumbo like himself. He felt he had stepped back into a scene as old as the human race itself.

"God be with this household," he said. "May God help and sustain you."

"Oh, Doctor Hobey," said Mrs. Colbey, "it don't move and it don't cry. Poor lamb. Poor little lamb. God doesn't intend it for this wicked world. But . . . just so its little soul makes a good end."

Dulcey was restless on her bed, half in and half out of her wits. "Where's Doctor Hobey? Did he come? Peter — where's Peter? Did Peter fetch him?" Then she struggled to sit up and cried out shrilly, "My baby can't go to Hell!"

"I'm here, Mrs. Flanneau," Hobey said, taking her hand. "Everything is all right."

"Oh . . ."

There was little paraphernalia necessary for baptism in Doctor Hobey's sect. He took off his greatcoat and muffler, drew a pitcher of clean water toward him. He wondered if the baby was not really dead already. If so, he'd go ahead and baptize it anyway. God, his own dear private God, Who knew all and forgave all, would understand. The bundle of flannel Mrs. Colbey put in his arms was warm. And as for coming early! He had never baptized a baby with such a complete head of hair. Dark, too.

"What name have you chosen for your child?"

Flanneau did not raise his head from his hands. "Petra."

"O Lord, bless this, Thy little servant as she starts out upon her path through this naughty world. Bring her through trial and tribulation, through the temptations of happiness as well as those of sorrow, triumphant and saved at last, back again to Thy Heavenly Kingdom. In the name of God the Father, God the Son, and God the Holy Ghost, I baptize thee Petra."

As the cold water fell upon the tiny dark head, the baby arched itself and began to snarl. It snarled and snarled. There was nothing human as yet in its noises.

Old Cora Colbey shrieked, "It's what we've been waiting for! We've slapped and shaken it and it wouldn't cry out. It's a miracle!" Tears ran down the tired old woman's face.

Flanneau stood up, flung out his arms. "A miracle! My baby was dying and at the name of God it lives!"

Nonsense, Doctor Hobey thought. It was the cold water.

"Dulcey" — Flanneau butted Mrs. Cunningham aside — "Dulcey, our baby shall live!"

Doctor Hobey had noticed, during his French lessons, the young wife's aversion for her husband's unending, tactless, tasteless caresses. He was forever after her, and she didn't like it. Now, however, she was smiling at him, with a weak, kind happiness, if not love.

Frances Cunningham had the baby. It was still snarling, but had also begun to hiccough. She was holding it close to the mother and saying how pretty it was.

How lovely, like a madonna, Frances looked, with her heavy russet hair loose on her shoulders and that sweet womanly look in her eyes! Doctor Hobey had seen her around for years, but she had always before hidden behind Mrs. Inman's skirts and her own half-mourning. As he looked at her now, he felt he saw her for the first time.

Flanneau was kissing his hands, and in very fast French renouncing something. Hobey was too sleepy to care what. He thought it was his French atheism. It might have been the Catholic Church. Hobey was ready to leave now, and so was Peter.

The boy didn't say much, but once again on the street he murmured his thanks. "We all have been through so much, Doctor Hobey. I couldn't have borne it if the baby had died . . . on top of everything." Then he turned toward his own house.

Doctor Hobey plunged through the moonstruck, snowy streets, longing for his bed. There is nothing, he thought, that brings every old superstition to the top faster than a birth. Unless it is a death. Combine birth and fear of death, and what a dark fog rises out of the past! He thought again of that ancient tableau he had walked in on, and completed. But one person was certainly out of place. What on earth was Peter Inman's part?

It might have been better for her if God had taken the baby's little unsullied soul back to Himself before her feet had even touched this naughty earth. Petra Flanneau. With one father too many. And Peter Inman! What a rascal! A villain! But what an innocent, lovable rascal the fellow was!

∼ 2 ∼

IT WAS MARCH in Salem, and winter over but spring not yet come. The harbor ice was rotting. The tall ships came and went, pouring their wealth into merchants' coffers and warehouses, and more shipyards and more ships, paying their enormous duties. Only a small part of the goods these ships brought in from all over the world would be sold in America, a sparsely settled, backward land. For instance, almost every picul of pepper carried out of Sumatra for years left in a Salem bottom. America could hardly absorb the pepper supply of the whole world. Almost all of it was sold, sometimes by hook or by crook, in Europe. And most of the European goods the ships brought in were resold in Asia.

'Sephus Hobey saw his first skunk cabbage, heard his first robin.

Mr. Africanus proudly slopped through the mud and slush of March in Hessian boots with red tassels on them. Once more his prodigious memory was earning him a penny here and a penny there. Several times a week he presented himself at the Inmans' kitchen. Linda, as Dorothy Belinda Gould was now called, wasted her young master's boot polish on his boots and fed him from her mistress's larder. Mrs. Cady snapped her parrot beak at Mr. Africanus and glittered her rectangular spectacles at him in disapproval. She told Mrs. Inman. But although Lucy Inman sighed and said she would have to "speak to Linda," she never did.

Peter met the new spring with a new confidence. For the first winter he could remember he had not been laid up with one of his devastating, month-long colds. He was putting on a little weight. Jack West told him that if he could gain like this every year until he was, say, twenty-four or five, he would promise him a long life. "And with your disposition, Peter, it will certainly be a happy one." Within a few months Peter would be nineteen. Twenty-four or five did not seem an unattainable goal. He'd do it. He was a handsomer boy than he had ever been before, and Jack West began to wonder if his sinful life was not agreeing with him pretty well. He would have been willing to swear that a young fellow with a weak chest shouldn't waste what strength he had running over to Essex Street, carrying on so indecently, and almost publicly, with that good-looking Mrs. Flanneau.

That winter Polly had had her second cousin, Georgiana Frick, for a long visit. She was quaint, bewitching, possibly plain. And yet as possibly beautiful. The one thing she obviously was not, was pretty. This forward, unstoppable miss had promptly fallen in love with Peter. Then she had returned to Cambridge.

Peter was writing pretty good poetry, but, as it was neither translated from the Latin nor the French but expressed his own ideas, he was leery of showing it to Doctor Hobey. And of what use to give it to Polly? She'd merely stick it in her album. Poems to her were like scalps to an Indian. Seemingly Georgiana knew much more about such things than did her cousin. Peter found for himself a perfect balance for his emotional life. One girl to write poems about. One girl to appreciate what he had written. His correspondence with the very young Miss Frick became voluminous.

Although he diagnosed correctly certain hostile, curious, and shocked glances he encountered, and although he knew that many mothers had stopped asking him to their houses to meet their nubile girls, he was not lonely. He knew that people were saying that he had had an illegitimate child, hired a Frenchman to marry the girl, and paid him well that he might continue the relationship. He guessed it was not the sort of thing Salem approved of. He did not know that, if he had been different, public opinion would not have been so bitterly offended. But public opinion wants each man to play the part assigned to him. To stay in the expected rôle. If it were Liz Inman who was leading so evil a life, they would at least have had the satisfaction of knowing he was as bad as they had always expected. There would have been some smug self-satisfaction in that. But it was almost unforgivable that Peter, a rather innocent-looking, inoffensive, not very strong young fellow, should refuse to play the rôle society had picked for him. He was supposed to be a great comfort to his grandmother, kind to his mother, a sort of harmless, necessary cat about the place. The one bad thing he was supposed to do was to "lack gumption." And here he had gumption enough to get mixed up in this scandal. So Peter not only was offending the sensibilities of his native New England town, but also going against the popular estimate of his character.

Yet Polly — she must by now have heard the worst — never refused to see him. In fact, she had given him that intimacy she was apt to withhold from her equals. He was a true confidant, almost a second Flip to her. And Mompesson, Peter believed, so loved to have her shrine crowded with worshipers — provided they did not touch — he would be loath to send even the least important of these away. That man would welcome Old Horny or Mr. Scratch if he'd sit quietly and do no more than admire.

Besides Polly and Georgiana, Peter had the Flanneaus. Not his mother's tears nor Doctor Hobey's sage advice had pried him loose from the Flanneaus. It had started with his obligations to Dulcey. Nobody had ever trusted him so. Perhaps nobody ever before had done what he had told them to do. He could not relinquish her completely to so strange a man as Flanneau was proving to be.

Monsieur Flanneau was tact itself. He wore his semi-public horns with dignity, and yet perhaps the situation was harder than he had expected. For one thing he had foolishly fallen in love with his "wife." He may have always had a tendency toward periodic drunkenness, but for six months he had worked inordinately for the Stackpools and never shown this weakness. Soon after he was married, every so often — about once a month — he would lay by his embroidery hoop, patterns, scissors, and silk, take off the pincushion he wore at his belt, and wander off to some alehouse or tavern, get drunk and stay drunk for about three days. Then he talked. "And who shall object," he would demand, "that I, a man incapable of having children, but wishing for such, permit another man to do for me that which I cannot do?"

This was a nice moral point, calculated to charm and fascinate the children of Puritans.

It bothered Peter that Dulcey was trying so hard to make herself over into the accepted pattern of gentility so that Dash could marry her when he came home. He would tell her and tell her to forget Dash. She did not. Of course, a coarse crock like Dulcey did not even understand the meaning of the word "love" as Georgiana or Polly did, but even so, he could not get the idea out of her head. She tended shop deftly and modestly. She minded the house well, and Cousin Frances, whom Peter was coming to admire very much, helped her and taught her. If you saw Dulcey running down the stairs with the baby in her arms, you'd hardly realize that less than a year ago she had been afraid of stairs. She had never been up and down stairs until she came to Salem. Often, as she served the ever-increasing number of customers, she had her pretty baby in a cradle beside her. Lady shoppers oh-ed and ah-ed over the ermine tails sewed to the baby's velvet bonnet, over the exquisite embroidery her father stitched on petticoats, dresses, and blankets. Even her diapers were feather-stitched, as Mrs. Flanneau would obligingly upend the baby to prove. They had never heard of a man so hysterically devoted to a baby. It seemed almost proof that the child was really his. As for his wife, she was a good enough mother. No love for this child had been created in her during pregnancy. But now that she was here, and good and cute, she tolerated her with some affection. Peter knew Cousin Frances loved her more than her own mother.

The unfashionable, aging Misses Stackpool appeared less and less often in their shop. Miss Clara had always had the asthma. Now

Miss Unity was down with what she called "my complaint." Although the sign still read Stackpool and Flanneau, the shop was firmly in the latter's hands. He was now renting the entire house from Mrs. Cunningham except her own back stairs and two upper rooms. And her barn as well. This he used for a warehouse, for he was branching out, a middleman who bought his fine ladies' goods off the ships and sold them at handsome profit inland. Flanneau's business acumen also helped ever so little to lift the cloud from Peter. Evidently Peter had been very smart to realize the man's potentialities, lend him the money for a partnership. He must be making a good profit. And perhaps the things Flanneau babbled when drunk were nothing but proof that he was a nasty-minded Frenchman.

Peter was not making profit from his relationship with Flanneau. He was put to it to imagine where — unless he gave up the two hundred he had ventured on the *Victrix* — he was to get that next five hundred dollars Flanneau was politely, but with increasing firmness, hinting was due him.

He would talk casually of removing himself perhaps back to France. "Eh, Monsieur Peter?" and his eyes squinted up at Peter; "for it is now that I hear if I so wish I may return. And of course my wife and my child they shall go too."

Peter knew it was only a threat and he should not take it seriously.

"I'll bet your wife won't go with you to France. You couldn't make her."

"No?" said Flanneau. "No. I cannot make her go. But my baby she shall go with me."

He never would risk losing Dulcey. He couldn't go back to France. Salem profited him. But what he politely threatened to do legally he might.

Flanneau loved the baby so much Peter was afraid sometimes he might kill her with his affection. Peter hated to see him kissing and kissing her until he left red marks where he had sucked the soft flesh into his mouth, straining her little neck in his exuberance of love. Of course he hurt the baby, made her cry. In fact, the baby would scream when she saw Flanneau approaching. Sometimes it froze Peter's blood. Perhaps, really, Flanneau hated her.

Although Peter might have abandoned Dulcey, he could not abandon the baby. He had never really looked at one before, not having considered them quite worth looking at. He had not known that every nail was perfect, that there were eyelashes, that soon babies began to smile. He was sure that, at three months, Petra recognized him and laughed and flayed her arms at sight of him. In his imagination she already looked like Dash. A very little Dash, so young and weak he could encompass her in his arms, hold the unattainable to his heart. Sometimes, as he held her, he could even forget Polly. Perhaps the best thing Dash could do when he came home was to marry Dulcey and lay claim to this fragment of himself. And yet, if Dash did so, then Petra would be Dash's, not Peter's any longer. Now she was his. No one doubted that, and he himself least of all. He had never thought the baby's arrival and development of a personality could make so much difference to him.

The *Victrix* had been gone almost a year. But, curiously, she had not been reported since last September. It was not yet time to begin worrying about her. Yet that was what his grandmother was doing already. She was always wondering where the ship might be.

～3～

NIGHT CAME, incredible, silent. There was no twilight in Java. The sun disappeared as though it were blown out. Then the black velvet curtain of night came down, spangled with stars.

Van Heelu sat with his guests on the back gallery. It was on the back galleries in the Dutch country houses that life was mostly lived, or endured. Here food was eaten — sambals, fish roe, palm shoots, salted eggs, and fruit. Piles of fruit — pineapples, bananas, purple mangosteen, velvety rambutan, smooth-skinned doohooes. But there were times when the two Yankees would have given them all for a bite of one good red apple.

All four men on the back gallery wore the accustomed dishabille of Europeans in the Dutch East Indies. They had flowered cotton coats, bare chests, flowing and flowered muslin trousers. Nothing on their feet. On the well-built, tanned Inmans, the odd flowery dress sat well. It gave them the look of Persian princes. But Doctor Vreed's years, tropical pallor, and thinness made him look like a dishonored corpse, amid his posies. Lids and lips were like parchment. He was an exhausted man, drained of blood as though host every night to Java's vampire bats. Probably a sick man, sick of body, sick of soul. Dash had found Vreed stranded on Isle of France, longing for passage to the Dutch islands. It was he who had shown him certain back-door passages into Batavia Roads.

Van Heelu was as stout and heavy a man as any prosperous Amsterdam burgher. But he was not so rosy. His skin was gray from his long life in the tropics and the many fevers he had endured. His fat did not lie upon him as a jolly exuberance, but like a disease. He was continually wiping the sweat from his obese bare chest, sopping it up as it ran down his flaccid jowls.

The back gallery was lit by lamps. Because the wind died so utterly with nightfall, slave girls stood by to fan the men as they sat in their creaking bamboo chairs. Barefoot boys came and went, silent as the bats in the hortus beyond them. And beyond the hortus, with its trees and flowers, was the bathhouse, the stables, the servants' quarters. The fireflies were so large and the lights in the servants' quarters beyond the garden so feeble, it was hard to tell which was which. The natives were playing softly, and singing sad, slow songs. Queer music it seemed at first, as senseless as the day-long crying of the wow-wow monkeys. But if you listened long enough, did not resist it, it got under your skin, into the blood and bones.

Miss Porteous, the one woman — for the half-naked cat-faced native fan-bearers did not seem quite like real women, more like cats — sat stiffly upright in her chair. She had not made one concession to the tropical life. No flimsy Javanese cottons for her. Tonight she had on a hot purplish silk gown, with a black velvet ribbon tight about her freckled neck. She was the English governess Van Heelu had imported some six years before to educate "his little wards" — there was quite a parcel of half-Dutch, half-Javanese children about the place. She was a bony, stringy woman, red-haired, with a high-bridged nose and an amazingly proper English accent. She was by no means young, and had obviously never been pretty, but she fascinated the Inmans. They had never seen a woman who could drink so much and show it so little. They were used to the sipping of ladies and the roistering drunkenness of the girls of, say, Marseilles. Here was something new. They had been watching her with intent, naïve curiosity ever since Van Heelu had invited them, through Doctor Vreed, out to his country place — to escape the fevers of Batavia and for a most private conversation.

But now that, at last, after four merely social days, Van Heelu was beginning to talk business, it disconcerted the Inmans that the woman was there. Both the Dutchmen spoke English. They needed no interpreter. And the fact was her country was now at war with Holland. This had not been the case when Van Heelu hired her. Most of the time she sat silent, every so often merely lifting a finger. Then a boy, silent as a bat, materialized out of the night and once more filled her glass. When she spoke, she was always sarcastic or unpleasant.

The *Victrix* had successfully evaded, with Doctor Vreed to guide them, such British ships as were attempting to blockade Batavia. And so, they found, had other bold American merchantmen. There was even one British merchantman in the Roads. By and large the Batavians were for England against their Frenchified fatherland. But the *Victrix,* being so smart and fast, had been chartered for two brief voyages by Doctor Vreed. He was working, he said, for a "certain party." Now they knew that Van Heelu was that mysterious party. The Dutch habitually built enormous clumsy craft. They were no longer sailors but merchants. They dared not venture their ships out to sea to face even a weak British Navy. But the *Victrix* had her small size and her speed to help her, and her American flag to protect her. On one charter they had gone to the Spice Islands for pepper. On the other, across the bay to Bengal, to sell coffee.

The great, gluttonous Dutch East India Company, "Jan Compagnie," which had held Java, Sumatra, Ceylon, in its grasp for over two hundred years, was no more. Greed and sloth had almost finished it. Then Napoleon had ended Jan Compagnie's power. Dash had learned in Isle of France that Napoleon was sending out from Paris some sort of a government. But it had not yet arrived. For the moment, there was utterly no government in the Dutch East Indies, but what power there was lay in the sweating, fat hands of Van Heelu.

When Dash had been here first with the Crowninshields' *Belisarius,* and later in command of the *Antelope,* one could not trade, nor anchor a ship, nor move except on the orders of Jan Compagnie. Yet a very handsome profit was allowed the foreign traders. He had not been permitted to stay anywhere except in the gaudy "Inner Lodgement," as the Company's hotel in Batavia was called. Now all this stale and stifling order had collapsed, but no new order had arrived. The British had already bitten off Ceylon from the Dutch Empire. But they were too weak in men and ships to attempt as yet the seizure of Java and Sumatra. French ships there were none. And the fat, slow Dutch ships rotted in the harbors.

Van Heelu had gone on now for a half-hour at least, suggesting to them what their next charter would be. They had known it would be important and secret and probably dangerous when Doctor Vreed had told them the "certain party" wished to talk to them face to face.

"And it will be well," said Van Heelu, sopping the sweat from his chest, "if they ask you if you are Christians, to say no — you are Dutchmen. When they say Christians, they are thinking only of Portuguese and Spaniards. These they hate and fear."

"With reason," said Miss Porteous from the dark. Her father was an English rector. "And they will ask you to stamp upon the cross as proof that you are not Christians, only infidel Dutchmen, who never think of anything but their ledgers, their schnapps, and their gulden."

"No, no, Miss Porteous," Doctor Vreed corrected her. "You forget I was for two years Company doctor on our island of Dechima — which the Japanese have permitted us. You are repeating the usual folklore, not fact."

"What would happen," Dash asked, "if we said, yes, we are Christians?"

"And Yankees — not Dutchmen — and proud of it," added Liz.

"They'd crucify you," said Miss Porteous, with a well-bred little sniff.

Van Heelu threw up a despairing hand. "My dear! Let me or Doctor Vreed answer any questions." And to Dash he said, "Perhaps nothing. We do not know."

"This is the time you will find out," suggested Liz.

"Japan, a hundred and fifty years ago, decided to throw out all the priests or kill them if they would not go. Then shut themselves off forever from the rest of the world. But they realized that there were certain goods they must have. They permit a few ships a year from China. And we — at least the Dutch East India Company — have ever since been permitted to send one ship a year, carrying in our goods and taking a cargo from them. And we do maintain in Japan one tiny trading post — Dechima. But now our annual ship will be seized by the British. There is only one way, and that is to charter a neutral for the great yearly voyage. Well, the American is almost the only neutral flag left in the world."

"I understand that," said Dash.

"It will be necessary for that neutral ship to show the colors and papers of her country if the British bespeak her. But I assure you, if she comes into Nagasaki Harbor under any flag but the Dutch, she will be turned away or destroyed."

Dash said bluntly: "And yet there is no longer a Dutch East India Company. Old Jan Compagnie is dead."

"Very true. But who will have told the Japanese? They have no news of the outside world from anyone — except by the yearly Great Hollander ship."

"So, in a way, your long treaty with them has been abrogated."

"In a way — a very unimportant way, I assure you. How can they guess?"

"They will find out," Miss Porteous said. "They are smart and sly as devils. And cruel."

"Of course, we must not let them know that old Jan Compagnie is no more. Dissolved — after two hundred years — by one sentence written by an upstart Corsican. And of course they will notice at once that you are not Dutch. We trust they will not see in you the ship of a forbidden nation — only a servant of the Dutch. Perhaps," he added hopefully, "it would be well if you hint, at least, that Holland has conquered America?"

Dash laughed. He looked down upon the Dutch. No sooner had the French overrun them than they had sided with their conquerors — and against England, who, at the moment, alone in all the world, had the fortitude to fight back against this monstrous, swollen, bloody, all-conquering France. He looked down upon Van Heelu, who seemed to him the very personification of "Jan" —

ruthless, powerful, money-seeking in its youth; obese, cruel, sick with the sickness of thee white man in the tropics, in its age.

"So — as you ask wisely what your reception in Japan may be — I must answer honestly, I do not know. But" — and one wet fat fist struck the other — "this I can promise you. You risk your ship. I will risk the cargo. If you succeed, I promise it will prove the richest single voyage possible in the world today."

"You pay well?" Liz asked. He knew Dash was off on a dream of seeing wonders, being the first American ship to enter the forbidden waters. This pleased Liz, too, but he could always think about money at the same time.

"Very well. Fantastically. First, because we admit you risk your ship . . ."

"And your lives," added Miss Porteous.

"And partly because of the value of the trade. Partly — and this is most important — because the Great Hollander ship must arrive, and exactly at the prescribed time. They must not guess that Jan Compagnie is . . . weakening."

"Weakening!" said Miss Porteous in her precise, upper-class manner. "Nonexistent. Face it, Van Heelu."

"Captain," said Doctor Vreed, "one thing more. As you know, I love my country, my Holland, so much I fled away rather than live under a foreign flag. I have come here, because here again I see the flag of Holland flying. Where else in all the world does it fly? Only here and tiny Dechima, our little island trading post in Nagasaki Harbor. Nowhere else. Very well. It has always been the Japanese copper we have wanted most. And now copper we must have. We must. If we have it we can cast cannon here on Java. Defend ourselves whenever it is that the British attack. For they will. France has no possible way of sending a fleet or supplies to us here. We must have copper. Rubies and emeralds, diamonds and pearls — all that fabulous wealth did not save Ceylon. In war all of the jewels of the world are not worth one cargo of copper."

Van Heelu looked embarrassed. He was not a patriotic man. What Doctor Vreed suffered from the extinguishment of his homeland he could not guess. For there was no Holland, only the Batavia Republic, a part of France.

"Why," Liz was asking, "did the Japanese shut themselves off from the world? Everyone knows trade is the life-blood of a country. They must be a stupid folk."

"No! No!" cried Doctor Vreed, with passion. "They are merely patriotic. How can you blame them? No people in all Asia so welcomed the first Europeans as did they. No people so heartily embraced Christianity. Why, certain Christian princes traveled as far as Rome to pay allegiance to the Pope."

"What then?"

"They were smart enough to look about them. They saw that everywhere in Asia the Europeans began with missionaries and trade — and ended with conquest. They saw India swallowed by England. We Dutchmen seized these islands and Ceylon. The Philippines disappeared into Spain's pocket. Mr. Inman, if they had not swung shut their gates, the same thing would have happened to them. So they went into complete isolation."

"That's what Mr. Jefferson is talking about at home," Dash said. "He thinks a country can cut itself off forever from the rest of the world. But sailors, who get around and see things, don't think so. I suppose the Japanese have never been sailors."

"Two hundred years ago they sent ships as far as South America. Then the edict came. Never again can any Japanese ship be built big enough to leave home waters. Nor may any ship ever land there — except a few junks from China and the yearly Hollander ship; and never again shall 'Kristo' as they call him set foot upon their shores."

"But if once they were so Christian, what happened to them?"

"They say that more Christian martyrs died in Japan in the seventeenth century than ever died under the reigns of Nero or Diocletian. Fortunately, they do not class Protestant Dutchmen as Christians."

Dash shifted quietly in his chair. He had made up his mind as soon as the word "Japan" had been said. It was almost unknown, even the shape and size of the islands. He'd go. He'd risk it. But he had spoken lazily and had sat back much of the time, with his lids half-closed over his fine eyes. He knew enough not to show eagerness. He was drinking in all Doctor Vreed had to tell. Let Liz, a monstrous smart fellow, who could figure faster in his head than most men on paper, carry on. He left to him the discussion of so-and-so much pay for the charter. So-and-so many tons were allowed as ventures for the captain, and so much for the mates.

And strangely, suddenly, as he often did, he thought of Polly. He could shut his eyes and see her. It was for her he'd risk any-thing — his grandmother's ship, probably his people, his brother, and his own life. For her he'd sail beyond the string tied to him by his ship's insurance, go to the strange land forbidden him. If gold was the key to unlock the barrier between them, he'd have the gold.

"But our people?" Liz was saying.

Van Heelu did not, at first, recognize a "crew" in the word "people." Then he said that the crew had no ventures. Liz and Dash exchanged quick glances, and Liz began to argue. Not that he really cared, as did Dash, about the success and happiness of the crew. But he knew that Dash meant him to fight out this small, and very Yankee, point with the Dutchmen.

"I think" — Dash at last spoke as master, taking the matter over from his bargaining, haggling mate — "that if all this looks as good tomorrow on paper as it sounds tonight in talk, we'll sign with you. And Japan will be something to see."

"Heh!" whinnied Miss Porteous. "What will you see, shut up on that island from July until November? Treated like a slave. You'll have to grin when spoken to, crawl upon your stomach."

"Miss Porteous, you exaggerate."

"Pah! And if they discover you are not Dutchmen, they will torture and kill you."

"Really, my dear . . ." But Van Heelu could not stop her.

"Oh, *you!*" she said to him, and no wife could have spoken more rudely — "you care for nothing except money. Money — pah! You've got it now, haven't you? Can you drink your pearls and gain your health? Can you run your rubies in your veins and have red blood once more? But they" — she pointed at the Inmans — "they are so young, so gallant, so brave, so handsome. And they are not really thinking *that*" — she snapped her bony fingers — "of money. Only of glory, adventure. To see them is like seeing once more the beginning of the world. Once more Jason seeks the Golden Fleece. Ulysses sails beyond the gates of Hercules."

As she spoke — to the intense embarrassment of both young men — she leaned forward into the light of the lamp and smiled first at Liz and then even more lingeringly at Dash.

"Stay here," she whispered, "my dears. I am old enough to call you my dears. Stay and be safe."

Good God! thought Dash. That's how the gin affects her. She had given him the most lascivious smile he had ever seen. How could she do it, handicapped as she was by her years, her bony, high-bridged nose, freckles, and upper middle-class breeding? That smile, so toothy and so lascivious, froze his blood. But he had an unpleasant picture of her with her stays off and the wet black ribbon about her neck untied.

"My dear young captain, I beg of you . . ."

"Miss Porteous . . ."

"Captain Dash — if I may be so familiar — refuse to go. Absolutely refuse. It is forbidden by all the laws of Japan. Van Heelu is sending you to die — because he envies you your youth and beauty." She was getting hysterical. "He has sent many to death — and he old and rotten and half-dead."

"Miss Porteous," her employer broke in with quiet finality, "I must ask you to retire."

She did. Her feet (the only leather-shod feet for miles around) never wavered. She was not drunk.

Not until the young men got to their bedroom did they realize how hot and wet they were. Not a dry hair on their heads, nor an inch of dry clothing on them. Naked they flung themselves on their couches. Neither could sleep. Then sent Meeda, the silent, calm-eyed slave girl, away. It was her duty to sit all night between their couches and fan them. It was she who, every afternoon at five, went with them to the bathhouse and poured buckets of water over them. She was obviously ready, any night, to spend half the time with one of her herren and half with the other.

Although so far from New England and the God of the white meeting-houses and other New England decencies, a shared mistress appealed to neither young man. Miss Porteous, who was housekeeper as well as governess to the "little wards," had been too pinch-penny. But perhaps she was tired of so vast a supply of little wards and wanted no more. Meeda was a beautiful golden girl. Seeing her always so near and attainable, and yet so far, had bothered both Dash and Liz. So they had sent her away. Then, too, tonight they wanted to discuss the voyage of the *Victrix* to Japan. They talked in whispers, Dash thinking mostly of the wonders to be seen and Liz of the money to be made.

Even the native slaves beyond the hortus had ceased their singing. The tropic night was soundless. Not a leaf stirred.

~4~

In the tawdry, purple, gilt, and faded grandeur of the old Inner Lodgement, the final arrangements for the loading and sailing of the *Victrix* were made. She was out at Omroos Island, and her crew kept aboard her. The city of Batavia, with its endless dirty canals, its filth and its fevers, was considered the most lethal city in the world. Then, too, on Omroos Island Van Heelu could keep private what was going forward.

Slowly, because secretly, the *Victrix* was lading with those things the Japanese could not themselves produce and without which they could not exist. Japan grew no sugar. The ship was floored with sugar. Elephants' tusks. Woolen goods. They had neither. Cloves and spices of the Dutch islands. Spectacles (Doctor Vreed told Dash they were a short-sighted people) by the dozens. Watches and clocks — Liz had done well to take half his clock collection thus far. Glass mirrors, for they had none. And they were great dosers Doctor Vreed said. It was the Dutch themselves who had long ago taught them to prize "unicorns' horns" above pearls. Faith in the efficacy of these Greenland narwhals' horns was all but dead in Europe, but the Japanese princes still believed they prolonged life and potency, protected them against poison. The fifty pounds of this sovereign remedy would, Vreed said, sell for toward ten thousand dollars. Quinine and choice camphor they also must have for their stomachs' sake. Slowly the *Victrix* took on her strange cargo — with either the captain or a mate always standing by to watch it properly done. It was being said, everywhere, that this year the Great Hollander ship would not make its ancient, annual voyage to Japan.

Dash had been almost ready to give the whole thing up when he found how close the restrictions would be upon him. He could not enter Nagasaki before a certain day in July. No matter what hurricanes, typhoons, or calms, he would be forced to clear the harbor on a certain day in November. He would hardly set his foot on the mainland, but pass his time either with the Dutch hoeffs and upperhoeffs, clerks and doctor of Dechima, or aboard his own ship. He'd be spied upon, night and day. Luckily, Doctor Vreed was being sent with him. He would relieve the doctor now marooned on Dechima. Dash had come to like the well-informed, wraith-like doctor.

Next day they would make their departure. All the papers, the infinity of papers required of the merchant ship, had been handled by Vreed. And endless palms had been well greased. The *Victrix* was cleared from Batavia for the Philippines, and it was east, toward Luzon, that he would start out.

At last, when all was set to go, Dash wrote his owner a long letter. He did not dare say that he had been sailing for the last few months under Dutch charter. If this became known to the British, he was afraid no American flag would save him. He dared even less hint that he was now heading for Japan, a land as unknown to America as the mountains of Tibet. Then, too, it would needlessly worry his grandmother. But he did write telling her of his second voyage to Mocha for coffee to sell at Isle of France. He let her know that he was in Batavia and that financially the voyage was a success and would be "many times more so" before he came home again.

And he wrote Polly, not as lovingly as he might if he had not known Van Heelu would read his letters, but he had so completely recovered from the shame he had endured when he last saw her that he wrote with confidence and hope. He would not be home soon, he said (for already he thought it might be worth while to make this same passage again next year — if all went well), but it was because he loved her so he was determined to make his fortune.

Van Heelu promised to start the letters on their way. He read them. Truly Captain Inman had said little enough, but that little Van Heelu thought too much.

He quietly destroyed the letters.

5

Two DAYS BEFORE, Dash had had a good observation. And yesterday, through scud of rain and lift of cloud, he had seen floating before him peaks of mountains, looking as though cut from cardboard. This was Japan — the land of gods and ogres and of flowers. The land of the monkey people — as the Chinese said. He felt a prick of excitement along his wrists, knowing he was in forbidden waters. Then rain came and more rain, gray sea, gray sky, and silver rain. At nightfall he anchored.

He was on latitude 26, yet next morning as he stood in sunshine upon the quarterdeck, the ancient Dutch East India Company's charts in his hands and Doctor Vreed beside him, he was doubtful whether or not the indentation the *Victrix* was feeling out would prove to lead him into Nagasaki's long harbor. He trusted Vreed's memory more than the charts that had been lent him.

Now they were beginning to see fishing boats and Doctor Vreed was confident they stood in the harbor's mouth. He swore he remembered a certain village.

"We'll see," was all Dash promised. "It isn't that way on the charts. No wonder Jan Compagnie has been losing one out of every five ships."

The *Victrix* seemed to feel her master's unsureness. She was picking her way gingerly, like a horse going downhill over rolling stones. And she'd better, thought Dash. The land struck him as something like the coast of Maine and even more like a Norwegian fiord. A dangerous landfall.

"This is it," Vreed said confidently. "Look at that little red fort; you'll find that on your chart."

Dash did. "Yes, I guess this is it."

It was a fair day, the breeze fair and following. The *Victrix* filled and leaned upon the wind with that trusting almost childish way she had. Her master was sure of himself and so was she.

Two days before, the guards on Cavallos Island had sighted the tall ship. They had signaled the next guardhouse and they the next and the next. On every rocking headland, facing out to sea, suspicious slanted eyes were eternally fixed for sight of foreign sail. Cruel "Krishto" must never set foot here again. From the red tower of the Emperor to the white tower of the Empress, and so inland, the news had gone. Now the governor of Nagasaki had started an imperial tattooed messenger on the long road to Yedo to tell the Emperor the news.

Nagasaki was thrown into a paroxysm of excitement. For weeks tourists had been crowding the inns to see the "red-hair" ship come in sight. It was one of the wonders of the year. Kimono-ed women with nodding babies on their backs giggled as they ran. The guild of print-makers, who for generations had been making prints of these foreign ships to sell to tourists, were already hiring boatmen to scull them out so they might sketch the new ship. Mountain priests forgot to beg. Old monks laid down their prayer beads. Upon the three-acre island of Dechima, Dutchman almost went mad with joy. Only twice a year — when the Company ship came and when she went out — were they allowed to use their barge. At other times their jailers kept their oars and rudder. The Upperhoef, Heer Waadenaar, buttoned his long-skirted red velvet coat about him with trembling fingers, put his plumed and jeweled hat upon his head. Not for a year had any of them had word from the outside world nor a letter from home. Last year news of the fall of Holland to Napoleon had made them fear no ship would come this year. No ship, no letters, ever again. But even now she was coming in.

Aboard the *Victrix* Doctor Vreed was seeing to the setting up of what he called the seat of honor — naught but planks laid across chicken coops with a rich Turkish rug and cushions on it. Two officials, he told Dash, would come aboard — two and their retinues.

"They'll come out in the Company's barge — and, by the way, it may look odd to you. It is about the date of your Queen Elizabeth. A gilded state barge — but if we used anything else, they wouldn't like it. Nothing must ever change here — ever."

"You lean over backwards to please them?"

"Oh yes — over backwards in one direction and flat on our faces in the other. I see you have your gun crew on duty. I will tell you when to begin the required salutes. There are many."

Now Liz, as "the" mate, was crowding among the men, collecting every bit of paper, written or printed upon, even playing cards. These were being packed in a barrel which would be headed and turned over to the Japanese until the fifteenth of November, on

which day the ship would make her departure. More than anything else the Japanese feared western learning. All powder (except
what had been measured out for the interminable saluting), all
weapons, ammunition, and money, must also be given up. Lists of
everything had to be prepared: of the ship's people, their ages,
names, station in life — everything about every man — even the
fact the captain had a knife scar upon his chest and the ship's cook
was a black man with woolly hair. There were lists of the cargo,
and even the strings and jackknives in the men's pockets were
listed. This was Mate Liz's business.

Dash said to Vreed, "You are sure they will know we are not
Dutchmen?"

"Their guild of interpreters speak good Dutch. The art is handed
down from father to son. But, after all, *once* New York did belong
to the Dutch? If you will permit me a slight exaggeration?"

"Of course." Dash would have permitted him to say America
belonged to the Devil rather than miss the excitement of seeing
even a tiny bit of Japan.

"The interpreters would know in five minutes you are not
Dutch. Ah, those interpreters! Fastened upon us like leeches. You
know how tiny Dechima is. Fifteen Dutchmen live there (unless
some have died), and for each Dutchman twenty parasitic Japanese.
Every Japanese except the Otona (that's the governor of the island)
goes home by night — thank Heavens. And the courtesans which
their law has always allowed us. They are a guild, too — of course.
Sometimes I think the entire imperial city of Nagasaki is supported
by us and our one ship a year. That's one reason why I am sure
they will not make trouble. They must have the things you are
bringing them. Too many of the guilds are dependent upon the
yearly ship for their livelihood."

"You must like them, to be going back to them once more."

"No," Vreed said mournfully, "no. But when I fled Holland to
escape a French flag over me (and I was well suited there — I am
not a young man — I had the chair of botany at Leyden — a wife
even — but I fled), I thought, although my country does not exist
in Europe, but yet she does in our Indies. But Captain — for how
long? You've seen Van Heelu. In a way he is all that's left of old
Jan Compagnie. Will such fight off the British? No. Java and
Sumatra will, like Ceylon, soon be under a foreign flag. Then
no place in the world will my flag fly — only upon tiny Dechima."

Dash was only half-listening He felt wonder and pride because the landfall he was making was so strange. He was not saying to himself, I'm the first American master ever ro enter Japan, but the *Victrix* is the first American ship. He felt very proud for her.

Liz stood on the deck below him, standing so smartly at attention; for never (before the men) did these two brothers relax an iota of discipline.

"Sir, all money, all powder, shot, have been stowed. Of written matter there is only the ship's papers and lists still out. Of printed, only the ship's Bible. The barrels are ready to head. Sir, shall I fetch the ship's Bible?"

"It is Sunday," said Dash, "Mr. Mate."

Nor had his people forgotten it. Every man had on a clean checked shirt and spotless white canvas pants. But like himself, they had been too excited to think much of it.

"Mr. Mate, summon both watches. We'll have service now. And I've a word or two to say to them. So slip wind and back sail. We'll stay where we are for a few moments."

Dash, also in white canvas pants, stood at the break of the poop with Doctor Vreed and his two mates beside him. The men stood below looking up at him. He noticed how healthy and shipshape they looked. Even little old Doctor Zack always put on a clean calico apron for Sunday.

"My people," he said, "by the time we round yon island to larboard, we will fire our first salute — to a people no American ever saw and who never saw an American. And then we will officially be in Japan. Soon after, Doctor Vreed tells me, we'll come up to the East India Company's barge. It will have not only Dutchmen, but two Japanese officials — and their train of young men. Some thirty people will board us. Now one thing, boys. These Japanese may look like funny people to you. But you're not to laugh. We've got these coops fixed up and a carpet spread for them. This is to honor them. So it has always been for two hundred years. You are to honor them, too. Not a smile. You hear me? Those are orders. And mind your wheel, Lem Ovington! If you can't listen and steer, for God's sake, stop listening. On the fifteenth of next November we leave — even if it's a hurricane blowing, or such dead calm it takes a hundred rowboats to tow us. Out we go. For that's the way it has always been. That's the way the eight thousand gods of Japan want it and our employers want it. So do I, for I've given my promise. And so it shall be.

"As for shore leaves. One officer and half the crew will always be aboard ship. Two officers and the rest of you on Dechima. That island isn't much bigger than a ship. And not much more fun." He paused. No need to tell them about those courtesans. "You may get pretty bored. But if you get bored, mind you, you are also getting rich. I wouldn't sign any charter with the Dutch until they agreed every man among you was to have share in profits. And remember . . . this is the first American ship ever to get to Japan. There's great honor in that."

They had not cheered him when he had reminded them of the money each would make. Now they did.

"We officers will keep a school of navigation. By November every man among you will know enough to go as master himself. Mr. Mate here and I will teach you languages — best we are able. All you want to learn. There are two lads among you that cannot read nor write nor figure. We'll fix that for 'em. For four months there will be no religious service. I had to promise that to get the charter. Doctor Vreed here says you boys hadn't better even swear. God and Christ sound about alike in Dutch and English. The Japanders might think you were praying. So mind you. Those are orders. But upon every seventh day you are to put on your white trousers. And Doctor Zack — don't forget plum-duff every Lord's Day — even though we are in a land where He is not. So, for the last time until next November, I'll read from the Bible, and soon's I'm done, it goes in that barrel and gets nailed up."

He stood, an impressive, sturdy figure on his quarterdeck, his bare dark head bowed, the heavy old book cradled in his right arm, hunting for the place he wanted. Robin, the ship's calico cat, rubbed about him smirking at him, drooling with feline love. Not even she, nor the fact he could not quickly find his place, could whittle away jot or tittle of his dignity. His young crew gazed up at him spellbound.

"I've got it," he said at last. "Seems it was the 139th psalm I was searching for. I got to thinking about it. Last eight bells."

. . . whither shall I flee from thy presence?
If I ascend up into Heaven, thou art there,
If I make my bed in Hell, behold, thou art there.

He was not reading prose as did most clergymen, but poetry. His low voice caressed the words.

> If I take the wings of the morning,
>> and dwell in the uttermost parts of the sea;

("And that's just about where we are now")

> Even there shall thy hand lead me,
> And thy right hand shall hold me,
> If I say, Surely the darkness shall cover me;
> Even the night shall be light about me . . .

And so on until he reached the end. He closed the book, laid it in the barrel. "It doesn't make any difference," he said. "God doesn't live in meeting-houses — nor in any book. Not even a Bible. We don't have to talk about Him — nor swear — to remember Him. God is in each one of us, telling us what to do. Don't forget. Mr. Obrian, set sails and break out the whole collection of flags the Dutch lent us. Nine salutes as we breast yon island. Now, boys, be smart and mind your *p's* and *q's,* and don't laugh. That's all."

The *Victrix* began to pick up the lightest of light winds. Her larboard guns boomed and in the midst of the cloud of gunpowder, flags broke out all over her.

"The barge!" cried Vreed. "There's the barge waiting us!"

And Dash couldn't believe his eyes. "Why, if that thing's a fact, I guess New York *does* still belong to Holland."

Soon hailing them, clambering on board came Heer Waadenaar and his clerks, dressed in velvets so old-fashioned he felt he was meeting men out of portraits by Rembrandt. But as Vreed had told him, the Japanese fashions had never changed. Neither were the Dutch upon Dechima supposed to. And Waadenaar and Vreed were embracing and Vreed was trying to explain the situation before the Japanese came on. They were last. For your greatest men came last in this strange land. Neither the two officials nor their train began to startle Dash as much as had the Dutchmen. He realized he should have warned his people not to laugh at the Europeans.

The great men scuttled for the seat of honor, sat down instantly, and producing tiny gilt-paper fans, began to fan themselves energetically. True, they had shaved heads (all but the quaint little topknot), but their dress of gray was modest and businesslike. But at the end of four hours Dash had been almost exhausted by their curiosity and the way they had smacked and regurgitated with pleasure over the fish chowder Doctor Zack had been told to prepare for them, the way they could drink brandy, but mostly by their unending childish curiosity. At last their smiling became vague, their questions stopped, their little gilt fans fluttered and fell. But cold sober (for no brandy had been fed them) the twenty-odd young interpreters, spies, and servants of the great men were everywhere and exactly as curious as their betters. To Dash there was something laudable about their passionate desire to know of the world beyond their locked-up islands. But they seemed unable to arrange things in their minds. Zack's woolly hair interested them much more than the cut and rig of the *Victrix*. The fact that Holland possessed an enormous colony called "America" they dismissed as of little importance, but Liz's French clock (with a goat-footed satyr and an undressed nymph on it) keeled them over. And yet every one of them had marveled over the *Victrix's* pumps. Which was right. They should, thought the captain. Yet how did they know enough to admire so intelligently? So his first meeting with the Japanese left him a little confounded. One thing he knew. Smile and bow and bob and all but curtsy, yet they hated the white men. And there is no good living hate in this world without its iota of fear.

He kept an eye out at the quaint little forts topping the great hills (almost mountains) that rose so sharply on either side of the long narrow harbor. They weren't any good. Three American frigates could blow the pretty things off their rocks in ten minutes and end forever for them Japan's boasted seclusion. Yet he had a certain sympathy for these people. They had not been seized by any European Power — like the Philippines, the Dutch Indies, India. They had been smart enough to look ahead. It might be a land of paper and flowers, cliffs and bamboo (but gold, silver, copper, and silk as well). Oh, let them have it! he thought with half his mind, and the other half wondered if the little *Victrix* herself wasn't strong enough to knock over their forts for them. And now his guns were firing the last salute. Thirteen salvos in honor of the imperial city of Nagasaki. There it was, the steep-sided city of wood and

tiles and pine trees and temples. Sticking out of it was Dechima —
shaped like a fan, connected to the city by a humpbacked stone
bridge coming exactly where the handle of a fan should be.

"Look, Vreed," he said, handing the spyglass to him, "there's your
flag." From all the pleasure boats that had crowded out to see the
ship, from the thousands gathered along the shore, he heard the
chattering of what the Chinese called "the monkey people."

The *Victrix* hull was lost in the smoke of her salutings. She
seemed to the people of Nagasaki to float upon air, a rare bird of
incredible plumage. For she was dressed — overdressed — with
flags from stem to stern. Her clean white sails were lost behind
the bunting. From her mizzen floated the flag of Holland. But
many of her flags were fantastic things, striped or checked, or pic-
turing strange birds or dragons. She carried the flag of her own
country and of France, Norway, Denmark. Any flag except those
of Spain or Portugal, for the Japanese would never forget. She was
(in other lands) signally the most contradictory things — mutiny
and fever aboard; the ship was in distress; it wanted fresh water,
firewood; it was now making its arrival or departure; it asked for a
pilot. But the Japanese saw only the gay flutter. And they, who
did not know a proper Becket-built ship from a Dutch dogger,
knew a thing of beauty when they saw it. She was greeted with
silent wonder and laughter and gratitude that beauty existed. The
tourists, who had walked hundreds of miles to see a great sight,
felt rewarded.

"So that's Dechima," Dash was saying. He looked at the stucco
houses and warehouses beyond the sea wall and the mass of green
tiled roofs. No bigger than a ship it looked, and here close by
upon her anchorage the *Victrix* would sit the summer out. The
ship of wood beside the ship of stone.

THAT FALL, Miss Georgiana Frick again left Brattle Street to visit her Cousin Polly. She had not been urged to come. The two girls were of such opposite temperaments that it might be wondered what brought her again so soon to Salem. It was Peter's translation of Villon's *Ballade des Dames* that had persuaded her, Peter's intelligent, somewhat literary letters, and the fond memory of Peter's calm eyes, serene broad smile.

Peter could hardly have realized that this bright, bewitching, odd-looking girl was, as the novels had it, "his proper fate," the woman selected by angels in Heaven for him. He could not know that as long as he lived he would never meet another girl so appropriate for him to love. Georgiana was not as good a poet as Peter — in those days many romantic girls were turning to writing (even Marcy had her ambitions), but she was good enough to know her weaknesses and generous enough to realize that Peter was far beyond her. But then — she was in love. She had found in Peter Inman what girls like her always crave — someone something like themselves, only much more gifted.

She had fought and won her own little battle among the teacups of Cambridge — the right to go ahead and be queer in her own way and to go as far as her ability might take her. The tragedy of her battle was that she had not much ability. She was left a somewhat forlorn vine without the strength to raise itself, longing for the pedestal it could entwine. Obviously, Peter was the proper pedestal. Less emancipated girls might see as clearly as she what they wanted, but they would never have dared pursue so frank a course. Both she and Peter were very young, but instinct had told her it was with this man and no other she might be happy. Instinct did not so tell Peter.

Miss Georgiana Frick was sallow, but her complexion never looked so dull or her hair so drab as when she sat next to Polly. Like Peter, she was too thin. Perhaps it was a biological wisdom in him that made her thinness seem not like a maidenly delicacy, but "just so much skin and bones." She was a little jerky, perhaps "too bright," in her manner, but it is hard for young girls to act naturally when they are in love. Especially in the presence of so devastating a belle as her Cousin Polly.

Yet there was something in her to which Peter responded. When he saw her without her cousin, there was quaintness and charm in the oddly shaped, narrow face. Her manners seemed easy and natural. But as soon as Polly would say to him, "It was such a pity dear Georgiana is so plain and sucks in her breath when she laughs," all her charm vanished. Georgiana fed his egoism, but better alone than when Polly was present. He had not quite his full masculine quota of egoism. It was good for him to hear her recite to him certain lines he had written. She had a tender voice. She forgot herself reciting poetry. But Polly's look of amusement — when she was there — made him feel a fool.

Although Polly talked much of "her young lovers," she would always make Georgiana seem an outsider and something unfitting for a henchman of hers to love. It was at such times that the girl sucked in her laugh and looked really plain. Polly did not let Peter forget that the reason he came to the Mompessons' house was not to begin courting any Georgiana Frick, but to keep up the courtship of Polly Mompesson by Dash Inman.

Sometimes they sat by the pretty white fane, close by the little pool in the allegorical back garden. Seemingly Peter needed only to have stooped down and drunk of the waters of love and been saved. He did not. Georgiana sadly, but completely undefeated, went back to Brattle Street in November. She knew more than ever what she wanted, but she was ready to retreat for the moment.

He really liked it better after she was gone. He was more comfortable, corresponding with her, than seeing her about, always overshadowed by the predatory Polly.

"Of course," said Polly one day, "I've loved having Georgiana here these last months. I know I have *her* to thank for your faithful attendance. But honestly, do you know, I did get tired of feeling like a chaperon with all this loving and doving going on about me." Perhaps this was the reason she had unconsciously but neatly greased the ways under her dear Georgiana.

"Not a love," said Peter, "not a dove."

"But I thought — that poem you wrote 'To Her' — wasn't that to Georgiana?"

"No," he said, thoughtfully. "No, it wasn't."

So Polly dimpled and laughed. But she was wrong. It was not even to Polly — not that one. In it he had expressed all his longing for Dash and worry over him and his willingness to "die for him" (which was a most poetic way of saying he'd be pleased to father any illegitimate children he had). "Poetry," he went on, almost to himself, "is not quite the fact — ever."

"I'm sure I prefer poetry to fact. Why, if we — you and I" — and she dropped her voice — "and Dash — were people in a novel, I'd be sure the reason why nobody has heard from the *Victrix* for so long was to create suspense. But now — how long since she was reported, Peter?"

"Ma'am heard direct from Isle of France — a letter written last year October. It's November. Well, yes, that's a long time."

"Over a year."

"Over a year." He steadied himself, determined not to pass on to her the worry all of them felt.

"Since then she was said to have been seen in Batavia Roads. Ship *Ellen* of New York. But we don't really know if she was there."

"Nobody knows where she is."

"Golly — yes, they do. Dash knows. He always knows where he is. Trust Dash."

And yet, if all was well, why had he not found a way to send letters home? The *Victrix* was acting as though she had simply sailed off the map.

"Dash can get through anything — I know him. So do you. And, Polly, he's coming home this time so rich . . ."

"So rich he'll never have to go to sea again," she agreed happily.

~7~

DASH KNEW things were not right on the ship. Three days before, when custom demanded the departure from Nagasaki, he had had the humiliation of seeing the *Victrix* towed out by the entire boat-towers guild. She had looked like a hawk deviled by sparrows, but there had not been a cat's-paw of wind. Once free of the harbor she had, indeed, filled away and a northeast breath of air had carried her, but she seemed listless without any of her old gaiety. Sluggishly for three days and nights she had tacked back and forth, but as if she didn't care where she went. Even to the bottom. Those three months' imprisonment had done something to her. He thought a little guiltily of all the copper he had burdened her with. She was no pack horse. God (and 'Tirey Becket and Dash Inman) had designed her for lighter work — coffee and spice, fine silks and teas. She was sluggish with the copper, which in a way would buy for her master the girl he loved even more than he loved her.

No, the trouble was with the people. They lay aloft when told to, but all the smartness was out of them. Dash stood on the poop deck and heard from forward (but pretended not to) the Dexter boy being pert to Mr. Obrian, suggesting that a second mate is nothing but a sailor's waiter — and he could go do it himself. And Danny, instead of paying no heed, but merely repeating the order quietly (and taking into consideration the infernal heaviness of the air), had clouted him one.

Dan had been clouted and kicked through childhood. Kicked and clouted before the Derbys' mast. Now he wanted to clout and kick anyone under him. He wanted to stalk the deck with clenched fists, all ready to knock blocks off. But Dash had thought he had cured him, explaining to him again and again he wasn't going to have a "bellering mate" on any ship he commanded. But when things went wrong — even after a year and a half the monkey in him did sometimes show its tail. Dash believed Dan had the making of a very fine captain. For one thing he knew his business, and for another he was always absolutely fair. Certainly that Dexter boy did deserve to be knocked down. He'd let it pass. Anybody might do anything in weather like this.

It was hard to describe the weather. Liz, who as "the" mate kept the log, had written down that it felt as if all the air had been taken out.

There was enough wind to carry them, but the foretopsail began to lift, back and fill. The cross-swell was enormous. Terrific. The *Victrix* was lying down in it wallowing like a little old pig. She'd lost her sea legs and the men had lost theirs. He saw Billy Bates, ship's boy, leaning on the taffrail, sick again.

Hab Parker and Cy Narbonne were slouching about like a couple of hayseeds, with their hands in their pockets. He thought he had broken them of the habit. A year before he had had the sailmaker sew up every pocket in their pants. No, he wasn't going to say anything about it to them now. But if they dared sit down on that windlass they were leaning up against, he would.

Yet what was going wrong he found hard to define. It was Robin, the ship's calico cat, that had given him the first inkling there was something serious to worry about. Instead of lying flat out on the iron strong-box in the cabin, as she usually did in hot weather, she had been following him about as he perambulated the ship. Now she followed him to the quarterdeck as he fell to brief, thoughtful pacing. Back and forth, back and forth, on the weather side. This was always the captain's promenade. And the mate has the lee side and the second only the weather gangway. It was as if she had known for hours now that things were not right. There was trouble ahead. Usually it was Doctor Zack she hung about — he and his galley. Now it was the captain she was trying to wheedle.

"Dad blast you," he said, as he picked her up, for she would weave between his legs, "I'm of half a mind to drop you overboard, seeing's you can't behave." He never would have. Like most men of intricate nature and only a healthy amount of male egoism, he was fond of cats. . . . She clutched him and purred confidently, for now she had the captain's entire attention. But she irritated him a little, and he found himself yelling at Cy Narbonne and Hab Parker to get their hands out of their pockets, although only the moment before he had decided not to.

He went down the poop ladder to the cabin, which was under the quarterdeck, put Robin where she belonged on the strong-box, wiped the sweat off his forehead with his fingers, and looked again at the weather glass. It was down so low the mercury hardly showed. He had never seen anything like it. He went to his bookshelf and took down a book.

In the bunk opposite his lay Liz, usually a profound and charming sleeper. He never got himself in awkward positions or snored, sweated, and smelt like other men. There was something almost feminine in Eleazar Inman's ability to look so innocent and beautiful in his sleep. But now he was muttering and tossing. After all, his watch would be called in ten minutes now to relieve Dan's. Your good officer is almost awake when his watch is coming. Dash studied the glass again. He felt as if it, the ship, the cat, his people, and himself were all going crazy. Robin jumped into his lap, He put her down. She jumped again, and stared at him out of intense green eyes. It was really her advice he followed. He woke Liz and yelled for Billy Bates to send Mate Obrian to him.

Liz woke with parted, smiling lips and lingering delight in his eyes — as though he had been dreaming of kissing his Japanese mistress.

Obrian came into the tiny cabin, looking bigger than life. He was sweating and breathing hard. "God, sir," he said, "I'll never be so glad in my life to have my watch end." His eyes gave off blue sparks. "That damned Dexter boy. Lucky I didn't kill him. The men won't work and the ship won't sail."

"Look at the glass, Danny."

"Heh? Broke, is it? Or what's happened?"

"Don't know. But I wanted to talk to you and Liz privately. I'm not a-going by the glass — only. There's a dirty weather ahead. Even the ship and the cat know it. And the men. Not with their heads. Bowels, maybe. Did you ever hear of a tuphan?"

"No, sir. Never did." For Danny, with all his admirable abilities, never had heard of anything he hadn't seen with his own eyes.

"They have them. China Sea. Real bad blows." But Liz, saying nothing, looked at him and nodded.

"Bad, sir?" said Dan, listlessly.

"Real bad. The Chinese call 'em 'tai fungs' and the Japanese, 'Taifus.' If you meet one — same latitude — t'other side of the world, West Indies, we'd call 'em hurricanes."

Then Danny brightened. Hurricanes he had seen. "I've got old Dampier's *Voyage* here in my hand. It comes on fierce and violent, he says, at N.E., lasts several hours. Then flat calm and it begins again — S.W., and lasts as long as first visit. Well — that's that — boys. It looks a little like the slant-eyed godlings don't want us in these waters. So the Japanese keep a god called Taifu to get us if it can. It's November now. They usually are over by October, but anyway — that's what I'm looking for. Guess we can lick old Taifu and all his baskets full of little wind gods." He lifted his square short chin. "We can do it, of course. But I'm taking all proper precautions. Liz, as you go on duty, take a squint at that cloud following us. And I'm ordering all sails down that aren't drawing. Everything battened down. Get a better lash on the longboat. Do it yourself. And life lines up."

"*Life* lines, sir? —— "

"When Mr. Taifu comes aboard, we'll need 'em. I haven't ever lost a man overboard, and I get life lines up before — not after — it's too late. Those are orders. It looks to me" — and he smiled — "the *Victrix* is resting herself just now. Getting ready for it. So I may as well do the same."

"I can't believe it will come up so quick. We've hardly enough wind now to carry us," said Liz, and added, "sir," for even in the cabin he maintained (more than Dash himself) every punctilio toward the captain.

The ship's bell struck 4. They heard a pounding on the forward hatch and the familiar crying of the change of watch. "All larbow-lines ahoy! Four bells there below! Do you hear the news?"

Liz stepped over the coamings, meeting Billy Bates sent to tell him it was his watch, and stepped forward to his men to pass on the captain's orders. He looked back at the quarterdeck where the helmsman was being relieved. And beyond the expanse of seas he saw the cloud Dash had told him of. Northeast, pressing after them, a bank of dirty, greenish cloud. It looked as impenetrable as a city wall — as if the Great Wall of China (for Liz always knew a lot about things he'd never seen) had broken loose — was floating out to sea after them. My God, he thought, Dash doesn't exaggerate things. Never saw nor heard tell of anything like that. Then he studied the west. The sun was making a ghastly attempt to set through murk and haze. Its yellow light reflected in the faces of the men. They looked down with fervor. Toward this unearthly sunset the *Victrix* was languidly rolling.

Dash, standing at his cabin door, watched the men going aloft, the idle sails coming down. The *Victrix* plodded along — as though she knew this was doomsday; that God was about to roll up the seas once more and put them back in His pocket. Before such an enormity of fate, it was not worth while struggling. Or maybe she thought the time had come to think of her soul. Maybe she was, as he had said, merely resting, getting strength for the time to come, and so would he. "Mr. Mate," he called, "notify me instantly of any change."

From his West Indy experience, from what he had heard tell, he did not expect much change for four hours more. Until then, he, like the ship, would rest. Liz was as smart a mate as he had ever had. He'd watch out. Suddenly the sun was indeed set and the yellow light was gone.

Two hours later, Liz stepped into the cabin to look at the glass. Nothing — not one thing had changed, and the log showed the ship was almost standing still. The lantern that lit the cabin swayed with the heavy rolling of the ship, throwing its light from one bunk to the other. Danny's face was wet with sweat. Face and hands clenched, suggesting that he was grasping sleep to him, had taken it by main force. The captain, however, was wide awake, fully dressed except his boots. He lay on his back languid, content. He looked up at Liz with knowing eyes.

"People seem nervous?" he asked.

"Yes — a bit. But at least they're wide awake and on their toes at last. It's just the same, sir — but the stars are going out fast."

"Put on a lee to help the weather helmsman. Who's on the wheel?"

"Rickie Locker."

"All right."

"And there's still hardly wind enough to move the ship."

"There will be. Now, lookee, Mr. Mate, any change comes, let me know. Till then I'll sleep."

"Aye, aye, sir."

But as Liz shut the lighted cabin after him and stepped out into the dark of the deck, he felt a moment of intense loneliness. He wished Dash had put on his sea boots and come with him. Well, it's his business — not mine, he thought — thus relegating the responsibility to the captain. For whether the Taifu sank the ship or not wasn't any mate's business. That was the captain's funeral, and the thought gave him a sense of relief — hardly at the moment was he realizing that if worst happened he'd be as drowned as the captain.

The night was queer — like wet black blotting-paper, and one by one the stars winked and went out. He saw the last one go. He thought of Dash, relaxed and peaceful in his bunk, with those knowing eyes and certainly not afraid nor bothered. Just waiting. It gave him a great feeling of confidence merely knowing Dash was there — just as a Chinese junk captain feels safe, knowing his joss is aboard.

~ 8 ~

IT CAME AT LAST so violently that Dash was thrown out of his bunk. The lantern jumped its gimmal, and he was after it. The slate on which he made his daily calculations fell and broke. Why hadn't Liz called him? Nothing in the world (he had believed) came as suddenly as this. He bumped into Danny as each tried to collar his sea boots that were playing about like a litter of puppies. They heard the screaming of the wind through shrouds, but it was not until they tried to open the cabin door that they realized how incredible was the gale. As they stepped out, it was like entering a funnel.

Dash was thrown against the mizzen-pin rail, but his hands cupped his mouth.

"All hands aloft!" His voice carried down wind, confident and calm. Liz had already ordered out the larbowlines. Dash could see them crawling up out of the forward hatch. Some on hands and knees, some grasping at stanchions and life lines, or each other.

He turned, ordering the helmsman, "Hard a lee!" and as she came up into the wind, "All hands furl sail!" There was no time to take it down. Now he knew he must save his canvas. Everything was ordered furled except only the head sails to steady the ship.

There was a soft flash of lightning, and he saw the men in the almost naked spars clinging like rats, struggling frantically as sails were smothered and kept in by clewlines and buntlines. He recognized Danny's formidable bulk, standing in the slings to make the bunt on the mainmast. This was where second mates belonged — the most difficult, most dangerous task in furling sail. And no smart second ever let anyone get ahead of him to this small post of honor. Second mates habitually went aloft. Captains and the mate did not. The difficult, dangerous task was performed in a few minutes. His men were still smart all right. . . . Another flash, and he saw naught but bare sticks before him and the slim white crescents of the head sails.

"Hard up!" She spun around before the wind. A great wave broke over her. The ship was washed from stem to stern. It looked as though cauldrons of soapsuds had been poured over it.

The wind came out of the roaring blackness, whistling, screaming, intent upon destroying them — and nobody else. The waves crashed against the ship and washed the decks again and again. The *Victrix* seemed bewildered by the cruelty of the attack, like a pet animal, who had never known anything but affection, is at first merely confused by unkindness. She was almost cringing, as though anxious to make herself so small the angry gods of sea and wind wouldn't notice her. Dash felt a hand on him. Someone had crawled back to report to him. Then a shock went through the ship ten times as violent as the one that had cast him away on Cape Cod.

As he put his hand out to meet the one on his arm, he almost lost balance. He and Danny were thrown into each other's arms. And he knew Danny was afraid. He knew it with the same instinct a horse may know its rider is frightened. Of course, Danny was scared. He had not enough imagination to have thought such a storm possible. Your imaginative man meets so many disasters in his mind, he may sometimes be better prepared when they befall than your real simple fellow.

Dash had a leg about a stanchion, felt the wet lips pressed to his ear trying to deliver some message. The ship was yawing frantically as though trying to leave her own element, climb out onto some nonexistent dry land. And he thought how long she had lain so safe in Becket's Yard.

"All snug aloft?" he asked Danny.

"Yes, sir, so it is, sir." The big fellow wasn't shaking, but he didn't feel real easy about things.

"So, Dan," he said, holding his head close to him, "you get forward now. You done a right smart job." And he hadn't called him Mr. Obrian, as he usually did anywhere except in the cabin. And Dan felt the light strong touch of his captain's hands.

Another great shock of water roared over the *Victrix*. This time she seemed to have recovered from her first incredulity, numb wonder, and fear. She was almost angry, but jerking about hysterically. She had not yet quite begun to fight.

Dash had a foot against the mizzen-pin rail, his back braced against the cabin door, his arms in a stanchion. Almost as though he were still talking to Danny (or was back in Salem talking to Polly), he said, "Easy does it, girl. I know you're pretty young —

and mighty scared. But you've got me here and naught's to harm you. So be a brave girl."

A third great blow and she was ready to meet it. She lifted herself, shaking the sea from her flanks. It was a gallant gesture. And he knew she could carry the great load of copper he had put on her. She was through with her resting and her sulks. Through with fear and panic. For the first time since they had weighed anchor at Nagasaki, he felt she was herself once more.

Then the rain came. It poured down to meet the flying seas. It was like standing under a waterfall. No air left. Dash breathed with open mouth, but sometimes it was fresh water he got and sometimes salt. Little air.

The lightning came less frequently and fainter. He could see little of the ship. The night whirled and roared about him.

He found the poop ladder and went to the wheel. The protected binnacle light still burned. He saw the statuesque figures at the wheel, Rickie Locker, weather helmsman, Cy Narbonne, lee. In their still, powerful intensity they and the wheel seemed one figure. He touched Rickie's arm. He should have been relieved long before this.

"Rickie — want relief?" It was only by pressing his face close to a man, you could make him hear.

"By God," one-third of the statue spoke, roared down the wind without taking his staring eyes off the compass before him, "ef you go jabbering at me, I can't steer."

He had reached that interesting state of determination, exhaustion when nothing but the problem at hand exists. He did not know it was his captain offering to relieve him. He did not know that there was a captain aboard, hardly that there was a ship or a storm. He was incapable of feeling any danger. He did not know whether it was night or day or the sea was the China Sea or Vineyard Sound. He knew nothing except that he was going to hold on to that wheel. Men, Dash knew, often could keep on almost forever, working to perfection in this vacuum of intensity. If the ship did break up, doubtless Rickie Locker would not notice. He'd go down still holding the wheel exactly so.

As often in times of greatest danger there was literally little to do. Everything that might save them had been done long before. Once again the diminishing lightning flashed. He saw the bare masts and spars, but out on the bowsprit the thin crescents of the head sail — holding. And he knew they would. The hemp of their rigging he himself had brought from Kronstadt. Amos Partridge had spun it. And the sails themselves were cut from canvas he had brought from Russia. The best in the world. He could almost see Salem sailmakers, cross-legged in their sail lofts, thimble on palm, cutting and stitching those head sails. So it was all over the ship. There wasn't a weak spot on her.

If the head sails went, he'd throw out the sea anchor, but if the rudder went, it was the end. And he thought with warmth and content of that rudder. It was of New England oak. One piece after another had been examined, tested, discarded. It was flawless, and would never break. He thought of the wiry black-haired arms of Mr. Crofts, forging its iron pintle straps, its braces, chains. Mr. Crofts was always saying, "I got that real good." In a way it was the smith's bulging arms that would now save the *Victrix,* and the oak trees of New England, the hemp and canvas of Russia (and he recalled with pleasure the hemp market in a St. Petersburg Square). And he thought gratefully of Mr. 'Tirey Becket. For the *Victrix* was "honor built." It was because of the honor of many artisans that now she would live through — even this. There was not a weak spot on her.

He alone of the twenty men aboard felt content, almost at ease, for he was in his own element — born to look the cyclone in the eye, set his hand upon the name of the whirlwind, or, as the teeth of the storm snapped at him, show his own teeth back at it.

Foam crests of water were flying by, sometimes beyond the rail, sometimes over the deck. When the lightning flashed, he could see the black, distorted figures of his men either lashed to the rigging or clinging to anything they could wrap themselves about; each apparently was frozen to the spot where disaster had overtaken them.

The whole fury of the China Sea, all the latent hatred of yellow men and yellow gods, seemed concentrated to but one purpose: the destruction of his ship. She had laid her bowsprit where it had been forbidden her and dropped her anchor where she did not belong. The seas that crashed over her seemed like kicks, the wind pummeling her down into the ocean like fists. Aye, aye. Once more the gods were athirst.

Then, far above him, infinitely far and high away — he heard the terrible screaming of the typhoon. It seemed almost unconnected with the storm enveloping him. It even seemed to be going in a different direction. Some horned and hairy Japanese wind god. Taifu himself. But he was gone.

Good God — thought Dash, as a bluish flame lit up the deck. The galley house has gone! It was a little structure he had put on while at Batavia and not as well done as the too-small galley Becket had built him. It was here that Doctor Zack cooked, slept, and worked. Dash had expected that it might go in a bad storm and he had warned Zack, but what surprised him was that it could utterly disappear and make no sound. It was like magic.

It meant that he must find out what had happened to his cook. The black fool was so proud of his spacious galley, probably he had disobeyed orders and thought to sit the storm out in it. His feet felt for the poop ladder to the deck. That, too, was gone. Grasping a life line, he inched toward the spot where the house had stood.

Suddenly he heard a great roaring in his ears and a heavy blow was struck between his shoulders and the back of his head. At first he thought the mainmast had come down on him, and then, as he found himself swimming, that he had been washed overboard. His hand touched a heavy round object rolling in the scupper and instinctively he grasped it. He felt the deck under him, as, like a diver, the ship seemed to be struggling to swim back to the surface. It was the cook's head he had grasped — he felt the woolly scalp — but he was not conscious that it was attached to a body until the body began to coil around him in the manner of a drowning person. It coiled slowly, respectfully, as if knowing that he and his captain were about to drown together, and apologizing for the liberty. Locked in this embrace, they rolled over and over across the deck. Dash got a leg hold on a stanchion, swore at the cook to wake him up, make him hold on for himself, not hamper him so. The oath went from his lips at some ninety miles an hour. Of course, Zack couldn't hear him when he yelled. And he couldn't bring himself to whisper his abuse in the poor fellow's ear.

He felt the Negro's enormous lips pressed against his ear. "I prayed, sir . . . I was about done praying. Good Lord, He answered my prayer . . ." So he thought that God himself had sent his captain.

Then they discovered that God also sent Mate Liz, with the same idea of saving Zack, if possible. For, struggling to hold fast in the infinity of water rushing about him, Dash felt another body, and knew it was Liz who bumped against him. They had washed against the freeing ports in the waist.

"Dash . . ."

"Aye."

"She's done for."

"No, no, no! She'll live!" Dash did not whisper these words soberly in the mate's ear — he flung back his head and yelled them into the face of the storm, into the very faces of the yellow gods. And Liz heard him, and heard the confident, ringing quality in his voice. That voice had held men to frozen rigging, it had put heart in men dropping at the pumps. Liz felt the magic of Dash's confidence, but resented it.

"Where's Zack?"

"I had him . . . but . . ." Had he at last washed overboard?

"Hold fast."

"Aye."

Liz knew there was not one thing that could be done. The ship would live through or she wouldn't. If the head sails held, they'd steady her. If the rudder went, they'd all go. The helplessness of the situation angered him. He knew Dash believed in the impossible. Dash wasn't facing the fact that the ship was doomed. And because he would not face it, the ship still had a chance. Somehow Dash's confidence was keeping her afloat. Nothing else could.

Dash was whispering again. "Becket . . ." was all he got out. He was reminding Liz how good were the ships built by Becket.

There was such a heavy numbness to his legs that Liz wondered idly, and without much interest, if he had broken them. He moved a little, and found there was a man clinging to them.

"Zack . . . here . . . Zack . . ."

"Good! Hold fast."

How long the three lay together they couuld not guess. The storm had struck about midnight. It might be two o'clock or four. Or time might have stood still and be but little past midnight. They longed for the coming of day, although to see light again was incredible.

Now the ship seemed to be losing her head a little, because she was tired. She wasn't fighting with the same intelligence But she was still fighting. She seemed a living thing thrown to a pack of hounds, twisting, turning, looking for earth — with the hounds' teeth on her flanks. But she still lifted her bow gallantly as if attempting to summon her last strength. Once more she tried to leap to safety, but her leap was not high enough. She pitched, as if carried downstream over a waterfall, striking on rocks as she went. But again she rose, staggering and groggy, barely able to shake herself free. Would she still be able to take another such wave?

"Helm!" Dash was disengaging himself from his brother.

"Idiot!" screamed Liz. "You can't possibly . . ."

"Must!"

What good to go on the helm now? Doubtless the rudder was gone, anyway.

"Idiot! Idiot!" Liz screamed into the night.

Dash was gone. He felt deserted. He put his hand out and touched Zack's head. It was well not to be too alone at times like this. Zack's face was so cold he thought the man must be dead. He felt along the wet jawbone clenched as if with *rigor mortis*. The man might be unconscious with fear, but he still clung to his only hope — the officer God had sent him. Liz could feel with his hand that the man's teeth were clenched into his trouser leg. Clenched into the flesh of his calf. He felt no pain.

And then, out of the nightmare of fury, out of the very blackest heart of the night, came the greatest wave. Liz thought calmly, "That one got Dash."

He was a fool to try to make the helm. But Liz had a superstitious feeling — the kind of thing he was the quickest to ridicule in other men. If Dash was washed overboard, the ship would sink. As long as he was aboard, he'd hold her up.

Liz had a sudden picture of Salem, of his home and the lilacs in blossom. His mother's face. He saw his mother weeping because her boy was dead. And in the rush and hiss of water that enveloped him, he heard the sound of fiddles. He saw himself prancing forward to salute his partner. I guess that left leg's broken, he thought. Can't feel anything in it. At the moment he was more worried about a possibly broken leg than what looked like inevitable death.

Chapter Six

~~~~~~~~~~~~~~~~~~~~~~~~~~~~~~~~~~~~

On Inman Wharf a white, old speckled horse walked round and round the capstan as *Fox Fire's* cargo came up from the hold. Already master sailmakers had gathered, were gazing hungrily at the great bales of Russian canvas and duck. Word had got about that *Fox Fire* had brought Swedish steel on her last trip to the Baltic. Instrument-makers, too, were looking at her longingly.

Peter and Tom stood side by side. Circumstances, more than natural affinity, had created intimacy between them. Tom, master of the *Fox Fire,* who had come back only the day before, said to the men watching canvas and steel unload upon the wharf, "It is not until tomorrow, gentlemen, the goods will be auctioned. Here upon this wharf."

There was no steel in Salem fit for the work of instrument-makers. Two sail lofts had closed for want of canvas, and yet the town was booming. More ships, more compasses, more sails, were needed. The merchants were so impatient at any delay that they would sometimes pay fantastically.

Fox Fire, a clumsy little old brig, had always been lucky. And once again she had brought her goods to a seller's market. Although so slow she couldn't get out of anybody's way, and so weak — she was less than one hundred tons — she could not stand to fight, she had never been seized or sunk. Her men cursed her because she leaked so they were always at her pumps. No man could take pride in commanding her, she was so old-fashioned and ugly. Yet, for twenty years, year after year, *Fox Fire* had crawled off looking as though she couldn't clear the coast, and then had come back grinning because she had, in her own little way, "done it again."

"Only two ships," Tom said contemptuously, "and *that* one of them. Magee back from Goa with the *Mermaid?*"

"Not yet. But she's reported on the coast. Ma'am's right. Magee doesn't do anything very big, but he hauls home the bacon, little piece by little piece. And, of course, Ma'am thinks he may have picked up news of the *Victrix*. Tom, you're sleepy. You always sleep when you first come home. You go home and get to bed. I can tend to everything here."

"Maybe I will. Peter . . ."

"Aye?"

"Peter, I think we've got to face it. You and I at least . . ."

Peter was silent. He knew what Tom had in mind. Face it! Night after night in tears, lying upon Dash's bed, he had faced it.

"What, Tom?"

"Of course, Ma'am can't. And Mother . . . I don't know about Mother. But it isn't sensible not to look the worst full in the face. The *Victrix* has been gone three years next month. She hasn't been reported, nor has any word come from her, for eighteen months. Now you know and I know, and Dash knew, too, she was a mighty ticklish ship. It wouldn't be too hard to sink her. She never seemed real steady, little I saw of her. She's gone. And that's that."

Peter said slowly: "Don't bring it up to Mother unless she mentions it, but I guess she's given up, too. At least, Captain Crowninshield wants to buy our house. And she's going to say yes. All of us are going to move down here. Live with Ma'am, in her house. There isn't very much money. We'd better pull in a bit, I guess. But Ma'am's house will be crowded."

"Not so many of us, these days."

"No, not so many."

In the long silence that followed, each mourned the lost brothers, but neither would put into words the heart-break he felt. About the financial loss they were ready to talk, yet to neither of them was it anything compared to the loss of Dash and Liz.

"Have her underwriters paid off?"

"They want to. And they're being decent. That ship wasn't insured beyond Batavia. That's where last she was reported, but she may have gone on from there. You know Dash. He doesn't stop for much when he gets going. Yet they'll concede the point, seeing it never can be proved, and pay off. Ma'am won't even let them talk to her. So they approach me. I tell 'em we want no money yet, no nothing. Of course, our ship's coming home safe. I can't take insurance money. You see why. It would about kill Ma'am. Look, Tom. There she is already, up on her captain's walk, watching for the *Victrix*.

They gazed upward at the tiny figure close by the stacked chimney. Looking almost like a witch, except that she carried a brass spyglass instead of a broom.

"She certainly hasn't given up hope. Not she."

Peter did not tell Tom the many "signs" about Salem that the ship was gone. For instance, Widow Bates, mother of Billy, the ship's boy, had awakened one night, hearing somebody at her pantry cooky jars. Billy had been passionately devoted to his mother's cookies. But still, she knew it might be a rat. In the morning, when she went down, she found strange wet seaweed on her kitchen floor. People said such seaweed grew nowhere in the world except north of Borneo. Captain Hardy had come home by the unusual Cape Horn route. Amid frozen icebergs, not he, but men of the lookout, had seen a ship appear and disappear in the cold fog, locked in the icebergs' death embrace. Spectral men had wrung their hands and wept from gull-pecked eyes. Dead . . . all of them. Such was the story along the grogshops of the *Victrix's* end.

"She waits up there," Peter said slowly, "and in the counting-house. And all through Doctor Hobey's sermons on Sunday. Three times lately she has asked for prayers for grandsons at sea. I guess nights are worse. It's killing her. And all of us. Polly, too."

"She cared that much for Dash?"

"Oh, aye. Aye. I thought you knew."

Both young men were silent for a moment. Then Tom said: "Dash had a funny way . . . do you remember? It was something he did with his nose when he didn't think a thing worth laughing at and yet couldn't help it."

"Dash didn't laugh so easy."

"No. And he never laughed at the men because they were ignorant. He helped them, and didn't laugh. I remember when I was naught but second under him, we had a landlubber so grassy-green that when I told him to cat the anchor he went after the ship's cat. We all laughed at him, but Dash didn't . . . But Liz, now . . . Liz had a real sharp way with him . . ."

"Liz was too tarnation sharp, sometimes."

Tom broke out desperately: "I'd give my right arm to see them. See them once more standing up the harbor, all sails set and the homing pennant apeak on that damned, tippy, crazy *Victrix.*"

"I've got Liz's clocks out," Peter said thickly. "All wound and going for him. God damn Liz Inman's clocks! They go chitter-chatter at me all night long." His voice broke as if in anger, but Tom understood.

The two brothers went on, remembering this and that of Dash and Liz, saying little, feeling much, using the past tense only.

"Ma'am," Peter said at last, "has her theory and it keeps her spirits up."

"What?"

"She says they got cast away on some island. Of course, the ship and investment's lost, but they are safe. Like Robinson Crusoe. Sometime they'll manage to build a ship. Or get picked up. That's nonsense."

"Yes, that's nonsense. But maybe."

"Maybe. Tom, I guess by now Dash is king of that island. You know Dash. He would be. Now he is."

"But Liz has the harem."

They both laughed because they were beginning to believe this nonsense, could actually see Dash kinging it among corals, canni-bals, and coconuts. And see Liz — looking very doggy, if dressed in naught but palm fronds and sharks' teeth — followed by his bevy of dusky beauties. And now they were using the present tense.

Tom yawned again and admitted that, if Peter didn't mind hang-ing about the wharf, he would go home and go to sleep. Then next day to Newburyport to see Miranda Fields.

"Miranda is wonderfully understanding," he confided in Peter. "She sees how we can't marry and I go into partnership with Mr. Fields, power-weaving. I've got to stick to Ma'am, and the ships. Until *they* come back. *They* both of them love this traipsing around the world. I'd a lot rather settle down and see if we can't make decent cloth over here."

Peter knew Tom was not a born deep-sea adventurer. Of course, he was so competent he could do it, command a ship, and make right smart profits. He really wanted to stay at home and make cloth. But he couldn't desert the House of Inman. For now he was probably the only captain left.

Peter watched him lounging off toward home. He didn't even walk quite like a seaman. He was always saying that greater fortunes awaited the men who could make cloth, canvas and spin the thread over here than the men, who, like the captains, merely imported those things. But Tom wouldn't desert even if it meant postponing and postponing his marriage and the start of his and Mr. Fields's mills.

Peter stood a long time on the wharf. He had hoped somehow he could touch Tom for a loan. But Tom, he knew, was so honorable he was putting back every cent of captain's share into the business. Tom hadn't a ready cent.

The year before Peter had paid Flanneau by giving him his two-hundred-dollar venture on the *Victrix*. Two hundred wasn't five hundred, but Flanneau had been good enough to accept it, if Peter would see to it that he got just what he wanted for himself from the cargo. Flanneau was obliging, up to a point. For instance, here it was May. Four months of the year gone, and only lately was he really insisting that Peter pay the five hundred dollars, and very evasively he was threatening that if he did not he and Dulcey might go to France. Taking Petra of course, with them. Peter would never see her again. He was forced to admit chances were that Petra was all there was left in the world of Dash. He couldn't lose her. He loved her and she loved him. Peter had given the Flanneaus an enormous Sumatra clam shell. It was set up by their barn-warehouse and Dulcey bathed the child in the shell. He thought of Petra standing and laughing as he poured water over her and Dulcey soaped her. And the difficulty the two of them had together of catching the slippery little thing to towel her. God knew . . . God would understand why he had to keep Petra. Even if it meant getting money out of Ma'am. Which he shouldn't.

Only lately Ma'am had sold to Billy Gray the warehouse he had a mortgage on. This meant ready cash. The *Mermaid,* Magee master, was coming in. The *Fox Fire* had had one more lucky voyage. This was not a bad time to touch Ma'am for a loan. She must be feeling fine about *Fox Fire*. No . . . she'd never feel fine about anything again . . . unless the *Victrix* came back. He'd probably get the money from her because she was in such despair that nothing mattered much any more. And he couldn't tell her that the money would be used to hold on to a great-grandchild of hers.

As usual, having had her look-about from her own roof, she was back at the counting-house. Of late Rose had fallen into the habit of bringing her mistress tea at eleven every morning. Now it was eleven. He heard the cry of "grog-o" going up along the shipyards and waterfront. Workmen habitually stopped at eleven to drink grog, which, habitually, the employer paid for. And there came Rose and her waiter. Her enormous mobcap seemed to grow out of her white face, white hair. She looked as tall from her chin up as from her chin down. Peter stepped forward and offered to carry the waiter up the ladder-like stairs. She thanked him in her great man's voice so at variance with her gentle character, and, seesawing a little, headed back for the house.

He watched his grandmother stir in cream and sugar, pour the tea into the saucer and set the cup on the cup plate. If she knew why he needed the money, he guessed she'd be glad to give it. He felt brutal to add to her worries, but no need to beat about the bush.

"Grandma, I want to borrow some money."

"I don't believe I've ever lent you any, Peter. Although once I used to lend small sums to your brothers all the time. Liz" — he noticed the hand that held the saucer shook a little, but her voice did not — "Liz was only fourteen when he borrowed from me to buy ginseng. Sent it out to China on the *Brazilia*. Made one hundred per cent on the venture. Now Dash . . ." and she went off on several minutes' reminiscences of borrowed money and big returns. "But I've never lent you, Peter, a cent. Not that I can remember."

"I'd like half as advance on my salary. That's two hundred and fifty. And two hundred and fifty more, on loan. I hate to ask. It sickens me to ask. But I've got to."

"Five hundred dollars! But what on earth?"

"Please don't go questioning me, dear Ma'am. Nor thinking questions, either."

She put down her tea. Resumed her spectacles and began to study a ledger.

"Is it that you've decided to go to Harvard, after all?"

"No. I've lost interest."

This pleased her. She loved having Peter sitting there in the outer office as she sat in the inner. And so often he went home with her, sat and had Madeira or tea with her, played checkers and smiled. When Peter smiled, she always had the feeling there was nothing to worry about.

"I've never quite understood . . . but I know you have some sort of business deal with Flanneau. I've been told on 'Change."

He flushed slightly. Thank God, no one had told her more. "It is true," he said.

She stared soberly at him. His face looked a little confused, but in the midst of the confusion the steady calm of the dark eyes begged her not to go on quizzing him.

"You want me to trust you?"

"Yes, I do."

"But if you'd only say why."

"I can't say why. You can question me, but I can't answer."

She was thinking how well she had known him all his life. There had never been anyone as good as Peter Inman. Probably lots of people had done more good. Given organs to churches and snug harbors to derelict mariners, firewood to the poor, homes for fallen girls. Sometimes it seemed to her that Peter did not do much either bad or good. But goodness existed in him, quite apart from any deed.

She said: "You always have been a good boy, Peter, and because you are, you have earned the right not to be questioned about your motives. They are good motives. But are they wise? Frankly, Peter, you have done amazing well these last two years. I couldn't have got on without you. But still I do not think you have an inborn money-sense. Like Liz and Tom. I can't have the same confidence in your wisdom as in your goodness. You see the point?"

He saw it all too plainly.

"Are you making a wise investment?"

"You mean more money than I started with? Right off — no. No, it isn't wise. But you've always been hammering at us that money isn't everything."

She smiled. "No, it's Liz and Tom I've hammered at. Not ever at you you or Dash."

"Sometimes there are things more important than profit."

"Yes." But she had grown absent-minded again.

He knew she was not thinking of money, only of Dash and Liz.

He felt how little and old she was, and how much he loved her. It was so wrong to take money from her. Money that she would give him because she was in such despair she didn't really care any more. He put out a hand and touched the ribbon on her cap, but she did not know. He loved her so his throat ached, and yet he would sacrifice her, if need be, for Petra.

"Yes," she said slowly, "I'll lend it, Peter. But I don't want you to put your *Victrix* venture on 'Change. She is a family ship. None of her paper has come up for sale. I don't want it to now."

It was over a year ago that Peter had given his to Flanneau. He said nothing. Now none of the *Victrix* paper was worth a cent.

She motioned him to get out her strong-box and carefully counted out the money. She'd miss it, unless *Fox Fire's* canvas, duck, steel, and iron sold amazing well.

She could not regret her brash trust in Peter. He was twenty and a grown man. Good, but not wise. Goodness is rarer than wisdom. Goodness is more important. Wisdom, at least as merchants used the word, she thought was often little more than low-down cunning.

～2～

DULLY, STUPEFIED with the sleep he had not had, Doctor Hobey wondered what time it was. He had been at his desk all night.

Yesterday an express had arrived from Washington, haste, post-haste. President Jefferson sent to him state papers from the Bey of Tunis to translate and return. There was not one person in Washington who could read the classical Arabic in which they were written. Doctor Hobey had told the rider to put up at the inn, return at nine next morning and the work would be done. And done it was. But his watch had run down. He had been too concentrated to hear a clock strike. He looked out the window. Day lay broad and golden upon the harbor. The sun rises early in May. He could not guess the time by staring out and yawning at the ships.

His clothes had not been off all night. He saw a candle was still burning and blew it out. Well, now for a shave and fresh linen. As soon as the express had come and gone again, he would walk out to Juniper Point. Such a walk would rest him more than the few hours he might spend in bed. Day after tomorrow was Sunday. He realized with horror how soon he would have sermons to prepare. Mrs. White had sent word to him she must see him. He only hoped Mrs. White had not had another holy vision. He felt more unable than usual to deal with holy visions.

He was so tired he staggered as he rose and looked outside his door. Madam Inman's Rose always left him a can of hot water and his breakfast on a tray at six o'clock. The sight of the cold coffee, gruel, ham and eggs, nauseated him, but the shaving water was still lukewarm. He called down the back stairs to Rose. Might he have some hot coffee? Then he went into his bedroom and lathered up to shave.

Above him, over his head on the captain's walk, he could hear the light tapping of feet. Footsteps so light they might almost be the stepping of a gull. Poor Madam Inman, up there with her spyglass, watching for the *Victrix*. Watching for a phantom ship. She had been gone three years. And now the underwriters had conceded her to be lost. They would pay up. Squire Mompesson in particular was insisting that he wished to write off the loss, balance his books. He was a finicky neat bookkeeper, that Squire Mompesson, with his real estate and his underwriting and his ship ventures. Red ink on one side of his ledgers. Black on the other. The *Victrix* written in red. A line drawn at the bottom of the page. And she was "written off."

Standing before his glass, his razor cutting a wide swath in the thin cold lather, he felt an overwhelming pity for all of those many "written off" young men of Salem. Ships that had been reported thus far, and no farther. It was childish of Madam Inman to cling to hope when really there was no hope. But in the midst of his godlike pity was a slight unchristian envy of those brave, doomed young men who know glory and die before youth and glory can be dimmed. He looked thoughtfully at his own face, half-shaved, round-eyed, intelligent, and *timid*. Such men as himself were good enough to translate Arabic state papers. Not good enough to fight the pirates. They grow bald early. He sighed. He was not yet thirty, but already his hair was receding and thinning. And die very old. But never, not once, do they look into the bright, wild eyes of danger. Never do they carry their lives as lightly as a man may carry an old sixpence.

A country, any country, must always have plenty of those other young men — hawks to fling from the wrist, fling away in times of danger. From them came legends and heroic stories. They died young, and lived forever. Dash was that way. You couldn't imagine his outliving the charm and valor of his earliest manhood. How could Dash ever be middle-aged, old? No, let him die in the golden glory of youth. Storm or pirates might defeat him. Time and the slow humdrum of the years never. And with the end of Dash and Liz, of course — if Ma'am would face it — ended the House of Inman. Tom was raring to marry, set up mills with Mr. Fields. Peter certainly could never carry on by himself. Only Peter and old Ma'am.

There was a tap on the door of his study. "Come in," he yelled through his lather. "Just put the tray on my desk, Rose, but mind you don't touch a paper." The coffee smelled so good, he felt slightly faint. He hurried and, as often happened, cut himself. Then he went into his study, holding a piece of paper pressed to his cut chin.

Standing patiently in the middle of the room was Marcy Inman.

"Doctor Hobey," she began, a little reproachfully, "I couldn't put it on your desk without touching a paper. Nor on the table, nor on a chair. You've papers everywhere. Shall I put it on the floor?"

"There." He made room among his French-Arabic dictionaries and other paraphernalia of his night's work on the table. "It's only that Rose is so destructive. Why, I only asked for fresh coffee — she sent everything. How good of you to fetch it up to me."

Tired as he was, Marcy did not tire him even further, as she did her grandmother and mother. She rested and refreshed him. Because she had slept so well, he felt he had himself. He caught some contagion from her exuberant well-being.

Rose was calling up the stairs that the express rider had come for the papers.

"Marcy, will you take these down for the rider? They must start immediately for Washington."

Marcy received the heavy folded and sealed bundle of papers with a flattering awe in her eyes. "Doctor Hobey, you are wonderful."

She did not come back for ten minutes, but when she did, she had a plate of meringues still hot and damp from the oven. They talked a moment about the express rider.

He heard a slight noise behind him and turned. Standing by the open door, looking as though she had seen a ghost or was a ghost herself, was Madam Inman, her old brass spyglass in her hands. She formed words with shaking lips, but could not say them.

"Oh, Ma'am . . . you are ill!"

"No."

"There . . . sit, do. Marcy, get brandy from my little red cupboard."

"No."

But she drank the brandy. " 'Sephus . . . I have seen her. Leastwise, I think so."

"There . . . there."

She was shivering all over, although the spring day was warm. "She was just being written off."

"Marcy, fetch the comforter from my bed for your grandmother."

"I've seen the *Victrix*."

Evidently the long, despairing vigil, the abandonment of hope even by the underwriters, had broken her mind. "There . . . there," he said again.

"Yes," she said calmly, quite herself now. "Out beyond Juniper. Topsails only, but I'm sure I saw our house flag. I'm sure it is the *Victrix*."

"There . . . a little more brandy?"

She got up quickly, not merely herself once more, but years younger than she had seemed for the last year. "Listen!"

They heard a yelling and a calling along the wharf, along Derby Street. They heard the name *"Victrix"* shouted from mouth to mouth.

"Others have sighted her," she said. "Oh . . . the boys. We always give fifty cents to the first boy who sights a ship of ours."

All rushed to the windows and stuck out their heads. Three or four breathless boys were shrieking and jumping about the counting-house. And Fessenden was coming down those outside stairs, handing out money to all of them, so excited he wasn't trying to find out which boy had come first. They saw Peter racing up the wharf toward them, his quill pen still over his ear. He saw faces at the windows and began to yell.

"Grandma, Grandma . . . the *Victrix,* the *Victrix!* Grandma . . . the *Victrix!*"

"Doctor Hobey," said the old lady, "let us give thanks to God."

For a moment the three of them knelt on the study floor. Doctor Hobey's lips were shaking. Tears ran down old Ma'am's face. Marcy was sobbing loudly, gulping and laughing.

~ *3* ~

As ONE OF THE *Victrix's* principal underwriters, Squire Mompesson, on his way home from a salubrious country walk, was stopped and congratulated by several people. The ship was standing up Salem Harbor. "I'll believe it when I see it," he had said.

But he had stopped on 'Change, heard the bell ring and the official announcement. Bedlam broke loose. Staid merchants, men of property, were yelling and hurrahing, running for the waterfront. *"Victrix! Victrix!"* He heard her name tossed from mouth to mouth. Mr. Hiller, collector of customs, wasn't thinking about how much she'd pay. He was racing for Union Wharf and the customs boat, bareheaded as an egg. In his excitement, he had forgotten his wig. The harbor master's tiny sloop had already cast off, going out to meet her and order her to her anchorage.

Suddenly Squire Mompesson saw the lovely, stately thing. Her return had saved him considerable money, but he felt a slight bubble of gas rising to his lips. He turned toward Federal Street and home, the bells that had announced her arrival still ringing in his ears. At least his ears rang. Why he was so upset over having saved so much money he was not self-analytical enough to know.

It was quiet here along the elms in that part of Salem, so beautiful it was sometimes called "Paradise." He walked in at his own front door. Aunt Birdseye's old poodle crawled out to smell of him. He pushed at it angrily with his cane. There was no sign of excitement here. Word of the ship's return had not yet come.

"Philippa," he called. He never condescended to call her Flip. She came quietly out of the dining room, curtsied, took his hat and cane. Polly had told him Flip was going to marry the *Victrix's* second. Of course, this was why Polly had been so depressed and so — well, he couldn't think of any other word for it — so *queer* about the loss of the *Victrix*.

"How's your mistress, miss? Slept well?"

"Yes, sir."

"How's she been busying herself?"

"She isn't up yet. She'll be down now and bear you company and toast your toast."

"Rest is the best thing for her. I wish she would stay in bed every day until noon."

"Yes, sir."

"Oh . . . and tell George to harness up the pair. Have the carriage around. Please to inform Mrs. Birdseye and Mrs. Brattle it will be a pleasure to Miss Polly and myself if they will drive out with us. Say twelve-thirty."

"Yes, sir."

He started toward the dining room. For some reason he could not understand, he added, over his shoulder: "There's great excitement along the waterfront. On 'Change. A presumably lost ship, long overdue, is coming in. I believe my ladies will enjoy the sight. So go tell 'em."

"There *is*? Oh, Mr. Mompesson!" She was not obeying him. The spoiled minx followed him into the dining room where her service was not needed.

"Squire Mompesson . . ." she begged. He turned. Her eyes trembled, meeting his, her hand caught his sleeve. "Squire Mompesson, could it happen to be . . . the *Victrix*?"

He turned on her angrily. "Never so long as you are in my employ dare lay a hand on my sleeve." He shook it off and flicked at his broadcloth as though she were contagious filth. One temple now was throbbing. Two would mean he had walked too fast.

"Now go, Philippa. Fetch your young mistress. The hall clock is striking twelve. She's late. Tell George to harness up. I don't pay you to stand there and gape at me. I pay you to mind."

The small hearth fire had broken down to perfect embers for toasting. He sat at the table.

He heard Polly and Flip meet on the stairs. Exclamations, shrieks. He had not denied that the long overdue ship was the *Victrix*. Now both the girls knew. Of course, Polly was only sympathizing with Flip. She was so oversensitive, in this romantic, modern manner. Aunt Brattle, an old-fashioned gentlewoman, was often putting up her visual and staring coldly at Polly. She thought there was too much sensibility and not enough self-control among young people these days.

Polly, her face vivid, wild, was rushing at him. Hugging him. Upsetting him on an almost empty stomach, spilling the boiled milk he was pouring for himself.

"Papa . . . it is the *Victrix,* isn't it?"

"My dear," he said, coldly, "I've told you, and Doctor West has told you, you must not so excite yourself. Of course, all Salem is gratified. The delicacy of your feelings does credit to you. I know that Peter and Nanny are among your chosen friends. And I'm afraid, Philippa as well. But please . . . please sit and compose yourself."

"Yes, Father."

"My toast, dear?"

"Oh yes, Papa."

She crouched before the hearth and drew on heavy gloves kept there for the purpose. In one hand she held a toasting fork. In the other, shielding her famous complexion, a fan. This difficult, complicated pose would have seemed awkward for any other woman. But he had first taught her when her mother died and she was but seven. Natural grace and long practice gave such subtlety to the bending back and neck, such discipline to the slim arms and hidden, twisted legs, it seemed like a movement in a ritualistic dance. He noticed today that she was trembling a little as she carefully kept the pose. For once he resented the sensibilities of which he usually boasted.

"Papa?"

"Yes, my dear."

"Two pieces?"

"You know my habits as well as I do. Two pieces, always, my dear. And no more."

"Does it matter if one is scorched . . . a little?"

"I do not eat charcoal, my dear."

She toasted a third piece, put them on a silver plate, rose, laid them before him, and took her usual place. Her hands were quietly folded in her lap. Her face shut up, shut away. In her determination that her excitement should not further vex him, she went too far. There was an expression of remoteness, hauteur, that offended him more than her usual girlish exuberance. And yet how beautiful she was! She was so animated he rarely saw her face so still. It was a different beauty, and, by its strangeness, moving.

"Papa, you are one of her principal underwriters, aren't you?"

"Yes. I and Mr. Crowninshield senior. And frankly, we had decided she was a gone goose, my dear. This is very good news for your father."

"It must be a load off your mind."

"A *very* great load. I've ordered out the carriage."

"I heard tell."

"Your aunts?"

"Across the street with old Mrs. Orne. I've told Flip to fetch them."

"My idea is not to waste our time along Derby Street — the water-front is a little boisterous — but to celebrate her return by a drive into the country. The day is lovely. We will drive to Nahant. Friend Brown has a neat ordinary. Fresh air, country food, will be a treat for us all. The unworldly Quaker atmosphere a solace."

"Papa . . . do you mind if I do not go?"

"But of course you will go. You must be well rested by now. Doctor West very much recommends carriage exercise for you."

"I don't think I will go. I'd rather stay here."

"Why?" he asked, coldly. He stared at her with incredulity, daring her to say, "Because Dash Inman might come here to see me."

She did not accept his challenge, but answered, a little evasively, "I think I'd rather stay here."

"You are to go. It is my request. You have been far too mopy of late, Polly. Frankly, I've been a little worried. Now, child, I hear the carriage. Run upstairs and fetch your bonnet and shawl. And a parasol. We don't want freckles, do we?" She looked at him as if she were going to obey him. "And tell cook that if Mate What's-his-name comes courting our help, he's to be sent packing. No followers is the rule."

"I don't think Flip is here, Papa. She went to fetch the aunts and then I think she has already run to the wharf."

She knew that before she left for the wharf, she'd come back to see her mistress — once again they could laugh and cry together.

"Papa, she loves Mate Obrian a lot, you know." Her wonderful eyes begged his sympathy.

"I don't know. And I don't want ever to know. And you, Polly — must you so cheapen yourself as to accept the amorous confidences of a servant? Well . . . bless me, here are the aunts."

Together, they put their heads into the dining room to call good morning. Aunt Brattle was a handsome dame, evidently Mr. Mompesson's sister. She was dependent upon a cane. Great-Aunt Birdseye, tiny, shrunken, toothless, and much older, was the spryer of the two. She owned the smelly old poodle. They did not look to be likable old women.

Polly let each kiss her as she asked for the gout of one and the dog of the other. When they left, she absent-mindedly wiped their kisses from her cheek. She went back to her father with an ungirlish, possibly unattractive stolidity. Unknown to either of them, she usually flirted with her father. Now she did not.

"Papa, what did you say — exactly what did you say — when Dash Inman asked . . . You told me he asked, but you never said what he said and what you said."

"Why, miss," he answered, in a falsely bantering tone, "you should have asked me at the time. Naturally, I've forgotten now. You are a flirt, Polly. I've often had the embarrassment of explaining to young gentlemen that they have . . . ah . . . gotten ahead of themselves."

"Ahead of themselves? Oh . . ."

"Now, when your Great-Aunt Birdseye was a young person, a gentleman would ask the father's permission to pay addresses before he began. But today — and I blame the Revolutions, French *and* American, for a complete downfall in the niceties of life — he usually *first* is confident he has the lady's affection, *then* asks the father. Polly, I've been meaning to talk to you. I don't" — his voice grew gentle — "want to reprove you for your natural playfulness, but a number of . . . ah . . . rather *queer* impossible suitors have come to me and imagined they had already gained your heart."

"Like Mr. Briscoe."

"There was nothing impossible about Fred Briscoe. Except you didn't fancy him. That's your affair, miss. I will certainly never urge you to marry anyone you do not fancy. But I will not encourage the impossible."

"I suppose you mean, like Dash."

"Well, frankly, yes. He'd lost a ship. Stove in his family fortunes. It seemed an odd time for a man to speak to the father. Then, too, I knew, Polly" — his rich, deep voice pleaded with her — "I knew that, although you had kept him dancing attendance when in port

— he wasn't in much — you had not the slightest serious interest in him."

"I know. But what did you say?"

"Really, how can I possibly remember? Not much was said on either side. No, not much. And Polly" — he did not care if he hurt her — "he made, as I remember it, very little *protest*. Put little heart into it. Made his offer, I refused, and he left without another word."

"But Papa, suppose the *Viatrix* has made a fortune? She's been gone three years. She might have. You know she might. Suppose he asked again, Papa?"

"There's an old adage, miss — don't count your chickens until they are hatched." The boiled milk he had been drinking tasted again in his mouth.

"But I've always wondered. I thought you must have something . . . something special against Dash Inman. Why are you so against Dash?"

"I am not. You are to marry, within reason, as your heart dictates. I refuse to be drawn into such a serious conversation at table. Table-talk must always be light and easily digested. But I'm amazed at your even bringing up Captain Inman's name. Did he not completely, and by his own volition, some months before he left on this last voyage of his, drop out of what the vulgar call 'the running'? And now, dear, the carriage waits."

She shook her head.

He was so furious with her he could hardly trust himself to speak. Until this moment he had always pretended to himself that it was Polly who had turned Dash away. Not that Dash had jilted Polly. His egoism demanded that that should be the situation. But in bad temper as in wine there may be *veritas*.

He stood and looked down at her averted face. "Captain Inman was not bidden by me to stay away. Nor by you, I gather?"

"Oh no. Never, Papa."

"It doesn't occur to you that he may have found another girl more to his liking?"

She smiled suddenly. Her eyes shone with faith. "That isn't it. And then, too, all of us Salem girls go to the same parties. And we do gossip. If Dash had someone else, I'm sure Nanny would have told me. That's not why."

"There are girls — girls right here in Salem — who do *not* go to your parties. There are girls — not ladies — who before this have bemused our young gentlemen."

Her face turned white and her pretty mouth fell open. "Papa . . . tell me . . . what do you know?"

"Nothing." He was honest enough to admit it.

"You are making things up to torment me." Her hands clenched, and she looked at him angrily.

"I can hardly see why you should torment yourself over Captain Inman's private life."

She made no answer.

He left her. Once more the boiled milk came gurgling back into his mouth.

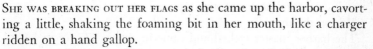

SHE WAS BREAKING OUT HER FLAGS as she came up the harbor, cavorting a little, shaking the foaming bit in her mouth, like a charger ridden on a hand gallop.

"Peter, tell me . . . You can see farther than I. Is her pennant apeak?"

If the homing pennant was apeak, it meant not one life had been lost.

"Aye, Ma'am, apeak it is."

"Thank God! Thank God!"

"And see how white her sails are."

They had been tawny when she left, and Peter thought how it was Dash who had pointed out to him that timid young things are apt to be tawny. Only with the boldness and pride of maturity do they dare to be white.

The harbor master's little sloop was running under her prow, ordering her to her anchorage. She trembled as if from excitement as she tacked.

"Look what he's carrying," Peter said. "Everything he's got. More than he started with."

"He shouldn't," said his grandmother, and surreptitiously wiped her eyes.

"Dash always carries all he's got," Peter boasted; "and if it's not enough, he gets more."

"And he shouldn't come in so fast. He shouldn't." She was shivering and holding to 'Sephus Hobey's arm for support.

The *Victrix* had turned on her tail like a cat. Her sails dropped. It was as pretty, almost as delicate, a gesture as a young girl slipping down her shift. Her anchors rattled out, grasped the muddy bottom. She swayed. The anchors held.

"Oh, why didn't they write?" Ma'am wailed. "Why couldn't they have let me know? And now it will take an hour to clear her. I've waited and waited . . . and this last hour I'll wait to home. Peter, run tell your mother they're coming in and the pennant's apeak. No, wait, Mr. Silas has word for us."

The harbor master was heading his sloop toward Inman Wharf, standing at the tiller, yelling, "She's been to Japan, Ma'am — JAPAN! JAPAN!"

The owner looked dazed. "Japan, 'Sephus? Why, I'd as soon have thought of a ship going to the mountains of the moon. I wasn't even sure there was such a place."

"It's on the maps."

The harbor master tacked and came in again. *"Twice* to Japan! Great voyage. Real smart."

"Now, Peter, go tell your poor mother. Those boys are safe."

As Peter left the wharf, where people were already gathering to enjoy the excitement, he saw Flip Dawson in a bright pink frock and the starchedest of white caps. Her eyes quivered with joy and her cherry-red lips shook. They hugged each other.

"Danny's safe," she gulped, "and I guess he's made a lot." But she was even then almost more interested in her mistress's happiness. "Mr. Peter, Miss Polly wouldn't drive out with her papa. He was real mad, too. She's waiting there, alone. You know for who?" He nodded and went on.

Tears came to his eyes. He couldn't help it. Never since he could remember had all Salem rejoiced so over a ship's return. People he hardly knew were stopping him, shaking hands, slapping him on the back. Congratulating him. And because they were Yankees they were talking more about the financial gains — everyone was saying it was going to prove one of the richest voyages ever taken — than the lives and health of the men. But Peter understood. I'm so lucky to live in Salem, he thought gratefully. Everybody knows us, and everybody's glad.

On Essex Street, standing before what was now "Flanneau and Stackpool," he saw Dulcey. Now she was fashionably dressed in pale blue, and because she had heard that Dash's ship was coming in, she had put off apron and cap and had put on a devastating shiny black bonnet and short black gloves. Flanneau saw to it that she advertised his taste. Peter knew she had heard the news, dressed up, and then just stood there because she didn't know where to go. He felt sorry for her forlornness and ready, but useless, courage. He had been running, but stopped, coughed, and said, "You've heard tell?"

Her gray eyes were brimful of happiness, her red cheeks dimpled with joy. She was so happy, and confident. God damn her confidence, Peter thought. Now she thinks she'll be shut of Flanneau and all that French cooking he makes her do, all that slobbering and pinching she has to put up with because he loves her. She thinks that's over. And Dash will marry her.

"Do I look nice?" She beamed at him.

"You look fine. Up to top notch."

"Like a lady?"

"Absolutely like a lady."

"I guess he'll be surprised."

He sniffed and left her.

Lucy Inman had never been one to run to wharves like a fisherman's wife. Gentlewomen, be they wives, mothers, sweethearts, often did not. They waited quietly at home as the man went through the rigmarole of making port, customs, officials, and owner, of course.

Marcy had brought the first news. Lucy, externally at least, refused to believe it. "Oh Marcy, it's just the *Mermaid* putting in or one of a dozen other ships. They look so much alike."

Her mind refused to react. Slowly, and in a daze, she went to her room, put off the morning calico and put on a beautiful becoming silk, gray, striped with yellow. Her hands were trembling so she could hardly fasten the clasp of the seed-pearl and topaz necklace against her throat. Liz had brought it to her from Paris. I must be calm, she said over and over to herself. Calm.

Then Mr. Africanus came to tell her, and earn a penny. He said the bell on 'Change had rung and that it had been officially announced. No, ma'am, those gentlemen had never been mistaken.

Frances ran over, but had the tact not to stay. She loved Lucy so much she understood her sudden petulance. She wanted to be alone. Not talk.

Standing at the front window, twisting her white hands, she saw Peter coming at a run. He shouldn't run. It always made him cough. She resented his frailties and futilities, his dreadful mistress, and most of all his cough.

He burst in. "Mother . . . her pennant's apeak! Mother, she's made a great voyage!" Then he coughed.

"Where have they been to, all this time?"

"Practically off the map, Mother. They've been to Japan. Twice. That's all I know."

"Oh."

"They're the first Americans ever to get there. And . . . "

"Peter, *walk,* don't run, back to the wharf. As soon as you see them, come back to tell me how they look. And why, why didn't they write? Why, we thought they were dead!"

"Yes, Mother. Mother . . . everybody in Salem's happy. Mother, everybody cares . . . a lot. I mean, for Dash and Liz. Us, too."

"I don't care a thing about everybody." She sat there, rocking back and forth.

"Yes, Mother. Mother . . . " He couldn't possibly find the words he wanted to say. He burst out: "Mother, you look awfully pretty. I guess you know it. Mother, you're so pretty." Then suddenly they kissed each other and cried, and felt the better for it.

At last, and it seemed to take forever, the *Victrix's* longboat was rowing in, smart and fast, toward Inman Wharf. Ma'am, Peter knew, was in her own house. That's where Dash would have to report now. First thing.

Jack West and Nanny, carrying what Peter thought was a most second-rate baby, and Marcy, were waiting on the wharf with him. And Tom, too. Peter drew back a little and shut his eyes. If he fainted now, people would never get over it.

Then Peter saw Dash, standing there. Because the day was so warm he had his whitish beaver hat pushed far back on his head. He was drenched in sunlight, surrounded by people. He looked handsome, amazingly alive, and his face glowed. Of course, he was being modest about everything, but Peter knew how proud he was inside. He did look considerably older. But three years is a long time. The blaze of sun on tropic seas had narrowed his eyes, put crow's-feet at the corners, deepened the parenthesis marks he had about his muscular mouth. It had done so before, but this time — now he was twenty-seven and not young any more — they might not ever leave again. So Peter pondered on his face. And the quick, high turn of the chin — like he wasn't used to taking much from anybody — and the wide smile glittering in the sea tan. He certainly looked fine, but not much like Peter's Dash. He no longer belonged to the sad fraternity of young men who lose ships, make missteps or even have weak lungs, clerk and write poetry. I guess they really have made a lot of money, Peter thought. He looks like he'd made a lot.

Liz was hardly stopping for anyone, pushing past people, heading for home. He'd go and report to his mother while the captain stopped to report to the owner. As he ran, he grabbed Peter by the arm, shook him and said, with deepest affection, "Idiot boy."

"Liz . . . your clocks. They're all running good."

"Aye, Pete. We can put a gold cupola on that house, if Mother wants . . . " And he shot along to tell her.

Dash saw Peter, hurried to him and had him by the hand. Then one of his solid arms was laid about his shoulders. But there was Mr. Crowninshield senior to congratulate him, and Captain George junior. Of course, he had to stop and talk to them, but he kept his arm on Peter's shoulder. It said, You were my friend in adversity. I will not lose you now I am myself once more.

Peter had never been more conscious of Dash's warm animal attraction than during the brief walk up the wharf to the gate before Ma'am's old house. Yet he felt him a stranger, vastly removed from the small and sniveling ways of the least of the Inmans. I bet he's forgotten about Dulcey. He hasn't asked me. Peter felt scared of him a little, and he loved him so he thought he might burst.

At Ma'am's gate, not even Marcy dared suggest she'd follow. Dash dropped Marcy's hand, for he had had her on the other side of him. Nobody could follow a captain about to report to his owner. "Pete, can you come with me? Help with figures? And where's Billy Bates?"

Billy, at fourteen years old, had started as ship's boy. Now he was clerk of the vessel, a tall, manly-looking fellow. He had the ship's books.

"Aye, sir," he said smartly.

Ma'am was sitting there before her hearth drinking tea, a cat in her lap, looking as though she had not and never had had a worry. Peter admired her seeming nonchalance, acting as though the *Victrix* had been away three months only. She'd never let on the waiting had almost killed her.

She accepted Dash's kiss without too much emotion, told Billy where to set a table and place his books. Bade Rose fetch rum, water, lemon, and sugar, also pipes for Mr. Bates and Captain Dash. Then she put on her spectacles. There was no reproof even implied. Peter, knowing what she had been through, couldn't believe his eyes.

He was too restless to sit and follow Dash's careful report. He felt he could not yet take in anything except the fact of the return. Certainly not figures. Grandma, he thought, is a better man than I am. She's a lot tougher. Hers was a pretty tough generation. He went to the kitchen, and there Rose gave him hot grog. He was shivering a little. Then he wandered back into the sitting room and heard enough to get the gist. Seems they had written regularly, although not very much about what they were doing. They had promised somebody called Van Heelu, somebody very important, not to say what they were doing and to send all letters through him. Well, that . . . and Dash almost said "son of a bitch," but changed in time and said "rascal" . . . evidently had been destroying the letters.

They had met real foul weather on their return from the first trip to Japan, but the *Victrix* had pulled through. Mighty smart ship. She could pull through anything. Dash had continued to work under charter. Piling up "plenty" until it was spring once more and once more the Great Hollander ship — "that's us, Grandma" — was due to set out for Japan. It was then the name *Victrix* was really lost. She was getting too well known. He renamed her the *Hope* — there were so many *Hopes* — and gave her a bark rig, so she wouldn't be recognized too easily by the British who were laying for her. That's why no one had reported her to Ma'am. They had bespoken two or three American vessels, but had always given their name as the *Hope* of Baltimore.

Peter went out into the kitchen and Rose gave him more hot grog. He was so restless he went back again into the sitting room. But he couldn't sit and really take things in as Ma'am could.

"Yes, Ma'am," Dash was saying, "as Liz and I and Billy here figure it, we've been clearing one hundred thousand dollars a year profit. She proved herself a very fine ship." And his eyes went to Peter and softened and lingered, because Peter would understand how he loved that ship. "But I couldn't take the money in drafts on London in my name or yours, Ma'am. War has upset everything. It had to go to Amsterdam and Paris and then to London. It's in the name of Roger Rowson. I made that up." He was smiling and looking proud of himself because he had made up so fine a name. "Baring Brothers, Ma'am. Once again. It's all there. And there's more to come."

"More to come?" faltered Ma'am.

Seemingly the "more to come" presented a problem. It was in goods in this Van Heelu fellow's go-downs at Batavia.

"Soon as we can clean and — well, sort of *rest* the *Victrix,* I'm taking her back and get that cargo. 'Fore any of those damned Frenchmen of Napoleon's can get around to saying those goods belong to them — not to Van Heelu and me, as he and I say."

Peter went to the kitchen. And had another hot grog.

"Rose," he said to the dwarf, the heavy drink steaming through him, "how'd you like to be rich, for a change?"

"Me, sir?" She had a child's rocking chair which she always sat in, and she stopped rocking in amazement.

"Well, have Ma'am rich. It's the same thing, isn't it?"

"Yes, Mr. Peter. There isn't any difference. What's mine's hers and what's hers is mine. It's always been like that, you know." She spoke in her great gruff voice, and started to rock again.

"You can buy some new caps, Rose. Caps so high you'll hit the doortops as you go through."

Her white, sensitive face, set so far down in her thick, shapeless shoulders, was peering at his incredulously.

"Yes, Rose. It's a lot of money. I mean a lot. No ship, ever, made one hundred thousand a year for three years, and even so had more to come. And Rose . . . listen, Rose. She's been to Japan. So tell your children" — she had none — "and your grandchildren, and don't let people ever forget the *Victrix,* Dash Inman master, was the first American ship to get to Japan. There's great honor in that, Rose."

Dash was leaving at last and Peter walked beside him. There was more of a crowd than ever on Inman Wharf, along Derby Street. And more hurrahing and fuss being made over Dash. This he took very well. Lots of young ladies had arrived and all looked ready to melt into his arms. Dash was shaking hands with some of them, but everyone who called him "cousin" expected a kiss. Probably they were "cousins" — Salem was so intermarried. But Peter noticed that Dash's eyes were always going beyond them, looking for someone else.

At last, upon Essex Street, they were alone except for the small admiring boys trying to make him promise to ship them next time.

"I say, Dash."

"Aye."

Those three hot grogs had given Peter great confidence. "Dash, Polly didn't come to the wharf."

"I noticed." Dash's responsive face clouded. "I guess she's married. Go ahead, tell me. Right off. Who'd she marry?"

"Nobody. She couldn't marry anybody else."

"I thought she might feel well shut of me. I did write to her . . . I wrote — well, as loving as I cared to, knowing Van Heelu would read it first. And I did ask her to hold on, a little longer. Till I came home. But she never got that letter?"

"No. She never got anything. But she knew. Dash, she's waiting for you now. She'll wait for you forever. I know."

Peter knew that men who do not love women resent such patient Griseldas. Those who do, do not. There was no resentment on Dash's face, only gratitude and wonder.

"She's sitting there in her house, alone. Waiting for you."

"I'll go. Soon as I've kissed my mother. Liz will be telling her everything — she won't need me. I'll go right off. You're sure she wants me to?"

"I'm sure."

❧ 5 ❧

IT WAS NOT ONLY FLIP who had run pell-mell to the wharves, but the cook, the second maid, and the rheumatic, cross old woman whom Aunt Birdseye had brought with her fifteen years ago and who did nothing but care for Aunt Birdseye and walk the poodle. She wouldn't even wash the poodle. She said that was not her business. And the Mompesson staff said it wasn't theirs. The poodle never got washed.

The gardener and his men had dropped their hedging and run. Her father and her aunts were gone. Polly, for perhaps the first time in her life, was alone in the house. The beautiful May day blew in and out the windows, scented with lilac, full of sunshine, fluted with bird song.

Polly knew how to play the cards of love. Make yourself unattainable, force the man ever to pursue. She thought of stories she had heard, plays seen, novels read. She wished she had gone to Nahant. She did not quite want Dash to come and find her waiting as though she were already his. He must not be so sure of her. She walked back and forth through the lower story of the house, from the little creamy sitting room which she considered her own into the wide parlors, through the dining room. The maids had left so fast the remains of second breakfast still littered the mahogany, to remind her of how she had opposed her father. And he had been right. She wrong. Dash wasn't coming to her. It was Peter who had kept telling her and telling her he loved her. Perhaps he had tricked her into believing what was not so. And if Dash did come, how stupid of her to let him find her waiting.

She went upstairs and took off the malachite brooch he had brought her once from St. Petersburg. It was the first thing he had given her. She had always loved it and thought it clumsy and ugly. She looked in her mirror. Her gossamer white dress was as delicate and as exquisitely embroidered as a baby's baptismal robe. She did not look at it. Only at her own face. She hardly recognized it as hers — those flaming cheeks, the parted lips, the burning intensity of the eyes. And how queer and wild they looked back at her from her silver mirror! Dash mustn't come and find her in such a state. The blood was throbbing in her throat. She could feel her shoulders shuddering.

"You must *not* excite yourself, my dear," she said, unconsciously this time mimicking her father. "There, now, lie down. Rest a moment." She tried it, but couldn't stand it. She washed her face again, brushed the golden tendrils of curls. Put on a lavender bonnet. She had decided to go out. Go anywhere. But there was no place to go. She took off her bonnet and slowly went down the stairs, holding her head high, making "an entrance" as she often had at balls. She found this did help, for she was pretending a hundred eyes were upon her and her pride responded to the imaginary audience. Then she went to her own sitting room. She was calmer now. She'd be able to meet him with coquetry and the proper feminine resistance. He must not be too sure of her. *If* he came, she'd tell him she had had a headache. That's why she was here alone. He mustn't guess she had waited for him. She flung herself on her couch and closed her eyes. The Iphigenia clock chimed a sweet two o'clock.

Far off, like a bugle call, she heard the whinnying of a mare, asking the old vernal question — where is my mate? She heard again the clip of the gardener's shears. The others might be back soon. And of course they must also think she felt too poorly to drive out. She thought of drawing the shades, shutting out the sunshine, to create a proper illusion of a headache. Now it was two-thirty, and still Dash did not come. She was sure now he would not. The young mare whinnied again. How sad and sweet was the cry! That's like life, she thought. At least I'm sure it's sad. I don't know whether it is sweet or not.

Now any moment Flip would be back to tell her that she had seen "him." And him was not her Danny Obrian. But when she heard a soft footstep, she knew it was not Flip. Flip would come running and calling her name. One of the other maids. If she peeked in, she would think she was sleeping.

The front door had been left open. Dash walked in. Glancing into the sitting room, he saw her. He said her name.

"Polly?"

All the blood drained from her face, returned again, flooding face and neck, mottling her bare arms like a baby's. She stood and stared at him. Her excitement was so great she forgot the most elemental of social usages. She forgot to smile. Her beautiful eyes widened and stared.

"Polly," he said again, in the well-remembered voice that had so much banked fire in it.

She could neither speak nor put out her hand to him. He seemed to realize how the shock of the meeting had upset her. He went to her, put his arms very gently about her, and pressed his shaven cheek to the mushroom smoothness of her own. It was the most delicate of caresses. His hands went to her hair, stroked the proud little nape of her neck. His fingers traced the curve of her lips. He did not kiss her right away. Then his arms tightened and she was clinging to him, laughing and whimpering.

"You really knew, all the time, my girl?"

"Yes, yes. I knew."

"You do love me?"

"Oh, Dash, darling! Darling Dash, sometimes I've wished I didn't have to love you. Sometimes I've wished I could stop."

"No," he said, swaying her back and forth. "No, and I won't ever be able to get clear of you. Nor you of me. I guess we have to. It's our hard luck, my girl, isn't it?"

She was smiling at last. She was over the shock of the meeting. And then he kissed her. He was so slow she had time to feel the inevitableness, the heaviness of passion. She felt it was something she could not escape. Love was not like this. Not the love Peter had talked about in Dash's name, the love one sang of in songs, read about in novels. She did not quite like to feel so torn up from her conventional roots, pushed back into some primordial slime. After a long moment, she sat weakly on the edge of her French couch, and he sat beside her. Her hands trembled to her face and covered it. Everything about him frightened her a little. For one thing, it was three years since they had met. And the roughness of his cheek, the muscular sweet mouth, even the hairy texture of his coat — all this frightened her. She was sensuously aware of the weight of bone and muscle which could be used against her. He was strong enough to crush her, kill her, if he wanted to. She almost wished he would. Half of her longed to jump up and escape, half of her that he should use his full strength against her, even if it annihilated her. She looked at his face. It was suffused with a curious innocent radiance. The eyes, light for brown eyes, now seemed almost golden. His kisses and caresses drew all resistance from her, all gentility, all coquetry, and without those ancient feminine barriers she could not feel herself. But it was not he she feared so much as the melting of her own fastidious delicate flesh, the longing she felt pulsing through her veins.

The young mare whinnied again.

It was as if her body, her heart, soul, mind, were not hers any longer. Only part of his. She thought of crying out for help against his "violence." No man could have been gentler. Then why could she not escape? She did not want to.

"Dash!" she cried, and took his square hands, still chapped from the sea, and fitted them about her throbbing throat. "Kill me now, Dash, please kill me . . . if you want to."

There was nothing he wanted less, but the wildness of the idea and the passion in her eyes brought him to his senses. Her little hands were pressing his tighter and tighter about her throat. "I wish I could die now," she whispered. He kissed her gently, almost in renunciation. And stroked her and murmured to her and tried to quiet her down a little. Then they both heard footsteps in the dining room. The maids were back.

"Oh," she said, rousing herself with difficulty, seeming still half-conscious, "I forgot to tell them. Papa and the aunts are dining out. Excuse me, Dash. I must tell them before they set the table."

When she came back, he had himself well in hand, and seemingly she had herself as well. Suddenly she looked much more as he remembered her, pretty and captious and hard to please. That other woman, the one he had held in his arms and only he knew about, was gone. But that was the one he loved most. This one all sorts of men had been in love with for years. Himself included.

"Polly," he said, standing well away from her, his hands in his pockets, "will you marry me?"

"Guess," she laughed. "What do you guess?"

"When?"

She had not entirely liked it when all the power had been in his hands and she had felt herself pulled up by the roots and a primordial darkness closing in upon her.

"Of course, it is not for me to set the day. The young lady's father does that."

He moved a little restlessly.

Suddenly she felt quite herself again, and ready to have fun with him. Make him wince a little. "Have you talked to Papa?"

"I did . . . once."

"Not really!" Her eyes widened with teasing incredulity. "He must have been so pleased."

"No. You know I was down on my luck a bit — just then."

"You've mended that?"

"Yes. Oh yes. For sure. He can't throw money up against me this time. And Polly, that's one reason I stayed out so long.. I was determined, absolutely, he'd never be able to throw that up against me again. But . . ."

"But what, my faint-hearted swain? Why, my darling?"

He looked at her thoughtfully. The innocent golden light had left his eyes. "We can decide for ourselves. We are of age."

"You're afraid of him," she mocked. "A tiny little old man not half as big and strong as you are."

"No. But he doesn't like me. Nor I him. He's smart. He'll think of another reason."

She colored in amazement and anger. "Dash, you didn't say you didn't like my father!"

"I don't want any secrets, ever, between us, Polly. I don't want one of those halfway marriages other people have. There's nothing I feel or do or have ever done I want secret from you. Well, yes, I said it. We've both got to accept it, Polly. I tell you he hates me."

"Whyever should he?"

"He's been afraid — for some time — you might come to care more for me than for him."

"Well, when you talk like this, I'm sure I do not. Be sensible, Dash. Just go to him, again. He has never taken you seriously. When he knows how much I care, he will love you for my sake." But her self-confidence faltered. "Dash, I must have a few days . . . to prepare his mind. I mean, don't come, say, tomorrow. Give me five days. Ask him five days from now. And by that time I'll have brought him around. I'll have kedged him, as you say."

"But Polly," he said slowly, "that's five days out of, say, two weeks."

"What's two weeks to do with it?"

"I've got to go back to Batavia. Right off."

The flirtatious mask she had drawn over her face fell away. He saw utter incredulity.

"No, wait. Don't get excited — dear girl — I'll be back fast."

"You can't go! I've waited so long. Dash you can't go!"

Her hands clenched. He was afraid she was going to cry. But when he tried to comfort her with his arms, she pulled away angrily.

"I never heard of anything so cruel. And you don't have to go.

Dash, aren't you rich enough to send other men — employees?"

"I'm the only man that can do it this time, Polly. It's not a matter of seamanship. The Government may try to say that cargo isn't mine. If they do, I'll have to talk fast."

"You care more for money than for me."

"It's Ma'am's money, not mine, sweet. I'm honor bound. We can marry and have a few days together — you and I."

"What's a few days? After I've waited three years! And it would shame me so — married and then abandoned."

"Polly," he said, with a slight exasperation, "I don't abandon you when I'm away. I long for you so — dream of you waking and sleeping." He had almost said that when away from her he was more in love than when with her. Her captiousness, her unreasonableness, had often brought on misunderstandings when they were together. This was a side of her he did not have to cope with in his dreams. Then she was always lovely and serene as a ship sailing a summer sea, beautiful as a ship. She would not have cared for this metaphor. He smiled suddenly. "Marry me and go with me. Wives have sailed before this with their husbands."

"I'd be seasick." He knew his suggestion was nonsense, but she, too, smiled, and she did not look so hurt and angry. Actually she was accepting the fact he must leave her.

"Anyway, I'll be back in eight months. I swear it. That's not long. We'll be officially engaged before I leave. You and your papa and the aunts can have eight months to prepare the most monstrous fine wedding Salem ever saw. January — I'll be back in January. Polly, I'll buy the silk for your wedding gown myself. Tell me the house you want and I'll buy it now — before I go — and you can fix it up and . . ."

They sat close together now. She was being unexpectedly good about his leaving.

"Papa's always said he'll give me the little house next door — then I won't be far from him. It's so sweet."

"Then I want it, too — and eight months is not long. Long to look forward to — not long to look back upon."

"Dash." She ran her hands through his hair because she knew he didn't like it. Too many times his mother had almost pulled it up by the roots trying to unsnarl it. To this day he didn't like to have even the woman he loved combing his hair with her light fingers. But she was herself again and wanted to tease him. "Aren't you afraid that in eight months I might find someone I loved as much as you and could manage better?"

"No."

"Conceited creature! Or you might find another girl. But the Dutch girls are all fat, aren't they?"

"In Amsterdam, perhaps, not Batavia. They're a sickly lot in Batavia, I promise you."

She suddenly remembered her father's cruel suggestion. During the long months after losing the *Antelope,* he had found someone else. She started up.

"Or perhaps you have already."

"No, never. I'm a simple fellow, Polly. I don't fall in love easily. I love hard."

She went to him and rubbed her face against his coat. "I knew it," she said simply. "It was my bad ogre of a father, as you think him, put such an idea in my head. He said perhaps that spring when you never came near me, you had another girl up your sleeve. I'd die if I believed that. And one thing you're right about, Dash. Let's not have just an ordinary marriage. But a wonderful, perfect one. I'll never have a secret from you. And you will never have one from me."

Her eyes were not on his face. Luckily for her peace of mind, she did not see a baffled, odd look come into it. That girl over in Marblehead. Here he had told Polly there must never be a secret, and now she told him the same. Yet, inadvertently, he had lied to her about that girl in Marblehead. No, no. It was the truth. He had never longed so for Polly as during those last few months before the *Victrix* sailed and he had had a simple-minded, pleasant entanglement with that nice little girl. But sometime he'd tell Polly even about that. He'd tell her everything. Just now she had enough to think about.

He made his farewells very delicately, rather afraid to arouse in her once more that hidden tigress which he felt in honor bound unable to satisfy. He must be careful not to let Polly get so excited. Not until they were married. But he almost laughed out loud, thinking of, say, next January.

He was going past Deacon Sam Pickman's pasture. A young sorrel mare, with pretty white feet and a crooked white blaze on

her forehead, was galloping back and forth, striking at the green
blossoming earth beneath her — innocents, violets, white clover,
five-finger. Tossing her head, lifting a forefoot as animals do when
they listen intently, and then calling. But the ingenuity and selfish-
ness of man had made it unlikely that there would be any answer
to her passionate calling.

~6~

ON THE FIFTH EVENING, Dash dressed himself handsomely in palest
silk nankeen, with a scarlet linen waistcoat and half-boots of glittering blackness. Under his square, tanned chin nestled the proper
amount of starched and fluted white cambric. So he stepped out the
side entrance of his house.

He was apt to wear his high hat pushed back at an unconsciously
rakish angle — an angle that had long been copied by lesser young
captains about Salem — or to carry it in his hand. Today he was
carrying it, and the gloves it was too warm to wear, and a handsome malacca cane. A very proper suitor he looked, now about to
ask the father for his official approval of an eight-month engagement. How could consent possibly be denied to such a paragon?
Handsome and famous, rich, of excellent report. Yet his boldly
confident exterior hid misgivings. He expected to marry Polly next
January on his return. He did not expect ever to have her father's
approval. But he'd force him into at least agreeing. He had forced
lots of other men into agreeing to that which they did not wish to.
Dash knew he could do it.

Lucy Inman saw him go. How could any housewife think to
send so much fame, magnificence, and simple dignity on a paltry
errand? But Lucy had always loved to send Dash on errands. He
might have made the family fortune — already McIntire had
agreed to set to work next week finishing the house — he might
have honorary dinners given him by the East India Marine Society,
small boys might follow him on the street, Washington might interest itself in his pioneering voyages, but his mother would see to
it that, when home, he never got too big for his pantaloons.

"Dash," she called from the window.

"Mother?"

"Dash, if you are going out, anyway, do stop by and tell Cousin Frances that yes, we are going to Derby farm tomorrow, weather permitting."

"Of course," he agreed readily.

Liz, sitting in the living room with his mother, laughed to himself. Dash was God himself at sea, and here his mother sent him on schoolboy errands.

"And you won't forget, dear?" Dash had a way of forgetting half the things his mother told him to do. "Keep your fingers crossed until you've done it. Then you can't forget."

So he did not turn left as he went out the driveway, but to his right, around the corner and into Essex Street.

He had passed Flanneau and Stackpool's several times before, and now he noticed that *Victrix* goods were already being displayed, a little overdisplayed, he thought. Adventurous and always longing for new things at sea, when he got home he wanted no changes. Already he was regretting that his mother's old barn was about to be torn down. The new white stable was going up at last, due to the money he had made. But he had liked the old barn and all the dirty talk with Mullins. It had always been there and he would have liked it always to remain. So now he did not care for the changes at the Stackpools'. The new show windows were the biggest in Salem. He did not like the elaborate large new sign over the shop, nor the strange name leading off. He wanted old Miss Clara and the even older Miss Unity to be sitting in there, selling thimbles and thread and horehound drops, making a living but not doing real well. That's the way it always had been. He wanted them to go on forever thus. While he was away, he thought, Salem should stay as it was without any change, so that even if he were in Japan, he could shut his eyes and see it all.

As he approached Cousin Frances's door to the rear, he noticed that her old barn had been repaired. There were locks and bolts and even iron bars at every opening. That was like a Frenchman, he thought. They always thought about thieves and not of fire — coming as they did from a stone-built country, half-full, ever since the Revolution, of light-fingered folk.

Before the door of this warehouse, if you could call it that, was a Sumatra clam shell, four feet long. Those clams were so big they could, and did, kill men. That's as big as my shell, he thought.

And he had a strong idea that it was his. He was always bringing useless curios home, and before this his mother had thrown them out.

Around the corner, running and laughing, came a stark-naked little girl, leaping and squealing: the prettiest baby he had ever seen. She leaned over, splashing in the water the shell held, jabbering and calling to someone who was following her. Like other men who have lived their lives mostly among men, Dash was sentimental about children. Now she was kicking and splashing in the water, yet, when her mother, carrying a bucket of water, soap and towels, came up to her, she leaped out and away, drops of water flying from her. Her mother caught her and dragged her back. She was flipping and flopping up and down, but evidently she was going to get that bath.

Doubtless this was Flanneau's family. The young woman, he noticed idly, was built much more like a French peasant girl than an attenuated, small-framed Yankee. He stood at the back door, half-hidden by honeysuckles and trumpet vines. Neither had seen him. Then he saw the woman's face, broad, healthy, ruddy, with a lovely big mouth, handsomely curved and curled. He looked at this face for a long time and in complete incredulity. He knew it wasn't Dulcey. Dulcey belonged in Marblehead, and the past. So it could not be Dulcey. But he knew it was. He'd have to stop a moment and think before he spoke to her.

Cousin Frances had seen him turn up her path. She was opening the door for him now, even before he had knocked.

"Cousin Frances," he said, "Mother says you and she are going to Derby farm tomorrow, weather permitting."

"Oh, thank you, Dash. For all day?"

"She didn't say. I don't think so. Yes, I suppose so. It's quite a drive. Fact is, I haven't any idea. If she said, I've forgotten."

She twisted her head about like a bird, and looked up at him out of her dark, pretty, beady eyes. Dash was a moody fellow, just as his mother always said. Here he was supposedly at her door, but he might as well be in Java. He didn't even seem to know quite what he was talking about. I suppose all he can think about is Polly, she thought, a little sadly, regreting her own, so quickly ended, youth. He's so dressed up, he must be going to call on Polly. She was unprepared for his next remark.

"Cousin Frances, how old would you guess that baby is — or is it a child?"

She could not see the little child, squealing and gurgling. She was a happy thing. Poor child. Not yet had the bar sinister begun to cast its shadow upon her.

"The Flanneau baby?"

"That one. Having a bath."

She colored slightly. She guessed no one had told Dash just how he was related. "I don't have to guess," she said, with forced gaiety. "It was born in this house two years and — let me think — over two years and six months ago." He said nothing, and she went on. "I love having her here. When Dulcey goes to market, or Flanneau . . . I hate to say anything against him, he is such a superior man . . . but when he *drinks,* I take care of her."

"Dulcey?"

"That's Mrs. Flanneau."

"Aye."

He looked as solemn as an owl. This sudden solemnity made him appear very young. Frances longed to put her hand out, rumple his already rumpled dark hair, shake his cravat or take some other liberty, such as older female relatives take with handsome young men. She did none of them. Nor did she mention his doggy appearance or make any coy remarks about going courting. There was good reason why the Inman boys tolerated so easily their mother's "young friend."

"Aye, Dash," she said, repeating the word after him. "But I'll be like your mother and tell you to leave sea talk to sea. You'll be saying lay forward or belay to me next."

"Belay's right," he said, a little cryptically, and stepped off with his shoulders so handsomely tight and flat, head up, and that smart quick step of his.

Dash was not a man who gathers much gossip. Liz was. Liz hadn't been home two days before at least six people had told him about Peter and Mrs. Flanneau. Frances knew that Lucy, as unable to cope with Peter as Doctor Hobey himself, had wanted to tell Dash. Dash could make Peter do anything. But she and Liz had said, no, let him have these two weeks home in peace. Dash was a worrying man. It was time enough to bother him about the family scandal when he next came home.

❧ 7 ❧

As if he could not command his feet to go slowly, they got him to the Mompessons' front door before he had had time to collect his wits. What he had inadvertently discovered, and at exactly the wrong moment, had thrown him off his course. Now he had nothing by which to make new observations, no moon, sun, or stars. He couldn't throw out a sounding lead even, or go dead reckoning. He hadn't a chart. His quick feet had got him ahead of himself. He was coming in too fast, and in his ears rang the long low roar of surf.

Flip was there to take the hat and gloves he had not worn, and the malacca cane he had almost broken against a tree in a spasmodic moment of frustration.

"Captain," she whispered to him, casting one eye toward the parlor, afraid Mr. Mompesson might guess she was chatting with guests again, "has Dan Obrian been awfully busy?"

"Why, no. No, Flip. He's signed off, of course." Then he saw her sorrowful face and went back to kindly pad the truth. "No more than all of us *Victrix* officers. You know, honorary dinners almost every night and folk flocking in for miles to see the oddities we brought from Japan. And even just to see the ship. We've all been so busy we haven't had time to blow our noses."

Ah, well . . . it was like Danny. Now he was an officer and had struck a rich voyage, he'd be forgetting about servant girls — no matter how pretty.

"Miss Polly," she went on sadly, "used often to plan how when the ship came in you and he were to come courting together. You front door, and Danny back. But . . ."

Dash said honestly, "Success has gone to his head . . . a bit. Just wait a little and give him time, Flip."

"Yes, sir."

Then he was entering the parlor, bowing formally to the ladies and shaking hands with Squire Mompesson. This was not what he had expected. Polly — in his imagination — was to receive him herself and then usher him into the little back library where her father so often sat and leave him to have it out. Alone. He had not visualized a whole family conclave. The aunts, who in the old days had scarcely looked at him, he quickly gathered were now firmly on his side. He'd struck it rich.

They expressed their pleasure in him in odd ways. He wasn't even seated before Great-Aunt Birdseye was hoping that sometime he might procure for her an Indy shawl the color of a flea. But she said "flea" in French so as not to sound too vulgar, and pronounced the word so badly he couldn't make it out. "Pucey," she said. Aunt Brattle slapped the chair beside her with her fan, indicating that was where he was to sit. She asked him to mend her visual for her, and "La," she said, putting the now mended visual before her eyes, "you're a proper-looking young fellow, I do declare. As well as such a clever man of business. Understand you've put the House of Inman back on its feet. Your grandmother is an old friend of mine. Glad you boys are beginning to be some help to her."

So the aunts crowded in. He did not feel their espousal of his cause was helping him, but cutting him off from Polly.

Mr. Mompesson sat bolt upright on an uncomfortably straight chair. Usually he dominated any conversation. Tonight, after his first formal, correct greeting, he said absolutely nothing, but he watched Dash, entangled with the aunts, out of unreadable, china-blue, china-hard eyes.

Polly seemed a little brushed aside. She sat well away from them all, as though what might be going on between her father, Dash, and the aunts was of small concern to her. She was nothing but the prize. She smiled at him a little mockingly, as if to say, See the obstacles you must overcome even before you can approach me. I'm the princess in the old fairy tales. First the lover must climb a glass mountain, then cross a sea of fire, or a magic stream. Next, acres of brambles with thorns as long as swords, and blood-sucking flowers. He fights dragons and ogres. But it is all worth while because, after every obstacle is overcome, the unattainable princess is his. And they live happily ever after.

At this moment Dash felt too confused to scale any glass mountain or even fight the dragon, Mr. Mompesson, or free himself from the doting ogre-aunts. So Dulcey had had a child. And if Cousin Frances was right about the age, it was his child. Somehow, sometime, he thought, I want Polly to know. And before we are engaged. I don't want secrets from her. So he had no force left in him to overcome obstacles.

Aunt Brattle had been telling him all she could remember about his grandmother. She had been a very bright child at dame school, and so on. And once she had lost her pocket . . . he was hardly listening. Something about her hornbook. This must have been amusing, for both the old ladies cackled with mirth and Aunt Brattle was slapping him with her fan. This evening he discovered that Aunt Brattle always slapped her favorites with her fan. There must have been great coquetry in that — fifty years before.

"And now," Aunt Brattle was finishing her long tale, getting it up to, and through, the loss of the *Antelope,* and to the present, "you'll be staying at home all the time, and taking all the worries off your granddame's shoulders. I do declare, I never could understand Mercy Inman setting up as a she-merchant."

"Not quite yet, ma'am," Dash said. "I'm heading out to sea next week."

At last, Mr. Mompesson spoke. "Yes, I've heard that news on 'Change. I see the necessity. But Polly assures me this will be your last voyage. After that, you will be ready to retire?"

Dash glanced at Polly. He had never even suggested such a thing. The poor girl had been so anxious to assuage her father that she had said something not quite true.

"Whether . . . after marriage," he said softly, not wishing to upset Polly's fabrications, "a man continues at sea or not is a matter 'twixt him and his wife only."

Well, at last he had got somewhere. Those two words, marriage and wife.

There followed a vast silence. The rattle of Aunt Brattle's fan and the snap of Squire Mompesson's jeweled snuffbox. Dash saw clearly what the next obstacle was to be. The first had been money. He'd made that. Now it would be this retiring-from-the-sea business. He knew that Squire Mompesson looked upon the working captains as not quite settled, really not quite gentlemen. It was only when they became full-fledged merchants that he would consider them in a position to marry.

Damn them all, he thought. I'll retire when I'm ready. Good and ready. Mompesson isn't going to get me to promise anything. It's nobody's business but Polly's and mine. And she won't ask it. No girl who loves a man could ask it of him.

Mr. Mompesson, having sneezed twice and brushed the snuff

from his frills, said mildly: "Oh yes, yes. But it has seemed to me — sometimes our men, our seafaring men, are a little too unregardful of their wives. The long waiting, the never knowing, for a nervous, sensitive lady . . ." He broke off, but glanced thoughtfully at his precious daughter's averted face.

Aunt Brattle said nervously, for the silence was becoming appalling, "Polly, do play for us, dear."

"If you wish, ma'am." She obediently went to the piano and played as neatly and stupidly as a schoolgirl.

"When I was young and in my prime," she sang, squeezing every bit of sentiment she could out of her ditty, ridiculing the silly words as she sang them —

> "In gathering flowers I passed my time,
> In gathering flowers, red, white, and blue.
> I little knew what love could do,"

and she nodded at the aunts, suggesting they join her in the chorus of —

> "Fol de rol rol rol, fol de rol de ra."

The aunts' heads swayed with the rhythm and their hands tapped the tune, but neither sang. At their request she sang some more love-songs, and something about angels, but she sang without feeling. Dash wondered if anybody knew the latent passion in her. It did not come out in her music. She could not, like some young ladies in Salem, sit and caterwaul her heart out at the piano, releasing pent-up emotions on or off key. She couldn't yell out, for all of those who understood such primitive language, that she was a nubile girl in need of a mate. And he remembered the bugle-like calling of the young mare.

The aunts were beaming with pleasure. At least they had stopped any discussion of Captain Inman's retiring. They praised her skill to Dash as though to say, "See what an accomplished young lady." She sang again, this time something sadder and softer.

These minutes gave Dash time to think, but he could not think because he longed for her so. Not so much for the high-toned young lady singing just barely so-so and languishing a little into the fashionable, heart-sick posture. But for the dark-blooded, helpless, passionate girl hidden somewhere beneath all this decorum and pose — hidden from the sight of everyone except himself.

He glanced at Mr. Mompesson and thought, You don't know a thing about her. I can have your precious daughter any time and on any terms — in marriage, or outside of it. You can dress her up like an angel, and she sings songs about angels and looks like one — but she has clay feet. For me, at least, she has clay feet. And he thought exultantly of her clay feet and loved her for them.

Then he was saying how much he liked that last song.

"Peter wrote the verses," she said. "My Cousin Georgiana set the tune. Pretty, isn't it?"

"Very pretty."

Again the silence was so long that Aunt Birdseye remarked that an angel must be flying over the roof. And Aunt Brattle, doubtless remembering Polly's song, suggested that Polly fetch her herbarium. Seems Doctor Hobey had interested her in the gentle art of botany. She was so absorbed, dear child. Seemingly she hadn't done a thing except pick and press flowers all the three years Dash had been away. He had already heard about Fred Briscoe. It had never occurred to him that Polly would content herself with taking nature walks with Doctor Hobey, pressing flowers. Of course she had been out raising Hell — with her father's help.

It was a long time before Polly came downstairs. Then she looked about her, evidently interested in what might have happened in her absence. I guess I should have said something while she was out of the room, Dash thought. But it was too late now.

She listlessly dumped her herbarium in Dash's lap.

"But, come, dear, show your flowers to Captain Inman."

She obediently took the chair Aunt Brattle vacated for her, and made a small *moue* at him as if admitting she had no interest in dead flowers. Under the wide quarto their hands met and clasped.

"Robins' plantain, *Erigeron pulchellas,* jewelweed, *Impatiens pallida* . . ." Her spirits and her color began to rise and she was casting sidelong glances of amusement at him, drawing strength and confidence from his hand. She mocked the dead flowers, her aunts' determination to show her off, her own erudition. She shut the herbarium, shook her head, and was almost Aunt Brattle herself in a cushion-sized turban and a visual.

"Really, Captain Inman," she mocked, in a throaty voice, "did you ever see a more accomplished young lady? She can sing, dance, and play, she can press flowers and learn Latin names. Why, she made the dress she has on, and the nimble cake you are about to eat."

Flip was, at the moment, entering with a tray of refreshments.

"My dear *child!*" Aunt Brattle did not want to call her a liar before so desirable a suitor. Dash laughed.

But Mr. Mompesson was not amused. "Polly!" He reproved her with a gesture of his frilled hands.

"She can paint on glass," Polly went on, in spite of him; "at least I'm sure she could if she ever tried. She could make wax flowers — except the wax always melts . . ."

"Polly," her father broke in irritably, "you are talking nonsense!"

" . . . she writes little letters — which her papa always corrects for her. She knows everything a gentlewoman should know, and, what's more important, nothing she shouldn't." Her sidewise glance at Dash assured him that certain things he had taught her in their brief reckless moments of love-making were among the things no gentlewoman should know.

"Polly! Enough of this levity, miss." Her father spoke sternly, and she sobered.

But Dash was still laughing. He felt her and himself together now, mocking at the rest of the room. And under her breath she sang to him alone, "In gathering flowers I pass my time, my time. In gathering flowers red, white, and blue."

The refreshments were served. Tamarind water for the ladies and Mr. Mompesson, extremely good brandy for the guest, and a large light nimble cake for all. Someone had been to the confectioner's and bought pink sugar hearts to set in the cake's frosting. Doubtless one of the aunts. So this was supposed to be a celebration of his and Polly's engagement.

When they had eaten and the plates had been cleared away, Polly humbly reopened the quarto. The young couple looked at flowers and looked at flowers until they began to feel that they themselves had been picked long ago, put between blotting-papers, gummed to cardboards, and labeled in Latin.

The Iphigenia clock across the hall struck a soft ten o'clock. Aunt Brattle had gone to sleep, Aunt Birdseye was feeding pink sugar hearts off the nimble cake to her old poodle. Mr. Mompesson still sat erect and correct in his straight, uncomfortable chair. Polly sadly whispered to Dash, "Please go home now. Papa wants to go to bed."

Never had Dash spent a more uncomfortable evening, and now it was ending and he knew that Polly felt as frustrated as he himself. What should he have done? Told Mr. Mompesson he must speak to him privately? This would have been a discourtesy to the aunts. Spoken out before them all? He could not. And yet, if he hadn't seen what he had seen on his way over, hadn't known what he now knew, somehow he would have cleared his decks and moved into action.

Walking home through soft, cloudy moonlight, hitting his cane at trees as he walked, he realized that before he could take one step forward, he must learn from Peter what had happened. Perhaps when Polly knew everything, she would not wish him to go to her papa and get his assent. She might turn on him with loathing and send him packing. He wouldn't be surprised if she did. And as for Mompesson — if he knew about that child, never would he consent to his daughter's marriage. Polly was too nervous to have a husband still going to sea, was she — she'd certainly be much too nervous to cope with a scandal. He didn't see how he could give Mr. Mompesson this information about himself. It would be like handing an enemy a loaded pistol, then standing back and saying, "Blow my brains out."

One thing was sure. He wasn't going to take Polly's permission to talk to her father very seriously until he'd heard the truth from Peter. Then, too, this business of retiring from the sea. Not until he came back in January would he have to make up his mind about that. This next voyage looked to him now a little like a reprieve. He didn't have to face anything until he had been to Batavia again and back.

～8～

PETER, STILL AS A MOUSE on his high stool, next to old Fessenden on his high stool, worked on the customary routine papers. Now all Ma'am's creditors, who, only last week, had been snapping at her heels demanding ready cash, were asking to be allowed to extend their credit. They wished to have shares and ventures on *Fox Fire* and *Mermaid*, which were already loading *Victrix* sugar, spice, coffee, cottons, and silks for Europe. It was in the final sale of East Indy goods to Europe that the greatest profits were made. The American market could absorb only a portion of what her ships brought in these days.

He knew that in the inside office Dash sat at Ma'am's desk. Ma'am had not been coming in much this last week. She said it was because she had neglected her flower and herb garden, and this spring she was going to get everything in her back yard in apple-pie order. This was not the reason. She wanted Dash and Liz to have the illusion, at least, that they were top dogs, merchants. And that she had retired. It was an illusion only.

Peter knew something had gone wrong at the Mompessons' the night before. He had read it in Dash's sober eyes this morning at breakfast and in the slightly drawn mouth. He looked ever so little as he had during those months after he lost the *Antelope* and before he took out the *Victrix*. If only a few days before he had looked as though the world was his oyster, now it seemed that that oyster was tainted. Something wasn't sitting on his stomach real easy.

Not once had he held Peter spellbound, long after the others were laid abed, telling of the wonders of the world. Perhaps this time he had been gone so tarnation long he felt homesick no more for them. The nostalgia, the longing to be off, was absent. For a time, at least. So he had no need to talk with Peter.

At breakfast that morning he had caught Dash's eyes on him, staring at him, speculating on him. He had felt scared to death. "You and me, Peter," Dash had said softly, "have got to do some talking. Soon. Sometime today."

But as long as Fessenden sat beside him, Dash couldn't quiz him. He was thankful for this chaperonage. If only Dash could go one more week without asking questions!

Peter, in the brief course of his life, had already broken some secret eggs and made some odd omelettes. He had to. There was no other way he could protect his own identity from the weight of so many surrounding superiors. But he had no idea whether or not Dash would sit and eat one with him. The whole business was, as Flanneau had said, in his excellent English, "skulduggery." A thing like this might make Dash mad. He had never seen Dash angry, but he knew he carried anger inside of him, ready to use. He was like a man with a pistol. He may never pull it, but one is conscious of the bulge.

He could hear Dash moving a chest, rattling papers, stepping about a bit in the inner office. Then he appeared on the connecting threshold, not even looking at Peter.

"Mr. Fessenden," he said, "here are three papers I'd like Ma'am's signature on. And, 'long's it's eleven, step along to the Happy Sailor and treat yourself to grog. They'll chalk it up against the House." As easily as that did Dash rid himself of Peter's chaperon.

Fessenden gone, Dash pulled up his pantaloons and pulled down his waistcoat. He had a long clay pipe in his hands, and for a moment he bothered with it and his tinder box. It would not light, but it gave him something to toy with. Peter thought how often his mother reproved Dash for his fiddling. He'd fiddle with this, and fiddle with that. But only when he was upset inside. Probably on those long, strange voyages that he took he went month after month with serene and empty, quiet hands. Nothing to fiddle with — and often break.

The silence was so long that Peter, having no pipe to toy with, was the first to break it. Dash had confided in him that last night was the time he would settle with Mr. Mompesson.

"How'd it go?"

"It didn't go."

"Still not rich enough?" Peter grinned.

"No. But I see the quarter winds setting. Real smart blow, I guess. There's talk about my retiring — and there's going to be a lot more. Maybe I will. After January. No choice now."

"You talked it straight out with Squire?"

"No. No opportunity was made for me. Seems like I couldn't go ahead and make one for myself. Couldn't push."

"Mompesson isn't the sort you push."

"Yes, I could. With Polly on my side. Yes, I could. But there were too many aunts and pressed flowers and nimble cakes. And in the bare spots in the conversation — there were a lot of them — I got to thinking. Peter, what . . . exactly what happened in Marblehead after I was gone?"

Peter studied the invoice in his hands, but his ears grew crimson.

"Nothing much," he muttered.

"She had a child?"

"Yes, she did."

"Well," Dash said reasonably, "why didn't she show my letter to the selectmen? Bring charges against me? I did it."

"I kept thinking and thinking of Polly . . . and you, too," Peter blurted out. "If that letter ever came to court, Mompesson would never think you suitable for his daughter. What's more, *she* wouldn't either."

"So you told Dulcey not to show it?"

"Yes."

"It was good and kind of her, of Dulcey." He worked on his pipe for a while, for at last he had it going, going beautifully. "And it is true that if she had demanded it of me, brought in those charges, I'd have felt that I had to marry her. It isn't as if I were mixed up with a trollop."

"But you don't love her."

"No. And now I can't ever remember what I felt toward her. But I do recollect how I couldn't cope with Polly. She was a gadfly to me and yet I loved her. Sleeping or waking, all the time I did, and do, love Polly."

"I knew that."

"Why did Dulcey marry that Flanneau? Fell in love with him, or scared I'd squeak out somehow? Leave her holding the baby? Scared into it, was she?"

"I fixed it up, Dash." And he added, with a belligerent lift of the chin, an unconscious parody of Dash, "And it was I who scared her."

"Told her I wouldn't marry her?"

"Over and over, I told her."

"There's no one I want less to marry, and that includes Aunt Brattle and Aunt Birdseye. But it doesn't hurt a man to do what he ought, sometimes. Not always what he wants."

"That's all right for you, Dash. No matter how you came to loathe her, you could always think what a fine upstanding fellow you were. Making your bed and lying on it — fine things like that. But what of Polly? If you jilted her, I think she'd fold up and die. Or, what's worse, go crazy. Can't you imagine Polly going crazy — like Ophelia?"

"That's jewelweed," Dash said, dreamily. "That's for remembrance. Here's pressed robins' plantain — that's for thoughts."

"Don't be quite so funny." Peter did not feel afraid of Dash any more, now that at last they were talking straight out. That bulge in him, the hidden pistol, the bombshell of anger, was lessening. "You courted Polly for four years. There isn't anything, anything real, in her whole life but you."

Dash was still trying to recall lines from Hamlet. "'I'd have brought seaweed,'" he went on, "'but it withered the day my father died.' No. Now I've forgotten. Mind, Pete, I want to take Shakespeare with me next voyage again. Put that down on your slate." Peter did so. "Go on. You persuaded Dulcey that a bird in hand is better than in the bush? Married her to Flanneau?"

"It is more mixed up than that. It is very mixed up."

"How so? For instance?"

"She never did marry him."

"What?"

"I was almost out of my head, Dash, and so was she. My God, Dash, I offered to marry her myself! She wouldn't hear of it. Because she hung on to the idea that you might. So I fixed it with Flanneau. For five hundred dollars, he took her in, said she was his wife. Yet it's one of those marriages — in name only sort of thing. She did agree to that."

Dash walked about restlessly.

"So," Peter went on, "if you still feel you have to marry her — even if it kills Polly — you can."

"They call each other man and wife?"

"Yes."

"And he admitted the child?"

"Absolutely."

"I can't marry her," Dash said slowly.

"I'm glad you feel that way about it." Peter relaxed with relief. Dash was going to sit humbly and eat that odd omelette Peter had cooked up.

"I can't marry her for the good and final reason that she is married already. And that's that."

"No. That's the point of the whole thing. You've missed the point, Dash."

"Flanneau's a Frenchman. He doesn't know common law. Dulcey doesn't know anything . . . but Peter, you didn't think. Did you?"

"What?"

"If a man and woman live together that long and say they are man and wife publicly, by common law they are. And if he admits the child, legally it is his child."

Never in his most optimistic moments had Peter dreamed of a solution so simple and final. He had steeled himself to Dash's rushing off, doing the honorable thing — let the heavens fall — no matter whom they landed on. Now Dash wouldn't and couldn't, legally, marry Dulcey. And Petra was Flanneau's child. No. For as long as Peter could pay five hundred a year, Flanneau, as well as all the world, would admit that she was Peter's.

But Peter had been so screwed up to resist Dash's anger that now that there was none, he felt slightly let down. Like a man who has studied Revelation so long, he thinks on a certain day the world will end. The day comes. The world does not end. That's fine. But he feels let down.

He had to go on talking to Dash, explaining more and more details of the transaction. Dash caught at the five hundred dollars.

"That's why you didn't go to Harvard."

"That's why."

"From now on, you can have all the money you can spend. You can go to Harvard from now on to the end of your life. If that's what you want."

"And, as for you," Peter said, "there isn't a reason in the world why you and Polly can't marry."

Dash tipped back in his chair. He said slowly: "That retirement thing I can . . . well, I can do as I please about. Polly will take it, and he'll have to, I guess. But this other business. Peter, sometime it will catch up with me. I'd rather she knew before, than after, marriage. Then, too, I don't want an ordinary, lying marriage. Nor she either. I don't want a secret from her. Ever."

"Don't think to tell Polly!"

"I'm going to be square with her."

"How square with you is she? She and her Fred Briscoes!"

"Perfectly square. It's an unfortunate mannerism, that's all." He firmly put down the paper weight he was monkeying with.

"But this matter of my retiring," Dash went on. "Mompesson almost said no engagement to a working captain. So I don't have to take a decided step until January, and, God willing, I'm back again from Batavia."

Peter said sadly: "Somebody's got to tell Flanneau and Dulcey that they have been getting married . . . by inches. I guess Flanneau will be pleased. He's daft over the child. He loves Dulcey, and she works for nothing."

"She doesn't love him?"

"No."

"Well, if money will sweeten the situation . . ."

"Oh, forget money. No. But I can hardly bear to tell her."

"All right, I will."

But suppose, Peter thought, that Dash and Dulcey meet again and "this thing" flares up again. "No, let me," he muttered. "I'm your clerk. And for one thing . . ."

"What, for one thing?"

Peter had been on the point of saying Flanneau, and everybody else, thinks Petra's *my* mistake. He went on lamely, "I can handle it better than you. Trust me."

"I'd like a little time to think things out. I don't mind any I'm to be gone for a while," Dash admitted. "At sea you have time enough to think."

At sea? Peter had a realization that at sea a man may think of the biggest things, of eternity brooding on the vast lonely waters, of space going on beyond the farthest star. Of God, and of man's fate. Or of the daily minutiae. Sails set to best advantage. Must pick up some onions before the people have scurvy. Is Goa open to neutral shipping? And that far-off topsail — is it attached to a friendly or a hostile craft? Will the pleasant breeze continue to follow? A seaman might think at one end of the gamut, or at the other, and never give much mind to all that lay in between. As, for instance, to what was he to do, what ought he to do, when he got back to Salem?

Peter sat alone with mixed feelings. Maybe he had saved Polly, and Dash, too. But he certainly, and inadvertently, had tricked Dulcey.

FLANNEAU WAS NOT by nature a noisy Frenchman. Now he was noisy, and Peter was thankful that his excitement had upset his English to such an extent that Cousin Frances couldn't understand him, even if she was upstairs.

Flanneau would not believe that Peter had been so ignorant of the laws of his own country. He swore he would engage a lawyer. Surely a marriage so easily come by would be as easily dissolved. His voice rose to a scream. Peter knew he was only pretending. He didn't want to lose Dulcey, whom he loved in a perverted, queer, sometimes cruel way. Nor the child he was so besotted over. Yet he held one trump card, and now, smartly, through his crocodile tears, he was playing it.

"I shall now leave Salem. I and my wife and child. We leave Salem. I shall return to my own land. I shall not be a figure of scorn for these yokels here. For you I have worn the horns and it shames me. Inside I am honorable — I accept the terms under which I have lain down. But you have tricked me . . . now I go away. To start once more."

"But Flanneau," Dulcey said quietly, "Peter didn't know."

"Didn't know, hah! Didn't know, heh! I do not care. But I shall go where no man shall look down upon me. No man shall say my wife is mistress to *that* . . . young gentleman . . ."

He looked at Peter out of his hot little red-rimmed eyes. For the first time Peter wondered if Flanneau was really as fond of him as he always pretended to be. They say, he thought, truth comes out in anger. But does it in pretended anger? Peter tried to control his face. He must hide the fear he felt of losing, not his mistress, but his child.

"You've done real well here, Flanneau," he said.

"It is shame. Not to be borne."

"And anyway," Dulcey put in flatly, "if you do go to France, or I don't care where, *I* won't go."

"Very well, ma'am. Very good. But the child goes with me. It is the law of every land. The child goes with me. You hear me, Mr. Peter?"

"Hear you! For God's sake, don't yell so. They can hear you down to the wharves."

Peter had not once been able to look Dulcey in the face. It was she — not Flanneau — he felt he had betrayed. Here she was, tied forever to a man she had not chosen, did not love, and who often exasperated even her easy temperament to tears and reproaches. And she had not once doubted that Peter told the truth. She was sitting by the window, her hand shading her face. Poor girl. The bent head, the silence, suggested a sad acceptance, as if she knew instinctively that nothing went right in this world, especially for poor girls. You build your sand castles and the next tide carries them away. No matter what you try to do, you are always trapped at the end.

When Peter took his leave, Dulcey followed him to the door. She did not look especially cast-down now.

"When is Dash coming home next?" she asked.

"January. So he says."

"I guess I'm so fixed I can't ever marry him."

"No. Never."

"But he'll come over to see me sometimes?"

"No. I'm sorry . . . I don't believe he ever will."

"He might," she suggested, and smiled her broad, easy, curly smile.

"You tend shop — you must have heard. He's going to marry. Someone else."

"Oh yes, I've heard about that. But what hasn't happened mightn't happen. Miss Mompesson is always real nice when she comes in. But will you tell Dash I'd like to see him sometime?"

She believed in herself and her power over Dash so much, she ended up with making Peter almost believe in it, too. He muttered something polite, but he would certainly have to get that idea out of her head before Dash was back again. Then he remembered how, no matter what, he had never been able to get the idea shaken out of her that Dash might marry her.

Now she had something else in mind. Dulcey was a real good, biddable girl — but only for just so far. And when she was sot and stubborn, nothing made the least impression upon her.

Chapter Seven

D ASH BROKE BY THREE WEEKS the previous record from Batavia
to an American port. It had not taken even the eight months he
had promised Polly. This fact might charm the waterfront — it
meant nothing to his mother. The black and gold lacquer box, the
silk inside, did. It was not often these two sat thus, confidentially
and alone. Dash knew what he liked, but had been so often told
his taste was unfashionable that he decided to show his mother the
silk he had brought home from Bombay for Polly's wedding gown
before he gave it to her. A smart, bright, smelly fire burned on the
hearth before them.

"Did you select this *yourself*, Dash? Didn't some lady help you?
I've never seen silk spun so fine. And usually you bring home
dreadful things."

"Is it right for Polly?"

"Nothing could suit her better. It's for her wedding?"

"That's my idea."

"You know she and her father are now in New York. But they
have promised to be back in time for my ball tomorrow night."
And she went on generously, wishing she could like Dash's girl
better: "It wouldn't seem like a ball in Salem without Polly Mompesson. She is beautiful, Dash. I think she is the most beautiful
woman I've ever seen."

"Aye," he agreed, but his expressive eyes warmed and thanked
his mother. She had said something nice about Polly, and from
her heart.

"Tom and Miranda are to marry next week. And I suppose you and Polly will be next. I'm having Miranda receive with me. Her parents aren't coming, thank Heavens. They are very strict, old-fashioned people. I wish I could have Polly, too. But of course her father and aunts will wish to do the announcing. Now let me tell you, dear, about my ball."

This she did. It had started out as a housewarming only. For at last the house was complete — inside and out. Had Dash noticed the new fences, gates, new front portico, cupola? Had he crossed the hall to see the finished double parlors? Of course he had not. He had not even as yet been upstairs. And they heard the heavy feet of porters coming through the hall carrying his gear to his own room.

"The old barn is gone, thank Heavens. You must see the new stable and coach-house. This is the old one we are burning now. It gives the whole house a barnyard smell, but even if you did make a fortune, I can't imagine wasting good firewood merely because it smells. Dash, throw on a sliver of sandalwood."

He went to the cupboard, took out an eight-inch little stick and laid it on the fire.

"I've used the silver papers with waves on them Liz picked up in Japan for the double parlors. I thought of putting new papers on the hall. You know how your Cousin Frances and I patched and labored and used three different designs for the hall? But Frances said, Don't change it. She thought all of you liked to think of old Ben Franklin there under the stairs, sneaking off to a grotto full of naked nymphs. So I left that."

The barnyard smell of New England had fought its losing fight against the sandalwood of the South Seas. It was always so, Dash thought. Only a sliver of sandalwood and the whole room smelled like the Far East. He had long since stopped really listening to his mother. It was one of the things about him that most irritated her.

"Liz told me if I ever change those hall papers, he'll move out and never come home again. Where's Liz?"

"Out in the kitchen. He's getting Linda to shrink his pantaloons for him. He'll cut a handsome figure for you at your ball."

"And I suppose soon he'll be wanting to marry, too. First I lose Tom and then you. Liz will be next." Mrs. Inman had never made any bones about the fact that Liz and whomever he married were to live here with her. Let all the rest of them scatter. "But Tom hasn't decided exactly where he and Mr. Fields will set up their knitting mill, or whatever it is. Something that makes cloth by power. Like the English. Until then, he and Miranda will live with me. Of course," she added, with transparent hypocrisy, "it will be *lovely* having Miranda here with me. Even if Tom has to be in Pawtucket or somewhere."

Liz walked in from the kitchen with Little Joe at his heels. He had on a Russian dressing-gown, fur-trimmed. Over his arm he carried his chamois pantaloons.

"Dad blast Linda," he said. "Mr. Africanus came in and took what mind she has off her work. She's shrunk my pants so tight I'll need boothooks and a shoehorn to get into 'em." He kept on walking, utterly absorbed in his own elegant problems.

Little Joe stopped to sneer at Dash, pattered into the hall, and began barking fiercely and meanly at Robin, the *Victrix's* calico cat, still in her basket. He wouldn't dare if she were loose.

Lucy's heart had sunk when she saw a porter carrying a basket. She was sure Dash was bringing home a monkey again. He had always been bringing home monkeys. He liked them. His mother did not. No sooner was he at sea again than Dash's monkeys began to fail and soon died.

Linda came in on Liz's heels. Her pale, frightened eyes went to her loved mistress's face, as if only from her did she gather strength enough to speak.

"Yes, Linda? Tell me, child, what you want."

"Ma'am, Mr. Africanus would like the honor of a word."

"Dash, do see what the old man wants."

"Ma'am, it has to be you. In person."

"Oh, well, then . . ."

Mr. Africanus looked even more enormous in a room than on the street. He emerged slowly, frowning thoughtfully. He knew Dash was home and that he was sitting in this room. He smelled the pipe. Mr. Liz smoked cigars. Neither Tom nor Peter anything. Besides, he "felt" Dash. He always did. Official business, however, came first.

"Mrs. Inman, on account this is the nineteenth day of January, eighteen hundred and four, permit me to congratulate you on your fifty-third birthday."

"Oh," she laughed. "I'd forgotten. Dear knows I wanted to forget. I can't believe I'm fifty-three. Am I fifty-three?"

"Yes, ma'am. I totted it up in my head."

"Lordy! Time flies! Give him a penny, Dash. Mr. Africanus, if you'll tot it wrong — I mean knock off a year every January nineteenth instead of adding one — from now and forever, you shall have two pennies."

"No, ma'am. I can't. It has to be just exactly right."

Dash said, as he gave the penny and shook hands, "Mr. Africanus, will you be here ten minutes longer?"

"Yes, sir, Captain Dash. Miss Linda is agoing to clean my boots for me and press my neckcloth."

When he was gone, Dash interrupted his mother's complaints that the old fellow might just as well leave the Charity House — move in here, he was around so much — by saying, "There's someone I'd like you to invite."

His mother lifted her arching eyebrows. She knew it would be somebody dreadful. And it was.

"I want my mate — Dan Obrian."

"Not, I trust, one of the *Salem* Obrians?"

"Who else?"

"I know a tipsy old woman who pushes a barrow and buys bottles and rags. Raggity-Meg, the children call her. She blows a tin horn."

"That's the family."

"Her grandson?"

"Worse. She's my mate's mother. I doubt she's older than you, but she's had a different sort of life. And as for peddling — Mr. Mompesson is always throwing it up against us it wasn't long ago Inmans peddled the fish they took."

"But why on earth do you want him?"

"Dan's a fine, smart officer, when it comes to handling a ship and men. But you know how we Yankees trade, Mother. We're not like the British. They have ambassadors and agents and consuls and commission houses and ministers and things like that everywhere. Their captains work through them. But a Yankee captain has to do all that for himself. Dan's got all the seamanship to go as a master, but he's not up to his land duties. He was for three years my second. These last eight months, my first. He can't be a master for us until he learns deportment. So he can talk to the head of any government in the world and be listened to. From Napoleon down to cannibal kings."

"You are seriously suggesting you want him to learn on girls like Polly, Miranda? Your own sisters?"

"I think if he was invited here, right in Salem, he might get interested in improving himself. He's a monstrous big, handsome fellow. All he needs is a little spit and polish."

She tapped her ringed fingers. All this newcome, welcome wealth was due to Dash. "Is he married?"

"No."

"A party can always swallow a queer man or two, provided he isn't pushing or noisy."

"He'll be too scared. He'll be terribly scared."

"I'll write him a note for Africanus to carry. Is that your idea?"

"Yes."

She was still sitting at her writing-desk, idly tapping her teeth with the quill of her pen, when Dash came back from the kitchen.

"Thank you, Mother."

She felt his gratitude, and now that she had just done him a handsome favor felt closer to him than usual. Sometime she had to tell him about Peter. She knew it was already agreed that Liz was to take out the *Victrix* next. Dash would be at home for some months. Marry Polly and perhaps be home forever. If Dash couldn't manage Peter, no one could. Now there was no hostility between her and her oldest son. Now was the time.

"Dash," she said slowly, "one more thing about my ball."

"Yes, mother?"

"Some people . . . some people in Salem are very critical of Peter. I mean, girls won't dance with him. Their mothers tell them not to. Things like that."

"Peter!"

'You're the oldest son. I suppose, head of the family."

"Why didn't he go to Harvard?"

She flushed uncomfortably. "I'm afraid he was too . . . too *concerned* with a woman. I've *tried* to talk with him. I can't — it's like trying to argue with a *feather* bed. You sink in and get *no*-where."

"He's not too young to marry. He's twenty-one. What if he hasn't any money to speak of? We as a family have a plenty."

"The woman's married."

"Good God!"

"Don't swear, dear. I mean, off a ship — at home."

"I can't imagine *Pete* mixed up with a married lady. Why doesn't her husband get after him with a little birdshot?" The very idea of Peter in such a position amused him and he laughed. "But I guess the husband needn't worry too much. I'll bet all Peter wants to do is write his lady a few poems. Oh, he'll get over it. Don't you fret. Leave him alone."

"Dash, it's so much worse than anything you can imagine. It's not a question of *poems*. Oh, he has a child already. And I can't stand it. And he doesn't make any *bones*, Dash. 'Sephus Hobey says that's one of the worst things about it. Peter doesn't make any *bones*. He says that's proof of moral depravity."

"But the husband . . . surely . . ."

"I'll have to begin at the beginning. It's been going on for four years. I decided not to bother you when you were home last time, dear, but now I'm going to. Well . . ." She sighed wearily. "A long time ago, when he was seventeen or eighteen, he fell into the clutches of a Marblehead girl. You know the sort, bouncing and bounding. You know how they stand about the fish market, straddle-legged . . . Dash, *don't play with those candle snuffers!* You'll break them. Are you listening to me?"

"Yes, Mother."

"He got her in the family way. But at least he had sense enough not to marry her. Anyway, he found a Frenchman who would. That man is real smart. Not only does he make clothes and sell goods here in Salem, but he goes off in a hired rig and sells inland. He's gone a lot. That makes it easy for Peter."

"How?"

"Oh, Dash! Don't you see? It isn't just one slip on poor Peter's part. This thing is going on now. Today. Peter *pays* the husband money — people say five hundred a year, but I think that's a lot of money to pay for Mrs. Flanneau. Well, he *pays* the husband for his . . . acquiescence, I think the word is. It's a most dreadful scandal, and, as I was saying, people snub him, and I don't blame them, especially the girls' mothers. Peter has made himself very *persona non grata*. It has got to stop. It's worrying me to death. Dash, don't go fingering that silk gauze. Your hands are so chapped . . . I'll give you some of my quince lotion."

Lucy had never known how morally, or immorally, her boys behaved, once out of Salem, beyond the shadow of the white New England church spire. Dash was looking straight at her. His face had suddenly grown thin. The muscles about the mouth stood out in unattractive lumps. The eyes, in spite of all the narrowing the sea had done to them through the years, were as wide-open as a child's. Certainly he must always have been a decent, well-behaved fellow, he looked so shocked. Shocked! He looked as though someone had hit him a body blow.

"Well, dear," she went on, "I'm sorry to have so upset you, and this your first day home. But you will use your influence with Peter? He will always do anything you say, and nothing for me or Liz. You'll talk to him?"

"As God lives," Dash exclaimed through clenched teeth and his right fist crashed into the hard palm of his left hand, "I'll talk to him! That damned Peter Inman! That damned fool of a Peter Inman!"

Red surged up over his jawbones, stayed there. Then very slowly the color moved up over his whole face and flamed under his eyes. His usual pleasant, light brown eyes — without a trace of hazel in them — had turned to molten metal. They hardly seemed like human eyes, but those of an avenging god. She felt literally, almost physically, afraid of him.

"Oh, *Ralph*," she said nervously, "I don't want you to take it *too* hard. Don't be so angry with Peter. He's very young and he simply *adores* you. Perhaps it is not entirely his fault."

"My God, no! No, it is not!"

"There, dear, please *sit down*. You upset me so, towering around in such a temper. Mercy, Dash, can't you relax a little? You look like an avalanche, or a tidal wave, or something too dreadful to have in the house with one. Don't you *dare* to tower — except at sea, of course. That's a good boy. Please fan me a little. I feel faint."

Whether or not she felt faint, she had made it impossible for him to tower and glare. Neither is possible for a man with a fan in his hand, fanning a mother who feels faint.

She went on quickly: "I'll say this for Squire Mompesson. He lets Peter call on Polly. Not like some of Salem's parents. But you know, admiring her is just the same as admiring him. He is a vain little man. So any man, roués — that's what people call Peter, Dash — and cripples, morally and physically and financially — or married men or old men — anything in pantaloons may come and admire, so long as they don't get too near her."

Dash said, "Mother, has Peter said flat out the child is his?"

"Practically, yes. And they named her Petra, for him. Isn't that shameless? Peter is so crazy about her. But why did she have to look just like all of you at the same age? I mean red cheeks and white skin and so bright and *active*. And she has a mop of the same sort of absolutely uncombable black curls." She thought a moment, and suddenly her emotion overcame her. "I used to be so proud of my babies" — she whimpered and sniffed. "Everybody said they were the pre . . . pret . . . prettiest babies in Salem." Lucy burst into tears, not the slow tears suitable to a fifty-third birthday, but loud sobs like Marcy's.

"I don't care," she stormed, "I don't care if you do wrong. I don't care if you have cann . . . cannibal children — in the proper place. But here in Salem! Right around the corner from this house! Everybody is talking about it. And daring to feel sorry for me. And Jack West says Peter simply hasn't the physical strength for what I think he called a liaison. He's never been robust. That dreadful woman will kill him."

"Everybody says it, Mother?"

"Why shouldn't they? Flanneau does — when he's drunk. He can't have children of his own. Ma'am's the only person who says it isn't so. She won't let anyone *mention* it to her. But you know she's so partial to Peter she would not believe it if he cut her own *throat*. Now, Dash — don't say anything to Peter until after the ball. Then you will, won't you? I can't tell you what a comfort it is to me that you are taking this so seriously. Liz is worse than nobody to me. He says everybody in Russia and France and Asia have mistresses. And what of it — as long as Mr. Franneau and Mrs. and Peter are all happy. Dash, I'm awfully afraid Liz thinks it is a *joke*. I see you don't."

"No, it's no joke. I swear I'll put some wind in Peter's sails for him!"

Now she was mopping up her face. She looked at Dash gratefully. For the first time Dash had proved more of a comfort to her than Liz. "Dash, when you get through talking to Peter — and don't be too hard on him, he's still very young — I wish you'd talk to Liz."

"Who's going to talk to Liz?" He came in, dressed in his chamois pantaloons. "I'm trying on my ball clothes," he announced. "Look at this waistcoat, Dash. *Victrix* silk. I paid Flanneau more for a piece of it, enough to make a waistcoat, than we paid for a bolt of it in Batavia. It was nonsense letting Peter have the whole lot for his two-hundred-dollar venture. Flanneau got it and is clearing a hundred per cent profit."

"Liz," his mother said, "you are not going to wear that waistcoat tomorrow night. I won't have it. Advertising the family shame. Dash, I haven't got around to telling you, but that silk — and Flanneau sells it everywhere as *Victrix* silk — was what came back on Peter's two-hundred-dollar venture. And he gave it to that man to pay for . . . to pay . . . you know, so he can go on . . . carrying on with his wife." She burst again into tears.

Liz went to her kindly, for hidden in cracks and crannies and sometimes hard to find there was a kindness in Liz. "Mother, when there's a family scandal, it's the family itself who decides how bad it is to be. If we act as though we don't care, why, nobody else is going to care . . . much. But Dash, don't you think it's funny? Why, it's the funniest thing that has happened in Salem since they hung the witches."

Dash was carefully and a little clumsily, for he was conscious of his chapped hands, folding the silk gauze from Bombay, putting it back in the lacquer box. Liz was actually making his mother laugh, even as she wiped her eyes. So Dash left them and went upstairs.

He went to his own bedroom and closed the door. This was the first moment since his return that he had been alone. The situation seemed incredible to him and yet obvious. He sat on his bed with his tired, aching head in his hands. Only his little old grandmother had been bright enough to realize that there were certain things Peter did do and certain things he did not. She knew this — no, she really only felt it. For with people you love, what you feel is often truer than what you know.

Not until after the ball. Mother's right about that. I won't do a thing until after the ball. And I haven't seen Polly yet. When I tell her, I guess that will end everything. I guess I'll leave Salem.

I'll set up as an agent — Bombay, St. Petersburg, anywhere. I'll tell her, and then I'll go. But I'm going to dance with her one night through. And then . . . that will be all. Polly . . . my girl. His desire for her was so great, he turned and clasped the pillow on his bed, stifling the cry of her name on his lips. He'd lose her now — and for ever. But he certainly couldn't let Peter be harmed because of anything he himself had done. "Upon my head be it," he whispered with twisted, savage lips, and struck at the pillow which only the moment before had been his dear love in his aching arms.

He had been ashore so briefly he still could feel the toss and surge of the ship beneath him, that living pulse of the sea beating through him, filling him with its own unending life — lifting him and carrying him. But it gave him a slight sense of nausea. He was more apt to be "landsick" the first day or so ashore than seasick when first aboard a ship. His mouth felt dry and harsh. He went to his ewer, but there was no water. He opened the door to cross the hall to Liz's and Peter's room. He stood a moment in the upper hall. His strong-set body remembered the rhythms of the sea and rocked him a little to and fro. His mother must have told Liz to cast on another sliver of sandalwood. Why, it filled the house with its incense!

There were islands in the Pacific where simple-minded natives burned sandalwood to light their pots. Sometimes coasting by such an island — and say the night is dark and there is phosphorescence in the wake and the strange stars of the South Pole are like unshed tears in the sky — sometimes there comes, soft, soft, through the night, the enchanting fragrance of sandalwood. There is the sky, the sea, the ship, the night, the fragrance. That is all, and perhaps that is enough.

～2～

WHEN DANNY SAW Mr. Africanus sounding his way down Daniel's Lane into Puddle Alley, the morning sun glittering on his famous boots, he thought there must have been a hitch over at the wharf and that Dash or Ma'am had sent for him. He steppped out of the lopsided old house where he lived, when ashore, with his mother and her assortment of roomers. So he stood, hatless and anxious, in the snowy street.

Danny was the only child of Raggity-Meg to outlive infancy. He was, as his captain said, monstrous handsome and very large. He was also very blond. As was right for a man of his size, his face was large and the features a little coarse and rough-hewn, his nose like the prow of a ship, his very blue eyes narrow and a little calculating. Many an old Salem family had produced their black sheep. It was even being said the Inmans had, in young Peter. But it was rare for as squalid a flock as the Obrians to toss off anything as magnificent as Danny. His father may have helped. Who his father was he did not know. All he had was his mother's name.

He was never glad to be home again. In other ports he could escape from shame. In Salem the only way he could do that was by sensational success. Let him only captain a great ship. But Dash had told him straight out that he could not even yet advance to master. He wasn't good enough in dealing with people ashore. And he was too prone to make fists at the men. He yelled too much. Dash wasn't going to have a yelling captain on any Inman ship. Yet he promised to help him. Danny had seen Dash's urbanity with damn foreigners succeed where he knew his own blustering would have got him nowhere. So he knew Dash was right, but he was too lazy to want to bother to learn.

Dash would put him ahead just as fast as he was good enough. And Old Lady Inman, too. What little time he had had ashore between the *Victrix's* first and second voyages he had spent hanging about the Inman Wharf, boasting to all the sightseers who came to view the ship which had been to Japan. The way he stuck out his great chest and strutted, you'd have thought he had been the captain, not just a "sailor's waiter," as they called a second mate. Little had his widowed mother seen of her handsome son. It was Ma'am Inman who had told him that now he was so well started on the quarterdeck, he must have new clothes. And a different haircut. He was to get one of those blue broadcloth coats with brass or silver buttons. Give up his sloppy sailor pants, checked shirts and kerchiefs. His mother had laughed at him for thus aping his betters. She had shrieked over his new haircut. She thought all sailors should wear pigtails and put tar on them.

Mr. Africanus's delicate nose trembled with aversion at the vulgar smells of Puddle Alley. He stood in doubt — not quite sure in which of these wretched, overcrowded tenements lived Mate Obrian.

"Hey, black man," Danny bawled at him, "looking for me? I'm Dan Obrian."

"Yes, sir, Mate Obrian." He handed the delicate note to him. Dan turned it in his big rough hands. "I don't guess it is for me."

"You're Mate Obrian, Puddle Alley. That's a most genteel invitation I've got you."

It was the sort of alley which easily assembles crowds. Three children with hands and noses purple with the cold, a woman carrying a basket of wash, the rheumatic old seaman who usually sat in his daughter-in-law's front window and watched the goings-on, but could hobble out fast enough at the smell of excitement. The woman who made gingerbread elephants and who now had a little time between batches to step out, get fresh air, and see the world. The night hostler from the Star, just coming home to sleep the rest of the day. Three fancy girls who also looked upon daytime as a period of pleasure and relaxation. In this mean crowd Danny stood tall, blond, clean, and deadly serious.

"Read it to us, Danny," one of the girls suggested.

> Mrs. James Inman requests the honor of Mr. Obrian's company at a ball Thursday evening at seven o'clock, the twentieth of January, 1804. R.S.V.P.

"What's that R.S.V.P. in the corner mean, Africanus, heh?" He had not the least idea of going. Everyone in Salem knew the Inman house. Dan couldn't imagine himself inside it. But sometime, he thought, I'll have a wife and we'll be rich and I want her to send out little notes just like this.

The Negro knew that it was always "trash" like this who called him "black man" or merely "Africanus," but he answered kindly. "It's just a hint that the lady of the house wants to know who's coming and who's not. Port towns like this sometimes can't scare up enough young gentlemen for all the young ladies. The last moment the lady of the house has to hunt around fast."

"She must have been finding herself pretty short of gents."

"Maybe. But you only got in early this morning, like Captain Dash. It was he himself said his mother had to ask you."

"Aren't you going, Danny?" one of the fancy girls asked, leaning heavily on his broad shoulder, playing with the buttons on his blue coat. He had every reason to be grateful to Mary Bull. When he was hard up, she never charged him anything. But he shook her off.

"Sure, I'm going. Wait a second, Africanus. What do I do next? Do I send something back?"

"You go to the Widow Pretty's Stationery, on Essex Street."

"Yes?"

"You buy superfine notepaper. It comes by the quire. And sealing wax." Then he told him what to write. Mrs. Pretty would lend him a pen and show him how to fold and seal his note.

"I've got that."

"Then you send your note. You don't carry it yourself."

His mother had come unsteadily up the street. She did not give a word of greeting to her son whom she had not seen since his return. "The handsome sailor," she sneered, "handsome sailor." If not exactly drunk, she was at least far from sober.

"Lemme take the note for you," said Mary Bull, known professionally as "Molly the Heifer."

"Me! Me!" cried the children.

"I'll carry it for you, Danny," his mother said when it had been explained to her what the excitement at her front door was about. She grabbed the invitation out of his hand.

"God blast you!" Danny got his note back. "Get out, all of you. Africanus, come along. You're going to carry it for me."

He headed for Essex Street, escorted by two fancy girls, three children, and his mother, all hanging on him and jubilant over the social honor done to a Puddle Alley boy. Mr. Africanus followed a long way behind. He did not like the company.

Dan himself moved forward in a dream. He was glad now Old Lady Inman had told him to get new clothes; glad he had cut off his tarred pigtail. He saw dirty weather and high seas ahead, but, like the brave fellow he was, he had no idea of avoiding them. He was going to carry full sail, and, by Jesus, go whipping right over the reefs. I'll get to the top of the Salem crust, he thought. But first, he'd clear his own decks. As he, his mother, and his escort approached the very genteel sign of the lady stationer, he turned angrily on his admirers, shaking his head like a tormented bull.

His narrow blue eyes gave off cold sparks and his great yellow-furred hands clenched.

"You get off this decent street. You get off my deck and you stay off. Go back to your stews and your filth — you low-down scum. I'm going ahead, and I'm going it alone."

~ 3 ~

Mrs. Inman stood up to receive with her two daughters and Miranda Fields. If she added four sons and a son-in-law, she felt it would make the line too long. Then, too, she wanted her boys to circulate — keep her party from stagnating before it had begun. She knew that certain Federalists were chilled at the sight of certain Republicans. For three years now the feeling between the two parties had been so strong they were rarely asked to the same occasion. She, as a woman and supposedly innocent of politics, dared do what no man in Salem would have dared. Then, too, quite recently, only since he had come back from France, Liz had gone over to the Republicans. And where was he now? He must keep an eye on his fellow Republicans and their ladies. They were in the minority.

Miranda stood beside her. She was a little girl with a big head, long-bodied and short-legged. There was nothing of the panther in her stride and something of the duck, but, although a man may love a woman for her feline grace, he does not keep from loving her for a slight waddle. The girl had fair hair of such infantile softness the pink skin of the skull showed through. In temperament she was cheerful, even to the unpleasant extent that is called "sunny." Yet, like many another person determined to see only the best, she often saw nothing at all. With all her sunshine, she could cast black shadows. Although she had every virtue, they all added up to make nothing, like an unfortunate punch into which have gone the choicest wines and fruits, yet the result is flat. Nanny clung to her, but Nanny had never been, by instinct, a member of her own family. She had been a lonely child. The only way she could keep herself in the family circle at all had been by peeking and prying at them.

Lucy Inman, with a plumed and jeweled turban on her head and wearing a sweeping dove-gray satin, stood with a tuzzy-muzzy in her hand, happy and well at ease. She loved parties, and this was the housewarming. With all her heart she hoped everybody would be happy, be they belles or wallflowers, Federalists or Republicans, Lamb and the hired-in waiters, or the richest merchants in town.

"Nanny," she whispered, "you do look so pretty tonight. How do you do, Mrs. Crowninshield."

Nanny was not a pretty girl, but at her mother's words became prettier.

"Nanny, no one would guess you were a married woman and a mother . . . How do you do, Mr. Gray, and Madam . . . oh, Madam, you have not been here since the house was done . . . (And Nanny, don't be old-fashioned and think you can't stand up to dance because . . .) Why, Mrs. Derby, to think you came all the way over from Danvers, and in the snow too! Yes, Mrs. White, this is my youngest, Marcy. She is only thirteen, but she is so big I decided it was time for her to *start* living up to her size instead of her *age* . . . (Marcy, don't offer your hand to gentlemen . . .)"

There was a little flurry as Polly Mompesson entered on her father's arm. She always made a handsome entrance.

"Sir, you are good to come and lend us your darling Polly. Polly, are you really a human being? You look like an angel." She did look like an angel with her silvery ballgown and silver stars in the gleaming blondness of her hair. Her face glowed with expectant rapture, burning like a candle inside alabaster. "And Tom's fiancée, Miss Fields. But, of course, you girls have met before."

The young ladies curtsied. Lucy Inman could understand why Dash had fallen in love with Polly. Frankly, any man might — men were such fools. But what on earth did Tom see in Miranda? Half the nice girls in the world were like Miranda. Why should she appeal so much more than the next one? Yet, five years before, Tom had met her at a funeral over in Newburyport, and he had never glanced at any other girl since. But of course Tom was so competent — so efficient, he wouldn't waste years making up his mind. Changing it, and making it up again.

"(Marcy, don't wriggle) . . . Mr. Mompesson, there are card tables set up. Loo in the parlor. Whist in the dining room."

Squire Mompesson was looking at her coldly. "I wish to congratulate you, ma'am."

"Yes?" Everybody had been congratulating her on something, the beauty of her house, the charms of her daughters, Tom's engagement, the return of the *Victrix* and her record-breaking speed.

"To mix wines and get precisely the right punch is an art. But to hope to mix Federalists and Republicans in Salem!" He marched stiffly away, cutting two Crowninshields and Doctor Bentley as he went. Oh dear, she thought, oh dear! Well, at least Liz will be nice to my poor Republicans.

Thank God, the darky fiddlers were tuning up. "Yes," she said absently, "this is the snowiest January I ever remember."

Now the fiddles all came together, calling the young people to dance. So sweet, so gay, these dancing fiddles, yet so sad and transitory. They would remind anyone, at least any woman who had passed her fiftieth birthday, that we are young but once and that but briefly. She felt a little tired and her tuzzy-muzzy was already fading. Well, apparently there were no more guests coming. The receiving line had best break up now. Ah, but there will always be fiddles, she thought, other dancing feet, passing on from generation to generation.

Old Monsieur de Herriot — it was said he was ci-devant marquis, but he had been teaching dancing to Salem young folk now for ten years — had been hired in that night to act as master of ceremonies. He was commanding the young people to come up and draw their partners for the first dance. Lucy and her girls had stood just within the doorway of the double parlors. She could see the old Frenchman tapping at his little kit-fiddle, no bigger than a soup ladle. He looked so fresh and happy it was hard to believe he had ever been under the shadow of the guillotine or even was a true marquis. Of course, nobody knew.

Excited young voices were crying, "I'm six . . . six! Who's six? Four, four! I want a lady four."

Well, one thing was certain. Young Federalists and young Republicans wouldn't care whom they stood up with. She glanced across the hall into the living room. Already Squire Mompesson had seated himself next to Madam Inman, who looked so pretty in her best black silk and laces, telling her that the country was going to the dogs, what with Jefferson President. Or giving her, once more, the grisly details of his family tree, boasting once more how "one" Inman carried Cecil, the First, piggy-back into Cat Cove.

"Peter," she grabbed him as he went prancing by, hoping for a partner — "you must rescue your grandmother."

"Aye."

"And don't go saying 'aye' to me. I don't like it. You're no sailor. Peter, don't forget the wallflowers. I can't count on Dash and Tom, of course. And Liz wouldn't be seen dead with a wallflower."

Nanny and Miranda were already off to take part in the dancing.

"Peter," Lucy went on, "somebody has got to look out for them and it will have to be you."

He looked very sober. "Blainey's here. I'll tell Blainey he's got to help me."

"It's your duty." And, she thought, the wallflowers will be so grateful to get a nice partner like Peter they won't *dare* snub him. Wallflowers wouldn't snub the Devil if he asked them to stand up and dance.

Marcy hung back, staying close to her mother. She was not sure what she was supposed to do. She longed to dance. All Lucy's children loved to dance.

"Marcy, I don't want you to take part in any of the draw dances. I don't want any gentleman disappointed to find he has drawn a fourteen-year-old child, built like a woodchuck. If you didn't eat so much, Marcy, you wouldn't be so fat."

"You mean I'm not to dance at all?"

"Let me finish my sentence. We are having a draw dance and then a voluntary, half and half, all evening. If any gentleman *invites* you for a voluntary, you may accept."

"Nobody will ask me," she said, mournfully. "Except Peter."

"Peter will have his hands full. We've got those three plain Miss Perkinses. He's got to keep them rolling. And that sallow girl from Baltimore that came with Mrs. Derby. She may be rich in Baltimore, but nobody cares in Salem."

"Mother, I might as well go to bed now."

"And mind . . . Emmy and Bibby and Veronica have been invited to be your little guests. Where are they?"

"They're peeking through the balustrades. They're scared to come down."

"In the back room there is a little table set for you. You will be given your refreshments there — early. Then they are to go home, and you to bed. But don't you children go hanging around looking as though you expect grown men to dance with you. For nobody will."

Then, bearing down upon them, she saw a desperate, stalwart, very blond young man in white pantaloons and brass-decked blue coat. His shoulders were braced as though expecting a cold blow of rain. In his eyes was a look of danger bravely met. Molly the Heifer had told him it was fashionable to come late. He had overdone it.

Mrs. Inman thought, If he only came from somewhere else. Anywhere except Salem. He is terribly handsome.

Like a condemned man walking a plank, Obrian bore down on Lucy and Marcy. Molly had prepared him for a whole line of family to receive him. Dash would be there. Dash would help him through this dirty weather as he had before at sea. A quick grin, a few words of command. But Dash was not in sight. Or Madam Inman. She would understand. She would help. But only the terrifying Mrs. Inman and fat Marcy stood to greet him.

He knew Marcy by sight. Every seaman in Salem knew Marcy. She had an unladylike quality of being noticeable and well-liked by common people.

His big red hands clenched, real foremast hands, hanging loosely out of his sleeves, always ready to grasp something.

"You must be Dash's friend," Mrs. Inman said kindly, putting out a hand to him. "Aren't you Mr. Obrian?"

"Yes, ma'am."

"Dash has told me so much about you. I'm glad we have at last persuaded you to come to the house — meet his family."

"It's a big house." Sweat gleamed on his forehead.

"If you had to dust it, you would think sometimes it was too big. This is my youngest girl, Marcy. Marcy, you lead Mr. Obrian to join the lines. This is a draw dance," she explained, to Danny's bewilderment. "But if you two just slip in and join the lines . . ."

"Whee!" said Marcy, leaping lightly into the air for such a heavy child. "Whee, Mate Obrian!" She gazed up at the rugged face, the narrow, ferociously blue eyes, with the admiration that only a child can give.

"No, this isn't shipboard. Not Mate Obrian. *Mr.* Obrian. And

Marcy" — Lucy put her ringed hand on the girl's white muslin shoulder — "I'm making you responsible for Mr. Obrian's enjoyment. It is up to you to see he has a good time. At least, you are to start him off."

"A good time! Oh, Mother!" She grasped Danny by the hand and led him away.

Little girls wore white muslin. The effect was supposed to be touching in its delicate purity. It had not that effect upon Marcy. Rather suddenly she had begun to develop. But Nature had played a trick on her. She had developed hips and a bust before a waistline. The result was a travesty on childhood and a caricature of womanhood. Well, 'Sephus Hobey was always saying, Marcy is far ahead of other girls her age. But he didn't have to dress her. All Lucy could do was shut her eyes and hope she'd outgrow it.

She hoped Marcy wouldn't be rough. Or forget her little friends entirely. Well, thank Heavens, the party would all be over by midnight. The fiddling no longer tempted her tired feet. She was glad she was too old to stand up. Now for a quiet evening of cards. Supper at nine. More cards, and so, thank Heavens, to bed. Perhaps she had better take this moment to look into the kitchen? But, of course, with Cousin Frances in charge and little Lamb and his friends, nothing could go wrong. Smiling a stereotyped hostess smile, already drying a little at the corners, she went into the living room. She passed among her guests, a smile here, a word there. Not a single Federalist sat with a Republican. And now she noticed that all the Republicans had got into the dining room and were playing whist and all the Federalists were in the living room and were preparing to play loo. What was she to do? She hardly knew or cared, but, as she preferred loo to whist, she sat with the Federalists.

But the sweetness of the music, the excitement from across the hall, oppressed her. She had never cared for cards. Then, having been looed three times, she heard such screaming and squealing from the girls and such a roar from the young men across the hall that she decided to see what had happened.

Squire Mompesson's curiosity had also been aroused. He was standing in the hall, looking in at the double parlors. She wondered if he had been standing here all the time, watching. She had not noticed him at the loo tables.

They stood together, peering in. The ballroom was pretty beyond belief, with the young girls' flower-like dresses, plumes, scarves, jewels, and gauze. The young men were brave in dark broadcloth, with identical pale pantaloons, festive waistcoats, and snowy neckcloths. But it was not the clothes which made the sight so pretty. It was the radiant faces, lovely young bodies, light feet, light hearts.

She glanced about and saw Liz with a casual arm lingering about a partner's waist. Such a pretty young girl. She couldn't think who she was. A bride newcome to Salem, but she didn't know whose bride. Yes, a married woman. Of course Liz shouldn't . . . Dash should talk *seriously* to Liz. And his pantaloons might be fashionable, but they were shockingly tight. She noticed that half the men had copied that one Napoleonic lock Liz let fall across his forehead. He had been the first man in Salem to adopt his style. In spite of herself, Lucy felt proud of him.

Chairs had been lined up against the wall for such of the old people who preferred to sit and watch. Oh, how could they? When you are too old to dance, how can you ever bear to sit and watch!

The rumpus she had heard was due to the fact that for the third time Dash and Polly had drawn each other. Both stood at the head of the room holding cards marked "one." Not only had they drawn each other, but were first couple. Old Monsieur de Herriot was being accused of accepting bribes and Dash of giving them. Marquis or no Marquis, old Monsieur was enjoying himself. "Mes enfants!" he would protest, and tap his little kit-fiddle, "mes enfants!" But the pretty girls were gathered about him, pulling at his neckcloth, shaking the lapels of his coat, squealing at him and loving him. There was hardly one here who had not been his pupil. They wouldn't let him explain. "You're cheating! You old rascal!"

Dash looked amazingly bright and innocent. He had exactly the expression she had so often caught on Peter's face, when he was doing something he shouldn't. Polly stood beside him. She seemed on fire, a secret, beautiful, dangerous fire. Some day it might really break out, consume her and everyone about her. So goddesses of love had burned in the past. Ashteroth or Aphrodite, Venus — but never, once, a nice sensible New England girl like Miranda Fields. But it gave Polly a breath-taking, inhuman beauty.

And how fascinatingly vivacious she was! Such a witty creature. Not really witty as gentlemen are supposed to be over their port, but just as witty, and no more, as a belle should be at a ball.

"Oh, Mr. Mompesson," Lucy burst out, "I've never seen nor imagined such a handsome couple!"

"Yes, yes. One so dark and one so fair and all that. But I do not understand the excitement."

"You don't?" And she explained.

"You are not suggesting that your son, in fact the host of all these young people, has descended to corruption?"

"Oh, fie! It's play only."

"I was taught, ma'am, that in play as well as in love and war there is honor."

"How happy they are!" she murmured.

"Happy? Hardly. Merely excited. It disturbs me sometimes, as a father, that Polly is using up so much of her strength. She is not a very strong girl. She'll pay for it tomorrow."

"Mercy, Mr. Mompesson, I never saw a girl yet who, given the right partner, couldn't dance all night and be the better for it."

"The *right* partner?"

She resented, for Dash's sake, the slight implied criticism of him. She tossed her head, for this great night wrapped in crimson brocaded tinsel, mounted with ostrich. "Well, they are happy now, and tomorrow is always tomorrow. I mean it's never really here. Not for twenty-four more hours."

Even she, at her age, could feel the excitement which radiated from Dash and Polly. It flooded the ballroom. It was so contagious wallflowers began to tremble upon their stalks. Even Maria Perkins, on Peter's arm, was losing her angles. Peter's best friend, the unappetizing, bespectacled Blainey Phipps, was evidently helping Peter out. He had Anna Perkins. Monsieur de Herriot stamped his feet, and arched his old neck. Liz was twirling in his long, tight chamois pantaloons. And miraculously, they hadn't burst yet. The Negro fiddlers were swaying and shuffling their feet. It was as if a furnace door had opened and the heat was great enough to consume everybody at the ball and touch even her and Mr. Mompesson. Love, love, everywhere. And all she had to concern herself about was the practical aspects of the entertainment.

"You'll excuse her, sir," she said, "if the housewife now goes to the kitchen to assure herself the supper is ready to be served?"

Mr. Mompesson bowed beautifully. "Indeed, madam. It is said the master's eye fattens the calf. But it is the mistress's eye that serves it."

❧ 4 ❧

OF COURSE, with such a tower of strength as Lamb and his cohorts and dear Frances, there was no need for her to go to the kitchen, but she had been angry at Mr. Mompesson, and the heat radiating from the ballroom had upset her. For a moment she wished to escape her guests.

As she went down the hall, she noticed that there was too much noise coming out of the back room, usually for storage, but tonight prepared for Marcy and her little friends. It was far past nine o'clock. They would have finished supper long ago. Time now to get them out of the house and Marcy to bed. She told herself it would not be fair to use up on Marcy the bad temper engendered by Mr. Mompesson.

As her hand turned the knob, she heard Marcy cry out, "Do it again, Danny, do it again!" She pulled open the door.

Dan Obrian was stripped to his shirt. Tied about his waist were bundles of straw, brought in from the stable. He was shaking his hips and curling his arms lasciviously, and his feet were beating the floor like a tom-tom. Emmy Crowninshield and the homely Veronica Valpey were trying to imitate him, but Cry-Baby Bibby was in tears. Marcy was on the table, now cleared of their supper. Her grass skirt was going in perfect time to Danny's beat and like him she shook her haunches and curled her arms. It was worse for her. She had haunches to shake, and her curling arms emphasized that she had a bosom.

To confound matters even more, Linda had dropped her duties and was spiraling about with a candle on her head, in a vague Ophelia-like way. Thank Heavens, it was not lighted. Linda saw her, a quick hand shot up and took off the candle.

"*Linda!*"

"Yes, ma'am," and Linda shot for the kitchen like a rabbit for its hole.

"Marcy! *Marcy*! Marcy!" The girl had seen her, but was off on one of her wild tears. She had stopped dancing when she had seen Danny stop — which was the moment he had caught sight of Mrs. Inman's face. But Marcy was laughing so hard she would not have heard the last trump.

Mrs. Inman reached up, pulled at and shook her. The straw fell from her. Suddenly Marcy sat down on the edge of the table, but she kept on laughing.

"Marcy, will you listen to me!"

Marcy stopped laughing and looked blankly at her mother.

"Oh."

"Marcy, what on earth are you up to?"

"Nothing, Mother, nothing. But Danny couldn't dance in there. He doesn't know how. He said he could dance like Ohayee girls. I got the straw. Danny said . . ."

"Mr. Obrian . . . Marcy . . ."

"Mr. Obrian said that was how he liked to dance. Mother, you told me to do *anything* to give him a good time. You said I was to dance with him. Mother, you did. If you say you didn't, you are lying."

"Marcy!"

Veronica, Emmy, and Bibby had never heard a child speak thus to her mother. Their jaws dropped, and they froze like children playing statues.

"Don't look at me like that!" Marcy roared. "I can't stand it! And I won't!"

Mrs. Inman collapsed into a chair and went on staring at Marcy, whose mouth squared suddenly. She burst into tears.

Linda, light and unreal as a wraith, but now with her candlestick put away and an apron on, silently began to pick up the straw.

Mrs. Inman went on sitting, saying nothing, letting her contrite daughter roar. How could a sensible woman like herself ever have had a child like Marcy! She was forgetting her own childhood. She herself had been a romping tomboy.

"Linda," she said at last, "please get Veronica, Bibby, and Emmy into their wraps and walk them home."

"I'm not sure I can walk, Mrs. Inman," Veronica said, with a martyred air. "I think I have twisted my ankle."

"Stuff, Veronica. Stuff and nonsense. You and your sprained

ankles. Linda, if Miss Veronica can't walk, pull her home on a sled."

"Yes'm."

They were gone, and Marcy only sniffling. "I'll put away the rest of the straw," she was promising. "I know where it came from."

"Yes, put it away and go to bed. Marcy, I can't seem to think what to do with you. But I may have to send you away to a very strict boarding school. But I'm too tired to think tonight. You go to bed."

"Yes, Mother. I'm sorry."

"It isn't just this . . ."

"I know. It's everything. But Mother, if you do send me to boarding school, I'll run away or die."

"Rubbish!"

"I'll run away to sea. To Ohayee."

Mrs. Inman shook her head, got to her feet. Then she caught sight of Dan Obrian, perishing in a corner. He had got his coat on again, but had forgotten to remove his grass skirt. Well over six feet, virile, bold, handsome — and scared to death.

She looked at his stricken face. "I could hardly reprove a guest before children," she said, coldly, for she was afraid she would laugh. "But Mr. Obrian, I consider this entire shameful affair your fault."

"It is my fault," he croaked. "I should have known better."

"I hope you realize that in inviting you to my house — the son of your mother — to meet my daughters and their friends, I did you some small honor?"

"You did me a very great honor. Molly the Heifer said . . ."

"Molly the *who*?"

"Just a friend of mine. Nobody you've ever met. And Old Lady Inman . . . oh God, I mean Madam Inman, but all the forecastle folk call her Old Lady. She and Dash both thought I ought to get around, learn to do better . . ."

"And what have you done?"

"I guess disgraced you folks — and Dash, too." His eyes cooled and darkened. "I guess I disgraced Raggity-Meg — even."

"I see you realize what you have done. Now, may I bid you good night?"

"Good night, ma'am. You were good to think to teach me better than I was born."

He was so humiliated he decided he could not go upstairs to the chamber where he had been told to leave his greatcoat. He could not face any more gentry. He thought that in the kitchen he might find and send Linda.

It was past nine. The kitchen was in a flurry of cakes and sandwiches, puddings, tipsy parsons, jellies, coffee, tea, and iced fruits. He saw a woman with lifeless heavy russet hair skillfully unmolding what looked like a hundred squabs, boned and jellied. She glanced at him, but was too busy to ask what he wanted. White folk and black folk were scampering about like mad.

The confusion and the heat swam about him. And then, there in the midst of it, he saw a too-familiar face. Flip Dawson! Of course, she could never have expected him, now that he was a mate and soon to be a captain, to pay any more attention to her. Not once had he sought the Mompesson back door and her company. He was going to fly a lot higher than servingmaids.

She was staring at him, unsmiling, and straight in the face. He looked back at her, but gave no sign of recognition. It was a direct cut. The woman with the russet hair and blue apron was now asking what he wanted. He mumbled an apology, backed out, and by luck found himself in the gun room.

The smoke of tobacco, the fumes of wine, rum, fruit from the punch, the fact that here only gentlemen were present, calmed him. Many knew him. Sam Derby did. Here in this man's world his self-confidence returned. Gentlemen were asking him about Japan. Was it true they were part monkey? As long as he lived, people were going to be asking Dan Obrian about Japan. At the punchbowl, he felt himself again. He had one glass of punch, another, then two more. Here were no stout little girls to make a fool of him. No haughty ladies to make a child of him. No pretty servant girls to remind him of his fickleness. He expanded, and at last dared ask Lamb to go upstairs and fetch him down his things.

Sam Derby strolled into the hall with him. "Baltic next?" he asked.

"Not sure. Dash hasn't said a word about where he intends to venture next. But I guess wherever he goes, he'll want me for his first. Dash and me, we get on good."

"Is it always going to be 'Dash and me'?" Captain Derby was smiling slightly. "Aren't you ever going to go as master yourself?"

"Sometime," Dan said, gruffly. "Sometime it's promised me."

"You've never thought of returning to the Derbys' house flag?"

"No, sir. Dash Inman took me up out of *your* forecastle."

"How old are you, Obrian?"

"Twenty-two, sir."

"H'm, yes, yes. And you've had almost four years under the Inman flag and still only a mate. Can't understand why they haven't put you forward."

"I'm up to the sea duties, sir. But not the trading, and what's called the diplomatic end of things."

"If you sailed as master for us, we would put on a supercargo."

"Old Lady Inman doesn't do that."

"No. Mr. Obrian, our *Asiatic Prince* goes out a week from Saturday. India."

"Yes, sir."

"If you can fix it with Dash Inman and his grandmother, I believe we could give you captain's berth. You'd do no trading. Your supercargo will do that. Navigation and command only."

"Captain Derby, Dash Inman has taught me everything I know. I can't go back on him, if he's counting on me." Yet his loyalty to Dash had been shaken this evening. Dash had not been at hand to help him through the perils, as he always was at sea. Only a first warm welcome, then off he had gone without a thought for anyone but himself and his own girl.

"Would you like me to talk to Dash?"

"If you think it's right."

"My dear boy, nobody's going to look out for Dan Obrian but Dan Obrian. We Derbys did not think you disloyal because you left us for the Inmans. They offered you a mate's berth before we got around to it. Now we want you for a master. The Inmans can't object if you leave them for a better berth with us."

"No, Mr. Derby."

"As for loyalty — you were a Derby man before an Inman."

"Since I was twelve, sir."

"Obviously, you owe more to us than to them."

It would be almost a relief, Dan thought, to get out from under Dash Inman. He was always after him, trying to make him better than he was. "Don't yell, boy, keep your voice down." "Dan, here's a book, history of your own country. Read it. Take my word, it will help you as captain." "Look-a-here, sir. If I ever catch you again slapping my people just because you got up on the wrong side of your bunk . . ." "Dan, for God's sake, practice your hand-writing. You write like a child of eight." "Now, if you want, I'll give you a French lesson every day. French you must have to trade Europe and Russia."

The Derbys wouldn't think, because you sailed their ships, you had to go to their parties — to be made a zany of.

❧ 5 ❧

By agreement, Tom and Miranda ate supper quickly and crept upstairs. They wished to study the two front rooms which Mrs. Inman had promised them. One was her own bedroom. But she had offered to remove herself to the little sewing room in the ell. Neither of the young people had any conception of the sacrifice she was making. If she had not offered it, they would have felt no resentment. They felt no gratitude that she had.

Tonight the white-canopied beds, the chairs, the chests, were covered with ladies' wraps and the warm socks they wore over their slippers to protect them from the snow. And with muffs, fur hoods, and mittens.

Sitting abject and alone on a stool by the fire, in a pretty pink calico frock, her face in her hands, was a little maid. Neither Tom nor Miranda noticed that it was Polly Mompesson's Flip — trying hard not to cry. Flip often accompanied her mistress to parties, and when she got there worked as hard and twice as deftly as any of the household's servants. It was not until supper was served that she could face, and alone, the meaning of Dan's direct cut of her.

Now she was on her feet, curtsying, taking it for granted that Miss Fields was looking for her wraps. But Miss Fields was taking a tape measure from her indispensable, and a notebook. She did not need Flip, and the maid vanished. She must find another place to hide her tearstained face.

First, they measured the space between the two front windows to see if the sofa Miranda's father had promised her would fit in. Yes, just, and barely. Both were agreed in not liking the pale, wreathed, exquisite French wallpaper in the room. As Miranda said, you could hardly tell what color it was. She liked colors and designs "you can really *see*." She would prefer a good solid bright green. Her sofa was crimson. The effect would be cheerful. So, carrying the tape measure between them, they covered window frames and floors. Miranda continually wrote in her little book. And then, as they moved out the commode to see if there would be room for her rocker, she discovered a scandal.

"Why, Tom, *look!* Why, dust!"

Mrs. Inman had always taken to beauty and comfort more readily than to the grimmer aspects of a housewife's labors. She had never been above sweeping dust under a rug. Nor was Linda, who admired her very much, any better.

"Well," said Miranda firmly, "I can see *my* work cut out for me. But I suppose your mother is getting too old to see if the girls do their work properly. Tom, do fetch me the brush from the hearth. I'm going to sweep it into the fire." She had on her best ball dress, turquoise-blue velvet, but she was happier now, sweeping Mrs. Inman's dust into the fire, than she had been all evening. Then they began measuring the wall to see if there was room for the gilt mirror her aunt was giving her. There was.

Both were as happy as nesting birds. Each got from the other what each craved, and greater love there is not. The girl was a born housewife. Tom, alone among the Inman brothers, was born to be as good a husband as he had always been good son, brother, captain, man of business, citizen. He never had had much credit for his virtues. Everyone took them for granted. So did Miranda. That he had never looked at another girl at home or abroad since first his eyes had fallen upon her did not impress her. Why should he? He got little credit for the fact he never drank himself silly, or played for high stakes, never missed church on Sunday or his bath on Saturday night; that he was incapable of a dishonest act or word and would never tell a fib, even to a wife. On Tom's part he never appreciated that for Miranda no other man could exist, not even the gallant Liz nor the famous Dash; that no matter how much money she had or how much more her husband made, she would rise, every morning, at five-thirty to set the help a good example and see to it breakfast was properly served. Not one meal would ever go to the table that she herself had not glanced at in the kitchen. Every bit of porcelain and glass would be washed by her own careful hands. Not a sack of salt, loaf of sugar or bread, would be bought and not written down. And she would never tell a fib, even to a husband, over household expenses.

They were deeply in love, but their love expressed itself differently from other people's. Not like Polly and Dash, for a moment and a moment only in each others' arms in that "back room" where Marcy had entertained her friends. Not like Flip Dawson crying for her faithless man in the privacy of the necessary, with Little Joe barking at the door. Nor Liz, making much too much of a married lady, his dark eyes telling a great deal, mostly lies. Not like Peter, who would descend to any trickery so only the man he loved might find no obstacle between him and the girl he wanted.

They crossed into Tom's bedroom, which, in a week's time, would be their bedroom, and here Miranda faltered and her modesty got the better of her. "Oh, Tommy, should I go in — do you think it is proper?" It was the sight of the strange men's greatcoats, mufflers, hats, that had aroused her modesty. Not the fact that so soon she would lie in this very bed with the man she loved. This was an aspect of marriage that she had hardly thought of. She wanted children. And there are few things you get in this world for nothing.

Soon she was happily measuring the bed and deciding that her mother's alpaca bed-dress would fit it. She called out the good news to Tom, who, at her orders, stood in the upper hall to warn her if he saw a gentleman coming upstairs, searching for his greatcoat. Then she joined him. "It is six by five and a half, dear," she said, and he kissed her.

They stood for a moment on the landing. From there down, the stairs were filled with people still lingering over their suppers.

So they stood and waited, their arms stiffly about each other, as correct as lovers in a print. Couple after couple left the stairs or crossed into the parlors. The music was beginning. Finally only Peter still sat, surrounded by the three Miss Perkinses and all their plates and napkins. Blainey, his best friend, seemingly had at last deserted him.

Miranda laughed. "Look at Peter. Three girls! But I suppose no *one* girl would want to find herself alone with him."

Ruddy as he was by nature, a slight flush spread over Tom's face. "Why did you say that, Miranda?"

"Why, Tommy, even over in Newburyport people are talking about . . . it."

"It?"

"My dear. Now that I'm practically a member of your family I think I might be expected to bear, in a way, the family's burdens."

"Peter isn't a burden."

"Even Mama has told me that when we are married and I am living here, I must be so careful not to as much as let his shadow fall on me. You do want your wife, like Caesar's wife, to be above suspicion."

"Miranda, I want you to do me one favor. Don't go gossiping about my family. You're never to say to anybody else what you've just said to me about Peter."

She bridled slightly. "Of course . . . if you command me." It irritated her that the bond between the four brothers was so strong. What was she? Only a stranger?

Music on their left. Card-playing upon their right. Blainey Phipps had appeared and was taking one Miss Perkins while Peter took another, and the third vowed she was so exhausted she'd rather sit out for a dance. Blainey was rather short. His eyes were bright and intelligent behind his spectacles, but when Dash called him a "weasel" there was some truth in it. Peter already did not care for Blainey as he had four years before.

When at last, well after midnight, the last guest was gone and the best porcelain and silver washed and put away, Cousin Frances, still in her blue apron, sat in the sitting room and munched over the remains of refreshments she had not had time for before, and also munched over the party with her friend. Oh, it had been such a success! But Lucy Inman, remembering how Republicans and Federalists wouldn't play cards with each other, would not agree that the elder part of her ball had been entirely successful. In the ballroom, yes. What did they care who was President? John Adams or Thomas Jefferson? And in her swollen feet — these new heelless French slippers were hard for her, she had grown up on heels — and in the aching middle of her back, all through her exhausted body, she still felt the vibration of the fiddles that would never play for her again.

Becket's shipyard was snow-filled and silent, the waterfront itself almost silent, so blocked was it with snow, cold, and ice. Dash and Peter went to Becket's house. There they found the greatest of shipbuilders sitting by his kitchen fire, curled up and drowsy as a hibernating bear. Shipbuilders had little choice but to hibernate through cold wintertime. Yet the kitchen was filled with models and half-models of ships, diagrams of hulls, drawings, paintings, and plans. And, Peter guessed, unpaid bills. Old 'Tirey Becket was not much of a businessman.

If February brought its customary thaw, maybe, he admitted cautiously, a new keel might be laid down then, and suppose — that old dream of the Yankees — spring came early.

Dash was telling him the new ship was to duplicate exactly the *Victrix* whose handsome model the old man held in his hands. Mr. Becket suggested improvements. The *Victrix* had never balanced quite right. No, no, the new vessel was to copy her and he had best forget improvements. Mr. Becket shook his head. Both men knew it was no more possible for a shipbuilder to duplicate a ship than for a violin-maker to duplicate a violin. They talked of width of beam in relation to length of ship, of shear and waterlines.

Peter let his mind wander. But not far, not farther than Dash sitting there. Of course, it was his mother who had told Dash about the family scandal. He knew Dash knew — all about Peter's mistress and illegitimate child, and how many people didn't think Peter was a desirable young man. But she couldn't have told him — for how could she know? — that Peter was content to bear for Dash any disgrace, give up anything. He felt a shiver almost of delight as he thought about what he had done for Dash.

As he watched Dash so softly, gently, arguing with Mr. Becket, who was sure he could improve even upon the *Victrix,* he loved him more than ever. And with that intensity and possessiveness of emotion one feels toward those for whom much has been sacrificed. Because he had done all this for Dash, Dash in a way belonged to him, proud and free though he might be to the rest of the world. Forever there was a secret corner which Peter possessed. The time had not yet come, but it was coming, when Dash would insist that Peter tell him all. Peter feared it, for Dash might be angry. Yet he half-longed for the moment he might say, "But I wanted to do it, for you."

Leaving Becket's, neither could help a glance down Inman Wharf. The navy house flag, cut diagonally with white, before the counting-house was a solid piece of ice. They saw old Mr. Fessenden out with a scuttle, cautiously scattering ashes on the ladder-steep stairs. The sun had come out at last. Soon the *Victrix's* sheath of ice would drop from her, but now, at this moment, she seemed rigged and cut from glass. She sparkled blindingly, beautifully, in the sun. She was headed in. Her figurehead faced them — a woman of ice who held a wreath of crystal before her. So beautiful a thing! Peter thought, sighing as people do at the sight of perfect beauty. And he remembered the despair and desperate hopes, the passion, the longing, that had gone into her building. Now Dash was so successful there were no more of these commodities to put into any ship. So how could he blandly say, "Mr. Becket, I want another vessel, just like the *Victrix*"? It couldn't be done.

Behind the ship, stretching like a long serpent out to sea, was the narrow black ribbon of open water boatmen had broken for her, three days before. Everywhere else, the harbor was deep with snow, for it had frozen in that winter, a smooth plain that reached from Naugus Head to Juniper Point.

As usual, children dragging sleds and grown people in sleighs were out to enjoy the novelty. The sleighing was wonderful. Now it was the horses' bright cold bells they heard from everywhere, not the shipyard men, the porters, the sailors sing-out. Liz was always saying neither Boston nor New York Harbor ever froze in like this. Salem did not very often. It was inconvenient when it happened. Perhaps even before the *Victrix* was made ready for sea once more, the ice would melt. Liz was to command her on her next voyage; he was already signing his crew. Dash would have a little time at home, and ashore. The first real vacation he had had for almost four years. Also he would oversee the building of the new ship which was already referred to as the *Wanderer*.

As they plowed up the sunny, snowy streets toward home and dinner, Dash suggested that he and Peter drive out together that afternoon and call upon their last night's partners. This was the custom. Gentlemen, the day after balls, called on every girl they had danced with the night before. There were six years between Dash and Peter. Never before had they thus stepped out together. Peter felt flattered, offered to go to the livery stable and bespeak a rig. Neither of them wanted old Dolly, and Lucy was using the pair, driving Miranda to call upon the dowagers of Salem. That possibly Dash might prefer to go alone — for there was much of the lone wolf in his makeup — Peter did not guess. Nor that Dash might like protecting Peter against slights.

The hired sleigh was scarlet. The robes, black bearskins. The hired horse, an arch young thing, black-coated, white-footed. The bells were all in tune. Dash, wearing the Russian coat and astra-khan cap that only men who trade the Baltic had the arrogance to wear, held the reins. But the first thing Peter knew, the red sleigh and the bells had carried them beyond Salem and into the country, out to the turnpike already packed and smoothed for sleighing. The world was white and enchanting about them. Yet all their last night's partners lived in town. Dash was saying very little, and Peter's heart sank. He was being taken thus far out because Dash wanted to talk with him, and privately.

Dash felt a trap had been sprung on him. Behind his back Peter had set the gin. There was some justice in the fact that it was upon him, not Dash, that it had sprung.

At last he said abruptly: "Peter, I know why you didn't go to Harvard back a few years ago. You had to take all the money you had saved to buy Flanneau. But since then, during these last eight months, why didn't you go? I put at your disposal plenty of ready cash. Last time I was home."

"I'm pretty old now."

"You're twenty-two."

"Most students are under twenty. For instance, Blainey Phipps has graduated. He's back here now in Mr. Storey's law office. Blainey is going to be a lawyer and . . . "

Dash interrupted him. "There's some other reason. Come, man, speak up."

"I didn't want to leave Ma'am."

Dash shook his head impatiently. "All right. If you won't tell me the truth, Peter, I'll go to 'Sephus Hobey. He knows more about going to Harvard than anyone else here."

"No need. It's only this. To be acceptable to Harvard, or any other college, you have to bring a letter from your home town. Clergymen — and such — vouch for you as a young man of good repute. Dash, I know it's funny, just as Liz says, but I couldn't get such a letter. Not even from 'Sephus Hobey. He tells me not to try. Not that I want to," he added, a little too airily to be convincing.

"Now *that* settles it." Dash stopped the horse, turned around, heading back for Salem. The arch young horse tossed her head and her bells, and sped over the dazzling snow. Peter waited a long time to hear what Dash might say next, but he said nothing.

"Dash," Peter finally suggested, "everything is settled — you're right about that. Just so you don't start meddling, getting your paws into it." And he went on to explain at length and in some detail all that had happened and all that was to happen — if only Dash kept his mouth shut and his paws to himself.

But Dash's gorge rose. He was accustomed to ordering his own life. The course he found himself sailing was contrary to everything instinctive in him. Granted Peter's suggestions were expedient, it wasn't right and it wasn't honorable.

"Don't try to be honorable, Dash. Try to be kind."

"Kind to you, for instance?"

"Yes. It isn't so much. You know Liz says it's the funniest thing that has happened in Salem since they hung the witches."

"Most people don't think that too damn funny. Fortunately. Or unfortunately."

"I'm doing what I want," Peter cried out sharply. "And it's nobody's business what I want to do. I want to do something that really counts. I'd like to have something I really want I can give you. I want . . ." He was almost incoherent. "Dash, I want to be the one that gives you Polly." And he stopped talking.

They drove on for some time.

"I haven't any girl to lose," Peter broke in on the silence. "I haven't anything — except you, Dash."

"Should have." Dash rebuffed his enthusiasm.

I might as well decide now as ever, he was thinking. Suppose I get Mr. Mompesson off in a corner — tell him I withdraw all pretensions to his daughter's hand. Tell him why. But Peter's right when he says it would break my Polly's heart. And he felt, not for the first time, a slight antagonism toward her. She was a girl guaranteed to understand nothing. Yet, no matter how clear might be his occasional flashes of seeing through the enchantment of her flesh, her smile, her passion for him, to something he did not admire in her, it made no difference. If I told, he thought, I'd not wait for the *Wanderer* to be built — I'd take the *Victrix* again and be off. And, damn it, I'd never come back again. On t'other side, I can do just as Pete wants. Then I'd marry Polly and . . . He had a sudden idea so helpful he put it in words before he had had time to think.

"This thing needn't be decided yet awhile, Pete. I've a mind not to retire yet awhile. Not till I'm ready to — but if I don't, would Mr. Mompesson consider me fit to marry his girl — or she either?"

So the sea that had nurtured him, made him famous and wealthy and the man that he was, now offered him a small loophole. This need not be a quick decision. He could take a little more time before he made up his mind what he would do.

Dash sensed something of Peter's willingness for martyrdom. He did not like it. He saw Peter's eyes, eyes almost literally blind with affection, fastened on his face. All this love, adoration, willingness to die for you, is hard for one man to take from another. Peter, he thought, should grow up. Yet how to extricate himself from the gin Peter had set him, he did not know. It was as if the compass within him had stopped pointing at the cold, pure North. Was racing about, chasing its own tail.

"I won't say I will keep my mouth shut," he at last admitted, "and I won't say I won't."

By then they were back in Salem stopping before the Pickering house on Broad Street. Yet Peter knew that for the moment at least he had won. Dash wouldn't act too quickly. He was going to take time to think.

Dash did see the truth in everything Peter had been telling him. And Peter? Well, somehow he'd "make it up to him." He can have money to burn. Yet he knew Peter did not want money nor the things it bought. He didn't want a yacht like the Crowninshields' *Jefferson,* nor a yellow curricle like George Crowninshield's. Nor a great house like Billy Gray's. He didn't want a talked-of, great country seat with everything you could think of growing under glass and Dutch gardeners, like the Derbys'. He didn't want women or wine. He was like a suit of clothes with no pockets in it. There was not a place where you could slip money in. Yet Dash felt he could not let Peter make such a sacrifice and go unrewarded. That was too humiliating.

Evidently the Pickerings were among the people who did not encourage "roués" calling on their girls, for Peter modestly insisted he'd rather sit in the sleigh. Dash got him out of it. Nobody was going to insult his Peter, his jaw said. Love me, love my dog. Not even the most pernickety parents, he quickly proved, as they went from house to house, would tell the famous Dash Inman that their daughter was not receiving. Dash was probably the most eligible bachelor in Salem. If they couldn't have him calling on their girls without the sinful Peter, why, they'd swallow Peter. They had better, Dash's eyes proclaimed.

Some dozen houses were visited. Polly they had decided to save until the last. She would be the reward for, for instance, the fifteen minutes they had allotted to the three Misses Perkins. Blainey was there before them and after they had gone. He had sat in a corner with the air of a household fixture holding up a skein of knitting wool for Miss Maria to wind off.

Peter knew that at four-thirty, and the day after a ball, Polly's house would be jammed. There were endless rakish greatcoats, handsome hats, in the hallway, among them Liz's. I guess that's why Dash fixed it for us to come just at teatime, Peter thought. He doesn't quite want to see her alone. And there was an odd look on Dash's face when Flip, in an excited little whisper and dimpling with pleasure, told him to wait in Polly's own sitting room — not in the great parlor where she, her father, and aunts were all receiving the cream of Salem's young manhood.

No sooner had they sat, a little stiffly, than Polly joined them. She was on her father's arm.

"We can't desert our guests but a moment, Dash. Dash, I want to tell you first, and then we'll all go across the hall. But I must tell you right off. Last night, after the ball, Papa did consent. I talked and talked. I cried. I was still crying at two o'clock this morning. But Papa did consent."

Her lovely face was trembling as aspen leaves tremble when no other tree can feel the breeze. Mr. Mompesson, or rather the porcelain image of him — for never before had Peter seen him look so exactly like a china figure — was managing a smile, holding out a lace-frilled, fragile hand to meet Dash's roughened one.

"When *I* was young, and that goes for Sister Brattle and my first wife's aunt, Mrs. Birdseye, young ladies did not take things into their own hands to quite such an extent. Frankly, the aunts were appalled by Polly's boldness. But, as I told 'em this morning, I had to consent or send for Doctor West. Still, it used to be the young *gentleman* who had the vapors and said he'd die unless papa permitted the engagement."

He looked at Polly with amusement. If, thought Peter, "amusement" was the right word for it. He looked at her with something, something Peter distrusted. Polly tossed her head. Not even this careful suggestion that her lover might be less ardent than herself humbled her.

"So it is settled, Dash."

She left her father's arm, and seriously, as though he were a Catholic kissing a holy image, Dash kissed her.

"I swear," he said, "you will never regret it, Polly."

"Polly, you forget the one condition," her father suggested.

"I have? Oh yes. Dash, we'll never keep anything from each other. I from you, or you from me."

Dash, so quick in his ordering, so accustomed to instant decision, felt an unfamiliar paralysis come over him. It was Polly's reminding him how often they had promised never to have secrets from each other. It was the awareness of Peter beside him, Peter who wanted nothing more of life than to be his doormat, and he felt such resentment against the lying position in which he found himself, he could say nothing.

"Very pretty. 'Twould read well upon the stage. But that was not the condition."

"Oh yes. And we'll live right next door to Papa forever. He is giving us that darling little house next door. So pretty and convenient. I'm sure Flip and I can manage it all by ourselves. I promised Papa we'd live next door."

"But," Mr. Mompesson added firmly, "the condition is that Captain Inman will see to it that his . . . business interests do not take him away to sea."

Here was the life raft tossed to him. Not until he was ready to retire might he marry Polly — not until then did he have to decide what to do.

"Oh, Papa, I know Dash won't want to leave me. He won't be going off for a year or years at a time. Let's not even discuss that, Papa. And then, it's *my* business and his business. It isn't yours, Papa."

She rushed to him and kissed a cheek hardly less perfect in its porcelain youthfulness than her own. And she talked fast about how she would be living only next door, never leaving him, and how he was the dearest, kindest, sweetest father a girl ever had — in the hope that the crux of the matter, Dash's retirement from the sea, would be forgotten or abandoned under her flow of words.

Squire Mompesson said carefully: "The world is upside down these days, and I blame the Revolutions, French and American, for that. Fathers, these days, seem to give their consent before the young gentleman has asked for it."

"Papa, don't. Dash did ask, years ago."

Mr. Mompesson went on: "Now, Polly, you and I must return to our guests in the great parlor. I believe we should never have left them. I am afraid you have let me into the embarrassing position of having promised your hand — perhaps a little prematurely. Got a little ahead of ourselves, eh?"

Polly's face looked confused. This time her father's suggestion that she and he had acted previously drew all the blood from it. This was the moment when Dash should do something tremendous. Oh, no matter what — cast himself at her feet, swear never to go near the sea again, never to leave her, not even for one night. This was the split second when he should act. Dash did nothing.

Peter's heart ached for Polly. She had humbled herself. Done all, and perhaps a little more than a girl might.

They were gone. And the two Inman brothers straightened from the low bows they had bestowed upon their vanished host and hostess.

Peter turned on Dash angrily. "Why didn't you say something, Dash? I mean, insist the wedding day be set, or even thank him for the house? Or *do* something? You just stood about. Poor Polly! She was so happy when she came in. You hurt her feelings horribly. Acting almost as if you didn't want her."

"You hardly expected me," Dash said, coldly, "to go into certain details of my private life? I'd rather tell Mompesson alone."

"God, Dash! Forget it. You've got the memory of an elephant and the sense of . . . of a baboon."

"Look-a-here, I've told you I'm not sure how I will act." Seeing Peter's distraught face, he added calmly, "Of course there's a way out. There's always a way out. Only . . . just now I can't seem to find the channel. Give me a little time."

～7～

LIZ WAS OFF on the *Victrix*, and once again she cleared for "Isle of France and beyond." Yet it had been decided that this was to be a brief voyage. When the *Wanderer* was completed and had gone, say, as far as the Mediterranean or the Baltic and back, merely to try her, these two sisters, commanded by two brothers, were to go out together, so each might support the other one. Peter knew of this plan. But evidently Dash had not seen fit to tell the Mompessons. Polly, so Nanny said, was telling the other girls that Dash had decided to retire. And they were to live in that pretty little house next door to her father's.

That spring, as the *Wanderer* was building, Dash did seem the settled merchant, taking, as people noticed with approval, "a great load" off his grandmother. He was every day at the counting-house and most careful and mindful of the duties of the home office which every year seemed to grow more complicated than the year before. He watched over the coming and going of the Inman fleet. The *Ajax* had been bought the year before from the Whites. And the *Shepherdess* Liz had picked up at Isle of France when he had been there with the *Mermaid*. She was a French-built brig, originally called *La Bergère*. He had sent her home laden with French colonial goods and given her an odd crew, half of whom couldn't speak English. Her captain was a renegade British naval man. All she had done in Salem was stop and get some American papers, then on she had gone to Bordeaux. England had been lenient about permitting American ships with American cargoes to enter France, but everything the *Shepherdess* stood for was illegal. Dash expected they'd have trouble over such a "broken voyage." Such things worried him much more than they did his grandmother.

No one had realized before the devotion between the oldest and the youngest Inman brothers. You hardly saw Dash without Peter beside him. If Dash as much as went to Boston to see about a cargo, Peter went with him. If Dash went to call upon young ladies, even Polly Mompesson, or to see a balance master, Peter went too. It was some time before Peter realized that this was not entirely because Dash so doted on his company. Dash had, in the long course of his masterhood, found ways of keeping himself alone, untouched, aloof, in the midst of the closest companionship. There was much that was solitary in Dash's nature, much more than in Peter's. A little slowly Peter guessed that Dash kept him close to him because he felt sorry for him. No, he thought, studying his older brother's almost inscrutable face, he feels guilty about me. That's worse.

By the time the *Wanderer* was fitted for sea, Peter was trying to make Dash talk about "it," as he called the Flanneau mixup. He felt it should, between the two of them at least, come up again and into the open. It was pressed down too hard inside of Dash. It was making him trouble, or it would, sometime. Actually what Peter had done for Dash was not drawing them closer. He felt less close to Dash than once he had.

When the *Wanderer* was ready to go, Dash suggested Peter go with him as his clerk. It would be an exciting voyage, straight into the Mediterranean, amid the rookeries of the North African pirates, fighting and running and doing all the tricks Yankee captains understood. Peter shook his head. Of course Dash didn't really want him along, reminding him forever of the injury he felt he had done him.

But all Peter said was: "Polly has been sure you weren't going off like this. When she knows, she'll be upset. I think I'd better be around."

True enough, next day Polly read in the *Gazette* that the *Wanderer,* Ralph Inman master, was clearing for the Mediterranean. It was on Peter's shoulder that she cried. She did need him, even as he had prophesied.

"I can't see why. Peter, I don't understand. He never said anything at all to me. Peter, if Dash does want to keep on to sea, doesn't he know I'd marry him just the same? And Papa would come round. He'd have to. Yet Dash hasn't even suggested such a thing. He thinks we had better just let things slide along until the House of Inman is so well-established he can really retire. Or," she added angrily, "until he's so old he can't go to sea any more. But oh, Peter, then I'll be old, too. Dash doesn't think of me. I won't wait forever. I don't see why I should. And if he doesn't really want to marry me, and sometimes I wonder, I'll marry someone else. Peter, something's wrong. Tell me, what's wrong?"

Peter knew, but he could not tell her. So he suggested she ask her papa to take her to Ballston Springs. It was April. Polly had always loved the gaiety, the new faces, new conquests, at this fashionable watering-place far away in New York State.

Two days after the *Wanderer's* topsails disappeared upon the horizon, there was once again that familiar scene enacted before the Mompessons'. The great traveling coach was trundled out, packed with boxes and trunks and more trunks and more boxes. This would be dragged through the muds of April by four hired horses. Mr. Mompesson's own fancier pair were tied on behind. Then a light chaise containing Flip, a groom, Aunt Brattle's serving woman, and the poodle which not even Aunt Brattle thought should ride with the gentry inside the stuffy closed coach — and more hatboxes and Polly's little writing-desk. And a large bouquet Polly received the last moment from an admirer, and the sheaf of poems Peter was so foolish as to press into her hand. So they took off for the wild roads and posting inns and all the beauty of the spring and the horror of broken axles, washed-out roads, bogs, bedbugs even, before they reached that fashionable haven, Ballston Springs.

It was well into July — for Polly seemed determined to stay away until her intimates had forgotten how much she had talked about that house next door and Dash's retiring, for her sake — when word came to the Inman counting-house that the *Wanderer* stood upon the coast. Within three days she would make port. Peter, as always, went home to tell his mother, but he knew that this news would mean little to her. It was only for the *Victrix's* topsails that she yearned.

As he left his house and turned idly into Essex Street, he saw Petra sitting under a currant bush in her own yard. Beside her was a naked, discarded wooden doll. He stopped as he always did to

speak to her, but she hid her face in shame and would not look at
him.

"Petra, what is it? Why are you unhappy?"

"I'm not unhappy. I'm bad."

"Why, no, I don't believe you are. At least you're the best little
girl I ever knew."

"I'm so bad."

Then he saw that there was a rope about her waist. She was
staked out like a lamb at grass. "You've been running away again."

"I ran away. I ran away to see you."

"I guess you shouldn't have." He sat down beside her, took her
in his lap. His hand rested on her curls, so hot and damp in the
heat of the midsummer day. "No, you mustn't run away. And not
to see me. You don't need to. I come to see you every day. Would
you like some rock candy?"

"Yes." She was a volatile child. Her spirits recovered, she took
the candy, and began to wriggle about in his lap. She did not want
to be held any more.

Dulcey came up the street. Many an eye followed her these days.
It was sad about Dulcey, Peter thought. As long as she herself had
thought she was going to marry Dash, she had been quite genteel,
even though everyone thought she was a mistress. But now she
began to look like one. Or at least to look subtly immoral. Perhaps that was Flanneau's fault. He knew it was ridiculous to try
to make her look really aristocratic. He had created a new style for
her. Very French. But not in the least like the little marquises
and such. She looked like one of those women Salem had been
reading about not many years before. Some of their seafaring men
had seen them. Women who had whooped and laughed as the
tumbrils rolled past, or had formed long dancing lines and sung
the *Carmagnole*. "Sansculottes" they had called them in those days.
Now many such had risen to the top of the immoral hurly-burly
of Napoleonic society. Now they had money to spend, but had not
lost the earthy, strong, common look, the broad peasant stance and
gestures. They did not wear their clothes like the old aristocrats.
Flanneau, the artist, had done nothing to hide the new-risen woman
in his wife. She seemed, nowadays, to scorn to imitate the refine-
ments of a passée society, confident that one world was swept away
and that the next, the future world, belonged to such as she.

"Peter," she called sharply, "let that child be. She's been naughty and I'm punishing her. There, come in, do." Petra was so depressed at losing Peter, she put down her rock candy. "And I'll tell you some news."

Peter followed her arrogantly swinging, handsome hips into the shop. There were no customers. She took off her flamboyant bonnet. From behind the door she took down a black apron. Flanneau always insisted that she wear a black apron as she tended shop, but hers was silk. The Stackpools had always worn black cambric.

"It's only," Dulcey said, "that the Mompessons' traveling coach has been sighted at one end of town — just as the *Wanderer* has been announced on 'Change."

"I knew about the *Wanderer*. So the Mompessons are back, too?"

"Yes. I'd been hoping and hoping the ship might get here first."

"She won't. It may still take her three days."

"I thought if Dash was here and *she* still away, he might come to see me."

"Oh, Dulcey, *no*. I tell you, and have told you — forget Dash. He isn't coming to see you — ever."

"I don't know about that. I guess . . . sometime."

"You forget Dash. Now you've got a nice child and a good husband and you forget everything else."

She was whistling happily as she rearranged fans and trinkets on her counter.

"Dulcey," he burst out, for her absolute confidence that Dash would sometime come back to her frightened him, "you know he's engaged, practically, to Miss Mompesson. And you certainly are married to Flanneau. What's the earthly good of his coming to see you?"

"No good." And a dimple eddied in her thick, firm cheek. "But sometimes things that aren't good do happen."

"So don't go pushing yourself forward."

"Oh, no," she agreed, smiling readily, "no, I won't."

She certainly hadn't pushed herself forward. She was simply there. Waiting.

~8~

AFTER HER RETURN, Polly invited her cousin, Georgiana Frick, to visit her "for a fortnight." This emancipated young girl came up on the next stage, without relative or servant to protect her. She knew all about such things, when stages run and whether or not you tip the hostler. But seemingly she did not know how long was a fortnight. Neither did Polly, but by the end of the third week, she began to wonder.

Polly had endured, more than enjoyed, her cousin's earlier visits. Before this summer the odd-looking, quaint child had been a toy for her, surely never a rival. But at eighteen, Georgiana had developed both personality and charm. She was one of those girls each generation calls "old-fashioned," yet the earlier generation to which they are consigned would in turn call them "old-fashioned." There was nothing modish or Grecian about Georgiana. Her dark hair was smoothly parted and pulled back to a knot on the nape of the neck. She did have, as Polly had pointed out to Peter, a coffin-shaped face, and was slender to the unfortunate extent that might be considered skinny, but she had spirit and wit, kindness, sympathy, imagination, and self-forgetfulness. A few years before, she had been so scared of her fashionable cousin that she always had seemed awkward when with her. Now she had poise and self-confidence that amazed and displeased Polly. Georgiana had certainly flowered. She was not one of those rare roses Mr. Derby grew under glass, but rather an odd, hard-to-find, delicate wild-flower that delights the finder by its rarity.

That summer, Dash and Peter, Polly and Georgiana, had many a pleasant water party together. Polly sometimes was piqued by the attention which the Inman brothers paid to Georgiana. Hour after hour the *Red Herring,* with Dash's hands forever on the tiller, skimmed the coast. Sometimes other young couples went with them, but usually the four of them were enough. Georgiana had, among her accomplishments, a richer singing voice than one would have expected, and a guitar from Spain. She made up many of her tunes. She had set Peter's poems to music. And when she sang in that rich, low voice of hers, the moon did seem enormous as it walked upon enchanted seas.

That Peter and Georgiana were in love, Polly accepted. She could see nothing lovable in Georgiana and she was piqued that before her very eyes an ever-devoted slave was deserting her for another and obviously far less attractive woman.

But it was Dash's pleasure in Georgiana that irritated her. He treated her like a loved younger sister and called her "Mouse." She knew he hoped nothing would come between Peter and Georgiana. But if he was playing a merely brotherly part, Polly thought he overdid it. The fact was that on their somewhat rustic gambols the young girl showed up a better companion than the belle. She could get wet, or becalmed, go hungry or sunburn, without fuss.

For the first time in her life Polly went to her father's library and took down a book to look up a word. The book was a dictionary and the word she was curious about was "fortnight." Fourteen days! It had already been over a month, and still Georgiana showed no inclination to leave. Well, perhaps she would after the Perkins wedding next week. The four of them were going together.

Dash had been grateful to Blainey Phipps for one thing. He had not let the scandal about Peter interfere with their old friendship. Of course, a bachelor does not have to be so finicky about such things. But now that he was marrying Maria Perkins — or her money — he had asked Peter to be his best man. Peter, too, was pleased. He knew that his friendship with Blainey was wearing a little thin. Harvard, or the law, had done something to Blainey. He had been a shy, poetic, idealistic lad, but now that he had decided to "descend to the marts of trade," he was ready to descend lower than your average, less imaginative young lawyer. His marriage to Maria Perkins was part of this new side of him. He was always talking to Peter of "getting on." Yet apparently he had not entirely forgotten the boy he once had been. He wanted Peter Inman for his best man.

You can't put four young people, all in love, into a chaise designed for two without some amusement. The Perkinses were at their country seat. It would be a long drive out. Peter was dressed to a tee — they had all seen to that. The girls wore their prettiest muslins. It was so warm they needed neither cloaks nor shawls.

So there were no wraps to pad the gentlemen's knees and even the daintiest pelvises became sharp-boned after an hour's sitting in a cramped position. But the physical discomforts, for the day was hot, much too hot, only added to the fun. They laughed and sang all the way over.

Theirs was the first vehicle that turned in the Perkins' driveway, passed gates, gazebos, great elms and lawns, box-edged gardens and imported gardeners. It had been agreed to deliver the best man early, so he might get his instructions before the pell-mell of guests arrived. All four felt happy. Georgiana was happiest of all. No one was going to be nasty to her darling Peter.

Blainey himself let them in. He had been watching for them from an upper window. There was something unpleasant about seeing Blainey surrounded by so much wealth, the fine, costly furniture, the Chinese papers upon the walls, the great pallid Aubusson rugs. He had a little the look of a man who had stolen them.

Polly was on Peter's arm, and they marched in almost as if they were the bride and groom. Blainey was alone in the hall. The rest of the bridal party was still upstairs.

"Aren't you proud of Peter?" Polly demanded. "See how beautifully we have him dressed. Peter, where's that comb I told you to carry?" She took it from him and he bent his head so she could comb and pat his dark curls as close to perfection as they ever got.

"Oh yes. It is good of you to come so early, Peter, especially because . . ."

Blainey took off his spectacles, remembered not to wipe them on his neckcloth as he usually did, and slowly pulled from his pocket an enormous Chinese silk handkerchief embroidered all over with insects, birds, and flowers. Without his spectacles, he no longer looked like the weasel, with which Dash had for years been comparing him, but lost and blind as a mole. Because they were all so happy, they began laughing at his handkerchief.

"Oh yes, I know," Blainey agreed, "but it is the one Father Perkins gave Mother Perkins on her wedding day. Maria says it is larger than ladies carry today. But she insists *I* carry it. For sentiment."

Dash, who, when in good spirits, was easily amused, seemed unable to get over Blainey's handkerchief. "It's lucky you don't have to wear Mother Perkins's veil."   ,

"Oh no," Blainey said seriously, "Maria is wearing that. But Dash, you understand the sentiment . . . it's very fine sentiment." He wanted his handkerchief back, but Dash was examining the pretty embroidery carefully.

Polly went to the piano and began to play. Georgiana, in the lavender she so often wore, was standing before a pier glass taking off her bonnet, patting her hair, putting her bonnet on again, and straightening her dress which was somewhat crushed by the long, sticky drive. She was a frank girl, even in her primping.

"Look, Polly," Dash said, "I've made Blainey's handkerchief into a rag baby."

Blainey saw a chance to speak to Peter without being overheard. "Peter, I'm sorry. You know how nervous girls get on their wedding days. But Maria . . . I mean, she isn't the nervous type. Only this. I mean today. It's too much for her nerves. Well . . . it was only this morning she told me that if you stand up with me as best man, why, she won't . . ."

Peter blinked as if from a physical blow. "Oh, that's all right, Blainey. I see what you mean." The rebuff had hit him, but, like the feather bed his mother compared him to, seemed to make no indentation.

The piano stopped. Georgiana swung around from the pier glass. Dash thrust the rag baby into his pocket. All had heard. There was embarrassment and consternation on every face except Peter's.

Polly was on her feet. "Maria Perkins objects to Peter Inman? Neither she nor her sisters objected, did they, when again and again he asked them to dance with him! Yes, and made you ask them, too. And many is the time they'd have had no suppers, unless carried to them by hired waiters, unless Peter had pitied them."

"Nonsense, Polly," Peter said, his face frozen into a queer smile.

"It's true. I've seen it." Polly slapped her hand down on the keyboard. "Come, Georgiana. Let's not stay. Peter? Peter, come with us. We are leaving."

"I'm staying."

"Stay where you're not wanted!" Georgiana cried. "Peter *we* want you."

"But," Blainey gulped out, fingering his neckcloth which suddenly seemed much too tight, "he is wanted . . . as a guest."

"Yes," Polly said viciously, "so there'll be one man you can count on to dance with the bridesmaids — the Misses Anna and Marianna Perkins!"

"Miss Polly, please try to understand. I can't help it, can I, if Maria gets nervous on her wedding day and doesn't want him for best man? I've told her how indebted I am to the Inmans." There was a sudden, touching look of dignity on his face as he went on. "I was poor and an orphan. When I was little, I'd never have had decent clothes nor unbroken shoes if it hadn't been for Mrs. Inman giving me what Peter outgrew. Please stay. All of you. And Maria says that if I wish to show my gratitude to the Inmans, perhaps I can persuade Dash to be my best man."

"Count me out. If Peter is not good enough for you, neither am I. I'm worse. And if my girls don't care to stay, I'll drive them home. Aye, Peter, are you coming or staying?"

"I'm staying."

Georgiana went to him, put her hand in his, but he would not budge. It was Maria, not Blainey, who had objected to him. He'd back Blainey, his words implied, even into the jaws of Hell or matrimony.

A servant was sent to fetch the chaise, but just as it had started down the long driveway, Blainey came running after them.

"My handkerchief," he begged.

Dash found it in one of his pockets and tossed it to him. He looked ridiculous, jumping into the air to catch the rag baby. They all three of them got to laughing, and led by Polly, none of them cared to stop.

Now the other wedding guests were arriving. A procession of carriages with flashing wheels, gleaming horses, lulling springs, stretched almost all the way from Salem to Danvers. A full tide of fashion was running. There was only one skiff going contrary to it. People leaned from carriages, chaises, curricles, whiskies, and gigs, in amazement. Was the wedding called off? Why were they heading back to Salem? They met Bacchus and Ariadne pulling the Inman carriage, Mr. Mullins on the box, Mrs. Inman, Cousin Frances, Marcy, Tom, and Miranda inside. They met Old Doctor West, Jack and Nanny, and Nanny screaming the questions others had been too self-controlled to ask. Here came the Mompessons' somewhat old-fashioned, stately equipage bearing aunts and Squire. Polly's father nearly fell out in his agitation. Polly had a handkerchief over her face, giggling and giggling. He couldn't imagine what was amiss. Aunt Brattle almost broke her visual, trying for a better focus.

Then Dash saw his chance to turn into a country lane and

escape the startled eyes. So they went west, and the lane became a cart path. They turned around and received directions in a farmer's yard and soon came out on the turnpike. It was not until then that the girls stopped their chattering and giggling. Dash had sobered down long before this. He was a man, and not accustomed to go off into laughter because he was angry. Then, too, he felt a sense of guilt the girls could not share. Why on earth any man wanted to put on his best clothes and be best man for a Blainey Phipps marrying a Perkins girl he could not understand. Yet, seemingly, this was what Peter had wanted to do. So Maria would not have objected to himself as best man! She would — if she knew the truth. And he thought grimly of what Polly's reaction would be if she knew. And Georgiana's. It was partly Dash's heavy mood that quieted the girls.

All three were dressed in their wedding finery, but now had no party to attend. The summer's day was oven-hot. Joe pyeweed and asters, goldenrod and thoroughwort, hung dustily along the turnpike and drought and dust enveloped the chaise. Polly, who had insisted before that the top should be down, now wanted it up. Here upon the turnpike they met other travelers. The mail coach rattled by, horses plunging against the collar, breasting the hills at a canter. They saw a tin peddler rolling toward them like a meteor, for his gig and horse, hung with samples of his wares, glittered in the sunshine. Surely that lank, black-clad, vinegar-faced man astride an antediluvian horse was an itinerant preacher. And there were farmers trudging beside ox teams, drovers herding sheep to market. Fine sights to see upon the turnpike. Yet the mood settling down on them was far from light-hearted. Dash was sneezing a good deal. Horses and dust had always made him sneeze. Polly was saying she'd suffocate if the top wasn't now put down. And all were thirsty.

There upon the pike Polly spied an inn sign. Hanging from an ancient oak was a dusty board and on the board was painted a pair of blue sleeves. About and under the trees stood drovers resting their cattle and refreshing themselves. They saw two sailors drive up in a hired gig, with enormous cigars in their mouths.

"Dash, I'm dead of thirst. Do let's stop here."

Dash knew of the Blue Sleeves. He couldn't tell the innocent girls that it was little better than a brothel, or "slaughter house" as sailors said.

"There's a better place half a mile from here. I don't think ladies come to Blue Sleeves much. It's for carters, peddlers, drovers, sailors on the lam, and such."

"Well," Polly insisted, "I see a lady at the upper window."

Of course there was, or, at least, a female. A doxy at an upper window was a more effective and a more ancient sign than anything selectmen would allow to be painted on a signboard.

Polly put her hands on the reins Dash held and the horse came to a stop. "I never heard of an inn called 'Blue Sleeves,'" she said. "Look at them, there on the board. They are frightfully old-fashioned."

"It's an old-fashiond sort of place."

"Oh, see, Dash, everybody is waving at us. I like it, I *love* it. I like simple people — now and then. Dash, I never knew you were a snob before."

The carters, drovers, and the two sailors were staring avidly at the man and his two handsome girls. Had he a doxy left over?

Dash got the horse started again, but Polly was almost standing in the chaise, craning her neck, looking back. She was still saying how cozy it was. It looked so cool there under the oak trees. The men waved at her and she waved back at them.

Georgiana had guessed why he would not stop. "Come on, Polly," she said quietly, "I don't like its looks either. Dash says we'll stop at the Red Lion. It's only half a mile along."

"I don't like the Red Lion. Papa often drives me and the aunts over there for an outing. It's so stuffy and dull. The Blue Sleeves didn't look stuffy. Dash, will you *please* turn around? I want to go to the Blue Sleeves."

He wouldn't. Why not? At first he wouldn't say, then came out with it. The place was a brothel.

Polly had a way of forcing conversation out on the most delicate limb, and when, as now, the limb broke, gasping with outraged innocence, or was it curiosity? She was so upset she refused to stop when they reached the respectable Red Lion. The long dusty drive had parched them all. But Polly wouldn't stop. All she wanted was to be taken home. She had a headache. The horse was tired. Polly cross. Georgiana silent. Dash's bad conscience made him glum. They had started out with high spirits and festivity. They drew up before the Mompessons' with nothing festive about them except their wedding finery.

Polly ran up the steps with hardly a word of farewell.

Georgiana lingered, watched her disappear, then said to Dash, "I've got to talk with you."

"All right, Mouse." But he felt as if he were seeing what he had taken to be a friendly brig suddenly break out the colors of an Algerian pirate.

"Now, please?"

"Now . . . of course."

"I've got to talk with someone. I've got to talk with you — first of all."

He tied the horse in the shade, halloed for a servant to bring it water, and followd her into Polly's sitting room. Here the shades were drawn, the windows closed against the heat.

They sat facing each other in the soft semi-darkness. On each face was a similar expression, a ruthlessness which said, "I will tell the truth, let the axe fall where it may."

"Dash," Georgiana burst out, "I want to marry Peter. I'm terribly in love with Peter. And he . . . I think he is almost in love with me. But I don't know what to do." She twisted the black onyx and pearl bracelets on her delicate wrists.

Dash said quietly, "And you feel there is an obstacle?"

"Yes, that's the trouble. That's where you must help me."

He thrust out his lower lip at her and answered soberly, "I will." But let her talk, he thought warily, lying low as he had learned to do, making the other person show his cards, lying low yourself and pulling out the ace when the time came. And, poor girl, he thought, studying her — so beguiling, so far from pretty. Of course she is suffering, thinking always of Peter and "that other woman." Peter . . . he thought of him as he had last seen him, so spruce and fine in his pale broadcloth and flowered waistcoat, slapped in the face by people like Maria Perkins and Blainey Phipps. He felt a tide of love for Peter, something he hardly wanted to feel because it shamed him so.

"Go ahead, Georgiana," he said, mildly. "Now as for this other woman . . ."

"I don't know what to do about her."

He was silent. Not yet had he seen her cards. Not yet would he play his trump.

"Why won't Polly let go of him?"

"*Polly?*" He was dumbfounded. "There's nothing . . . not a thing between them."

"Yes, there is. That's why she hates having me here. She wants Peter to go on forever following her about. And he . . . " She went on rapidly: "It's not exactly love with him. No, it's a sort of dream. A *real* woman would not bother me so much. Polly has told me about the *real* woman. It's Mrs. Flanneau. I know all about it. Did you know it's only the child he cares about, now? If ever she meant anything to him, it's all in the past. And I don't care. It's Polly's hold on him that's so terribly tight. And not real. She does it on purpose."

Dash had steeled himself to discuss Peter's mistress with Georgiana, and to dispel that shadow forever. He was completely unprepared for this frankly unkind attack upon Polly.

"I never gave it much thought, Georgiana. No, Peter is not in love with Polly."

"You see, he sends me his poems. Half of them are really about her. Hidden behind the lines, but I can guess. Yet it is not *really* Polly — just a fancy picture of her. And it's only because he cares so much for you. I'm not a fool," she announced, as though he were contradicting her, "and I'm a grown woman of eighteen."

"You mean you don't care at all about what is called 'the Inman scandal'?"

"No, I don't, because . . . Dash, aren't women supposed to go by feeling more than reason? Aren't they thought to be intuitive? I've never felt Mrs. Flanneau was any barrier at all between me and Peter. You're one and so's Polly."

At that moment Polly came down the stairs, surprised to find Dash had come in with no invitation from herself. Obviously not pleased that he had been sitting here so long with Georgiana. She was in a dressing-gown, and freshly bathed, her hair still pinned tightly on the top of her little head. Hardly dressed, surely, to receive gentlemen by any standards less lax than those of the water-front girls of Marseilles. Or those of the doxy hanging from the upper window of the Blue Sleeves. Dash's eyes went to the Iphigenia clock. Her father and aunts would not be home for a while yet. The dancing was about ending over in Danvers. Georgiana muttered a little crossly and left.

Knowing that Polly had talked freely about his family's skeleton with Georgiana made it easier for Dash. She couldn't pretend she hardly knew what he was talking about. His mother had always told her sons that there were some things men never mentioned to any lady, even to a wife. He supposed those were the things Mullins often mentioned. Some things may be discussed with a married lady, especially a wife, but never with an unmarried girl. Mistresses and illegitimate children belonged in that category, obviously.

"Polly," he said, sitting close to her, smelling the fresh soap and lavender water of her bath upon her, very conscious, even if she were not, that she shouldn't be receiving him with so little on, "Georgiana and I have been talking. About something that inadvertently concerns us all. You and I as well as Georgiana and Peter. But Peter, most of all." He took one of her always ringless, subtle hands to play with. Fiddling with it in an almost impersonal way as though it were a little thing he had picked up off his mother's sitting-room table.

"She wants to marry Peter?"

"You've guessed it."

"Guessed it!" She laughed. "That's no conundrum. She certainly hasn't been hiding her love under a bushel. She was just sixteen when I had her here with me and she first laid eyes on him. She told me that night she loved him and was going to marry him. And she has been saying so ever since. Do men really like such bold girls? I've thought sometimes her tactics were all wrong."

Dash had never thought of Georgiana as a "bold girl." Nor did he now. Polly this time had been a little too transparent.

"If there's deep feeling, honesty, behind the boldness, yes. And Peter does care for her. Perhaps more than he himself realizes. Of course, there are obstacles. But I think Georgiana is brave enough to go over or through them. With all my heart I hope she succeeds."

Polly said, almost callously: "It is only lately I've taken her infatuation seriously. But I told Papa when he went to Boston last week, he must talk to Cousin Frick. You know he's a Harvard professor. I don't think they notice things much. Papa talked to Cousin Frick."

"Was that necessary?" he demanded coldly.

"Of course. And Cousin Frick was flabbergasted that Papa had permitted her to receive so much attention from an absolutely impossible man. He's writing her she must come home immediately.

I think she'll have to leave by the end of the week. Really, Dash, I only invited her for a fortnight."

"You'd say any man who had had a mistress was impossible?"

"Of course. But it's Cousin Frick's fault. He has always given Georgiana so much head. It's not Papa's fault she fell in love with a man she'd never be allowed to marry."

"Georgiana is a determined girl. She'll do as she pleases."

"Yes," Polly assented languidly, "she's very masculine."

There was nothing masculine about Georgiana. Dash thought of the delicate hands and feet, the bright, shining, mercurial spirit behind the almost prim facade. Unwisely, perhaps, he began to defend her.

"I see nothing masculine about a girl's wanting a man and going after him. They all do. So do all she-animals. Happens only that Georgiana shoots a little straighter than most. I take it you're tired of her visit?"

"I wish she'd go home. She and her songs and her guitar." She smiled suddenly. "I wish Peter would give her his 'no.' But there, if she doesn't go, I promise you Cousin Frick will be up himself and drag her away. He may not be able to *keep* her away — Georgiana is so unmanageable."

"Let's go back where we started from. If I could prove that Peter never had a thing to do with Mrs. Flanneau . . . "

"But you couldn't. For one thing, the child looks exactly like him."

"No. She looks like all of us Inmans. Polly, did you ever stop to think that Tom and Liz and I were home nine months before the child was born? Any one of us could be its father — chronologically. I might be."

"But you are not. Peter has practically said he is. And Flanneau has told everybody."

"Polly, suppose it was not Georgiana, but you, who loved Peter. Couldn't you, somehow, rise above an early mistake? Take things into your own hands . . . even if your father disapproved?"

"Oh, fie! I never take things into my own hands. I'm not Georgiana."

He looked at her critically. "I wish you were more like her in some ways, Polly."

She gazed at him in blank amazement. Not believing her ears.

"*I*, like Georgiana?"

"At least she can understand a man. Even the bad in him. Say, 'I love him and nothing else and nobody else matters. I'll marry him anyway.'"

Polly still couldn't believe he had wished she were like that dreadful Georgiana. She said, knowing it was not true, "I think you are in love with her yourself."

"No. But I love her. And I love Peter. I'm not going to let any obstacle I can remove stand between them."

"What can you do?"

He looked her straight in the face. "I can say that Peter was never involved with Dulcey Flanneau, except as he acted for me. I can say I seduced the girl — left her with child, went to sea . . ." She sat stiffly, staring straight ahead of her. " . . . Left Peter to stand by her, and so on. Of course, it looked as though it were Peter's child. I *could* say all that, Polly."

"Dash" — her voice was drawn thin and tight with emotion — "what you really mean is that you care more for Peter and Georgiana than for me. You're ready to *lie* to help them out. Oh, that's awfully gallant of you! You're going to help them — even if it kills me. I think . . . I think . . ." Her voice broke, and she was crying.

He came close to her, holding her tight in his arms. She would at first have none of his blandishments.

"I won't have it!" she cried. "If you really loved me you would never have thought of such a . . . a *disgusting* thing. And you never do anything I want. You won't give up going to sea. Why, even little things. I did so want to go to the Blue Sleeves. And you wouldn't. And now you've said plain out as a man can say you care more for *them* than for us. All right, you can have Georgiana. I don't care. I don't care what happens to me. I wish I were dead, Dash!"

But even as she railed, his arms tightened and tightened about her. His shaven cheek pressed close to hers. "Yes?" he whispered, encouraging her to go on. And when she was ready to stop, he again urged her on with his whispered "Yes?" Now there was less and less conviction in her words and they came farther and farther apart, until at last she was spent and speechless lying in his arms and there was nothing more to say. Nothing left but love. What if she thought he was ready to toss her aside to help Peter, what if she often irritated and even offended him! It did not matter as they lay locked in each other's arms.

It was, as always, Dash who had the sense to know when to stop and the strength to get up and leave her.

"Polly," he said, at last, miserably, standing beside her, looking down upon her, "why have you and I never been able to talk?" His voice shook slightly.

"Don't talk," she murmured.

He walked away from her to the window, pulled up the curtain and pushed back the shutters as if determined to let in fresh air and light on a situation that was too much for him.

"It's as if words," he began, speaking as much to himself as to her, "the usual medium for ideas between humans, mean nothing to us. All we have is a deeper, more primitive language. Perhaps the truest in the world. Like this . . . like now. I start out determined to talk to you . . . but . . . oh, Polly, I think I'd feel the same toward you and you toward me if you spoke only Russian and I Hottentot. But now . . ." He smiled his wide, sudden smile, "Polly, let's try to talk. And at arms' length."

She yawned as engagingly as a kitten and closed her eyes. "I love to hear your voice. Dash, if you won't go home — and I think it's time you did — let me lie here and relax and have your voice flow over me. I'll not bother about the sense."

He laughed ruefully. It was so hard for him not to go back to her, fling himself down beside her and say nothing. He braced his body as though a heavy wind had caught him.

"If you don't like what I say, you can pretend not to hear. Polly, I'm not going to let Peter lose a fine girl like Georgiana, be snubbed by people like Maria Perkins and that Blainey Phipps; not be considered nice enough for Harvard . . . because of anything I've done . . ."

Certainly he had said it straight out at last. She did not drop dead, faint even. She wasn't going crazy as Peter had promised. She sat upright and looked at him curiously.

"You heard what I said?"

"And I can see by your face you are lying. You look so ashamed. If you still cared for me, you'd never have thought of doing anything so dreadfully gallant — and loathsome." She did not break into the hysterics he dreaded so much. Seemingly she had herself well in hand. "Very well," she said, staring at him, "help Peter out of his mess. Why should it be anything to me? You and I are not engaged, Dash. But what there was — there was always something between us — oh, Dash, it's broken. It's breaking now."

"My dear."

"Go to sea, then. Please go to sea again. Right off. I don't want to see you for months."

The doorbell rang. Polly wiped her eyes and gathered her voluminous dressing-gown about her. Dash admired the self-control she was now summoning. Usually it was much easier for her to turn her emotions on than off.

Flip came in. "Flanneau has sent the eggshell bombazine cloak you ordered, Miss Polly."

Polly said stiffly: "It was promised this morning. For me to wear to the wedding. And it wasn't here in time. Tell him I refuse to accept it."

"Yes, Miss Polly." But the little maid hesitated, her bright, pert face turned reproachfully toward her mistress. "But today was so hot you wouldn't have worn it anyway."

"That's not the point."

Flip went away, and came back immediately. "Can't you take it, miss?" she pleaded. "It was made to your order and so expensive I don't believe he could sell it to anyone else. You could wear it all summer."

"No." Polly's emotions seemed to have caught up with her rather late. She was obviously holding on to herself with great effort. "I won't have it now. It was *not* done when promised. Send Flanneau in."

"It's Mrs."

"I never expected to receive *her* in my house. And why did she come to the front door? Well, send her in."

Dulcey, in spite of the brave, bright ribbons in her bonnet and the elegance of her green and white striped summer silk, stood a little timidly on the threshold. Over one bare, solid round arm she carried the pale cloak.

"Mrs. Flanneau," Polly said languidly, "tradespeople usually ring at the rear of a house."

"Excuse me, Miss Mompesson. I didn't know. I don't often deliver. *He* does that himself. I didn't know. But today he was so tired I said yes I would."

"My servant told you I would not accept the cloak?"

"Yes. But I don't believe it. I know it was promised this morning. It would have been done if only yesterday you hadn't changed your mind about the cuffs. He was up all last night, sewing. And when he brought it over this noon, you had already left for the wedding. You left very early, miss."

Polly colored angrily. Dash felt all the anger she had manufactured within herself to use on him was now about to explode on Dulcey. He was still standing, back to the window, little more than a silhouette in the darkened room.

"I believe I may leave my house when I please?" Polly asked sarcastically.

"Steady!" Dash interrupted, speaking as he might speak to a nervous mate in a storm.

Dulcey turned her eyes, and saw him. Her worried face immediately smoothed. Again and again they had met upon the street, and every time she had looked at him thus confidently, but never had presumed to address him. She did not speak, but smiled at him with confidence and admiration, sure, now that he was on her side, that all would go right. She at last said firmly to Polly: "Long as it's late, I'm sure Flanneau will shave the price. Mr. Mompesson can settle with Flanneau on that."

She laid the cloak on the lounge beside Polly, bobbed a curtsy and turned to go.

"I don't want it, anyway. It's ugly and badly made. Take it away with you."

Dash walked toward her. "Take it, Polly," he commanded. "Don't let innocent people suffer for your . . ."

"My what, please, Dash?"

"Upset temper."

"My temper is not upset. The contract was not fulfilled. I don't have to accept it, and I won't." Nor could he budge her.

At last Dulcey, the cloak over her arm, her bravely ribboned bonnet hanging in dejection, left.

There was a long silence in the room. Finally Dash picked up his hat and walked out the front door.

Outside, standing forlornly on the street — and the bravado of her clothing increased the impression of forlornness — he found Dulcey with the cloak over her arm. She did not seem to be waiting for him. She simply had not the heart to go home and tell her husband.

"Come, Dulcey," Dash said. "I've a horse here. I'll drive you home. Jump in."

"I don't feel like going straight home. *She* doesn't understand how hard he worked. And he'll be disappointed and get drunk and . . ."

"Jump in and I won't take you straight home." He turned the horse west on Federal Street. "And I'll buy the cloak."

"Will you?"

"Yes. And you can keep it to wear."

"Mayn't I say it was Peter who gave it to me? He's used to the idea of Peter, but he wouldn't want any other man to give me things."

The horse had confidently expected to go home. He was bored to be once more headed out and away from Salem. Dulcey was drawn far back under the hood of the chaise.

"Dulcey," Dash burst out, "I . . . I've treated you like dirt."

"I don't care if you treat me like dirt, Dash. Just so long as you treat me like anything at all."

He felt his temples begin to throb. His hands on the reins were sweating.

"Dulcey . . . do you want to drive over to the pike with me? And have supper?"

"I can all right. He's so tired he'd gone to sleep before I left. He won't wake up for hours. He won't miss me."

"And you want to go with me?"

"Yes." She gave him again that look of utter confidence. He reddened in spite of himself.

"There are two inns over there. The Red Lion is fashionable . . . and respectable. But the Blue Sleeves . . ." His longing for her was suddenly so intense he was literally speechless. It flowed through his whole body, making him feel weak as water, yet tingling all over.

"I guess the Blue Sleeves," she said, with finality. She knew what he meant. Probably she, too, had heard of the inn.

They did not draw closer as proper lovers who had made such a decision might have done. Dash felt the blessed relief of her, after Polly's captiousness. And the endless love-making that always stopped short. He did not have to tell Dulcey he loved her, or say anything.

He did not even kiss her, as the horse took them far out beyond their neighbors' eyes. There was no need even to kiss her until the candle was blown out.

~9~

ONE NIGHT, months after the *Victrix,* Ralph Inman master, and the *Wanderer,* Eleazar Inman master, had left Salem, Peter woke hearing the doorbell. It was a blustering December night. He hardly saw the burly men before his candle blew out. One said ominously:

"Peter Inman . . . couldn't stand to see this child's foster father mauling her so. Down at the Sun. He always does when befuddled."

For every so often Flanneau's natural melancholy overcame him and he drank. Unless Dulcey would hide Petra with Mrs. Cunningham, he would take her with him.

"Sometime he'll kill her with his love. Took her first to her mother, but she was entertaining gentlemen friends. Brought her here — where she belongs."

So they landed Petra in his arms and off they staggered. It was not only Flanneau who had been enjoying the Sun's liquor.

Dulcey had told Peter how Flanneau would get the child away from her and take her drinking with him. Then sometimes captains, enured to the sight of young Hindu wives burned alive with dead husbands, the drowning of girl babies in China, or the eating of grandparents by cannibals, would feel they could not enjoy their liquor and look the other way as they could in heathen lands.

Petra was wide enough awake to cling to him and she smiled.

I hope Mother doesn't wake up — or Miranda. Good Heavens! Suppose Miranda! . . .

Half of him longed to be rid of her. The other half wanted her never to leave him. She said his name. His arms tightened and he said hers.

Now he must sit her somewhere while he stole upstairs for his clothes. He carried her to the kitchen, lighted a candle at the glowing hearth, sat her in Mrs. Cady's chair.

"Petra," he whispered, "be a good girl and don't budge."

"I'll go with you."

"No, wait here until I come back. I'll take you home." For if Dulcey was still entertaining, he could hand her over to Cousin Frances.

"I'm going with you, Peter."

Robin, the little cat who had already gone out three times with the *Victrix,* had by now swallowed the anchor. She lay by the hearth encircling her kittens.

"Here's a kitten for you to hold, Petra, until I come back."

By the time he returned, it was already hers. She had no idea of leaving without the kitten.

"All right, you can have it."

"My kitty?"

"Yes."

"What's its name?"

It had no name he knew of, but the mother was called Robin, so he answered "Wren." "And look," he said, "we'll put him in this basket so he can't run away."

Then she was delighted to go.

The gentlemen callers were gone, for there was only one light at the Flanneaus' and that was in the shop. Dulcey opened before he could knock and she was already in a dressing-gown.

"I couldn't stay abed, I was that worried," she admitted, and stood by to let him pass her, go into the shop where the candles burned.

The first thing he noticed was her concern over the child. Sometimes he thought she cared little enough for Petra. His second thought was . . . my God, she's pregnant again! This was a subject that had been discussed for over a month in Salem. But no one had been so indelicate as to mention the fact to the supposed father. He noticed her heavy backward leaning.

"Sit, Peter, do," Dulcey said. "Tell me what happened. Flanneau came home first — but the constable had to lead him. He'll be like this again tomorrow. It always lasts about three days with him. I've been that worried."

"Put Petra to bed, Dulcey. And here's a kitten to go with her."

"A kitten? I'm glad to have a kitten. Real pretty, too."

While they were upstairs, Peter had a moment to get used to Dulcey's condition. He was still thinking about it when Dulcey joined him, and he mechanically told her how he had happened to have Petra.

"So they landed her on you, Peter," she said, with a laugh. "Thought that's where she belonged. Well, at least they got the right *house*."

Peter said: "They brought her here first. They said you didn't hear them. Too busy entertaining gentlemen friends."

"That was spiteful of them. I suppose, as long as they think you are paying for me, you ought to know if I'm keeping company with anyone else."

She went on: "You know there's nothing wrong with my parties. If there was, Flanneau wouldn't stand for it. He's that particular about the company I keep. He won't let any men, except you, hang about me." Then, noting a look of knowledge in Peter's eyes, she flushed. "So he isn't mad about your having a new baby. He hopes it will be a son."

"You can get the real father to finance this one," Peter said, stiffly. "I'll not accept anybody's brats as mine."

"Maybe I will," she agreed. "But it would break Flanneau's heart if he thought I was immoral. And the *real* father could pay plenty." She looked at him oddly. "Is that what you want?"

He had an intuitive realization of the truth. But he said, "How can I tell if I don't know what you're talking about?"

"About Dash . . . of course."

His heart went to his boots. He tried to say, "I don't believe it," but he knew she had said the truth.

"All last summer, ever since the Perkins wedding, it went on."

Yes, Peter realized, Dash had drawn in to himself last summer, and it had started at the time of the wedding. He had not confided in him. But Peter had known that he and Polly had had some sort of misunderstanding. Dash had been crazy for Liz to get the *Victrix* home, so he could go to sea once more.

"And don't you ever go telling Flanneau. Will you please promise, Peter? He says it's all right because it's your child. I think he might kill me if he knew it wasn't. Or — and that would be worse for you — just take Petra and go off to France and leave me. He could, legally. Legally Petra is his and he can do anything he wants with her."

Peter gave no promise. Her tone changed, and there was a slight threat in it. "And I've still got the letter."

Peter had almost forgotten it.

"If Flanneau finds out Dash is this child's father and turns on me because he can't trust me to have the same father for all my children, I'll show him the letter. In fact, I might show the letter to anyone who's interested."

"Why don't you destroy it? You ought to have, long ago."

"I might," she offered, "and I mightn't." She meant, Do as I ask you or take the consequences. "You agree?"

"More or less. I'll think it over."

Wren came down the stairs, ready to go home with him now.

"No, you don't," Peter said. "You're Petra's cat now. And don't you forget it."

But in the days that followed, Wren did forget. The back yards of the two houses adjoined. And Petra followed him. It was possible for a child her size to squeeze under the boundary fence. First Wren would arrive, and then Petra, at the Inmans' kitchen door. It was in vain that Dulcey slapped her and tied her up. Whenever she could not find her kitten, she went to the Inman back door and asked.

When Frances told Dulcey how offended Mrs. Inman was by these sudden appearances, Dulcey began punishing the child with a heavy hand. She slapped and shook her, locked her for hours in dark closets. Petra began, for the first time, to grow a little timid, to lose her bright trustfulness. She had nightmares and sudden fears. These fears always took the form of worry for the kitten. When her mother locked her up, she would sob for hours, sure this time that something awful had happened to Wren.

Late that spring, Wren once more ran back to his original home. Then Flanneau did an ugly thing. He put him in a sack, carried him to North River, and drowned him. Petra now became a mournful figure. She was four and at an age children are apt to run away. Over on the Marblehead Road, far out on the Neck, along the wharves and upon the common, people not only could see her but hear her and her sad cry of "Wren, Wren, Wren."

❧ 10 ❧

Lucy Inman could have taken the unpleasant situation philosophically if it had not been for Miranda and the fact that Nanny took Miranda's side in everything. The two young matrons were great friends. Both were agreed that it was shameful to have Petra about the house, almost that it was shameful to have Peter living with decent people. Nanny's son, Boots, was almost three, Ruth was eighteen months. And Miranda was "expecting." These young women insisted their own children, born or unborn, were being contaminated by the elfish, pretty love-child.

"Mother Inman," as Miranda called her, neither asked nor desired Miranda's help in running her own house. She had always run it pretty well. Everything — no matter how little money she had — was always comfortable and gay. Her children had been happy, and her servants. She was an easy employer, never able to keep after people. Nor did she herself always set them a good example in housewifery. Miranda couldn't believe her eyes the first time she caught Mother Inman brushing dust under a rug. She could not understand a woman who would spend an hour arranging bright leaves in a copper kettle. Copper kettles belonged in the kitchen. And leaves were something Mullins was supposed to sweep and burn. Yet Mother Inman would concern herself with such nonsense when she must realize that *nobody* had really "turned out" the attic since the house was built. Nanny, who for the first time possessed an intimate in her own house, stood by Miranda and the two of them together were stronger than Lucy. Mrs. Inman went off to drink tea, sew, and gossip with her own little circle of admiring ladies — and let the two girls "turn out" the attic. They threw out into the yard great heaps of things, paddles carved and painted like tattooing, strange idols of wood or clay or basketwork, for the boys had been using the attic for years for their curiosities. Luckily, before Mullins got around to throwing them away, 'Sephus Hobey and Marcy arrived. Doctor Hobey saw the great value of the collection and installed it properly in the East India Marine Society where it belonged, to be known forever after as the Inman Collection.

Not only did Miranda rise early, but she took upon herself to supervise the care and cleaning of the second floor. Mrs. Cady, these days, wasn't supposed to do more than cook and mind the kitchen. Linda was so slavishly devoted to her own mistress she'd pay no heed to Mrs. Miranda's requests, for she was as quick at getting her dust under a rug as Mrs. Inman, and she too, liked to spend hours on the useless part of a ménage and give but a lick and a promise to those fundamentals which Miranda insisted were all that counted. So Miranda, at least once a week, got herself up in enormous cleaning caps and aprons, looking much more like a servant than the deft, neat Linda, and did a good, thorough job on that second floor. She would begin on her two rooms, proceed through Dash's, Liz's, and Peter's rooms. It was agreed that Mother should be allowed to have her room just as she wanted it.

Mrs. Inman gave in gracefully. She found she had more time than ever before to be out of her house sitting about with her women friends. She told all of them — except Frances Cunningham — how lucky she was to have dear helpful Miranda living in the house with her. She took so much off her shoulders. How she would miss Tom and his wife when they finally made up their minds where the mill was to be built! In a household it is always the most selfish woman who wins. Mrs. Inman did not.

Lucy did not accept Miranda and swallow her up as "a young friend," as she had Frances Cunningham. In fact, Miranda's rigid courtesy made Mrs. Inman feel even older than she was. She treats me like a grandmother, not even a mother, she thought. Never as a friend. Why, she suggests I can't *see* the dust Linda left behind the gilt vases in the dining room, and that I'm too *stiff* to climb the stairs to the attic storeroom. Well, she was a grandmother, twice over. And Miranda would be delivered this spring. Then, of course, there was Petra. She thought with shame of Petra, and a little covetously. I hope Flanneau doesn't love her to death, she thought. And I can't help it if I'm really glad that second child died. (For a boy had been born in April and immediately died.) I hope Peter didn't mind too much. I don't think he did. I can't understand Peter. That second child made everything twice as bad. I don't see why . . . I do rather miss Petra now she never comes over looking for Wren. But I suppose the kitten stopped coming as soon as its mother got tired of it and began to spit . . . I never thought I'd have this sort of trouble with Peter.

Peter was locked out from the usual round of young people's life. There was a definite dark shadow of disapproval, disgust, outraged decency, about him, but it did not fall across his face. That was clear and untroubled. He was working harder at his clerkship now that he had given up all idea of college. He had his share of the family's love of parties, dancing, merriment — this they got from their mother. Also his share of the family's ability to turn in on themselves and live alone — this from his father whose face he could hardly remember. Now he took the latter course.

He wrote many poems. Not very good poems, but better than anything being written by other young men of Salem or even of Boston. If it had not been for Georgiana, he would have had no one with whom to share them. She wrote such lovely letters and he knew her criticisms were good, as well as loving.

He wrote often about a sleeping girl lying in her crystal coffin, waiting always for the coming of the one man who might wake her into real life. Sometimes this same girl was awake and greeting her home-come man in a rapture of love and understanding. He wrote magically of almost magic ships. And a good deal about early death and the frustration of love. Sometimes about God. But not as often about God as his great-grandfather had who had been a clergyman and an extremely minor poet.

Miranda and Nanny, too, read his poems. They would pause with feather dusters in their hands, and shake their heads. It was strange to think anyone could be so in love with that dreadful Mrs. Flanneau. They wondered idly who the dead girl in the coffin was. Some sort of allegory, they supposed. They spent little time on Peter's poems.

Marcy was supposed to keep her third-floor room clean herself, but she was so dawdling Miranda felt she had to take that over, too. So it was that she read Marcy's novel. Marcy was writing not half as well as Peter at the same age. She was writing horribly, furiously, secretly — sentiment piled on sentiment. Ghosts in Scotch abbeys. Dukes in the highest English society. An elfin love-child that haunted people. That Salem itself had its own romantic charms she had never guessed. She preferred to write about titled ladies dying of broken hearts, with doves fluttering about their lonely graves.

Shoddy and exaggerated as these efforts were, they were good enough to fool Miranda and Nanny. They believed Marcy was making a copy of some novel she had borrowed. They could hardly wait from one cleaning day to the next to find out just what had happened to Lady Tritona and Lord Everfast.

Chapter Eight

ALL OVER SALEM one could feel the rising tide of spring. Coming down Essex Street was Mr. Africanus, beating a strange rhythm with the malacca cane King Derby had given him so long ago. 'Sephus Hobey noticed his new rhythm, but did not know that the old Negro was remembering the witch doctors' drums, the shaking of black ostrich feathers on their heads, the rattle of bone anklets and the hiss of shaken shells. He was almost a child again in the childhood of the year.

A Derby ship was to be launched that day and 'Sephus was to attend. Madam Inman, however, was tired of so many launchings, and though she had closed her counting-house so that others might go, she herself had decided to stay at home.

Madam Inman did not approve of all the wealth that was pouring into Salem faster than ever, of the big houses going up about the Common, along the newly laid-out Chestnut Street. Once again she was saying the houses were too big and the horses too fast, the servants too many. Since she felt that way, why would she wish to walk over to South Fields to see the Derbys' *Rose* launched? It would only bring back more of this accursed wealth.

'Sephus Hobey felt how young Salem was, how like its own shipmasters. True, as American towns went, it was very old. It had had its days of the witches, and many of its black, peaked old houses, like Madam Inman's, still stood. There had been steeple hats on these streets and Lord's Day had been kept most solemnly. But this earlier town seemed only like an ancient, half-forgotten ancestor of the lusty, rampant young town he saw about him.

Everywhere lilacs were in blossom and new leaves spread a delicate lace of shade. Grass had never been so green nor hopes so high. Hopes? It was not hope merely. Salem had had every success. She was said to be the richest town of her size in the world. Boys of twenty-four and twenty-five could retire — if they wished — wealthy men. No one but Salem knew the route to the Indies. The pepper trade of the world was hers. The wealth of the seven seas poured in upon her wharves.

And yet, there was something in Madam Inman's complaints. There always was. People, doubtless, were neither better nor happier than they had been before. They had won success, wealth — but is that where true victory lies? He thought of the figurehead of the *Victrix,* holding her wreath so disdainfully out of the reach of poor mortals.

With Mrs. Inman upon one arm and Frances Cunningham upon the other, his eyes threatened by both their parasols, he made his way to South Fields. As they turned into Mill Street, they paused, not to disturb a small procession. This was Mrs. Rogers and her girls. They carefully did not keep step, for keeping step would have made them seem too manly. All were dressed in white muslin, for the May day was warm. But their whiteness was relieved by blue hats and pink bonnets, scarlet sashes, or yellow beaux-catchers. The little girls walked in front and the very littlest had her hand in Mrs. Rogers's. Big girls brought up the rear, and there the young drawing mistress was in command. Marcy was one of the last couple.

She was fifteen, and the amount of ribbon it took to make a sash for Marcy Inman was a scandal among the teacups. The flimsy, short-waisted dress suited her poorly, yet there was a gorgeousness about her. She alone walked as though her ankles would never buckle. Her rosy, freckled face seemed so living, it made the others look dull and anemic. She had the unmistakable "Inman look." A few years ago 'Sephus Hobey would hardly have realized there was such a thing, but since various dramatic entrances of Petra upon the Salem scene, he knew that there was.

Marcy's quick eyes recognized her mother, her teacher, and her Cousin Frances, and she grinned quickly. Doctor Hobey realized her eyes were too quick, her smile too enthusiastic. They take young girls, he thought sadly, and knead them and roll them out like so much dough. They take cooky-cutters and cut out as much as they want and throw the rest away. Poor Marcy . . . poor Marcy! He knew that, now she was fifteen and almost a young lady, she was not quite so happy, so carefree as she had been. He did not know why.

In childhood Marcy had been immensely popular with her own age. Little boys half her size had adored her. She liked belly-whoppers on their sleds. With a pair of her brothers' skates and boots, she could skate like a streak while other little girls stood about and cried because they were cold. She dared climb ships' rigging, and once it had taken two able-bodied seamen to get her out of a crow's-nest. At dancing school she had so loved to dance and had had such fine rhythm that she never lacked a partner. But already those same little boys, with changing voices, long legs and pimples, were coming back from Dummer, Exeter, Andover, or even from the sea and Harvard, and were preferring more conventional specimens of her sex. All her life she had been told, Don't be forward, don't talk so much — or you'll be left an old maid. Comb your curls, cross your ankles, look down when you are introduced. If ever I find you dancing hornpipes again down on the wharves with the sailors! Your dress is mussed. Change it. Do all these things or, the implication was, the boys won't like you. In the past she had been right and her admonishers wrong, for the little boys had liked her just that way. This was no longer true. Why, timid little Emmy Crowninshield, Cry-Baby Bibby, complaining Veronica Valpey, were all forging ahead of her in the strange new game of young womanhood.

There were, however, two groups of masculine admirers she could still count on, although neither did her much good. Her sturdy good looks, her beguiling wide mouth, twinkling greenish eyes, the size and freedom of her conversation, fascinated older men. Even as Mrs. Rogers's crocodile minced past them, men old enough to be her father were saying to their wives that Marcy Inman was going to be a real woman and they wished their own Peg, Pamela, or Betsy could put on a little weight.

Men of the lower classes also admired her. They always had. Ropewalk men had given her blond curls of hemp to make wigs for her dolls. Sailmakers would cut out tiny sails for her toy ships. Carters had let her ride the horses they led. Or fish peddlers would let her blow their tin horns. She had none of the nice girl's fear of workmen. Ever since Marcy had been at Mrs. Rogers's, when the little girls had been walked to the wharves to see educational things, like a polar bear or an Egyptian mummy, or had gone to the yards to see a launching, the sailors had noticed Marcy Inman. Their interest in her took the form of winks, coughs, or even small whistles — most unsuitable to even a very young gentlewoman. Behind her teachers' backs Marcy had responded. And such favors were dearer to her than ever, now that the boys who should be making much of her were beginning to ignore her.

Close by the ways, drawn up in almost military order, was the crew of the Derbys' *Fame*. Their ship had just come in, and they had been ordered over under a young mate to dress the occasion. They were brown young men, in their best white canvas pants, checked shirts, and beribboned, varnished hats. In this line of set young faces all eyes went to the right as Mrs. Rogers took her place close by them with her fairylike troop of little girls. Marcy, whose curiosity included everything to do with ships, mouthed to one of them, "What ship?" and he mouthed back, "The *Fame*." Then she began to look about for the *Fame's* captain, for she knew Danny Obrian had commanded her. She had read it in the newspaper. Ever since that time, two years before, when she and Danny had disgraced themselves together, she had always acknowledged him on the street a little surreptitiously. He had never been to the house again. She knew Dash had washed his hands of him and said ridiculous things about silk purses and sows' ears. She knew he hung about the Inman counting-house too much, talking for hours with Madam Inman, who did still like him — he was such a figure of a man — but who complained she'd got nothing done today because Captain Obrian had taken up all her time.

So her eyes went about until she had located him, standing with a group around Sam Derby. He did look like Lord Everfast and also like Alfred Lynnecroft, the hero of *The Vigil, or the Female Dilemma*. She tried not to look at him, but at the ship, all of a flutter with bunting and flags, waiting for the blocks to be knocked from under her. It was a long wait, and she began to look at the people of the *Fame* and wonder if they knew how fine a captain they had. The people of the *Fame* had already been casting bold glances at the young maidens. Then it grew hotter, and the launching did not come off, and a little game began between the two groups of young people. Authority, in the shape of Mrs. Rogers and in the shape of the nineteen-year-old second mate, had commanded that all hats were to be kept on all heads. But as soon as authority turned its back a sailor would take off his hat and a girl would take off hers.

"Marcy," Mrs. Rogers would say, turning to them, but having no idea what the giggling was about, "put on your bonnet, dear. You know how you freckle." And not far away a mocking masculine voice would say to a sailor, "Jack, put your hat on, dear. Don't coarsen your complexion."

By then Mrs. Rogers was busy talking to the friends she had run across. She couldn't understand why her girls were tittering. Soon even some of her best-behaved girls were taking their hats off, but trying to get them on again before she caught them at it.

"Marcy, if you feel the heat, take my fan. It is vulgar to fan yourself with your hat."

"Yes, Miss Penelope," Marcy would answer the drawing mistress.

"And Veronica, Bibby, Emmy, I know you're just copying Marcy. But hats are designed for heads."

"Yes, ma'am."

The girls stopped their fanning, but did not put on their hats. Four sailors also stopped their fanning and held their hats exactly as the girls had held theirs. And they, too, put their noses in the air and stared at the ship on the ways. Marcy began, unthinkingly, to tap the ground with her foot. Ten of the *Fame's* young men did the same. Bibby was shaking with laughter, and even Veronica was too amused to sprain an ankle. Behind the square back of the young mate the sailors shook. Soon the girls were holding on to each other, trying not to laugh out loud. The sailors did the same.

Mrs. Rogers turned around suspiciously.

"It's only the hiccoughs, Mrs. Rogers," Marcy defended the gulping Bibby. "I'll fix her." She did so with a slap on the back, and every sailor slapped his fellow on the back. The mate knew exactly what was going on behind him. He didn't care. He almost wished he was a foremast hand so he could join in, and half-wished he could knock the heads off his people.

Mrs. Rogers had not guessed. From where she stood, she had little view of the sailors. Now she was almost in tears — her girls were so wriggly and giggly. It was this distressing long wait. But, thank Heavens, the ship had at last been launched. All the younger children had been invited to the Derbys' for a little party. The older half of her school was to be escorted home by Miss Penelope, and was to go on with its lessons.

The season was spring. Miss Penelope was not a good disciplinarian, and also she was in love. From the entourage about Sam Derby came the pale clerk she loved. It was nothing for the dozen older girls to lose her. But they could not lose the crew of the *Fame*. The mate, his duties over, dove into the nearest grogshop. Soon began a slight exchange of words.

"Excuse *me*, Miss Marcy," as the crowd pushed a sailor against her. "Oh . . . may I carry your hat for you, miss?" The ribbon on a sailor's hat caught Veronica's parasol. All stopped to untangle it. The girls hardly looked at anybody except each other and they tried to pretend all this jostling was unintentional.

South Bridge by the Mill Pond was so crowded they could merely inch their way along. Below them the pond was full of mahogany, teak, satinwood, rosewood, ebony. The girls began to boast to each other about whose father or brother owned it. Momentarily the sailors were so far ahead, they thought they had lost them. The girls walked up Central as nicely as though escorted by Miss Penelope or Mrs. Rogers herself. And there at the corner of Essex they saw the crew of the *Fame* waiting for them. If they had progressed proudly past them, unabashed, nothing would have happened. But the moment they decided they daren't walk past them and took to back alleys and running, they were lost.

The game began to get exciting. The girls ran and the boys ran, but the boys never really let themselves out. Had the girls been actually caught, the boys would have been embarrassed. Once, led by Marcy, they struck a dead end behind a blacksmith shop and shinnied over a high board fence. They knocked down a clothesline, upset a coop with a brooding hen in it, and got to laughing so that they could hardly find their way to the street. Now they were sure they had shaken their pursuers. They had not, and once again they had to run. Of the original number of girls, only five now remained, but the *Fame* had not lost a man.

At last, having turned and twisted and hidden like hunted hares, been found again and run on and on, they came out by the ropewalks and tanneries on the east side of the Common. There, beyond the five muddy pools and the trees, was Marcy's house and safety. The girls were so winded they had no breath left to laugh with. It seemed impossible they could ever live to get across the Common. They had fallen down and got up again, climbed fences and splashed through mud. Their dresses were torn and filthy, their hair loosened on their shoulders. Marcy had lost her little French lavender bonnet, her very best bonnet. A sailor had it on and was now offering his in exchange. Another sailor had Veronica's broken parasol. Skirting the muddy pools, dodging from tree to tree, the girls began to weave their way toward the safety of Marcy's house. It was amazing that Veronica had sprained no ankle, Bibby had not cried, little timid Emmy had been able to keep up. The fact was, they had enjoyed themselves, as their feverishly bright faces showed. Buttons had burst, dresses had been ruined, parents would be furious, but it had been fun.

From the beginning, Marcy had been the leader, and she had had more than her share of the excitement of pursuit. As she had lost her own hat, the sailors began throwing theirs at her. And she picked them up and threw them back. Whish! You could send the flat varnished hats out like skipping stones. The other girls got behind the watch house on the Common and were almost forgotten. It was wild Marcy Inman the boys were really after. Feeling herself thus suddenly alone, she was a little frightened. She made a tactical error, for she reached down, picked up a clod of mud, and flung it smack into the nearest face. Soon hats were forgotten and muddy turf filled the air.

Marcy darted from tree to tree, but was successfully approaching her goal and safety — her own house. She stood at last, heaving, by the glittering whiteness of the Inman carved gates, an urn on each side of her.

"Don't you dare throw mud at me!" she yelled. "Don't you dare, you dirty bums!"

From across the street came an avalanche of torn-up turf. None was aimed at her. They meant only to desecrate the exaggerated purity of the gates. But a sod hit her in the mouth, burst, and streamed down her, inside her frock and outside her frock and down her throat. Suddenly she thought of her mother's anger — she was so proud of these beautiful, urn-topped gates. It looked as if one of the sailors, at least, was daring to cross the street, chase her right into her own house. She couldn't bear it. She was frightened and angry, and she went into a paroxysm of rage.

"Go away!" she stormed, as a muddy hat sailed past her up the walk. She stood, a young and gallant Primavera newly risen from primordial slime. She stamped her foot.

"Go away, you . . ." and it was what she said next that people were soon declaring was the worst thing any girl in Salem had ever said. Soon it was whispered that the mud the sailors flung at her was nothing compared to the bad words she had flung back.

～2～

THE HOUSE was quieter without Marcy. At least once a day Lucy Inman said what a relief it was not to be worrying all the time about what Marcy might be up to. The Misses Riggs of Boston were being well paid to do that. Girls who swore at sailors should be sent away to school. She would speak as though she was glad the girl was gone. She really missed her badly.

Peter came and went. Sat at table, saying little. Then off he went. Either to his own room, books and poems, around the corner to see his mistress and child, or over calling on Polly Mompesson. He made Lucy no trouble, if you accepted his unfortunate infatuation as philosophically as Liz advised, but gave her little amusement. And he made no noise. It was the silence of the house that irked Lucy Inman.

Miranda's baby Thomasina was but six months old when Miranda proudly whispered to her that she was expecting again. Having had six babies of her own, Mrs. Inman was in a position to know whether or not she liked them. She didn't. Children, if they were pretty and bright, yes. But not babies. She did not like the smell of regurgitated milk or damp flannel.

Surely, sometime soon now, Tom would be in a position to take his wife and child and set up for himself. He and Mr. Fields had almost settled on Danvers. But Tom, so cautious and intelligent was he, decided to hire himself out as the merest workman in Pawtucket and Providence, where the strange new art of power-weaving, spinning, and knitting was better understood than anywhere else in backward America. He, a good, domestic fellow, would have liked to have Miranda and little Thomasina with him. But considering what his life would be as he learned the arts of the textile industry, he could not drag them around with him. He felt he was being generous to his mother in leaving his wife on such a long loan. Miranda had often told him what a help she was to his mother. It was true. She did twice the work of Linda, who was a kind, sweet girl, but a vague and fiddling servant.

So now the quiet of the great house was broken by little except the howling of the baby and Miranda's sharp voice reprimanding Mrs. Cady and Linda, the cats and dogs, and, inadvertently, Mother Inman. No dancing, no laughter. No excitement. Cousin Frances came faithfully every day. She admired and consoled Lucy and received back plenty of correction, but also much genuine love.

It was October when the *Victrix* was reported on the coast. But not the *Wanderer*. Her absence did not worry even Lucy. Doubtless she was putting in at New York or Boston, not wishing to flood the local market with copper, if that was what she was carrying. More and more Salem ships were using other ports these days, although Madam Inman didn't like it.

The *Victrix* made port so early that the first meal her captain sat down to at home was breakfast. Yes, he had ordered the *Wanderer* — he was senior captain — to New York. Lucy Inman noticed that Dash did not want to talk about her. Nor of Liz either, except for a bleak admission that Liz was "all right." She jumped ahead in her imagination. Of course it was Liz, a much smarter fellow than Dash, really, who had insisted on taking his ship to what Dash and Ma'am thought of as a rival port. They had had an argument and Liz had won. Dash went on to say that the *Wanderer* might not only sell her copper, but rest herself in New York, clean and grave and sign a new crew there. But Liz, he said, would in a day or two come up on the stage.

It pleased Mrs. Inman secretly that Dash obviously had not ridden over Liz, but she was too anxious to tell him her news to linger long over the fact that the *Wanderer* was in New York.

"Dash," she said, "there's something I want to tell you before you go roving over to the Mompessons'."

"It's a little early for me to go calling."

He went on eating his breakfast. Miranda had finished long ago and left for the kitchen. Lucy Inman and Peter still sat with him. Peter was pretending to eat, but only to keep Dash company. She had always resented the younger brothers' childish — so it seemed to her — worship of Dash. Tom had escaped by going into textiles. Liz had, of late, shown plenty of will to oppose Dash, go his own way. These days it was only Peter who still — actually like a schoolgirl and a favorite teacher — hung upon Dash.

Peter, knowing what his mother was about to say, gave her a quick, reproving glance.

She tossed back her gray curls impatiently. "I wanted to tell you myself. I didn't want you to have the shock of picking it up anywhere else."

"Well, then?" Dash prodded her gently. He knew it could not be as bad as her introduction suggested. Peter had walked up from the wharf to the house with him — Peter would have told him if anything terrible had happened.

Although she herself believed she wished to spare him an unpleasant shock from strangers, she really wanted the pleasure of seeing him squirm. She never had been able to keep from bedeviling Dash. "Dear," she said, and her voice sounded hypocritical in spite of what she thought she felt, "Polly is engaged."

If she had hoped to break through his habitual aloofness with her news, she was disappointed.

"Oh?" Dash helped himself to more cornmeal mush and poured on maple syrup.

"The engagement has been officially announced. She's been to Philadelphia to visit his family. He has been here with her, half the summer. He's here now."

"A Philadelphian? That gardening fellow?"

"Oh, no. That was years ago. And besides, he was a Baltimorian. And Briscoe. This one is Pringle. He's a wealthy Quaker."

"I can't see Polly dressed for the plain people."

"Why, they aren't so plain these days. At least, not the wealthy ones, in Philadelphia. Flanneau has made her the most exquisite gowns, grays, and drabs and white and rosy tans. I'm sure they are very becoming. She has never worn bright colors. I mean she has so much color herself that soft shades set her off to best advantage. She knows that. I'm sure Mr. Pringle is quite worldly.

He's a mature gentleman. But as her father said to me, she needs someone mature and settled down. Someone who won't excite her any."

Peter spoke for the first time. "Dash, he doesn't excite her *any*."

Lucy Inman had half-hoped to see Dash blaze with anger, or even tears come to his fine, enigmatical eyes. He did what she least expected. Burst into laughter. And Peter, of course, laughed too. They did not look at her, but at each other, leaning back in their chairs and laughing.

"What a cheat that girl is!" Dash said at last, affectionately; "what a minx!"

"That's what I've always felt myself," Lucy admitted. "But I couldn't say it to you. I've been waiting for years for you to see through her."

"I always have. Well, if that's what she wants. At least, such a mature gentleman will not always be leaving for the sea." Seemingly he had accepted this blow to his pride, his heart, without a quiver.

She was glad he was at last over his long infatuation, would be ready now to think of someone else. She ran over in her head Salem's supply of unattached girls. She had often done this with Liz in mind and had never found one good enough for him. But she could name a baker's dozen good enough for Dash. This brought her mind again to Liz.

"I hope Liz won't raise Pursey Nichols's hopes again," she said. "Pursey is a nice little girl. And pretty. Dash, did Liz talk about any one girl more than another while you were at sea together? Sometimes I think more Salem men have found out which girl they fancied on a long voyage than when they stayed at home and courted them. But I'm afraid Liz likes to *court* better than dream of a girl."

Now that she was back again on Liz, she once more felt Dash stiffen. "You are sure Liz isn't sick?" she demanded.

"No, no. Not *sick*." But he emphasized the word "sick" in a way to arouse her suspicions. Peter, too, sitting idly over his coffee cup, stiffened a little. Something had happened to Liz, and Dash had already told Peter, but no one else.

"You're being a little mysterious about him, aren't you," she suggested.

Unlike himself, Dash went to the tantalus on the sideboard and poured out rum. Then he called for Linda to bring him a lemon. He never began on his "slops" at breakfast.

"Well . . . not exactly, Mother. I've been meaning to tell you. Sometime, before he arrived."

"Dash," she burst out, "tell me now, right off, and don't squeeze the life out of that lemon. Put it down, I say. Is Liz all right?"

"He's not sick at all, but . . ."

"Something has happened to Liz!" Her words fell into a terrifying vacuum. "What's he done? Married a Turkish lady, or . . ."

"No, no. But his ship got to fighting. At Smyrna. He got boarded. We didn't expect a thing. Had no nets up. All was serene —but the *Wanderer* got boarded." He added, a little sternly: "Women. He'd rather court, if that's how I should put it, than dream, any day. I know he didn't kidnap a girl, but that was the talk in the bazaar. The *Victrix* boats came off to her. But there was already quite a pack of 'em aboard. We fought them off, of course. But he lost a man — rather, I lost a man, I was senior captain — the Darling boy from Ipswich. I'm going to call upon his mother. And Liz got a nasty cut."

"Oh!"

"It's all healed up now. Why, that was three months back. But it delayed us. I hadn't the heart to write you. I thought I'd rather tell you."

"Dash, you say it was a nasty cut, where?"

"Smack in the face. Mouth mostly."

She set down her coffee. Her face looked greenish and flabby, but her voice was still calm. "Did it leave a scar?"

"Leave a scar!" Dash said, miserably. "Why, ma'am, his face was split open like a melon."

"Oh . . . don't!"

It was lucky for her that she was already seated. The room was swaying about her, and in the midst of this confusion she saw Liz's face, that mischievous grin he had had as a little boy. She had never been able to punish him. When he looked like that, everything seemed like a joke between them. Dash had been a sullen boy when punished. Tom scared. Peter had never needed much. She heard Dash's voice going on, precise and a little hard.

"I wanted to tell you before he gets here himself. Break the news myself."

And the moment before she had been breaking news to him. How little did it matter who Polly Mompesson married compared to this!

"I ordered him," Dash continued, "to bring the *Wanderer* into New York. I thought it might be pleasanter for you if . . ."

"*Pleasanter* for me?" she said, coldly. The fog lifted and Liz's face vanished. There was only Dash, looking tight and hard as he had when she whipped him when he was a boy. "What are you talking about? Is it really disfiguring?"

"I'm afraid so. Yes, it is. It is disfiguring, Mother."

Peter had not moved his chair, but it seemed to her that he was sitting closer to Dash. Being sorry for Dash, hardly thinking at all of Liz's gay handsome face. She couldn't stand the sight of them, and their united front. Peter spoke softly to Dash. She sprang to her feet.

"Stop it! Stop it!" she screamed.

Dash was on his feet, too. "Don't take it like that, Mother." His abrupt chin was thrust out, and in the midst of the pity in his eyes was a pin-point of hostility.

"You were the elder. You were in charge of those two ships. I trusted Liz to you. Not to let him get hurt — mutilated, that's worse than being killed. A mother . . . a mother of sea captains . . . oh, she has to face it. She knows her boys may die . . . die young. But not this. Oh, I wish you had told me he was dead!"

"I came on ahead just so you'd say that to me, not to him. I guessed how you'd feel. But I don't want him ever to know" — his hard eyes were unfriendly — "that you'd rather he were dead than not pretty."

"I never said any such thing . . . never. But where is he? Tell me."

"Now look-a-here, Mother. I had to put his first, Billy Bates, in as master. Liz isn't up to command yet. He's getting there. He has lots of guts. He wants to see some doctors in New York, or he may stop in Boston to see Doctor Warren. Maybe they can do something for him we couldn't."

"What did you do?"

"Patch and I sewed him up best we could. We kept the wound clean and it didn't fester much. It healed pretty fast. Three weeks later, I bespoke a British frigate, the *Thunderer*. The captain lent me a naval surgeon. He said Patch and I had done pretty well."

"Patch? Who's Patch?"

"Our sailmaker, of course. Joseph Hartley."

"You and a sailmaker sewed up *his* face! You dared!" Her voice shrilled. "You clumsy creature!"

"Captains have to turn surgeons in emergencies. Mother, Liz has taken it like a man. I've been proud of Liz. Can't you be proud, too?" He went to her with a sudden feline grace so unlike his stiffness of a moment before. At last there were tears in his eyes. Dash is going to cry, she thought, in belated triumph. "Mother, please don't ever let him guess you care so much about what he looks like."

He put a hand on her shaking shoulder, but she jerked away from him. It was his fault. He was the senior officer and should have seen to it women hadn't been taken aboard — not in a Mohammedan country. She almost hated him.

"Do you think I'm an ogress?" she cried. "Of course, never to Liz . . ." She was twisting her smooth ringed hands together. "What was it you said about a melon? You said something about a melon." She was chattering with sudden cold, yet she could feel the sweat starting all over her.

"That's the way his face looked."

"Peter, tell Linda to pack for me. I'm going to New York. I've got to find him."

"No, Mother, don't. You stay here and get used to the idea. Wait for him to come . . . when he feels like it. Just look him in the eyes. They are just the same as ever, Mother."

Suddenly she was in tears, clinging to him. Sorry for him, too. "It was hard on you, too, Dash," she faltered.

"It most killed me, Mother. And I thought of you and I wished it was my face. It didn't look so bad when we first got it sewed up. Later, it began to twist a little. But good doctors can do wonders these days. Somebody will have to make him a few teeth — but they can, nowadays."

"I might meet him in Boston. You said he might go to Doctor Warren?"

"No. Sit quietly. Wait for him as you've always waited for us. You know when we are off at sea and think of home, why, we think of you sitting here waiting for us . . . and Davy Jones out barking in the yard and Little Joe scratching at the necessary. If it's wintertime, we think of hearth fires — and maybe someone has tossed on a bit of sandalwood. We think of the gray and white wallpaper in the hall — and Ben Franklin chasing nymphs under the stairs. Or lilacs in blue vases." He talked softly, his arm about her. There was a persuasion to him.

Peter saw his mother, usually adamant against his charm, melt a little. Her anger at him was gone. She'd end up by doing just what he said. She was relaxing, letting that low voice carry her.

Peter slipped away. Dash was doing mighty well. He decided, privately, to go over to Cousin Frances's, tell her the bad news. Suggest that it might be a good idea if she just happened over early this morning. His mother was going to need her.

~ 3 ~

Not even Dash's warning had prepared them for the sight of Liz.

He did not come up from Boston on Manning's stage. It arrived with bustle and tootings, and everybody who had nothing else to do ran to see it. He had hired a chaise and driven up alone, and he arrived after nightfall, as if hoping candlelight might be kinder to his disfigurement than daylight.

Peter had come home from the counting-house too late to have tea with his mother, so he sat in the kitchen with Mrs. Cady and Linda. This he often did. For a long time Mrs. Cady had been the only hired help in the house. She had been as much an aunt to the children as a servant. It was natural that the boys hung much about the kitchen. Perhaps Linda's coming should have changed Peter's habits. It had not. There was nothing in the world this young girl would not have done for Mr. Peter. If he was something of a pariah in his own social group, he was a divinity to her. She prayed for him — and his sins — every night, for Linda was very pious.

Peter heard the front door open and a queer, thick voice calling out, "Anybody home?" Little Joe was barking. He knew his mother was alone in the living room. She had to see him first. Dash was absent, Miranda visiting her people in Newburyport. Mrs. Inman would get used to Liz best alone.

Having finished a second cup of tea and mended the mechanical jack for Mrs. Cady, Peter went into the living room. Dash hadn't told half the truth. Only the smooth black hair, broad manly forehead, snapping black eyes, were unchanged. The broken nose, the lips twisted and fixed forever in a brutal smile, the bare gums . . .

"Petie!"

"Aye, Liz."

"Petie . . . the idiot boy." Peter realized he couldn't speak clearly. Of course, he could not yet command at sea. But if you looked straight into his eyes, as Dash had told them to, you could almost forget. It was hard to forget when he talked. Liz had always been the most talkative of the four brothers, and now he seemed to want to talk all the time. And so did his mother.

By now she must have had a good look at him and she was taking it marvelously. She had a fixed, determined smile on her face. Liz was smiling, too. Poor Liz. He couldn't do anything else but smile, with that split mouth of his. Both were behaving so "naturally," Peter felt the strain was almost more than he could bear.

Ever since childhood Liz and Peter had shared a room and a bed. That night, as they were getting ready to go to bed — Liz had not run about town calling on his girls — Liz said: "If you don't mind, Peter, I'd like the outside of the bed. Sometimes I couldn't sleep. Then I'd get up and walk about the ship. I used to go to the galley and talk to Doctor Zack and get something to eat."

"Sure, Liz. Sure, you can have the outside of the bed."

"You know Dash had Zack for himself. Soon as I got hurt, he didn't say anything, but he gave me Zack." He was quiet for a moment, then said, "I might want to get up and read. I don't want to have to go crawling over you."

Liz had always been a phlegmatic sleeper.

He was unpacking his chest. Seeing only his long back and dark, shapely head, you could almost forget. But not entirely, for Liz kept on talking.

"Mother's taking it pretty well. I did stop three days in Boston to see Doctor Warren. I thought if he'd promise *anything,* I'd have that to hold out to her."

"He couldn't promise?"

"Not a thing, really. In fact, he thought Dash had done surprisingly well. But he sent me to a dentist, who thinks he can fix me up with some front teeth. Chemical ones. Funny-looking. Better than nothing."

"Dentists are getting to be pretty good."

"I'm going back next week to see him again. Pete . . . did you suppose Dash could cry?"

"No."

"I was in such shape after the fight was over, I could hardly feel the needle going through my flesh. It wasn't till afterward I remembered I'd felt wet splashes on my face. Did you ever see a man cry?"

"Don't think I have."

"Well," said Liz, positively, "sometimes they do, poor devils. But if I were a girl and got smashed up like this, I'd have something to cry about. It doesn't make much difference to a man, really. You going to bed now?"

"Not yet. Dash is going tonight to the Mompessons' — to clear the decks of that Quaker, I suppose. I'm sitting up till he comes in."

"Tell Dash the dentist can make me new fore-teeth. They may click, but I won't hiss so when I talk. Tell him Mother isn't as upset as we were afraid."

These days Peter did not take the liberty of sitting on the edge of Dash's bed to wait for him. He picked up a candle and went downstairs.

WHEN HIS MOTHER had told him of Polly's engagement, Dash had tipped back his head and laughed. There had been nothing else to do. Then, too, it had been wryly comical, the way Peter had croaked, "He doesn't excite her *any*." Yet now, home six days, he had had time to think the matter over.

He was trying to think of Polly impersonally. Not from his own point of view. Or hers. Not with her father's morbid affection, his mother's hostility, or Peter's mooncalfish adoration. He tried to pretend he was merely an old friend who wished her well. Surely a staid, not too young, Quaker might be the very thing for her, if one considered Polly's own tragic instability. Even his mother, never too good at human relationships, had been smart enough to understand that a man who "didn't excite her any" might be the best husband for her. It was true, Dash knew, that he himself had always brought out the most hysterical side of her. Once he had felt that he also was the only one who could control her emotions. He was not so sure now. Another man might not be able to control her hysterics, but might not ever drive her to them.

If he called forth her most hysterical side, he also called forth her most sensual. He hated to use this word in connection with a lady. He was enough of a child of his era to be willing to set his love upon a pedestal. The fact was, she was always slipping off. Yet her latent sensuality, hidden under all her fripperies and pretense at a fashionable sexlessness, was what had always bound him to her, and her to him, in an unholy alliance. She was completely full of original sin. Nobody else knew this.

So . . . Polly was to find calm seas, fair sailing, with a different sort of man from himself. He must wish her well. Not merely with words, but from the bottom of his heart.

There was another, stronger reason why he was ready to steel himself to her loss. So ill had his life been ordered, he deserved nothing. Except the reproach now heaped upon Peter. A man who secretly lets another man bear his burdens should not be rewarded by possession of the girl he loves. He ought to be disappointed, punished. After all the evil he had done — and his return to Dulcey was not the least of it — his sense of honor would have been outraged if the prize had been his.

He chose the evening of his sixth day home to call upon Polly. Sleepless nights had he had. It had been harder than usual for his body to accept the motionlessness of a bed after the toss and rocking of a bunk. So he had lain restlessly in the bed in the dead, unmoving house, waking every four hours when the change of watch should come, waiting to hear the three blows on the hatchway, the mate's cry of "All starboard lines ahoy! Eight bells below." But here in his mother's house it was never eight bells, only midnight. Then sleep again. Four hours of it to wake again, but here no change of watch was ever called. The sea did not lull him and the clock upon the landing lugubriously told off its landlubber hours. And to this tune he firmly and, as he thought, forever renounced Polly whom he had forfeited, but his longing for her he could not control. It was so intense in him, he felt almost as though she belonged to him more truly than she ever might to any husband. Far off on distant seas, under strange constellations of southern skies, he had held her in his heart, his arms, in a phantom embrace which nothing, no mere fact, might ever weaken.

And now, as he walked the prosaic streets of Salem, he swore to himself (hitting at tree trunks as he swore) he would do nothing — no, not one thing — to call her back to himself. Not a word, not a glance. He knew how strong his hold was upon her.

He wanted the sharp stab of pain he knew he would feel, seeing her as soon he would, happy (God willing) with the man she and, of course, her father had chosen. But before the Mompesson gate he stopped, took a long breath. God help me, he thought, but so shall it be.

She was sitting in candlelight as he had often dreamed of her, by the piano. Her back was to the keyboard, her head tossed back. She was refusing to do something. Play, or sing, of course. Her refusal to furnish music was often more enchanting than her compliance.

The group in the parlor was not one to call out much merriment. A plain, elderly couple was there — they had rented the house next door which Polly had always insisted was to be hers when she and Dash were married. Her father, aunts, and the poodle. Old Doctor West, Jack, Nanny, and their oldest child who was always called Boots. Boots was as red-headed, prickly-haired as his father, and already at only five extremely male. Such a collection, Dash knew, had merely happened in. He was interrupting no party.

As Flip said his name, Dash bowed and entered. Mr. Mompesson rose to shake his hand. Then Dash noticed the one strange face.

"Mr. Pringle, Captain Inman."

Their hands and eyes met. Mr. Pringle must have heard of this erstwhile suitor. He flushed slightly under his extremely thin skin. Dash did not. He looked imperturbable, manly, aloof.

Then Polly was off her stool, flying to him, looking as if she expected him to take her in his arms. Mr. Mompesson felt called upon to explain to Mr. Pringle the close intimacy between the *families.*

"Oh, Justin," Polly cried to her fiancé, "I've so wanted you to meet Dash. Yes, this is *really* Dash Inman. I suppose he's Salem's most famous captain, isn't he, Papa? But he's hard to catch. Never home. He's something of a Flying Dutchman. Dash, I heard your ship was in six days ago. But you didn't come and you didn't come. Justin, you will be friends . . . for my sake?"

Justin was an attractive man. He said to Polly, as if from his very heart, "Thee know thy friends will always be my friends, Mary."

Dash was puzzled. He had forgotten long ago that Polly had been baptized Mary. A stranger calling her by a strange name made her seem a different person. Perhaps plain people did not care for nicknames. There was something quaint, serene, about the man's words, his voice and manner. Dash felt the honesty of his handshake and liked him.

Polly, like many another much-touted belle, had had more than her share of impossible suitors. Some were too old, most of them too young. Or too poor. And if rich enough, too foolish. There had been more quantity than quality among her admirers. It was as if your really desirable men do not wish to be one of a belle's entourage. Dash himself had been far too young to be acceptable when he had first fallen under her spell, and then too poor. He had lately had the habit of looking down upon Polly's "mice," as he contemptuously called her suitors. But here was Mr. Pringle, only slightly too old, perhaps, a man of standing, worth, intelligence, sensitivity — he had flushed when he met Dash Inman — and genuine charm. Although of less than middle height, he carried himself without any of the highfalutin often associated with the short man. He had a slight almost frail body, but his face was strong and clear.

Dash had been expecting naught but another mouse. Mr. Cabot had been a mouse to Dash. And Fred Briscoe another one. Mr. Pringle was a real man. No mouse. Polly was standing close to him, and he had one gray-clad arm lightly about her waist, even as her eyes flared toward Dash.

I'll not come between them, he thought to himself. But he felt an aching longing for her, a spasm of jealousy. He could not have been jealous, ever, of the mouse he had expected. This serves me right, he thought. Damn it, this is what you deserve. The book's closed now. All right, this is my punishment, and I'll take it like a man. He found himself offering congratulations to the Quaker, playing a proper part.

The conversation was general. Mr. Mompesson was even boasting a little to his future son-in-law of Dash Inman's deeds. He was sure now that Dash would never come between him and Polly and so ready to like him at last. And Dash felt that Justin Pringle liked him also.

Polly, never one to sit back and be ignored, had been left aside a little in the conversation. She interrupted it to ask if Dash had brought back from the Near East any very fine silk. Flanneau himself had said he could not find any suitable for her wedding gown. There was something teasing in her eyes, but also something desperate, as she reminded him of the silk he had promised her, long ago.

Dash hesitated, thinking of the black and gold lacquer box long hidden away in the glory hole in his baseboard behind his bed. He had never told Polly of the Chinese silk he had bought in Batavia.

"No," he answered. "Near East silk is flimsy stuff. Neither Liz nor I bought any for our home cargoes."

She bit her lower lip and looked at him strangely, as if she knew what was in his glory hole. "But haven't you, hasn't the House of Inman, something superfine? Put by for a great occasion?"

"Yes," he said. "Once I bought some Chinese silk gauze. And never put it up for sale."

"Oh?" She went on boldly: "And I suppose you don't want me to have it? You are saving it for the girl you marry?"

Nanny gasped. Mr. Mompesson said, "Ahem." The aunts' two turbans shook and quivered together as they exchanged whispers. Dash was too used to Polly's proddings to be entirely caught off balance. He felt suddenly sorry for Mr. Pringle. Why would Polly push so at delicate situations, and make them worse?

As he did not answer, she shrugged, and tried to make Aunt Birdseye's ancient poodle stand on his hind legs for a piece of nimble cake. Fussing over the dog she really hated.

Nanny, next to Dash, clutched his sleeve. "Don't give it to her, if you really have it. Don't," she hissed.

Dash went on evenly, "I don't know much about such things. My mother told me nothing finer ever came into Salem."

Polly, still crouched over the dog, exclaimed, "Then it's exactly what I want." She stood up, pushing over the poor old poodle, who, with infinite labor and many rheumatic pains, had at last managed to rise to his hind legs. Polly forgot to give him his reward.

Mr. Pringle put a fine hand to his neckcloth. It was odd that a man past forty, and a most successful banker, could flush so easily. "If it is what Mary wants," he said, controlling his voice as expertly as Dash himself, "may I not, sir, buy it of thee?"

Polly shook her head. "Why, Justin, I thought Quakers never wasted a penny. Don't you see I'm trying to get it for nothing?"

Mr. Mompesson saw his chance. "My dear Mr. Pringle, I don't know how it is with the plain people, but *hereabouts* it is the father who provides his girl with wedding clothes. Captain, it's hardly the time now to talk business. May I not consult with you tomorrow at your counting-house? It is true that Polly has thus far found nothing to her taste."

Dash saw Polly's eyes commanding him. He was not to sell it to her father, but to give it to her. No one in this room should ever doubt Dash's devotion to her.

"Yes, Mr. Mompesson" — Dash's voice was like silk itself — "if it proves to be what you and Polly wish, you may buy." He could not help adding, so determined he was that there should be no romance left for Polly to feed on, "You may think the price rather high. It's rare stuff."

"Oh yes. Yes, of course. But I'm sure your price will be right. Yes, my dear fellow, yes," Mr. Mompesson exclaimed warmly, "I'm sure any price you set will be right." And once again he was almost boasting to Mr. Pringle about what a fine man Captain Inman was and how honorable the House of Inman.

There had always been a childish lack of self-restraint in Polly. Her eyes wavered, her teeth bit into her lower lip. Anyone could see, feel, her disappointment. With a surge of emotion, Dash thought, My poor, dear girl. Why had he not done as her eyes commanded him? Even if it did hurt Mr. Pringle's feelings. As he looked at Polly's distraught face, he felt he still loved her as much as ever. She alone existed for him, foolishly, passionately, a living part of himself. He felt a tug at his heart as though an actual hawser connected her to him. Very well. He'd cut the hawser and cast off. Let the *Mary* sail upon her own course. Wish her fair seas, fresh winds and happy voyage.

When she looked at him, he almost wondered if she did not really hate him. Perhaps. What of it? She also loved him. And Justin Pringle had never fanned within her any emotion.

Once in the street again, he felt his longing for her almost as a physical sickness. But he wallowed in his sense of loss — a loss which certainly served him right. Still mooning over Polly, he stopped before Flanneau's. He knew where Dulcey slept and he tossed a pebble against her window. Then another. It was not until the third that he was sure he had awakened her. The old sign came — a hand pulling-to the shutter. Soon enough she'd be at the warehouse, with the key to it in her hand.

At the Inman house, Peter had fallen asleep over his book. He awoke, looked at his watch. It was one o'clock. Mr. Mompesson believed in early hours. It was not there Dash was tarrying. He sighed, closed the book, blew out the candle, covered the hearth, and crept upstairs. He was almost sure where Dash was.

❧ 5 ❧

ON THE STAIRWAY, one after another, hung the four portraits of the Inman brothers. Lucy had never been satisfied with them. Ever since the money had come in, hand over hand, she had been insisting her boys were to sit again, and this time to a proper portrait painter. The limner who had done these had arrived in a tipcart. He did inn signs and arms on coaches, he could japan trays. He said he could "take a likeness," and he hadn't cost too much. But the portraits weren't worth even the little she had paid. For, curiously, they did look like the boys, but caricatured each one.

Dash had that broad, square lower lip stuck out as if saying to Hell with everybody, especially the limner and his mother who had made him sit. Tom — it was true he had come home from sea but the day before — looked ready to go to sleep and fall out of his frame. Peter's ears were not on straight. He looked like an innocent, wide-eyed schoolgirl. And Liz looked like a clown. It was Liz's portrait, especially, that had dissatisfied her. But now Liz would never sit again. Now the face the limner had seen was destroyed, it did not seem quite so bad. At least, he'd caught the mockery, the casual self-assurance. But posterity now would never know how handsome a man Liz Inman had been.

Although Lucy talked to her favorite son as much as or even more than ever, she soon gave up trying to look at him. She was a good enough human being, but she was not a very maternal woman. Such instinctively love best the weakest of their flock. If she had been maternal, she would have loved Peter most. Instead, it was the happiest, handsomest, and, she believed, smartest, of her boys who was her favorite. Now he was no longer happy or handsome. This made a gulf between them. She had been so proud of his rakish appearance, had so loved to drive him out and show him off. Luckily the question of driving him out need not come up. Bacchus and Ariadne had at last been retired. Mr. Mullins, too. All three would end their days in Tewksbury. The new coachman, a young Irishman called Michael Shean, had not yet found the pair he considered handsome enough. When Mrs. Inman complained to Liz how hard it was for her to get along without her pair, he suggested hiring from the livery stable. She told him livery-stable horses were not safe. He looked at her with a wary knowledge narrowing his eyes. Nothing could be safer than the usual livery-stable plugs. He had always submitted to his mother's driving him out, showing him off to her woman friends, rather than enjoyed it. Now he knew he would be spared such expeditions and forever.

They were most at home with each other when moving furniture about, rearranging things. Liz had a fine sense of color, proportion, style. It was usually the Salem men who did the buying for their women. When he drove to Boston to see his dentist once more, she went with him. Together they had happily shopped for furniture, clocks — Liz never could get past a handsome clock — Irish linens, and fine silver. The only thing that went wrong was when she forgot once and asked him to please let her do the talking. She could have bitten out her tongue. The talkative Liz lapsed into a long brooding silence, and when she tried to pat his hand and be sorry for him he was angry.

Thus far, she had noticed, he was most at ease when engaged in business. Only a little unnatural when with women of her own age, though he did seem somewhat forward, too bound to talk and laugh a great deal, so no one could feel sorry for him. But young girls he avoided. His mother had done wrong in suggesting that they drive out to the Misses Riggs', call upon Marcy. She had already warned Marcy, and of course the young girl had not batted an eyelash at the sight of him. In spite of her unladylike spontaneity, you could count on something as solid as rock in her. It was her schoolmates — all finding an excuse to walk past the drawing room and peek in — whose little gasps at the sight of Liz's face made Mrs. Inman's heart pound and her hands clench. She hoped Liz hadn't noticed. Marcy, being Marcy, of course had boasted of her famous brothers, but had not prepared her friends for the sight of Liz. So young girls he avoided. His mother pinned much hope, however, on his promised chemical teeth.

It was to help him she arranged a small dancing party. Surely, among the young ladies he had known all his life, girls who had long pursued him and he them, he would not feel awkward. She would invite such old flames of his as Josie Orne and Pursey Nichols. They were happy discussing the details together. But the morning of the party, he told her that he must visit his dentist in Boston that day.

"But Liz . . . you have always loved to dance."

She could not make him change his mind.

"They might not like looking at me, Mother," he said cheerfully. Too cheerfully. She felt him slipping away from her. Hardening. He was growing to be as hard as Dash himself. She knew she was losing him, but couldn't think what to do.

The night after the party, Peter woke up. His bedfellow was gasping and choking. He remembered Liz saying, "Did you ever see a man cry — sometimes they do, poor devils." Peter froze, at first pretending to be still asleep. Then "Liz," he said, and put his arms about the shaking shoulders.

"Oh, for God's sake, Pete. Get up and go to bed somewhere else."

"Liz . . ."

"I can't help it. Nights are worse. She tries so hard. She tries to look at me, but she can't. I'd stand it better if she didn't try so damned hard."

"Liz, let's get up and go downstairs to the kitchen. I'll make some coffee. I know there are new doughnuts."

"You go, if you're hungry."

"You come along."

Peter built up the fire and made the coffee, set out the doughnut crock. Liz looked very smart in his Hindu silk dressing-gown. He was sitting there calmly stirring cream into his coffee, soaking the doughnut so he could bite it. It was hard to think he had ever had a moment of weakness.

"I've been thinking," he said. "She never could stand anything not new or nice. Cracked teacups or mended dresses. Do you remember that lapdog she had — Foxy? It got scalded, and the hair wouldn't grow on its back. She had doted on Foxy. Then she didn't."

"I remember Foxy. Grandma didn't care. Mother gave her to Grandma. Half Grandma's teacups are cracked. And *she's* prouder of you than ever before."

But his recent conquest of his suspicious grandmother's heart meant nothing to Liz.

"Well, to Mother I'm a cracked teacup."

"You'd just about as well face it. She loves you as much as ever — but she can't feel the same way about you."

He supposed Liz was smiling. It was hard nowadays to be sure.

"Liz," Peter said suddenly, "why don't you grow a beard?"

"Nobody wears a beard."

"You could set the fashion. You'd look fine with a black beard — like a Spanish captain."

"I might."

"You could, you know. I doubt if Dash could, although he's four years older. I think he's got bare spots under the corners of his mouth, like pictures of Christ, or like me."

"I might grow a beard — and turn pirate." Liz had always been proud of his hirsute gifts.

"I'll bet in a couple of months you could grow a fine beard."

"Less time than that. But who wants a beard?"

"Folk never get just what they want. They just about have to take the least objectionable thing that comes along."

"Quite the philosopher, eh?"

Liz came back from a long stay in Boston armed with some large, ferocious, very white, brand-new teeth, glittering in the midst of what was going to be a remarkable black beard. His mother told him how marvelous were these teeth, but she felt like little Red Ridinghood confronted by her grandmother. Probably he would rather be feared than pitied. He had, before this, gone through life scaring foremast hands, careless servants, foreign agents, consuls or natives. But never before, his mother and young females. Now he scared them, too. But nobody could pity the ferocious face Liz Inman turned upon the world. He no longer looked so much mutilated, as an entirely different sort of man. And in a way he seemed ageless. Liz was twenty-six, but he might as well have been forty. That fresh, audacious, charming young face, so woodenly presented by the clownish portrait upon the stairs, was gone forever. His expression now was hard to read, for it was not formed by the character of the man, but by injury and chemical teeth.

He did not expect to go immediately to sea. Those great wolf fangs the Boston dentist had made him did not satisfy him. He'd try another man, and if the next did no better, he'd try another. In the meantime, even as he came and went, hunting for the perfect dentist, he devoted himself to his grandmother's counting-house. He said he was going to make things hum, and he did.

For the first time in thirty years old Fessenden trembled for his job, and Peter dared not fail to get to work on time. Liz had indeed got out from behind his mother's skirts, but had gone off again behind that black beard of his. Madam Inman had long thought of retiring. Now she dared not, for fear Dash and Liz might fall to quarreling. Liz, who had always been secretly somewhat abashed before his oldest brother, really a little scared of him, was getting completely over this earlier childishness. He was contradicting everything Dash said. He was saying that Salem Harbor was too poor and Salem too far from a rich hinterland. He'd prefer Boston or even New York. Madam Inman considered this treachery. These two great ports were rivals of Salem. She wished to do nothing to enrich them. Dash, too, loved Salem. But, as Liz pointed out, Dash cared little for money and too much for "glory." He spoke the word contemptuously.

Dash took all this bumptiousness of Liz's like an angel, never losing his temper, giving in and giving in. Actually Madam Inman was afraid Liz would get the upper hand. Such a thing had never occurred to her until Liz's accident. In the old days Dash had to say no more than "Belay, Liz," and the younger brother certainly "belayed." Whatever that was. She never had been quite sure.

Madam Inman was afraid that if she retired, he would move the whole kit-kaboodle out of Salem to deeper water, richer hinterlands. Sell off even the wharf in Salem. So, nervously, she kept an "upper hand." Liz had his desk next hers in the inner office.

She felt he was really laughing at her behind that black Spanish beard of his. All her boys were expected to rise as she entered or left the counting-house, but Liz's bow was so punctilious, so sarcastic, it bothered her more than the times Peter forgot. So Liz was top dog, champing those big teeth at her, talking so fast of hold-backs, split voyages, and adding more quickly in his head than anybody else could on paper. His talk was of money, and that he was producing. Although he dressed the dandy as ever, he certainly wasn't wasting any time upon the girls.

Dash was soon off to sea once more, Bombay this time. It looked like a long trip. Nor did he take the *Victrix*. She went out with Billy Bates master. It was as if he felt he must fight off his superstitious feeling about the *Victrix*—that she was part of him and he part of her. He commanded the good old *Mermaid*. His mother was relieved as she saw him go. Tom would never sail again. Liz was darting about making business deals for the House of Inman up and down the Atlantic coast, and trying new dentists. It would never do if Dash retired just now, and captains' shares forever went out of the family.

Then, too, poor Dash, Polly had jilted him. It would have been too hard for him to have been around when Polly married Justin Pringle. She was glad he would be away. But there never was a wedding. Two weeks before the date set, Mr. Mompesson calmly announced that Polly had found it "impossible" to leave Salem, all her friends, and himself.

❧ 6 ❧

ONE BRIGHT SUNNY AFTERNOON Lucy was sitting on the broad landing sewing. With her were Frances Cunningham and Miranda. Since she had lost her own bedroom to the Tom Inmans, she had taken more than ever to the landing as the place she liked to sew, or watch Cousin Frances sew. The women were shortening ugly purple poplin bed-curtains Miranda wanted for her Thomasina's crib. And she was about to have another baby. Lucy had not the heart to tell her how ugly she thought the curtains were. Poor child, she had no taste.

Marcy, home at last for a few weeks' holiday, and a half-dozen of her special friends were downstairs in the double parlors around the piano. The girls were comparing dance tunes and dance steps. They'd dance and stop and go on chatting as girls do without partners.

She heard the front door open and Liz's step. A sad, heavy step. By glancing through the balustrade she could see him standing a moment outside the door, watching the young girls dancing. These girls, recently naught but children, were now suddenly becoming young ladies, and of a not too inappropriate age for Liz. Go in, she wanted to call down to him, go in, Liz . . . why not?

He came up the stairs, looking a little tired. She knew it was not bullying his grandmother, outsmarting his fellow merchants, or the many sudden business trips he took to Boston, New York, even Washington, that tired him. It was dance music and young girls.

Before him were the three women sewing, blocking his way. Miranda rose with difficulty to let him pass. Her parents had warned her against Peter Inman and his mistress and Liz, who had never had a very good name where women were concerned. They always told her that Dash seemed a respectable citizen and that her Tom was a good, moral man, but she must not let the shadow of the two younger brothers ever fall across her. Liz was piqued by the fearful glances Miranda always turned toward him. Some day he was going to say "boo" to her and see her jump. If she was scared into a miscarriage, he didn't care.

"Liz," his mother suggested, "why don't you go downstairs and help the girls?"

"No, I guess not."

His mother did not want him once more to go to his own bedroom, fling himself upon his bed and do nothing. Nor did she quite want him to join her and her friends.

Liz stood irresolute. The sight of Miranda, gaping at him like a fish, holding back her chair for him to pass, settled him.

"Don't get up, Miranda."

"Oh, you don't want to go upstairs?"

"No."

She sat timidly on the edge of her chair, her eyes still glued to his fierce face, ready to rise again if he changed his mind.

"Boo!" he said suddenly. Miranda jumped.

"Why, Liz! What a funny thing to say to Miranda!" But both Lucy and Frances were laughing.

"I like to say 'boo' to pretty girls and see them jump." He sat himself idly on the last stair before the landing with his back against Cousin Frances.

"Boo, Cousin Frances," he said.

She smiled down at him serenely. "Boo, yourself, Liz. Whatever that means."

"I told you. 'Boo' means you are a pretty girl."

"Oh fie, Liz."

She did not jump, and because, of course, she was only an elderly female relative, she tapped him on the head with her thimbled finger, like a sewing mistress correcting a little girl. Nobody had for years even suggested that she was a pretty girl. She always dressed in such drab half-mourning, and her heavy, dull chestnut hair was done in so matronly a style that people forgot that she was, if not a "pretty girl," at least an attractive widow woman in her thirties. Her dark bird's eyes were her best feature and these were on Liz's face.

He leaned his black head so it rested against her thigh. Cousin Frances began threading needles at a great rate. Miranda and Lucy went on about the virtues of blind stitch in comparison to French seams. Cousin Frances's usually ivory-colored skin acquired a pretty color. Liz's head lay heavy against her, as loving Davy Jones laid his against those few he completely trusted. He was enjoying emotions as simple as a dog's. As if he were one, his eyes half-closed. And Frances's thimbled hand went out and stroked his hair. He could have rested for hours with that tender, caressing hand on him and the warmth of the woman's body under his cheek. He had not felt such content for months. He straightened and slowly opened his eyes. Then he yawned — the perfect expression of relaxation, and often so curiously related to physical desire.

Below, the piano was going well. One of the girls had tuned up the old fiddle from the gun room.

"Don't you want to help them out, Liz? You can play that fiddle much better than they can. Do give them a little fun — go down and dance with them — they have nothing but themselves for partners. Go, dear, do, and join the dancing."

"Cousin Frances" — he rose, took her hand and pulled her to her feet — "come, stand up with me."

"But — I haven't danced for years, not since Captain Cunningham died . . ."

His mother reminded him that gentlemen did not ask ladies in mourning or even half-mourning to dance.

"Then I'm no gentleman."

He pulled Frances past the pregnant, gasping Miranda and up the four stairs to the upper hall. He was using actual physical strength against her efforts to grab the balustrade and to straighten her mobcap. It fell off. She wasn't being coy. She did not want to dance. Yet, once he had her where he wanted her, she completely acquiesced, smiling into his face — and he noticed it was his face, not merely his eyes she looked at — smoothing her little black sewing apron. Eagerly she picked up the bright steps of the contra dance from the piano and squeaking fiddle below, bowing, turning, and curtsying. They did as well as a single couple might. The wretched fiddle squeaked, and the music stopped.

Miranda watched in amazed disapproval. Lucy did not look especially pleased that at last Liz had taken to dancing again.

"Why," said Cousin Frances, sighing and joining the ladies on the landing, "I haven't danced since . . . let me see. It's over ten years ago Captain Cunningham died." Her face was pretty and pink, her always bright eyes fluttered like a bird's. One forgot the soft, slightly receding chin, losing itself in the too plump neck. She was shining with either perspiration or pleasure.

"Why do you always wear black or gray, Cousin Frances?" asked Liz.

"Why not?"

"I'm tired of it."

She thought a moment. "So am I."

"I do think it is time" — Lucy Inman gave permission to her satellite — "for you to add a little color."

Liz went whistling off to his room. Frances took her place with the sewing ladies, half-apologetically and half in triumph. There was a dimple that came and went as she leaned over and bit a thread. Lucy could not remember seeing it before. Could it be that Frances was setting her cap for Liz? No. She had resisted Liz as nobly as ever the Sabine women had resisted the Romans. But the Sabine women had, of course, at heart, really wanted . . . But Liz had always done those teasing things that women love. It might have been *me* if I had been nearest him. Or Miranda. Except Miranda can't dance, just now.

Yet one thing happened after another. Lucy could feel a tightening of intimacy between her son and her "young friend," and behind her back. Her special worry was that Liz might callously break the older woman's heart. She had always vaguely known that Liz was selfish and heedless about women, but his girls had been very young and very pretty. She could not understand his changed attitude toward Frances. He had stopped calling her "Cousin Frances" and now she was "Fanny" to him. She bridled and protested that nobody had called her Fanny since her school days. She said she did not like to be called Fanny, but she did. Liz would make her sit and play checkers with him after supper. And at this rate the boys' stockings would never be mended. Lucy tried to hint to him that often as women get older they get sillier. As they pass their courting years, they lose all sense of proportion. Casual attentions from a young man might be misinterpreted. She would not, she said, name any names. Liz smiled. He didn't say anything. There was not much that Lucy Inman had seen.

Frances now rented rooms from Flanneau, as he had bought the house from her. She had nothing but the back stairs and two second-floor rooms, but Monsieur was hinting politely that he might soon like these also. Frances knew that if she moved out, there would no longer be any reason she could think of for not moving in with Lucy, and be swallowed up forever. She'd sew her life away, to the continual accompaniment of "Frances, don't bite threads, dear." Here in her two little back rooms she was her own mistress. To a certain extent she could do what she pleased, not what Lucy pleased. Nor did she always tell Lucy just what she did do, under her own roof. For one thing she spent many a pleasant evening with the Flanneaus. How the man could cook! And Peter would be there so often, so much too often. He played cards with Dulcey and her friends. He'd sit for hours with Petra sleeping in his arms, or she'd wake and he'd make cat's-cradles of string for her, people going upstairs with his fingers, and the minister saying prayers with his thumb. He was clever with shadow pictures of swans and begging dogs. He made caps and boats out of paper. Of this Frances did not speak to Mrs. Inman.

Nor did she tell her how often Liz came to her little back tenement. Neither did Peter say a word.

Sometimes Peter and Liz would walk home together from the Flanneaus'. Neither poked or pried at the other's private business. In fact, Liz actually had more respect for Peter than formerly, although he had his suspicions, from what he heard around town, that Dulcey might be cheating on him. He believed Mrs. Flanneau was carrying on with other men — in spite of the good sum paid her husband by Peter.

"Fanny," Liz said one day at his mother's tea-table, "why don't you ever wear your pretty dresses over here?"

She still dressed everywhere except under her own roof exactly as formerly.

She fluttered. "Oh, those!" To Lucy she explained that Flanneau had persuaded her to accept some of the interest on her mortgage in dresses.

"But Frances . . . why haven't you shown me? I'm dying to see them."

"I was afraid they were a little gay. I'm not a young girl."

"But, these days, even quite old ladies are gay. What colors?"

"I let Flanneau choose. The last he made me — he has only made me three, Lucy — was mauve striped with pink."

"And she has pink ribbons for her hair, Mother."

The idea did not please Lucy. "Pink ribbons for your red hair, Frances?" she asked bluntly.

"It's not red any more. Flanneau says it's chestnut. And what Liz calls pink isn't exactly pink."

"Oh, I suppose his taste is always right. Or perhaps he uses up on you lengths of cloth no one will buy. Did you stop to think of that?"

"No, I didn't. But, anyway, I'm not fussy. I suppose it doesn't matter any more what I wear."

At Lucy's insistence Frances came to supper the next night dressed in her newest gown. Perhaps not even the softest of shell-pinks suited her. Miranda did not care for the dress because the stripes were so narrow they did not show. Mrs. Inman's admiration was perfunctory. It was possible that she preferred Cousin Frances drab.

She had always insisted that one of her boys must walk home in the evening with Cousin Frances. This had been started, frankly, to teach her boys their manners rather than to give protection to a widow no longer in need of such guarding. Through the years, behind her guest's back, she had many times grimaced and gestured to Dash or Tom, Liz or Peter, trying to start one or the other of them toward the door with their Cousin Frances.

Tonight was a snowy night. Frances sat in a chair in the hall and Liz pulled on the warm white stockings over her thin slippers. As she stood up, he wrapped her in her Cashmere shawl. Then he put on his cloak and hat.

"Oh, it's only a step, Liz. The walks are all shoveled and the moon is bright. I'm sure your Cousin Frances will excuse you," his mother said.

It was Frances's cue to say of course she wanted no escort, she wasn't afraid. But she said nothing, and Liz drew her arm through his.

Mrs. Inman sighed and went back to the fireplace, hoisting her skirts for warmth where warmth is most appreciated. Already Peter had his nose in a book. She wished she could talk to Peter — to someone. Liz shouldn't . . . Liz *must* not flirt so with the poor silly old thing. And Frances had not looked nor seemed quite herself this evening. Quite ludicrous. I wouldn't *think* of wearing pink ribbons in my hair. And she laughed so much. I wonder how much wine she drank. She had quite a little pink in her cheeks. Has she taken to painting? I must tell her how much more attractive she looks without color. That simple pure ivory. I don't think Liz quite realizes what a tizzy she is in about him. Oh, well . . . what of it? She's old enough to know better, dear knows. I can't blame Liz for everything. She does make eyes at him.

She felt quite relaxed. It wasn't Liz's fault. It was poor Frances's. She told Peter she was going up to bed. He was to see that the cats were out. Linda was so soft-hearted she'd let them in to sleep in the kitchen after Mrs. Cady got to bed. And he was to lock up the house, except the front door. Liz would be back in a few moments, of course.

It was only Peter and the cats who knew that Liz did not come back for over an hour. Peter had seen many a straw blowing. His mother would be furious. Dash might have his hysterical Polly, Tom his dull Miranda, Peter himself what was usually referred to as that dreadful woman, but Liz was too good in his mother's eyes for anything Salem had to offer. Peter counted up. Liz was twenty-six, Frances, he thought, about thirty-five. Nine years. But ever since the agony and humiliation of his mutilation, Liz had been an ageless man. He did not look nine years younger than Frances. How pretty and young and sweet and girlish she had become to-night! Every time she looked at Liz, her eyes were beautiful, like the darkest topazes. And Liz, spurned ever so inadvertently by his mother, did need desperately some woman to admire and be proud of him.

Maybe Liz's attentions to Frances were more honorable than his mother feared.

❧ 7 ❧

AT NIGHT, as she lay sleepless upon her bed, Frances Cunningham knew she was doing wrong. For ten years now, ever since word came that Captain Cunningham was dead at Surinam, she had been Liz Inman's aunt. Now the threads had tangled. He was not a nephew any more, he was a suitor. Why not? Why on earth not? There was no reason why a man of twenty-six might not marry a woman of thirty-five — if he and she had a mind to it. And I've had so little out of life, she thought, wiping away a tear of self-pity. Captain Cunningham always seemed more like a father than a lover to me. Oh, so little! I've had so little. I love him so much. Why can't I say yes? Oh, please God, if I can only make him happy, I'll never ask for any other thing. Oh Liz . . . Liz, beautiful Liz. Lucy will be furious. Furious with him, and most of all with me. But think of any woman, any mother, who actually loves a son less because he has been marred! Oh Liz, I love you so much. I'd never have loved you at all if this dreadful thing had not happened. I'd never have dared to.

She sat up in bed. He needs me. He needs me terribly. He loves me just as much as I love him. Don't be a fool, Frances. Don't be an old fool. He needs you, just for now. He doesn't really love you. Not forever and for keeps. Face it, face it. Don't be a fool. You'd be a fool to marry him when all he needs you for is now. If only Lucy had been able to help him, he'd never even have looked at me.

The thought that Liz was rich and obviously going to be a lot richer, that she, a poor forlorn widow woman, would be making a most profitable marriage — if she agreed — hardly crossed her mind. But she did have a pleasant vision of herself driving up to the Inmans' house in her carriage, taking Lucy out to drive, and she decided that if she married Liz, she was going to do a lot for her dead sister Kate's two little girls. Aside from these fancies, though, money did not enter into her calculations. It was only of love that she was thinking, a love on her part half-maternal, half-romantic, and utterly unself-seeking. Yet that night she had the strength to face the fact that on his part his love was most fleeting. His self-assurance, resilience, indomitable courage, would in time win out without help from her.

Never again, she decided, would she let him whisper those loving, unreal words to her. When he walked home with her, he was not to stay on and on, his arms about her, kissing her, saying he wanted to marry her. "You are the only woman I love now," he had said. He had not obliterated past loves — and Frances was sure it was he, not Peter, who had seduced poor Mrs. Flanneau — he had promised nothing for the future. Now, now. Is that enough for a marriage? She knew it was not. Another thing. She was going to stop his calling her Fanny. He was, even when they were alone — except, of course, she was never going to see him alone again — to call her Cousin Frances. I've got to be brave. He is brave. I've got to be brave for him, and keep on saying "no." Until he is back on his feet. Then he won't think *that* of me. Frances, don't be a fool. Don't be mean. It would be mean to marry him — it would be taking advantage of his misfortune.

She heard a cock crow and another answer through the dark cool dawn. She saw the posts of her bed, the chest of drawers emerging in the half-light. Her nightcap was off. Her heavy chestnut hair streamed about her. Her bed-linen had worked loose at the bottom.

"I'll give him up," she whispered, and limply began to cry. "I'll cry a lot more than this if I don't," she said to herself. And her mind, she was sure, firmly made up, she fell asleep.

She woke almost instantly. Her back bedroom was full of light flickering and dancing on the walls. Then she smelled smoke and ran to her window. The old wooden barn which Flanneau used as a warehouse was afire. He had put on locks and double locks. It was impenetrable to thieves. Not fire. Frenchmen always thought in terms of thieves, Yankees of fire. She leaned out — it was almost light — and tried to scream, "Fire! Fire!" but no sound came from her. But others had seen it. She heard the terrible cry of "Fire!" up and down the street. Already she guessed the old barn was beyond the aid of any bucket line. Perhaps the house would go, too. She ran to her desk. All she thought to save was the handful of little notes Liz Inman had written her. She dashed down to the street in her nightclothes with only these bits of paper in her hand. Even as she did so, she wondered why. They were true now, she knew. They would not be true always.

Chapter Nine

~~~~~~~~~~~~~~~~~~~~~~~~~~~~~~~~~~~~~

T HE KITCHEN offered much solace to a young man not welcome in his own level in Salem. Lucy Inman agreed with Miranda. Peter shouldn't hang about the kitchen. It had been different when he was a child and the aunt-like Mrs. Cady the only help. Nowadays Mrs. Cady rested afternoons, leaving the kitchen to Linda and Miranda's Becky, who tended Thomasina and the new baby, Tommy. On cold days old Mr. Africanus sat here for hours. Michael Shean, unlike the dour Mr. Mullins, would desert horses and stable for the kitchen and the girls' company. Flip Dawson and Linda Gould were fast friends. Flip, too, was always about. No wonder — and his mother understood, but approved no more than Miranda — Peter often spent time in the kitchen, especially when his family was out and presumably would never know.

Peter came back from the counting-house and glanced about him. Parlors, landing, and living room were empty. He looked in the Chinese cloisonné bowl in the hall where the mail was left. There was a letter to his mother from Liz, who had gone to New York the week before. He put down the letter and without stopping to take off his hat dove for the kitchen. Mother and Miranda, babies and all, were gone. Nobody was home to disapprove of him and his low company.

Linda and Flip sat alone.

"Where's everybody?"

"Michael has driven them back to Danvers, Mr. Peter," said Linda, "to see Mr. Tom and his factory. Becky's gone, too, to mind babies."

"Aren't *we* anybody?" Flip demanded pertly.

"Sure, Flip. Is tea being served?"

"We were half-expecting you, Mr. Peter." Linda's expressionless eye fastened on his profile. Even yet she did not dare look at him full face. Three cups had been set out. When the cat (to all of them that was Miranda) was away, the mice certainly did play, for Peter saw they were not using the cracked cups and nicked saucers Miranda had put aside for them, but something pretty and flower-strewn. I hope Miranda doesn't catch them, he thought.

Linda poured out his tea. She was as skinny as ever and as graceful. There was something poetic about the way she handled herself, even her thin hands. And she was as shy and blank-looking as ever, and no prettier. It was laughable how she couldn't pour out tea without raising her eyebrows when she asked, "Sugar?" There was no reason for it except that his mother always did. No two women could be less alike, yet Peter knew how closely she and his mother were united. Together they formed a secret but unshakable front against Miranda, with Nanny always backing Miranda.

Flip also imitated her mistress. When Peter said he was sorry Michael was away, she tossed her curls and said, "Begorrah, and who was she to be after chasing a bogtrotter." Her voice flicked with mirth, exactly the way Polly's did when she mimicked people. The minx had recoverd from Dan Obrian. She was going to marry Michael Shean, and soon, but only on the condition that he would permit her to go on working for Polly by the day.

"But I thought you were running after him, Flip. And had caught him."

"Me? I never ran after a thing in my life. Things catch up with me," she boasted. "Now it's Linda who does the running after."

"Oh, Linda," Peter said, with mock severity, "are you running after New Lighters again?"

"Yes, sir."

"Shouldn't, should you?"

"No, sir."

"I thought you had promised Doctor Hobey not to."

"No, sir. Didn't promise anything." Her voice squeaked a little as it always did when she was perturbed or very pleased. Now she was both.

Of late Linda had become too religious. It was not in the formal dissertations of 'Sephus Hobey's church she had, as she admitted modestly, "seen God," but in the disorder, weepings and shoutings, of the New Lighters. Ugly sects, many thought them. No trained clergy. No church buildings. On street corners, in barns, taprooms, holds of vessels — in fact, wherever two or three were gathered together in their Master's name — there they were. Linda herself had been baptized in North River last fall. She had caught a bad cold, but this seemed a slight malady compared to having caught "religion."

The old passion of the Puritans was dying down into what might seem like cool embers. There was little left in it to appeal to the poor and despised. The New Lighters were sweeping much chaff before them, and it was in vain for proper folk to say it was chaff only and that the good wheat had already been gathered into Congregational and Episcopal bins.

Doctor Hobey had, at Mrs. Inman's request, talked to Linda. She shouldn't go traipsing off after New Light preachers. She shouldn't dance before the Lord — and was it true she had once danced with a lighted candle on her head? Were there not pews set aside, rent free, in the gallery of his own church, for servants and such? Linda had squirmed and nodded, but promised not a thing.

As far away as Newburyport, Linda Gould could be found swaying gracefully and shouting weakly with her fellow enthusiasts when she should have been home paring potatoes for Mrs. Cady or washing cellar stairs for Mrs. Miranda. But when the mood came upon Linda, she was off. Then she'd come home as exhausted and as at peace as the Inmans' returning tomcat. Mrs. Miranda would cuff her and threaten to discharge her. But Linda was too sure of Mrs. Inman to let that frighten her.

Once Peter had gone with her. He did not quickly forget the singing, exhorting, stamping. The speaking-out in "foreign tongues" and the sins confessed in plain Anglo-Saxon. He could not understand the "peace" Linda got out of it. Peace! He had never heard such yowlings. It was his fault, Linda had dared tell him. "You have to let go, Mr. Peter. You didn't let go — any. But you've a soul to save. Some folk haven't any. I pray sometime you may be called."

"If anybody saves my black, stinking, damned soul," he said, making a terribly lecherous face at her, "it will be you." And "Please God," she had squeaked back at him, thrilled to pieces and scared to death. Part of Peter's fascination for her was his "sins."

Drinking tea and carrying on a gossipy banal conversation much more suitable to servant girls than to a young gentleman, he passed a satisfactory half-hour. Then, like a passing bell, Davy Jones boomed, announcing the return of the carriage. It was stopping at the side entrance.

Now Flip would make her well-timed exit to palaver a little with Michael as he unharnessed the new pair, Froth and Foam. Mrs. Cady would rouse herself from her afternoon nap and be down. Worse yet, Mrs. Miranda might be upon them with bonnet and gloves still on and catch Linda using good china, and Peter — once again — sitting sociably with servant girls. Surreptitiously the little group scattered like mice before dawn.

Peter found his sister-in-law and his mother standing in the hall. His mother had Liz's letter open in her hand. Becky, carrying the two babies, had already reached the landing.

"You may as well read this," said his mother, in a queer, drawn voice.

My dear Mother,

That this, my announcement of marriage, will surprise you, I do not doubt. But Fanny has at last consented to be my wife. This morning the Reverend Mr. Jordan united us here in New York. It was no feeling of shame that has prompted us to act thus privately. But neither of us felt a necessity to go through the arguments we felt inevitable if we previously announced our decision. I know you — everyone — will say Fanny is nine years older than I. But in actual fact it is I who am her senior by all the true measurements of time. I must have a few more weeks here to complete my business, and for Fanny to complete her wardrobe which, I assure you, will compliment her greatly. Then we shall visit Charleston to enjoy a more delightful climate than New England offers in January. In two months' time we shall return. I have already engaged from Mr. Mompesson the little house next to his on Federal Street and owned by him. Before I left, I ordered its re-doing. I hope I can count on your advice and help about this house. If you are passing by, do drop

in and see if the paper I'm sending up from New York is not too
drab a gray. The curtains will be primrose yellow.

I am most gratefully, most obediently, and affectionately

your son,

ELEAZAR INMAN

January 17, 1806
5 Bowling Green, New York

P.S. Fanny sends love and filial respects. She is apprehensive this
marriage may be unwelcome to you. I assure her you have always
loved her so much as a friend you will gladly welcome her as a
daughter. Be pleased to write her a brief welcome.

LIZ

"I still *can't* believe it! I don't believe it yet. Peter, what did
you know about this?"

"Nothing, Mother."

"And to think he writes she has at *last* consented. She's been
after him hammer and *tongs* all winter. She'd have given her eye
teeth to get him. And that simpleton thinks he had to persuade
her!"

"I guess Liz knows what he wants, Mother. And Cousin Frances
is nice."

"But what could a boy Liz's age see in an older woman like
that?"

Miranda, who by now had read the letter too, pronounced por-
tentously, "She'll pay for her folly."

This Peter could not deny. Pay for the folly of marrying Liz
Inman? He guessed any woman who did would pay — but it might
be worth it.

"Of course, Mother Inman, you will not receive her?"

"*Miranda!* Don't be *stupid.* I'll have to. Now listen to me, you
two. We must take this attitude. We are all so *pleased.* And for
Heaven's sake, don't let anyone guess we were *surprised.* We are
all so *happy.* It is terrible — but a family does have to stand together." And she remembered Liz's own earlier words, "It is the
family itself decides how bad is a family scandal."

"But Mother Inman, she has behaved so treacherously toward
you. Do you think it is right to pretend so?"

"I don't care what's right. We've got to make the best of it.

Now, let me see . . . I'm going right over to Mrs. Crowninshield and tell her before my bonnet's off. They're our cousins. They'd expect to be told immediately. Miranda, Mrs. White — I don't mean the old one, I mean the young one — is the *worst* gossip in town. Do run in and tell her our 'good news.' And don't *dare* wear that look on your face. Look *happy*. Peter . . ." There were not many places she could send Peter. "Dear, you go tell Polly and the aunts. And on the way home stop in for a grog at the Sun. Tell everybody. Oh, dear . . . I suppose by tomorrow it will be in the *Gazette*. But luckily my sewing circle meets in the morning. I'll tell them all."

"Just as you think best, Mother Inman."

"And I suppose" — Lucy's face screwed up — "*she* will begin calling me 'Mother Inman' too."

"She could hardly presume now to call you by your given name. And Mother Inman, I promise Nanny and I will accept her exactly as we would any other sister-in-law. If this is your wish. We'll do anything to help you. I know how hard it is at your age . . ."

"Thank you, Miranda," Lucy said tartly.

She did not feel she had merely lost a son and gained a daughter, as the old saying went. She had lost a son and her dearest friend in the world as well.

❧ 2 ❧

Mrs. Liz sat in her parlor. The gray paper was not too drab. The primrose curtains gave even a north room an illusion of sunshine. She was happier than she had believed possible. Married for six months and not a single rift in her lute. Her hands flowed down over the rust-silk dress. She studied the tips of her bronze sandals. These sandals cost more than any dress she had ever bought before. She was a little too plump, as the long French pier glass told her, but it also said that she had a neat waist. It was only a pretty, very feminine plumpness. But sometime, of course, she'd have to begin "watching out." Having a man to feed properly and an excellent cook in the kitchen did mean she herself ate more than when she lived alone and never bothered to prepare proper meals.

Her chestnut hair was parted, waved back from her little ears, tossed up high behind. It had lost that wig-like look. Love and happiness or good food had lubricated it a little. And her complexion did look more like the ivory Liz compared it to than the tallow candle Lucy had once suggested.

Sitting properly on mauve velvet hassocks close by were her dead sister Kate's two girls — Jeany just sixteen; Devotion two years younger. She looked at them through quick tears of love. As long as she had been only a poor forlorn widow woman herself, she had not been able to do much for them. Brother Thorndike — a miserable fellow who had sunk to the journeyman level of his craft of silversmith — had not wanted to lend her his girls even for these few weeks. Jeany was already his housekeeper. He had told Fanny that as soon as Devotion was old enough to "mind the pot," he was going to put Jeany out in service. He had sent them to her with a firm illiterate letter telling her she was not to "spile them — they was pore girls."

All Frances had done was to spoil them. And Liz had been just as bad. She knew he loved to come home from the counting-house and tease and charm and forget himself with the pretty demure young girls. She had dressed them from their shifts out in the daintiest clothes. She had washed and brushed and loved them. Oh, she thought, I wish I could keep them forever. If only Brother Thorndike would die. He has bowel trouble. I wish he would die — then Liz and I would have them forever. But day after next she had promised to start them on the stage home, back to that alley in Providence.

To add to her momentary happiness she also had Petra Flanneau. The night before Mrs. Flanneau had come running to her, dragging the child. Flanneau had been drinking a good deal ever since he had lost his warehouse. He seemed utterly unable to get over his loss or think or talk of anything except the fire. But last night was the first time Dulcey had hidden the child, as once she had often, with Frances since the latter's marriage. She couldn't do anything with him. She was afraid of him. Perhaps, Frances thought, she shouldn't have hidden Petra in the house. And only this morning when she woke up, she had heard her prattling and talking to herself and had gone to her and wished she might keep her forever, too. The arms of her maternal passion went out in all directions like the tentacles of an octopus reaching for what it might seize upon.

The young girls, on their identical mauve velvet tasseled hassocks, in identical white muslin dresses, bent almost identical faces over the delicate handkerchiefs their aunt was helping them to hem. Both had straight flaxen hair which fell forward over their bent faces. When Fanny spoke to them, they raised almost identical enormous gray eyes with black lashes so long they looked stitched on like fringe on a curtain. The girls were all eyes, like insects. And almost insect-thin. Their aunt thought, in pity, If only I had them a little longer, I could fatten them up. Whipped cream on everything — and she generously did not stop to think what whipped cream might do to her own plumpness, only of the girls.

Were they not tired of their hemming, their aunt asked them kindly. No, no, they were not. And Devotion smiled. Both Frances and Liz had agreed that Jeany was the "pretty" one. But there were moments like this, when Devotion smiled, gravely as she did everything else, and there was something so sweet, so womanly, on the little thin face, she had an almost madonna beauty. Lucy thought, with amazement, Jeany is much prettier, but Devotion is going to be a beauty. In four years' time nobody is going to even look at Jeany if Devotion comes into the room.

The maid Liz had engaged in New York — and she still frightened Fanny by her unfriendly ways — announced that a gentleman had come to the kitchen door, asking for her.

"At least, madam," the maid said starchily, "whether he's a gentleman or not I daren't say."

Flanneau, of course, sobered up and repentant. Dulcey — she had noticed how kind Dulcey had been to him since his misfortune — had evidently confided in him where she was hiding Petra. Frances skewered her needle in the sock she was darning. First she must send away the young girls.

"Dears, I want you to go to your room now and put on fresh dresses. Wash your face and hands, brush your hair fifty strokes. Your Uncle Liz will be home soon now and he likes to see you fresh for supper."

"May we wear our blue sashes?"

"Yes. Or would you like to wear your Roman stripes?"

"Oh, yes. Please."

Then she told the maid to bring the gentleman in. She dreaded seeing Flanneau. He was becoming so desperate and depressed. People were saying he'd never get his affairs in order again.

Now he was entering with the shame and arrogance of the defeated man. The evenings they had shared so cozily — always behind Lucy's back — were so much over, she was surprised he sat down in her presence, and instantly ashamed of her surprise.

Once again he was telling her of his financial loss. Oh dear, how could he be so boring? He had grown very gray, his face as lined as a closed accordion, his little eyes red-rimmed. His voice droned on.

"But Flanneau," she interrupted him, not unkindly, "you don't seem to say anything. You just talk on and on. What is it that you want?"

"A loan, Mrs. Fanny."

"Oh . . ."

"If I can get a loan, once more I can buy here in Salem, silks. And sell elsewhere, to profit. But I have no money to buy goods. There are three ships in harbor here from the Far East. The auctions are posted. But I cannot buy, I cannot begin again. And yet now at last I feel the courage, the will rises in me. The courage" — and he struck his meager chest — "has returned home to roost, as you say here."

"A loan . . ." she repeated. "Money?"

"I must have it. And who is it will dare to say I am not a good risk?"

But Liz had told her that Flanneau had gone to pieces so, was drinking so stupidly, that not a merchant in town had any more confidence in him. He knew Peter would have lent it — if he could. Liz was much smarter about tying up what Peter did with his shares of profit than Madam had ever been. "He can have that five hundred a year for his woman," Liz had told Frances. "I guess she's worth it to him. And no more. I'm holding on to it for him." There were plenty who'd say Flanneau was not a good risk. And now he was asking for a "character loan" — he, a man of no character.

"You have become a very rich lady?" he suggested, hopefully.

"No. Not really. I mean I can buy and charge anything I want, for myself or my household. Literally anything. Captain Liz is the most generous man in the world. But Flanneau, I haven't one cent in the world to put into business."

"You would not wish to speak to Captain Liz?"

"I don't see how I can."

"I have already approached him," Flanneau went on, with sad honesty. "He says no."

"Then I certainly can't. You must understand. And I'd never dare presume to talk business with Captain Liz."

"Then, my little girl, please," he said quietly.

So Dulcey had taken him into her confidence, told him where Petra was. Yes, Dulcey had given him an excuse to call upon her. Ask for money. Seemingly his adversity was arousing some loyalty to him in her.

"I will go elsewhere. I will get the loan. My little girl, please?"

Once more Petra would leave her. Fanny couldn't bear it. She thought of the diamonds Liz had given her, and then he had decided she was not the type to wear diamonds — and she was not. Did she dare suggest to Flanneau that he take them to Boston and pawn them for her? They were worth a little fortune.

"Flanneau . . . I'm unused to business, but . . ." She was frightened by the enormity of what she knew she must say next. Her fright showed on her face and in her tense hands.

"But what, my dear Mrs. Fanny?"

"There is something you have I want. I'll do anything to get it."

"Yes, madam?" He was standing, bowing. "It is yours for the asking."

Her face twitched with emotion. "I want Petra."

"Petra? Oh, madam!"

"Yes." The perspiration stood on her waxen face. "Everyone knows she is not your child. We can talk frankly."

"We shall talk frankly, yes. Yes, always, Madam Fanny. I have never said she was."

"I don't know if I'll ever have any children or not. I've a feeling . . . I'm awfully afraid not. I was married before, you know. Five years, and didn't. And Liz and I . . . actually we've been married six months. Flanneau, without a child, especially a little girl, I can't ever hold him. He so loves everything young . . . and pretty. Do you not think that I, who am nine years older than he, have not thought of it?"

"But she . . . the apple of my eye! The soul of my heart! I cannot live or ever work again if I have not her. My Petra."

Frances sat dejected, her hands loose in her lap. "I was thinking . . . next time Liz is on a long voyage he'd come home and find Petra here with me. And she'd call me Mama. Then I know he would admit her. Give her his name . . . as he should have done. Long ago."

"Madam," he spoke softly.

"Yes, Flanneau?"

"Madam, Petra is not Captain Liz's child."

"Oh, don't tell me again," she said angrily, "that she is Peter's."

"Madam, in strictest privacy I will tell you the truth. It shall go no farther. But you shall not eat out your heart for what you have thought your husband's child."

"I swear."

Flanneau paced the room and finally sat on one of the mauve tasseled hassocks. A very caricature he did look of the young girl who had so recently left it, for his lank hair hung forward at the same angle.

"When the fire was," he said, not looking at her, "the fire brigade, they told us the house next would go."

"Yes, I remember."

"And to us each we take the most valuable?"

"Yes."

"So after Petra is safe, I ran, I run back and forth and forth and back, carry, carry, carry. My wife, she too."

Fanny nodded.

"It was this that I did notice. She, who never reads a book, she clung to a book. It was never once put down. I saw it was dearer than all else to her. She would not put it down. Next day I so angry that she cared most for a book she never read, I struck it from her. And then . . ."

"What, then, Flanneau?"

He did not answer her questions. "Madam Fanny, for five years he, Mr. Peter, and she have fooled me. She had glued together certain parts of the book. And cut out others, to make her a box. There was a letter. Mr. Peter is not the father of Petra. Half of your guess is right. My wife should have told me long before, especially as this is in part a business matter. A little affair of the heart, perhaps, a wife and husband need not share. But business must be shared always between husband and wife."

"I don't see any business connection."

"Do you not think that Captain Dash, who has so slyly hidden behind Peter, would, if he were home, give me a large loan . . . lest that letter appear, say, in the Salem *Gazette*?"

"Oh, Flanneau! Not Dash! Of all men! I love my husband for what he is — not for what I wish he were. I've faced it. Captain Liz could behave dishonorably toward a poor girl. Could let Peter take the blame. I'll say that of the man I love. I don't love Dash, but I'll pay him the compliment to swear he could not. He might have had an illegitimate child. But he couldn't have harmed Peter so."

"Madam," Flanneau said, not arguing with her, "how wise to love a man for what he is, not what you wish he were."

"I'm no young girl. And a woman may find advantages in her increasing years — if she has the wit to look for them. Shouldn't a man get some advantages for marrying someone much older than himself?"

"Madam, madam, may I kiss your hand?"

"Still I cannot believe you."

He shrugged indifferently. "But if it were true, if that which I know and have proof of is true — would it not alter my financial condition? If only supposing Captain Dash was in? For Peter, there is nothing he has left. No money left in Peter."

"Flanneau! You're not talking of *blackmail?*"

"A blackmailer? No, madam. Never. It is not money that I ask. It is a loan with good interest. I do not blackmail." He seemed fiercely proud of this fine point. "If only Captain Dash were home . . ." He paused and asked suddenly, "It is true, is it not, Captain Dash is engaged to marry Miss Mompesson?"

"Oh, deary me," she said, hardly following his thoughts, for she had gone back more firmly than ever to her idea that Liz was Petra's father, "everyone always says so. At least when he's ashore. Yes. I suppose it's settled between them. Somehow. For some time."

"It is obviously to the greatest of Mr. Mompesson's interest no blight shall be attached to the name of any son-in-law."

"Why . . . as far as Polly is concerned, he's very fussy." She had not the least idea what he had in mind.

She went into the hall and called to Jeany and Devotion to bring down Petra. A pretty picture they made, the young girls in fresh muslins and hanging, flaxen hair, the vivid, flaming-cheeked child between them. Petra made not the slightest secret of her aversion to Flanneau. Even as he kissed her and chatted his French endearments to her, she stiffened and stared calmly at him. She had Peter's eyes.

It was close on suppertime. Next door to Liz Inman's house was the Mompessons' stately gate. Flanneau stopped before it. He clutched Petra too tightly by the hand.

"It is very rich, these people. This Squire Mompesson," he spoke in French.

"Oui, Papa."

"And a little of so much they have, can they not share?"

"Oui, Papa." Now his hand was so tight on her arm he was hurting her.

"But I am not a blackmailer. I spit and stamp on the word." And he spat and stamped. "I do not say 'give,' I say 'lend.' "

"Oui, Papa."

The front door was opening and from the hallway he heard voices and a slight bustle of departure. Two slender women in dark muslins — Aunt Birdseye had died that spring — were stepping out together, attended by Mr Mompesson in all his elegance. It was only he who saw the man and child staring through the bushes at his daughter and her cousin and himself.

Flanneau had made the dark muslins Miss Mompesson and Miss Frick wore and Mompesson had paid him for them. The thin fine silk of Mompesson's coat had been bought from Flanneau. So Mompesson knew him well, indeed. But he stared straight at him and through him. His expression said, "You insolent cur, you and your misbegotten, filthy child, how dare you lift your eyes and stare at me and mine?"

Flanneau watched them as they disappeared down Federal Street, one lady hung upon each of the gentleman's arms. Once they were out of hearing, he burst into a spasm of rage. He grabbed Petra, tense fingers sinking into her flesh, twitched her back and forth. *"Cochon!"* he hissed. "But he shall eat humble pie. My little girl shall have everything she wish."

"Stop it, Papa," Petra said, with an amazing amount of authority for her age. "Stop it."

He relaxed his grip upon her. More and more he was beginning to obey her. He was sometimes afraid of her. So there was love and fear on one side. And dislike and scorn on the other.

~ 3 ~

HATLESS, Georgiana flung herself out of the house, still in her morning calico, her eyes circled with sleeplessness. Polly had been sick, desperately sick, with soaring temperature, shaken pulse, almost out of her mind, for three days.

Of course, poor Old Doctor West was puzzled as to what had brought on this brain fever. Nobody had told him about that dreadful letter. Georgiana did not know how Cousin Mompesson had got it. She did not care. But she now realized that Peter was the best, the most self-sacrificing of men. And quixotic. Her heart bounded with the speed of her running and her love for him. And she could almost laugh at him, and love him even more. He was so quixotic.

At first Polly had taken the letter very well. She had immediately pointed out the obvious fact that it was not in Dash's usual handwriting. She went to her desk and fetched certain notes of Dash's. Not even a good forgery, as she told her papa. Flanneau had realized, she said, how much more money he could get out of a wealthy man like Dash than from the impecunious Peter. That was why he and his wife had cooked up this letter. She had been so positive she had almost persuaded her father. Not Georgiana. The fact was that Dash had written out for her words of certain sea songs, printing them beneath the music. Georgiana said nothing, but her heart began to beat hard. She could, she might, produce these samples of how Dash printed and end the argument forever. She did not. So at first Polly took it very well.

The next night Georgiana woke to hear Polly sobbing. She was feverish and almost literally out of her head. Moaning and crying out. Doctor West had been called in the night. And could make nothing of her ailment. Three days later, and she was only weaker and her voice gone. Then her father had said he would send for Peter himself and let him say yes or no flat out. So

Georgiana ran down the streets. At this hour, eight in the morning, surely he would be at his grandmother's counting-house. She did not notice the curious glances that followed her. Or, as she streaked down the waterfront, the pleasure she aroused in foremast hands and porters who like to see pretty girls run fast in tight calicos, with hair jouncing down their backs.

At last she stood by the counting-house stairs. "Peter!" she called. His head immediately popped out his upper window, like a cuckoo out of a clock.

"What is it, Georgiana?" His face whitened. "What's happened?" Everyone knew that Polly had been struck down by brain fever. Evidently he feared the worst.

"Georgiana," he demanded again, as he stood beside her, "what is it — not Polly?"

"No. Yes. I mean she's not *dead* or anything. Peter, you must come with me. She wants to talk with you. Peter, she's going to ask you . . . whether a certain thing is true or not. Walk slowly. I'm out of breath and there's a lot we must talk about before we get there." For even at such a moment she remembered that it was bad for Peter to walk fast.

He did not go back for a hat. He took the quill pen from behind his ear and, as he walked up the wharf with Georgiana, broke it deliberately, scattering the pieces. There was an air of finality about this simple gesture. As if he was saying, Well, that is that. That settles it. Georgiana glanced sidewise at his profile. Perhaps only she, in all the world, had noticed that it was growing thinner and thinner. She hardly saw him oftener than every six months. And every six months he was a little thinner. So she looked at his profile and almost cried — it looked so thin, wasted, and lost. Her heart cried, Oh, my dear, don't, don't get so thin. Darling, you're not lost. You have me, Peter. Don't lose hope.

Out loud she said, "Cousin Mompesson has a letter."

He gave her a quick, comprehending, baffling look. So she saw he knew what letter. That proved it. It was not, as Polly claimed, a forgery, just cooked up.

"Oh?"

"It is supposed to have been written six years ago. It says flat out that if Mrs. Flanneau — she was Dulcey Delaney then — has a child within the next nine months, Dash is the father. And he wrote it and signed it. So nobody else is the father of Petra. Not you, for instance." She never minced her words.

"Well . . ." he gazed at the horizon.

She stopped on the street and stamped her foot. "Peter Inman, look at me! I won't go on talking to a profile."

He looked at her. "I love to look at you, Georgiana." But there was such a baffling expression in his eyes she could read no more from them than she could from a profile.

"And not like that, Peter!" she cried out, almost in anguish and wrung her hands. "Peter, Peter, don't do it!"

"Whatever mustn't I do?"

"Go on as you've been going. Lying!" She was intensely conscious of the mask over his face. She felt it as something so real she could almost see him holding it up before him with his two hands. She grasped him by the arm and shook him, determined to shake off the mask.

"Begin at the beginning, Mouse," he said gently. "You have me all in a fog."

"No, I haven't. I can't help notice you knew all about it — that letter. Wait . . . don't move. Stand here and answer me. The time's come when you have to go to Polly and her father and swear before them whether it's true or not."

"I guessed it was something like that. Right off."

"Why did you guess? I didn't really say anything. Why did you guess?"

"I always knew that sometime this was a thing that would catch up with me. When I saw you, I thought, now's the time."

They stood in the middle of Essex Street, almost blocking the sidewalk. People had to crowd to get past them.

Then she cried out in sudden passion, "Peter, if you go in there and lie, I can't love you any more. I can't love a liar."

The ensuing silence would have hurt a far less sensitive girl than she. He had never asked her to love him. He did not now. He put a gentle hand under her elbow. She was terribly hurt.

"Come on, let's get moving. That woman with the oyster barrow can't get past us."

And she felt, with sinking heart, the disillusioning, cool kindness of his hand on her. They left Essex for Court Street, which was almost as crowded, and came out into the serenity of Federal.

Here was peace and privacy. But here they walked in silence, arm in arm, as lovers walk, but they were not lovers. As they reached the Mompessons', Georgiana stopped and did something with her handkerchief. He was afraid she was crying. But she looked him in the face, defiantly and dry-eyed. "I never cry," she said, proudly.

Lying across the open doorway, breathing asthmatically and smelling to high Heaven, was Aunt Birdseye's poor old poodle. Now there was no one left who loved him. Great-Aunt Birdseye was dead. Nobody left that he loved, and he had already made up his mind to linger on but little longer in so hostile a world. He did not raise his head as they stepped over him into the house. A servant told them not to go up quite yet. Mrs. Shean would come down and tell them when. They sat together in Polly's sitting room.

Georgiana went to an inlaid card-table and picked up a pack of cards. She seemed determined to make no more appeal to Peter. She dealt herself a hand of solitaire. Independent in all her ways, she didn't do embroidery like other women — "catch-up work," they called it. If she had a spare moment, she played solitaire or read a book or thrummed on her guitar.

Her action and his silence suggested there was no more to be said between them. But, in a moment, she asked, "Do you play solitaire, Peter?"

"Not with cards," he said, smiling. He had always been more frank with her than with anyone else about his position in Salem.

"Do you like two-handed games? I know a nice new one."

"I'd prefer to sit. And talk."

"There isn't one thing left for us to talk about." She shuffled, cut, and slapped down her cards.

"Tell me about Polly."

"Yesterday, she lost her voice. She won't be able to question you. Cousin Mompesson will do that. Except with her eyes." She dealt again.

"Has Polly seen the letter?"

"Yes. She says it's not in his hand. It is almost printed. She says she knows it's a forgery."

He said nothing. She got up from the card-table, flung herself on her knees before him, covering his thin hands with kisses. Then she threw back her head and looked into his face. In spite of Polly's comments on her appearance, at this time she was beautiful. Love shone through her, transfigured her.

Peter was not unmoved. He put a hand on either side of her head and swayed it gently back and forth. "Mouse," he said, "get up off your knees and sit in a chair, like the proper girl you've never been."

"No. I've never knelt to anyone before. I never will again. I want to now. Let me. Peter, I'm saying good-bye."

And to herself she thought, You never loved me, but thank God you've liked me. But whatever we might have had couldn't have lasted long. Peter, Peter, I know it, but I hope you don't. You're not getting better all the time. But weaker, sicker. The tears she boasted she never shed swelled in her, smarted in her nose, ran down her face and choked her. She hid her face against his knees and he put his arms about her and kissed the part in her hair.

"Mouse," he said, but his voice, too, was choking, "you've told me a hundred times, No, you don't cry, ever. No more'n a man. You're a big little girl and stand on your own feet. Why are you crying now?"

"And I don't fib, either — like most girls. I won't now. I do love you. I've loved you for so long." He held her so close her face was against his throat. "And now, any minute, you are going upstairs. Polly will look so beautiful. Every curl in place. You'll pity her because she can't speak above a whisper. So then, I know it, you'll forswear yourself. Forever, because . . ." she choked, "you've always loved Polly, although you like me best."

And she felt him pressing her closer and closer to him and such an ecstasy she hardly knew where he began and she left off. She felt there was nothing she did not wish to share with him, her soul and body, his shame, his foolishness, his disease, even — which only today she had admitted would conquer him — his poetry, his early death.

"You *do* like me better than Polly?" she whispered.

"I've liked you best of any girl I've ever known. And as for Polly, you don't understand. Nor I . . . I never thought of her quite by herself — I always think of Dash and Polly. Together."

"Oh," she looked at him in a sudden amazement of understanding. "I think I see . . . It does make it different, having you say that. It's for Dash you'll do this dreadful thing — not for her — it's Dash."

They heard feet coming down the front stairs.

"You feel you have to, Peter?"

"Yes."

"Even if it is a lie?"

"Even if."

"Peter, kiss me quick. Kiss me now. My dearest."

He had never kissed her like this before. The wealth of love he held in his arms kindled him, but it was for only one moment.

"Good-bye, good-bye," she whispered to him, and by the time Flip — called officially Mrs. Shean these days — entered, she was sitting once more, idling over her solitaire.

~4~

THE BRIGHT SUN of June streamed into the fragile white room, flowed across the little bed. It was a French bed, without any of the old-fashioned, ponderous tester and bed-dress, and as slim and delicate as the girl who lay upon it. This was the first thing Peter noticed, and next that — even as Georgiana had promised him — every curl was brushed and lay just so upon the pillow. Her flushed face did look beautiful, and he read in her eyes the anguish she had been through. She smiled wanly and mouthed a welcome she could not speak. About her neck was a stiff white poultice. This seemed to decapitate her, disconnect her from the reality of her body, sheets and satin bed-quilt, free her head so it might float about the room following him forever like the haunting face of a dream. Her eyes were begging him. And he knew for what.

Flip was arranging pillows, helping her to sit up a little, curtsying and leaving. Little Mr. Mompesson greeted Peter formally, but did not rise nor ask him to sit. For once he seemed almost an old man. Too stiff to rise.

"Mr. Inman," he began, "recently a letter has come — er — come into my possession."

"Yes, sir. Georgiana told me."

"She did? She shouldn't have. I instructed her not to breathe a word. But, anyway . . ." He was still at a loss for words. Peter could smell the rank, sweet, almost pleasant but entirely nauseating smell of linseed from the poultice. I'll never smell linseed again, he thought, but I'll think of this moment. "Although," Mr. Mompesson went on, "there has never been a public announcement of intent to marry between my daughter and your brother Ralph"—he was twisting the silver buttons on his blue velvet coat—"there has been . . . talk. Plenty of talk."

"Yes, sir."

"If what this letter states is true"—he had it in his hands—"I will never even consider giving my daughter to so worthless and dishonorable a man. Never. I'd rather see her dead in her coffin than married to so—so"—he struggled to find a word bad enough for Dash and not too bad for Polly to hear—"so depraved a monster. Polly and I discussed this matter frankly before she unfortunately lost her voice. She is in complete agreement with me. If this letter is true, and no forgery, she chooses by her own volition never again to—to tolerate such a"—again he was at a loss—"such a monster in her sight. I am not, of course, referring only to the original—*slip,* shall I say—after all, I at least know young gentlemen will sometimes act like they oughn't—but to the disgraceful silence he has kept. To the great injury of—but I need name no names. All this if this letter proves true."

Polly tried to speak. Georgiana was beside her, bending to catch her whisper. Peter wondered vaguely when she had come in. He had left her downstairs playing solitaire.

"Polly says, Cousin Mompesson," she announced, in a queer, flat voice, "that it isn't true. She knows."

"Polly, please don't try to talk. And you must not interrupt. As I was saying to Mr. Peter . . ."

Once more Georgiana bent over the pillow. "Polly says it is a forgery."

"Now, Polly, I command you. Your vocal cords, dear. Mr. Peter, she and I have agreed to send for you. There are two things I wish to hear from your own lips."

"Yes, sir."

"First, I beg you to consider carefully and answer me honestly. Is this letter in truth your brother's hand?"

How well he remembered Dash tearing a flyleaf from a ledger, writing this note, not in his usual illegible, quick hand, but very carefully, almost printing, because Dulcey did not read easily.

"Flanneau," Peter said deliberately, but very conscious of Georgiana staring at him, "or whoever did it, was very clever with the signature. That 'Dash' is pretty good. As for the rest of it, it doesn't look like Dash's hand at all. He writes so fast — I see you have some other samples of his hand here. He writes fast and all in a heap, sort of. Doesn't form any letter very carefully."

"Yes, yes. But to me it looks like the same hand, deliberately disguised. Look at those L's."

"Why should Dash have wished to disguise his hand, if this was a sort of almost legal letter he was writing so a girl could show it to selectmen?"

He felt blood pounding in his throat and was afraid. Mompesson was smart. Would he be smart enough to make the next, perfectly obvious, remark that this letter was written for an almost illiterate person to read? Peter felt Mompesson could scarcely miss this. But he had. In the long silence, the smell of the linseed was sickening. He had not been asked to sit. He was standing and suddenly felt dizzy. He looked straight at Mr. Mompesson's face, for by focusing hard on something he could keep his feet.

"For years I've not denied the Flanneau child, children — one died — are mine. And it is true I've been paying Flanneau, just as people say, to support the child and to gain his . . . acquiescence. But there's little money in me these days. Liz keeps it all reinvested. Flanneau has had a calamity. He wants ready cash. He knows Dash has struck it very rich. That's why he has swapped horses — I mean fathers."

"Please don't joke about this matter."

"I'm not joking. Flanneau couldn't wait for Dash. He tried you, sir, thinking Dash Inman's good name would be dear to you."

"Dear to *me?*" He had a handkerchief in his hands. "I don't care *that* for Dash Inman's good name" — and he tore the handkerchief in two and threw it on the floor — "as long as he is in no way allied to my family."

Polly gestured. Georgiana went to her.

"She says, Cousin Mompesson, please ask Peter to swear — flat out — Petra is his child." Georgiana looked at Peter disdainfully as she spoke, and yet with beseeching love. Will you swear it? her eyes demanded of him.

"Yes, yes. That's my second question. Is she or not?" He turned to Georgiana. "Run to my bedroom. Fetch me a Bible."

She brought it in. Once again Polly wished to speak and Georgiana's flat, seemingly disinterested voice repeated her words. "Cousin Mompesson, Polly wishes to remind you that you have said one gentleman's word means more to you than a dozen knaves like the Flanneaus."

"Why, yes. Yes, of course."

Peter had always ridiculed Mr. Mompesson's snobbish insistence upon the virtues of the gentility, the evil of the commonality. Now he had reason to be thankful for it.

"Put your hand on the Bible."

Peter wished he'd been invited to sit. It was the smell of the linseed, he felt, so sickened him, and he was drenched with sweat. Phrase by phrase he repeated what Mompesson demanded of him, beginning with the fact that he had had guilty carnal knowledge of one Dulcey Delaney, fathering a child upon her, and so forth.

"This is your Bible word, so help you God?"

"So help me."

Georgiana was in a rocking chair, her hands over her mouth. The noise of the rockers sounded incredibly loud. Creak-crock, creak-crock. He wished she wouldn't.

"Now," said Mr. Mompesson, "there is only the question — should I go on permitting Mr. Peter to call upon my daughter?"

Georgiana was not at hand. Polly raised herself up and said clearly, "Of course, Papa."

"I'll think this matter over."

"Papa, he's *got* to come."

"Hush. Do not strain your vocal cords. I suppose we may consider this . . . farce over. How you, or your brothers, comport yourselves is no affair of mine. So only the subject of an alliance does not come up. If Captain Dash should ever ask my permission for any young lady under my guidance, I would expect him to be ready to give the same assurances you have, Mr. Peter."

"No!" Peter exclaimed, in fright. But he caught himself. "You've as good as said, sir, you doubt my word."

Such high-spirited concern over one's word, Mr. Mompesson understood. "There, there," he said, mildly, "calm yourself. Forgive a doting father. But if, as I was saying, the subject of an alliance does come up, I will consider it my duty to question him."

Question Dash? Dash couldn't ever stand up, put his hand on a Bible and swear a falsehood. He'd fling everything overboard, Bible and Mompesson and Peter's careful web of lies, and Polly too. In such a pinch he'd fling away Polly — so he might selfishly hold on to his own honor.

He was glad no one went downstairs with him, that Flip was not there to bow him out or notice how he held on to the rail. He sat a moment to recover himself, if he could, in Polly's sitting room. There were Georgiana's cards tumbled over the table. He saw the rug was rumpled. That was when she had flung herself at him and knelt to him. He was sitting in the same chair and by shutting his eyes he could almost believe that, any moment, she might join him, tell him again how much she loved him. And he almost loved her. For a moment he was forgetting Dash.

Once more on the street he felt stronger, but had not the heart to return home nor to face again the counting-house. It was a fair June day with a promise of rain in the clouds on the horizon. His heart was still pounding and he dripped with sweat. Suddenly he decided he'd take a long country walk. Fill his lungs with the fresh spring air, get that terrible smell of linseed out of them. He had to be alone for a little and he had to think. He had crossed, and he knew it, a ghastly Rubicon.

❧ 5 ❧

PETER'S APPETITE had never been good. That evening at supper he could eat nothing. He had walked fast, and stopped to rest, walked fast, and rested again through much of the long June day. Nor had he eaten since breakfast. The rain came to wet him and the sun again to dry him. As he walked on, this small fact seemed marvelous to him — that rain comes to cool you and next moment the sun to warm and dry you. Earth and woods are fragrant. There was a row of turtles sitting upon a log. He heard the ecstasy of a thrush's song and the cynical cawing of a crow. Blue sky and sudden silvery downpour — oh, how good was this earth! How very good and fair!

He had exerted himself enough physically to make straight thinking impossible. He thought only in little tags. How lovely this earth is, and, I must do something so final that when Dash comes home, Mompesson will never think to question him. Georgiana . . . I don't see how anybody could help but love Georgiana. That laurel looks like girls' white muslin dresses. It's not a woodchuck's digging — that's a fox's. That's an oven bird. It seemed to him as if the whole earth was opening up, letting him look down deeper into herself, see a new unperceived layer of beauty. Once he stopped to wipe his eyes. It was so beautiful.

But, four miles from home, he had suddenly become so exhausted he had sat by the roadside almost unable to move. Jack West had told him he must not ever overtax his strength. Obviously he had — and what of it? He had found a queer lyric peace in his long ramble. Yet there were four miles yet to go. His legs were as weak as water, and this time, no matter how long he sat, his heart would not quiet. It was racketing around inside him as though it had broken loose from all moorings, sometimes beating low in his stomach, sometimes high up in his throat.

Coming toward him at a snail's pace he saw a plump, slow old horse drawing a little covered gig. A man as plump, slow, old, as his horse asked him if he would like a lift to Salem. Peter got in. Then he realized the old man's calling. He was an itinerant limner. There were boxes of paints and brushes, rolls of canvas, frames he would sell. All winter, he said, he had been painting bodies and backgrounds, leaving only the heads to do from life. He spent winters with his daughter-in-law in Leicester. And as he talked, Peter's excited imagination saw the daughter-in-law, doubtless hating to have the old man mussing about her kitchen with his paints all winter long. The old man would long for warm weather and the open road. "And so would Trot," he added, flicking the reins at the placid old horse. And I'll bet that daughter-in-law would, too, Peter added to himself. He began to love the old man and unreasonably despise the daughter-in-law. And yet, why despise anyone? Why? He saw her patiently tending her children, washing the old man's clothes, preparing his food. He saw her thin, sallow, overworked face seamed with care, her hands swollen and coarsened by hard work. He saw her standing in the barnyard, waving good-bye and wishing the old limner well as he started forth once more, now spring had come. He was ready to love her, too.

As the old man talked, he felt how deeply he loved, not perhaps his art — Peter guessed he was but a poor old dauber — but free blue sky and rustling green leaves, springtime and harvest, night and day, and every person he met upon his travels. He loved everything and resented nothing. Why, thought Peter, suddenly excited, what a wonderful old man! He is really a philosopher. How I could love him! He felt as if the Heavens had opened and dropped down to earth, for his solace and stay, this marvelous old limner. He was almost too moved to thank him properly for the ride when at last Salem was reached. He wrung and wrung his hand and the old man beamed upon him and seemed to understand.

At supper he had tried to tell his mother and Miranda something about the old limner. Already he could feel stirring in him certain cadences which meant that upon this subject there would be a poem. He could feel the poem struggling in him toward birth.

Miranda thought all traveling folk should be locked up. His mother was pointing out, truthfully enough, that no matter how little she had paid for those portraits of her boys, she had paid too much. She swore sometimes she was going to take them down and burn them. She did not want posterity to think *her* sons had ears one higher than the other, and eyes not matching.

Only Linda noticed Peter played with his food and did not eat it. When she served him, she bent close to him and whispered encouragement. Mrs. Miranda noticed this, but she did not quite dare reprove her in Mother Inman's presence. Mother Inman had a curious predilection for Linda.

He went to his bedroom early, hoping to get down something on paper about the old limner. Miranda and his mother had almost drowned those lovely slow cadences he had felt pushing up through him. He wanted to get them back. Linda secretly carried to him hot milk and the thin toast she had often found he would take later when unable to eat at table. He ate them and found he was ravenous, and praised Linda extravagantly — there was still a lot of the queer secret rhapsody left in him. She looked at him with eyes that would have been loving except they were so expressionless.

But when he tried to go to sleep, he found he could not. He was so cold. Where now did the poor old man lie? He hoped by some warm hearth, wrapped in his own blankets, for Peter knew he carried them with him. And next morning he'd pay for his night's lodging, horse bait, and food, by doing a portrait of a grandson. His imagination was so vivid he could even see the scene, hear the argument before it was decided which child would have its picture made.

Fragments of the day before kept passing and repassing before his eyes. Yet everything was exaggerated, decked in trailing clouds of his own imagination. Nothing was exactly as it had happened. That row of six turtles upon a log became hundreds of turtles, and the log stretched to infinity. He saw Georgiana shaking him upon Essex Street and telling him she couldn't love a liar. And the ferocious softness of her eyes. Her eyes grew to room size. That daughter-in-law of the limner's — what a plain, cross, overworked slattern she was, and yet how worthy to be loved. It was sorrowful that she had to work so hard all her life. And get so little back. He saw her put a tired hand to her forehead to brush back the stray wisps of hair.

The wood thrush sang again in his half-dreaming. Polly's decapitated head rolled after him like a Medusa.

He had been asleep. He woke with a start. Golly — that was odd. To think of Polly as Medusa. Turning all men to stone. He wished he hadn't thought of it. He felt that this moment, when he had seen Polly's head with the snake-coiled hair, the dead, parted gray lips, meant something — something that might go on into his waking life. And no sooner had he settled back and calmly told himself, yes, now he was going to sleep, than he smelled linseed, and once more Georgiana was on her knees to him and he embraced and kissed her and this time knew that never, never would he let her go.

So he slept. But Polly's head had rolled into the sitting room where he sat with Georgiana in his arms. He heard a lisping hiss of the snakes. It was Georgiana who turned first to see. And there in his arms he could feel her beginning to turn to stone. He looked, wondering what he would see, wondering what it would do to him. The head was rolling closer and closer, and first his feet grew cold and the cold went up and up, and he, too, was stone.

Then he woke. He was sodden with sweat and shaken with nightmare. At first he could hardly move arms or legs and could almost feel the heavy weight of Georgiana, cold stone in his arms. He had had night sweats and horrors before. They didn't mean anything. First he'd put on a dry nightshirt, then go to the kitchen, get some water and sit by the fire. Perhaps read a little before he went back to bed. His heart was beating hard and high up. He felt a tickling in his throat, and once more that not unfamiliar, far from piercing, dull pain in his chest.

The salamander eye on the kitchen hearth blinked a welcome. He lit a paper spill from it and then a candle and pulled Mrs. Cady's favorite red rocker close to the heat. Creak-crock, it went. And he remembered Georgiana rocking and rocking all the time he had taken that oath.

The cold that shook him came from within, not from without. The kitchen was warm. The teapot he had put on began to sing. The cats purred in drowsy bliss. It has never been as bad as this before, he whispered to himself through blue lips. And now at last he was shaking all over. Then he felt a rising in his throat like nausea. It had come at last — a torrent of bright blood. It flowed over his linen, the silk of his dressing-gown, dripped and ran on the bricks of the hearth. His first thought was, I'm glad it happened here. It will be easy to clean up here. And his second, Why, this is what people have been talking of for years. He could hear Jack West's voice asking, "Have you spit blood yet?"

Spit blood! A curious expression for the torrent that had burst from his nose and mouth. He coughed. Little more came. It was over. There was a feeling of relief, half-physical, as though the blood had long been stagnating in him and now he was better off, having got rid of it. Half-psychological, because something long dreaded had happened and was not as bad as he had expected.

Now to clean up. He managed to get to the back entry, got a bucket of water and rags. The bucket's bail clinked in his weak hands and he cursed it under his breath. But almost immediately he heard soft bare feet coming down the back stairs. He was caught, so he went back hopelessly to his rocker. It was Linda.

"Don't say anything to anybody," he murmured, anxious that their voices should not wake Mrs. Cady and Becky too. "But help me clean up."

"Yes, Mr. Peter," she said, in her squeaky voice which might mean pleasure, amusement, or fear.

She went back to her room and got a quilt from her bed to wrap him in. She took hot bricks from the hearth, wrapped them in flannel and put them under his feet. The fire began to blaze and at last he felt he was thawing out. She took warm water and washed his face, throat, and bloody chest and hands. She said nothing, neither did he. Finally he heard her washing up the hearth, but he was dozing.

It was light when he awoke. Birds had begun to sing, and she was leaning over him.

"Take my arm, Mr. Peter. I'll help you to your room."

"I don't need help." But he took her arm and found he did. She inched him gently up the stairs and into his own room.

Tomorrow, he thought, I'll have to go to Jack and tell him, Yes, I have, I have spit blood. Oh, God, why tell? There's nothing they can do. I've got to take it like a man. And alone. He thought again of the happy, wise old limner and drew strength from him, or rather from his poetic conception of him.

Even after he had closed his eyes, Linda still sat beside him, murmuring a prayer. Surely God would not take Peter until he had repented and confessed and had washed himself in the blood of the Lamb.

She looked at his watch. Past time for her to be in the kitchen. Oh, please God, make Mrs. Miranda, just this once, oversleep.

But God did not hear her prayer. Mrs. Miranda was there ahead of her. Her eyes and mouth grew rounder and rounder as she realized Linda had not come from the back of the house. As she was soon confiding to Nanny, you could have knocked her down with a feather. Linda had been spending the night with Peter. Miranda had been so aghast she had been able to say nothing to the girl. And Linda had not even had the grace to blush. This was proof to both of them, not of her innocence but of her depravity.

~6~

WHAT HAD BEEN WORKING in him for years almost invisibly now had been manifest. Peter gave more importance to his first hemorrhage than Jack West would have, if he had confided in him.

The end, he believed, was now in sight. All right, and what of it? He squared himself to meet whatever Fate had in store for him. And who wanted to live to be old, or even middle-aged? Like most people of twenty-four, he feared death the less because he had no conception of the pleasures of middle-age and the serenities of old age. So he squared himself to meet it like a man. Suppose that, even this summer, he had one more, and that a fatal, hemorrhage. He could see, for he had a romantic, self-sacrificing attitude toward life, one advantage. With himself out of the way, there would be no reason, not the slightest reason, why Dash would feel he must tell the truth. He had a shrewd idea why it was Dash kept himself to sea so much. And yet, even as he told himself Dash would indeed benefit by his death, he dropped tears upon his own, as yet unfilled, coffin, half-pretending they were not his but Dash's. And he wrote a number of good poems. Yet the best he had done so far — in fact, it was so good he could not have borne that anyone but Georgiana should read it — was "To an Old Limner." He had not forgotten the queer loving ecstasy of that long walk, and the old man had come as the climax of it. But he had made no effort to seek the old fellow out again. He knew he had got from him all he wanted. For your true artist does not want fact in all its entirety, but only his own awareness, response, vision, of the fact. Too much fact might spoil everything. And Peter had his poem.

Thinking much of death, he began to consider his will. Unless he outlived Ma'am, which he thought unlikely, he would have little enough to leave in money. But it would give him a chance to mention right out and before the world "my natural daughter, Petra, called Flanneau." Then, even if Dash did try to say something, who would believe him?

His mind made up, he went to Blainey Phipps's little pumpkin-yellow law office. Behind it was the handsome dwelling-house Father Perkins had given his son-in-law. The law office was flush with Essex Street and looked scarcely larger than Davy Jones's kennel.

It was hard even for Peter to recognize in the somewhat pompous, very legal young man behind the spectacles his old chum Blainey Phipps. Ever since two years before, when Blainey had told him Maria wouldn't have him for best man, a friendship that already had been growing thin had progressively weakened. Was this really dear Blainey, the boy with whom he had read Latin poetry, had talked for so many hours all that adolescent talk about the beauty, the sadness, of life?

Blainey had done very well for himself. Because he was a stranger now, Peter felt little embarrassment. The business seemed easier than Peter had feared. "I, Peter Inman, of Salem, being of sound mind and body, but knowing that all flesh must die, leave and bequeath two-thirds of all of which I am possessed to my natural child, Petra, called Flanneau, and to her mother, Dulcey Flanneau, I leave one-third." And so on. The whole thing covered a half-page of foolscap.

"Can I sign it now?"

"I'll copy it off on best legal bond. Then, too, there must be witnesses. You are looking so well, Peter, I can hardly imagine there is any great hurry." Peter those days had a bright girlish flush high up under his dark eyes. "Take home this rough draft of mine and ponder on it for a little. You are sure you are doing a *wise* thing? Have you talked it over with any of your family?"

"No. But when Dash comes home, I'm giving the will to him. If I die, remember that he has it. And Blainey, can't we get the business over with now? Can't we get some witnesses?"

"H'm. I'll run back to my house, Peter. Surely I can find three witnesses there."

Peter watched a fly buzzing against the window-pane until Blainey reappeared with his wife, Maria, and her two older sisters, Anna and Marianna. They knew the signing of a will was a solemn moment only to be compared to a funeral. They treated Peter half as though he were the corpse already, and half as though he were the bereaved.

He watched their angular bodies bent over the document and felt ready to laugh. At last they were repaying him for all the times he had pitied them and asked them to stand up with him; for those plates he had carried to them. It was delicate, but unnecessary and probably un-legal of Blainey to keep the blotting-paper so they never quite saw what they were signing. Peter thought of saying straight out it was no secret and the whole world could not know too soon for him. How could fortune have produced a stranger trio to witness his will than these three, Anna Perkins Silsbee, Marianna Perkins White, Maria Perkins Phipps! They tiptoed off together, back to their sewing. Mrs. Silsbee still had her thimble on.

"Now," said Peter, when they were gone, "I have legally admitted paternity, haven't I?"

"In a way, yes. In a way, no. The will, of course, will not be published or probated yet."

"Not until I die?" Peter looked disappointed.

"Come, Peter, don't talk about dying. By the look of you you'll outlive us all. To a hale and hearty old age. Jack West is telling me these days it's not considered healthy to put on flesh. Says I've put on too much — sitting here at my desk all day. Bad for my asthma. Says he thinks thin men healthier than stout." But Blainey puffed himself out proudly. It was true that he already, at only twenty-five, had a middle-aged look. There was not a suggestion of youth left in him anywhere. He looked very "sound."

He reached behind him and drew out a bottle of brandy and some glasses. He poured two generous drinks.

"That's an old custom, my dear fellow. *Tengomenas faciamus.* How'd you translate that, eh? Petronius, if I recall . . ."

" 'Let us wet our whistles,' " Peter said.

"So here we are for old sake's sake. Tell me, Peter, do you still have time for Plato and the Iliad, Theocritus, and all that? Do you remember how, at Exeter, we loved our Horace?"

Peter did not answer with the obvious fact that his time was hardly as well filled as that of a rising young lawyer. "Yes," he said, "I've kept up pretty well with the classics."

"Ah, how I envy you! But a young lawyer trying to get started, especially nowadays . . . it's often a fourteen-hour day for me."

The mood between them lightened, for Blainey did, in a way, envy his old friend his leisure and the great company he could keep in books. They began to chat as they had not for years. Blainey still could recite line after line from Horace and when he failed, Peter quickly capped him. "Now is the time for drinking," he'd say, and Peter would add, "And with sportive foot to beat the air." And violet crowns, wine cups and girls, the sweetness of love, the sharpness of death. How quickly life passes, and your wise man grasps boldly the pleasure within reach on his long sad errand to the grave.

"And you did it," Blainey admitted with admiration. "You had the courage. It never occurred to me, as I read all that, that it had any real connection with my own life. Nor yours, either. But all the time you dared. I couldn't understand at the time why you didn't join me at Harvard. But by then you had that woman, eh?"

"Yes . . . she was the reason why I didn't go."

"I'll say this for you, Peter. You were not merely a poet in philosophy, but a poet in action, eh?"

Peter knew he had been called many a foul name, but never "a poet in action" before. Blainey refilled the little glasses.

"*Carpe diem!*" he cried with a flourish, laughing and gesturing with his glass.

"*Carpe diem* is right," said Peter, gesturing back handsomely.

"Wine, women, and song, eh, Peter? Eh, Peter, my lad?" He gulped his brandy. "To tell the truth, I've kept my nose pretty close to the grindstone these last years. Stuck in my law books. And, by George, those are no books of poetry. Now, what if, sometime . . . not around Salem, my position in society, my reputation as a very steady young man makes that impossible . . . you could show me around a bit. Of course I'd never do anything to hurt Maria . . . best wife a man ever had. All I have I owe to her. But surely the most model husband should sometimes be allowed a holiday, eh?"

"You've earned it," encouraged Peter.

"Wenham . . . I understand there are some mighty pretty obliging girls over at Wenham."

"Farmer's daughters?"

"Ah, I see how you know your way about. I believe their father is a farmer."

"At least I know a lot of dirty stories about farmers' daughters."

Peter got up to go, eluding his erstwhile friend who was eager to set the very evening for a "holiday." There had been almost a half-hour when they had talked poetry and had verged, at least, on coming close again. Now they were poles apart. He didn't care in the least how this absurd, bespectacled little man betrayed his unlovely Maria, but he wanted no part in it.

Peter knew Miranda sometimes went through his papers, doing what she called "turning out his drawers." But he had not forgotten Dash's secret glory hole in the baseboard behind his bed.

Banks were so good nowadays, specie was no longer kept here. It was there he hid his will. It lay beside the black and gold lacquer box with the silk for Polly's wedding gown.

❧ 7 ❧

"JACK," SAID DASH, "something happened to Peter while I was gone. Something pretty bad."

"It was back in June, yes."

"But what?"

"Being a doctor, I believe I should limit myself only to the physical side."

"Not so good?"

"No, not so good."

Dash had taken his brother-in-law's case of lancets from his desk. Was opening it, fingering the knives. I don't care if he cuts himself, Jack thought. And he will — he's that keyed up. But just so he doesn't break one.

"No one seems to have noticed," Dash blazed out angrily. "Liz is too busy. Tom's got his knitting. Mother . . . she's a born optimist. Optimists are apt to be cruel, inadvertently. Won't face facts. My little old grandmother is the only one that's worried. Little old Ma'am."

"You've been gone over a year. You come home and of course you notice changes more than they do. I'm afraid his disease has advanced. A little."

"He's thinner."

"Yes. And more feverish. Coughs more. And you know, last June he had a first hemorrhage. I wish he had told me right off, not worried about it alone. But he didn't until he had a second one — right at table during supper. Couldn't hide it. That was July. But I've known many patients to hemorrhage and get well."

"You mean *many*," Dash demanded suspiciously, "or *some*?"

"I should have said some."

Jack moved about his office. It was hard for him to face Dash's quiet despair. Jack had one of the front offices of the big brick double house the Wests had recently built facing Washington Square. His father had the other.

"I don't like anything about Peter's case," he burst out at last. "He's not fighting hard enough. He's meeting death like a hoary old philosopher, not fighting it like a young man. He doesn't fight."

"Does he do as you tell him?"

"Oh yes. As far as medicine goes. Yes. But the most important thing — I tried to touch on it last month — he won't do. And since then he hasn't even come to see me."

"What do you consider the most important thing?"

"He's got to give up his dissipations." Dash moved miserably in his chair, but said nothing. "After all, he's kept that woman for ... what is it ... seven years, I think. And yet that poor, consumptive fellow, without strength enough for one woman, is sporting, on the side, with another."

"Who?"

"You know I'm no gossip. It's Miranda that tells Nanny and she tells me. But this does have medical bearing on the case. It's that young girl your mother took from the Charity House some time back. I forget her name."

"Dorothy Belinda Gould. We call her Linda."

"Yes, that's the name Nanny told me. Linda. Taken up for lewd, lascivious conduct at fourteen. Well, Miranda says she goes to him pretty often. She watches."

"And tells everybody?"

"She tried to tell Mother Inman." Jack suddenly laughed. "You know your mother likes Linda. Although Nanny says she's a real shiftless little servant, she won't hear a word against her."

"But Peter isn't having an affair with Linda. Jack, you *couldn't* have an affair with Linda — no more than a paper doll. And Peter isn't the sort."

"Consumption is queer that way. And, after all, he's had this Mrs. Flanneau — for years. I know it may be a hard thing for a pretty strict, self-controlled fellow like you to understand. But you're not sick."

Dash colored slowly.

"I've told him he's not only got to cut out Linda, but this Mrs. Flanneau, too. Got to. But as soon as I began to talk to him about his women, he stopped coming to see me. I told him, 'You've got strength enough to live a very quiet, but perfectly normal life. You can't go wenching around so.'"

Still Dash did not speak. Jack went on, half to himself. "Medically speaking, the old moralities are often right. Sinners do pay for their sins. I don't mean merely by a certain ostracization — the normal desire of a healthy society to quarantine itself. That's happened, of course, to Peter. But, speaking as a doctor, not a moralist, Peter's immoral craving for women is catching up with him."

Dash cried out angrily: "I've had enough of this, Jack. For God's sake, stop talking morals to me. I'd have gone to Doctor Hobey if I'd wanted to talk about sin. Jack, I want a medical opinion from you. And nothing more."

After this rebuff the young doctor kept a dignified silence. His feelings had been hurt. His red hair looked a little crestfallen. He hadn't intended to, but he knew he had prodded some sore place in Dash.

"For instance," Dash went on calmly, "I've been home only four days, but Peter's after me. He's determined that I take him on my next voyage. And that is to be right away — so he says. Jack, I've heard you say you don't believe in sea voyages for people with weak lungs."

"My father is quite as good a physician as I am," Jack lied blandly. "He has always been for them."

"I know it."

"I've always felt the best help — I don't think there is a cure — is a very simple life. Plenty of rest, fresh air, good food. Little worry. Perhaps not even a wife — certainly not what are called 'women.' Think for a moment of ship life. Soaking wet one moment, and the next shut up in a tiny cabin. Men packed in, all breathing the same air. Terrible food, and little rest. But still, I can see one thing. This case is different."

"In what way?"

"If you took him on a voyage couldn't you keep him away from women?"

"Of course. No shore leave. No women."

"Then, Dash, I'm not sure . . . yes, I do believe I'd give my consent. If there is anyone that can cure him," Jack went on, "I think it is you. What you can give him. He has always hung on you. Yes, take him."

"I will."

"His life here about Salem is forlorn enough, you know that. If only he'd gone to Harvard, found his own niche. But he didn't. Could you get into the Baltic, or is it too late?"

"With a good ship I could. And with good luck in and out and home again before the ice closes the Baltic. As you know, all of Europe from Brest to Elbe is blockaded now by the British. The Baltic ports are about all we have left to us, legally. I was thinking of trying for them. Even now."

"Lübeck?"

"That's east of the Elbe. That's easy."

Jack sat down, clasped his hands behind his head, and looked at the ceiling. "A few years ago a German doctor invented a new method of examining chests. It sounds childish. He does it by tapping. I've read about it, tried it myself, and can't hear a thing. But there are doctors, mostly in Germany, who have learned how. From him."

"But tapping doesn't cure a chest."

"No. It tells how far the disease has gone. But this Doctor Groete of Lübeck — I've heard great things of him. Medical gossip — and, Dash, it is no more than gossip — says he is working out cures."

"That's where we'll go."

"Wait. I said gossip. He may have found something. He may be lying. He may have been lied about."

"No matter where that blockade may spread to, I'll get Peter to see him."

"It would do no harm. The Viennese and German doctors are far ahead of us. I know that."

Dash was pretty excited, for him, a usually self-controlled sort of fellow. "I can't take the *Victrix*. She's getting new copper. The *Wanderer* is back. And loading for Goa. I'll unladen and put on Baltic stuff. I'll be out of here . . . Jack, I can and will. I can get her out of here in three days. And Peter with me."

He took the Wests' stone front steps with one bound, moving so fast he never noticed Becky with Thomasina and Tommy who had come over to play with their cousins, Boots, Ruthie, and Phineas West. All these small nieces and nephews stared with fascination at Uncle Ralph's long leap.

But confound it, he thought. He'd forgotten to ask Jack about Polly's health. Of course Old Doctor West was her physician, but it was Jack's opinion he wanted. She had had brain fever or something last spring, or early summer. And Old Doctor West had persuaded her and her father that now she ought to lie down about all the time except when she went to parties. Flip had told him privately that she often, at night, had crying fits. And she had seemed strange, very strange, and looked at him queerly the two times he had been to see her. She had said the reason why she had decided against Mr. Pringle was that she wasn't sure she was strong enough to marry anyone. What nonsense! And yet, if she was so nervous and hadn't yet recovered from that brain fever, it was certainly no time to go pushing his suit. His first duty was to Peter. Get Peter to hell out of here.

～8～

DASH HAD ORDERED a coach-house built on the forward deck. In it he had put his two mates, Cal Lessing and Jim Porter. He and Peter, written down as "clerk" of the vessel, shared the cabin. A cabin of a ship was far more of a home to Dash than ever his mother's house had been. And he proved a delightful host. Seemingly there was nothing of this, his real life, he did not want to share with Peter. They talked and played chess for hours. Peter felt himself held and wrapped in Dash's affection and understanding. And how happy and carefree Dash seemed at sea! And how serene and empty his hands! How easily command sat upon him! — so easily one never thought about it as one doesn't about the most obvious facts in life.

The *Wanderer* spread her sails. Fair winds carried her, but off Dunmore Head in Ireland they were stopped by a British frigate and ordered to Falmouth. There without shore leave the ship tossed at her dangerous anchorage while Dash went on to Portsmouth to make his plea. When he came back, he not only had permission to sail, but was assigned his place in a British convoy. And he brought the news that Napoleon had crossed the Rhine. He had invaded the German states.

Dash fretted over the dawdling. At this rate he had no chance to leave Peter at Lübeck, get himself in and out of Kronstadt (which was port of entry for St. Petersburg) before the ice came. He broke loose from the slow-moving convoy, although by so doing he might be attacked by the British, made his own time and took his own chances flashing through Skagerrak and Kattegat, not stopping to take on local pilots. Had he not, as he told Peter, cut his milk teeth on the Baltic route? And he was always making more and more sail. The *Wanderer* came in about Fehmarn's Island, her sails cracked, and one more long tack and she stood for Lübeck Bay. It was nighttime when he nosed into Travemunde, dropped anchor, and ordered the longboat cast off. Through the dark Peter heard him yell, "Bend your backs and break your oars, lads," and the longboat leaped as though shot from a gun. Peter felt the excitement of it. Next moment he would for the first time set foot on foreign land. Dash was hurrying him up strange medieval streets with houses so high on either hand their foreheads almost touched. I never thought it would be so wonderful, Peter thought, for even through the dark he could see he was in a city such as he had never dreamed of before.

At the British consulate, Dash knocked, for Mr. Castle was an old acquaintance of his. Next moment they were inside the vast Gothic ground-floor hall where the consul did his work. Dash was explaining how it was he would leave his brother to see Doctor Groete. Did Mr. Castle know a pleasant inn? And he himself would push on for St. Petersburg that very night.

The consul was a sandy, bony man, slow in speech and prone to add "what?" to the end of his sentences. He looked at Dash quizzically. "I doubt if you have heard the news, Captain Inman, what?"

"No. Only Napoleon had crossed the Rhine."

The consul put his freckled hands together tip to tip. "Napoleon defeated the Prussian King at Jena two weeks ago. Beastly luck, what?" And by his adding of "what?" he made the whole thing seem like a rather well-bred not very funny joke. "Blücher — and what's left of the Prussian army — are drawing back, northward. And three French armies are after him. Blücher may try to make a stand on the Baltic. Beastly mess, you know. Rather a beastly mess."

"But Lübeck is a Freie und Hansestadt city. Neutral in every war. Prussia's nothing to them. Lübeckians don't fight. They grow rich."

"She's rich. Well-stocked with provisions. She has ships, what?"

"Yes?"

"Now this may be a mere fancy of mine. But Blücher may try to get here, take his men off — to, say, East Prussia, on those ships, eh? And Napoleon will be after him."

Peter's heart stood still with an excitement almost of delight. He might see great doings. Of the horror and filth of war he had little conception. He was thinking, I might see Napoleon himself! Not even Dash has ever seen Napoleon. All his young manhood had been overshadowed by one gigantic name: Napoleon; a figure of such evil not even Beelzebub himself had ever loomed larger to his Puritan ancestors. Napoleon may get to Lübeck before Dash can come for me.

"So," Dash was saying, "you expect him — even here?"

"Oh, we English expect Napoleon everywhere, except in England — and what of it?" Mr. Castle announced with the bland, sometimes irritating self-confidence of his race. "And the last battle, sir, will be ours. We British are a little sluggish — would you say? But we win last battles."

"I've never doubted that. If anyone can stop this mad dog, it will be you English," and he added (forgetting the insults and delays he had gone through at Falmouth and Portsmouth), "I've wished sometimes I was actually fighting him with you."

"But you understand that, although it will be a pleasure to me and my wife to offer such hospitality as we can to Mr. Inman, we may have to pull out in a hurry — what?"

And they were again at the consul's door. "You won't budge from here, Peter," Dash commanded. "You hear me? You're not to go traipsing off — even if the French do come and Mr. Castle goes."

So Dash tore off.

~9~

THE ICE came early. The harbor was frozen.

But spring came early too, after long nights, short days. The ice was rotting, breaking up, the harbor opening.

Peter began to long passionately for sight of the *Wanderer's* topsails, standing in. Many people in Lübeck, German burghers and French soldiers as well (for the city fell to Napoleon soon after Dash left), knew how it was one brother waited for the other. Six or eight ran to his little old inn on Holstein Strasse to tell him a tall white ship, carrying the bright and hopeful flag of his young country, had been sighted, was coming in fast.

But now it was the French who held Lübeck, and they knew these so-called neutral American merchantmen often called at an English port before they went to the Baltic, often accepted British convoy. Indeed the *Wanderer* had — although much against her will. Yet Peter got his chest to the quay. Nothing, not even Napoleon, would stop Dash, nor did it.

Dash, leaping from his longboat to the quay, hardly glanced at Peter. He was doing something to the French soldiers, something with money, of course. The conquerors had itching palms. In five minutes Peter was in the longboat, the oars flashed, they were rounding old rosy brick warehouses, rounding the city, and suddenly there, behold! the *Wanderer* was standing, sails backed and unanchored, looking as light and bold as the gulls about her. Dash caught her boatline and they were climbing aboard.

Then, not until they stood upon her deck and she was already filling, leaning upon the breeze, did Dash relax, really look at Peter and take time to grin.

"You look good."

"I feel good."

"When I heard Lübeck had been taken by that rat Napoleon, I thought to buy a sleigh and come back. But I knew you'd slip through all right. You've always been good at slipping through things."

"I saw a lot. Learned a lot."

"You saw the sack of a city."

"Yes. It was pretty bad, Dash. You know — women and children. Dead people piled into the Trave. It was certainly bad. But . . ."

"But what?"

"Well, it made me realize I wasn't very important. No. So many got it worse than I. It sounds mean — my saying the sorrows of others gave me courage to bear my own. Somehow it did. God . . . I hate war! I hate Napoleon!"

But Dash was already thinking more of his command.

"There's a clumsy sort of British brig-o'-war standing by Fehmarn's Island. She tried to stop me coming in. Now I've *been* in, the damned old tub will chase me. They'll say I'm trading with the French. Well, here's where we get chased!" And he was off, happy, it would seem, to be chased, so sure was he of his ship's speed and his own uncanny knowledge of reefs, shoals, tides and of himself. Sometimes Dash's self-confidence frightened Peter — who was modest by nature.

He could tell by Dash's face that he had had a merry winter, although he had been so quickly frozen in. Peter guessed he had been sleeping with some woman. He knew, unlike Liz, he would never tell him a thing. Some Russian snow-princess, white-skinned and very fair. Peter could almost see her, her little furred boots, the sable cape and hood, her coachman rolled up in a cocoon of overcoats. The bright snow, the galloping horses; on the yoke of the middle horse the bells shaking out elfin music across lonely wide white plains. He could almost see the snow-princess's piquant profile. Polly's, of course. It was as if he could not dream of a fair woman except in Polly's image. So the snowflakes fell like tattered lace on the girl's bright cheek. The horses galloped through sunlight and pink sunset and dark night. That was why Dash's face looked so unknotted, simplified. Peter was glad that so mysteriously and far away as St. Petersburg Dash and Polly had met and loved, without hesitation or one backward or forward glance.

Although Dash questioned him about Doctor Groete, Peter felt no need to tell him. Dash's easy well-being made a barrier. He could have told a broody, unhappy Dash, but not the well-contented master of the *Wanderer*. So how tell of Doctor Groete?

He remembered and shivered to remember his one visit to Doctor Groete.

The cold stone room. Sleet rattling upon window-panes. The suck and lashing of the wind through the narrow medieval street. (Lying safe and warm in his bunk upon the *Wanderer*, he chilled to remember it.)

It had seemed to him incredible so distinguished a man should know no English; no French. Everyone in Europe spoke French. Perhaps the doctor had refused to use the language of his city's conquerors, for Doctor Groete did not come back to Lübeck until after

Lübeck fell. He was a morose small man, seemingly little interested in the sick body exhibited to his skill. He had tapped and listened, listened and tapped, his fingers cold as the sleet on the windows. Cold as the dead men Peter had seen grotesquely frozen and heaped along the Trave. Doctor Groete blew out his lips and shook his head.

This was an unfavorable diagnosis in any language.

Over and over, lying in his bunk (for nights were worse) Peter could not help but go back, see himself, see Doctor Groete, hear the words. He could see himself pull on his shirt, moving closer to the green porcelain stove for warmth. The doctor's cold hands and eyes, the sleet, the ancient fallen city, even passing drunken Frenchmen outsinging the storm, singing of their emperor — all these things, and what the doctor knew but had not the words to say, depressed him.

Once in the night the fear had been so strong in him, he had put out his hand and grasped the bedding of the bunk close to him. "Dash, Dash," he had whimpered. Dash did not wake. "Dash . . ." yet he knew his brother was the lightest of sleepers. He got up, thought to shake him by the shoulder, but the bunk was empty and Dash gone to the quarterdeck. Yes, those feet he heard, quick sure feet, pacing above him, were the captain's. The brother had left him. He could not confide in the captain. No.

Picture after picture, word for word, it came haunting back.

"I have been told you have medicine . . . ? On dit . . ."

"Je ne parle pas français."

He almost slept. Je ne parle pas . . . je ne parle pas . . .

He woke roughly, remembering the idea he had had. He asked his question in Latin. For the first time Doctor Groete had looked pleased. He bushed out his coarse black beard with one hand and answered (in Latin) almost happily, "There is no medicine that will help you."

Peter saw himself buttoning up his shirt, shoving in its tails, shivering with cold.

"Quantum?" (How long?)

Doctor Groete shook his unkempt head. He looked at Peter as though not exactly seeing him, only through him to the diseased lungs. He held up a grubby hand. One finger went up. "Uno anno."

The next came up readily, "Duo ..."

The third very slowly, and Peter was never sure whether the fourth meant to come up or got out of control.

Then he lifted his symbolical hand toward the ceiling. Upon the whitewashed wall it cast an enormous shadow. A great black hand moving toward him. The very hand of God it looked. Steady, steady, he whispered to himself. It's nothing to get excited about. And he was glad that, the night he had thought to tell Dash, Dash had been gone.

❦ 10 ❦

THE HOME VOYAGE was through high rough seas, but the winds always favored them and the *Wanderer* lay down, sometimes almost on her beam ends, for tacks of a hundred miles or more. They were chased by strange vessels they never identified.

Cal Lessing and Jim Porter, the two young mates, were gleefully prophesying that the *Wanderer* was going to break the old record from Baltic port to America. "The Old Man" certainly could sail anything. "The Old Man" was damned lucky.

Dash was thirty. Younger masters than he had been called "the Old Man" behind their backs by young mates, but it gave Peter a strange feeling. Perhaps he seemed a little old to lads younger than Peter himself. He noticed how much these boys spoke of his "luck." Dash Inman's luck was getting to be a byword among sailors the world over. Cal and Jim spoke less of his skill, resourcefulness, and wisdom, things which, along with his daring, had made him a great master. But Dash seemed, even to a landlubber like Peter, a little too confident of his luck. He knew that masters who lean too much upon the Bitch-Goddess are eventually betrayed by her.

Once, as they lay idling in their bunks, Peter asked Dash to admit that the *Wanderer* was every bit as good as the *Victrix*. Peter had grown devoted to her.

"Perhaps," Dash said, absently. "But she might let me down. The *Victrix* couldn't. Ever. She'd sail through seas of fire if I asked her. She'll never sink until I want her to. And she is so smart she can sail herself." He was smiling, admitting with that smile that he didn't believe what he was saying.

"Cal and Jim think the *Wanderer* is the better ship, Dash. The *Victrix* jibs. The *Wanderer* doesn't."

"Perhaps. I never have found a way to stop the *Victrix* jibbing. I guess I sort of like it."

"Just how does it feel?"

"She'll be galloping along, nice and handy, sure of herself. Then plunges downward, as though she had suddenly snatched the reins from your hands, got the bit in her teeth. Then she flings up her head. It's the freest, wildest gesture imaginable. It says, 'I'm boss. You're here on my back only because I like you, but I'm boss, so don't forget it.' Then she goes slick and steady for weeks, months even, and doesn't do it again. But you don't forget."

"You ought to write a poem to her," said Peter, a little scornfully, but as Dash had spoken, he longed more to ride the *Victrix* and feel her free ecstatic plunging than anything on earth.

"I might, if I could make anything rhyme. Lookee, Peter, sometime you and I and the *Victrix* . . . No northern route — tropics." And he slowly named strange city after strange city from Bombay to Hong Kong. Peter was speechless with longing. Then Dash went back to the ships. "The real difference between the two sisters is this: Jim and Cal are set on breaking the record. Well, if we had the *Victrix,* she'd do it. When you want anything, she begins to want it as much as you do. The *Wanderer* won't."

"Whyever not?"

"She hasn't any real soul. Watch and see. I'll bet she'll come in on the coast, and get herself becalmed and go dead and dumb and lie there wallowing like a hog. Because she don't care a damn thing." Seeing wise skepticism on Peter's face, he added: "I know I'm talking nonsense. I don't believe everything I say to you. That's one reason why I enjoy gamming with you. I can say what I feel. Not facts."

And what Dash said came to be true. Off the New England coast the winds died. Sails flapped. The *Wanderer* lay down in the long troughs of the waves and wallowed.

Cal and Jim were heart-broken boys. No record. But how the tarnation had the Old Man known? He'd said right off the *Wanderer* wouldn't do it. The two youngsters stood at the open door of the galley, waiting for old Doctor Zack, Dash's favorite cook, to light their pipes for them with live coals. The thin pale old Negro, looking so motherly in the checked gingham apron he always wore, did not see Peter waiting for them. The three were close friends now.

"Young gentmen," he said, "some folks do say Captain Dash sold his soul to the Devil, but that's evil talk." He added, with pious satisfaction, "No, sir, I'd never say anything like that of my Captain Dash."

"You'd better not, with me and Cal around," little Jim Porter said, manfully.

"They say there's a curse upon him. He can sail where he likes. He has foreknowledge of weather. No weather, no sea, ever going to get him. But to get the way he is, you understand, he had to pay for it by agreeing never to stop off sailing. Not until his feet have grown into the quarterdeck and his hands are dead upon the wheel. And a hundred, two hundred, three hundred years from now Captain Dash won't never be able to leave off sailing. Not to no quiet grave. He'll be sailing the seas still."

"Well," said Cal, laughing at such sailor superstition, "please God, if I've been a good boy He'll send me back on earth again to go on sailing with him."

"Me, too," said Jim.

Peter saw Dash leaning over the taffrail. He did, as captains often do, seem a solitary but formidable figure. He'd been conversing with the man in the mast. Hadn't he sighted land? Yet he wasn't really interested enough to go to his cabin and fetch his spyglass. Peter noticed that his face had already lost the bright, clear audacity he had come to believe was his characteristic expression at sea. He looked a little broody.

"Chess?" Peter suggested, going up to him.

"Might as well." And he yelled to Mr. Lessing whose watch it now was, then followed Peter to the cabin.

For months Dash had made Peter feel he was on his honor not to more than mention Salem, the Mompessons, the Flanneaus. It was as if he said, You are my guest. I will do everything I can to charm, instruct, amuse, and care for you. I will be a perfect host. But in return you are not to talk of subjects I do not like.

But now land lay there behind the haze on the horizon. Peter felt he was no longer a guest. And he must talk. Had he not forced this sudden voyage upon Dash because he didn't dare to have him find out things for himself in Salem? He had to talk to him first. Wrestle with him, and his conscience. Argue. And, once more, persuade.

Dash seemed to realize Peter's wish. He took out the chessboard, but, instead of setting up the men, he began toying with them, as, to his mother's utter weariness, he often toyed with little things at home. Peter knew he didn't at sea.

"While you were out last voyage, Malay, Manila, things happened. In Salem. I thought — sometime before we got back — I'd better tell you."

"I guessed it. Go ahead. Clear away."

Peter told him easily and methodically as he had told himself the story over and over, waiting for this chance.

The chessmen were carved ivory, curiously threaded and screwed together. It took four or five parts to make each man. Dash took up the white queen, screwed her crown off. Unscrewed the whole thing as Peter told him how Mompesson had got the letter, and how Peter had forsworn himself, his hand upon the Bible. Before God. He did not add, and also before Georgiana Frick. It was no longer merely a case of letting people say — and that included Flanneau — what they pleased, lying low, and saying nothing. Before God and man Peter had forsworn himself. Then that night he had hemorrhaged for the first time. He did not make much of that fact.

"Yes," Dash agreed to all of this. He had the red knight in his hands, took the tiny horse's head off it, laid it next to the white queen's crown. "Peter, where's that damned letter now?"

"Your glory hole, Dash. I didn't see Georgiana again. I guess maybe she doesn't want ever to see me again. But we write. And so I asked her to steal it from Mr. Mompesson. She did so and sent it to me." His eyes, dark and brooding, upon his brother's face, said, See, Dash, I'll lie for you, I'll steal for you. I'll make Georgiana steal, too. What now do you say to that?

He almost wanted to see happen that which he most dreaded. He wanted Dash to be angry at him. Tell him again a man can't build a decent life upon a tissue of lies. A man can live without his girl, without wealth, and without fame. But he can't live without honor. For it was not only his own honor Peter knew he had cast away but Dash's with it. So Peter steeled himself for a blow that did not come. Then he went on again with his story. After that first hemorrhage — which later Jack had told him hardly meant anything at all — he had thought he was going to die real soon. Perhaps before Dash came back. So he had made a will.

He watched Dash's hands, skillful, strong, chapped as always when he was at sea — and he could almost see his mother in a dressing-gown, remembering, just before she blew out her candle, to carry quince lotion to set on Dash's washhand stand. More and more chessmen were coming to pieces, but Dash said nothing. Literally not one word. Why, Peter thought, in amazement, relief, disbelief, Dash isn't going to say anything. He approves. When Peter got to the signing of the will and was enlarging on the comic aspects of his witnesses, Dash's eyes began to crinkle. He was amused. Thus encouraged, Peter told about Blainey's desire for farmers' daughters and Dash laughed aloud.

Yet this was not how the old Dash would have taken it. The clear white light came in off the sea and struck through the cabin. Dash's face showed not merely the marks and mars of his profession. It looked a little worn and corroded. There was a shadow of shame about the fine eyes, a look that nowadays only came and went. But if ever it came and did not go, that would be the end of the free, bold, adventurous man, Dash Inman.

"Your idea of the will," Dash said finally, "is nonsense. I'll bet you outlive me by years. Yet I see your point. It certainly would settle things so no question would ever come up again. Sometimes I have wished it might come out, flatly and publicly, and be settled forever."

Peter paused. This was not the old Dash speaking. "If we lived in the old days, it would be easy," he said.

"How?"

"People used to stand up in church and make public confession of sin. Ask for prayers. But can you imagine Doctor Hobey!"

"As I see it now, you're sure of Mompesson, Georgiana, and Polly?"

Peter did not answer directly, but added: "Blainey Phipps, too. Not the Perkins girls. He never let them see what they were witnessing. And none of those people will blab. They'd feel duty bound not to."

"That's the trouble."

Dash jumped to his feet, went to the porthole and opened it. They heard the slap of water against the sides of the becalmed vessel, the sad flap of sail, the creak of the rudder post. "It's hot in here," he said.

Peter looked at him, for the first time in his life not as an acolyte, but as one man measuring another. Dash was taking it exactly as he had supposed, he hoped, he would, and yet, by so doing, was becoming somebody else. The stranglehold Dash had always had on Peter, Peter had never realized. Dash had paralyzed his emotions, made it impossible for him to go ahead and love others as he might have loved them if Dash had not bulked so large in his heart. Perhaps his disappointment in Dash was freeing him a little. For he suddenly thought with love and longing of Georgiana. Thank God, Georgiana knows the truth, he thought.

"Leave the whole thing to me, Dash," he said, aloud. "Sometime I'll fix it so it will all come out. Flat out and publicly. Then Mompesson wouldn't dare ask you to take one of his fancy oaths."

"Don't you dare think about dying," Dash said.

Peter felt he meant it. But did he? The probate of the will would smooth everything. But even more important was the fact that Dash would never again have to look at Peter. Never again have to wonder . . . Suppose he had gone to Harvard . . . he couldn't have helped meeting Georgiana . . . Perhaps he'd have had a happier life . . . not cough and talk about dying. For Peter supposed that Dash did wonder, sometimes.

"I've had a happy life, Dash," he said, abruptly.

"No. Not exactly. Not what I'd call happy. Bearing other people's burdens, and so on."

"It has suited me."

"Blessed are the easily pleased, then, for they shall be satisfied."

There was a new note in the creak of the rudder post. A sail flapped. The breeze was a-coming up.

Dash's face had lost its shamed look. Suddenly it was flooded with awareness as though he possessed some sensitive, secret, inner knowledge. He was thinking of nothing now but his ship. He reached for his spyglass. His inertia and heaviness of mood were dropping from him. As he stepped over the coamings onto the deck, he said sidewise to Peter, "One of the pleasures of a sea voyage is that it's something of a short-term suicide."

Mr. Lessing was ordering the setting of the sails. And the people were singing out, "Yeo-ho-ho." Then, from above them, like the voice of an angel, the man in the mast sang out, "Land-ho!" The ship's people threw their caps in the air and hurrahed and hurrahed. Peter felt a prick of joy and nostalgia and tears in his eyes. Not until this moment had he realized he had been homesick.

Dash was adjusting his spyglass so that Peter might see the land his own trained eyes needed no glass to make out. Yes, there it was.

Between the clean, empty eternity of the sky and the unending depths of the sea was a little mean smear of something solid and very narrow on the horizon. And that was land. As Dash saw it.

Chapter Ten

~~~~~~

OUT OF THE SORDID TALE Peter had told him, Dash fastened on
one fact. This was that Dulcey had kept his letter all these years,
had looked upon it as her most valuable piece of property when fire
threatened, and had been so acquiescent when Flanneau got it in his
hands.

He nursed this grievance against her for several weeks, trying to
make it grow so large that he might quarrel with her and be done
with her forever. Feeling ashamed of everything that had happened,
he felt that here, in one respect at least, he might clear his decks.
For a man who feels himself wrong in almost every respect will
cast about to find someone else he can criticize.

Since the burning of the warehouse, the Flanneau and Inman
houses seemed much closer together. Each family could look into
the other's back yard with unobstructed view. Formerly the dwell-
ings had felt well away from each other — now they were drawn
close.

One evening, when Dash had been back several weeks, coming
home late from a men's dinner party, with "Landlord fill the flowing bowl until it doth run over" still running in his head, he passed
Tom Briggs's grogshop. Through the open door he saw Flanneau
peacefully asleep with his head on the stained oak table. "Tom,"
Dash said, entering, "here's a coin. Don't put that fellow out at
closing time for the constable to pick up once more. Let him sleep
it off here, will you?" Tom grinned and agreed. Of late Flanneau,
in his cups, had been saying that it was Dash Inman, not Peter, who

had so long loved his wife. But he had switched too late to be believed, and now for over a year was getting queerer and queerer.
All that Tom Briggs thought was that Captain Dash was being
mighty kind to a fellow who had of late been blackening his name.

It was almost midnight. As he stopped at the Flanneau door,
Dash heard laughter and rather loud conversation from the back of
the house. Dulcey was entertaining. It took raps and a smart pull
on the doorbell to tear her away from her guests. Doubtless she
thought somebody had steered Flanneau home to her, and doubtless
she wasn't pleased. As she opened the door, he saw a shrewish,
hard look on her face — perhaps appropriate for a returning,
drunken husband. As quickly as possible she made it over to one
of pleased surprise — more suitable to a lover.

She was magnificently dressed. Overdressed, surely, for a simple
shopkeeper's wife, especially as everyone knew her husband was
having a hard time. Her satin dress was emerald and, as she moved,
paste sparkled in her ears and hair, about her somewhat stout red
neck and along her too-heavy arms. For the first time he felt an
almost physical revulsion against her. And for the first time he
could neither see nor feel any connection between Mrs. Flanneau
and the young girl — stupid and dirty, of course, but sweet — he
had betrayed seven years before.

"So you're entertaining tonight, eh?" he asked.

"Just a few old friends, Captain, and a little whist. Peter's here.
You've been home three weeks, and this is the first time you've
been near me. I'd about decided you weren't coming, ever. But
there" — and she flashed him a smile — "slip along upstairs. If Flanneau comes home, he'll be too besotted to know what's happening.
So make yourself comfortable. And I'll send those folks home."

"Dulcey, it won't take me a minute to say all I have to say. Go
back and tell your friends you'll soon join them."

The doors were open through the house. He heard an obstrep-
erous voice calling her name. And a woman laughing. He could
smell the wine punch. Poor melancholy Flanneau doubtless was
not being invited any more. And yet he had started out with choice
little groups coming in of an evening to talk French.

Dulcey ushered him into the shop and gestured him to wait for
her on a stool. When she came back, she too sat on a stool, and the
contrast between the shop and shop stools and her own magnificent

appearance was startling. Flanneau, when he had the money, had made her dresses as elegant as any woman's in Salem. But as Dulcey never went to fashionable occasions she, had no place to wear them. Yet she loved to dress up, put on her paste. This she did for her own back-room parties, as elegant parties as she was eligible for.

The candle was between them. He noticed how it reflected and caught in the paste along her plump arm. She noticed it flickering in dark, hostile eyes. There was no love left in them. If there ever had been any love. Now at last there was not even any desire left.

"You're tired of me," she announced.

"No. Not tired of you so much, Dulcey, as I'm tired of everything. You've been very good to me. I'll never forget that. I'll always be grateful. But the time has come, hasn't it?"

"Time for what?"

"To call an end to a thing that never should have been started."

"But there's never an end to anything, once it starts."

True enough. And Dash was uncomfortably aware that had Dulcey never met him she would not now be what he saw. In a way he'd done it to her. Give a dog a bad name and you get a bad dog. For years everyone in Salem had thought her a kept woman. Now she certainly looked it.

"No," he said. "I realize that. Nothing once begun ever stops."

"So you came over just to talk philosophy to me, like Peter?"

"No. I wanted to say good-bye. I'm not coming again. So it is good-bye, my dear," he added, in afterthought, and took her unresponsive hand.

"I guessed you'd be gone for good, sometime. And you've always been so ashamed of me, it shames me too. Now, any of these gentlemen" — she gestured toward the back room, and suddenly he heard and recognized Dan Obrian's great guffaw — "would be mighty proud to — well, you know what. What you're so ashamed of. Nor has Peter ever been ashamed to be seen with me."

"He's here now?"

"Yes. He comes over now and then to play cards and laugh. He has never been in the least ashamed of what people said of him and me."

Dash remembered his wrongs. "Dulcey, it was an infernal trick of yours — letting that letter I wrote you, and shouldn't have, get to Mr. Mompesson. Whyever did you do it?"

"Why, Dash, Flanneau had it. Peter told you how."

"Yes."

"He had it, and what was I to do? Then, too, he had worked so hard and done so good and nobody'd lend him anything. It wasn't fair, really. I thought maybe I owed him . . . that much."

"It was a dirty, low trick." Dash said the words sharply, trying to make himself feel anger. He couldn't. He felt nothing toward her.

"No more than some of yours," Dulcey shot back at him.

"I'm not in a position to contradict you," Dash said, but the muscles tightened about his mouth. He was on his feet. "It's a lot easier to talk about money when there's no love left. How much do you think I owe you for a farewell present?"

"Two thousand dollars," she said firmly.

"All right. In gold?"

"I certainly don't want it in goods. Flanneau always takes his pay from Peter in goods. And everybody knows, of course. Gold isn't so easy to trace as silk, for instance. I'd like to lend it to Flanneau," she went on thoughtfully, "but he had a nice loan from Mr. Mompesson and even so he couldn't get his mind on things. Really get started again. I can't count on Flanneau — not since the fire. And his finding out that you and I and Peter had tricked him. He's sort of broken. I've got to have something laid by of my own — for a rainy day."

Both were standing. They talked over the payment as equably as two merchants. There was nothing, Dash felt, left with which you could get mad or make love. Peter and I, he thought, have pushed her into what she has become. She's dead right in saying what's started never ends.

But as he was almost at the door, she put a hand on his sleeve.

"Kiss me once more, Dash," she said. "It was wonderful once. So wonderful I didn't think it ever could end. But although things don't end, they change."

He kissed her. "And now you've got another gentleman?"

She did not deny it, but looked at him roguishly. Whether or not this was true, he knew she wanted him to think so.

The thing that bothered Dash most about his farewell to Dulcey was not the two thousand dollars in gold he must part with, but his certain knowledge that Peter was not above sneaking over back-yard fences and sitting to cards with what low company Dash could well imagine. And yet he could not mention it to him. He knew he was in no position to criticize Peter in any way. Let him get his forlorn amusements as he could. Again and again Dash would see Peter engaged in long conversations with Petra. He brought her toys and dolls. He took her walking with him. There was a calm indifference about the two of them as they made their peregrinations through Salem. Neither paid the least heed to the lifted eyebrows and the slight smiles that followed them. Sometimes Peter even took Petra to the wharf to sail the *Red Herring* with him or to row about the harbor. No, Peter was not ashamed.

The news from Europe also bothered Dash. He even thought of offering his services to the British Navy. Napoleon had enslaved the Continent of Europe. Only England still stood. Dash, who had cursed at the British warships that had stopped him to see his papers, had sent him into Falmouth or wherever to await their pleasure, had chased him with their frigates, had made him endless trouble, was painfully conscious that if they were conquered, there would be little hope for freedom anywhere, not even in America. Then, too, no matter what he might say about them, he liked the English.

Then, that June, the Americans launched a new frigate — the *Chesapeake*. She put out, armed but unready for battle, from Norfolk. There the British *Leopard* bespoke her. Insolently demanded the right to search her for their own deserters. Commander Barron refused. The *Leopard* fired a broadside into her, killing and wounding twenty American seamen. The British boarded her and did indeed not only find deserters, but Ratford, the very man they were after.

After this insult to the American flag and injury to American citizens, there was a great demand for war. But President Jefferson would not yield to it. He was determined somehow to keep his young, poor, ill-prepared country out of the holocaust that was consuming the rest of the world.

The *Leopard's* attack upon the *Chesapeake* finished for Dash his momentary desire to sign up under the flag the *Leopard* had flown.

❦ 2 ❦

By December, having crossed the Equator twice, Dash was home again. He had taken the *Victrix* to Surinam. War, British Orders in Council, Napoleon's Berlin Decrees, had upset everything. The British were impressing American seamen and France was confiscating American ships. South America was less disturbed and there one might find tropical goods. He brought back rare woods for cabinetmakers and dyers, sugar and coffee, but the bulk of his cargo was cotton for Tom's "knitting" as Liz always referred to Mr. Fields's and Tom's efforts at power manufactory. Surinam, with its long mud flats and fevers, orchid-choked jungles, parrots, alligators, and hidden death, was no new route for Yankee seamen. They had been trading there for over a hundred years. And Dash stopped, as Inmans always stopped, to gaze at the gravestone of his father. Dead of the lung fever, here in Surinam, eighteen years ago.

Things had never been the same between himself and Polly since her attack of brain fever a year and a half ago. She was less captious with him, but subtly more remote. He often found her looking at him oddly, smiling a sad, secret smile, but her eyes as loving as ever. One day Old Doctor West had stopped Dash on the street to tell him that she was recovering her health but slowly. Plenty of rest, little excitement would do it, he promised, and yet neither he nor her father could persuade her to give up her dancing and night parties. Surely Dash would understand that at the present time there must be no talk of marriage? The old argument about his retiring would come up again, and excite her. Best say naught. Dash said naught. Then Tom had run short of cotton. Dash had been pleased to go for it.

Upon his return in December, he had not rushed to her impetuously, knowing she was his girl and would be waiting for him. He sent her a little note, received a little note back asking him to call next day at four-thirty. When he came, she did him the kindness of receiving him alone, not attended by the one remaining aunt or her father. They sat in her little sitting room before the fire. Shutters were closed and curtains drawn to keep out the cold.

It was of her own health she wished to speak. She had never

been interested in any man's voyages. Nor in the assorted heathen a man might meet on his travels. Doctor West said she was doing marvelously. He did not think a year, and over, of convalescence from brain fever so very long.

"But," said Dash, "why did you have it in the first place?"

"You know. I've told you. It was when Papa got that dreadful lying letter. Blackmail, of course. And Peter took that silly oath. It upset the fibres of my brain, Doctor West said. I suppose I have to sit back and take it patiently and grow new fibres, or something."

Dash gave her a long, slow look. If I should tell her the truth now, he thought, and sometime I must, it would shock her ten times as much as anything Peter could do or say. No, I can't, yet. Not yet awhile. I'll wait until she's real strong.

"And how's your health been, Dash?"

He almost laughed. Nothing was ever wrong with his rugged good health, and nobody ever asked of it. Yet her question did suggest an ugly truth. He and she never had had much to talk about, except in that most primitive, wordless language. Well, obviously when Doctor West had told him he must not excite her, he had meant no more love-making, for a while.

Then she brought up the Derby ball next night. He knew she never missed a ball even if it did mean resting in bed the entire next day.

"Liz and Fanny and I plan to go together. Will you be the fourth? They have been dear neighbors to me, Dash. At least Fanny ... I love Fanny. She is so sweet and self-effacing. Liz" — she laughed and pouted and shrugged — "he's exactly the same old Liz. But he's in Washington now. Fanny expects him back today. Dash, have you heard — is Liz back from Washington?"

The doorbell rang sharply. Both turned their heads. It rang again and someone began to knock.

"He always does that," Polly said. "That's what Liz always does." No servant was going to the door.

"Oh, I forgot. Today's Tuesday. Flip stays home on Tuesdays to catch up on her own house. But wherever is Patty?"

As Patty did not materialize, and as another impatient knock sounded, Dash went to the door. It had begun to snow. Liz stood there in riding clothes. His great cloak was white with snow, and snow was on his hat and beard.

"Well, I found you. I've been hunting."

"Come in."

"No. Lookee, Dash. It's important. I've got to see you. And now. Make your farewells and come to my house. Yes, I've just come from Washington on horseback, and stopped off at Danvers and found Tom. There'll be just the three of us. We've things to decide. Tonight. Ma'am is not invited. Emphatically not invited. My respects to Polly, of course. And my apologies. But come, immediately."

Dash found Fanny standing in the hall in a wordless flurry. She knew something important had happened, and that in the dining room, behind shut doors, a great decision was to be made by the three oldest Inman brothers. And of course, being men, they'd never tell her a thing. All her husband asked of her was to send them a tray of rum and Madeira and lemons. Things like that. And she might never know.

Liz had already cultivated a nice palate. He poured Madeira for himself and Tom — who always took whatever was set out for him — and left Dash to concoct his old-fashioned "slops."

"I've told Tom," Liz said, keeping his voice carefully low-pitched. "In fact, even Tom got so excited he's almost forgotten he's an old woman and knits for his living. He remembers he was born and bred a deep-sea man."

Tom smiled. Nothing ever upset his ruddy, calm face. Certainly no sarcasms from Liz. He was too used to them.

"Have you told Dash yet?" he asked.

"No. Dash, here it is. Have a drink first, you'll need it. Here it is — and mind you swear to secrecy?"

"I swear."

"Mr. Jefferson is going to scuttle the entire American merchant fleet. Break every merchant."

"Is Liz crazy?" Dash demanded of Tom, not believing his ears.

"No. Mr. Jefferson is." Tom placidly finished his glass, and poured some more.

"Jefferson is going to pass an Embargo Act. Not an American vessel is to clear. Now let me tell you two Federalists — it's lucky one of us is a Republican. For I've got the news in time." Liz was pacing up and down, his white chemical teeth flashing in his dark beard. "Jefferson thinks he can make both the British and the French treat us right, treat our ships right, by boycott. He's thinking back to the old days. Before the Revolution, even. Boycotts were tried then."

"And didn't work," Dash put in. "It·didn't stop the fighting, did it?"

"No. I don't say it will work now. But he's set on trying it."

"So we'll shut ourselves up — like Japan?"

"Yes. Just like Japan. And pretend nothing is happening anywhere elese in the world."

"We've had a chore of it," Dash admitted, "steering a course for ourselves between Napoleon's Berlin Decrees and British Orders in Council. But we've done it. That was hard enough, but to think now we're scuttled by our own Government. You mean literally not a ship?"

"Even coasters and fishing vessels will be put under such heavy bond no one can afford to meet it. Not a vessel. Literally."

Tom said, "But he must know that last year Salem port paid one-fifth of the entire Federal income. He daren't cut off his own revenue so."

"Yes, he dares. He'd rather impoverish the whole country than fight a war. And if he decided on war, which side would he fight, and which join? Both have put upon us shamefully. You and Tom would rather fight the French. I'd like to finish off England, myself — she's a gone goose anyway. Jefferson is trying to keep us honorably neutral. He thinks he can't if our ships are streaking all over the world. You know — getting into trouble and fighting back and breaking regulations and both sides roaring that we are supplying the enemy. So, no ships."

"He's no seaman. He cares more for that Louisiana Purchase of his, and all that waste land Lewis and Clark walked over, than for world trade."

"Maybe. Yes, he's no seaman."

"Has Jefferson thought this out?" Dash demanded sternly. "He's dead set against the British. And we're their only rival left in the Far East. Withdraw our ships and we give England a monopoly in Far East trade. We may never get in there again. I can see why he might forbid us Europe, but why Asia?"

"He doesn't care a snap for world trade."

"And, Liz, you voted for him."

"Lucky I did. Lucky I spent the last three weeks hanging about Washington — and a damn rickety sort of hog wallow it is — and hanging about cabinet ladies. But now look here. This Embargo will be declared December twenty-second. It will take four days beyond that for official word to reach us here in Salem, even by messenger riding haste post-haste. Today's the fifteenth. We've got eleven days, for any ship already to sea will be allowed to remain out. She can go on working for her employers, making profit, and no questions asked. It is only when she returns, she will not be cleared again. Laid up for as long as this damned thing lasts. And so — to sea."

"How many merchants know about this? Liz, let's call a meeting and publish the facts and let every ship get out of Salem in time."

"Can't, Dash. You see it was Billy Gray tipped me off to go hang about Washington and see what was coming. He knows. And he let us in on it. Nobody else. And I've sworn secrecy. So've you."

"The Crowninshields are Republicans. Do they know?"

"Not through me — nor Billy Gray. He and I are in this to-gether — sort of. Yesterday, when I stopped in Boston to tell him what he'd guessed was a fact, he helped me buy a Medford brig, the *Dolphin*. Very fine vessel. And he's signing me a crew for her. I'm taking her to Europe. We've rigged it, Mr. Gray and I, so it will profit both him and us — mightily. The *Dolphin* goes to Europe. Now I want to get ships to the Far East. Luckily both the *Victrix* and the *Wanderer* are in. That's one for each of you — I'd hate to trust a hired master for such ticklish work."

"Count me out," said Tom. "I've got a wife and two children, and am having a third."

"And your knitting?"

"Yes. It strikes me this Embargo may help the knitting. Folk have always been able to buy better and cheaper cloth from England than any we can make. Now for a while they'll have to buy American goods."

Dash poured himself another drink. "It will ruin Salem, Liz. We're going to see soup kitchens and bread lines. I've seen them in Europe. There's only one trade in Salem. Ships. Not a man in town whose livelihood doesn't come from deep-water ships. The Charity House won't hold the paupers this Embargo will hatch. Everyone will go down together in ruin."

"This damned nonsense won't last forever."

"God grant it doesn't. With our ships rotting and our people starving."

"Don't look so far ahead, Dash. All this will happen if the Embargo lasts too long. What I'd like is to have it last just long enough for us to make a killing."

"You don't care what happens to anybody else?"

"No. And so, Tom, you won't go, eh? Dash?"

"I'll go fast enough. Don't worry. Anything I can do to grease the ways under this last bright idea of Mr. Jefferson I'll do with pleasure." He slowly poured himself another drink. Neither of the younger brothers spoke, for they knew Dash was thinking. "I'll get Dan Obrian for the *Wanderer*; he's getting tired of the Derby house flag. I'll take the *Victrix* myself. Be senior captain of the two ships. Bombay," he said. He thought with affection of the hot island city — the finest port in India and the only India port with sufficient tide for proper repair docks. He remembered the cool breezes of Malabar Point, the sacred sandalwood fires that the Parsees had burned "forever." The conchs of the Brahmins blowing through the night. Rice paddies and wooded hills and the strange myriad-headed teeming Indian life.

"I could settle down in Bombay," he added, "real comfortable."

"Hell, who wants you to settle down? Think of what Indy goods are going to fetch in America — after the Embargo has been on a year! Look at Tom, here; he's longing for Guzerat cotton already."

"Soon after I get there, I'll laden the *Wanderer,* send her home. But if I can get me an English partner, I'll start a graving yard and repair shops for all the American ships that are going to get stuck out there and don't want to come home. You know the trouble we always have repairing and fitting in the Far East."

"You've got something," Liz admitted, with grudging admiration. "And you can help them with their cargoes and take the usual ten per cent."

"I can. Lucky for me Mr. Duncan is governor. He and I are old friends."

"What cargoes do you want to take out?"

"Rolled copper for ships' bottoms. Bolts, spikes, dovetails. Things like that. And Baltic steel. No oakum. India cotton's as good for caulking. Most Yankees don't know it. I'll learn them. I want masts. Don't trust tropic wood for masts. But dammar is as good or better than tar." He went on, explaining what he would do.

An American yard and agency in Bombay was mighty smart business, Liz thought. He had begun arrogantly by giving all the orders himself. Now he was almost silenced. The business man in him was pleased with the idea and he was generous enough to admit that once again Dash had been smart. Dash was through talking.

To sit in the cool of the evening, on a long veranda, one's work done, one's soul at rest, thought Dash. What if Peter did cough himself to death — way off in Salem? But so contrary was his temperament that, even as he thought this shameful thought, he found himself saying, "Guess I'll take Peter with me. For clerk."

"That would be a fast way to kill him. India!" Liz exclaimed, and Dash quickly agreed. He did not want Peter.

"I'll rent a bungalow — on Malabar Point. And near-by there is a cleft in the rocks. You can get rid of your sins if you can wriggle through it." He was smiling. "Not many Europeans can. We are too bony and muscle-bound. Hindus haven't any bones."

But Liz was interrupting him. He cared nothing for sins nor the weird bonelessness of Hindus.

"Where's the *Mermaid* now?"

"Probably at Batavia, Bates master. If I have luck I may bespeak her, say Isle of France. Turn her back."

"The *Shepherdess*?"

"Napoleon has grabbed her at Naples. But I guess the American commission can talk her free again. And *Fox Fire* has been broken up."

So they discussed the situation and made their plans.

⁓ 3 ⁓

DOCTOR HOBEY often stood upon the captain's walk atop Ma'am's old house and viewed the harbor. He had never seen it so jammed with shipping before. The ships were tied up three deep along the wharves. An ignorant man might believe prosperity was in full swing, for here was indeed the traditional "forest of masts." But inverted on each masthead was a barrel to prevent rot. These were called "Mr. Jefferson's nightcaps." The ships were dismantled, stripped. Decks cleared, sails and cordage stowed. The only living, moving vessel he saw was a clumsy Government gunboat sent to Salem to keep an eye out.

There was no bustle along Derby Street and a green fuzz of grass had grown among the cobbles. No fine young fellows crowding about the counting-houses to sign off or to sign on. No boy came running to say he had sighted a ship and where was his fifty cents. No loading and unloading. No clatter from the anchor-smith's forge, nor tap from shipyard. In the sail lofts sailmakers had unfastened their leather thimbles from their palms, uncrossed their legs, and gone. The ropewalks were deserted. He missed the countryman hawing to his ox team, bringing masts to Salem that might have been cut as far away as Maine. He missed the sluttish girls yelling at the sailors from upper windows. Respectable coffee shops, convivial grogshops, were shut. From where he stood, using his spyglass, he could see that certain warehouses had For Let signs tacked to them, and some wag had written below, "See Mr. Jefferson."

As a natural philosopher he had begun by summer to notice that the great number of ships crowded in together was interfering with the flow of silt. Usually the harbor silt was carried into the Mill Pond. But now he guessed that shallow Salem Harbor was growing shallower with every tide. The *Mermaid* had come in from Batavia five months before and been given good anchorage off Inman Wharf, but already she was resting on the muddy bottom at every low tide. Given another year of silting about the ships and she'd not float even at high. There was a hideous and growing stagnation about the scene.

And as a natural philosopher there was another thing he had not noticed before. There were not half, no, not one-third the number of gulls. He had never thought the time would come when he would miss the inordinate number of pestiferous gulls that habitually haunted the waterfront, living off the rich ships and their rich garbage. Madam Inman's house had always been whitened with their wings and their guano. Rose had often complained that she couldn't spread sheets in the back yard, the gulls flew in and soiled them. Well, a good many more than half of them seemed to have turned honest fishermen again. Given up scavenging a town that had not one crust of bread it might throw away. So he missed the fancy girls and the gulls — both were symbols of Salem's prosperity.

By late summer that time had come which Dash had foreseen before he and the *Victrix* and Danny and the *Wanderer* had headed for Cape of Good Hope and beyond. One-fifth of Salem's entire population was being fed in public soup kitchens and bread lines. In Salem, so recently the richest town in America! Here, always, a good man had got good wages and there had been work for everyone. The town had always had an enormous proportion of skilled artisans as well as sailors. Skilled artisans — everyone knew how little Mr. Jefferson sympathized with them, how little he understood seamen. He was at heart a farmer and a fine gentleman. Seemingly there were few other classes in America he did understand. Now sailors and artisans stood twice a week in the long lines as the free bread was doled out. But 'Sephus Hobey knew man does not live by bread alone.

The very poor and the very disreputable were living better than ever before — such people as Raggity-Meg — and 'Sephus had never noticed that she had profited any by handsome Danny's success. The hardest group to help were the young mates and masters, too proud to stand in bread lines now or accept the fuel and warm clothes that would be doled out next fall. Doctor Hobey was on the committee to relieve suffering. He knew how hard it was to help proud folk.

Sometimes there were near riots. It was said that the Government gunboat crew were scared to stop ashore for a drink. There were many petitions sent to Washington, but, by and large, this sudden unemployment and poverty were accepted philosophically. There had always been ups and downs in New England, beginning with the weather. Men were used to accepting evil days and planning boldly for better. Certainly the well-to-do in Salem had given openhandedly. No, not even yet was anyone hungry who would accept charity. 'Sephus had sometimes felt he should hold Ma'am Inman back. She and Rose had many a meal of gruel and poor man's pudding, so determined was the old lady that no one in Salem should be hungry while she had food to share. 'Sephus guessed she felt embarrassed about her own ships. It had been amazingly lucky that her grandsons had not been caught in harbor. The *Wanderer* and *Victrix* had gone tearing off, three days before the Embargo was announced. Liz had bought that Boston brig, the *Dolphin,* just in the nick of time. When the *Mermaid* came in from Batavia, her Far East goods had not needed to be reshipped to Europe for a better price. They sold, and at best market, right on the wharf here. Napoleon had disgorged the *Shepherdess.*

Yet it was a little strange. Strange, too, that the Crowninshields had got so many ships to sea in time. But Billy Gray, who usually used Boston as his port, had been "luckiest" of all the Republican merchants. He'd got his whole fleet to sea. None of the Federalist merchants had. Ma'am said nothing, but did not like it. Her loyalty to Salem was far greater than any party loyalty. That was why, 'Sephus knew, she gave so prodigiously to the unfortunate.

But Tom and Mr. Fields were, for the first time, prospering. People said American cloth wasn't very good and was very dear. But it was all they could get.

Another group besides the struggling industrialists that had profited by the Embargo was the New Lighters. Many desperate people were turning to these new religions as they always will in adversity. Doctor Hobey, unlike most regular clergymen, had not the stomach to preach against them, although the suicide rate among these religionists was shockingly high. He had a humble knowledge that what he had to give was not what they needed. Of course, egged on by Mrs. Miranda and Mrs. Inman, he did now and then "talk" to Linda. And she'd nod and squirm and seem to agree with everything he said. Then off she went.

One October day — and now the grass that had grown on Derby Street was bleached to hay — Peter stopped his curricle before the Mompessons'. Polly had yesterday told him she longed to drive out and see the glory of the autumn coloring. And talk of Dash. She always wanted to talk of Dash.

Ten months after his departure, the first letter had come from him. He and the *Victrix,* Dan and the *Wanderer,* had arrived safely in Bombay. The two sisters had been making short voyages picking up India goods, and at the moment he had sent the *Wanderer* to Canton for teas. As soon as she returned, he'd send her back. He had rented a bungalow for himself, found an English partner, and was setting up graving-yard repair shops already much patronized by American ships. It all looked "real profitable" to him. And the agency end of his business looked "real good." But Polly was not, of course, interested in his business — only in him.

The autumn day was so chill and threatening, Peter was not surprised when Mr. Mompesson told him Polly would not drive out.

Foam arched his silvery neck, pawed, and longed to go. Peter decided he himself would see the glories of the season. The clouds were close and dark, but through them struck a long finger of suplight. Of course, Jack was always warning him not to overexpose himself to the elements, not to let himself get too tired. But surely there was no harm in a country drive.

Ahead of him, running pell-mell down the street, he saw two women. He recognized his mother's old green Cashmere shawl on one. That was Linda. A black velvet bonnet with a plume which had looked so devastating on Polly's head three years before still looked devastating on little Mrs. Shean.

"Girls," he called, bringing his green curricle to a walk beside them, "what's your hurry?"

They stopped, panted and giggled. "We're late."

"Late for what?" They were certainly leaving their domestic duties like bats out of Hell.

"Don't tell Mrs. Miranda," Linda begged.

"Of course not. Well, get in if you are in such a hurry and I'll drive you to whatever mischief you are heading for."

They both giggled again. They always thought Mr. Peter very witty. Foam sidled. The emerald wheels turned. Riding in such a dashing curricle was no novelty to the girls. After all, Michael had to keep the horses exercised. It was hard to think of any reason why he should not take his wife and a friend of hers out with him. Although there was no reason, it had bothered Miranda very much.

"Flip," Peter said, "tell me where to go."

"To your right now, Mr. Peter." They were still panting.

"And then where?"

"Back of Gallows Hill. Do you know Brickell's great barn?"

"Of course." The huge red barn was a landmark.

"That's where, if you please, sir."

"A barn dance? Harvest Home?"

"Oh, Mr. Peter. You forget. Today's Lord's Day."

"So it is."

Before him was Gallows Hill, a rough and barren mass. Even a little sinister. It was here that distant Aunt Tabby had been hanged, and other witches and warlocks. It was a cursed and lonely spot and no cattle were pastured there. The trees were thin and drooping. But as he rounded Gallows Hill he came to pleasant fields and meadows. Obviously no witches' curse hung over Brickell's farm. Here elms were lofty, fields looked rich, dark and plump. Maples throbbed with color and the high winds whipped them. Peter felt so good he began to sing and the girls sang too. Bluejays squawked. A colt in pasture was racing back and forth behind his fence whinnying to Foam. Crows floated like bits of charred paper up from the corn shocks they were plundering.

In the midst of all this richness was Brickell's great red barn. Various conveyances were hitched to trees and posts about it. There were a number of old horses with sacks on their backs in lieu of saddles. People had come from very far. Poor people.

"Mr. Peter, let us out here."

"No, I'll drive you up in style."

"Oh, please, sir. You're making us conspicuous," said Flip. "Michael won't like it if he knows I've been off with Linda again to a New Light meeting."

"Everybody is in the barn. They won't see you." And he heard the hymn-singing.

"Flip, how did Linda get you into this?"

"Oh, I've gone a dozen times. It's fun, Mr. Peter."

"It's fun, is it, Linda?"

"Oh, Mr. Peter, it's sort of lovely, in a queer way."

"Can't I go?"

Linda looked at him doutbfully.

"Linda, you took me once and I swear I didn't laugh."

"No, sir. You didn't laugh straight out, but you spoiled it for me. Because you looked as solemn as though you were in a real church. Never letting go a bit."

"I *might* let go."

Linda said, "Oh, if you only would! If only it would please God to move you and wash you clean of all your sins before it is too late."

"He might. Can't I go in? I might get that cleansing bath today, right in public."

"It could happen, sir. It happens strangely for some disbelievers. I've seen it. But if you go with us, you've got to do like them. When they yell, you yell. When they praise God, you praise God. I won't have you sitting there looking like you did the other time. If people dance, you get right up and dance."

"Dance?"

"Not exactly. But before the Lord. Like **David** did."

"It's awfully exciting," Flip added.

"It certainly sounds exciting."

He tied and blanketed Foam and warily the three of them crept in a side door. The beasts had been put out to pasture, but otherwise it seemed like any other barn except for its great size. The hay lofts were full of hay. Stalls and bays were crowded with people. At one end, standing on a freshly painted blue farm wagon, was a man.

"Who?" Peter asked in a whisper.

"Don't you really know, Mr. Peter? Why, that's **Lover Birch** himself."

They settled themselves comfortably on a couple of empty cider barrels. He could feel the girls already tense beside him, waiting like race-horses to jump forward at some signal not yet given. The audience was about what he expected, the excitement less rather than more. The "exhorter" was as illiterate, ungainly, repetitious as Doctor Hobey had said they were, but considerably duller. He began to yawn.

"Please don't yawn, Mr. Peter. It hasn't begun yet."

He looked at his watch. He had been here over an hour. He wondered if he should go out and make sure Foam hadn't slipped his blanket. He gazed about him. To his surprise, very silently the barn had filled. Above the hay in the loft he saw hundreds of faces. He looked at the rafters. People clustered along them like bats. But all these faces were featureless now, for it was growing dark. Lover Birch, standing in his farm wagon, was silhouetted against the sunset behind him. Up and down he went, up and down like a jack-in-the-box.

"We'll have to go home soon," he whispered to Linda. "It will be too dark to see."

"No. No. Torches."

Then the torches came, great primitive orange towers of light. They were carefully set in iron brackets prepared for them. For the first time Peter saw Farmer Brickell himself. He might be a New Lighter, but he wasn't planning to see his barn burned down. He had everything well arranged.

With the coming of the torches what had been tedious began, in a way, to grow exciting, just as the girls had promised him. You could see it as the torches blew this way and that and brought one face after another into their ruddy, hellish light. You could feel it. For the last half-hour Lover Birch had let a younger man carry on. Now he knelt a moment in prayer and prepared to take again his bucolic pulpit.

"He always does that," whispered Linda, "and then he takes over."

The tired, rather old man with the glittering God-struck eyes took his place on the wagon. "Oh praise the Lord," he intoned.

"Oh praise my God," the people answered.

"Oh praise the Lord."

"Oh praise my God."

What had started almost as conversation was going off into a heavy chant. People were thumping with feet and fists like drums. Mr. Birch rocked back and forth and his flock rocked with him. Peter rocked. Not only had he promised Linda, but there was no room not to rock. They were packed in like herrings in a barrel.

The chant went on for some time. Then Lover Birch was clapping his hands for silence. "And now," he kept saying, "And now . . ." Silence came and he began almost like a regular divine.

"I want to say a few words. Them sanctified geld-cats, those regular ordained ministers, are trying to keep Christ's love from getting to you."

"That's why," Flip explained to Peter, "they call him Lover Birch. He's always preaching love, just like Christ Himself."

"They talk to you about Moses, don't they?" Birch went on. "And Abraham and Jacob and Isaac — rich men like that? They're scared to let you hear too much about dear Jesus Himself. Did He live in a palace? On Washington Square? Chestnut Street? Federal? He did not. He didn't know where to lay His poor head. But Solomon and David did. And Abraham had more flocks of sheep than he could count, just like, say, some men today have more *ships* than they can count. So of course those kept cats of the rich don't want us to ponder the words of Jesus. Or take a man like Moses . . . why, the King of Egypt's daughter adopted him. He lived like a prince. But Christ *was* a prince, a prince of Heaven. On this earth He was naught but a poor carpenter. And I guess, like some of you poor carpenters here tonight, He knew what it was to have no work and much sorrow. Because the rich every so often rig things — like they rigged this Embargo — 'cause they feel poor folks are getting too proud. So the poor get poorer and poorer. Christ understands folks like us, and all He asks of us is our love. That ain't much to ask, men and women, boys and girls, saints and you poor sinners. It ain't much and it is a joy to give. But I tell you them regular clergymen don't want us to know about Christ Himself. They're scared, if you knew too much about what dear Jesus really promised us poor people, you'd tear down the fine houses of the rich."

Peter thought he was preaching as much hate for the rich as love for Christ. He had heard that they were talking about the rich being too rich, their houses being too big. He was listening with more interest now. The fellow wasn't merely a "ranter" — he was an iconoclast.

"No, no," Lover Birch's voice, for the first time, rang out loudly, "He don't ask it of you. No. Only that you love Him — like He loves you. Like He loves you, did I say? No. Only a hundredth part as much, and repent your evil deeds and thoughts. Repent, He says. Open your hearts to Him and to His love and let the cleansing blood of the Lamb flow over you."

Even as Peter was thinking this was the most childish speech he had ever heard, the crowd was responding fervently. It was what they wanted. Here, to them, was that love past understanding. Comfort in a time of hardship.

Without waiting for him to reach a decent end to his sermon, a woman screamed.

"What may I do to be saved, oh Jesus?"

"What may I do to be saved?" Someone else echoed.

"Repent!" warned Lover Birch, showing no resentment at this interruption.

"What may I do to be saved?" wailed the women, alone.

"Repent!" roared the men. Evidently they had done this before.

For a long time this went on, getting faster and louder, fast and sharp as musket-fire.

"What may I do to be saved?"

"REPENT!"

The girls shrilled the question from either side of Peter and Peter roared "Repent!" with the men. The women were jerking backward, tossing up their heads, flinging out their arms. The men bowed forward with the weight of the heavy word "repent." He had to admit that in a curious way it was fun. This was indeed a real Witches' Sabbath. Hah, he thought, Satan is let loose once more on Salem. He felt a primitive evil magic. But he went with it. Oh, it had done no good that some had confessed their evil, others had been hanged so long ago. You don't really kill such primitive forces. Here they all were once more and Hell's pot was boiling.

The torches flared and he saw the beginning of what Linda called "dancing." With arms about each other they swayed forward and back.

"Mr. Peter, you do it," begged Linda.

He did. The simple jerks were exhilarating. He was laughing and so were most of the people about him.

A young girl, who had come over to the wagon, screamed and, as she fell, Lover Birch caught her and laid her upon the straw of the wagon bed.

"You all know . . ." he began, and then tried again, "You all know . . ." At last silence came rather suddenly.

"You all know what a sinner before the Lord Sister Suzanna has been. Yes," and he gestured at the seemingly unconscious body at his feet. "A great sinner before God and man. Many of you remember our meeting last summer in Newburyport. Remember how she came among us tricked out with paint upon her face, and false curls upon her head — to ensnare men. Brethren and Sistren, she came to scoff and she remained to pray. For Christ entered into her that night and caused her to speak out and confess and repent. And she saw God and from henceforth she has walked with God. And God bade her come to us tonight and tell us the way to salvation. Who else will follow the path to righteousness, the road to Heaven? Turn their backs upon that Hell yawning beneath them?" A modest young sailor was standing close at hand. "Brother Tobias, while we wait for Sister Suzanna to gain strength, you tell these good people your own experience with Jesus."

The young, blue-eyed sailor stood confidently beside Mr. Birch. "I can tell you somewhat about Hell," he admitted without a shade of embarrassment, "for I've been that close to it I've seen the fires and I've seen the devils and I've heard the damned, screeching and screaming. For I had led a depraved and blasphemous life. And I was dying and the devils were reaching out their pitchforks to receive my immortal soul — and then I saw a flash of light and I saw my Maker's face, so full of love and sorrow. And He said, 'Repent and cleave to me.' And so, God help me, I've clove. You just say I've done this and I've done that and I'm sorry and I won't any more. And folks, the joy you feel! Hell's fire backs away and you stand clad in naught but sanctity. Saved. Amen."

Sister Suzanna was now ready to talk.

"I guess I don't have to do much explaining," she began. "I guess, by now, all of you know me. And my baby hadn't any father. But now the Lord has touched me and made me His. Why, the Lord is my baby's father. I'm real sorry I've done wrong. And I'll confess and repent just as often as Lover Birch asks me to."

"And wherever there's a fallen girl," Lover Birch was saying, "there's a fallen man. It might be you or you or you. And in the sight of God one's as guilty as the other."

"Peter" — Linda was clinging to him — "Peter, he was pointing at you."

"No, he wasn't."

"I'll go up with you if only . . ."

"No, you won't."

"Peter, would you go up with me?"

"What?" She had spoken so low he had to lean down to hear her. She, so graceful in all her emotions, gave a sudden ugly writhe, as though a serpent was inside her, making her twist and coil.

"I've got to go. God calls me."

"Look-a-here. No, he don't. Flip . . ." He looked about for Flip a little desperately. The dancing and what-not had moved her from them and moved her away.

"I've got to! I've got to!"

Her plain little face was white in the torchlight. It was curiously wide open. Eyes, mouth, nostrils, all had opened and stiffened. He knew he'd best get her out of here. Fast as he could navigate, she was moving slowly away from him. At her touch, the crowd

parted courteously, almost reverently, as though they felt and respected the God in her. As far as he could figure, there was only
one exit for them still unblocked. That was the great door of the
barn against which the blue farm wagon, which was Mr. Birch's
pulpit, was placed. If he could steer her out of that, he'd push off
fast. Let Flip walk. I can't lose Linda, he thought.

He was sweating badly and could feel the fever rising in him and
a bad taste in his mouth. All about him he heard his own name
murmured. "Inman, Inman, that's Peter Inman." "A grievous sinner comes to God." She had him by the hand.

If he had been more egotistical, he would have thought of the
effect all this might have upon himself. He thought no more of
himself than Dash would have weighed his own life if one of his
people were in danger. The almost feminine instinct to protect was
strong in both of them.

As they came to the farm wagon, he took Linda firmly by the
arm, confident he'd walk her past out into the black night beyond.
He had her by the right arm, but Lover Birch leaned down and
took her left. Pull devil, pull tailor, flashed through Peter's head,
but he felt dizzy, stopped to mop his dripping forehead, lean against
a wagon wheel and regain his breath. He had felt something move
inside his chest, for every now and then his disease did move
within him almost like the quickening of a child. Well, let Linda
have her say, then he'd be able to handle her. Get her out of here,
if only, please God, he didn't hemorrhage first. Now he realized
she was standing on the wagon body, he below her like pagan
Ixion bound upon his wheel. And as she stood there he heard shouts
and hallelujahs for "Sister Gould." Evidently she had confessed
her sins before this, and now she must again. What might these
sins be? Doubtless something back in that lewd lascivious childhood of hers was still eating at her.

"It's only partly for myself, Mr. Birch," she said, in a low but
confident voice.

"Louder, please, Sister, louder. All these good folks wan'er share
your sins as well as your joys with you."

Her usually weak voice came out piping loud. "It's not for me
only, although I have sinned and sinned. But I'm nothing at all.
But I'm a-standing here for *him*!" she cried out clearly — "he, a
poor miserable sinner, come at last to God. And O God," she

prayed, "O God, take him and wash him clean as snow and forgive him that he's a fallen man and has lived in sin for many a year. And forgive his little daughter. He's led a wicked life, I know, dear kind father God, but he's pure inside him — inside the sinful raiment of his flesh."

Peter began to cough.

"He ain't a-going to be with us very long," she wailed.

"Shut up!" he managed, and coughed again.

"And he's real sorry and asks all of you — pray for the soul of Peter Inman. It's a good soul."

He stopped coughing, wiped his mouth. There was no blood. But he had no heart, no strength, almost no will, to deny what she'd been saying. It really didn't matter. No, it didn't matter at all. He only wanted to get her and himself out of this witches' brew.

"Linda!" he said sharply, and she obediently got off the wagon and came to him. He heard a murmur, almost a roar, of Hallelujahs and Amens as he pulled her into the dark night beyond the wide door.

Foam had slipped his blanket and was nickering at him in cold misery. He pulled it out from under his feet, tossed it into the curricle. "Get in, Linda," he commanded, his voice sad, compassionate, impersonal. "You better hold him as I unhitch. He's chilly and a-raring to go."

"Yes, Mr. Peter," she said shyly.

Neither had a word to say as Foam sped lightly homeward down a dark country road. Peter was grateful that she was no conversationalist. If she felt any elation that she had (in a way) brought him to God, she showed no elation. If she was remorseful at the liberty she had taken with the young master, she did not apologize. Feeling as she did about God, he could understand how it had happened. But whyever had he stood there leaning against the wheel (like poor Ixion himself) and never denied her words. He had not. His mind jumped back to months before. He and Dash standing up for Salem leaning on the taffrail. Dash with shameful eyes. If only Peter had lived at an earlier period, he might admit Petra by public confession of sin in meeting. It was curious, he thought, this human need for "public" confession. People weren't so vain as some thought. They didn't want to bury their sins with them. They wanted them pulled out of them into the open for all to scorn and wonder at — and forgive. Man wanted the forgiveness of God and the forgiveness of his fellow man. Then only could he forgive himself.

"Linda," he said softly.

"Yes, sir."

"Do you think those are northern lights?"

They both turned to stare. The lights came clearer, streaking up and retreating, shivering in cold ecstasy.

"They are the gates to Heaven. Great pillars of pearl and crystal a-shivering and a-shaking so," she whispered in wonder.

"No. Not to me. Linda, to me they look like the hand of God. See, he's got three fingers up."

"I guess it is the hand of God," she admitted readily.

"I guess so."

After a long time he added grimly, "I guess things like this get around fast, don't they?"

"Yes, sir. But don't you feel good and clean?"

"Not especially," he answered cryptically.

❧ 4 ❧

THAT NIGHT it was Linda who put him to bed. It was she who nursed him through three weeks of illness. Everybody was saying that Peter had not only admitted Petra as his child, but had stood up with Linda so admitting his guilty liaison with her. Even Mrs. Inman was inclined to agree with Miranda. Linda must go. But the girl's nursing would pull Peter through if anything would. Night after night, unobserved even by Miranda, as the fever raged and drenched him or the chills shook him, Linda would lay her almost nonexistent body beside him with the most sexless, angelic love. For the first time he was in considerable pain. Jack West said his pulse was up so he couldn't count it. And yet, in time, he grew better again.

Because of his sickness he did not quite have to face the disapproval about him. His mother was angry that he had made such a vulgar display of himself, and in such low company — escorted by two maidservants! It was felt in Salem, even by those who cared little for mistresses or illegitimate children, that he had acted in an ungentlemanly way and committed the unforgivable sin of betraying his own class. He did not know that Miranda took Thomasina and Tommy back to Newburyport and her father's roof because she was afraid that if she stayed on here she would lose the new baby, as yet unborn, but already kicking.

Every day Georgiana wrote him, sweet letters, dear letters, and he treasured them under his pillow and, when strong enough, wrote back. And Polly sent him notes, glasses of jelly, and lent him a potpourri jar. She never suggested that things were bad with him, but merely that colds at this time of year are hard to shake.

As soon as he felt confident of his strength, he went to see her. Flip, looking very serious, told him she was not at home. He went two days later. Once more Polly was "not receiving," and yet he knew somebody was in the great parlor and guests were being entertained. Of course it might be Aunt Brattle and the Squire. He still did not guess what had happened. Almost the worst thing that could have happened to him.

So he went a third time, carrying back the jelly glasses and the potpourri jar. Once again Flip opened the door. This time she flushed. "Mr. Peter," she said, averting her eyes, "Miss Polly isn't at home today. Master said to tell you if you came that she overexcited herself yesterday at the Wests'." Yet in the hall there were, once more, visible signs of visitors. Hats, cloaks, shawls, canes. And from among the pleasant murmur of voices in the parlor he heard Polly's nostalgic laughter.

"Flip, is it that her father says she's not well enough to see me —or does she?"

"It's her father. She doesn't know."

"Flip, what's amiss?"

"I can't say, sir, but . . ."

"Aye?"

"Oh, can't you guess, sir? There! They are ringing for me. I've got to go, Mr. Peter. Please go away. Go away from here."

"Tell me."

"I can't. But you might guess."

The bell rang again and sharply.

"Flip, dear Flip, please."

"Come round to the kitchen door and step in. There now, I've got to go."

He sat in the warm, toast-scented kitchen. He had no idea that his method of corroborating something which everyone had said for years was so offensive to Salem. He was thankful it was the Squire, not Polly, who had forbidden him the house.

Flip, the only servant on duty at the moment, joined him. She took off her pretty apron as if by this gesture to insist that now they talked as equals. She poured tea for him and herself and buttered toast.

"You promised to tell me."

"No, I didn't. But I will. Squire Mompesson says no gentleman ever would have done what you did, over at Brickell's great barn. He says no gentleman would ever have even attended such a meeting with a couple of servants. He says a gentleman is known by the company he keeps. He says he can forgive a gentleman a slip, maybe, but not his making an exhibition of himself. He says lots of the first families won't have you in the house because of that woman. You know what woman?"

"Yes, I do."

"He says he has been lenient because Polly has enjoyed your visits. He has let you come free as air. And from now on he won't. You're not to come here any more, ever, Mr. Peter."

"Polly?"

"He wants it kept from her. She can't be riled up and excited. He wants her to think you don't come because you are too sick."

"Pity I got well so fast."

"Don't go joking, Mr. Peter. It isn't a joke."

"No, it isn't. It isn't a joke."

It was true that during these last few years one door after another had been closed to him. One of the first, and the most shocking, had been Blainey Phipps's. But he had not wanted to go about much. He went regularly to the Flanneaus' for Petra's sake and because he liked the rowdy back-room card games and the low company Dulcey kept. He went very often to the Mompessons'. He had hardly noticed, until this moment, how many doors were closed to him. Why . . . he hardly had a friend in Salem except Polly and now she would be denied him. He was still so weak from his recent sickness that tears came to his eyes.

Flip saw them. She threw herself at him, her arms about his neck. "Mr. Peter, don't feel so bad. Please don't go off and die,

Mr. Peter. There, let me take your teacup, do. Don't cry. I can't stand it."

"Hell, I'm not crying." Nor was he. He tried to laugh and almost succeeded.

When the guests came to go, Flip was not in the front hall to curtsy as she handed them their outer wraps and curtsy again as she opened the door for them. Mr. Mompesson had never approved of her working half-time, as Polly called it. Actually she was here all day and still had her own room in the attic. Such conduct on a young wife's part seemed to him a very travesty on marriage. And secretly he had always disliked the servant girl who was, most inappropriately, his daughter's best friend and confidante. He had absolutely forbidden her young husband, Michael Shean, to hang about the kitchen, and yet, before this, he had suspected his presence. He tiptoed down the hall, listened. Yes, there was a soft murmur of a man's voice. He flung the door wide open, hoping to catch Michael. It was not the coachman embracing his wife. It was Peter Inman with the minx in his arms.

"Philippa!" he said, his voice pale with anger, "go up and pack anything you have still left in this house. You're to be out of it — and for good — in ten minutes."

"But, oh, sir . . ."

"Don't ask me where you are going. I would hardly expect that decent young husband of yours to let you in . . . after this."

Flip began to cry.

"Get out on the streets, where you belong," he said savagely.

"Don't tell Michael," she begged. "Oh, please, sir, don't tell Michael." Her words were almost a confession of guilt. To make things worse, she clung to Peter as the one protector at hand. "You don't mean what you are saying. Peter, Peter, tell him." She did not call him "Mr. Peter" as she usually did.

"I know, Mr. Mompesson," Peter said, "appearances are bad. But I can explain."

"Shut up!" Mr. Mompesson exclaimed, in his deep masculine voice, without a trace of his usual elegance. "And now, madam, if you will tear yourself from your paramour's arms and obey me. Harlot!"

Flip began to roar and stamp her foot. In spite of her usual pretty manners, scratch her a little and something of the servant girl did come out. Peter felt slightly revolted by her sudden commonness even as he pitied her.

"Harlot, yourself!" she shrieked at her employer. "There — you horrid old man with a face I declare like a wax doll's and no more heart in you than a toad! I'm going and not even Jesus-Christ-our-Lord-and-Saviour could stop me."

She bounded out of the room, her wails echoing up the back stairs as she sought her attic chamber.

"Mr. Inman" — Squire Mompesson looked Peter up and down and sneered at what he saw. Passionately concerned with his own health, he had a supreme distaste for sickness in others, unless it took the ethereal form of delicate sensibilities. "You're a consumptive, I believe?"

"More or less. Yes."

"I've heard that consumptives, doomed to early death, are apt to be lustful, libidinous, lecherous. The instinct to beget before they die. Mayflies, sir, mayflies. That you formed an ugly connection with a low woman I have overlooked. That you had so little of the gentleman in you as to seduce one of your mother's maids is, I believe, a business that lies between you and your mother. But a man is known by the company he keeps. Low company is evidently your taste. Otherwise how could you have stood up in . . . I forget the name of the barn."

"Brickell's, sir."

"I see you understand to what I refer. But *this* situation that I discover with my own eyes is insufferable. Carrying on with my daughter's maid even as you mooncalf about in the parlor after my own girl and her cousin, Miss Georgiana." He came nearer, shaking with rage. "Get out!" he said thickly. "Sickly, puny puppy! Get out by the back door you entered by! Or shall I call my coachman to throw you out?"

Peter barely heeded his anger. He was thinking more of the young wife than of himself. "I'll go, Mr. Mompesson, but first . . . there's nothing, not one thing, between myself and Flip."

"Philippa, please, or Mrs. Shean."

"Believe anything you like of me, but if you send away that good little girl without giving her a chance to explain . . ."

"I'll dismiss any damned servant I choose, and when I choose, and it's nobody's damned business. Damme!"

"She's Polly's friend, as well as servant."

"From now on you are to say 'Miss Mompesson,' sir. I won't have her pretty name on your dirty lips."

"You weren't honest enough or kind enough to tell me why I wasn't admitted here any more. But Philippa was both. Why did she hug me? Because she is so kind she felt sorry for me."

"Stuff and nonsense, Mr. Inman! Stuff!"

They heard slow and heavy feet coming down the back stairs, feet slow and implacable as the feet of doom. Both expected Flip and her box. It was Polly. She had heard the outcries of her maid-servant and run to her. She stood with folded arms and stared at her father. Her usually pink face looked cut out of snow.

"Polly! You'll make yourself sick. Please trust me to do what is right. You cannot thus break in on a gentleman's conversation. There are things I must discuss with Mr. Inman — alone. Things I would rather not have come to your ears."

"They have come, already." Her voice, which tended to be high and ringing, was now low and throaty.

"Then you understand. Mr. Inman cannot be received here. Mrs. Shean must go. I have never approved of her deserting her own home — no matter how humble — still earning wages over here, with a decent man to support her."

He was almost pleading with her. What he said sounded reasonable.

"I will not have Mr. Inman in the same room with you, breathe the same air."

She merely stared at him and said nothing. Her silence irritated him.

"And that goes for his whole family. Do you hear me, miss? Miss, are you listening to me? I won't have Mrs. Nanny. Nor our neighbor, Captain Eleazar, nor his foolish wife. Nor Dash — if he ever turns up again. I won't have an Inman in this house. They are pitch — all of them — and pitch comes off on the purest hand. Are you listening? Speak up, miss!"

Polly picked up a silver teaspoon, bent it double in her little hand, and flung it on the hearth. "Flip stays," she announced in the same queer, throaty voice. "Peter, Father doesn't mean a word he says."

"Polly, you cannot so set your will against me. There are some things which I, as head of this house, will decide."

She looked at him with curiosity as though she had never seen his face before. "Pooh!" she said wearily. There was nothing she could have said that would have cut her father more deeply.

That "pooh!" of Polly Mompesson's rang in Peter's ears. So she really did dare to oppose her father. She was not so utterly powerless as he had feared. The beauty sleeping in her crystal coffin could move and at least tap upon the heavy, transparent lid.

That she had won was soon apparent. Flip stayed, nor did she leave for her own house and husband until she was five months pregnant. Polly went for three days to Boston with Mrs. Nanny. When Captain Eleazar came back from Europe, he and his black beard and his jokes were never refused entrance. As for "his foolish wife," Polly was always doing this and that with Fanny. When Dash came home, he would not find the door shut firmly upon him.

But Peter abruptly ceased his calling. He waited for a written apology from Mr. Mompesson or a note of invitation from Polly. He often saw her, but not at her own house. He was at the Liz Inmans' and she would be there. She even, for the first time, began to drop in to see Miranda, and then she would seem so sweet and put on so few airs that his mother was saying how much better she liked her now that she was "a little older."

ᵔ 5 ᵔ

Lucy Inman was a little lonely. The main prop in her life for years had been her "young friend," Cousin Frances. She neither needed, nor wanted, one more daughter. What she needed was a friend, preferably a little poor and dependent. Fanny Inman came faithfully to her house, but dear Cousin Frances came no more. For the first time Mrs. Inman's problems were not Fanny's. One cannot discuss with a daughter the problems of middle age, and there, waiting for her, just around the corner, was old age itself. Let me see, she thought, next year, no, the year after, when Mr. Africanus comes to me on the nineteenth of January to wish me happy birthday, he'll tell me it's my sixtieth. But nowadays she couldn't tell Fanny how hard it is for a woman, still erect, handsome, rosy, and very healthy, to realize how soon sixty will be upon her. But Frances would have nodded her head and understood, because, in the old days, she had been almost as old as Lucy. Now, when Mrs. Inman began upon her household worries — clothes and curtains and servants and marketing — Mrs. Liz did not merely sympathize with her, but produced problems of her own. Often her problems were more elegant than her old patroness's. For instance, Mrs. Inman kept two maids, if you did not count Becky who did nothing but care for Tom Inman's children. And she had Michael, the coachman. But the Liz Inmans, with only that little house and the two of them, were keeping a Javanese butler, two maids, a coachman, and a yard boy. Of course Liz said it was everybody's duty in hard times to employ as many people as they might. Times were indeed hard, cruelly hard. And yet she knew the House of Inman, under Liz's direction, had profited amazingly. She guessed they weren't saying much about it — were really ashamed. Billy Gray, folks were saying, had made so much money by the Embargo he couldn't stand the look on people's faces in Salem. He was going to move to Boston. Liz, back from Europe on the *Dolphin,* was now in Boston half the time.

She wondered if perhaps it was not her duty to enlarge her own staff, but of course Miranda would not hear of such extravagance. If Mother Inman wasn't satisfied with the way she was running the house, she would get up earlier and work harder. For Miranda ran the house. Mother Inman must realize that Linda was not a very efficient maid, but Miranda understood that, in spite of everything, Linda was to stay.

Miranda always treated her mother-in-law most respectfully. Never did she kindly diminish the years that lay between them. She was always thinking that Mother might be tired, or needed her spectacles or a shawl, or, that crowning indignity, a nap. The early rising, the supervision of the servants, the unending cleaning, Miranda did happily, but her suggestion always was that Mother Inman was too old for such things, instead of always having been a little bored by them. No. Miranda's coming had in no way compensated for the going of Cousin Frances.

Nanny, too. Nanny refused, even now, to meet her mother merely as one adult meeting another. She was as filially respectful, as unconfiding, as she had been at fourteen. Every day Nanny crossed Washington Square, came in to call on whom she was rather horridly referring to as "Granny." Boots, her oldest child, was eight now. Then she had Ruthie and Dorcas besides, and they were all taught to "run to Granny." Mrs. Inman had had hardly her full share of maternal feelings. Of grandmotherly ones she had none. And yet . . . she couldn't help it . . . Petra Flanneau did rather excite her and she observed her, out of the tail of her eye, almost covetously.

Petra had outgrown running away, exciting sympathy by her wailing for the lost Wren — and never was Adonis himself bewailed more touchingly. She went no more to taverns with her father. When a fit of drunkenness and depression came upon him, Petra was now able to free herself. She almost hated her "Papa," as she called Flanneau. And already she knew Peter was her father. Boots West yelled "love-baby" every time he saw her. Not once — and his mother really admired his stubborn frankness — did Peter act or pretend that the child was merely what 'Sephus Hobey called "his responsibility." She was his darling.

Boots and his little sisters, Thomasina and her brother Thomas — and very good, pretty children they were, too — made Lucy Inman feel old and discarded, but Petra, to whom she had never spoken, never really acknowledged with a loving glance . . . why, the very sight of her made her feel young again. She was a heady child, and how poor Peter could have done it! All by himself, seemingly, for of Dulcey there was nothing in the little girl.

A little forlornly Lucy tried sometimes to share the interests of Nanny, Miranda, and now Fanny, and their talk of such things as interested young wives and mothers. Diapers, bellybands, teething! Children and husbands, children and children. Comparing notes on pregnancy. Why, Fanny was forty-one! It was not the changes wrought in a woman by pregnancy that Lucy Inman wished to discuss, but those changes at the other end of life which a woman of over forty should be thinking about. She had been sitting with the girls over at Nanny's, discussing whether or not Fanny could be "expecting." Lucy was so bored, she very unkindly and secretly was hoping she was going to be disappointed. Then suddenly she announced she was going home.

"Oh, Mother Inman," cried Miranda, "don't you want me to walk across the Square with you? You know there is a little ice and the thaw has covered it with water."

As a matter of fact, Mrs. Inman had her own feet under much better control than did Miranda, who was not very well co-ordinated and waddled a little like a duck. Lucy Inman was still strong as a horse. She stepped out into the delicious, soft, misty, melting day, a day of February thaw which promises spring just around the corner and raises man's hopes only to dash them.

She had recently added a two-story columned portico to the south side of her house — to give carvers and carpenters work during the hard year — and she was thinking that it looked too big and that Mr. McIntire, now dead, might not have approved of it. It was handsome. She liked it, but not really very much. Frances looks like an old fool, she thought, pretending she's as young as any of them. I'll bet she is too old to have a child.

Standing beside the white gates and looking toward her front door, she saw a little girl. She had on a lovely brick-colored corduroy coat with a three-tiered cape to it. Hanging down her back, suspended by the black satin ribbon under her chin, was the palest and largest of yellow felt hats. Mrs. Inman had by no means lost her interest in clothes. For years ladies had worn similar large hats in summer, made of straw, to keep off the freckles. And very becoming they were. She had never seen one before in felt, worn frankly in winter. Bonnets were worn in winter. Flanneau still liked to experiment with fashion and, as often happened, he had tried it out first on the eight-year-old little girl.

The child seemed a solitary figure. And what was she doing there? If she caught her swinging on the gate, she'd give her a piece of her mind. She wasn't doing anything except staring at the house. How familiar were those dark curls! Why, Lucy herself had had them at the same age. Fifty years ago, she thought. Half a century ago. Once her own cheeks had been as pink. Here was something she knew and loved coming out in the third generation, but somehow condensed and exaggerated. I hope she doesn't start hanging around here again. And she remembered those weeks, six years before, when Petra was always in the kitchen asking for Wren.

"What do you want, little girl?" she asked rudely.

"Nothing," said Petra, "nothing but to look."

"Well, you go over to the Common, child, and look at the squirrels."

"But they aren't sick."

"*Sick!* Why do you want the squirrels to be *sick?*"

"Peter is sick."

"Yes, Peter has had to be in bed this week. But he'll be out again soon."

"May I see him?"

Lucy thought a moment. "Yes." But she had not intended that Petra should put her hand in hers. There was something elastic, living, about that little hand. Not at all like Dash's hand, she thought. Even as a little boy Dash's hands were always so chapped and masculine and strong. And the West children and Miranda's had "paddy paws."

"Come," said Mrs. Inman, as they entered the house, "we'll run up the stairs and whoever gets there first will have a sweet."

Lucy Inman's cheeks were almost as pink as the child's when they reached the top, and of course she was one step behind. She produced from her pocket one of the sweets she had taken over for the West children, and then not given to them because Nanny had said too many sweets were bad for children's teeth. She suddenly kissed the child.

"There, that room is Peter's and the door is open. He's sitting up and, I suppose, writing poetry. Steal in on your tippy-toes. He'll be glad to see you."

Her outside wraps laid off, and on tippy-toes, the little girl seemed more like an elf than a human being, floating off, like the ghost of a happy child long dead.

Honorable or not, Lucy felt she must see this meeting and she too tiptoed down the hall. The little girl was already curled up close to Peter, with her black curls on his thin chest. They were both so extravagantly happy they had nothing to say.

This must never happen again, Lucy said to herself sternly. Miranda must think about her own children. Of course Petra must never come here again.

But whenever Peter was in bed for more than three days, Petra always appeared. Miranda, and even Tom when prodded by her, insisted that Thomasina was at an age to notice things. And the West children! Of course Nanny couldn't bring them over to see Granny and inadvertently be contaminated by that "dreadful little girl." Mrs. Inman said, yes, she saw the point. She didn't think it was nice to have the "disgrace" so in evidence. She certainly would "do something." She never did. She knew it was Linda who arranged things so deftly, for the child miraculously appeared only when Mrs. Miranda was out. Through the kitchen door up the back stairs she would materialize and be with her father.

These two together touched some half-hidden chord in Lucy. She felt a burning, second-hand love such as she had never experienced before. She scolded Linda, she told Mrs. Cady and Becky if the child came to the back door, she was not to be admitted. But she never told the child she could not come. In fact, she was always sending up cambric tea and gingerbread elephants. She gave her the turquoise and pearl locket she herself had worn at the same age. There was an excitement about Petra's secret, so well-timed comings and goings. You never knew when it was she would suddenly be there. It was a little like living in a house with a goblin.

Patiently Peter waited for the spring, for he believed that when sun and spring came and snow and winter went, he would be better again. About every day he heard from Georgiana, and she from him, but not once had she come to Salem since that ghastly business of the oath. It was as well, he thought. It was too late now.

He, too, waited for Petra's visits with almost held breath. He had not been about for three days. Miranda and Becky were getting Thomasina and Thomas ready to ride out on their little red sleds. He could hear the noises of their departure and then the house became still and Petra came on soundless feet to lie beside him. Sometimes they lay close and said little. Other times she brought her dolls and he and she soberly dressed and undressed them. He taught her nursery rhymes and told her old stories he had heard from his grandmother. His mother had rarely taken the time to tell her children stories. And next moment he'd hear Miranda and Becky and the good, legitimate children making good, legitimate sounds of happy children home from sliding — and Petra would vanish.

'Sephus Hobey came to him, lending him books, telling him of the wonderful things Napoleon's savants were discovering in Egypt, or reading newspapers to him. He was certain that Mr. Jefferson, who he swore was the best and wisest man in America, would soon realize his Embargo had been a ghastly failure. Come spring, he swore, ships would sail again. But of Peter's "responsibility" he never spoke. The subject embarrassed him.

Polly did not come to see Peter. He knew her father had a physical revulsion against disease. Perhaps Polly inherited it. Or perhaps she was more under his control than he sometimes thought.
He thought of her often, but missed her, he discovered, surprisingly
little.

His little old grandmother came. Her attitude toward Peter had
never changed, although there had been so much gossip at the time
of his "public confession." The story of his sins had at last reached
her. It had been Aunt Brattle who had called to condole with her
and explain why Brother Mompesson could no longer permit Peter
in his house. As she was soon saying to Doctor Hobey, " 'Sephus, I
don't believe a word of it." Like an ostrich, he had thought. Puts
her head in the sand and doesn't have to look facts in the eye. He
was glad this was so.

The day the *Wanderer* came in, she hardly stopped to listen to
Captain Obrian's report, see his books, although she had a fancy for
Obrian — like many old women she doted on handsome men. Here
was a letter to her from Dash — all business. More and more
money. And the dearth of coffee, sugar, and tropical goods was so
great in America the *Wanderer's* cargo would fetch an incredible
price. But Dash had also written Peter. She climbed down the steep
stairs from the counting-house and headed for Peter. It would
cheer the lad.

Peter was sitting up in bed. As his grandmother, still panting a
little, for she had hustled, handed him the letter, he felt such a longing for Dash his lips trembled. He had almost forgotten how Dash
had disappointed him on the last days of the voyage home from
Lübeck by doing exactly what Peter had hoped he would do. Now
he only remembered the free bold Dash of his boyhood and forgot
how he had seen him with shameful eyes.

"He doesn't write much, Grandma," he said, "only I'm to get
strong and he'll take me to Bombay. I guess I'd rather go to Bombay with Dash than to Heaven. You read the letter."

He handed it to her, and immediately shucked down in the bed
and closed his eyes. If resting was the way to get strong fast as
Jack had told him, seemingly he would begin this moment. Ma'am
did not have any spectacles with her. She couldn't read the letter,
but sat beside the bed in a rocking chair, holding it at arm's length,
squinting at it. She put it down.

"Peter . . ." His eyes opened slowly.

"Yes, Grandma?"

"Was he the reason" — she was looking at him with sharp scrutiny — "why you stood up, and — well, I must admit, made a spectacle of yourself in Brickell's great barn, last October?"

"Yes. You know what Flanneau's been saying lately about Dash?"

"No. Nobody tells me a thing. Except Aurora Brattle — she who was Aurora Mompesson — and I must say a born fool. Never paid no heed to her. Never will. Mind's going," she added with relish.

"Flanneau's been saying — well, Grandma, that what Mrs. Brattle told you wasn't so — that it was Dash, not me."

"Ah?" She stopped her rocking.

"Yes, Ma'am. I was scared people might believe it. I think it should come out."

"The truth?" she asked bluntly.

"You might call it that," he said listlessly.

She was whist and very still a long time. Peter's mind wandered to Bombay — he and Dash in Bombay together.

"And you might not?"

He had been so far away he answered stupidly, "Might not what?"

"Call it the truth."

He could not think of a proper answer. He could not lie to her — ever. He moved restlessly on his pillow. The moment before, he had almost seen Bombay — elephants and tigers, towers of silence.

"Don't go quizzing me, Grandma."

She went back and forth, back and forth, in her little rocking chair. He closed his eyes indicating that either he or the subject was exhausted.

"Do you want to read me the paper?" He did not like being read to. He was not so sick that he could not read. Still it might shut her up.

"No spectacles," she said briefly. "Left my entire basketful down on the wharf."

"Oh." He knew she was staring at him.

"Grandma — tell me stories as you used to do when I was a lad." It was years and years since he had sat at her hearth, listening to tales of ghosts and witches, demons and curses.

"No," she said, "no, not now. But, although a sensible person can't believe them, I think there's much truth in them. If they haven't an inner kernel of truth, why, they get discarded in a few generations." Then, relenting a little, she added, "Which story do you want?"

"Tell me about the man who sold his soul to the Devil. I always thought it happened in your house — long ago."

"There's a baker's dozen of those stories lying about Salem. And they all go something like this. A man is in a predicament. He turns this-a-way, that-a-way and don't see a way out. Then the Devil comes (we call him Old Horny and Mr. Scratch, Old Nick, maybe). He isn't at all terrifying. He comes smiling, plausible, and kind-seeming. Like a friend who loves you and wants to help. He says you do so-and-so (usually sign in my little black book) and I'll give you heart's desire. All the kingdoms of the earth. The admiration of your fellow men, riches of the sea and love of woman. No one needs know you've given your soul away. There'll be no public scandal. Only you and I will ever know you are a soulless man."

Peter was sitting up in bed, his mop of black curls on end. His grandmother was turning the newspapers she could not read.

"We've got many old stories about like that, Peter. And they are all true."

He felt the blood quicken through him, a ringing in his ears. For he had suddenly wondered if this was what he had done to Dash.

"A man must do what's right," she went on, in her sturdy old-fashioned Yankee voice. "No matter how hard. No matter how shameful. A man must stand up on his two feet and do what must be done. And if he hasn't strength to do it, God will give him strength. Shame, public shame, is not the worst of it. The worst thing that can happen to a man is private, secret shame — guilt. Nobody, not even with the Devil's help, gets out of anything. For that eats into him like cancer and destroys him. At least, destroys the god-within-him. Destroys his soul."

He wanted to cry out, "Don't say such things," but he said, as naturally as he could, "Grandma, look at the big print on the last page. See if Mr. Oates has any new books he's advertising."

She obediently turned the pages, held it at one angle, then another. "No," she said, "I guess not. Somebody's advertising p-i . . . p-i-c-k . . . pickles, I think. If there are any books they're too little for me to see. As you get old, all you can focus on is big things. That's one of the pleasures of old age."

She got up abruptly. "Good-bye, Peter," and she scuttled out of the room like a little old white rabbit.

Peter was still sitting straight up in bed, his lips parted, his eyes, made enormous through sickness, staring off into space. He felt sweat start and trickle. The blood flamed into his face, giving it a hectic, unhealthy parody of abundant good health. Was it chance, he thought, chance only that made her say all that? Liz is always laughing at her. Thinks it's stupid of her not to be able to figure in her head. But what she has just said is infernal smart. But why did she say it . . . just now? My God, what she said is true. And I don't believe she knows it. I can't talk to her. Maybe I can to 'Sephus. Things like that . . . souls and things are his business. And death, too. I can't die peaceful if I feel I've harmed Dash so. I've got to hold on. Hold on hard. I think I'll put on my clothes, he thought, for suddenly he was feeling strong and almost well.

~6~

"DOCTOR HOBEY," Peter asked, "how do people live who know they have not long?"

They were sitting upstairs in 'Sephus Hobey's study. Outside, the soft sodden March day was melting winter's ice. They could hear water running down the old-fashioned high-pitched roof. After his long winter's sickness, Peter had rallied valiantly. Once more he was dressed and about. Until this moment they had been talking of Russia. In all Salem there was but one little book on Russia, and that in German. Peter had come to Hobey to borrow it.

"How do they live?"

"Yes."

"Why . . . as kindly, as decently as possible. But I've always thought we should live each day as though it were our last."

"And not take up too much room?"

"I know what you mean."

"Not impinge upon and darken the lives of others."

"Well, yes. The sick must forgive the well their good fortune."

"That's what I have thought."

"Why let such things worry you? There's a lot of good sense in Horace's *Carpe Diem*."

But, Peter thought, you're a clergyman, 'Sephus. Shouldn't you always be preparing men's minds for the grave? What's *Carpe Diem* got to do with that?

"You may have years yet," Doctor Hobey went on.

"Yes. But not many. I'd like to live what's left for me manfully and well. If I have done wrong, I wish to right it. I don't want to take up too much room. Not be afraid."

"You are afraid?"

"Sometimes. Especially at night. Nights are the worst. Naturally I don't want to die."

"But death is the common fate we all must face. Yes, man is born unto trouble. As the sparks fly upward. It is a perfectly natural process. As natural as being born. And the fate of all living flesh."

"'As for man,'" Peter quoted slowly, "'his days are as grass. As the flowers of the field, so he flourisheth. And the wind passes over, and he is gone. And the place thereof shall know him no more.'"

It did not occur to Doctor Hobey to cap this, as he should have, with promises of life beyond that cold, passing wind. He did not speak of that other place which man shall know when this earth fails him. He was thinking of the soft, slow surge in Peter's voice. It takes a poet, he thought, to get the true poetry out of those great lines. Then he was also thinking of Peter's physical, not spiritual, health.

"What does Doctor West say to you, Peter?"

"Which one? Frankly, Doctor Hobey, I don't listen much to either of them. One says sea voyages. One says no. One says a breath of night air will kill you, and the other, get all the fresh air you can, night or day, summer or winter. Take Iceland moss to prevent a chill — and the other says blood-letting. Yeast, says Jack; syrup of mushroom seeds, says Old Doctor. They do both agree on gum tragacanth." Peter yawned slowly. "You see, I've listened to them. And neither knows a thing."

"You know, I have always interested myself in science and medical books. A new treatment comes up every year. I'm sure that out of all the experimentation now going on, sometime what you have will be conquered. Already we have smallpox beaten. And smallpox is the oldest, most deadly, of man's enemies. Consumption today kills more people in America than any other two causes put together. But sometime man will conquer that, too."

"I'd like to think so. Fact is, I'm only one person who wouldn't last very long, anyway. We flowers do get cut down pretty fast. And the place thereof doesn't know us any more. But it, the place, this earth, goes on and on. And everything man — say, you and I — sees, feels, loves, fears. They do not go out of the world with us. Not the blue skies nor storms, nor a girl singing, nor the turn of a hawk's head. Not the first skunk cabbage in the spring. Nor the way of a ship in the sea. Nor fear of death and war. The sack of a city. These things have been for always and are forever. Sometimes it seems to me man is but a nice instrument adjusted to catch at universal experience. He goes, they stay. Love, for instance."

He did not finish his sentence. He thought, My love has flown into strange channels. Not the clear old channels. Yet there were men before me, and men to come after me, who have loved a daughter who is not theirs. And a grandmother more than a mother. And a brother's girl more than their own. And Dash . . . my love for him has been "passing the love of women." David loved Jonathan that way. But he found the words to say it. I cannot.

"Love," 'Sephus interrupted his long reverie, "is the most important thing in the world. To be as little children and love one another."

Peter picked up the German book on Russia. "You've been good to listen to me." He stood to go.

'Sephus had a sudden resolution. "One thing more. Peter, I believe that all of us, sick or well, should so live that if Death comes this very night, he'd find our house in order."

Peter watched him with interest, but did not sit again nor speak. It was of such things as putting his house in order he had come to Doctor Hobey to speak of. But it was too late now. Now he knew he never would.

"You have — er — Peter . . . you have a certain . . . responsibility."

"Oh yes," he answered, almost gaily, for 'Sephus Hobey's embarrassment amused him, "I'm providing for Petra. In my will. No, I won't forget."

"Peter, I want to say . . . I think you have known . . . I've never felt differently toward you because of — well, a youthful slip. You have borne the consequences like a man. It is hard for us, all of us, to understand Nature. Nature, the great mother of us all. She gives us life. Then takes it away."

Peter was smiling as they came out to the head of Ma'am's old crooked steep stairs.

"Nature gives," he said, "and Nature taketh away. Blessed be the name of Nature."

Why, thought Hobey, that's almost blasphemy. It is God who gives . . . Peter shouldn't . . .

Peter was going down the stairs. Doctor Hobey stood with his hand on the newel, looking down after him. Then Peter had another bright, irreligious thought. "Thank you for justifying Nature's ways to man."

'Sephus Hobey stood at the head of the old-fashioned stairs, stunned, those last, almost flip, words of Peter Inman's ringing in his ears. He had not said Milton's great old words, "To justify God's ways to man." He had said Nature's ways.

Why, he had talked for half an hour with the doomed fellow and had not once thought to mention God. He had first given ethical advice. Then medical advice. A little milk-and-water philosophy. A suggestion about his "responsibility." He had not mentioned God. Very slowly he returned to his study and carefully closed the door behind him.

Christ, the Saviour of mankind, the promise of the resurrected life, life everlasting. He had not thought of Christ's "I am the resurrection and the life. Believe in me, and thou shalt have eternal life."

Oh, he had stood at a hundred deathbeds with those words upon his lips. The sick and bereaved were comforted. He himself was comforted as he felt these living words roll from his lips. Somehow Peter had caught him unaware. Had tripped him. Was he, himself, at heart, nothing better than a wicked French deist?

"In my Father's house are many mansions. If it were not so, I would have told you."

But actually, where were those many mansions? Think of all the funerals, all the tears wiped away from the widowed and fatherless, parents, children, as they saw the beloved dead ascending golden steps, mounting up to the infinity of those mansions in the sky. Peter . . . he could not, for the life of him, ever imagine Peter Inman up there with the harps and angels. He had not mentioned those mansions to Peter. And now it was too late.

Although he felt there was nothing now left of religion which he might say to Peter, he went next day to the Inmans', hoping to find him at home. But Peter was well enough to be at the counting-house, doubtless gazing out to sea, hoping to justify *Nature's* ways to man.

~ 7 ~

For close to a year, Dash had lived in his airy bungalow on Malabar Point above the hot, seething cauldron of Bombay. At dawn every day he rode his neat Arab pony to his dock, keeping an eye on his white-muslin Parsee workmen. They were, he thought, the most able men in the East, although it took a hundred of them to carry a mast twenty Yankees could handle (but in a different climate), and he never could get used to ships' carpenters who held planks with their toes as they sawed. Nor did he quite get used to the slow, tropical pace of life. He himself, come monsoon or drought, worked as hard as he would have in Salem. From a business point of view everything had worked out as he had hoped. He had quickly found an English partner. The many orphaned American ships in the East flocked to his repair yard. A large part of all India goods bought during the Embargo by Americans he was agent for, and he had sent ships as far away as Mocha and Canton to collect goods. Yet he was not content. He would lie upon his bed, listening to the break of the sea below the cliff. The sea beats slower than a man's heart, saying always, Forget your human rhythms, take mine. Nothing is as important as you think. He knew what it was saying, but he could not believe it.

Then one morning, suddenly, he felt he must go home. He had had a hideous dream. The punkah boy had fallen asleep in the night. The great white bats' wings over his bed stopped their fanning, and the hot sticky black night had stifled him. He had dreamed Peter was caught in that near-by cleft in the rocks the Hindus (lithe as snakes) were always wriggling through to rid themselves of sins. He had seen Peter was caught there, the rocks closing in tighter and tighter on him, crushing him. He got him by a hand and had his knees braced to prevent the rocks' contraction. Already the hand he had held was ground to pulp. He seized the head. It was squashy as a mashed melon, but the face was unmarred and the eyes looked at him with affection, almost amusement. "Let go your hold," Peter had said clearly. "I've got to go." So he had, and the cleft in the rocks had closed and the last bones ground to powder.

He woke up tangled in his mosquito bar, one knee braced against the wall, wet with sweat and panting, and enough of a sahib to be already yelling and cursing his punkah boy. Immediately the white wings over his bed began to flap. He lay on his back, heard Peter's voice still ringing in his ears. He was so exhausted by his efforts to save him, he was trembling all over.

Far less superstitious than the average seaman, he did believe that that night Peter had died. And because the night was so hot and in the tropics white men do strange things, he felt tears running down his face and the slow, tearing sobs of manhood shaking him. For a man cannot cry with only his face as a woman can — he cries with his whole body. So he knew he would have to go back again, almost as a murderer must revisit the scene of his crime.

The *Victrix* was waiting for graving and she needed it. Her sails were worn — even her rigging much chafed — but he ordered her laden. He was so obviously under a compulsion to get out that immediately people were saying he must have had some secret word that the Embargo was about to be lifted. He put everything he could on the *Victrix,* sugar and spice, cotton (for Tom), bales of Canton ware, silks and camel hair. And then he'd think suddenly of five hundred pounds more of this or that. A coach-house was built on the deck to carry all he was determined he could. When his mate demurred a little at this overlading of a well-known tippy ship, Dash looked at him with cold, unseeing, wrathful eyes. "Mr. Mate, this ship can do anything I ask of her."

Yet even he knew he had stayed too long, worked too hard, in the tropics. But he did not know that he was half-hoping the *Victrix* would sink. Unable to stay longer in Bombay, he sickened at the thought of Salem.

Five months later, he was conscious of that fragrance landsmen call smelling the sea and seamen smelling the land. He had not followed the usual route through Vineyard Sound and about Cape Cod, but struck in boldly from the high seas. Therefore, he had not been reported. With that first whiff of land, he began again to long for the scentless nothingness of mid-ocean. Night and day. Sun and moon. Wind and wave — and nothing more.

The *Victrix* was struggling, heavy and dull for her, almost helpless because of the great wealth she carried. She was so clumsy she could hardly have withstood a slight blow. (He had ordered water casks lashed alongside the hull to keep her right side up.) Never a gale. And yet Dash's fantastic luck had held. There had been serene and gentle weather. To his crew, this quieting of the seas before her seemed as great a miracle as the parting of the Red Sea before Israel's hosts. He knew his people were saying it was he who had made the fair weather — not God.

As the captain brooded at the taffrail, his second (an English lad he had picked up at Calcutta and probably a British naval deserter) was showing him the log — "Even laden as she is, sir," he said reverently, "the men say she's broke the record for India to Salem via Cape Horn."

Dash had broken so many records in his seventeen years as master, he had no more interest.

"Aye, maybe. But that's only because Salem ships don't go by Cape Horn. Cape of Good Hope's our route. It's better and safer."

"Yes, sir," but the young man's eyes questioned his master. Why had he chosen the unusual, unsafe Horn route?

Dash answered absently: "Never been round the Horn. Always wanted to."

Although the *Victrix* was drawing much more than usual, the captain ordered no sails taken in. No sounding leads out. He handled a ship like a god — or a devil — these days. I'm getting too old to command, he thought. Men either get too cautious like old Captain Magee or too trustful of their luck like me. I'm setting no good example to young men these days. Too old to sail? He knew forecastle folk had been saying for years there was a curse on him. He never would be able to leave off. But now Peter was dead (for he could not rid his mind of this fantasy) there wasn't a reason why he shouldn't retire, marry Polly. Not to take her after all Peter's sacrifice would reduce everything Peter had done to futile nonsense. Surely Peter must not have died in vain.

From Fort Pickering a cannon boomed in welcome. He saw flags running up. And he saw a sight he could not have believed. The harbor was a forest of masts, but every ship was dismantled. Every mast was capped with an inverted barrel. He saw the *Wanderer* tied up at the Inman Wharf and looked about him for the harbor master to direct him. So few ships came in these days, he was not on duty. So he called for a harbor furl on his sails, yelled at the helmsman to put about, and brought the *Victrix* in to moor against the *Wanderer*.

He walked across the *Wanderer's* deck and saw the crowds gathering to welcome him. A home-come ship was a rarity these days. Actually church bells were ringing, all was hurrah and excitement.

And the first face he recognized, with a sickening feeling of relief and almost angry amazement, was Peter Inman's. And he was looking almost fit. The expression on his face was exactly what he had remembered in his dream.

❦ 8 ❦

THE *Victrix* brought in the last cargo of priceless Indy goods before the Embargo was admitted at Washington to have been a failure and was lifted. Once more the sails of America floated out across the gray Atlantic to Europe or south to the Southern Cross. The world was theirs. Again Salem shipwrights' hammers rang, men crowded the wharves signing off or signing on. Masters and mates walked the streets proudly after a year and a half near starvation. Trade would boom and commerce flourish.

By mid-April the *Victrix* would also go out, Liz Inman master. Dash himself would go as a mere passenger. He had decided to leave Salem again, go back to Bombay.

No hand had been lifted to stop him as he announced his decision. Not even Polly's hand. Dash had an uncomfortable instinctive feeling she was aware that he could face neither her nor Peter. There were moments when he felt Peter had tricked him.

For Peter had not died the night of Dash's nightmare — November 5, 1808. He had carefully remembered that date. No, indeed.

He had been woefully ill in September and October (after he had let Linda make public confession of his sins before the New Lighters gathered in Brickell's great barn), and Dash, reticent and gentlemanly by nature, felt his gorge rise at the thought of it. But by November, in the curious manner of the consumptive, he had begun to mend. So it had not been Peter's spirit caught in the cleft rock of Malabar Point that had cried out to him, had lured him back to Salem and to a stagnation and paralysis he could not face. Sometimes he thought how easy it would all be for him if only Peter really had died.

He could not bear to be woken night after night by Peter's cough from across the hall. Sometimes he would make himself stay in bed, pay no heed. Usually he went to him, although there was nothing he could do. Now, he never told him of his travels, never held him spellbound by the wonders he had seen. Yet he was a gentle nurse. He couldn't be otherwise. So he faced his scapegoat, but the stones Deuteronomy recommended to be thrown at such, Dash felt bruising his own heart. And somehow Peter had changed. He seemed not so much older as more mature. For the first time in their lives they were meeting almost as equals. Now at last they had reached a point where Peter should be free to go ahead, lead his own life, but they could not pry themselves apart. They were knotted, welded, together by the secret they shared. Dash resented the secret and had moments of resentment against Peter.

Peter stopped coughing. Dash sat on the edge of his bed, his face in his hands, waiting to see if he would begin again. Jack had told him the disease wasn't cured and never would be. Only that now Peter was so well adjusted to it, he might live for years — if he did nothing rash. Peter did not cough again. Perhaps he slept.

Why couldn't Peter have gone to Harvard, lived his own life, married Georgiana (Dash knew these two corresponded, but had not seen each other for years). Dadblast Peter Inman, presuming to bear other people's burdens! He looked back with curiosity to that night on Malabar Point when he had "known" Peter was dead, and that he had to go back to Salem. But if he had really wanted to get home, he could not have so overburdened the *Victrix*. Was there some devil of self-destruction in him that had wanted her to go down? But no. She always did what he wanted. Take that typhoon, China Sea, eight years before. He had bade her stay up, and she had. So I guess, he thought, I didn't really want to drown myself and all my men. No.

He heard Peter softly going downstairs. Dash pulled on pantaloons over his nightshirt, thrust his feet into carpet slippers, and followed him with a spindrift of anger and a deep groundswell of affection.

The side door was open. He followed him into the dewy freshness of the garden. It was the unreal hour before dawn. The most lonely God-struck hour of all on shipboard, and he thought with nostalgia of the empty cleanness of the sea. Two silent cats watched from the back-yard fence. That's my little old Robin. The old fool is still out courting. The trouble with animals is they never grow up.

Dash said, not wanting Peter to feel he had followed him, "I thought I'd stroll down to the wharf. See if the ship watcher is on duty," and, "Damn the ship watchers," he added, letting all the pent-up anger he felt at a situation he could not cope with burst out against the harmless old men. "Laziest bunch of old derelicts I ever saw. Peter, did you have a bad night?"

"No, a fine night. When I get to coughing, I often get up. And it stops. I'll walk along with you."

The streets — almost Salem itself — were drowned in fog. Dash remembered to walk slowly, but his nervous feet felt they could not.

"You're leaving on the *Victrix* in four days?"

"Oh aye — Liz will be master. Leave me at Bombay — for a little while. Make his own voyage. I've never gone as passenger before, but — well, I was getting real careless."

"I know that. But to waste two captains on one ship. You're not planning to *stay* at Bombay?"

"Maybe. God, Peter, you can't understand."

"Yes, I do."

"And Liz has to go."

"Fanny" — and Dash was thankful Peter was pushing the conversation out of shoal water — "will be heart-broken that he has bought that enormous house in Boston and leaves her to move and furnish it and she doesn't know anybody there."

Dash laughed. "He's doing it for her — I mean leaving for a while."

"For Fanny?"

"She ought to be grateful that he leaves — Liz is in a mess with a woman."

"Liz has always been in a mess with women."

"With women, yes. Not with *a* woman before. That's worse."

"I'm sorry. Fanny's so nice."

"Liz knows that. He hopes a year away and he'll get over — the other little person. And she him."

"So," Peter said slowly, "when you at last decide to retire — you choose Bombay?"

"I'll choose any place I want. I've built up a handsome business out there. And Peter" — he wanted to say it, but his voice thickened a little — "I've got to leave off commanding. For a while. Perhaps forever. Or I'll get to be just another Flying Dutchman."

The fog was so heavy from the head of Inman Wharf, they could not see the end. The *Victrix* was tied up beside it, looking indeed a phantom bark. They saw the lantern of the ship watcher. He was on his duty.

They went to the cabin, and Dash flung himself on his bunk which was more his home than any spot on earth. Peter was standing by the little washhand stand. He was looking at Dash kindly, but almost pityingly, as though he felt himself the older and wiser of the two, not with any of his former blind adoration.

"If it suits me and suits the House, why shouldn't I settle in Bombay?"

"You couldn't ever stand it for long here?"

"No," Dash admitted honestly.

"But you've got to."

"What are you talking about?"

"It won't do any good — for long — to go streaking off to the ends of the earth. You can't escape. That way."

Nor had he.

"You do a lot of fancy talking, Pete," Dash said, almost irritably.

"I've got more coming. Dash, you can't go away. You've got to stay here."

Dash was unaccustomed to the tone of command, especially from his bootlicking little brother, his humble scapegoat. And Peter looked taller, bigger, more forceful than he ever had before.

"So stay here," Peter ordered him calmly, "and face the music.

Tell the truth. Not to save me. No, I don't want it. But to save your own soul."

Dash said nothing. He was sitting on the edge of the bunk, head in hands, as he had sat so many nights — waiting to hear Peter cough.

"I've been thinking for months," Peter went on, with that unexpected ring of authority in his voice. "It was something Ma'am said. She said old stories (you remember how I was always as a child hanging about to hear her old stories) are apt to be true. If they aren't true, they get lost off in a few generations."

"What are you steering for?"

"Wait, I'm tacking, but I'm getting there. There's one story comes up again and again — there's a lot of them. It goes something like this. The Devil appears to a man and says, Swear me your soul and I'll give you heart's desire — great fortune and fair winds, the admiration of the world, the love of any woman you want, all honor the world can offer. The man gets it. But he has lost his own soul."

"Helm about."

"I was going to helm about. I don't know what happens to our souls after we die ('Sephus Hobey doesn't either!). I guess some people are born without any. But if God gave you one, you can't live without it. Dash — you can't really live unless you get back your soul again."

Dash said nothing.

"It was I," Peter said, softly, "did it to you. Dash, let's face it. I was your Mr. Scratch or Old Nick, Old Horny. We've got a dozen pet names for the Devil in New England. Anyhow, I tempted you and you fell."

"Oh, cast off."

"Don't you remember in the old stories the Devil always comes smiling and loving? So did I. For we are destroyed as much in this world by those who love us as by those who hate us. I loved you a lot." The silence was long. Peter went on: "I'll bet that's why Eve gave Adam the apple. She loved him so much she wanted him to have it. But . . . Dash, I'm not a-hinting to you any more. I'm telling you flat out. You've got to stay here and the truth has got to out."

"Peter, it's too late. And Polly's frail. It gave her brain fever when she thought it was you. It will kill her."

"All right. What of it? You're killing her by inches as it is. Dash, you can't go flying off for God knows how long. Time's come for you to face it. And you've got to go it alone, Dash." His voice burned with his old love. "Dash, I could dig the pit you fell into. I can't pull you out — that you must do. And alone — I'm leaving."

"You?"

"Last night Liz (and he's master) agreed to sign me as clerk — I bade him not tell you. But I'm going to Bombay. Dash, I don't want to be around Salem — for a while. If I was, you might think you ought to do it for me. That's not so. It's your own self you must save. In the end each of us must save his own soul. I want you to be free to do as you must — your own way. I can't go meddling in your life if I'm in Bombay."

"Bombay will kill you." Dash sprang up. "Fever and heat — endless rain. You can't."

"Yes, I can. And I will. In fact" — and there was a flicker of a smile in his eyes — "Old Doctor West says tropics and a long sea voyage will help me."

"You're talking nonsense. And even if you go, I'm not going to stay here — and dig up old corpses. What's the good?"

"Plenty good. You know, even today, if a ghost walks, country people dig up the body, drive a stake through it. So it won't walk. Stay here, Dash, and lay the ghost. And," he added gently, "be yourself once more. I've been thinking, and now I know. Stay here and accept your punishment. And be shut of it. It's the only way. For a man — a man like you — must be punished if he's earned it. If not, he goes on and on punishing himself. And that's worse. Stay."

Dash looked Peter full in the face. He seemed almost like a disembodied force, serene, wise — old as the soul of man.

He said, with savage deliberation, "Half of all this business has been your fault, Peter Inman."

"No, more'n half. I was your devil — I set the gin and spread the net."

"You tricked and pushed me into this."

"Yes, I did."

"And even now you're going on with your infernal meddling in my life. I wish you would leave me alone. One thing flat — if you go to Bombay, I don't."

"I knew you'd feel like that."

"Nobody's going to tell *me* what to do."

Peter went on inexorably. "And when you have done as you must, write me and I'll come home again. If — if Bombay works out as Doctor West says it will. Not until then. You go it alone. And there's one more thing, Dash — before I went to Lübeck — you and I went to Lübeck" — and for the first time his voice shook and his eyes faltered. He and Dash had been so happy together on the voyage to and home from Lübeck. "I told you how I made a will — admitting Petra. Making her and Dulcey my heirs. It's still in your glory hole." He lifted his chin proudly. "I'm not destroying it. If you decide that once more — now — I'm tempting you to foolish action, you can (when the time comes) take it out and probate it. But if you do — remember you've truly lost your soul."

The two brothers looked each other full in the face and Peter read Dash's expression correctly. Unsaid words hung in the air between them. Terrible words, luckily unsaid. But the worst of it from Dash's point of view was that Peter did not resent them. Peter was understanding and forgiving him — as a mother might forgive the child that cries, "I hate you."

"*Mea culpa,*" Peter said softly, and laid his hand on the clenching muscles of his brother's arm, and Dash felt his anger subside.

Chapter Eleven

~~~~~~

THE HALF OF SALEM which followed Old Doctor West was sure Peter Inman would return cured. Jack West's half shook their heads.

Gone he might be, but surely he would not quickly be forgotten, for he had left Mrs. Flanneau expecting. Three months after the departure of the *Victrix,* Peter's mistress was brought to bed.

Once again that oldest of figuring games was played all over Salem. This child's keel had been laid last November. How miserably ill Peter had been at the time, yet had had the strength to crawl out of his bed and into Mrs. Flanneau's. And only the month before that, he had been standing up in Brickell's great barn getting religion, presumably forswearing evil ways. Catching hold of God's skirts. His hold had slipped off quickly enough. That was certain.

On the Sunday in July that Doctor Hobey baptized the child, his church was crowded. The Inmans sat stolidly in their square pews, pretending it was nothing to them. Only Nanny West joined the vulgar curiosity Hobey felt corrupting his flock — she was half-standing in her anxiety to see the color of this child's hair. 'Sephus kept the tiny skull, fuzzed with white, well covered. God's house was no place for such speculations.

Mrs. Flanneau presented the child. Flanneau himself, she told Hobey with frightened eyes, was "sick." Drunk, of course. And she asked him to baptize the boy Peter. But, on such occasions, the clergyman has the last and loudest voice. In the name of Father,

Son, and Holy Ghost, he pronounced the child's name to be Jacques. That poor fellow! he thought, as he once more ascended his pulpit. His drinking bouts came closer and closer together. Flanneau had thought, handicapped as he was, that he could bear the shame of an unfaithful wife. He had overestimated his own strength, apparently. He could not. Something was going radically wrong in his complex nature.

After the fire, Flanneau had only begun to make a new start before the Embargo came to break Salem. But now, once more, ships sailed. All seemed going well with other men. Not with Flanneau. Of the dressmaking part of his trade, he did little. For one reason, ladies did not care to be fitted by a drunken sempster. Worse yet, the artist in him had been destroyed. His wife ran the shop, now little better than a thread-and-needle business. Actually the three of them (and now a mysterious fourth) were living principally on that five hundred dollars a year from the Inmans.

One August day, as Flanneau stood with brooding dignity by his own door, he saw Dash Inman walking up Essex Street. Flanneau had been telling himself he had graciously accepted Peter Inman's relationship with his wife. To this, as a business man, he had agreed. Then he had discovered it was not Peter but Dash Inman. Of course, it had been wrong of Dulcey not to have been honest with him from the start. He knew five hundred dollars was all Peter could pay, and Flanneau had always been lenient and understanding of Peter's difficulties to raise that much. But to a wealthy man like Dash, five hundred dollars was chicken feed. A wife must be frank with her husband in all business matters. If he had known it was Dash, he would never have been content with a mere five hundred. Yet morally, all had been correct. He had permitted her a lover, one lover and only one.

But this new baby — and his gorge and hatred rose to think it was named for him — whose child, in God's holy name, was that? Not Dash Inman's. He had been at sea last November. It was not Peter's. He was sure of that. Who in the name of domestic sanctity was it? Surely a man has the right to know the name of his children's father. Yet Dulcey refused to confide in him. She told him to shut up, and reminded him that it was she, not he, who supported their ménage. She with her shop and her annual allowance from the Inmans. She had said only this morning it was no business of his, and called him a "froach" because she still used Marblehead words. And he had slapped her and she had "squaelled" him with her fist. So he had come to stand upon his stoop, get a breath of fresh air, and swallow his rage and confusion.

Then he saw the author of all his shame blandly walking up Essex Street. Flanneau literally saw red as he leaped forward to accost him. He had not the least idea what he wished to say. He blew and almost spat in Dash's face and, raising shaking hands to Heaven, began a long torrent of French. Dash was handy in French, for it was the international language of world trade, but he couldn't follow him. He knew a little group of onlookers was gathering to enjoy the spectacle. Of course, they thought Flanneau drunk. If so, it was on nothing more alcoholic than his own spleen. Dash smelt no liquor on him.

"You walk Salem," Flanneau at last shouted in English, his lank gray face and protuberant bloodshot eyes not three inches from Dash's handsome nose, "like you own it. You think for five hundred dollars a man bears the shame I bear? Pah! I am an honorable man. A man of highest honor. Keep your money. Pah! I do not wish money. No."

"What do you wish?"

"What it was I knew," he went on, failing to explain anything, "but next I do not know, nor next and next. I demand to know the name of the man that has last November debauched my wife. Eh?"

Dash had no idea. "Come, Flanneau," he said kindly, "let's get inside your shop and talk this over."

"If you will admit it was you, yourself, my honor is safe, yes. It is restored to me. But if you deny . . ."

This delighted the onlookers. If Dash was the father of that baby, it was either the shortest or the longest pregnancy on record.

"If you dare deny, you are as good as saying my wife is a wanton."

"I'll deny it, fast enough," Dash said, and yet he had a troubled feeling, for wasn't he the man who really had made a wanton out of what God had intended to be some fisherman's decent wife?

"You have dared to say it?" Flanneau screamed, jumping with rage. "You say my wife is a woman of loosenesses!"

Then, being a Frenchman and a sempster by trade and unused

to using his fists, he stamped on Dash's toe and would have slapped him if Dash had not caught his wrist. Dulcey could knock Flanneau down at pleasure. In Dash's powerful hands he was as impotent as a rag baby. His attack was like that of a woman, and the next moment, like a woman, he burst into tears.

Dulcey had been drawn to the door by her husband's screams and sobs and by the laughter of the spectators. Now she turned and called for Petra. She was always sending Petra to "bring papa home."

The child walked calmly down the front path, followed by a small white dog.

"Papa," she said, going to him. Her voice was as cold and clear as ice. Against the sordid background of her family life, the coarse scene she had been sent to end, she seemed untouched and untouchable. She had a patrician beauty unrelated to the woman who had borne her or the queer man whose name she bore. The onlookers made way for her respectfully and stopped laughing at her father. Some immediately moved off, down the street.

"Papa," she said again. This time he heard her, stopped in the middle of a sentence and looked down at the cold little face staring reprovingly up at him. Before she could even give him a command, he bolted for his own door, cringing and sick with shame.

Petra stood for a moment looking after him. Then she stopped and patted the little dog that had followed her.

"What kind of dog is that, Petra?" Dash asked, for now the two of them stood alone.

"Caniche," she said proudly. It was a killing little dog, slow, dignified, and already very old. It was anyone's guess what breed it was. It was curly as a lamb and had the intelligent dignity of the poodle which, in French, Petra was claiming that it was. But not the legs. It had almost no legs and the clown's ears of a Maltese.

Dash looked at the dog critically, trying not to laugh. "It is what we used to call a 'popcorn dog' when I was a boy. I had one something like it."

"It is *not* a popcorn dog," she flashed at him a little angrily, "and his name is Chien Caniche. Because that's French for poodle."

"I guess you're right, Petra." He knew he must not belittle her dog. He was almost afraid of her airiness, littleness, formidable strength. "I was wrong. It doesn't look at all like a popcorn dog."

She accepted his apology with a faint smile.

"Is he a French dog?"

"No. American."

"But he has a French name."

"Oh . . . " She had not thought of this before. Although her papa talked French to her, she did not like it. She wanted to be an American girl and talk only English. "I could change his name. He wouldn't care. I might call him 'Popcorn.' Popcorn," she said slowly, staring down at him to see if he liked it.

The dog jumped against her and gave a microscopic bark. He never barked louder than this. Some untended laryngitis, or embedded bone in his long-past puppyhood, had disabled his bark.

Dash had never spoken to Petra before. He was loath to leave her. Yet it was not as his child he saw her, flesh of his flesh, bone of his bone. She seemed to him more the soul of Peter's soul.

"He is *my* dog," she added, a little hostilely, as though she had felt something proprietary in the fine dark eyes fastened so soberly on her and her pet. The dog was drooling and wagging with admiration and love.

"Where did you get him?"

"Peter Inman gave him to me."

"I'm Peter Inman's brother."

"Write him to come back soon."

"I'll do the best I can." But not one letter had he written Peter.

"He left me Chien Caniche to walk with me. He said until he came back I wouldn't be alone because I'd have Chien Caniche."

Dash could think of nothing more to say to her. Now that she had decided to take her dog for a walk, she drew a blue satin ribbon from her pocket and tied it to his collar. It was only a symbol binding the two together. Chien Caniche was never farther than three feet from her. So these two, the one so young and springy, the other so old and stiff, had walked together ever since Peter left, week after week, month after month.

Nice children were not allowed to speak to Petra, much less play with her, but they watched and admired. Eyes always straight ahead, slipping lightly, silently, through the streets of Salem, alone except for Chien Caniche. Many pitied the child, but they did not need to, for they had forgotten how much company a dog may be.

And, in her imagination, Peter was just around the next corner. Any moment she might find him. She held long conversations with him. So she pretended a happiness for herself and Peter and her dog greater than any of the three had ever known.

She would pass through Washington Square, often filled with her own little cousins, their nurses and mamas. Thomasina and Thomas, Sarahlee Inman, Boots, Ruthie, Dorcas, and Phineas West. That summer Jack West had bought his children a goat and goat cart. Then the Inmans' Becky had rigged a cart and harness for old Davy Jones. Davy had at last come into his own and was a household pet. Two years before, Little Joe had committed his last theft —the carcass of a chicken from the kitchen table. And there on the kitchen floor he had choked to death, unmourned but certainly not forgotten. Davy, feeling the coast cleared of his old enemy, began inching himself into the house. First he asked if he might not have his meals in the kitchen. Linda said it was easier than carrying his food out to his kennel, now that Little Joe was not there to scold if he as much as put his nose into the house. When snows fell or rains came, he'd knock modestly at the back door. A cold kennel, he seemed to say, is all right for a young dog, but mighty hard for an elderly gentleman. Linda couldn't refuse. And even the cats liked Davy.

From the kitchen it took him almost a year to get up his courage to intrude into the front part of the house and go upstairs. He was thirteen years old before he felt that greatest ecstasy a dog may feel, coming in wet and muddy and rolling on a bed. Then he found his way to the nursery, and it was here his genius lay. For it was not to catch thieves Davy had been designed by his maker, but to care for, comfort, and amuse very small children. He lay in Paradise before the nursery hearth in winter and went to Washington Square to pull a cart or permit children to ride on him.

Sometimes the little cousins quarreled. Thomasina and Thomas insisted Davy was superior to any smelly old goat. The small Wests, led by Boots, defended their pet. Then Petra would pass by with her nonchalant little dog. What were goats and big clumsy Newfoundlands to them then? All they wanted was a Chien Caniche to lead about on a blue satin ribbon. It was in vain nurses and mothers told them that that "dreadful girl" was coming. They must not speak to her. They were to act as if she did not exist. But she fascinated them. They did not despise her as they were supposed to do. They looked up to her. There was something compelling, complete, about everything she did, the turn of her head, her gestures. She never hung about the small Wests begging for a goat ride, or small Inmans asking to be allowed to try her bonnet on Davy Jones, as did all the other children. She never glanced in their direction. Her little dog never paused to smell of Davy or bark at the goat. He, too, kept on and on and on without pausing or looking back. Petra's quick gait and eager eyes promised that where she was going were such delights as no other child in Salem could dream of. So she passed and passed through Salem and everybody surreptitiously watched her. Dash watched her, too.

He rarely spoke to her. She would not talk with him any more freely than with other fellow townsmen. No matter what conversation he brought up, she always asked only for Peter. Peter had been sick, he told her. He had gone a long way off to grow well again. Then he would come back.

The *Victrix* had been gone for over a year. It had taken four months for her to get to Bombay and five months more before the first letter came back. Liz planned eventually to sell the agency and yards, but first he would build them up so they would fetch top price. He was sending the *Victrix* to the Dutch Indies to collect spices, sugar, and coffee. He had sent a chartered vessel to Mocha for coffee, goat skins, and horses. Peter, too, wrote in a poetic ecstasy which might mean better health or higher fever or delight in seeing the world. Liz was sending him out with the *Victrix*. He did not write to Dash, only to his grandmother.

When the Crowninshields' *Favorite* cleared for Bombay, Dash wrote him six letters and every one he tore up. In spite of his promise to Petra, he did not urge him to come back again.

His mother was sure Old Doctor West was right. New England winters had been killing the boy. Other young men before this had cured their lungs in tropic climes. So she told Dash. He did not dampen her optimism. Perhaps in time he came to share it. For now he had made up his mind. If Peter came home helped or possibly cured, he'd certainly once and for all admit the truth. Then from being a pariah, Peter would be looked upon as the most unselfish of men, wickedly put upon by an older brother. Dash would stick out his lower lip, square his shoulders. He could take it — and leave for Bombay.

If Peter did not come back, surely nothing was gained by blabbing. For Peter's sake he might confess. Not to save his own soul. The business about saving one's soul was part of Peter's romanticism. Nothing to it. Yet there it was, forever biting at his own uneasy conscience.

He had become a fatalist. If one thing happened, he would act so; if another, so. Peter still ruled his life.

With Polly he was most conscious of the burden of guilt upon him. Polly — the lovely reward for all he had done — or Peter had done. Or permitted Peter to do. Or had done to Peter. Polly was always talking about Peter. Poor Peter, she would say with her eyes fastened sadly on his face. Sometimes he felt a remorse so intense it was almost physical pain. And she often hurt him. Her power to hurt him (as she talked of Peter) was one of the things that bound him to her. He wanted his own secret Golgotha.

He did not turn to younger, healthier women, even if Doctor West was saying he doubted Polly would ever be strong enough for a normal woman's life. Dash knew all this was nonsense. Polly accepted her semi-invalidism with patience, but it always seemed to Dash as though it were a part she was playing on a stage rather than anything real.

There was a certain opprobrium fastening upon Polly. If she might never marry, she shouldn't keep a man like Dash Inman, Salem's most eligible bachelor, dangling after her. She shouldn't go to balls and still be the most graceful, beautiful, and most living woman on the floor — and then go home and collapse for four days in bed. By now she should be ready to retire into spinsterhood. Leave the field to younger women. And why on earth didn't she fade? She was thirty-two. She should have the tact to fade. But she did not.

Dash's devotion to Miss Mompesson seemed most honorable. Very gallant. He had not dropped her because she wasn't strong, probably might never marry him. His devotion was as romantic as the last French novel and yet very Yankee — to be so stubborn in his steadfastness.

❧ 2 ❧

PETRA WOKE knowing her papa was in the room. She could smell the liquor and she could feel Popcorn stiffen as he lay beside her, hear him growl. When Flanneau told her to put on her clothes and walk with him, she did not hesitate. It was late August and very hot. Before this, he had called her from her bed to bear him night company. She was not in the least afraid of him, although she knew her mother always hid Jacques when he was "like this." Her mother feared he might harm the baby — he hated it so. But of course he would do anything Petra told him.

She could hardly remember the times he had taken her to taverns, kissed her, pinched her, and bitten her until someone had taken her away from him. But the night she had been carried to Peter and he had given her Wren, she remembered well. Papa had drowned Wren. But now that she was a big girl, he'd never dare touch Popcorn. Then, too, Popcorn could growl.

Papa was talking French. She hated French. Lately she always refused to talk French to him.

"Get up, now, ma chère petite, get up and go with the Papa. Yes?"

"If you want, Papa." She sleepily got into her clothes. Once she stopped to scold her dog, who had growled steadily since Papa came into her room.

Flanneau walked her first to Washington Square. The night air seemed wonderfully cool and fresh after the hot little bedroom. Her spirits began to rise and she felt wide awake. He was pausing before the Inman house. There it stood, so white and huge in the bright white moonlight. The night was so still not a leaf rustled.

"Sometime it will be the dear God Himself will lean to you and He will say, in his dreadful voice, 'Little girl, whose little girl are you?' Then it is you must answer God truthfully."

She was bored. "I'll say I'm your little girl, Papa."

"Ah, no, no, no. That is my sorrow. It is that which eats at me. That you must not say. If He asks you who is your father, you are to say —— "

"Peter. Peter is my father."

"That will be a lie before God. Although I believe God would forgive your ignorance. Still, it is better you go to Him knowing exactly what to say. Now listen." He shook her. "Do not forget. You say, 'Dash Inman is my father, Lord.'"

She turned on him angrily. "Papa, it isn't true."

"Yes."

"But I won't have anyone but Peter."

Flanneau was almost happily rubbing his dry hands. "Peter! Pah! Peter is nothing to you, nor you to him. You have been mistold. It is Dash who is your father. And if God asks you, you are not to forget."

She was frozen where she stood. "All right, Papa, I won't forget."

Popcorn put his paws on her. She looked down and saw his, to her, pleasing face in the moonlight.

"Popcorn," she said, thoughtfully, "you're not a popcorn dog." She had not quite taken in what Flanneau had said to her. "Papa, I'm going to go back and call him Chien Caniche."

"It does not matter, ever, what you call your little dog."

At last he was speaking English, which was always a relief to her. They went down to the wharves. There was every reason why anyone so foolish as to fancy a night ramble would go to the wharves. The moon was enormous upon the sea. The rigging, masts, even the hulls, seemed beaten out of silver. First they went to Crowninshields' Wharf, but two ships were in. They veered away when they saw the lanterns of the shipwatchers. They went to White's. Here also a ship was in. At Union they almost ran into the town watch. They turned and trudged back up Derby Street until they came to Inmans'. Not a ship was in except old *Mermaid* in the graving yard. She needed no watching. Caniche was going slowly and hopelessly, not at all with his usual daytime aplomb. He could not bark, but he whined and gave his little cough. Petra was growing sleepy, but it was as if the dog felt a danger the overself-confident child did not. Peter had taken her here, she remembered, and they had gone rowing or sailing. When her papa said they would take a rowboat ride, she was pleased.

They crawled down the slimy ladder, pulled in the painter, and dropped into a dory. Caniche stood above them at the head of the ladder, a halo of moonlight about his white woolly fleece, and tried desperately to bark.

"Oh, Papa, you are so silly you've forgotten the oars. Peter keeps oars under the counting-house."

"Mon Dieu, the poor head aches and aches and cannot think." The tide was going out, pulling at the rowboat. Flanneau went back to the counting-house. He returned and dropped his heavy burden in the boat. There was a clank of chains. Then he untied the painter.

Caniche almost barked in his despair.

"Papa, wait. Caniche wants to go with us."

"No, no. Nothing . . . no one shall share our last moments together. Our last trip."

She was glad it was to be a last trip. Her papa had not brought any oars, after all. He didn't know a thing about boats and she was enough of a Salem child to look down upon such nautical ignorance.

"You didn't get the oars?"

"We need none for the trip we are taking. The tide will carry us far."

There was truth in that. The dory was rapidly leaving the wharf. She felt sorry for her dog standing so forlorn at the ladder-head, so white and shining in the moonlight and unable to bark.

Flanneau went on in a torrent of French. But she was not listening. What he had told her about her parentage had not really impressed her yet.

"Papa," she interrupted him, "please don't talk French. If you talk French, I'll put my hands over my ears and not listen." She did so.

He was sorting the chains and things he had taken from below the counting-house.

"Papa" — her hands came off her ears, and for the first time she had a sudden tingling awareness of danger. "Papa, why have you all those ropes and things? What are you going to do with the anchor?"

He lifted his face, and at the sight of it, emphasized and exaggerated in the moonlight, all her nonchalance vanished. It was the face of a devil. He did not answer her question, but was creeping toward her. Now she could not see his face, but the memory of it increased her horror.

"Papa — keep away from me! Go away! I want to go home!"

She was frozen with terror when nothing but serenity, courage, could have saved her.

"It is right that we go together."

"Don't come near me! Mind what I say! You're tipping the boat!"

"Don't fear, little one. Your papa has always loved you. And you have loved the poor papa, yes, more than Peter, yes. It is so. Is it not?"

"No, no!" she cried. "I hate you! I hate you! I hate you! Don't! Don't!" She was hysterical with the knowledge that she had lost all power over him.

He had knotted ropes about himself and fastened the anchor chain to them. The anchor was already balanced on the gunwale. He paused, looking at her thoughtfully. Surely he would not need to rope her. He could hold her in his arms. One long, last embrace.

She saw the long arms sneaking toward her, the encumbered, crouching figure about to fling itself upon her. Once again in the moonlight she saw his terrible face.

"The world has been cruel to you, my poor angel, and cruel to me. Together we shall turn our backs upon it. Spit upon it, yes?"

Then she screamed. How could such little lungs, such a tiny throat, form such a volume of sound. The rowboat had drifted a hundred yards from the wharf. There were three terrible screams before Flanneau got his hand over her mouth. The anchor splashed. The calm sea closed over the heads of the man and child. Caniche trembled and coughed and finally jumped from the head of the ladder. The rowboat filled and slowly righted.

It was two o'clock, but Madam Inman was still dressed and downstairs. Sitting up, dozing over a book, she was more apt to go to sleep than if she went to bed. As usual, it was the Bible she held on her knee, but she had been thinking of Peter. Dreaming of him. It was not the face of the grown man that she had before her eyes, but Peter as a little boy. The red cheeks, the crisp, dark curls, the slow, engaging smile, the serenity of the eyes. It was not she who had picked him from among his brothers and sisters to be her favorite. He had picked her. He had always been running away from his house to hers. There he would be at the kitchen door. "I've come calling, Grandma." Then he'd sit as she peeled apples and told him old stories. He never refused cookies from the pantry jar, or the barley candy she kept for children in the silver pitcher in the sitting room. But it was not for such things that he stayed. He stayed because, as he said, he loved her, and he loved what he had called her "conversation."

She still had the blue cooky jar in the pantry and the barley sugar candy in the sitting room, for other children who came. Only yesterday lordly Boots West had said, as he took some candy, "Why does great-granddame keep candy in a pitcher? Mama . . . don't you think it is a funny place to keep candy?"

The banshee scream woke her from her reveries. She stood paralyzed, then ran to her front door. There were two more screams, and from her own wharf. She hurried over the cobbles, calling for shipwatchers as she went.

"Jarden! Jarden! Pickman! Brown!" she cried, forgetting there was no Inman ship in. The old shipwatchers were sleeping at home that night. The wharf was deserted, and almost as light as day, so enormous was the moon. There were no more screams, but all up and down Derby Street windows were going up, doors flying open, voices calling back and forth. The years had dimmed her eyes and ears. She saw the empty dory, but not the little figure clinging to it. Nor did she hear the choking gasps.

Others had. Two young seamen rushed past her, throwing off their clothes as they ran, diving off the wharf. She saw their heads dark against the moonlit water and the white flash of their long strokes. When they reached the dory, one of them yelled back to the shore, "It's a child!"

It had been years since old Madam Inman had climbed down a slippery, slimy ladder from the floor of the wharf to sea level. Now she did. The sailors were approaching. Holding on with one hand, she reached out to receive the rescued child. That face! That mop of dark curls!

"Why . . . Peter," she said in wonder.

People said later it was the sailors' fault. They should have recognized Old Lady Inman, known the burden they handed her would be too heavy for her. The child's arms went about her neck, pulled her from the ladder.

It was nothing to fish them both out of the shallow water, for by now there were many about to help. Madam Inman was joined by her faithful dwarf, Rose, and by her boarder. Although she was shaking and shivering from the shock of her immersion, she was saying that it was nothing. And what was that white thing floating about in the water? Had the little girl lost her hat? So Chien Caniche was also rescued.

Rose and Doctor Hobey supported Madam Inman the few yards to her house. She was put to bed with hot grog and hot bricks for her feet. She seemed exhilarated and talked a good deal, laughed easily and moved restlessly all night. Her two friends sat up with her. She would not relax.

Wrapped in warm blankets, followed by Chien Caniche, coughing in his minute but distinguished way, Petra was carried back to Mrs. Flanneau. The child answered the questions put to her readily, told how Papa had come to her room and suggested a walk. They had first gone around the corner to Washington Square. But she said nothing of what he had told her of her parentage. They had walked to Inman Wharf. He had taken ropes and an anchor, but no oars. He wouldn't let her dog go with them. And she had felt sorry for her dog. But of the terrible conversation in French, she said nothing.

Next day she seemed none the worse for her half-drowning. By then, Madam Inman was delirious. She even thought sometimes that she had swum out and rescued the child. Half the time she thought the child was Peter.

❧ 3 ❧

AT FIRST they tried to convince her that the child had not been Peter.

"Why, bless me, no," Madam Inman would agree. "Peter's a grown man now. And it was a little girl, wasn't it? I remember the feel of her wet frock."

Although she really knew it wasn't Peter, as soon as she weakened and went off again into her vagaries, she kept congratulating herself that it was he whom she had saved. She was rational a good deal of the time and completely clear in her head about her business. Her mind was sound when at last she signed the papers which ended forever the old House of Inman and created the new firm.

Then she'd doze off and come up wondering how poor little Peter had been left to drown in the harbor. "Lucy is very careless about Peter," she would say. "He is a delicate boy and should not be allowed to go swimming in the middle of the night." But as soon as she was fully awake, she was at first quite sensible.

Her lungs began to fill. Her old heart trembled, paused, and yet went on. On the third day, Old Doctor West and Young Doctor West for once agreed. She could not last long. She had begun the terrible breathing which, in pneumonia, often means the end. Yet the slight, worn body was strong. Day after day she lived through suffocation, exhaustion, and agony. She was in most ways sensible enough. She knew which of her grandchildren were to have which of the ancient silver porringers or black family portraits. She took great comfort in 'Sephus Hobey and his many mansions and promises of a risen life.

Marcy was too disturbed, too frightened, and, although now a young woman of twenty, too young to cope with the situation. Out back in the necessary, down in the kitchen trying to help Rose prepare a gruel her grandmother could eat, Marcy cried without ceasing. She cried for her grandmother and she cried for all flesh that withers and dies. The weeping girl could not be trusted more than a few minutes in the death chamber. She had always been rather disturbing to her grandmother. Now, as soon as she entered her room, her mouth began to square and her eyes to fill. 'Sephus Hobey, watching her, would gesture at her to get out.

Madam Inman asked oftener and oftener for Peter. Had he suffered so much from his near-drowning that he, too, lay sick and at death's door? Her own approaching end she accepted, but Peter, she felt, was too young to die. For she had gone back firmly to her delusion that the child was Peter.

Marcy, her face swollen, her eyes blind with tears, was blundering homeward down Essex Street. Passing the Flanneau house, she noticed the black crêpe on the door. There in the yard, looking no worse for her recent ducking, was Petra. She wore a blue linen dress with a white collar. Her dark hair was tied on top of her head with a red ribbon. She was idly throwing a ball for her little dog to return to her. She looked almost more like Peter than Peter himself.

"Petra," said Marcy, "come with me."

"No, thank you."

"Petra, why, you know me."

"No," said Petra coldly.

"But why won't you? If you'll come with me I'll give you a cake. I'll give you a barley animal." She put her hand to her throat. "I'll give you this locket. Please, Petra."

"Thank you very much. No, thank you."

Petra knew Marcy Inman, but the urgency in the familiar voice, the signs of weeping, revolted the hard heart of childhood. She held out firmly that she did not know her and would not go with her. What had started as the merest whim with Marcy grew to direst necessity. She was determined to bring Petra to Ma'am. Ma'am would see nothing but the head, the stiff boyish collar. And once you took off that hair ribbon and brushed the hair back over her shoulders as even little boys often wore it, Ma'am would die happy, thinking she had seen Peter and that he was well. To accomplish this kind purpose Marcy was ready to use force. She almost hated the child for the havoc which, one way or another, she had brought into her family. But for her Ma'am would now be as well as ever.

"Don't you know who saved your life, you horrid little rat?" she exclaimed, stamping her foot. "You've got to come and thank her."

Petra looked at her. Perhaps she remembered the last time she had seen so naked a face. She picked up her worsted ball, called to Caniche, and started to go inside.

"Petra . . . Petra . . ." Marcy put a hand on her shoulder.

Petra had been upset by what she had been through. Usually she would have shaken off the hand and kept on going. Now it took minutes for her protest to form itself. At last she gave a long, heart-breaking wail.

"What's about?" a cheerful voice called from inside the house. "Good morning, Miss Marcy." It was Captain Obrian. Now that he had left the Derbys and was once more an Inman captain, he always exchanged greetings with her. He came out the back door and stood beside them. Petra ran to him, sobbing.

"I wanted . . ." said Marcy, in a shaking voice, "I wanted Ma'am to see her 'fore she dies." And she explained the confusion in the dying woman's mind. "And Petra *won't*, Captain Obrian. I can't make her."

"I can. Petra, do you want to go walking with Danny?"

"Yes."

"Now I'll hold one hand and Miss Marcy the other and Caniche can come along behind and pick up anything we drop."

"Thank you. I don't think so."

"But Miss Marcy is a very old friend of mine." His narrow blue eyes flashed to her sidewise. "You love everybody I love, don't you, Petra?"

And so he got her started. Suddenly she, who had walked the streets so much alone, seemed happy to have such distinguished company. She laughed and chatted, and her dog, forgetting his usual sobriety, coughed joyfully at her heels. So they came to Ma'am's black old house at the head of the wharf. Danny's eyes noticed that the house flag on the counting-house was not at half-mast yet. They sat in the living room and Petra ate candy from the silver pitcher and cookies from the blue cooky jar. She was quite ready to leave Danny and go upstairs with Marcy.

The terrible breathing grew louder as they approached the room. Tom and Dash were there, Lucy Inman, Nanny, Miranda, both doctors, Rose, and the kind old woman who went out to nurse. They all turned and stared at Marcy and the little girl.

"Grandma," Marcy said, "Peter has come to thank you. You can see how well he is."

She pushed the child in front of her against the bed so her skirts would not show. Madam Inman smiled even as the roaring breath went in and out.

"It's Peter, Grandma. Don't you remember? You swam out and saved his life."

She looked at Petra sweetly. "It's a . . . ver . . . pretty little . . . girl. But whoever . . . told you . . . it was Peter lied, my dear."

Petra was only slightly abashed by the deathbed scene which would haunt her whole life. Her quick eyes had taken in every detail.

She said, with no prompting from Marcy, "Thank you very much for not letting me drown, Ma'am."

"Thank you for coming to see me." Madam Inman sank back and closed her eyes. She was glad she had saved such a nice pretty little girl.

Marcy took her hand. "Grandma," she said, "I guess you're right. It wasn't Peter. But it is Peter's daughter."

"Peter's daughter."

"Yes, Grandma."

The old woman's eyes opened and fastened on the child's face. "Perhaps yes, and perhaps not," she said to Petra. "My dear, nobody but God can save Peter and it was God who saved you. Not I."

Next morning folk stopped in the street to count the tolling of the passing bell. Old Clerk Fessenden could be seen running up the Inman flag before the counting-house, navy with a broad white diagonal. It went to the top and fluttered down to half-mast. The other house flags, all over the waterfront, fluttered down to half-mast, Derby and Forrester, Perkins and Pickman and Crowninshield. The ships' flags followed them, and there were many ships in the harbor that day. Old Madam Inman was dead.

~ 4 ~

Madam Inman was carried to her tomb in the old-fashioned manner, on the shoulders of men, and every bearer had commanded an Inman ship. Every one was an East Injun captain. There were three on either side, and behind them walked two more to spell them. Over the coffin was a black velvet and silver pall. Carriages followed. Most of Salem was there. Children from the schools and poor paupers from Charity House, foremast hands with their varnished hats and checked shirts.

Marcy, among the chief mourners, was in the first carriage. She saw the burdened men slowly approaching the tomb. It had been built only this last year. The name Inman had been cut on it, but not a single date. The earth which covered the little secret stairs leading down to the vault had been shoveled away and the iron door was open. Since her grandmother had died, Marcy had stopped crying. For two weeks she had had nothing but lugubrious thoughts. But the day was beautiful, the most beautiful of September days. Oh, how bright and pretty a day! A lovely day for a funeral. She took a deep breath of the fresh air and felt better.

But the sight of the men with their burden descending the granite steps chilled her. Grandma couldn't have weighed much of anything at the end. It was the heavy lead that wrapped her. She had a vision of the unendingness of this procession, going on and on into the tomb. One Inman after another. Ma'am first, as was appropriate, for she was the last of her generation, her mother, and then her own generation. She got to herself, and this thought depressed her most of all. She sniffed, but no more tears came.

The black-clad bearers were reappearing like trolls out of a mine. They all looked like reprieved people. They had been a brief moment underground with death itself, but for a little while they were allowed to return to sky and earth, warmth, light, and sun, feel the soft air blowing in off the sea. Marcy looked to see who they were who had been thus reprieved. There had been much talk about who should be the bearers, but she had not listened. Of course, Dash and Tom. Their distant cousin, Captain Dick Crowninshield. Old Captain Magee and Captain Locker. Captain Billy Bates. And the eighth one . . . it couldn't be, and yet, yes, it was — Captain Obrian. At the church Captain Gibault, who was to have been the eighth bearer, had asked to be excused. His bad knee was bothering him. Dash, seeing Dan Obrian's solemn face and remembering his grandmother's interest in him and his devotion to her, had asked him to take Captain Gibault's place. He had not had a moment to consult his family. If he had had, it would not have been so arranged.

Dan had the misfortune to be related to many of Salem's humbler citizens. Even as he emerged from the tomb, one of the grave-diggers was trying to remind him of this fact. His handsome face darkened, there was an ugly look on his mouth.

Marcy thought, Danny shouldn't have carried Grandma. He is a snob. He isn't fit to. For years she had felt vaguely sorry for the time he had disgraced her and she had disgraced him and they both had worn grass skirts. Then she had written that dreadful first novel. Lord Everfast had looked like Dan Obrian. Only three days before she had walked with him from Essex Street to Derby, with the family "disgrace" between them, and he had got Petra started with that silly joke of his about her loving everyone he loved. Yet, as she went on staring at him and disapproving of him, she felt a tiny prickle of awareness. The sun glittered on his heavy silvery-blond hair, his rugged face turned proudly away from the gravedigger's importuning. His blue eyes were hidden by lashes that not even Lord Everfast could equal. He was taller, broader, than any of the other men.

'Sephus Hobey, in his black gown, was pronouncing the last words. Soon the iron gate would shut, the little stairway vanish, gone until the next family funeral. She remembered her grandmother telling her the story of "little table come, little table go." So would this little stairway come and go through the years.

Now the family would return to the home of the deceased, eat the funeral meats, and hear the reading of the will. She did not want to go. There was a slight reshuffling among the carriages. The Crowninshields were taking in the member of their family who had been a bearer and had therefore arrived on his own feet. The Derbys were taking in Captain Magee. Dash and Tom had shouldered off together. Seven of the bearers had disappeared. Dan Obrian was left.

"Mother," Marcy cried, in excitement, "Captain Obrian hasn't a ride."

"A *ride?* Can't he walk to wherever he is going?" It had not pleased her that such an honor had been done to the son of Raggity-Meg.

"But he's left all alone."

"Not as much alone as he ought to have been left," said Miranda starchily.

"Where do bearers go after funerals?"

"Home, of course, if they are not close kin."

"Do we all — all close kin — have to go back to the house and hear the will and eat?"

"Of course."

"Mother, I can't do it. I can't. And I won't. If I eat anything, I'll throw it up."

"Oh, hush yourself, Marcy. Don't begin to make *more* trouble. You must learn to consider *other* people. I think a lot of the things people do at funerals — and that goes for weddings, too — are foolish, but it takes less *energy* to go along with them than fight them. Of course you have to go."

"I want to get out and walk. It's this shut-up carriage and the smell of black crêpe. I think I'm going to be sick."

"Marcy, if you are too upset you can go home now."

"Thank you."

"Dear, pull the black veil over your face and just go home quietly and rest. I know things like this bother you. I used to mind awfully when I was your age. But there — the nearer you get to the grave, the more hardened you are to it, luckily. I know how you will miss your dear grandmother."

Marcy felt hypocritical for all the tears she had shed. She knew that no more than half of them were for a loved person lost. The rest had been for the mortality of man and for herself. Out on Brown Street she decided to go back once more to the grave. She had a morbid compulsion really to see with her own eyes "little table go." Actually see the steps filled with earth and the sods reset.

On her way she met Dan Obrian. He planned to pass her with nothing more than a bow. The black crêpe that hung upon her did not invite a more intimate approach. But she stopped him. Her hands went to her heart, much as the hands of her heroines often went to their hearts.

"Captain Obrian, I want to thank you. I'm speaking for my entire family. I want to thank you so much for all the . . . work you did for us today."

He could hardly follow her exaggerated thinking.

"Of course, you are so strong it wouldn't seem like much to you." Her eyes were glued to the great spread of his shoulders.

"Oh, Miss Marcy, it was nothing but honor to me. The greatest honor of all my life. I don't think I deserved it, but I was standing by — and Dash saw me. That was all."

"You were so very good" — and her rich voice trembled — "I wanted to tell you."

She pushed aside the black crêpe through which she had been speaking, with expressive black-kid hands. Her face was quite white and the lingering hazel eyes looked enormous. With the years had passed her unfortunate overplumpness. The fastidiousness of the bony structure of her face, characteristic of her breeding, was at last fully apparent. Perhaps she would never be as handsome for a woman as her brothers were for men. The pattern of broad mouths, short, slightly aquiline noses, square chins, high cheekbones, produced amazingly good-looking men, and merely good-looking women — until Petra had come along and proved how it might be etherealized. There was nothing ethereal about Marcy, but Captain Obrian was not unmoved by this sudden parting of the black curtains of mourning and the emergence of this vivid, passionate, woman's face.

He spoke from his whole heart as they walked down the street toward Washington Square together. He told her of his first meeting with Madam Inman. He said all the merchants in Salem had agreed that they wouldn't be bothered with boys swimming off the wharves. King Derby had begged that she, too, would post her wharf — the boys were such a nuisance. "Why, Mr. Derby," she had said, "these boys have to learn to swim somewhere, don't they? Who's going to sail our ships ten, twenty, years from now? It's these boys. And I always hate to ship a lad that can't swim." Danny hadn't forgotten. He hadn't forgotten when he was thirteen or fourteen and home from his first voyage — he'd seen her struggling with some enormous big ledgers, trying to get them down the stairs of her counting-house. He'd carried them for her. "And she asked me in to sit, and talked to me. You can't imagine what it meant to a poor boy. She didn't tip me. She gave me barley candy out of a silver pitcher, and she said I was a good boy and that sometime I'd be a captain."

So he talked of her grandmother. "She always called me 'Danny,'" he added, as they stood at last by her front door. He told her how it was her grandmother who had persuaded him to cut off his tarred pigtail. "She was always good to me," he said, thoughtfully. "Dash, too. But at first Dash was always after me to go farther than I was born to. But while he and I were out over the Embargo, he gave up. He sets a powerful store on book learning."

"Book learning!" Marcy laughed as scornfully as though she had never seen a book. "Ha, ha!"

"Ha, ha, ha!"

She fingered the latch of the gate. To ask him in at such a time she must not.

"Tell me," she begged, "just one more thing about Grandma. I think the things you say about her are so much more important than what Doctor Hobey said in church."

"She was the finest woman and the kindest and the wisest I ever knew," he went on, willingly.

Why, she thought, as long as people feel so about her, she is not really dead at all. She's still alive — inside all of us who knew her. The grave did not seem to have its victory and the sting was drawn from death.

"Captain Obrian," she said suddenly, "where do bearers go after a funeral?"

"Close kin to the deceased's house."

"Mother said I needn't."

"Folk like me" — he smiled broadly and every tooth was perfect — "we go and get a drink."

"May I presume," she began, in the stiff manner of the well-brought-up young lady, "to invite you in? And *I* will give you a drink."

His eyes narrowed. To Marcy he was as attractive as ever, but there was something a little calculating in his caution.

"Yes, Miss Marcy," he admitted, softly, "you might."

The house was utterly empty, for the servants had gone to Ma'am's to help Rose with the funeral meats. It didn't seem quite like her house, so empty, silent, mysterious. Her heart began to beat hard. That queer bright look he had given her before he had accepted her invitation had told her that he, as well as she, knew she should not have asked him in. Now was not the time. She knew it. And Danny was not the right man.

She went to the dining room to fetch a decanter and glasses and then to the kitchen. Davy Jones's tail thumped a welcome, but he was nowadays too lazy to get up and greet her. There, surrounded by a promising batch of fall kittens, was dear little old Robin, the calico cat who had been to Japan. Marcy flung herself on the floor beside the rocking chair and buried her face in the warm mass of soft, purring fur. "Oh, Robin," she cried, "it's wrong and I shouldn't." Robin purred more loudly.

She got to her feet and thought wildly of running out the back door to Ma'am's house to join her protecting family. She couldn't — any more than a fly can leave treacle. She had, but not as suddenly as she believed, fallen desperately in love with Dan Obrian. "I've got to go through with it, Robin," she whispered. "I can't stop. No, I can't stop."

Resolutely she prepared her silver tray. Now she must return to him, put aside the beloved dead, give the lie to the black which hung upon her, disgrace the sad, silent house. It was with more a feeling of fatalism than of joy that she returned to Dan Obrian.

Her green eyes did not flash — they were wide open and sober
as she gazed at the face she could not help but love. Many women
in many climes, including Salem, had loved that face and coarsened,
not refined, it with their love. He was very conscious of her. He
liked her generous size, the animal daring she had always had.
Her black became her marvelously. I don't know why she has
taken to me so suddenly. He had made love to so many women
who did not speak English, he had grown clever at reading a
woman's eye. Gosh, he thought, I can certainly get the girls without even half-trying. So he took his seat beside her on the couch.

"Marcy" — and for the first time he did not call her "miss" —
"I've always wanted to thank you for being so good to me that first
— and last — time I came to this house. Do you remember, I came
here for a ball? Scared! — I've never been so scared at sea."

"And I've always wanted to apologize to you. Mother was so
mad at all of us. It was my fault. I'll never forget those straw
skirts."

Dan threw back his head and laughed. "Ha, ha, ha! Forget
them? I laugh every time I think of them."

He jumped lightly to his feet. His hips were slim and trim in
contrast to the vast chest and great shoulders. He began to sway.
Hands and arms flowed about him as he fell into the lascivious
rhythms of what Marcy only knew as a cannibal dance.

"Oh, Danny, you are so killing!" And she began to laugh. The
two laughs, one so broad and masculine, the other so girlish and
getting higher and higher all the time, rang through the sad and
empty house. Danny threw in one step after another. Marcy was
laughing so hard it was no longer any real pleasure. It was like
being tickled.

"Danny! Don't! Stop it!"

Gracefully for such a big fellow he came to a posturing end.
She wiped her eyes.

"What do cannibals do next, Danny?"

"Make love."

"Oh, ha, ha, ha!"

"Ha, ha!" he echoed. But he couldn't imagine himself making
love, ever, to an Inman. To him "making love" was a simple,
biological fact. To her it was something vague, lovely, romantic,
for she was, in spite of bad words she might once have used and a

quick, perceptive mind, an innocent young girl. He was thinking simpler, and not half so poetic, thoughts. Now he knew he might put his hands on her. But he thought with burning loyalty of the old woman he had help lay in her tomb. He had not been loyal to much. He had a generous compunction against the young girl's own helplessness. Still . . . it would be a great thing for him to be married among the Inmans. But he thought of Dash and was almost physically afraid.

It was he who got the conversation off on more conventional lines. He who watched the clock and was well out of sight before anyone could be back from the funeral feast.

Lucy Inman hurried home. She was worried about Marcy. But the poor girl looked so happy, she felt like slapping her. What a moody thing she was! For two weeks she had flowed like Niobe. Her tears must have been sheer hypocrisy or never could they have dried so fast. Left no trace. There she was, running upstairs, singing — singing of cockle shells and silver bells, mussel shells that will not grow on every tree. At least not until "my love is true to me." Everybody in the house was tired, saddened, and depressed. Only Marcy looked radiant.

～5～

THE DAY Flanneau was finally fished from Salem Harbor, black crêpe hung on the shop door, nor was the shop ever open again. Mrs. Flanneau decided to rent rooms. After months of painting, papering, hemming sheets, haunting second-hand stores and auctions, a neat notice appeared in the Salem *Gazette*.

> Mrs. Flanneau of Essex Street, near Washington Square, begs to announce she is in a position to Accommodate choice Gentlemen Lodgers, neatly, and at Reasonable Rates. By Week, By Month, or By the Year.

Dash wondered if she was the woman to be trusted with bedfuls of choice gentlemen lodgers, but she seemed to have turned over a new leaf. Public opinion swayed toward her. Of course, it was the wicked Frenchman who had sold her to Peter Inman, who had encouraged her card-playing and tippling in the back room. Who had overdressed her to advertise his own skill. It was hardly her fault.

Now she was rid of Flanneau, she knew the only thing that stood between her and a good marriage was her reputation. She was ready to play the part of the respectable widow woman, interested only in the support of herself and her two children. Certainly, from among her gentlemen lodgers she might find the proper man.

The first gentleman to establish himself under her roof was Dan Obrian. It had been years since Puddle Alley had seen rosy hide or gleaming hair of the handsome sailor. When ashore, he usually boarded with any reduced gentlewoman who could stand his easy ways about a house. Evidently he was confident that Mrs. Flanneau could. He engaged her two best upper rooms by the year. Others, mostly unmarried captains and mates, but with a sprinkling of clerks and customs men, came and went, but Danny had obviously come to stay. Dulcey, who combined the usually contradictory qualities of landlady and love in his life, might nag him, but he was supremely comfortable. She thought he should go to sea right off and make more money. He pointed out that he'd already done pretty well. She insisted that the next time she married, it would be a rich man. As he was already getting all the advantages and none of the disadvantages of marriage, he was hard to move. They quarreled a good deal, but both enjoyed that. Dan was smart enough to realize that if he did, as he expected, make a great deal of money, Dulcey would not be the wife to show it and him off to best advantage.

Now a girl like Marcy Inman would. Since the barn had burned, from the upper windows of what had once been Frances Cunningham's rooms was a good view of the side entrance and stable yard of the Inmans. He certainly liked the way Marcy walked, the way she held her head. She seemed a bold, free, adventurous spirit, something to frighten a namby-pamby man, but challenge to a real conquering male. She aroused something ruthless and hard in him, not perhaps farther removed from love than was 'Sephus Hobey's sentimental desire to protect her. And yet, knowing how extremely unwelcome he would be to her family, knowing that to get her he'd have to fight, he was too lazy or too indifferent to take any steps himself. All he did was admire her from his own bedroom window. He also had a vague sense of loyalty to Ma'am Inman and to Dash. But he would have liked to make a monkey out of Liz. Liz would be furious to find him his brother-in-law.

The August before, Napoleon had tricked American ships into Naples, seized them and their crews, and Salem was, for the moment, short of captains. Although the Continent of Europe had never been more dangerous, the Far East trade was returning safer and greater profits. Having lost, temporarily, two masters to Napoleon and forever two ships, Dash was anxious to get the *Dolphin* heading out for China. He sought Danny in his lodgings.

It was ten o'clock in the morning when Dash went to see him, but he was still in a bedgown, unshaven and yawning. He was not a riotous fellow, understandably sleeping off a hangover. He was merely inert ashore. What a great lump of muscle and bone the fellow seemed anywhere except on a ship!

"No, Captain Dash," he announced, almost yawning in his face. "I've set my heart on a good long spell of landlubbering." The sun, reflected from the dazzling, new-fallen snow, glittered on the gold dragons and silver waves of his fantastic dressing-gown. "I'm so tarnation comfortable right here, I hate to move."

"Liz writes me there's never been such an opening for American merchantmen before in the Far East. The British are so pressed by Napoleon they have not been able to replace their trading vessels. We've pretty near got the Far East, as well as the West Indy, trade in our pockets." But he could not tempt him.

"Oh, I can make more money any time I feel like it," Danny admitted airily. He was completely indifferent.

"Danny?" a voice called outside his closed door. "Danny, shall I come in?"

It was Petra's voice, but Dash had never heard it so unguarded before.

"Sure, sure. Come in, Pet."

She was carrying his breakfast to him. How could anyone call such a choice little spirit "Pet," or burden it with such a heavy tray of sausages and steak, mush, mulled wine, coffee! Like her voice her face was unguarded. When she saw that Dan had a visitor and who he was, she stiffened. It was Dash who took the heavy tray from her and found a place in all the litter to put it. She did not look at him, but went confidently to Danny. Dash had tried in little ways to make friends with her and once he had thought he was succeeding. But ever since Flanneau's death, she seemed to have a distinct aversion for him. If he offered her anything, she thanked him and said she had more of the same thing at home. She usually shot past him with her nose in the air as though he were Boots West's goat or Tommy Inman's Newfoundland. She would not even stop for news of Peter. Yet Danny, he saw, had her confidence. Dan kissed her heartily, as he evidently did every morning.

"Petra," Dash said, "where's the dog?"

"What dog?" she asked, staring at him in chilly wonder.

"Chien Caniche."

"Oh, I thought you meant *your* dog."

"Well, you know my dog, too, don't you?"

"No."

"Don't you know the big black Newfoundland that pulls a little wagon and lives right over your back-yard fence?"

"No."

That's a fib, thought Dash. But at least you've ended the conversation. You trump every card I play. And yet he was amused. He did not take her aversion to him seriously. But it puzzled him and he often wondered why. She had been quite friendly, for her, with him once. And had always been asking for Peter. Now she wouldn't mention Peter's name.

Having promised to come to see Danny later and saying something about the sled he had fixed for her, Petra left.

Half an hour afterward, in Washington Square, Dash saw her again. Everywhere the beautiful fresh snow was piled in shining, blinding drifts. Beyond the bare purplish tree branches the winter sky was turquoise blue. He saw that various nieces and nephews of his had been making snowmen, sliding, tunneling in the drifts. All of them now stood staring in one direction, as unmoving as children playing statues. Becky, in a red knitted hood and mittens, supposedly sent to mind them, was as paralyzed as they were. They were gaping at Petra.

The little girl had taught her bright but inert little old dog to ride on the red sled Dan had given her. She had often been seen about Salem before, leading her dog with one hand and dragging her sled with the other. She never stopped to slide because it is no fun sliding alone. Now someone — and he supposed that it was

Danny — had contrived a box on her sled. In it the old dog sat and she pulled. It was a triumphant progress. Davy Jones boomed in wonder at so odd a sight as a dog riding and a human furnishing the traction. Boots West, just her age, was yelling, "Lookit! Lookit!" He forgot, in his admiration, the snowballs and the sneering "love-baby" he usually cast at Petra.

Petra and Chien Caniche did not so much as turn their heads. But no sooner were they out of sight than Boots was trying to persuade Davy to sit on his sled and be pulled. And so it was all over Salem. Children gaped with admiration and envy at Petra. They dropped all their usual snowy pastimes and tried vainly to teach their dogs to ride on sleds. Not one would except Chien Caniche.

Then the snow thawed, alewives began to run. Sleds were put away and the time of marbles and hoops, kites and skipping ropes, was come. Dash wondered what new idea the child would have. Of all the familiar childish sports of spring, nothing is more solitary than kite-flying. Probably it was Danny who had made Petra the kite, before he left for Sumatra and the enlargement of his and the Inman fortunes. The kite was a beautiful and terrible thing, something like a dragon, green, yellow, and gilt. It had yards and yards of tail. No one actually saw Petra flying her kite. She'd leave her house carrying the fascinatingly hideous, frail body in her arms, the tail wound carefully about her neck. Her dog followed her. So did the eyes of all Salem children and many adult eyes. Dash asked once if he might see her kite. "No, thank you," she had replied, and kept on walking. But he'd seen enough to be sure the thing would never fly. Danny had known that she needed it for display, not for more practical purposes. Although no one ever saw Petra standing upon a hill flying her kite, children were always claiming that they had seen the dragon in the sky, flying so high it was almost out of sight, and large as a sloop. Many asked her if they might handle it or even fly it for her. Petra had the same cold, courteous answer for everybody. "No, thank you."

She was never snubbed — she was too wary for that. She did the snubbing. What humiliation lay behind her cleverness Dash was quick to realize and kind enough to regret. It seemed to him that something, sometime, must be done to help this brave bright spirit. He knew his mother also often thought of Petra. Perhaps she coveted her as a beautiful, exotic possession she might show off. Once she had felt that way about Liz. That spring, the spring of 1811, she and Dash were driving back from calling upon the Tom Inmans over in Danvers. For six years Miranda and her children had lived with "Granny," while Tom and his father-in-law tried out one site or another for their mills. Not until the year before had he known exactly where he wished to build them and a handsome residence for his family. Thank God, Lucy was always saying to herself, they are gone. But the fact was she missed them. The house seemed so empty. Now she was always getting Dash into her carriage, to drive over and call upon them. He was infinitely less stubborn and broody than he had been in his earlier days. If he was not as doggy as Liz, at least he was one of Salem's most successful, most famous, captains. People were saying still, "But you went to Japan!"

His mother herself brought up the subject of Petra. "I wish, before Peter comes back, something could be done about Petra."

"What, for instance?"

"Well, she's his daughter. I can't help but admit I do rather admire him for never, not once, trying to hide the fact. Somehow he ought to have her."

Dash was silent. He had had a private letter from Liz written eight months before, but only lately come to hand. Things were not going as well with Peter as his letters to his mother suggested. He had begun bleeding again. But his mother, Dash thought, without bitterness and with some admiration, had always preferred to live as long as possible in a fool's paradise. So let her.

"Dash, sometimes you're impossible to get a word out of. I wish Frances was here. I could always talk to Frances."

"Why don't you go to see her in Boston?"

"Oh, no. Never. But I know you stay with her when you are in Boston."

This he always did. The firm had broadened its interests so much in the last five years that while Liz was away Dash had to go often to Boston, New York, or Baltimore. He had seen plenty of poor Fanny. She had followed her husband's commands, closed the little Federal Street house that she had loved so much, moved everything out of it to the great brick mansion on Mount Vernon Street in Boston. And herself, too. Then she sat down to wait for Liz's return. She was still rather camping out and seemed a trifle dazed by the change. There was not half enough furniture for the new house. All the curtains were too short, but she did not trust herself to buy a thing until Liz came back from Bombay. Nor, seemingly, to make a friend. She had none. She lay low and waited, reverting a little to the forlorn widow woman she had been before Lucy Inman had made a place for her in her household and heart. But evidently Liz's mother felt that as long as she had chosen to be a daughter-in-law rather than a friend, she must face the consequences.

"Yes, I go to see her," Dash said. "Nobody else does, Mother."

"If Fanny chooses to live in such great style in Boston, I suppose she can. But you see, she had the Flanneaus for tenants, and then they had her. I thought she might know if Mrs. Flanneau . . . I'd like to ask her if she thinks we could *buy* Petra. For money."

"No. I'm sure she never would sell her."

He spoke surely for various reasons. Dulcey might be a careless mother, but there was no question but that she loved her own child. And Dash had seen enough of that ménage to realize that Dulcey would like to marry Dan Obrian. Dan was so fond of the little girl — much more than he was of his own son, as Dash considered Jacques — she would lose her trump card if she lost Petra. There was another reason, known only to himself. If Peter never came back, and that will was probated, Petra would be an heiress. Dulcey would never part with a daughter who was an heiress in her own right.

"But I don't like to think of my own grandchild growing up like *that*. Everybody kicking her aside. Except, of course, they can't — she's too spunky. I don't see where she got her spunk. Not from Peter, surely. She's just as spunky as you were. Peter was always a good, biddable boy. No, he wasn't. Of course he wasn't, at least about Mrs. Flanneau. Well, as I was saying, in case you don't know, Linda has made an over-the-fence acquaintance with the little black girl Mrs. Flanneau employs. And she says Petra takes up the lodgers' breakfasts to them. Men in their *night*shirts! I do declare! And not shaven. I don't think there's anything so unattractive as a man in his *night*shirt. And their big, bony, bare *feet*! I always made your father, Dash, put on his slippers before he got out of bed. I'm sure Peter would not like that." She was doubtless referring to those breakfasts carried to choice gentlemen lodgers, not to the slippers on his father's feet.

"Michael, do keep the horses at a trot." Ever since Dash could remember, coachmen were always letting horses slow down when the conversation behind their backs got interesting. And his mother was always leaning forward and telling them to trot, so they wouldn't eavesdrop. Mullins had had endless excuses. Michael Shean was less imaginative.

"There's only one way," Dash said, "to get the child. And that's by marrying Dulcey. She's a widow now." It was not of Peter he was thinking. He was thinking of himself.

"Dash, that's why . . . Don't you see, that's why we *must* do something about Petra before he comes back. I'm sure Peter never would . . . except to get the child. I hope we can think of a way. Oh, I couldn't bear it to have him *marry* her. But I'm so afraid. He's so quixotic, Dash. Dash, don't fiddle with your watch chain."

The horses trotted briskly home through flowering country lanes. Before them rose Gallows Hill and Salem just beyond.

"Mother," he said slowly, "we haven't heard from Peter for a long time." He did not want to shatter her optimism, but perhaps he had, at least, better prepare her a little.

"And I think," Lucy said, "that means they're already started back. Liz had almost wound up all the Bombay affairs. I'm glad everything has gone so well for both of them. Dash, I think I may change my doctor. I've always had Jack lately, because, after all, Nanny married him. But I think Old Doctor is the smarter of the two." He let her chat on and on, wondering vaguely what, if anything, his mother needed a doctor for. She was as healthy as a bear. But of course women liked to refer to "my doctor." The last time she had actually employed one was when Marcy was born.

She talked on almost as happily as though he were listening to her. As they turned into the driveway, it was Dash who noticed old Captain Magee standing bareheaded by the side entrance, waiting for them. As a custom-house employee he was often the first Salem man aboard a home-come ship. He had a letter in his hand. Dash knew that he must consider this letter of greatest importance, since he had dropped his official duties and come running to the house with it. And that hat, held so respectfully, so sadly, in his hands. Probably the captain of the *Good Report* had told him the news the letter confirmed.

"Give it to me, Captain Magee."

"It's for your mother, Captain Dash."

"Mother," he said, "we've a letter from Liz."

"Came in this afternoon on the Derbys' *Good Report* from Bombay, ma'am." Magee shook his head with sympathy.

"When will they be back, Dash? Does Liz say when? Dear, do open it and read it for me. I haven't my visual with me."

She walked gaily into the house, so dark in contrast to the bright day outside. Dash exchanged a quick glance with Magee, said nothing, and followed her. So Dash was free, absolutely free and forever to go his own way regardless of Peter — now beyond all hurt. This thought came to him through the surge of grief he felt. Why, why had he let him go in the first place? Why had he never written him once? Not one letter.

～6～

LIZ WROTE A GOOD LETTER, expressing more warmth on paper than he often did in words. Peter had grown steadily weaker and yet he had been so set upon going a voyage to Canton with Liz and the *Victrix*. So, thinking the sea air would make him more comfortable, Liz had agreed to it. Then one day he had been too weak to get from his bunk, but he seemed in good spirits. They had carried him to the foredeck and it had all been over soon in one torrent of blood. So they had buried him at sea, latitude 20°, longitude 120°. And Liz spoke of him affectionately and told how everyone had loved him.

In one respect Liz had been remiss. He did not give the actual date of Peter's death. From what he wrote, it was obviously some time last September. If Peter had died before his grandmother, he had little to leave. If after her, he died a wealthy man. But as Blainey Phipps pointed this out, Lucy Inman said it would make no difference. Peter had made no will, she said. He had had no heirs except his own family. Lucy had taken his death philosophically because, Dash knew, in spite of everything she had said to the contrary, she had never expected any other outcome.

When Blainey mentioned how important was the very day of Peter's death, he had looked sidewise at Dash, for Peter had told him that he was leaving his will with his oldest brother.

At this time Blainey, already a widower, was often about the house. He had married Perkins money once. He seemed to have no idea of sitting back and watching little Ben Crowninshield, the only meager specimen of his famous family, walk off with Inman money. It humiliated Marcy that her mother would laugh at Blainey and yet obviously did not consider him an impossible husband. He was respectable and had done very well financially. Tom, she knew, would be pleased. Blainey had specialized in the lawsuits the mill-owners were endlessly involved in. He was said to know more about water rights, factory law, than any other man in New England. Dash never expressed his feelings about Blainey any more. But Marcy knew he thought him a worm.

Her mother was insisting that any husband was better than ending up, as so many strong-minded girls did, an old maid. Marcy did encourage Blainey because she liked going to parties and needed an escort. Ben she could not encourage more than about so much. She was so fond of him she could not bear to hurt him. But underneath her toying with these two young men was the heavy fact of her attachment to Dan Obrian.

Marcy seemed to Blainey a little too straightforward, unabashed, to be really in love with him. Maria Perkins had been flustered by, first, his "respects," and then his "addresses." With Marcy there was nothing left now except to "declare himself," and yet he cannily hesitated. True, Fields and Inman, the weavers, were employing him to unsnarl their water rights for them. Textile companies needed smart lawyers and Blainey was smart. Seemingly these days all over New England wherever there was a fall of water a mill was rising. Wherever there was a mill, a lawsuit. He felt Tom was for him, Dash against, Marcy indifferent, and Mrs. Inman ready to jump either way the girl jumped. But he never yet had burned a bridge behind him. He wished to gain the approval of Dash and, when he returned, of Liz Inman as well. He knew that, although Dash was the oldest son, Liz would be the power in the firm. Perhaps he could go just a mite easy till Liz came home. And it was with Liz he would "talk money." Marcy, since her grandmother's death, had a lot, and he did not want to start his marriage with any strings tied to it. He was to have full control of her property. He'd put it in factories.

Never having liked Dash, Blainey got to the point where he

couldn't stand him. Dash paid more attention to Mr. Africanus than he did to him, and actually he was engaging his rival, Lawyer Orne, to unsnarl certain nice legal matters for him that had arisen over the insuring of the *Calypso*.

Sometimes he would look at Dash's unhostile but indifferent, almost unseeing, face and think how he had the petard by which to hoist him. Five people knew Peter Inman had made a will. It was true that his sisters-in-law had never read the document. They did not know Peter had acknowledged his natural daughter and had made her and her mother his heirs. Only he knew — and Dash. And Dash had the will.

Yet two months had gone by since news of Peter's death and that will had not been probated. Morally, Blainey held nothing against Dash that he had probably destroyed it in order to let Peter's share stay in the family. But he began to watch Petra Flanneau's silent but subtly conspicuous gyrations through the town. Little girl, he would think to himself as she flashed by, if your uncle gave you your due, your mother wouldn't have to run a boarding house, and you'd be quite the heiress.

Next time he wished to accelerate his courtship of Marcy — but not, of course, without the sanction of the young lady's family — he decided to talk with the oldest son rather than the mother. He went to the Inman counting-house and was told to look for him at a shipyard over toward the Neck. Blainey gingerly picked his way around hoists and spars, among porters and drays. Girls from what seamen called a "slaughter house" laughed at him from an upper window. He was easy to laugh at, with his spectacles, awkward, cautious feet, and roly-poly build.

Dash was standing bareheaded and in his shirt-sleeves beside the *Wanderer*. She was having new masts set.

"What's that again?" Dash asked, and yelled at the workmen, "Mind now, easy does it." Near-by the ox team that had hauled the masts stood chewing their cuds. One of them had drooled on Dash's sleeve.

"Captain Dash, you must have noticed that for these last four months I have devoted much of my time to your lovely sister, Marcy."

"Hey!" Dash yelled, dissatisfied with the way the workmen were handling the mast. He ran lightly up a shipwright's ladder, took a heavy mallet from a workman, and was showing how it should be done. Why, Blainey thought, in contempt, the wonderful Dash Inman! Take off his captain's coat and high beaver hat, put him in his shirt-sleeves, and he looks like any other carpenter. These captains Salem is so proud of really are little more than workmen. Master craftsmen, perhaps, but laboring along with their apprentices. He knew he was seeing a way of work that had existed for centuries and was already doomed. It was not thus the new directors of the factories looked, gathered about mahogany tables at directors' meetings. Many of them knew nothing about the actual work of the mills — they merely had the ready capital. Liz was something of a connecting link between the old methods and the new. Doubtless, now that Old Ma'am was dead, when Liz came home they'd get the House of Inman, or rather J. Inman's Sons, organized in the modern manner. It was ridiculous, repulsive even, to Lawyer Phipps to see one of Salem's wealthiest men working thus with his own hands.

Dash returned to him with a shaving hanging to his bare, brawny arm. Blainey felt almost afraid of him.

"Now my mind's free, what were you saying? Come on, eleven o'clock and time for grog." He cupped his hands and sang out to the workmen that old call, "Grog-o!" The cry echoed and rang down Derby Street, and other workmen in other yards picked it up. "Grog-o!" Riggers, smiths, porters, all waterfront men had, from time immemorial, thought it their right to fling down their work every morning at eleven and drink grog, which the employer paid for. In summertime they needed it, for they started work at sunup. In winter they needed it even more, to get themselves warm again. The question had come up among the mill workers. Blainey, and all directors sitting about mahogany tables in long-tailed broadcloth coats, were utterly opposed to it. Many of the shipbuilders would have been glad to let the old-fashioned custom be forgotten. Fellows like Dash were obstructing the march of progress by holding on to that eleven-o'clock grog. As long as masters worked with men, the custom would hold.

Dash led the way to a grogshop, a very humble place, with bulging glass in the tiny windows and strong smells. The strapping girl at the bar was showing gums and bad teeth at Captain Dash. The five men who had been at work on the *Wanderer,* seeing their host had a guest, sat apart. It was a warm summer day. They were dripping with sweat and so was Dash Inman. Blainey felt ill at ease. He wished he had got Dash in his own little pumpkin-yellow law office. It had been a mistake to accost him on his own Derby Street.

"I've spoken to your mother," he began, almost in a whisper, "about Marcy. She has honored me with her approval."

"That's too strong a word, Blainey. Mother simply means that Marcy is a grown woman of twenty-one. She's to decide."

"Yes. And I believe that Marcy has done me the great honor of showing some preference for me."

Dash was watching him with those fine, disturbing eyes of his. Actually, thought Blainey, his face is a little dirty.

"But of course I would not want to intrude myself into a family where I am *persona non grata*. No man of honor could do so."

"No." Dash looked thoughtful.

"Frankly, Captain, I am a very busy man. I will not, I give you my word for it, push my suit against the wishes of the young lady's family. But I do not wish to waste time. If there is one commodity we younger men appreciate, it is the value of time." He was thinking of the fifteen minutes the shipwrights wasted with "Grog-o," the time Dash himself was wasting on work surely so unimportant any hireling could have supervised it. The fact that those masts were being set so they would never betray any man that ever sailed the *Wanderer* did not impress him.

He went on hypocritically, "Although there is no young lady in Salem as possessed of every charm, every virtue, as your sister, still there are other young ladies."

"I know," said Dash, "but I doubt if many of them have quite so much money."

This was going to be easier than he had expected. Evidently right now the family were ready to talk money and settlements. He might not have to wait for Eleazar.

"So, you see, as one business man to another, I can hardly afford to waste my time."

"I'm afraid that's what you have been doing."

"Why?" Blainey colored slightly in surprise.

"Marcy, of course, will decide. I don't think she has ever once for a moment thought of you seriously."

Blainey was stung.

"Peter did not consider me unworthy of his friendship."

"Not at the beginning. But at the end."

"Captain Inman, I'm sorry to be forced to bring up old matters. Mrs. Phipps, my dear Maria, did not, because of the scandal . . . at least she felt she could not . . . I mean, she believed that the long, close intimacy between Peter and myself had best be severed — when I became a family man."

"Peter was good enough for me," Dash said, with a low-voiced passion. "Good enough for Marcy and my mother and Ma'am. And Liz and Tom. Nanny, too, I guess. But he wasn't good enough for you. Well, now he's dead. But I'd think you'd be ashamed to have even his memory for a brother-in-law. And, my God, I think he'd be ashamed of you. False friend if I ever saw one."

Blainey slowly empurpled. Now the shipwrights were calling their thanks to Dash and he was promising to join them in a moment.

"There are times, Captain," Blainey said thickly, and he could feel his heart pounding in him, "a man cannot be too fussy. Take this matter of brothers-in-law. There are some men who would be too fussy to wish to have one who deliberately has suppressed or destroyed a dead brother's last will and testament, to his own immense profit."

Dash looked so unmoved by this taunt, he wondered if Peter really had put it in his hands. Perhaps he had reconsidered and torn it up himself.

"I want to do what's right by Peter," Dash said, gesturing to the bar girl to bring him more grog. "And I've been thinking and thinking . . ."

"You admit that you have it?"

"Yes, so I have. It seemed to me that in this case the exact date of his death, I mean, whether he died before or after his grandmother — both died around the first of September, last year — makes so much difference that I'd not bring the matter up until we've seen the *Victrix* log."

Blainey saw that Dash, behind a stoical front, was more disturbed than he had ever seen him. "Well, perhaps before then the rats will eat it, Captain Dash? Eh?"

"Not where I've got it."

"Captain Dash, I sympathize completely with your point of view. It was a foolish whim of his. I did my best to dissuade him. It was the fantasy of a diseased mind. I think it would be the kindest, most decent thing if that will never sees the light of day. To think of all that money going to that guttersnipe of a girl! If, as a lawyer, a potential member of your family, I may advise you . . ."

Dash was sitting there opposite him, still and secret as a mouse. Blainey for the first time felt he had the upper hand. He swelled a little, toyed with the rich seals of his watch chain. Now he was himself again. He cleared his throat in a legal manner and went on.

"As a lawyer, may I advise you? Even if the will was probated, I believe it could be broken. Wasn't Peter most odd, surely, subject to *spells?* If it is probated, I will take pleasure in assembling the witnesses, handling the case for you. But why haul all this to court? If you follow my advice, that will was never written. You and I are the only ones that know. I felt the foolishness of it at the time. The witnesses to it, my wife and her sisters, never saw it. I promise by my honor to stand back of you completely in this matter."

"Your honor?" said Dash, in a queer, thin voice unlike his usual warm tones.

"Come, come," the lawyer answered, "honor is only a figure of speech. What's honorable in one decade is dishonorable the next. And it changes in every country."

"So you are ready to swear by a figure of speech?"

"Ha, ha! Very good. Very good indeed. I'm glad you are being sensible about this whole affair, my dear fellow."

"I've never been very sensible. About anything. Ever."

Dash stood up slowly and without the least sign of passion — and that was the most insulting thing about it — struck Blainey across the face.

After that, Marcy had to look elsewhere for an escort. Blainey came no more.

A month later, the *Victrix* floated up the harbor. Her homing pennant was not apeak. For she had lost a man.

Dash had the log in his hands.

Sept. 10, 1810. Fine light winds and those easterly. We set all sails and stood before the wind. Died Peter Inman, clerk of this vessel. Buried at sea Lat. 20 Long. 120.

Peter had died the day of Ma'am's funeral, and so a wealthy man.

Dash thumbed ahead through the *Victrix* log absent-mindedly, thinking of Peter alone so far away, lying forever in the South China Sea.

Liz took it from him. "I'd rather explain to you myself. There was a mutiny afterward."

Dash's face showed amazement. As far as he knew, there had never been a mutiny on a Salem vessel. It seemed to him shameful that men could be so maltreated, they'd turn on their officers.

Liz was explaining. He still wanted his oldest brother's approval. On this brief voyage he had only a few of the *Victrix's* Yankee crew with him. Lascars and renegade English and Frenchmen — just foreigners. The mutiny had been brought on because he had refused to let foremast hands share on profits. The damned foreigners had never heard of such a thing. So Dash saw it was the Yankee boys who had started it, merely demanding the old democratic rights of Yankee seamen. Here, on these white decks, people of the *Victrix* had died — cut down by their own officers.

"No," Dash interrupted. "You needn't explain. You can't. You treated your people badly, and they had the sense to turn on you. Yes, go ahead and explain and explain and explain — you'll never be able to change the facts."

❧ 7 ❧

THE MEMORIAL SERVICE for Peter Inman was held upon the first anniversary of his death, September 10, 1811. The day was so warm, so golden, the ladies of his household would wear white muslins, not black. For a memorial is hardly a funeral. A sad, but not a tragic, day. Already the tears are wiped away.

After the church services, the Inmans would walk over to Howard Street, carry flowers to the tomb marked with his dates and name — the tomb which did not hold him — then go back to their own house for a cold collation and the reading of the will that just yesterday Dash had told them Peter had left with him. Nothing more than a memorandum was expected — who was to have certain books or chessmen. If it had been a "real" will, certainly Dash would have had in a lawyer to read it to them all. Dash felt a grim amusement over the consternation the reading of this will would produce. He was glad to have this interlude of flowers and sunshine coming between the church and the will-reading.

As the informal little procession left the house in twos and threes, carrying their bouquets of asters, turtleheads, white boltonia, the last sweet williams and fringed bleeding hearts, it seemed almost like some rite off a Grecian urn. Peter would have liked to have them come thus with classic simplicity to the tomb that did not hold him.

Dash walked with his mother upon his arm. As they came to the cemetery, they saw that many other people had had the same idea. They had gone home after the memorial service, taken scissors, gone to their back yards and cut what flowers mid-September offered. Already flowers lay about the Inman tomb. And groups of people stood there. Voices were low and hushed, but the bright blue and golden afternoon suggested that nothing is too sad to be borne.

Mr. Africanus stood like a bronze statue, reciting Peter Inman's virtues to whoever passed him by. Dash saw Flip and her husband stooping to lay marigolds beside the stone. And a gaunt old woman who ran a cent shop, with only a handful of mint. Well, he thought, if her catnip attracts all the cats in Salem, neither Peter nor Ma'am will care. Many people were here already, and more were coming, and even now others were leaving. Evidently now that Peter was dead, all were ready to forgive him the shameful ordering of his life. The truth didn't seem buried in his empty grave as much as to rise triumphant from it. And yet, not far away stood his mistress and Petra, and both were hung in heavy black. Even Chien Caniche had a black ribbon on him. The three of them looked isolated and alone.

Mr. Mompesson arrived presently with two ladies, followed by a coachman with a basket of flowers. Now the servant was handing out nosegays, sweet williams and pansies, to Georgiana, late roses to Polly. The white-clad women approached the granite block where Africanus still stood chanting his threnody, bowing low and gracefully as they laid down their offerings. Please God, Polly would never know how much the dead man had done for her.

Then Dash noticed that Miranda was bedeviling his mother.

Calling her "Grandma," and suggesting that she must be tired after the brief walk. Nanny was on the other side, and between them they had summoned all their children about her, although they must have guessed by now his mother wasn't very fond of children. It was as though they were trying to point out to her that, although one generation passes, look, here comes the next. So Dash persuaded his mother to go home, and thought he would go with her.

But Dash was eyeing Mr. Mompesson and his ladies, now joined by Liz and Fanny, who had driven up from Boston in their own carriage. He longed to speak with Georgiana, who had loved Peter so much. He waited.

Of course, Polly was flirting with Liz. She always did. There was a radiance to Polly, a suggestion of abundant good health — no matter what any doctor might say. You could only account for her sick spells — and Dash knew this — by some sickness of mind. And yet he knew, as perhaps her father and physician did not, that inside her she was coming unmoored. There had of late been bursts of something primitive, savage, uncontrollable. He felt it might take little these days to unhinge her mind. And he was thankful that he had never weakened and told her the truth. Of course, it might save him from the feeling of emptiness, unreality, dry rot, he had suffered from lately. But if he destroyed her belief in him, she'd have but little to cling to. Unmoored, indeed, she would be if she knew the truth — floating off into what phantasmagoria he could hardly imagine. Wasn't he strong enough to bear the burden of his own dishonor?

With Peter dead, Dash thought, there was no reason why the secret should not be buried with him forever. Let the South China Sea, and this empty tomb, and Dash's own conscience, hold it. Curiously, it was Blainey Phipps who had decided him as to what he must do about that will. He had not been entirely sure, until the moment Blainey accused him of suppressing it.

So now, and soon, he and Polly would marry and live in the small house next Mr. Mompesson's which Liz and Fanny had left vacant. And every morning he'd walk from there to the counting-house and every afternoon home to dinner. And never go to sea again. He watched Polly almost with curiosity, as if he had not seen her before. This was the woman he would marry. If Peter was right, he had given his soul to possess her.

He had been so young, so very young, when he had fallen in love with her. He wondered, suppose now, today, this moment, I saw her for the first time. Would I fall so completely under her spell as did that twenty-year-old captain, just home on the Crowninshields' *Belisarius,* full of oats, full of beans, he thought almost contemptuously, with his tail over the dashboard? The talk of the town! What could have been more appropriate than that the young hero of the hour should immediately fall in love with the belle of the moment. But now he could feel little connection with that twenty-year-old marvel, he a mature man of thirty-five and now retired. Except that from that young lad — and he was perfectly willing to admit dispassionately that he was a real smart, bright lad — he had inherited the legend and the fact, the burden and the joy, the duty and the pleasure, of loving Polly Mompesson. Strange that now he could stand and look at Polly with simple appraisal. Was the time really past when the mere sight of her tingled through his flesh, set his heart rocking, his palms to sweating, and he felt the sick weakness and shuddering strength of unendurable physical desire? At least, as he stood this day at Peter's tomb, he felt little more than a connoisseur's admiration for a very beautiful woman. He could feel the same looking at a lovely ship. But it made no difference — he was bound to her. It was that twenty-year-old marvel that had bound him so that there was never any escape for him. Nor did he wish it. Surely, much evil had been done that the present moment might come, when nothing stood between him and Polly. It was his duty — and he liked the word — to marry her, rescue her from the psychic morasses which, he had always known, endangered her.

Georgiana had left the little group under the high elm, was looking at him and setting her course straight for him. Actually, he thought idly, Georgiana Frick, with her little green-apple figure and coffin-shaped face, was closer to what he might choose for himself — these days. But one doesn't escape the past. What's happened never does end. Even Dulcey had known that much. Peter . . . Peter had known. And he himself had learned it. A man doesn't escape what he has done. But he can bear it. This, too, he believed he had learned.

Georgiana was bearing down upon him fast, and he felt, more than saw, that she had all her guns shotted for action. She did not offer him her hand and his bow was as formal as hers.

"I'm glad, Georgiana," he said, "you happened to be in Salem the day we make our farewells to Peter."

She swallowed awkwardly. "No, Captain Inman, it didn't just happen. Polly wrote me. I haven't been in Salem, once, for years. And you're wrong in another thing. I'll never say farewell to Peter. He was the best man, the best human being, I've ever known. He will be with me always."

He noticed that she did not call him "Dash," but "Captain Inman," and that she was looking at him with frank hostility. "Of course, *you* will be glad to forget him, as soon as possible. Now he's dead. What a load off your mind!"

"You are at liberty to hold any opinion of me you wish." He bowed and turned to leave her.

"Stay! Wait!" Her emotions made her voice harsh.

"Miss Frick?"

"*Nothing* stands between you now. Between you two" — and she tossed her head in the direction of Polly. "How happy you must be that all the past now may be considered dead and buried! And you have come, and so have I and Polly, to lay flowers upon it. The past shall not rise again. Captain Inman, let me congratulate you on this happy occasion. For he's dead now. Wasn't it hard for you while he was still alive? No, don't look so perturbed. I'm not going to have hysterics, like Polly. And I'll never tell what I know to anyone. But I've always wanted you to know that I did know the truth. That's one reason why I came up today from Cambridge. And tomorrow I go back. And that's all." She made a weary gesture. "You don't deny anything?"

"No, I don't deny. But let me say one thing. You and I both loved Peter, and in his own way he loved both of us. Mouse" — he laid a hand on her arm — "do you remember how we used to call you 'Mouse'? For Peter's sake, forgive me if you can. At least do not hate me. Nor begrudge any happiness still left to Polly and me."

"No," she whispered. His voice had almost bemused the anger out of her.

"Do you remember what Faustus said to the Devil, at the end? 'Why, this is Hell — nor am I out of it.'"

Her eyes widened. "I didn't know you'd take it so hard."

"Peter knew. For I am a Yankee man. We take things like this hard. Do not fear, Mouse, that I have not had my punishment. I could not have escaped it, even if I had wished. Nor," he added, as an afterthought, "have I ever wished."

"And now you will marry Polly?"

She was almost saying, This will also be a part of your punishment. It gave him a feeling of treachery, for just at the moment she had come to join him, he had been wondering — suppose now for the first time I saw Polly Mompesson. There she was, laughing with Liz, so beautiful, so utterly desirable, and yet he felt cut off from her as though the angel with the flaming sword barred his way.

"It shall be as Polly wishes," he answered. "It is certainly my wish."

"How happy we might all have been," Georgiana said, smiling for the first time, but it was a sad smile, "if only everything had been different! Dash, I'll never forget that summer, and Blainey Phipps's wedding and the water parties."

"Neither will I."

"Every ship," she went on, "that came from Bombay brought me letters from him. And I wrote him every day and sent them when I could. So I guess he did love me. When it was too late."

Dash kept a guilty silence. Not once had he written Peter. There was only one thing Peter wanted to hear from him. He could not write that, so he had written nothing.

This, too, would be forever on his conscience.

"He cared so much for you, Dash. There wasn't at first any room for anyone else." She had not meant to call him Dash, but she could hardly go back and correct herself.

He did not deny Peter's devotion to him, but he said: "The time did come, Georgiana, when I . . . disappointed him. He saw through his fancy picture of me to something real. And not so honorable. That freed him a little. And he did love you — more, I guess, than you ever knew. But it was too late."

"I almost guessed it from his poems. But it was too late."

"And yet . . . may we not be friends?"

Her face melted and her lips twisted. "Yes . . . and one thing more. Something I didn't expect to want to tell you, but I do."

"What is it, Georgiana?"

"I'm going to be married. Soon. I'm going to marry a Harvard professor. I knew I had to, right off. Or I'd be nothing ever again but a . . . an empty cenotaph." She gestured at the flowery tomb. "We've got to go on living, all of us. That means not only me, but you, too, Dash, and Polly."

So at the end she did give a grudging approval. The hand she gave him was half-hesitant, half-affectionate. "Peter did love you very much," she said, and left him.

The cemetery was almost empty now, but he saw Dulcey still standing stolidly by, as though she, longer than anyone else, had the right to mourn Peter. Dash had a sudden idea.

"Mrs. Flanneau," he said, speaking stiffly as though addressing a mate on a ship, "would it be convenient for you and your daughter to come to my house for a few moments?"

"Me, Captain Dash?"

"Yes. Both of you." The child would not even look at him. She was fussing with her dog's black ribbon. "Peter had some property to leave. You and your child have been remembered. It is fitting that you should be present."

"But, you see, I thought it was a funeral and I'm in black and she is, too, and then all the ladies of your household wore white and . . ."

"It doesn't matter. You'll be along?"

"Why, yes, sir. Yes, we will."

The child still would not look at him, but he guessed she'd remember the next half-hour all her life. She was ten. So would everybody else present. He guessed that that will would prove a bombshell.

He went to the tomb a moment and knelt and prayed, not to God, but for forgiveness and understanding from Peter. "You told me to go it alone, Peter, and I have. But I miss you terribly, I miss you, Peter, Peter . . ."

❧ 8 ❧

It was a voluntary. Dash looked about for Polly. "I cannot live without you," the fiddles cried, then sobbed and softly answered themselves, "Why try — why try?"

Polly had been in an odd mood when he had stopped by for her this evening. Mr. Mompesson told him, as he waited for her to come down, she had been suffering from headaches, dizziness, crying spells, for three days. He had begged her not to go to the Crowninshield ball, especially as the snow and the wind raged through the streets. But she was determined to go. Dash promised to see she did not overexert herself, to bring her home early.

She was not in the ballroom. He wondered if she was among the card-players. Not seeing her in the card-room, he went back to the dancing and slowly circled about, looking for her. Already couple number one was standing up. Their host, Captain Crowninshield, had chosen Marcy. Marcy was always being chosen by men ten or fifteen years older than herself. And the more happily married they were, the better they liked Marcy. It was as if men liked to dance with her, talk with her, but not the idea of spending their lives with her.

Thinking of the uncle, Dash ran across a niece. He thought it was Emmy Crowninshield, but it was Emmy's sister, Anstis — only sixteen, and this her first winter. She was so afraid no one would ask her to dance, she was hiding in a corner. Dash might seem rather old to her, but surely better than no partner at all.

"Emmy," he called, bowing to her averted shoulder. "Come, child, give me the honor?"

She was too shy to tell him she was not her older sister, and delighted to have such a wonderful partner. Her eyes dropped, but a smile trembled on her lips.

Her uncle was calling to the fiddlers, naming the dance "Spanking Jack." As usual, some were saying they did not know it and others that it was their favorite. The two long lines of petal-pale dancing frocks, tinsel ribbons, faced the broadcloth, silver buttons, ear-high neckcloths, and fancy waistcoats. "Emmy" had not taken her place with the ladies. She was clinging to Dash.

"Do you know 'Spanking Jack'?" he asked.

"I learned it at boarding school."

Dash could have danced this well-known reel with his eyes shut, but he said, "Then perhaps you can steer me a bit?"

"Oh yes, of course I can help you."

She explained the steps so rapidly, in such technical phrases — and in French — that he could hardly follow her, but at least he had given her self-confidence.

The bows struck the strings. Monsieur de Herriot clapped his hands and called. Anstis, far more concerned over her partner's feet than her own, forgot herself and floated up and down the lines like a pink butterfly, helping her partner at every turn. In boarding school she had been the joy of her dancing master. But until tonight her shyness at a real ball with real men for partners had paralyzed her.

The next was a draw dance. Dash drew number one from Monsieur de Herriot, and looked about for the corresponding lady. He saw "Emmy" standing before him, pink with joy, but too shy to speak. She showed him her card. Number one.

They went hand in hand to the head of the room. "What dance do you want, darling?"

She whispered to the buttons on his chest, "Drops of Brandy."

"What?" He had only heard "brandy," and wondered if she felt faint. By bending his ear almost to her lips he heard, " 'Drops of Brandy' is the very latest thing out in Boston, Captain Inman." And she had the nerve to pat her back hair almost contemptuously, as if to say, Of course, these provincials may not know it.

Old Monsieur de Herriot did not. One of the Negro fiddlers did, and offered to call it. But the dancers were complaining.

"It may be the latest thing out in Boston," Dash said to his partner, "but it hasn't got here yet. Don't you want to choose something else? 'Sukey Bids Me' or 'Barrel of Sugar'?"

She shook her head. She's not wasting much time, Dash thought, before putting all the other women on tenterhooks. And she'll enjoy watching them galloping about like carthorses in pasture, and she so sure of herself. I wonder where Polly is. She always knows the latest steps. And she's been to Boston a good deal this winter. But Polly was not in sight.

Instead of being irritated that little Miss Crowninshield selected a dance no one but she and one Negro fiddler knew, the other dancers decided to be amused and agreed they all wanted to learn. Without the least sign of self-consciousness, "Emmy" gave them a lesson. How pretty she was, how sweet, how light-footed, how tactful — now at last she literally had the floor. Everyone was thanking her, even dear old Monsieur de Herriot. Dash told her she was wonderful and kissed her as men often did their partners. But he was thinking of Polly.

He left the ballroom and decided once more to look over the card-players. Not once could he remember Polly sitting to cards when the fiddles played. But her father had said she was not well. He stood at the door, his eyes going from woman to woman.

Here, in this room, sat those who already felt their dancing days were over, although they might stand up on family occasions for years. He saw Nanny and Jack West, soberly playing loo. Thyrza Birdall, and her husband. Thyrza had been a romping girl. He was vaguely surprised that she was not any longer. And there was Peggy Pierce! You might say he had been in love with Peggy before Polly had completely knocked out of his head, his body, his senses, every other girl. She had been as slow, sleek, and innocent as Polly had been vivacious and subtly wicked. Peggy had had enormous blue eyes to roll. She was rolling them now as she trumped her partner's ace. The fair hair he remembered had completely disappeared under a brocaded, feather-topped turban. Although he had been seeing her about for years, he had scarcely realized how large she had become. He could not blame her that she, married at sixteen, the mother of many, had not kept her figure. Her bare upper arms looked like masses of dough. Her many chins flowed down to meet the uprise of her bosom, a bosom so big and bare it reminded him of the backside of a baby, disappearing down the low décolleté.

As he stood by the doorway, he saw gathered together about the card-tables most of the "girls" with whom he had begun his dancing. Some were handsomer than they had been in their teens. Some heavier, or thinner, or smugger. Some obviously happier. Others not so happy. To add to the shock of this sudden revelation, he saw the real Emmy Crowninshield. She, too, was a matron now. But who on earth, then, had he been dancing with and calling "Emmy"? Here indeed were not only his and Polly's old friends, but even a sprinkling of Marcy's. Marcy was twelve years younger than Polly, he remembered. He began to feel concerned for Polly.

He went back to the ballroom. Marcy was clowning a bit. She shouldn't. Men did not like it, even as they encouraged it. His mysterious, erstwhile little partner was hopping about as happy and unself-conscious as a bird. But Polly was not there.

He decided to waylay a woman servant, ask her to explore regions forbidden to his sex. He recognized a stiff old woman, often hired in on great occasions, long a chosen chaperon for Salem's young girls — Old Abby Flack.

"Abby," he said, "where's Miss Mompesson?"

"She's a bit droopy, Captain Dash. I've got her fixed up in one of the chambers set aside for the ladies."

"What's wrong?"

"A touch dizzy. I've my eye on her. Don't fret."

"Which room? I want to see her."

"Fie, Captain Dash! When ladies go to upper chambers they don't want their escorts following them. Then, too, it wouldn't be nice."

"No," he agreed, grinning from ear to ear, "it wouldn't be nice. Well, keep an eye on her, Abby. And if she'd rather go home now, let me know."

But when he left Abby, he decided he would find her himself. Upstairs were two rooms, mountain-high with ladies' wraps. She was not in the first room. In the second, he saw first a pile of garments on the bed and chairs. A slow fire was burning, but the room seemed freezing cold. And here on the second floor he heard in all its force the shriek and howling of the wind about the house.

Then he saw a lock of golden hair above a dove-colored velvet cloak. Either she was asleep in her armchair before the fire, or playing 'possum. He went to her, put a hand on the back of the chair, and looked down at her. Her color was high, as though she had a fever. Her eyes were wide open, looking up at him. She saw who it was and smiled.

"Don't worry," she said. "It is nothing."

"Headache?"

"No. Yes . . . a little. All those fiddles!"

The crying of the fiddles vibrated in the room.

"I can't stand them. Please shut the door."

He did so. The fierce gale outside seemed to howl all the louder. He put fresh wood on the fire and stooped to draw her cloak closer about her, for one shoulder was uncovered. She looked at him with the gentlest, sweetest expression he had ever seen on a human face, put a hand on either shoulder, and lightly forced him down so that he knelt on the floor beside her.

"I'm not cold," she said. Her hands stroked his dark hair, ever so little weighed down his head so it rested in her lap. He wanted to stretch up his arms, hold her, but he dared not. The last few years she had become extremely captious. If he tried to embrace her, she would turn on him. He had begun to believe it was as important not to "overexcite" her as her father and Old Doctor West were always saying.

Her hands rested on his head. It made him think of a time when he was a little boy and his grandmother had taken him to receive the dying blessing of a pious old man.

Finally he lifted his face to her. "Polly, what have you been doing up here, all alone?"

"I've been crying, Dash."

"Crying?"

"Suddenly I felt — I can't explain it — so . . . trapped. And oh, so sad. I felt so sad. I had to cry. I think old Abby Flack understands."

"But why were you crying, my girl?"

"I've been to so many balls."

"You have always loved them."

"Yes."

"Then why did you cry?" He started to get up.

"No, no, Dash. Stay where you are."

He did, and felt again the remote, cool blessing of her hands upon his head. "But we can't talk this way."

"Why talk? There's nothing to talk about."

"Polly, when did you come up here to cry?"

"There was a voluntary. I think, the first one."

"Yes, and I hunted for you, and all I got was some little Crowninshield. I thought it was Emmy."

"Anstis. Just like Emmy five years ago. I stood behind the hall portières, watching. I did not feel like dancing. And I watched, and the next was a draw dance."

"Yes, and she chose 'Drops of Brandy' — and was the only one who knew it."

"I noticed."

Surely she could not be jealous of a little sixteen-year-old girl.

"I began to feel so sad," Polly went on. "I came up here and decided to figure out the number of times in my life I'd stood up to dance. Not dancing school and not just tossed-up dances on the spur of the moment. Say I began at sixteen, like Anstis Crowninshield. Now I'm thirty-three. Say I've averaged about twenty balls a year, counting Salem and the times I've been in Boston, and there's a ball most every night when Papa and I are at Ballston Springs. So that gives you thirty-three minus sixteen, and that's seventeen years. I'm not sure, doing it in my head, but I think that makes three hundred and forty balls, roughly. We dance usually about eight or ten dances. Say nine. But I can't possibly multiply three hundred and forty by nine in my head. Can you?"

"Three thousand and sixty, for a guess."

But still he did not see why this would make her cry. These surely were happy memories.

"Then I saw you dancing with a girl young enough to be my daughter."

"Oh, Polly, how could she?"

"If she had been born when I was eighteen, she could have been my daughter. Peggy Pierce was seventeen when her first was born . . ."

"But I wouldn't have danced with what's-her-name Crowninshield if you had been to hand."

She laughed confidently. "I know that. Of course. But I couldn't help but think what a child she was. Why, I never thought of *Emmy* being old enough for you to dance with! Emmy was a clumsy little girl. Nobody could teach her to button anything. Her *drawers*, Dash, were always falling off, all over Salem. And already she's sitting there playing cards and watching 'the young people' frolic. Because she's going to have a baby. It was when I looked in the card-room and saw Emmy, I began to count. Dash, that's where all the girls·— I mean, the women my age — were, and even women much younger. And they looked surprised to see me. Thought I was ready to join them. I suppose they thought at last nobody had asked me to dance. And Nanny was so 'nice' to me, she was the worst of all."

"Nanny wouldn't mean to be."

"She said nobody our age should try to keep up with the young people. And I said some of the men were forty-odd. She said, yes, she knew. And the older they got, the younger they wanted their partners. Hadn't I noticed you kissing Anstis Crowninshield?"

"Nanny doesn't mean to be nasty. She merely says her mind without second thought."

"But that's what they were all thinking. Yes. And Thyrza Birdall — she's Mrs. Sam Orne these days — and Peggy Pierce! Why, I used to be scared of Peggy Pierce! I was frightened when you'd ask her to dance. Dash, you were only eighteen then, but you always could look at every girl so each thought she was the only one."

"I never meant to."

"Peggy Pierce must weigh two hundred. She says every time she has another child, she puts on ten pounds. Why, she was as slender as a reed!"

"And you still are."

This she could not deny.

"Polly," he said, getting up off the floor, sitting in a chair beside her, "I don't think either of us is in the mood for more party tonight."

"No."

"So now I'll take you home. I think I can still get a sleigh through. Your father made me promise to take you home early tonight."

She burst out angrily: "I don't want to go home! I can't stand it! I can't stand Papa sitting up for me every night, and I have to drink tamarind water and tell him whom I've danced with, and Aunt Brattle comes down. And they treat me like a little child. I'm not a little girl. I don't want them to pretend I am."

Well, he thought patiently, here's a squall blowing up. But her voice quieted to the nostalgic tone it had had before.

"Did you ever know that we often use up a pair of slippers in one evening's dancing?"

"No."

"I was thinking about slippers. I figured close to five hundred pairs. Thousands of dancing slippers stretch behind me — white slippers and gold and silver. Black velvet, purple kid, green morocco. And when I first began going to parties — I think I was sixteen or so — we all wore red slippers. That was because of the revolution in France, Dash. People said the fashion started by women dancing in the blood about the guillotine. Ugh!" She shivered all over as if cold, then bent with her characteristic grace, untied the ribbons on her ankles, and thoughtfully pulled off her slippers. They were heelless, cream-colored, as flexible as gloves. "Ah, well . . ." she sighed, smoothed and caressed them, studying them minutely. "They are hardly worn at all." Her face suddenly contorted. "And I'll never put them on again! Never!"

He noticed that she was breathing hard. "I'm not going to another ball. Never, so long as I live, will I put on dancing slippers again."

He tried to put his arm about her, comfort her, but she turned on him angrily, and struck him across the face. She cried out, "Please go away! Please go away, Dash, and leave me alone!"

There seemed nothing else to do. He'd give her a few minutes to compose herself, then he'd come back again.

In the lower hall he saw Abby Flack. "Abby, will you be so good," he said, "as to inform Miss Mompesson I intend to take her home early? Tell her" — he looked at his big gold watch — "in half an hour."

"Yes, sir," she agreed, and he saw her mounting the stairs, heading for Polly's hiding place.

Captain Crowninshield came toward him laughing and mopping his sweating forehead. "Oh, Dash, Dash," he said, "a man can't go on dancing forever, eh? Come on, now. There's punch in the back room — stronger than is served the ladies. And we can have our cigars."

He wanted to corner Dash, to ask him what he thought of all this war talk. Or rather tell him what he himself thought. Once not so long ago America had fought her undeclared war against France. Now there was little injury France could do. She no longer had a fleet and so was in no position to impress Yankee seamen as England had been doing. Dash hoped the Government would not be so reckless as to draw the country into war at this late date. Surely war with England should have been five years before, if ever, when the British *Leopard* had shot up the American frigate *Chesapeake,* and everyone had been fighting mad. That had not brought war. Dash was saying that popular opinion now would not support a war against Britain. And as for impressment of American seamen, the fifteen biggest Massachusetts merchants had recently announced that, of the thousands of men they employed, there were only twelve *bona fide* Americans impressed by England. Surely George Crowninshield knew as well as he that American captains were always signing on British deserters. And, by international law, England had the right to seize them. Even upon the *Chesapeake* there had been four deserters from the British Navy. Not, of course, that the *Leopard* had been justified in killing Americans to get them. And talking of impressment, the worst either country had done to America was Napoleon's seizure of twenty-two Yankee sailors at Danzig. These he had marched to Antwerp and added to the French Navy. Surely both countries had put upon American shipping past all decency. But Captain Crown-inshield, recently back from Washington, was talking about the "War Hawks" in Congress. Frontiersmen from the wilds of Ohio and God knew where, who had never seen an ocean. *They* were talking about the conquest of Canada, saying England was too busy with Napoleon at home ever to send men to defend Canada.

Dash looked at his watch. Although he was talking well, defending his Federalist point of view against George Crowninshield, his mind was still on Polly.

❧ 9 ❧

WHEN HE SAW ABBY FLACK stick her head in the door, beckoning to him, he excused himself from the punch-bowl group. The half-hour was not up.

"Abby, is she ready to go home now?"

"Sir, I don't know. But perhaps she ought. She's been crying a good deal, and now she's stopped, it's worse. Shan't I call Doctor Jack? He's in the card-room. She seems sort of bemused, sir."

"No, I can manage her better than Doctor Jack. It was right to call me."

As they went up the stairs, Abby confessed. "I took the liberty of turning the key on her. I didn't want folk coming in on her. She's really odd-looking. When I tried to get her slippers on, she wouldn't. And I can't get her to pin up her hair. Tomorrow, when she's herself again, it would be mortifying for her to think other folk had seen her."

"Give me the key. See if you can find a hackney sleigh hanging about. She'd best go home."

"If you can persuade her, sir. She keeps saying she won't go home and that she can't get out. Over and over. It don't make good sense."

He saw that Abby Flack was a little frightened, but some sense of propriety was still left in her. She hesitated before the closed door.

"Shan't I go in with you, sir? She's real queer tonight."

"No. Coast about and see if you can locate a sleigh."

Polly was sitting so quietly, his first feeling was irritation. Servants always make mountains of molehills, he thought, even so reliable an old party as Abby Flack. Polly was sitting bolt upright, almost primly, hands locked together on her lap, chin up, gazing into space. Her fair hair stirred and blew about her. And next he felt cold wind blowing in and through the room. The curtain at the window was moving. Already a white triangle of snow was piling up on the floor. It was curious that the Crowninshields would assign to the ladies a chamber with a broken window.

Then he knew. In those few moments after Abby had left her and before he himself had come, Polly, finding herself locked in, had fallen into some sort of frenzy and had broken the window. She might have used a piece of firewood from beside the hearth, or a pair of tongs, but, anyway, she had cut herself. He saw that the quiet hands and arms were bloody. Realizing the frenzy of that scene which no one had witnessed affected him deeply. The mainmast's gone now, he thought grimly. But belying all his fears was Polly's utter quiet. He spoke her name. She turned her head indifferently. He had no reason to think she even recognized him.

"Polly," he said again, went to her and took a lock of the fair hair in his hands.

"Oh!" she cried, and winced. "How dare you lay hands upon me! No! Go away! Go away!"

The second he left her, she quieted again, ready to forget reality and go back to whatever dream now held her. He went to the door and locked it from the inside. Abby was right. He wasn't going to have some girl in search of her handkerchief come blundering in. Nor Polly suddenly break out, run down the stairs, frightening everybody half out of their wits. Lunatic. For the first time in his life, this ugly word came into his mind in connection with Polly. She had broken the window. She might do worse.

The slight click of the key aroused her — probably it had when Abby locked her in. That was when she had broken the window.

She was on her feet, crouching away from him and staring at him. "Why have you locked that door? Why do you retain me here?" There was a strange animal look in her eyes, a shocking, trapped, animal look. Then she began to walk back and forth, washing her hands, smooching the blood upon them until she seemed to be wearing brief red gloves. Apparently she felt no pain from her injuries. But the red gloves were hideous.

"I've got to get out!" she wailed over and over. "I've got to get out!"

"Yes, and I've come to take you home, Polly."

At the word "home" she gave a whimpering cry, flung her red hands to the ceiling with so exaggerated a gesture it seemed like mockery, and fell to pacing back and forth. She went from the door to the window and back to the door, but with the seeming indifference to her audience of a caged panther. There was a savagery about her every motion, the expression on her face, the soft stockinged-foot tread, a feeling of softness and power, and an indomitable energy, a hardly human energy. She moved like a whirlpool, and Dash felt he might be sucked in. She was eddying up and around him and his sanity. His longing for her had been slowly dying through the years. Remorse, despair, guilt, postponement, and remorse again, natural incompatibility, had done much to kill it. It flamed in him now — now, of all inappropriate moments. He felt her casting all moorings, floating off into what dark sea he could hardly imagine, begging him to plunge in after her.

He sat and buried his face in his hands, would have wept if only tears had come. I'll have to call Jack, he thought. And tomorrow he'll be calling Doctor Kittridge of Andover. The strait-jacket and the chains. And that will be all. If only now, this moment, he could say or do the right thing! Arrest her as she stood on the brink of the horror about to engulf her.

She had begun talking to herself incoherently. About her aunt and her papa, and again and again he heard his name said with longing and despair. He felt he was eavesdropping upon a dream. Yes, if I call Jack, this is indeed the end. But if he could steer her, mastless and rudderless as she was, ride out this storm, there might be calm seas ahead.

When she stopped talking, the shriek of the wind about the house, the throbbing of the fiddles, came closer. He noticed that the snow was piling up below the shattered window in a larger drift.

Now she was fingering the lock on the door. Suddenly she shook it wildly. "I'm locked in! I can't get out! Oh, God! God! God!"

"Polly," he said, going toward her softly, "look, I have the key. Here in my hand. Do you want me to open the door?"

Then she saw a strange man, terrifying in his strangeness, leaning toward her, smiling. It seemed a terrible smile to her. She gave a gasping shriek which she smothered with her own red-gloved hands and shot for the window. He was there at the same moment. And both of them were half out of it. He had no idea how strong she was. She was actually shaking herself free of him. Her precocious strength gave him more knowledge of her derangement than anything that had yet happened. Her dress was tearing to ribbons on the jagged glass, and the glass was cutting through into her flesh.

Before he got his hand over her mouth, she managed one cry, one terrible word which the winds took and the fiddles drowned. A word which doubtless in her right mind she could never have mentioned.

"Rape!"

Back inside the room once more, he tried to handle her as gently as possible. "You mustn't yell again, Polly," he said, as though talking to a child. "See, now, be my good girl." She was fighting him ferociously and caught one of his fingers between her teeth. He shifted his hold. Then came shrilling into his ears the most inhuman, terrible scream he had ever heard. "Help! Help! Rape! Rape!"

This would certainly be heard throughout the house. He stood back from her and looked at her with compassion and almost with loathing.

"Poor girl," he whispered. "My poor, lost girl."

Already he could hear running feet coming up the stairs, excited voices. Then for the first time she looked at him as though she knew him.

"Dash," she said slowly, in amazement. "Oh . . . " Her eyes grew immense with reproach, disbelief. "I couldn't have believed it of you . . . or was I dreaming? Perhaps I was dreaming?"

"Yes, Polly. You've been asleep."

Now someone was shaking the door and pounding on it, yelling, "Open up!" And the door was straining on its hinges. He took one moment out of all eternity, it seemed to him. He went to her and kissed her.

He started to unlock the door, but was too late. It burst inward and let in, seemingly, an avalanche of strangers. Strangers with murderous eyes, furious faces, fierce, parted lips. It was hard for Dash to recognize such as old friends and neighbors.

They had been expecting to find that some drunken foremast hand had climbed a gutter and attacked one of their women. Or perhaps a black waiter had followed a girl to this chamber.

Dash stood there, stolidly facing looks of amazement, incredulity, honest disbelief of what their eyes saw. Miss Mompesson, he explained, had had an hysterical fit. He was glad to see Jack West pushing through the crowd about the door.

Jack admitted to Nanny — knowing she would spread the news — that if it had been any other woman in the world except Polly Mompesson, he'd have been ready to go to court and swear at least attempted rape. Her clothes had been almost torn off her. Her shoulders were black and blue, her hands and arms cut. She had tried to escape through the window and had been cut badly by the glass. Apparently it was not until she had expended every ounce of strength that she had been forced to the humiliation of calling for help. But only "apparently." She had had hysterics, and no one can say exactly what an hysteric subject will do. Yes, he told his wife, she is prostrated and will be so for weeks. Perhaps she may never completely recover, and she is so ashamed it will be hard for her to go out and meet her old acquaintances. There is no one she wants to see but Dash.

This fact — that it was only Dash who was allowed to see her — did much to clear his part, whatever it might have been, in the mysterious thing that had happened at the Crowninshield ball. If she held naught against him, why should anyone else? Dash himself hardly knew what had happened — but he knew that it was something of an end.

Chapter Twelve

F IRST BY EXPRESS RIDER came the news long feared by Federalists, long hoped for by Republicans. A state of war was declared to exist between Great Britain and the United States. Next day Liz Inman arrived from Washington. Once again, as in the time of Embargo, he had guessed something was going to happen and was on the spot to pick up private information.

The three brothers sat in the old counting-house. Outside, along Inman Wharf, up and down Derby Street, yelling and hurrahing made sober thought impossible. The June day was hot, the windows open.

"Confound the damn fools!" Liz exclaimed angrily. "A man can't hear himself think."

No wonder the yelling irritated him. For up and down the wharf seamen were calling for Dash Inman. Apparently every man of them wanted to sign on whatever privateer he might command. That Tom had ever been a most capable master they had long forgotten. It was not Liz they wanted.

"Hey . . . Dash . . . Dash, show us your face, sir!"

"Stop your gamming in there and come out and begin to sign!"

An ambitious drunk had shinnied up the outside of the counting-house and was peering in the upper window where the three men sat.

"He's here all right, mates!" he yelled back, and presumably lost his footing, for his face instantly disappeared.

It was three years since Dash had been to sea, but he had lost not one jot or tittle of his great reputation. Other men, almost as able as he, would be forgotten in that length of time. But some, like Dash, would tend to grow into legend.

"Come on," Liz said impatiently, "let's go to Ma'am's. Doctor Hobey never uses the sitting room. And those rag-tails won't dare follow us there."

They passed through thrown caps and masses of pushing, sweaty, muscular bodies. Liz, absorbed in the larger aspects of the war, plowed straight ahead. It irritated him to see Dash stopping and stopping, calling this man by name, accepting claps on the back. Nobody was calling him "Captain Inman." Only a few "Captain Dash." In the great excitement of this afternoon he was merely "Dash." Well, Liz had noticed before that Dash never did seem to know how to keep discipline. And he was honest enough to admit to himself that Dash never had needed to "keep" discipline on his ships. It was always there.

"Have done, men!" Liz would yell. "Let us pass, will you?" Evidently he and Tom would have to wait forever at Ma'am's gate. Not until Dash said what ship he would command would the sailors let him go. He and Tom finally went inside to sit.

It was nothing to Liz who fought whom in what war. He had no settled convictions like Dash. He was a Republican, because, eight years before, he had been smart enough to realize Mr. Jefferson's party was the stronger. And his politics had paid off handsomely at the time of the Embargo. They might help the firm again. Actually Liz liked Napoleon. He had been the first young man in Salem to wear a Napoleonic forelock. He knew how Dash loathed the little tyrant.

Dash came in, his buttons burst from his coat, his neckcloth awry. Certainly his would-be crewmen had been mauling him, but there was a look of deep satisfaction in his handsome eyes. Perhaps at no moment of his long years of command had he received greater recognition than this afternoon on Inman Wharf. If ever he had trusted too much to luck, it had been forgotten.

He flung himself into a chair. "It's the bloody hypocrisy of the thing," he went on exactly where he had left off a few minutes before, "talking of free trade and sailors' rights. Yet it's not the seaports that have started this war. It's the backwoods. *They're* talking about wrongs done our ships and seamen. It's a mask to pull over the ugly face of a simple war of conquest. Canada is all those War Hawks in Congress care about."

"Something in that," Liz agreed, determined not so to oppose Dash he'd send him off on a wrong tack. "But don't forget that old Ben Franklin, years ago, said this country would never be safe as long as Canada was in the hands of an unfriendly power."

"All right, I agree. But why make England unfriendly?"

"Oh, Madison says we can conquer Canada in three weeks. How can England, just now, fight back? Napoleon has his teeth in her throat."

"You've been saying that for years. And I don't think our snapping at her heels will make much difference."

"So you care more for England than for your own country, eh?"

"Hell, no. Sometimes I don't like the bloody blighters, but . . . if she goes down, nothing can stop Napoleon from having the whole world."

"I'm not talking about 'the world.' I'm talking about J. Inman's Sons."

And he did. Dash lapsed into broody absent-mindedness as Liz read a list of their ships. It was perhaps the first time he had actually faced the fact that the ships Liz managed at the Boston office represented a bigger tonnage than the ones he controlled at Salem. They had better "write off" the three Inman ships now in Asiatic waters. The British would seize them. That's the end of the *Wanderer*, Dash thought. For the *Dolphin* and the *Nereid* he had no particular feeling. He thought suddenly of Japan, Dechima, and Doctor Vreed. For now the time had come Vreed had foreseen. There was not a place in the world the Dutch flag still flew except only on Dechima. England had seized the Dutch Indies.

"The *Calypso*," Liz went on, pulling ferociously at his long cigar, "is upon the coast. I believe she'll make port before the British naval officers get word there's a state of war. I've got the *Lightning* in Boston. Been holding on to her three months now. Guessed this thing was coming." The *Lightning* was the pride of Liz's heart. Boston built, Boston manned, but Salem registered, she was too big for Salem Harbor. Dash always referred to her contemptuously as "the Boston boat."

"She's four hundred and fifty tons. I've ordered her razeed to three hundred and thirty. Twenty guns. One hundred and fifty men. As a merchant she's been carrying thirty men. Now one thing, Dash. I'm not going to have any trouble getting naval stores. I belong to the right party. If you can't locate guns, munitions, and so forth around here, send to me. First thing get the old *Mermaid,* the *Victrix,* and the *Calypso* razeed and built over for fighting."

Dash was calmly drinking rum and water. He was listening, but not so much to Liz as to the humming and shouting and yelling along Essex Street; to the tootling of a fife and the beat of a drum. Already recruiting officers were abroad.

Liz edged his chair toward him. Too close. Dash was aware of the ticking of his watch in his waistcoat pocket, the fumes of his heavy cigar, almost the clink of money in his pocket. "One thing more, I've got to confess. I was so sure this war was coming that three months ago I ordered a keel laid at Medford. She's being built like a real little frigate. Four hundred tons. I thought I might sell her to Government. But you know how against a navy they are in Washington. We've only a handful of frigates."

"What's our fleet going to do? We haven't many frigates, you're right. Jefferson cut the fleet down and Madison has ignored it. It's little, but it's good. What will it do?"

Liz looked embarrassed. "Every ship-of-war is to be ordered to keep port. Government's going to build little forts to keep off invaders. And gunboats once more. You remember, the gunboats time of the Embargo? So tippy they had to stow the guns if they put to sea? We'll have them again, I tell you this is supposed to be a land war."

Tom and Dash looked equally blank and unbelieving.

"To comfort you, I think Commander Rodgers and the ships he has will get to sea before any *official* word gets to him. Once he is off the coast, it wouldn't do any good for Government to tell him to keep port."

Tom asked, "You sure Government will commission privateers? No point in our converting our merchantmen if they can't get commissions."

"Aye. That's settled. Privateers cost Government nothing. They can sink or make a fortune and it's nothing to them. All private risk. We are lucky to have first-class ships we can arm and send out."

They talked a little of the masters they'd choose. At the end, Liz said contemptuously: "Of course Tom will stay home, with his knitting . . . I'm going to take out the *Lightning* from Boston. Soon as her commission comes. Dash" — he leaned over and put his hand on his brother's knee, pleading with him — "which would you rather command, that new frigate-built vessel or your old *Victrix*?" The drumming and fifing were coming nearer — right past the house. "If we want men," Liz added generously, "all we'll ever have to do is give Dash a drum and walk him up Derby Street. Of course, you're the only master who ever got the whole strength out of the *Victrix*. Me . . . I nearly sank her." That's the way to get Dash, Liz thought. Put it on thick.

"The *Victrix* is still laid up," Dash said.

"Haven't you even *yet* got her seaworthy, Dash? Why, it was last year I brought her back. God damn it, a firm can't afford to lay up one of its best ships for almost a year."

"She's not suited to privateering. You know how balanced she is. By a hair. Soon as we razee her, put up four-foot oak bulwarks, give her masts like church steeples, she'd turn turtle."

Tom added, "Liz, if this war is as short as Washington says, I'd suggest we leave one first-class merchantman unconverted. Ready to set sail for the East the moment peace comes."

"Good idea," Dash added. "We won't send her out."

"Well . . ." Liz hesitated. He did not believe one word of the optimistic talk he had heard around Washington. It could not be a mere summer war. But he was anxious to agree as far as possible with Dash. Not offend him. The firm must have him for a master.

"Of course, our entering this war is only a small part of a big picture. But the second Napoleon breaks England's neck, why, we win."

"I'm not anxious to go hanging on to that blackguard's coat-tails," Dash said sternly. "Nor am I anxious to have the *Victrix* engaged in so dishonorable a war."

"I agree with Tom," said Liz, patiently. "No use converting all our merchantmen. The *Victrix* is going to sit the whole thing out, right where she is. Like an old woman."

"So'll I."

"Damn it, you can't. Haven't you heard them yelling for you? You're a born privateersman, Dash. They know it. So do I."

"Fight for Napoleon? Not I."

"Forget politics, Dash."

"It isn't that entirely. You haven't heard, of course. Yesterday Mr. Mompesson had a stroke."

"Good," Liz said, roughly. "I suppose it was this declaration of war gave it to him? You choose queer mates politically, Dash."

"I try not to be influenced by the men I don't like on my side any more than by the people I do like on the other. But you see how it is — I can't leave Polly. Just now." He got up to go.

Liz barred the way. "You've got to leave her. You've got to get yourself to sea — once more — or you'll rot. Why, she's been false enough to you. Didn't she tell everybody last winter you tried to violate her or something — crazy bitch!"

"Other people said that."

"I wish you had!"

Dash's dark eyes blazed, but he was rigidly silent.

"Dash, do something. What you need is a real woman. Not a ghost in a haunted house. You come back to Boston with me to-night. I'll fix you up. What do you do for women, anyway?"

"Nothing."

"Nothing!" Liz gestured weakly, unable to understand so unnatural a situation. "You were a damned forward little kid. You started early."

"And finished early, too."

"Look at me" — Liz pounded his chest. "I've got a wife. And as you both know, a mistress — and two sons by her. Now and then I catch hold of a stray girl besides, as I pass through this vale of tears."

"That's fine, Liz. But you leave me be."

"Going now? We've only begun to settle things and I have to ride back to Boston tonight."

"Yes. Doctor West told me this morning Polly's prostrated. But she wants to see me. He said four-thirty this afternoon. And he'll talk with me first. So . . . I'm expected elsewhere. You can have your war."

Liz raised smooth, expressive eyebrows. "I see," he said, coldly.

Liz and Tom stood at the window, silently watching him go through the crowd still gathered about Ma'am's gate. Every cap came off, but almost as men doff caps in the presence of the dead.

They knew Dash Inman wasn't going to sea. The brothers noticed that smart, elastic, quarterdeck step, now turning away from the waterfront.

Old Doctor West was waiting for Dash in the street before the Mompessons'.

"How is she?"

Doctor West shook his old-fashioned great wig. "Almost completely collapsed. She's a morbidly sensitive creature. Frankly, undue excitement like her father's sickness may unhinge her completely. And forever."

"I know."

"I must ask you, Dash, not to say or do anything that will, in any way, upset her. No talk of this war, for instance. Nothing violent or unpleasant. I found out last winter, sir, that you have a most uncanny control over her. I need not advise you, I'm sure."

Dash stood with bent head.

"But I recommend a short, daily visit very much. Remember, do not excite her."

"No, I won't," Dash said, sorrowfully. "No. I won't excite her, ever."

Even from where he stood, now alone, he could hear the fifes and drums along the waterfront and the hurrahing. It was a still day, June 22, 1812, the day news came to Salem that it was to be war. He thought he heard his own name called and lifted his head to listen. Yet if it were (and he was not sure), he might not answer. He had a painful moment of awareness and knew it. He felt himself a hollow and unreal man. Peter's warning came back to him, as he stood fiddling with the gate latch, not quite ready to go in even yet. But he had nothing to give the seamen yelling for him.

He went up the brief path and knocked on the door.

~ 2 ~

THERE WAS EVERY REASON why Dash and Liz might quarrel, but when they did, it was not over politics, but so ridiculously small a thing as the naming of the Medford-built, almost-frigate Liz had ordered when he believed war imminent. Liz had already taken the *Lightning* on two quick voyages and sent back seven prizes before the new ship was launched. Dan Obrian was to command her.

"Why don't we name her for Ma'am?" Dash said.

"That's been done. She's named."

"What?"

"The *Devotion*."

Dash's underlip thrust out. "That won't do. A man can't name a ship for his mistress. Call her the *Fanny* if you want to."

"I'll call her what I please. You've been in Boston again and again, yet you never came to see her on the stocks, nor to her launching."

"I'm glad I wasn't there. A shameful thing. And I suppose Devotion herself broke the bottle on her and gave her name to the ship."

"Yes. And was more pleased that day than by anything I've given her — except her sons. Why shouldn't a man name a ship for his wife's niece — I'd like to know?"

"I say no Inman ship is going to bear the name of a mistress."

"No Dulceys in our fleet?"

"No. No Dulceys. You'll have to get a new name, Liz."

Liz looked at him patiently. "It's done. She'll be to sea in three days now. She was launched all standing. I wouldn't think to go back on Devotion so. Fanny doesn't care. Why should you get your wind up?"

"Fanny does care. She'll never say so. But she cares . . . and now you shame her publicly."

"She certainly pushed those nieces of hers at me. Sometimes I wished I might come home and find Fanny alone. But no. She was always telling me Devotion was so shy, why couldn't I pay more heed to her, draw her out a little. When it came out Devotion was going to have a child, Fanny went off with her, stayed with her, found a place to board the baby. Fanny understands. I don't know how to say it, I love her so. And now there are my two sons to consider. Boarded over in Andover. Almost never see their mother or me. Doesn't this sound different, Dash, than when you say 'my mistress'?"

Dash had never believed Liz capable of falling in love with any woman. He remembered how anxious he had been to make that long voyage after the Embargo. He had wanted to get away, had hoped that absence would cure him and the infatuated young girl. Probably Liz was doing as well by her and her sons as a man might.

Yet Fanny was going downhill fast. He thought of the fat, shiftless, indifferent woman she had become, how ill-suited to the grandeur of Liz's enormous Beacon Hill house. Anybody to see her would think she was some auntie the owner had taken in from kindness; given her a back attic room and let her hem and mend for her keep, with the tacit understanding that she must not get underfoot. Dash had often seen her, had watched her face corrode away with secret tears, and knew why so often her eyes were red-rimmed at breakfast. Her oldest niece, Jeany, a smart, hard little thing, very stylish, kept the house, often received Liz's guests with him. And then, ever and anon, Devotion was there, so silent, so beautiful, with that straight flaxen hair and enormous gray eyes. Such a deathly serious young girl, without any of the gaiety and coquetry, not even the handsome shape he would have thought would have appealed to Liz. No wonder that, although there had been some talk about what Jeany's relationship might be to her Uncle Liz — they were always together about Boston — Devotion's occasional visits to the house were hardly noticed. It was Liz himself who, of course, had told Dash. Liz had always confided his love-affairs to his brothers, no matter how shameful.

"All right. If that's the way you want to fix your life. But you've got to change the name of the ship."

"Well, then, I won't."

"Look-a-here, Liz" — he sounded as if he were going to say next, Who do you think is captain of this ship anyway? "I've said it. And flat out. That ship's not to sail under that name."

Liz said nothing for a moment, but his color was creeping up from under his black beard, flooding his face.

"The fact is, Dash, I care no more than *that*" — and he snapped his fingers — "what you say. For years and years," he went on with difficulty, "I . . . cared. I cared too much. Perhaps that's why I don't give a God damn now."

Dash knew he had long ago lost the upper hand over Liz because he himself was hollow inside. You can't expect loyalty to an empty case. What had once filled that case had drained away.

"Well, there's nothing to quarrel about," he said, almost listlessly.

"Isn't there? You think I've treated Devotion shamefully. I haven't — I've made her happy. What about you and Polly? For God's sake, I wish you'd seduce her — and get it done."

"Belay!"

"Belay yourself, Dash."

Liz went his own way. The ship, one of the largest of all American privateers and built from the keel up for such service, carried her shameful name to great success. She, the Crownin-shields' *America,* and the Inmans' *Lightning* were the three most victorious of armed merchantmen.

Once light as foam, symmetrical as gulls, the old East Injunmen had been bedeviled by dockyard riggers and carpenters into clumsy, rigid fighting craft — as ugly, Dash thought, as Dutch doggers. Often the prizes piled up fifteen or twenty at a time in Salem, and the privateers themselves were continually coming and going. Not even the greatest success of the old India trade had brought in more money.

So the first summer passed with amazing ineptitude along the Canadian border, and with nothing but glory at sea.

There were comparatively few people in America who saw the connection between their own war against England and her infinitely greater war against Napoleon. But merchants who had ranged the world, like the Inmans, knew. Even Liz admitted he was making hay while the sun shone. He was not so confident of the "invincible Napoleon" as he had been ten years before. His Napoleonic forelock had disappeared.

Although the *Lightning* often sent her prizes to New York or Boston, the *Devotion* sent hers to Salem. This was because her commander, Dan Obrian, wished to impress the town where he had grown up as a poor boy. Late that fall, he decided it was time for Salem to see him in all his new glory. It took four tides, kedging and sweeps, to get the big ship into the harbor. Salem registered she might be, but it was the first time the *Devotion* had ever seen Salem.

All Salem streamed down, crowding Inman Wharf, yelling and hurrahing. This one ship, with only eight months of service, had paid back her original cost to the owners several times over. She had enriched for life many of her shareholders and officers. She had been from the beginning the most aggressive of American privateers and had, wisely or not, the week before engaged the British frigate *Tenedos,* off Halifax. Then, injured and withdrawing, had run into the *Banner* and *Hunter* and fought them to a standstill off Thatcher's Island. Now she was safe, but in need of repairs and fresh men. People gaped at her broken bulwarks, shot-torn sail, the slings or missing fingers of her crew. Even Obrian had a becoming bandage about his blond head.

Dan Obrian wore a replica of a naval captain's uniform except for the epaulets. He was covered with gold lace and he carried a sword. The blue, swallow-tailed coat was cut away to show snowy, skin-tight pantaloons, and, in his case, the flatness of the abdomen. His black boots glittered. Dash, waiting for him at the head of the wharf, glanced at him and grinned. Danny looked ready to blush.

The repair of the ship was discussed and the ship's business. Then Dash said, "Will you be my guest, Danny, the three weeks you're ashore?"

"Thanks, sir. But no. You see, I engage my rooms from Mrs. Flanneau by the year. And that's home to me now. Her children seem almost like my own."

Since Mrs. Flanneau and Petra had inherited Peter Inman's share of the firm, she had given up all her gentlemen boarders except Danny. Why doesn't he marry her? Dash wondered, as he walked beside him up Essex Street, with four porters following with handcarts carrying his gear, and half the town of Salem and all the small boys in their wake. I'll bet dollars to doughnuts that last child is his — that Jacques. As they reached Mrs. Flanneau's gate, Petra flew down the path to meet him, yelling, "Danny!" He picked her up and called her "Pet" and she hugged him. As usual she cut Dash dead.

At the moment Marcy was in Goodrich's bookshop across the street. She heard the commotion and saw Dash, so casual and at ease, with his hands in his pockets, walking along beside Danny. Danny looked like the god Mars himself, with his handsome build, bandaged head, proud step. The contrast between the two was almost laughable. No question now who was the hero. Like one of her own heroines, she felt a little faint.

Marcy had fought her feelings for Dan Obrian. She knew he was not the man for her. She couldn't imagine being married to him, nor could she imagine not loving him. Bad as her novels were, the writing of them had given her a certain awareness of human emotions and values. Dash, who had discovered Danny, signed him as an officer, was these days often belittling him. She longed to hear Dash say, only once, "That's a very able captain," or, "Dan Obrian is as good a master as we have." A few words from Dash would justify her predilection for him.

As Dash turned from Mrs. Flanneau's, he looked at his watch. Every day now, ever since Mr. Mompesson's stroke, Dash, unless he was out of town, had gone to see Polly at exactly four-thirty. That was where he now was obviously heading. Marcy decided to join him.

"Dash," she begged him, "don't you think Captain Obrian marvelously clever?"

"Oh, aye. Clever at getting himself up to look as much like a naval officer as he dares."

"But he has handled the *Devotion* wonderfully, hasn't he? Everybody says he has done wonderfully."

"So far. But I've warned Liz that give him time and he'll do the wrong thing."

"He's made lots of money, hasn't he?"

"Aye. Lots and lots. And he certainly is no coward. But this running around, fighting British frigates, is nonsense. He could have outsailed the *Tenedos* — why did he bump into the *Banner* and the *Hunter?* Should have run away."

"No, he isn't a coward, is he?" Marcy exclaimed in jubilation.

"No. Nobody ever said the fellow was a coward. But the monkey shows his tail."

"What do you mean by that?"

"Who but a monkey at heart would put on all that gold lace, carry a sword walking Salem streets? I almost laughed. Still, he's my monkey."

Somehow, Marcy thought, she must make Dash unsay those dreadful words. She would stay with him a little longer.

"I haven't seen Polly for weeks. Couldn't I go with you this afternoon?"

Marcy was so much younger than Polly, they had never been intimate. It was not weeks since she had seen Polly, but months. Not since the Crowninshield ball. People had said Dash pulled off most of her clothes; had attempted rape, or succeeded. She had tried to jump out the window, and Marcy would never forget that terrible, terrible cry for help, and men dropping their partners on the spot and tearing off upstairs. Her face burned with humiliation and anger. Dash, of all men in the world!

She slipped her arm through his, and was not the first woman to wonder how surprisingly muscular he was. He never looked heavily built. "Can I?" she begged.

"I'd like to have you go with me, Marcy. Polly will be pleased, too, I'm sure."

He was grateful to her, she knew by the softening of his eyes. His family had certainly never supported him in his infatuation for Polly. And since that dreadful scene of last winter, his mother had been hounding him and picking on him. Laughing at him because he wouldn't let go of Polly Mompesson, who had turned on him and made the ugliest charge a woman can bring against a man. Yet he had forgiven her.

Marcy knew the Mompesson house little, but even she realized, as soon as they were admitted, how it had changed. Like a run-down clock. It felt, sounded, different.

Not only had a Negro man been installed to carry Mr. Mompesson up and down stairs and even to his carriage on fine days, but Nurse Meeker had come. Aunt Brattle was confined to her room with gout. A man nurse and a woman nurse did not seem an exorbitant amount of extra help for a wealthy household with two elderly invalids, yet their presence cast a longer shadow than a casual visitor could realize. Dash knew.

Nurse Meeker, like every other woman servant, was devoted to Polly. She spent much more time on her than on the cross old woman she was hired to attend. She brushed Polly's hair, carried up her breakfast, mended her clothes, and because she was a capable woman, ran the household. Thus she combined the former duties of the aunts with those of Flip.

Yet how different it seemed now! Aunt Brattle and Aunt Birdseye had run the house because obviously Polly was too young. Nurse Meeker, because she was not well enough. When she waited on Polly, how unlike the services of deft, pretty Flip! Flip had made Polly seem too wonderful to move a footstool, but Nurse Meeker made her seem too weak.

Today Mr. Mompesson had been carried down to Polly's sitting room, and there he sat with a far more attenuated, delicate Polly than Marcy remembered. They had been playing backgammon. Marcy was surprised at the cordial welcome Mr. Mompesson gave Dash. Perhaps it had been only one of her own family's legends that he hated Dash. He was even calling him, through twisted lips, "my boy." That's because he knows now Dash won't ever take Polly away from him. Surely now she will never leave him. That's why, these days, he likes him. Immediately he was insisting that Dash sit with him and talk money matters. Since his stroke he had turned over his complicated financial affairs to Dash. So Marcy sat with Polly to finish the backgammon game he had abandoned. She picked up her dice box and shook it with the vigor of a terrier shaking a rat. Squire Mompesson looked at her out of china-blue, china-hard eyes with startled amazement. She had a guilty feeling that this was the loudest noise to disturb his household for a long time. So she almost whispered "doublets" to Polly and made her four plays so carefully not a piece knocked against the next. Polly would not be hard to beat. Her mind wasn't on the game.

"Why, Marcy," she was soon saying vaguely (and Marcy knew she was listening to Dash, watching him out of the tail of her eye), "what luck you are having!"

Marcy began rattling her dice loud as she could every time. She liked the noise, although she guessed nobody else did. She wished she could get Polly and Mr. Mompesson and Dash in a dice-box, shake them and shake them. Or, if only she might jump to her feet and shout, "You're not real, any of you! Just a lot of old memories."

But she was getting her own men home so fast, Polly looked bewildered.

"It's all over," Marcy said firmly, and got to her feet, preparing to leave, even as Nurse Meeker appeared with tamarind water for Polly, boiled milk for Mr. Mompesson, and suitable refreshments for the two guests.

"But don't leave now, Marcy. You've just come."

"I have to!" she cried out. "I've *got* to go." There was no elegance in her farewell.

She felt she must burst forth, knock down everything, chairs and nurses and people, decency even. She must escape.

And she thought of Dan Obrian with the sunlight on his blond, bandaged head, and the gold lace on his uniform.

~*3*~

BUT EVEN DASH was amazed when at last his monkey showed the full extent of his tail. This was no mere matter of too much gold lace. Dan Obrian and his *Devotion* had landed in the Admiralty Court in Boston. Dash, determined to back his own man, sat week after week listening to the evidence. He felt little doubt of Danny's guilt.

That fall, the fall of 1813, a captured British brig, the *Templar,* had almost reached Providence when her crew broke from below the hatches and were fighting to regain their ship. At that moment the *Devotion* had come up. Dan claimed the prisoners were already victorious. Therefore, she was once more a British vessel and belonged to him as fair game. But the *Templar's* prize crew said they had the situation in hand and the *Templar* and her rich cargo was theirs. So they had told him before he had boarded her.

The case dragged on until the following spring. A heavy fine was imposed upon Obrian and the firm of J. Inman's Sons. Dash half-expected another charge to be brought against his monkey — piracy on the high seas and a hanging matter. None came. But Captain Obrian was forbidden to command another privateer. He might ship as a foremast hand or he might go back to Salem and sit about Mrs. Flanneau's. He chose the latter course. And nothing in the world had he to do but talk about his wrongs and scheme how he might get himself whitewashed and to sea once more. He was sure if Dash would only use his influence this could be done.

He hounded Dash in the counting-house, on the streets, at the East India Marine Society, at church. But worst of all, he hounded him in his own house. Dan did not really believe in law courts and justice. He believed in pugnacity and pull. Over and over he admitted to his employer that — well — perhaps he had been just a mite previous in his attack on the *Templar*. But why on earth should this debar him from another command? The fine had been paid. Now if Dash would only write to So-and-So — see the right people in Washington? Dash heard him over and over and came to dread the sight of him. But he refused to lift his hand.

To make things worse for him, Marcy had decided Dan was innocent even before the case came into court. She had never (as she told him every day) heard of anything so dreadful as that wretched prize crew turning upon their gallant rescuer. Danny, the most wonderful privateersman in the world, must somehow be got to sea once more — and as a captain. She, too, pestered Dash. He was not ready to forbid Danny's long, boring visits, but he was not above leaving by the side door when he heard him asking for him at the front. So it was Marcy who sat spellbound listening to Danny's wrongs, until one day her mother suddenly blew up and told him to come no more.

To pay the fine, Dash was glad to sell the *Devotion* to a parcel of so-called peaceful Quakers in Providence where she lay. She was too frigate-built for a merchantman. The Inmans had lost most of their ships, whether of Salem or Boston, and most of their men. Liz Inman was a prisoner in England. His *Lightning* had never struck her colors. She had gone down fighting in the very chops of the Channel. Her captain and such of her men as had been picked up were held at Dartmouth. Beyond this nothing was known of Liz Inman's fate. The war was in its third year, nor had it proved the pleasant summer story Washington had promised. The entire coast was blockaded. All the famous frigates were either lost or unable to leave home ports. Only a few privateersmen still dared venture out. And the American merchant fleet was all but gone. The Inmans, for instance, had only two ships left — the old *Mermaid*, too badly sprung ever to go to sea again, and the *Victrix* that had never gone. There they lay, nose to nose along Inman Wharf.

Dash had little thought to give to Marcy. Surely the girl had not taken her mother's dismissal of Dan Obrian much to heart. Now his name was never even mentioned. She had immediately begun painting Doctor Hobey's portrait. She went again and again down to Ma'am's old house where he still lived on with Rose. When she had tired (as he supposed) of that, she hadn't done much of anything, but looked very handsome and happy. Both she and Danny had completely stopped their hounding of him.

That hot August the moon was wonderful — over in the Howard Street Burying Ground. The Inman tomb was pleasant to lean against as one watched the moon; listened to the tidal waters of the North River slapping the gravel banks of the graveyard, to the whoops and howls of happy drunks from the near-by jail. It was all so wonderful. Not Lucy Inman, nor 'Sephus Hobey, nor Dash knew that at nine every night Marcy slipped through her garden to Brown Street and in a moment was in Howard Street.

Everything conspired for the lovers — or against them. The moon, the lovesick summer nights. The secrecy of their meetings. Both were reckless and tumultuous. Nor did Madam Inman ever turn in her grave.

These two were meeting on the only possible plane they might, and if Marcy had the better mind, it cast no shadow.

～4～

DEAR MOTHER,

A word to allay your fears. First, I must beg your forgiveness for this desperate step to which I have been driven by the coldness of my family and my profound love for one of the choicest of Nature's noblemen —

Lucy glanced about the breakfast table. There was Dash lost in a newspaper, but Linda was staring at her with wide pale eyes.

"Linda where did you find this note?"

"I went up to see why she wasn't down. On her bed it was, Mrs. Inman — her bed hasn't been slept in."

"Nonsense, Linda. She made it before she left . . . for Portsmouth. Early stage."

By the time you read these words, Captain Obrian and I will be miles away. Please do not try to send after us. As soon as the final step has been taken and no man may legally part us, I will write again.

Your willful but affectionate daughter,

August 28, 1814.   MARCY

"Linda" — she could not bear the feeling of those glassy eyes on her — "go and feed the dog."

Linda was afraid of the watchdog, a cross, stupid mastiff, always chained by day. It would take her fifteen minutes to get the meat within reach of him.

"Dash," she cried shortly, "wake up and get your face out of that paper. I do declare sometimes — "

"What is it?"

"Captain Obrian, of all people!" And she forced the note on him.

She saw a half smile eddying about his mouth, then he burst out laughing.

"How can you — Oh, Dash, what is there to laugh about?"

"One of Nature's noblemen."

"But you must *do* something."

"God, mother! Let her alone. She's done enough. Done something even if it's the wrong thing." He flung down the note, looked at his watch. She knew he was taking the stage to Boston. "The trouble with people — some people" — he spoke softly — "is they don't do anything at all. Sort of stagnate. I'm real disappointed in her, and of course it's wrong, but she knows what she wants and she's gone straight out after it. All right. Let her go."

Actually he was stuffing his paper in his pocket, looking again at his watch.

"Dash, you're not still planning to go to Boston?"

"I am."

Mrs. Inman sat a moment with her head in her hands. She longed for Liz, and dear knows how he was faring in that dreadful prison. But most of all she wanted dear Frances Cunningham. Fanny Inman, living alone in that big Boston house, was nothing to her. She might drive over to Danvers — ask Tom? But he'd tell Miranda and Miranda would tell Nanny — and both of them so looked down from the dignity of their matronhood at poor Marcy. *They* look down on Marcy? She was worth the two of them — and all their children to boot. There was but one person in whom she could confide and that was Doctor Hobey.

She went upstairs for her bonnet and shawl, stopped a moment in Marcy's room. Oh, Marcy, how could you! You didn't need to elope. She saw slippers under the bed and wept as one does over the shoes of the dead.

Doctor Hobey, since Ma'am's death, had continued to use his upstairs study. The old sitting-room was usually closed and empty. But it was there she found him today. And there was Marcy's easel and paints and stretched daubed canvases all over the place. He looked sad and mopy.

"Josephus!" she cried, "Josephus, Marcy has eloped."

"No, no!" The blood drained from his face. "Dan Obrian?"

"Yes. But how did you guess?"

"She's been in love with him for years."

"But she got all over it. Never spoke of him — after I asked him please not to come. Months ago."

Then her eyes went to the canvases. Innumerable attempts at Dan Obrian. In some he waved his sword, in others held it nonchalantly on his knee. He smiled in front views and meditated darkly in profile.

"Then it wasn't *your* picture she was making — all that time?"

"No." He swallowed uncomfortably.

" 'Sephus — you let them meet here?"

"But really, Mrs. Inman, I thought nothing but that too much of him would cure her. And ... at last I got where I couldn't stand it. I told him flat out I couldn't stand it — or him."

"Well," Lucy admitted, "I know exactly how you felt. I put him out. Then you put him out. Where next did they go? No, that doesn't matter. Where are they now? I'll tell everybody she's gone to Portsmouth to visit my cousin. Of course he'll marry her. But if we can't make him? . . . I'm covering up best I'm able. And after all, if it isn't known . . ."

"You care more for the appearance of virtue than virtue itself?"

"Yes. Frankly, I do."

She met the two Mrs. Derbys as she crossed Essex Street: stopped to say what a pleasant day Marcy had for her trip to Portsmouth. Then wandered back, hoping for other acquaintances she might casually tell. But when she came to her own gate, there was Michael Shean white as a sheet. The new black mare had been stolen from the stable and the little black chaise was gone too. She was to raise hue and cry. Tell the constable. Order handbills.

"Michael, it isn't *your* horse and it isn't *your* chaise. I decide what I want to do. I want to simply forget it. I'm tired, and I'm not going to let anything upset me. I don't care."

5

So Mrs. Inman said how much Marcy must be enjoying Portsmouth, and that she didn't care who had stolen her black mare and chaise. But she knew there was talk going around.

Then, on the first day of September, such news came that all else was forgotten. The British had burned Washington. All summer they had been raiding along the coast almost at will. Not far from Salem, at Provincetown, two British frigates had their headquarters. Wareham had been attacked, the island of Nantucket forced to declare itself neutral. Yet the fact that they were able to land a force capable of destroying all the public buildings of Washington was shocking news. And seven thousand raw militiamen had been unable to defend it against a small force of well-trained sailors and marines. In fact, it was being said that the militiamen ran so fast the British lost more men by sunstroke, trying to keep up with them, than they did by gunfire.

Marcy, who had never done a sensible thing in her life, had at least chosen the perfect moment for her disappearance. Her mother was almost reconciled to the burning of Washington. Its lurid light had cast Marcy's small scandal in the shade.

But then Mrs. Flanneau arrived. She looked at Mrs. Inman oddly. The two women stood in the front hall. Of course Mrs. Flanneau would not expect to be invited into the living room and sit down.

"I wonder, Mrs. Inman," she began, "did Captain Obrian happen to tell Captain Dash where he's off to? You know he boards and eats with me. He left without a word."

Mrs. Inman's heart sank. She felt confident nobody had noticed that Marcy and Dan Obrian had both disappeared on the same night.

"Dash might know, but he's gone to Boston for a few days. To see the governor about the defense of Salem. Of course we have forts, but actually, Mrs. Flanneau" — and her voice warmed and became that of one friend discussing local gossip with another — "the regular troops at the forts won't speak to the militiamen."

"Does Miss Marcy know where Captain Obrian is?" Dulcey broke in.

"Of course not."

"Mrs. Inman" — she swallowed nervously, but her eyes did not falter — "*where* is Miss Marcy?"

"Portsmouth. But Marcy wouldn't know anything about Captain Obrian's plans. It is literally *months* since he's been inside this house."

Dulcey's face twisted, and she tossed her head belligerently. "Perhaps not in this house, Mrs. Inman. But who do you think she's been going to see over to Howard Street Cemetery? Ghosts? Black cats, ma'am? She's been going, and by night, to meet Dan Obrian."

Lucy was almost speechless with chagrin and anger. "I hope I know where my own daughter is nights."

"I'm glad for your peace of mind you don't," Dulcey flashed back.

"I trust you are misinformed, Mrs. Flanneau, and if that is all you have to say . . ." But she dared not take the obvious next step. She dared not open the door and say, "Good afternoon to you." She mustn't let this woman go ranging over Salem, ringing bells, demanding Marcy Inman and Dan Obrian. She tried to smile.

"I've been mistaken before," she admitted, with engaging frankness, "about what Marcy is up to." And she smiled until her lips ached and her gums showed, but by that smile accepted Mrs. Flanneau as an equal.

"Me, too," Dulcey said. "Seems like I can never keep up with my Petra."

"It is a responsibility, bringing up children. Boys are supposed to be worse than girls. But that's not been my experience."

"Nor mine, either. My little Jacques is good as gold."

"Why don't you step into the parlor and we can have tea?"

The day was warm, the parlor delightfully cool. Very diffidently Dulcey sat on the edge of a chair. This was the moment for which she had longed for years.

Her pleasure over her social success fought in her bosom against the faithless girl who had snatched her Danny from her. Snobbery against love. And apparently snobbery won out. With her first dish of tea and first helping of hearts-and-rounds, she almost forgot what she had come for. I'm sitting here, she thought, with awe. Like I was to the manner born. And Mrs. Inman and I are confiding in each other.

"Dreadful news from Washington," her hostess was saying in exactly the hostess tone of voice Dulcey had longed to hear.

"Dreadful, indeed, ma'am."

"I do hope the men of this country will now get their dander up. Fight them off our coast. There's no reason Salem won't be next. Our warships are gone now. And we've not more than a handful of decent privateers. Perhaps some of our privateers . . ."

"Dan was offered," Dulcey submitted, "a sort of secret commission — not from the Government, mind you — of the *Devotion*. You know Captain Dash sold her after the *trouble*. They call her the *Gray Goose,* these days."

"How *very* interesting."

"Some Quakers bought her. And they couldn't find a master they'd trust her to — she's too big. So they've been after Danny, hammer and tongs. You know. Very secret. He'd be *signed* just as a foremast hand."

"How *nice* for Danny." She was smiling until her teeth ached.

"Yes, Mrs. Inman. If he don't get caught at it. Privately — just between us ladies — he got notice last week he was to get to Providence, lickety-cut. The British frigate down those there waters was ordered to Halifax to repair. He couldn't wait for no stages."

"Of course not. So that's where he has gone. Obviously. Took a fast horse and rode down."

"But he couldn't have. Mrs. Inman, Danny couldn't take a fast horse. He doesn't know one end from the other. I think he's sort of scared of horses. But I've got an idea."

"Yes?"

"Mightn't he have presumed on old friendship and persuaded Miss Marcy to drive him down — with your rig? The one that's missing?"

Mrs. Inman leaned forward and put a hand on Dulcey's knee. "I think you have it!"

"You see, Miss Marcy was just trying to help out an old friend of her family's. And there wasn't anything, there really wasn't anything at all between them. Don't you think so, perhaps, Mrs. Inman?"

The mother grasped firmly at this straw Dulcey held out to her.

A disgraceful, foolish whim of Marcy's — but not that sinister "the worst."

"I'm so glad, my dear . . . I'm so very glad you came in to talk with me. She's always been such a rash, headstrong girl. She certainly didn't ask *my* permission. She knew I'd never have given it. Even if as *worthy* a man as Captain Obrian had to miss a ship."

"Mrs. Inman, you don't think, then, do you, they was in love? Or anything? And they wasn't eloping? And going to marry . . . or anything?"

"No indeed," she lied positively. "I've never seen any sign of it."

"I just didn't know. You see, Danny's been acting queer all summer. And he'd come home late and never say where he'd been to. Not to a tavern — he'd come home cold sober. Then one night not long ago — just for the kit of it — I followed him. To the cemetery, and he met a young lady and in the dark I thought it was your young lady."

"If it was, all they were doing was planning this trip to Providence. And yet" — she glanced shrewdly at Mrs. Flanneau — "don't you think, perhaps, we'd both best say nothing? It wasn't *right* of Marcy to go off like that. And it isn't *quite* right of Danny, is it? To accept a secret command of a vessel, after he was told he mustn't. Ever."

Dulcey looked at her sheepishly. She realized that she had talked too much in her passionate desire to be friends. "Yes. Do let's keep quiet. Both of us."

"Of course. And we'll not say a word to anyone — except each other."

"You bet!" Dulcey exclaimed fervently, and gazed with awe and admiration at this great and simple lady who had so easily accepted her as friend and neighbor.

She was jubilant when she left. It was lucky for her pride that she did not see Mrs. Inman opening windows to air the room — an unnecessary precaution, Dulcey no longer smelled — or heard her tell Linda to *scald* the cups.

Chapter Thirteen

~~~~~~

ACROSS WASHINGTON SQUARE Lucy Inman watched two blue farm wagons backed up before the Wests' double house. She had lent them her own carriage — Froth and Foam and Michael to drive them. Word had come from Maine that Castine and Eastport were captured. All of New England was going to be annexed to Canada.

So panic had descended upon Salem. Wherever you looked, old people, women, children, and valuables were being moved inland. It was already hard to find a farmer to take you in or a wagon to cart your goods. The roads for two days now had been blocked with refugees fleeing the port towns. And last night a cold gale had come in off the sea; the glass had dropped forty degrees in one night. The refugees were deep in mud and already shivering with cold.

Of course, Tom over in Danvers was insisting his sister and her household and his mother and her maids must forthwith take asylum with them. He had even been able to find farm wagons. Nanny, of course, was going and Old Doctor West. Jack would not; he was surgeon of the hastily organized Sea Fencibles. Lucy had told Tom Mrs. Cady and Linda would go with him, but she herself would not.

As she stood at the window, she was thinking, Suppose this should be the time Marcy came back? She could not bear to think of her finding the house locked and empty or, worse yet, full of British soldiers. Then, too, she had to think of Dash. He was at sea now commanding the *Heron,* Salem's one guard ship — only a tiny sloop. It had been sighted a few hours ago. Any moment he might run up to the house looking for pies for his crew or something he wanted. She must be here if Dash came. She had always been at home when the boys came back. She would not begin failing them now she was an old woman.

So she stood in her parlor watching the commotion before the Wests' double house across the square. What a collection of things were being piled into her carriage — Old Doctor West and flannel bags of silver; family portraits; choice silk hangings; silk gowns; furs and jewel boxes; more pictures; the silver-plated andirons. Heavens! they'll break the springs. Five children, Boots, Ruthie, Phineas, Dorcas, and the new baby India. As if anybody, she thought crossly, would steal *them!* Then she wondered where they would find room for Mrs. Cady and Linda. Both had seemed pleased to go when Mrs. Inman suggested it. Well, Tom had a pillion on his saddle. One could ride with him. The other must squeeze in somewhere. And she was angry at the abuse of her property; that carriage had never been designed for such an enormous load. Now it was stopping before her own front gate. Nanny was getting out. She picked up a magazine and started to read, pretending a nonchalance she was far from feeling.

A very refugee Nanny did look, with three or four coats on, one over the other, and jewelry fastened all over her.

"Oh Granny!" she cried, forgetting she was not one of her own children. "As soon as the wagons have unloaded at Tom's, they can come back for your things. But you come now."

"Nanny, I've decided I'm staying here. And my things stay with me."

"But Mother! Mother!" she wailed, "you haven't heard the *latest* news. They say *they* have already left Halifax. *They* might be here tonight. Tom says the gale helped them. Oh please come; come now. I'm sure there's room in the carriage for one more."

Her argument fell on deaf ears. "I've heard the 'latest news,' as it's always called, so many times in my life, and half the time it isn't so."

"Or by land even. They might march an army down from Maine, and think of the *soldiers,* Mother."

"What are the soldiers, anyway, Nanny, except a lot of small *boys* dressed up in uniforms? And if they do annex New England to

Canada, it certainly won't be for long. *Mercy,* don't get so excited.
But what of Mrs. Cady and Linda? I think they are both ready to
leave with you."

As Nanny went to the kitchen to get them started, Tom came in.

"Tom," she said, wanting to know the truth, "Dash says the de-
fenses of Salem are not too bad. He thinks we can fight them off
if they come; that is, if the men don't lose their nerve — go off
hiding with the women."

She had not meant to gibe at Tom. After all, he was a Danvers
man these days, but he looked down at his now soft hands and
was still a long time.

"Mother," he said at last, "Dash doesn't always make good
sense."

"Why, that is what I *always* said, but none of you younger
brothers would believe me. You all *hung* on him as though he
were God speaking from Sinai. But he says we've the men — if
the men will stay and fight. We've got cannon and pretty good
forts. From somewhere he's found powder and balls for the can-
nons. He says the British can't send in more than a raiding party.
That is all that burned Washington. He says it wouldn't have been
burned if people hadn't lost their heads."

"But what we need isn't more militiamen, but a fleet. All our
frigates are blockaded or lost now. We haven't a fighting ship left
afloat."

"What do you call the *Heron?*"

He was irritated by her stupidity.

"She's a guard boat only. If the British fleet does come this way,
I suppose the *Heron* may draw their fire so the militia will be
alarmed. She's nothing more than a damned target, Mother. Dash
knows that."

"Is that all she can do?" Lucy's face turned white.

"About all. Of course she might get away, back here in time to
warn, but probably she'd get sunk. So, Mother, be sensible. Begin
packing now. The wagons will be back after dinner."

Nanny joined them from the kitchen. Mrs. Cady in her best go-
to-meeting bonnet, her boxes neatly packed and corded, followed
her. Linda was still in her morning calico.

"Mrs. Inman," said Mrs. Cady, "I'm going now and I'm not
coming back. My grandniece has offered me asylum in Topsfield

— and a home with her for the rest of my life. So now it seems a sensible time to leave. I'm a real old woman, and I've been here twenty-odd years, and thank you for everything."

And she was going on with thanks and farewell, but what Mrs. Inman was thinking about was the shiftless Linda.

"You haven't changed your clothes, Linda. Are your boxes packed?"

"No, ma'am. Not going."

"You can't stay!" Nanny exclaimed; "why, we can't leave young women to the mercy of licentious soldiery."

"I don't care about the soldiery. I was thinking of Mrs. Inman."

"Don't be so *silly,* Linda; do go where it is safe. I know how scared you are; you'd *die* if you saw a redcoat."

"Yes, ma'am. No, ma'am. I stay here."

The door had closed on Mrs. Cady and Nanny.

"You're going to stay?" Mrs. Inman exclaimed in wonder and relief.

"Of course, ma'am."

Lucy hugged her. "Then from now forward to forever, Linda, you're going to be the cook and we'll call you 'Mrs. Gould.' Would you like that?"

She squeaked with pleasure. "Yes, ma'am."

"Now *Mrs. Gould,* dear, see if we have any pies we can give Captain Dash. The *Heron's* in. He'll be here just half a' moment and no more. You go pack them up."

Tom came back. "One thing I forgot to say, Mother. Miranda says, 'Well, if you won't come, perhaps you might send over a load of valuables? I mean especially *family* things.' She thinks you should think of your grandchildren."

"No. I don't care quite so much for things as I did when I was younger, and perhaps not so much for family even."

Nanny was calling for him, but he told her to go ahead — he'd overtake the carriage on his horse. Seemingly, he was loath to go.

Then Dash walked in. He had put in to Salem to report. As far as he could learn, there was no British fleet near at hand, and he must get supplies and another man for his crew.

It had been burly at sea and cold. He was dressed in leather jacket, sea boots, and on his head, a knit cap. He looked just off the quarterdeck. Tom had not seen him like this for many years

— a captain at sea, not a captain smartly turned out in going-ashore costume. The knit cap framed his face and gave it a Roman look. His face and hands were red and chapped from salt water. There was no reproof in the glance he gave Tom — Tom, a little pudgy these days from Miranda's too-good table and much sitting at an office desk. He did not say, as Liz would have done, "Tom, how's knitting?" — making him feel like an old woman.

He simply said, "Orne's out."

"Which Orne?"

"My second."

"That must be Jolly Orne, then."

"Aye. His wife's over in Ipswich — somewhere — going to have a baby. No place to stay. He says his first duty is to her."

"Women do feel that way. Miranda's expecting, you know."

"So," Dash plowed on, "I need a new second for the *Heron*."

He wasn't even looking at Tom. He was hunting through his pockets for his pipe, but Lucy saw the old miracle working. She wanted to cry out, "Don't let him take you in, Tom. You mustn't go. The *Heron's* nothing but a target. I've lost Peter, and I don't know what's happened to Liz. I can't stand it if my last two boys are blown up — just to warn Salem in time."

"Well, Dash, I haven't been to sea for — let me think — eleven years."

"No, but you were always good."

"Mother" — Tom turned to her — "haven't we still got a lot of sea gear up in the attic?"

She gulped and looked a little like a hen swallowing water. "Of course, Tom, yes — sea boots, tarpaulins — everything you might need."

Then, while they were in the attic, she went to the kitchen to help Linda pack up the pies, stood in the back entry a moment, her heart aching with emptiness.

~2~

Marcy Inman was gone for over a month. She did not once write, and little had she heard of the exodus from Salem, but her luck still followed her. Her return to Salem coincided with that of the refugees.

By October it was obvious the British would not try to extend their meager holdings upon the coast until the following spring. The hundreds who had fled Salem began to come back. Usually Marcy would have been curious about the great number of carts, carriages, wagons, barrows, and pedestrians she saw pouring into Salem, but she hardly lifted her eyes to see them. She moved slowly up Essex Street. The little black mare looked despondent. The pretty black chaise was encrusted with mud. Many of the other returning equipages looked equally bedraggled, yet hers was the one everyone commented on.

Everyone knew three things had disappeared from Salem on the night of the twenty-eighth of August last: Marcy Inman, her mother's rig, and Dan Obrian. They had been put together. Now, as she drove blindly down Essex Street, eyebrows did raise, a whisper followed her. Had she married the "handsome sailor," or was she "betrayed"?

"She looks pale — for her."

"But she doesn't droop any, like a fallen girl."

She didn't droop. She sat stiffly under the black leather hood of the chaise, not noticing when people tried to speak to her. She neither heard nor saw them. And she blew her nose a good deal; she had a bad and very unromantic head cold. The first person she really saw was Michael Shean running down the driveway to meet her.

"May the Saints be praised!" he murmured.

"Oh yes, Michael. I got the chaise awfully muddy and I didn't have the money left to have it washed. Michael, is Mother awfully mad?"

"More sorrowful. You've brought shame on her gray hairs, Miss Marcy."

This she would not deny. "I know," she said, in a tiny voice. "I'm sorry."

She went in at the side entrance. Seemingly, no one was at home. So she crawled upstairs to her own room. Her mother, thinking the steps she heard were only Mrs. Gould's, did not look up. She was sitting in Marcy's room doing nothing. Marcy did not lack imagination. She had known she had been cruel, but it was not until she saw her mother sitting there that she realized how cruel she had been.

"Mother" — she flung her things down on the bed as she ran to her — "Mother, I've come back home — may I?"

"Yes, any time — no matter what."

They cried together.

"Tell me . . . of course you are married?"

"No, Mother."

"Oh, Marcy, why not, whyever not? Why, this is dreadful!"

"It is dreadful, I know it. But I found I couldn't."

"You mean he *lured* you away and then refused to marry you?"

"No, Mother. Mother, I lured him, and he was ready to marry me, but I couldn't do it."

"Begin at the beginning; tell me everything."

"Don't ask, Mother. I can't tell. And I've got an awful cold."

"You do look sick. You're feverish."

Mrs. Inman fetched up the ewer of hot water and hot tea and toast. The girl was exhausted. Seemingly, all she had strength left to face was hot water, a little food, bed, and no questions. Even when her cold was better, she had no desire to leave her room. Her mother worried. Was Marcy going into a decline? And, worse yet, What are the first symptoms of pregnancy? Mrs. Inman had little backward-looking in her make-up. Although she had in all borne seven children, she had almost forgotten the first signs of pregnancy. She had her virtues.

Marcy refused to see anybody except Linda and her mother. She would not even see Doctor Hobey. Her mother got brief answers to her persistent questioning.

"But why didn't you marry?"

"He didn't love me, Mother. I loved him so much, I thought he did. But I think I really always knew; I didn't want to face it — until I had to. And so . . . after a while I came home."

"Marcy, do you still care so frightfully for him?"

"I don't know — even yet. That's why I stayed away so long —

in all those different inns in Connecticut; as long as my money held out, I had to get over it — alone."

"Marcy, exactly when did you find your true feeling for Captain Obrian and his true feeling toward you? I mean, was it then *too late?*"

"Do you mean had he seduced me?" Her eyes grew suddenly green.

"If you insist on putting it so bluntly."

"It isn't anybody's business except mine. I've forgotten. I don't care."

"Perhaps the best thing will be to have you marry Danny, after all, when he comes back again."

The *Gray Goose* had not got out of Providence until three weeks after Dan and Marcy had left Salem, for not until then was the night dark enough and the frigate absent.

"Anything," she said, "even death, is preferable to marriage with him."

The first week she nursed her cold. By the second, she began to grow restless. All she wanted to talk about was the necessity of leaving Salem. She had been much helped by the timing of her elopement, but not entirely saved. Lucy talked things over with Doctor Hobey. It would be much better for her to be somewhere else for a few months — perhaps a year or more. Both agreed.

Although Marcy would not see him, and he called almost every day, Doctor Hobey went industriously to work on her future. Among his parishioners were the Gaineses. Mr. Gaines had been summoned to Washington to assist in the Treasury Department. Mrs. Gaines was crippled with rheumatism. Obviously she would need a companion. And she was a sweet, worthy woman and childless. There were no children for Marcy to corrupt.

~ *3* ~

ALTHOUGH THE WAR ENDED officially the day before Christmas, word of peace did not get to Salem until into February; then the bells and the minute guns; the parading military, the martial music, speeches, flags. The terms of the treaty suggested a drawback to *status quo*. Nothing was said of England's rights of search, the impressment of seamen, although these evils had been the excuse for a war. Canada had not been conquered as the War Hawks in Congress had promised. After the peace, but before word of it had crossed the Atlantic, the Americans had had one stirring victory at New Orleans.

Salem went confidently to work, repairing wharves, cleaning basins, laying new keels. Most of her pre-war fleet had been lost, but the first year of privateering had brought in great wealth. Now soon once again ships would sail.

Liz came back from his imprisonment at Dartmouth on the ship which brought news of Napoleon's final defeat at Waterloo. So the long war that had covered an entire world was over. Men the age of the Inman brothers had no conception of a world at peace. Liz looked thin and tough. He was still sallow, and this made his beard blacker and china teeth even more startling. He was restless and bursting with ideas. Dash took him down on Inman Wharf. Everything there was in apple-pie order, but Liz was not impressed. He thought the new ship, the *Golden Fleece,* Dash had ordered built too small. He hardly glanced at the fresh paint on the counting-house, or the brand-new house flag that flew before it; neither did he notice the wharf had been straightened and the brick warehouses had been repointed. His imprisonment had increased his natural restlessness and, what bothered Dash more, his natural energy and ambition. Liz had spent close to two years planning what he was going to do when he got out. And now he was out. The *Mermaid* had been broken up for firewood the winter before, but there in the mud lay the *Victrix*.

"You breaking her up, too, Dash?"

"No, I hadn't thought to."

"Might as well — too small — or sell her."

"Maybe."

"It's useless putting money into Salem. Even before the war we were making handsomer profits on the Boston end. And I'm thinking of making a tie-up with White in New York."

They walked slowly to the end of the wharf. There lay the *Golden Fleece* ready to go out to Batavia in three days, and pretty as a dream ship.

Liz pointed to a gravel island. "So many Salem ships have gone out in stone ballast, there's not much left of Tinker's Island. One trouble is we haven't any natural exports around here. Too many of our vessels have left port in ballast. Picked up their cargoes elsewhere — along the coast. That's bad business."

"Yes, obviously that's bad business."

Liz burst out: "Nature didn't give Salem a thing — no inland to draw out-cargoes from nor rivers. Do you realize we're the only town in America that ever tried to be a great port and had no river? And we haven't even a real harbor."

The two brothers walked back and forth the length of the wharf in the bright June sunshine. As usual, Liz was doing most of the talking.

"The world, Dash, we grew up in, learned to navigate, is gone."

"The world a boy grows up in is always gone by the time he's man-grown."

"Yes. Our little old vessels were handy, to slip in and out and about a world forever at war. Then, too, the Pacific was hardly charted in the old days. Little ships could sneak about; find new places to trade; buy and sell cargoes; get where a large vessel never could have. It was good sharp business. Those days are gone." He paused. "The world's going to be at peace now for years and years. France is licked — England tired to death. She was even too tired to fight out the war with us, and, by God, she had us by the scruff of the neck. All she wants is to lick her wounds. So American ships have naught to fear from anybody. Peace now — for as long as you and I are apt to live. Well . . . it all adds up to this. Ships are going to be bigger and bigger. Salem can't accommodate them."

"We could dredge. I saw a new mud machine in Boston."

"O God, why waste money dredging? Eight to eighteen feet of water is all we ever had. There are a dozen better harbors just in New England, and the harbor is silting, ever since I was a boy. It will go on, and faster than any mud machine can manage."

To believe in the future of the old port was, as Liz pointed out, sentimental, and in the heady post-war years all sentiment was kept for songs and ladies' albums. It had no part in a man's life. Of course Salem could still make a living, and Liz was asking Dash about the new shoe factories over at Lynn — glue factories, too. That meant Salem masters had better turn their energies toward

South America — hides and horns. This was going to be "good business" for Salem.

Dash knew Liz was right. He understood why Liz wanted most of the money made on the first year of privateering for the Boston end of the business. Two truly enormous ships were to be built for the firm in Medford, the first of all the *Queens of the Sea* that carried the Inman house flag and a second *Devotion*. But he didn't do what Liz had all but told him to. He didn't order the *Golden Fleece* to Argentine to bring home hides, horns, tallow. She went out the old way around Cape of Good Hope and to Batavia. Perhaps she wouldn't make much money, but he loved to think of her out there in his old world. Money had never meant a thing to him.

～4～

THERE WERE A GOOD MANY Boston stockholders in J. Inman's Sons these days, but Dash was offended when the August meeting was held, not in Salem, but in Boston. He was not there (with his impressive block of stock) to vote against the official moving of the firm to Boston. He knew calling Salem the head office was rather letting the tail wag the dog.

"If you don't like it," said Liz, "why didn't you come to Boston? Tell me your side of the story."

But Dash knew he hadn't any side to tell. Liz, Tom, and the stockholders were right.

"One thing you'll be glad to hear, we've decided not to break up the old *Victrix*. We can kedge her out of where she sits in the mud, remast and rig her, cut her down. I've arranged to have the work done in Charlestown, so all you have to do is get her into towing order."

This was the first time the directors had ever interfered with what the Salem office might do. Dash stiffened. They were quite within their rights, and he knew it.

Liz went on, "She's good enough for the hide-horn-tallow trade."

"I wish the damned thing had sunk — years ago," Dash burst out.

"You do? And I thought you had sort of a sentimental attachment to her. Fact is, I thought I was heaping coals of fire on your head, Dash. You hardly waited for me to have disappeared into Dartmouth Prison before you sold my *Devotion*."

"Well," Dash said, glad to head the conversation away from the *Victrix*, "Danny certainly made a fortune on her and wasn't hung for piracy."

"Oh, he and his *Gray Goose* were holding up British Tea Wagons for months after peace had been declared, and it's been said . . . have you heard? . . . some people have said the *Gray Goose* has been seen off Africa — middle passage."

"Damn that fellow's hide! If he's taken ship of ours into slaving . . ."

"Not ours, don't forget. You sold her to those Quakers, but I guess you old-fashioned Salem gentry had better get used to the idea that when Danny Obrian comes home next, he's going to come home mighty rich, and thanks to Peter's will (what an idiot that lad was!), he's got a mighty well-to-do wife."

So Dash sent out the handful of ships over which he still had the say. Everyone profited — a little — but it wasn't like the Boston ships nor that "tie-in" Liz had arranged for the firm in New York.

The work he remembered longest that fall was getting the *Victrix* out of the mud and fit to tow. Her hull proved amazing sound for a vessel which had lain there doing naught for five years. She was, as Liz said, "a sound little apple," but Dash was glad the actual work of cutting her down, brig-rigging her, was to be done at Charlestown. She'd be a lot slower and, it was hoped, not so teetery. Perhaps at last she wouldn't fling down her head, take the bit in her teeth, or, in plainer talk, jib. He felt wrong was being done to her, but it was nothing you could explain to stockholders. Her hull, he noticed, was slimmer, trimmer, than other ships of her decade. Her length was greater than four times her beam. Ever so little she had foreshadowed the ships now coming, yet by postwar standards she was a mite chuckleheaded. He'd have liked to keep her — as something of a souvenir, but of course that would be a waste of money.

Why was everybody so set on squeezing the last drop out of every penny these days? Salem was still a rich town. Great brick houses were going up all along Chestnut Street and about Washington Square — money made on privateering. Yet things were not as they had been. Formerly money made in Salem was reinvested in Salem. This wasn't true now. It went inland to waterpower and turned spindles and made nails, wove cloth. It flowed into banks and insurance companies, turnpikes, canals. Money earned in Salem cleaned the mouth of the Mississippi. It might support an old man's home in Cincinnati or run a chain of brothels in Natchez. It was no longer local money. It was money on the loose, flowing out into any vacuum.

And many of Salem's most famous names were leaving — following their investments and turning their backs forever upon the sea. Billy Gray had been the first to go. Now he was being followed by Crowninshields and Derbys, Whites, Ornes, Pickmans, and Pickerings. The old names were leaving. He himself was the last male Inman left in Salem.

Salem had always been disproportionately full of women. The sea had taken the men in their youth and often claimed them in their death. Now there were more than ever. Some, like his mother, were very well-to-do. They did not care whether their money was made in Salem or Cincinnati. Some poor — these had run cent shops or sold gingerbread. Some queer — like that Mrs. Hawthorne down on Union Street — folk said she never once had left her bedroom since word of her husband's death came to her seventeen years ago. Now the young men were leaving for inland factories or deeper water, or even for western plains; and more women than ever were getting left behind. And the spinsters! He knew women lived along the waterfront, waiting for the return of the *Fortune* or the *Fame*, the *Endymion* or *Neptune's Car* or plain *Polly Perkins*, waiting for ships lost years ago — still showing (so it was said) a candle on the window-sill so Jack or Tom or Billy would know (when their ships came back) their sweethearts had not forgotten them.

So he had the *Victrix* ready for towing, and she was leaving, too. He thought, I might go; I'm thirty-nine — pretty old for a master, but I might. He could remember the surge and lift of the sea beneath him. The pull of the wheel and the sails' fill. The cutwater slicing eternity. Yet a man without a soul can't be a real good sensible master. A *Flying Dutchman,* maybe, but such should not be allowed loose at sea. For now what Peter had told him he felt had come true. It was a long time since he had honestly stopped to ask himself whether or not he loved Polly, or wanted to marry her. He'd never go back on her. So far as he was able, never hurt her.

She hadn't much to live for since her father's death except his daily visits.

He had been standing watching the workmen pumping out the *Victrix*. The pumps began to suck. He looked at his watch — four-twenty. He'd be late; so he gave his final orders to the men and turned to leave.

Then he heard a caulker laugh and say to a fellow, "I thought he'd given up going today. Captain Dash is going to be late."

It was the first indication he had had that Salem counted on his regularity. They were setting their clocks by him. It had been a long time since he had failed to arrive at Miss Mompesson's exactly at four-thirty.

Then within the week he stood at the end of Inman Wharf with a spyglass and saw the sailless, mastless hull of the *Victrix* quickly disappear in the trough of the waves. Oh, she'd be coming back carrying her stinking cargo, crawling along under her safe, slow new rig, but she'd never come home again wrapped in glory, smelling of the Far East, galloping so lightly before the wind, her homing pennant apeak and aflying, bright foam on her lips, trembling in ecstasy. Peter had died on the *Victrix* and so had men of her own crew — cut down by their own officers.

He stood until even the sails of the towing vessel were almost lost to sight.

Dad blast it! he thought, tucking his spyglass under his arm, why hadn't he taken off her figurehead? A mere scroll was good enough for a hide-tallow-horn brig. He'd write Liz. He wanted that figurehead. McIntire had carved it, and it was pretty nice, that white woman with the wreath of Victory in her hands. He'd write Liz to take it off, send it back to him in a cart. It would look fine in the back garden. But Liz (as well as Dash) would know it was sentimental to cart about a lot of old junk.

He would always be able to see her by merely closing his eyes. So she would be with him always — a woman, fierce and unregarding and beautiful, flying forward with the wreath of Victory in her hands 'cross the China Sea and not stopping; flying across the skies of Salem, but on and on and beyond. She had stood for something lovely and unattainable. She was no answer to man's longings — only a brief vision of what lay forever beyond his grasp. What she stood for was more important than the things that actually are.

~ 5 ~

AFRICANUS WAS JUNGLE-BORN. He could remember the witch doctors' black plumes shaking on head and haunch. He remembered the rustle of shells on wrist and ankle, hissing like snakes, and the beat of the great drums of Africa — Boom (shake)! Boom (shake)! Boom!

He had never been able to realize a white witch. To his blind mind's eye, the witches of Salem were black — every one. That was why he so often left the comforts of the fine new almshouse on the Neck to feel his way slowly to Gallows Hill — sit and brood there among his own people.

Here a hundred and many more years ago Salem had hung and buried her witches, but still in his darkness he saw them, fierce black faces tossing plumes — heard through his increasing deafness the lisping of shells, the throb of drums.

Boom (shake)! Boom!

Shake, shake. Shake-a-shake.

Shake-a-shake.

BOOM!

Then his rheumatic old body would sway with Congo rhythms. He had not been blind at birth. Not only could he remember the witch doctors, but his mama's smile and the ugly, greenish faces of the first white men, the sickish smell of them. Maybe he was five or six. The last thing he remembered to have seen clearly was his dead mother's face. They had taken up the hatches to fetch out her body, and because he'd clung to it and complained, someone had hit him on the forehead with a belaying pin.

He had seen the sunrise of his first day in America — so marvelous and full of promise — but soon after that, he remembered the anger of his American owner when he discovered a blind child had been foisted off on him. He remembered traveling about with a man who sold snake oil, cures, African and Indian remedies. He had changed masters several times before he heard a judge upon the bench here in Salem saying that the boy was to be sent to the Charity House and taught whatever trade possible for his affliction. The old Charity House by Pickering Hill had been his home.

It was hard, now, to be moved over the Neck, even if the accommodations in the new almshouse were so much better. Nor did he want to be buried in the new paupers' graveyard on the Neck. His mind was made up — he was to be buried on Gallows Hill.

Although he told nary a soul why he was so sot on this grisly eminence, he was forever stopping one after another Salem citizen, asking him to promise this should be so. When he came to the Inman kitchen, as he often did to have his great Hessian boots polished, coat brushed or mended, he made Mrs. Gould promise. The keeper of the almshouse gave him his Bible word for it — anything to keep the old man quiet. Deacons and selectmen, overseers of the poor, ministers — all promised him that, yes, he would be buried on Gallows Hill. With an animal cunning he knew his time had come.

Among the simple tasks suitable to almshouse inmates was coffin-making. There were plenty of decayed shipwrights, carpenters, cabinet or chaise makers among them. On foul days these knocked together coffins and stored them in the loft against time of need.

Then Mr. Africanus died.

That day and the next and the next day after every ablebodied man, including gravediggers, were sent out to make salt hay. It was late in the year, almost the end of October. The hay would not keep; neither would Mr. Africanus. When it was almost too late, it was realized not one of the stored-by coffins was big enough for his gigantic frame, but like Procrustes, the sleeper might be accommodated to his bed.

His head was cut off and set at the bend of his knees. His shallow grave was dug close by the almshouse. Then his fellow paupers began to protest. They said it had been promised him to lie upon Gallows Hill, but the gundalows waited at the wharf for the salt hay.

"Mr. Keeper, if you go back on your beholden word to him, he'll walk."

"Nonsense. Do as I bid you."

"You promised . . ."

"Of course I did. So did a hundred other people in Salem, but it was only to give comfort to a sick old man."

"Mr. Keeper, it weren't right and Christian to cut his head off him. He'll come haunting back."

"Rachel Rea, shut your trap, will you? Who do you think's runnin' this almshouse? I couldn't go wasting taxpayers' money, could I, for an old man's whims? He's dead now, ain't he? Let's forget him. He's forgot us."

"No, he ain't. He'll walk."

"He'll walk. He'll walk" . . . was whispered all over Salem, and he did.

Like all proper ghosts, within a few years he had established his own habits and his own beat. He was most apt to appear on chill, windy nights late in October, close to Halloween. He walked from his shallow grave upon the Neck, edged along Collins Cove, picked up the head of Essex Street, took Pleasant to Washington Square, crossed that (he had often been seen there); tapped his way patiently past the Inman house, into Brown Street, and so on down Federal, heading for Gallows Hill. In his hand was the malacca cane King Derby had given him thirty years ago; on his great legs, his famous Hessian boots with red tassels; and he carried his severed head under his arm.

Here a sailor, thrown out of a grogshop at closing time, felt the hair rise on his head, the flesh creep on his bones, as a huge headless figure bore down upon him through the dark, windy, cold night. A woman on Brown Street, who had "just run out back" before she went to bed, began to scream; no, she hadn't seen him exactly, but she had heard the tapping of his cane. There a child had a fit. A dog bristled, growled, and ran away, tail between legs. A cat spit and glowered at nothing human eye could see.

Mrs. Gould wished the Inmans did not live so exactly on his line of march. Again and again she had seen him materializing out of the night, had heard the tap-tap-tap of his cane. That for seventeen years he had befriended her, and she him, made no difference. She was deathly afraid of him.

It was in vain Dash tried to explain to her that, in the first place, there were no such things as ghosts and, in the second, how could she be so terrified of the kind old man, living or dead? She smiled her meaningless smile and knew better. Ghosts were ghosts, the one as evil as the next. The first anniversary of his death she had been so frightened she had got Dash up in the middle of the night. She had heard him turn in the driveway and knock on the back door — a soft polite knock. She'd know Mr. Africanus's knock among a million. The next year he knew she reverted to charms. Holy water she got from Michael, who was a Catholic; garlic and iron horseshoes and incantations from old Yankee women — but he came.

The yard dog, a stupid, vicious mastiff, howled all night. The cats were nervous and jumpy even next day. It was in vain Dash laughed at her. Well . . . let the old man walk, he thought. Why not? Salem has always had God's plenty of ghosts. There was certainly room for one more.

Chapter Fourteen

〰〰〰〰〰〰〰〰〰〰〰〰〰〰〰〰〰〰〰

A SUMMER'S SEA strained and sucked at the rocks of Nahant, and a summer's sun warmed them. Nahant was no longer a solitary spot inhabited by fishermen, Quakers, and seals. It had a hotel. In a small, and to 'Sephus Hobey loathly, way it had grown fashionable. But the sun was warm, there were rocks to sit on and the broad blue sea to look at. To both himself and Marcy such things were more pleasurable than rocking chairs upon a hotel veranda.

He was busy writing scientific memoranda. Marcy had her sketchbook with her.

"Look," she said, pointing to a black smooch on the shimmering horizon. "It must be another steamboat. The first time I saw one, I thought it was a ship on fire."

"Steamboats and sea-serpents," 'Sephus said, thoughtfully. "As the old craft leave Salem, stranger ones arrive."

For the last year, off and on a sea-serpent had been reported along the coast. Doctor Hobey had become absorbed in the sea-serpent, which the more scientifically minded referred to as a "Norway Kraken." It was said to have a horse-like head, carried some five feet above water, followed by a hundred-foot body which looked a row of buoys on a net. Although some of the people who saw the sea-serpent were the same ones who were always meeting Mr. Africanus and his head, many were as astute observers of sea phenomena as could be found, men who for years had commanded at sea.

'Sephus Hobey interviewed every observer. He pursued the creature in the customs boat, in sloops of friends. He borrowed chaises and hired rigs and drove back and forth from Gloucester to Nahant, writing down for the Linnean Society descriptions from the last man to have seen it.

Last night word had come it had been sighted at Nahant by a most reliable Quaker. No sot. No romancer. So today the Inman chaise headed for Nahant. The fisherman interviewed, Doctor Hobey sat ready to begin what he knew would be his final letter to the Society.

Salem, August 15, 1818, was all he had written. The fisherman had seen it clearly moving slowly on a flat sea at sunset time. Its body, he said, looked to him like a school of porpoises, the one following the other. Its head did not resemble a horse's head as much as he had expected. It looked like a seal.

"That was one of the best descriptions you've had," Marcy said, working idly on her sketch.

"No, Marcy, he told me exactly what a seal looks like — swimming ahead of a school of porpoises."

"You mean — maybe it wasn't really . . . ?"

"Perhaps. And never was. Perhaps all I've been following for almost a year now is porpoises, seals — and imagination."

"Do you mind — so very much?"

"Why, I've given half my waking thoughts to this monster. I was determined to get at the truth."

"And in your mind's eye you saw it caught. Studied scientifically for the first time in the history of the world. Named *Serpens Marinius Hobeysius.*"

"Ah, yes. Why not laugh at me? But if I have to give it up, I will. I've just written the Linnean Society. I say flat out I do not believe there is or ever was a sea-serpent upon our coast. And as you know, I have backed it with more enthusiasm — I'm afraid — than wisdom. I so *wanted* one. Well, it will be better so. I'll eat my humble pie."

He knew his parishioners were displeased with his absorption in the sea-serpent. A clergyman's time belongs to the souls and egoisms of his own flock. Hints had been dropped since Marcy's return from Washington that she was not in the least the woman they would welcome as a minister's wife. The fourteen years' difference in age no longer furnished chaperonage. The half-scandal of her elopement (if she really did elope with Dan Obrian) made her an unsuitable life-partner to a man of God. He guessed Mrs. Inman had long read his secret. It worried her, of course, that Marcy was twenty-eight and unmarried. She would rather the girl married anyone — even himself, she had implied — than become that saddest of things — a forlorn old maid.

It was this day, the day the sea-serpent slipped forever through his fingers, he decided not to propose to Marcy, but at least talk things over with her. She might prefer to marry him than let herself be pushed into marriage with some other man whom she could not even enjoy talking with. As for himself, he longed for, he hung upon, her bolder spirit, her rare gift for simple animal enjoyment.

"Marcy," he said, firmly shutting his sea-serpent notebook, "I have been so concerned with the 'horrendous worm,' as our Anglo-Saxon ancestors would have called it, I've hardly asked you how things are going with you."

As if she sensed a drawing closer to a subject she might wish to avoid, she squinted out to sea. "'Sephus, did you ever stop to think that nobody can draw a steamboat? The full-rigged proper ships are so lovely they almost draw themselves."

"I'm sure that's so. Marcy . . . your mother took it hard when you decided not to marry Doctor Perkins, didn't she?"

"Why, that was six months ago. She doesn't really take anything hard for long. Not Mother."

"Well . . . but tell me. Tell me, Marcy, how are things going for you? Your real life. Your inner life."

She brightened. "You mean about my novels. 'Sephus, I get a hundred dollars a novel now."

"No, no. I'm not interested in your novels. And I never will be until you stop writing about an England you never saw. And belted earls and ghosts. Are you satisfied with them?"

"No, of course not. I was born dissatisfied, and what I have or what I write is never so good as what I can imagine."

"The best people are like that."

"And long for sea-serpents?"

"And the people they cannot have."

"Are you throwing up Dan Obrian against me after all these years? You said you never would. I did long for Danny once. Not

for long. And how I'd have loathed him by now! He's really growing fat — as fat as Mrs. Obrian. And now they are so very rich, it
is all coming out — what they actually are underneath. That's the
trouble with lots of money. It makes people too natural. You know
he's buying Billy Gray's great house. I'm glad they've sent Petra
South to school."

"I wasn't throwing Dan up against you, Marcy," he said, dog-
gedly. "I was talking about myself."

"Yourself?"

"Aye — as your brothers used to say. Aye, Marcy."

"Don't, 'Sephus," she said gently, and touched his hand. "Don't
long for me. I'm not half good enough for you. I'd be awful —
not as a friend, but a wife."

"I've known, for years. It will have to be you or no one for me,
Marcy. I've faced it. We are not ideally suited. I know it, but . . ."

"Perhaps we will be better for each other than — nothing."

"I can't urge you. I'll never urge you. It seems to me Dan was
one extreme — and I'm the other. You are halfway between."

"So," she said, dreamily, "I took off too far in one direction and
now you are suggesting too far in the other? I have loved you
always, but not that way."

"Not like Danny?"

"No. A much nicer love than Danny."

The loved face she saw was almost shimmering with emotion.
I'd deserve to die if I hurt the best friend I've ever had. There was
nothing of the flirt in her. She had never exulted over this conquest
as Polly might have. She was hurt because she had hurt him. The
tears suddenly stood in her greenish eyes.

"Don't feel so badly if I can't," she whispered. "I wish I could
feel differently. You have been the keel, the rudder of my whole
life. If everybody in the world was against me, I'd know you were
there. Not even trying to understand me. Only forgiving and accepting me — and loving me. 'Sephus — without you I'd have fallen
all to pieces. I couldn't exist without you for my friend."

"We can go on — like that, Marcy, forever, if it is what you
wish."

She jumped to her feet, her hands clenched angrily. The wind
caught and whipped at her skirts. "No! No! No! And be just like
Dash and Polly? Oh no, not like that! Never!" The light breeze
tossed her black hair.

"Marcy, sit down again. We must talk this over as quietly as we can."

"Don't talk *quietly!*" she cried; "that's the trouble with everything. People talk so quietly. 'Sephus, face it. Married to me — I might do something dreadful again. Lose you your church. It might be Hell for you."

"All right, then. I know and I'll risk it. I haven't taken many risks in my life."

"Suppose we marry — because we are so fond of each other. And then someone else came along. I mean, someone with all your good qualities plus what . . . plus what——" She could not find the words for what she wanted to say.

Doctor Hobey said them for her, but with a sinking heart, "All of Dan Obrian's excitement."

"Have you ever thought I might meet someone like that?"

"Yes, I've thought of it a hundred times. I promise you, if that happens, I won't hold you."

She was still standing with hands over her face. He went to her and put a tender arm about her shoulders.

"You don't want to wait a little longer?"

"No. There isn't anybody — like that, really."

Her voice sounded so sad, he pitied her. "Marcy! Marcy!" he cried. She hadn't said no or yes, but now he knew the answer. Probably it was Dan Obrian who had taught her to kiss like that. Or only her own warm-running, living Inman blood. He thought desperately, perhaps this moment — now — is the happiest we'll ever have together. Don't look back. Don't look forward. There is only now.

Not fifty yards from the rocky inlet there was a strange long ripple. A mysterious head, truly like a horse — or was it more like a seal — suddenly lifted. Doctor Hobey's scientific notes, the draft of his letter saying he withdrew from further study of the sea-serpent, his acceptance that the world of every day is all that exists, were tossed and wafted by the random breeze.

And there still upon the horizon was an even greater wonder. A ship within whose bowels was the force to move it — not God's winds and tides. A steamboat with paddles turning, black smoke curling, on its way from Salem to Boston.

❧2❧

Many an erstwhile Salem wife returned in summer to visit the home town. The husband might be left at any of the hundreds of new industries on inland brooks or rivers. Or to the heat of New York or Washington. Some had even gone as far as Cincinnati or New Orleans, but the wife and children often returned for the summer to what still seemed like home.

Except for the fact Mrs. Eleazar Inman had not the excuse of children's health to consider, it did not seem strange that for the last few years she had been visiting her mother-in-law every summer. It was flattering to think this now wealthy woman preferred the salubrity of Salem to the stuffiness of Boston (as Salem said). She was a woman in her fifties. The pretty plumpness of her younger days had widened into broad indifference. Her chestnut hair had grayed at the temples. She still had a bright and birdlike eye, but now she reminded one more of a Rhode Island Red than a brown thrasher. At last the actual years between the two women seemed completely erased. Lucy was marvelously well-preserved for a woman of almost seventy. She was fashionable, vivacious. To see the two together, it was impossible to believe one was the mother-in-law of the other. Frances did not even look, as once she had, like Mrs. Inman's "young friend."

The two women would sit contentedly on the broad landing sewing and chatting. As in former years, it was Frances who did most of the sewing and Lucy the chatting. Although Mrs. Liz was now a far richer woman than Mrs. Inman, she was happy to sew for her patroness. Sometimes she was sent back to do her work over. For instance, the new silk curtains for the double parlors. Mrs. Inman looked at them critically. "Dear," she said, "I wonder if blind stitch wouldn't be better than a rolled hem, after all?" Frances was glad that the dull, tedious work was to be done all over. It was almost fall. Any day now she would be expected to return to her great Mount Vernon Street house — and Liz. But of course not until the curtains were finished. Now she had an excuse to prolong her visit.

She could smell the guinea-hens she had bought at market for dinner roasting. They would taste so good — if Mrs. Gould didn't get too much savory in the stuffing. Food — good expensive rich food — was Frances's only extravagance. Certainly her clothes were not. Lucy often harped on her clothes. Frances preferred old slippers (worn, but comfortable). Her stockings were never trim because she said tight garters shut off the circulation. She wouldn't even put on her stays except when hounded by Lucy Inman. She certainly liked to be comfortable. Ah, she thought, obediently beginning to rip out seven days' labor, I do love it here. I feel so safe. And after dinner we'll drive over to Danvers to call on Tom and Miranda and see the children. I suppose Lucy will want me to change my dress — get all fixed up in stays and everything. Well, I guess, as she says, it doesn't hurt me any. Frances knew Lucy was bossy. Put on your stays, dear; pull up your stockings. And she knew she loved her. Not even this badgering meant anything else. Everything in their relationship was secure and comprehensible to her. Nothing in her marriage had ever been that way. And a person does love the familiar, the comfortable, especially after fifty.

Lucy remembered every now and then to ask Frances about those nieces of hers. The subject did not especially interest her, but she was occasionally polite enough to inquire.

"I suppose by now your sister Kate's girls are getting old enough to repay you for all you have done for them?"

"Oh yes. Jeany really runs the house, you know. And if I don't feel like bothering to get all dressed up — go to the hairdresser and all that — Jeany receives our guests with Liz. I'd so much rather just curl up over a good book — upstairs."

Mrs. Inman had never been able to keep up with her children's love-affairs, but she had heard that some people about Boston were so thoughtless as to invite Liz and Jeany, omitting or forgetting the wife. She wished Frances would tell her more, but she couldn't press her. She quickly turned the conversation to the safer subject of the younger sister.

"What happened to Devotion?"

"I know you'll not believe me, but Devotion is a grown woman now — of twenty-five or six."

"Mercy! And I always think of her as a child — with flaxen hair straight as a poker, and the most enormous gray eyes. Where is she now?" And she hid a yawn. She did not care.

"Just now living in Shrewsbury as a widow."

"Left comfortably off?"

"Oh, *very*." Frances put down her sewing with finality. "Every time she is going to have another child, we have to go through the farce of taking her some place and saying she's a widow. Frankly, Lucy, Devotion has never married."

"My dear — and after all you and Liz did for her! Oh, I am so sorry. But what are young people coming to? I'm glad Marcy is so sensibly married to 'Sephus Hobey. Dick Crowninshield's girl eloped with two of her father's Irish weavers. *Two* of them, and —— " She was ready to drop the scandal of Devotion for others nearer at hand.

"Devotion has three children. All sons. I suppose this fourth will be a son, too."

"Twenty-five or six? She must have begun early."

"She did."

"Same man?"

"Heavens, yes. She really does deserve her name — Devotion. She loves him."

"But you must do something."

"I can't."

"Well, Liz can. He ought to go to the man. I suppose he's married? Any money?"

"Very rich — even."

"You can't stand back and watch your own orphaned niece being ruined by a — I think they call them protectors."

"Oh, please, Lucy . . . don't." She gave a sniffling giggle. "Devotion is certainly ruined already. I don't see anything to do."

"But you are so *inert*."

"Thank Heavens. It's my only accomplishment."

"Now, Frances — there is these days (although when you and I were girls it was pretended there wasn't) such a thing as a divorce. What sort of a wife is she? A woman of spirit?"

Frances's bird eyes fluttered and came to roost fairly on her friend's face.

"No," she whispered, "not very spirited, Lucy. Inert."

Lucy's handsome face fell to pieces — fell into the patterns of old age.

"No, no, Frances. Not Liz."

"I didn't want to tell you, Lucy. I didn't mean to — but I'm so glad now I have." Then she said the words Lucy had been waiting to hear for fifteen years. "Lucy, I shouldn't have married him." But Lucy felt no triumph, only pity. "It was I who for a short time should — well, I don't care who hears me say it — have been his mistress . . . It is Devotion who should have married him. She is truly his wife."

"But it must have hurt you horribly."

"Horribly. But, Lucy — I've got to decide what to do. Liz says he's going to have his own boys. He says he's going to adopt them — and I'll have to put up with Devotion living in the house with us. And he doesn't care what anybody says."

"No wife could stand that."

"Not even the most inert. At first I was so hurt and angry, and I didn't understand. But it was harder when I did understand. I wasn't so angry, but it hurt even worse."

"Oh, Frances, Frances, I am sorry."

"I used to cry a lot. But I haven't for years. I haven't that much energy left. I simply don't care any more. Don't you see, Lucy — that I don't care any more whether my stockings fit or *anything*? But I'm so lonely and half-dead all the time."

"Frances, please, please, dear. Don't ever go back to Boston. If Liz wants you to divorce him, do it. I need you so. I'm lonely, too. I try not to show it, but I am."

"How can you need me?"

"My dear!"

The two women embraced, and Frances did come to life again sufficiently to cry on her weeping friend's shoulder. So they cried and did not talk because there was nothing to say. They understood each other with the sad understanding of middle age, which knows enough to ask but little of one's friends and to cherish that little like miser's gold — not throwing it hither and yon like young people.

So Frances Cunningham came home at last. She had been Salem's Cinderella, but now her coach was a pumpkin once more and her horses mice. The blame of the whole miserable affair was laid on Frances's inert head. In Boston people were saying that she was really his mother's age. She had caught the poor fellow off balance. A thing no honorable older woman would do. It was lucky for her she had a place to go where she was loved and badgered, her stockings and her rich, enormous appetite for food criticized, and her company appreciated. And here she was permitted to fulfill that for which she was born — to be a lady companion to someone much more amusing, much more fashionable, than herself.

Nowadays, when Dash came home from the counting-house, he felt nothing had changed in twenty years. And yet how different! Not even Linda was a young girl any more. Marcy married and living in Ma'am's old house at the head of the wharf. There on the landing ahead of him he saw Cousin Frances and his mother sewing.

"Don't bite threads, dear," his mother was saying. "You'll chip your teeth."

In the Chinese basin on the hall table was an invitation addressed to him. He opened it.

Mr. and Mrs. Daniel OBrian requested the honor of his company at a ball to meet their daughter, Miss Petra Obrian.

~ 3 ~

DAN OBRIAN HAD PROSPERED in the South American trade. If ever people had whispered that his ships sometimes took the sinister middle passage, nothing had been proved against him. Nobody quite knew what he had been up to, secretly commanding the *Gray Goose*. There would always be a smell of piracy about his great fortune, but it was great.

"Dash," Mrs. Inman said, "after the way Dan Obrian treated poor Marcy and what that *dreadful* woman did to Peter, I'll never as long as I live cross their threshold." These were high and noble words, but he knew she was consumed by curiosity. "And I hope you won't *think* to accept."

"Not I. No, ma'am."

"Only . . ." He waited to see which would win out, her proper pride or her curiosity. "Well," she went on, "if none of us attended, it might seem as though we held a grudge. I mean, wouldn't it be almost an admission that what people have been saying is true? Of course, we don't want any more talk. Have you heard"—she veered off—"*what* they have done to Billy Gray's old house?" As she ran on, he knew (perhaps before she did) that he was to go and report back to her, for she was explaining exactly what he was to examine. At last, with a sigh of unconscious hypocrisy, she said, "I do think perhaps you *ought* to go. For the sake of your sister's reputation."

When the invitations to this first ball had been received, most of Salem's gentler citizens had said, of course they would not go. But curiosity won in the end, Dash guessed, by the great number of carriages prancing up to the door, and the steady lines of people arriving on foot, like himself. There was something comical about the gilt eagles the Obrians had perched on the outside of their house, and that row of liveried black footmen from sidewalk to front door, shaking their torches and getting in the way. Dan must have hired them from Boston. They weren't a Salem product.

Too many footmen, too many guests. It took many minutes for a man to make his way from sidewalk to house. People, presumably the nicest people in Salem, were yelling back and forth to each other stories they had heard about the size of the mirrors. The cornices all had been gilded. The price of the purple and crimson velvet hangings. The price of everything. Black marble fireplaces from Italy. A punchbowl which was (or was not) solid gold. Murals in the cupola, alabaster nymphs, naked as jaybirds, perched in niches.

There were two things Dash had been told by his mother he must tell her about. The punchbowl. Was it solid gold or only silvergilt? And the murals in the cupola. She told him it was an allegory, exalting the owner. And gossip said, not only had Danny posed for it, but his lady was the sea queen crowning him. Nor did she have on more clothes than one would expect of an allegory.

As he laid by his cloak in a room reserved for gentlemen, Dick Crowninshield was telling him that the chamber-pot (so his wife had informed him) was of solid silver. The commode door had been left open so anybody might notice this elegant touch.

"They won't last long at this rate," said Dick, hopefully.

"Well," said Dash, "at least they are having fun spending the money while they have it. Even if they don't lay by much."

An Italian orchestra (also hired from Boston) was squeaking and tuning up in the ballroom below. The two men parted at the bottom of the stairs leading to the third floor. And from the third floor one went up a still steeper flight into the cupola where the murals were. Already a slowly moving line was heading for the murals. They were getting themselves organized. The cupola was too small to accommodate more than six at a time. "Don't push!" someone was yelling as though at a public museum. "Don't push! Take turns and we can all see."

The big parlors were also jammed.

Captain Obrian and his lady were stout, commonplace people, but to Dash they looked less vulgar than their guests. At least, they weren't going around fingering other people's things, guessing how much this cost and was this "real." They seemed simple and kindly, honestly delighted and naïvely surprised, that everyone had come to their ball. Mrs. Obrian was draped in cloth-of-gold with black ostrich plumes in her turban. She tossed her head and diamonds (or were they, as Mrs. Derby behind him suggested, merely paste?) flashed cold blue flames. Diamonds also on her heavy bosom, about her neck, on her wrists and fingers. Her naturally high color had been killed for this occasion by rice powder. Dash inched slowly closer. Dan was crimson with hospitality and triumph. He had certainly put on a lot of weight lately. His roughly handsome face had coarsened, but there was an innocence in his eyes (and in his lady's, too) that made the avidity and contempt of the genteel guests ugly in contrast. It seemed to Dash incredible that any Inman ever had loved either of this extraordinary couple. And yet two had.

He felt little of his mother's resentment against Danny because Marcy had made him elope with her — as he guessed. Toward Dulcey he felt nothing — not even a feeling of guilt. Not even curiosity — so often the last thing left of love.

Then he saw Petra.

For the last three years she had been sent to Charleston, South Carolina, for schooling. This was because she had that so common failing, "weak lungs." She had the air of inherited wealth — so hard to define and so unmistakable. She was a tall girl, and very slender, with too square shoulders for the fashionable conception of female beauty. And very beautiful. A woman behind him was saying that the young girl evidently followed her own — not her mother's taste. Petra wore creamy velvet without one ornament in her dark curls. Only one jewel — a large pearl suspended by a tiny chain about her neck. But of course (as Mrs. White behind him was saying) the school where she had been sent was very choice. She had always spent her vacations visiting friends in the South. Her taste was formed by them — as fine taste as there was in America.

Dash bowed as he spoke to her and for the hundredth time that night the young girl curtsied. He noticed as she answered him she had a slight Southern accent. It was soft and pretty. She looked at him a little quizzically and he thought her color rose. He wondered — not for the first time — how much she knew. Her eyes had much of Peter's calm knowledge and inner self-assurance.

Already there was a slight piling-up of gentlemen about Petra. There was Boots West, a strapping fellow of nineteen. He seemed to have all of his mother's determination (it was he who was blocking the line) and his father's awkwardness and red hair. He was teasing her a little about the way she pronounced her name. Now she knew that "Obrian" was incorrect. It should be O'Brian — thus the kings of Ireland had been called. But as she answered Boots, her eyes went again, secretively, to Dash. He smiled slightly, and this time he was sure that she blushed. That this was his daughter he could not believe. It was as if the long acknowledgment that she was Peter's child had even convinced him. Because she was Peter's, he felt a wave of emotion toward her, half-love, half-sadness.

Jacques Obrian, now eight or nine, was present with his nurse. He was a blond, chuckleheaded lad. There was another child upstairs in the nursery — the only one of Dulcey's whose fatherhood would never be questioned. Dash had been offended by the gleam of curiosity in the guests' faces. Only Petra seemed exactly right. Much too well-bred, too much the lady, to go into anyone's house, laugh at the host and hostess, finger things. Speculate on who was the father of what child. And yet she seemed as transient a guest as anyone.

Having refreshed himself once or twice at the punchbowl (forgetting to find out for his mother whether or not it was merely silver-gilt), he decided to see the murals and go home. He had not done much dancing for seven years. Not since Polly had given up going to balls. And another thing, too. The waltz had come in, sweeping everything before it. Not many men his age had bothered to learn it. Nor had he. Having failed his mother on the punchbowl, he decided he'd give her a good report on the murals.

It was still crowded on the servants' floor, about the ladder-like steps leading to the cupola. He waited for some time, but at last there he was.

Ships coming in all directions led by sea nymphs and laden with pearls and gold (not the prosaic horns-hide-tallow in which Danny was so much involved, and surely no poor black men as gossip suggested). This wealth was being piled up before an idealized Dan Obrian, dressed in the classic manner. He, in turn, was being crowned by a sea queen — a great big goddess with breasts, thighs, stomach, all bellying out at you like the full sails of a ship approaching. The face was only one of those flat, allegorical things. He would never recognize the mellow, queenlike body as anything he'd ever seen. Or ever wanted to — any nearer than he now found himself, he on the floor of the cupola, she on the ceiling. A change of spectators was called. He and his group had to leave, and the next would take its turn. Had Mrs. Obrian actually posed for this naked queen? The argument would go on and on in Salem for another generation.

He went to the ballroom. The sweet, floating music of the waltz drew him. It lacked the gaiety of the old contra-dance tunes. It was, as many a clergyman had pointed out since its arrival in the ballrooms of America, of a seductive quality. Enchanting, unearthly, it wove its magic spell over the young people. Here were no two long lines of girls and boys facing each other. They danced close in each other's arms. It certainly wasn't much exercise. Why, nobody's feet even left the floor; it was a swooning and turning, a floating off into dreamland to a three-four tune.

He saw Doctor Hobey standing by the door and he joined him. Of course, he had come to watch Marcy enjoy herself. Some people thought it unfitting for a clergyman's wife to be so devoted to the waltz. Doctor Hobey should not be quite so willing to escort her, especially to the Obrian ball. Dash saw 'Sephus was watching her with eyes almost blinded by love. And Marcy was a graceful dancer. Well, he thought, that marriage seems to have worked out well — for two years at least. And she does look happy.

But she never looked as happy with her husband as she did dancing with younger, less loving, gayer, handsomer men.

Dash's eyes went over the floor looking for Petra. She appeared floating and turning toward him in Boots West's arms. Everything has been against her, he thought; the evil of her birth, the vulgarity of her parents; but her surprisingly square little shoulders seemed capable of carrying anything. How triumphant she looked! How burningly alive! Indestructible!

"Petra," said 'Sephus Hobey, "would certainly be the belle of Salem if she were staying here."

"But her schooling can't go on forever. Isn't she through yet? She's seventeen."

"Haven't you heard? Where were you when Dan Obrian announced his daughter's engagement — and we all drank toasts?"

"In the cupola, I'm afraid. Gaping at those pictures."

"Petra is engaged to a Hugh Blessington of Virginia. She only came back to say her hail and farewell to Salem. And to the Obrians, too, I imagine."

"At least she will be married here."

"No. From a friend's house at Winchester. The cut direct. And you notice she did not produce her young man for this one night? I suppose she is ashamed of her mother and stepfather. It's monstrous cruel. But the young have to be cruel. They don't know another way to get what they need. I suppose she's right. Salem treated her rather shamefully. Do you remember Boots West following her on the street yelling 'love-baby' at her? And look at him now! And she so alone walking and walking the streets. Always alone. Especially after Peter died. She used to pull a red sled. With a dog on it."

"Chien Caniche."

"How's that?"

"The name of her little old dog."

"There cannot be one thing to hold her to Salem."

"No, not one thing."

The music wound itself up to a finale. The couples stopped where they were. Dash went back to the punchbowl with some gentlemen, left them, deciding he'd had enough and would go home. It was ten o'clock. Considering how he had started out his life, he was surprisingly regular in his hours these days.

Nobody but himself was leaving now, for refreshments were about to be served. A perfect collation — everybody was saying. He put his cloak over his shoulders, had his hat and cane in his hand. Stood a moment at the head of the long stairs. From below came the high-pitched party voices, but the orchestra was still. "Look what we're going to have to eat!" He thought that was the voice of his old first flame, Peggy Pierce. "You've never seen anything like it! They say there's a molded elephant in the dining room three feet high."

He had chosen a conspicuous moment for his sneaking home. And his mother would be disappointed if he could not tell her about the refreshments. He thought of laying off his cloak once more, eat before he left. As he hesitated, he heard a sound from behind the closed door at his right that froze his blood. All evening long he had been thinking of Peter. Now, unmistakable from behind the door he heard Peter cough. This slight, solitary sound shook him. But he had been drinking a good deal of punch. He felt the loneliness of that little smothered cough, in the midst of gaiety and laughter floating up from below. How each man or woman faces life, death, eternity, utterly alone! He hesitated, his hand on the knob. The cough came again and he went in.

The young girl was flung face down upon a bed, lying in that same attitude of resignation and despair he remembered too well. There was blood on the white pillow. She did not turn to see who had entered. Her hands were flung out and clenched.

"Petra," he said gently, "wait a moment, child." He raised her head and wiped her mouth and nose with his handkerchief. He wet a towel in a ewer and washed her bloody chin and hands. She lay back on the pillows he built up behind her, and she looked at him with Peter's calm, considering eyes. Utterly unlike the eyes of the young girl he had just seen dancing—eyes that accepted everything with philosophical detachment. She was Peter's girl—and nobody else's.

"I hoped no one would hear me. Or know."

"Nobody needs know—if you wish."

He sat beside her and held one of her hands in his. With his other he stroked back the damp curls from her forehead. Now she would have a chill. He looked about and found a satin quilt lined with rabbit fur.

"Do you often?" he asked at last.

"No. Hardly ever in the South. It's this terrible New England climate. And perhaps I danced too much."

"Then it's a good thing you are going to live in the South."

She was staring straight in his face. "Hugh — that's Mr. Blessington — the man I'm going to marry — looks so much like you — or the way I remember Peter. Everybody who first meets us thinks we are brother and sister."

"And you like him very much?"

"Oh, very. Captain Inman . . . you're my father, aren't you?"

She hadn't given him a moment's warning.

"Yes, I'm proud to say."

He thought she was going to cough, perhaps hemorrhage again, for he saw a spasm shake her slight body.

"Flanneau told me the night he died. I didn't want it. I loved Peter so. I didn't want anyone else to be my father . . . But I always knew he'd told me the truth. That's why I disliked you so much."

"I guessed you disliked me."

"All I wanted was Peter. I was so lonely for him. Of course, by the time he went away, I was old enough to know he had gone. But . . . although I knew I'd never find him, I hunted and hunted."

"You'd put Chien Caniche on a sled and go out hunting for Peter?"

"And I didn't want you to come along and crowd him out. It wasn't anything against you — personally."

He put his arm about her and her head against his breast.

"You do remember him? I'm glad. You were such a little girl when he went away."

"I'll always remember Peter. All my life."

"So will I."

Neither felt there was much to say. After a while Dash said: "I didn't own you, Petra. Peter did. Somehow that makes you his girl — not mine. Now I guess you are thirsty? I'll get some water."

When he came back and pressed the goblet to her lips, she smiled at him. "You know just what to do."

"Yes, I've had plenty of experience. I often went to Peter in the night — toward the end."

"Nights are worst. He was lucky to have had you. Hugh knows. But I don't want *them*" — he knew that she meant the Obrians — "ever to know."

Then she sat up and began talking hopefully. She was never sick in the South. The vivid color flowed back into her cheeks.

She talked of Hugh Blessington and about how they had met and how happy they were going to be. The climate there, she said, suited her. The doctors said so. The doctors thought she would always be well — if she lived in the South. She would never again come to New England.

Softly, so very sweetly, once again the waltz music came up from below. She turned her head to listen. He was going to leave her now, he said. Would she promise to be a good girl, not go down again — not dance again tonight? But as her spirits rose, Dash knew it was only a courtesy promise. She would not obey him. Doubtless, no sooner would he be out of the house than she would be dancing again.

～4～

Novels were disapproved of by the old-fashioned. Most of the clergy preached against them about once a year. Doctor Hobey never did.

He had been badgering Marcy for years to write about the things she knew. "How many titled Englishmen have you known?" he would ask. "Not all disappointed lovers sink into early graves. If they do, the doves don't turn up next day to mourn them — nor willows sprout from their graves to weep. Write about what you know. Fielding did. And Defoe. Look about you. Look at Salem — for instance."

For the first time she began to see the old town, with its glorious waterfront, now definitely fading, its ancient peaked black houses, its crooked back streets, heady sea air, and even its fashionable bustle, with appreciative eyes. She wrote, not a very good novel, but as good as her young country had yet produced. And it was as indigenous to her own locale as ships and seamen, sumach bushes, corn fields and stone walls.

Her undoing was the elopement with which the book ended. It was so genuine that Dinah Lee, on the night of her elopement with Captain Joshua Hardy (who in no way resembled the flawless males held up for the admiration of American womanhood), was horrified to realize he did not know how to harness a horse. There he was in the stable swearing like a foremast hand and admitting he didn't know a thing about the rigging. Dinah had had to harness the horse herself. And drive it, too. The captain was so ignorant a man ashore he didn't know how to drive. There was a suggestion, at least, that this marine hero was afraid of horses. Also that both had moments when they wished they had not eloped — at least with each other.

Whoever had written this novel knew Salem inside out. The very smell of Derby Street, the hearts-and-rounds ladies of Salem so often had for tea. The fact they called "diet bread" what other communities spoke of as "spongecake," that what was called "tom cod" in Boston was in Salem "frost fish." Hardy and Lee are good old Salem names. Both families rose up to say they had been insulted. Giggles and Yell also were Salem names. Nobody had then thought them funny until they appeared in *It Hardly Ever Pays,* by Constance Libby.

But the cruelest injury had obviously been done to Mrs. Josephus Hobey. One person after another came to Doctor Hobey, insisting that he ought to find out who was hiding behind the name of Constance Libby. He must bring suit for libel. Then, too, the novel was morally amiss. It ended with the elopement — and where in the name of pure American womanhood was the ring?

Whoever this Constance Libby was, she not only knew Salem, but the Inmans well. Of course — who else could it be but Frances Cunningham Inman?

Then Marcy did what Dash had never done. She spoke out. She could not bear to see poor old Cousin Frances, all twittery and scared, being treated like a viper. Nobody could imagine why Marcy had done such a thing — dig up her own disgrace. Write a novel about it. Why had she?

Why had she, indeed? Curiously, she had, while writing it, written out of herself something which had long festered within her. She had never taken her abortive affair with Danny lightly. But now she had won almost complete release from it. It would no longer lie like a gigantic shadow across her marriage with 'Sephus. Vaguely, blindly, he tried to understand. The very fact that in her book she had ridiculed things, which had at the time hurt her, helped her to a new sense of freedom from the past. Josephus Hobey almost understood. Nobody else did.

There was a demand for her punishment.

Doctor Hobey wrote the State Department, asking for a consular appointment in Burma or India. He presented such credentials as were rarely seen, nor was his long service to that Department quickly forgotten.

He never blamed Marcy that she completely ended for him any possibility of continuing in the ministry. The world was young yet, and he himself not too old to begin a new life. Marcy and he would at last see the world together. Together! If only always and forever they might be together!

~ 5 ~

IT WAS THE INMANS' *Congress* that would take the new consul and his wife to Bombay. She would leave the Inman Pier in Boston the thirtieth of April, 1820. Crates of books, chests of linens, trunks, had been sent on ahead.

Marcy was grateful that her mother had never questioned this step around the world.

"But Marcy, when you begin your new life in India, do try to be as sensible as you can."

"Oh yes, Mother. I'm sensible underneath."

"No. I think you have a great many gifts, but good sense was left out of you. 'Sephus is a sensible man. You must, dear, let him decide everything for you."

"Of course. Husbands always do."

"Do hold on to him. Don't ever let *anything* come between you and him. You've no idea how hard it is to get the right husband for a girl as smart (and foolish) as you are, Marcy. There's the carriage, dear. I told Shean to be around early."

"You are so good to lend us the carriage to drive to Boston. Won't you change your mind? Please drive down with us and see the ship sail."

"No, dear. I'm going to say good-bye — inside my own house. The way I did to your father before you can remember and the way I always did to my boys — when they were still following the sea. I don't like to make a spectacle of myself down on a wharf."

"But Mother — you wouldn't make a spectacle of yourself over *me?*"

"Marcy . . . I don't know why it is . . . I've never been able to say, or, I guess, to show you how much I care. I'll miss you."

"You won't have anyone to scold any more."

The old combatants embraced. The bond was close between them. Lucy Inman had had little but heart-break and despair over Marcy, but she loved her. She had had nothing but filial obedience and duty and good sense from Nanny, and Nanny was nothing to her.

So Marcy was gone with that last whish of carriage wheels on gravel. Mrs. Inman got up a little heavily. She walked slowly down the stairs, wishing Frances had not gone out to market. It was only lately Lucy had fallen into the habit of holding onto the balustrade as she went up or down stairs. She noticed the four portraits on the wall. Why, she hadn't any likeness of Marcy. She must have a miniature painted and send it to her. Her children, she thought, had none of them turned out exactly as she had hoped — except poor Nanny from whom she had never expected much. Liz, she thought, looking at the clownish face before her, mocking her from the wall. Dear Liz. Dear Liz. Why, when she had built this house twenty years before, she had fancied that he (and of course his wife and children) would by now be living here with her. It was she that had failed him, she thought. And the breach had never healed between her and Liz. Widened rather. Those four little boys of his she'd seen but once or twice in Boston. In a way she had been forced to choose between him, Devotion, and the children on one side, and dear Frances on the other. She couldn't have both. Well, that's the way things went. At least, she had Frances.

Tom, of course, was a great comfort to her, so she assured herself. Living so close by in Danvers, doing so well with his mills, but she had not quite got over her amazement that one of her sons was a weaver — although people these days were calling him an industrialist. But between her and Tom was always, and always would be, the dominating, terrifying figure of Miranda. She literally hid Tom from her. She hid the children — Lucy's grandchildren, Thomasina and Thomas, Sarahlee and Dicky. She was like a semi-opaque curtain. Behind it you could see figures moving about, but never quite who they were or what they were like.

Nanny West, only catty-cornered across Washington Square. Boots almost a man now, and following after him were Ruthie, Dorcas, Phineas, and India. She tried to think sentimental thoughts about her grandchildren. But the only one among them for whom she had ever felt personal affection was forbidden to her — the enchanting, lonely Petra Obrian. And now Petra Blessington, and gone forever.

Thinking of Petra, her eyes stared at Peter's portrait. She really had known, even when that picture had been painted and he was only fourteen or so, that he would not live long. But it was very sad about Peter. So sad. She was glad he had had "that dreadful woman" if she had been any comfort to him. And Linda, too, if what Miranda said was true. But most of all, that he and his daughter had had a few years of closeness and love.

She walked back up a few steps and stood looking at Dash's picture. If anyone had told her that she would face her declining years with Dash the one child left under her roof, she would not have believed it. He had always been such a wild young hawk. The first to fly. The farthest to go. He had looked as though he would go on and on forever without one backward glance. The artist had caught something of what Dash had been — even if he had been unable to get the face quite straight. Something indestructible. A hardness few had realized because Dash had been low-spoken, non-argumentative. Probably Peter was the only person who had ever known him at all. Very self-controlled, he had been by far the most remote of her children. Of course, that was why she had always (and still did — so Frances told her) picked on him. I won't do it. I will let him alone — as Frances tells me I should. I won't laugh at him because he calls on Polly every afternoon at four-thirty. Or badger him if he's late to meals. But Dash had not been late to a meal for years. He had settled in comfortably, so far as his mother knew, as a bachelor son living at home. A far cry surely from the winged lad he had been. Seemingly no woman, surely no mother, could ever hope to have held him, and yet how tamely now he had come home to roost.

Not for the first time she wondered what had broken his wings for him. He had not been quite as indestructible as the artist and the mother had thought. How strange, she thought. How sad.

Life, she thought, is not so awfully tragic — but it is very, very sad. She sighed, and continued her way down the stairs. She had always been able to "take things as they came." She still could. Very sad — but exciting and — well, yes — fun. Strange, too. I'm glad life is so strange. I don't see how anyone could be bored by it or want to die.

She heard from the kitchen the sounds of Frances's return from the market. Of course she had bought some ridiculous extravagance. Frances did like to eat. Well, there was money enough these days. Of course, when she tells me not to nag at Dash, she's really asking me not to nag her. And I won't. If eating is the way she gets her fun, I don't care. It's *her* figure — not mine.

~6~

THE WIND was high and rising. It streamed and screamed through naked trees above him. All the color in the sky had gathered in an angry knot to the west. This would be a burly night at sea, and rain before dawn. Maybe, Dash thought, I'll get myself a pair of gum shoes. People who have them seem to like them. He disliked getting wet these days, although there had been a time when he had not had a dry hair on him for days on end. The time was not far off, and he knew it, when, on leaving his mother's house at four-twenty (the walk to the Mompessons' took just ten minutes) on such threatening days, he would not be carrying a smart walking-stick, but an umbrella. And he'd be wearing gum shoes.

Exactly the moment he stood between the Mompessons' gates, the church spire struck half-past. He saw himself, not as he stood this day, but as he would still be standing ten years, twenty years, from now. Perhaps thirty. He saw the somewhat bent but still determined figure of an old man in gum shoes. Carrying an umbrella.

Through the early twilight, three little ghosts shot out of the Mompesson driveway, tripping over their sheets, crying with fear. Dash had forgotten it was Halloween. He'd have to tell Mrs. Meeker not to scare small mummers so. Like many old women, she hated children. He called to them, but they squealed and ran faster. Doubtless they thought the half-seen figure in the gloaming was a spirit, and he smiled.

Ah, well, this shrilling, crying wind would seem to the superstitious full of the dead tonight. Perhaps it was — the dead almost living and the living almost dead, so the rough wind blew and whirled them together. As he stood, not advancing to ring the bell (as he should have), he thought, first thing you knew (for man's span is so brief), once a year upon All Souls' night he and Polly would, like the fallen leaves, blow hither and yon together through the streets of Salem. Those who were little girls now (like those tots Mrs. Meeker had scared so) sometime would be old women huddling close to fires as old women huddled, chewing over with toothless gums their witless stories as the next generation of children listened and stared. Every day at four-thirty — he heard the croak of ancient tongues — he called upon her. They loved each other all their lives — but never married, because — and the voice would drop and the children shiver — there was a curse upon them. Folk say he sold his soul to the Devil. As he stood, he could almost hear the lisp and mutter of the legend which sometime he and Polly would become. Why, he thought, still lingering against the post as the wind dragged at his coat-tails and almost unseated his hat, if they knew the whole of it, what a tale to frighten children with! Yes, there was a curse upon the man. Everyone he loved he blighted. Beautiful Miss Mompesson and the girl he betrayed and the child she bore him. His brother. Peter Inman — far away in China Sea Peter Inman died because of him. And yet it was Peter who had told him the incantation he might use — if he would break the web upon him and charm the soul back into his breast. For I gave my soul, he thought almost dully, to possess that which I never could reach out and take. A spasm almost of fury went through him. He drew a fist out of his pocket and crashed it against the gatepost. He bruised his knuckles, but the great white post did not move. "God! Peter," he said out loud, "you knew it — and you did your share in the catching of me, but you told me how I might free myself. I wonder if now — no, never now. But I might, by God, I might!"

The door was opening and Mrs. Meeker was cautiously peering out. The wind whipped at her mobcap and she had a hand on it. Of course, Polly was in a tizzy because he was by now five minutes late. He filled his lungs with the wild dark air of late October and entered the house and the dead leaves blew in with him.

"We was getting a little worried, sir," she admitted. One of the things he liked least about the admirable Mrs. Meeker was her habit of including herself and Polly in her "we's."

"The sitting room today, sir. We feel the first cold of the year cruelly, although we have on our warm underdrawers by now, sir. And I got nice fires burning through the house. I took 'em out of mothballs just this morning."

As Dash laid by his coat and hat, she whispered to him: "We didn't sleep very good last night. You know, it is almost the anniversary of Papa's death. Five years ago dear Mr. Mompesson died. November first, sir. It's still pretty upsetting to think about." And she left to announce him. He heard her cuddly voice saying that "our Captain" was here "at last."

Dash bowed as he crossed the threshold and once again as he bent over Polly's hand. The candlelight and firelight were kind to her delicate face. She had lost but little of her unexpended nymph-like beauty. Her smile broke enchantingly over perfect teeth and the beautiful eyes, with their sad downswept corners, went lovingly to his face.

Dash at forty-four was thicker all over and quite gray. He looked a prosperous middle-aged man, director of such and such a bank, president of so many charitable organizations, prime mover of the East India Marine Society, a most valuable and upright citizen, and the look of the sea only lingered on in eyes permanently narrowed by sunlight upon salt water, the unmistakable air of command about the carriage of head and shoulders. But his mouth, that had been so flexible and bold in his youth, had tightened and locked a little. Here obviously was a man who knew enough to keep his mouth shut.

Mrs. Meeker immediately brought in the customary tamarind water for Polly, rum, lemons, and sugar for "our Captain."

"Polly," he said, as soon as the door had closed on the heavy creature, "you must tell Mrs. Meeker not to scare the Halloween children so."

"Oh, Dash, didn't you know? I can't do a thing with her. She manages everything and me, too, thank Heaven. 'We won't worry our pretty head about *that*,' she says. And the children were being really naughty, Dash — hooting like owls and tapping panes. 'Just you lie here,' she says to me, 'and rest so's to look pretty when our

Captain comes. I'll fix them brats.'" Polly's spirits rose, as they always had, as she mimicked. "And you know, Dash, you have your troubles with Mrs. Gould, too. But does she decide when you put on woolen underdrawers?" — and they both laughed.

"No, but she swears the dead do come back on All Souls', and seemingly there's not a sperret (as she calls 'em) in Salem that misses coming to our back door and scaring the living daylights out of Mrs. Gould."

"Why!" Polly looked so shocked he was not sure whether she was playing or serious.

"Of course, by now every boy in Salem knows he can get a screech out of her. Last year I had to chase a lad down our driveway. He had a jack-o'-lantern under his arm and a cane to tap. She was sure it was Mr. Africanus and his head."

Polly's eyes widened. Her face stiffened, and then Dash realized he should not have brought up any subject as unpleasant as Mr. Africanus and his head.

She said slowly: "I know you will laugh at me — I *want* you to laugh at me — but don't you think if he was reinterred on Gallows Hill, he'd stop walking?"

"Nonsense, my dear. Nonsense."

"Don't you think the dead ever come back?"

"Yes," he said, slowly, "in a way they do. Things they have done — or said — bad things you have done to them. Sometimes it haunts you. All your life." And he blurted out: "Polly, I never told you, but all the time Peter was at Bombay, I didn't write him. No, not one single letter. I couldn't. I wrote and I tore up. But I didn't send him a letter. Because . . . there was only one thing he wanted to hear from me. And I couldn't. Well, then . . . that haunts me and always will. So Peter's ghost will stand beside me. Forever — sort of plucking at the sleeve of my conscience. And I can't lay him."

He wasn't comforting her any for her superstitions, for he saw a look of fear in her eyes.

"Peter isn't the sort that would ever walk, Dash. He was so polite and considerate of other people."

"God, yes. I wish he hadn't been."

She had not quite understood what he meant, for she went on, a little vaguely, "Peter wouldn't be so mean as to haunt anyone."

"Oh, Polly," he said, half in irritation, half in pity, seeing she little realized the sort of haunting he was referring to, "be shut of your worries. No. He won't come back to either of us. You may go out back any night — even on Halloween — and never see Peter Inman sitting on the ridgepole of the privy."

She gave a little shriek, meaning that that was a dreadful thing to say to a lady, and yet it was funny.

"But," he went on firmly, "he does haunt me — in quite a different way. For years. And night and day."

Their eyes met, and he saw she understood what he had meant. Some knowledge in her sharpened face made her for a moment almost look her years.

"Don't," she said. "Please don't."

"Polly, I did him a great deal of harm — more than not writing him letters, like I just told you."

"Dash — leave things as they are."

She was desperate now, and buried her face in the pillow behind her.

He bent over her, put a hand on her shoulder. He was so close she could hear a strange rasp in his breathing. "I've got to tell you."

Then she turned, lifted her chin. "Don't say it. For I know."

"You know?"

"Yes. You're going to tell me, aren't you, that Petra was your child, and Peter took the blame and you let him? Isn't that what you're going to say?"

He sat back in his chair, utterly deflated. "Why, yes, Polly. And when Peter went off to Bombay I really knew it would kill him. I know that climate. I let him go. I guess I wanted to be rid of him — so tired was I of thinking how I had injured him. And I thought — with him gone I could go ahead. Reach out and grab you. But it was worse after he was dead."

"But you couldn't, because . . . it was something like this, wasn't it? You felt you had been so bad you could not take what you did not deserve."

He had never phrased it so accurately before.

"No. I had to punish myself. A man who's done wrong must be punished. Publicly and by other people, if he's lucky. If not, he destroys himself — secretly. Like me. Peter knew before he left. I had to find out the hard way. But Polly" — and he looked at her curiously — "Peter and I were so sure that you did not know. That you'd be so shocked if you knew. I thought, perhaps — even now you might never want to see me again."

"Dash, when I first knew, it almost killed me."

"When . . . how?"

"Oh, years and years ago. You were at sea and Flanneau gave Papa a letter. The one that woman was to show the selectmen — you remember."

"Naturally."

"It didn't look like your writing at all. I told Papa it was a forgery. And Peter swore to it. Likewise that Petra was his child. So Papa was persuaded. But Georgiana and I both knew. Although we never spoke of it to each other. I knew she had guessed by the queer way she acted and she never came again to Salem, except for the Memorial Service."

"However — oh, Polly, however was it —— "

"Why, Georgiana had written down the tunes of some sea songs she had heard sailors singing. You printed the words for her. Under the music."

"I can't seem to remember that."

"Yes, you did. I guess you printed your letter because Dulcey couldn't read very well."

"Polly," he said, slowly, "I wrote that letter twenty years ago. That's a long time — twenty years."

"And you couldn't ever get over it, could you — that Peter got the blame?"

"No, I couldn't."

"You had to suffer, but, Dash, so did I. You weren't suffering alone. We've been together in the queerest way all these years. And that fact has made me feel content. I never, these days, have crying fits by night and brain fever and hysterics. I never will again. Everything's all right now — but I was hoping we never would even discuss it."

"Polly," he blurted out, "knowing all this, and being — well, sort of used to it, why can't you marry me now?"

She looked at him in amazement. "There's no good of talking about that now."

"Why not?"

She reached up and took his face between her frail hands, holding it but a few inches from her own. "Everything I had to give is gone, Dash. Dash, it is too late."

He felt tears start to his eyes.

"We can't go on like this forever," he said, impatiently. "To me it has been forever, already."

"And to me." She rocked his head back and forth in her hands. "Forever and ever," she intoned, like a clergyman; "forever and ever, Amen." She was smiling.

"Is this all you want?"

"It is all I have the strength to take."

"Polly, *I* did this to you."

He pressed his face into the coign between neck and shoulder. Her arms went about his shoulders, pressing him closer and closer. "My dear," she whispered into his heavy, graying hair, "lift your face. Why"—and she was laughing excitedly—"those are tears in your eyes—aren't they? Dash—it has been harder for you than for anyone else."

"It is not too late, Polly. Marry me. If you don't want to move, I'll come over and live with you here."

He grasped her in his powerful arms, as years before he had sworn he never would again. Then he kissed her, the slow, long, hard kisses she remembered so well. Women of forty, he knew, were apt to be more passionate than young girls, but he could not feel the old miracle working within—the ice melt and the fire burn. The embrace was as meaningless as the rehearsing of actors.

Above him the Iphigenia clock struck a delicate soft half-hour. He started up and glanced at it guiltily. He was not supposed ever to stay longer than an hour.

"When I first knew," she admitted, "I couldn't stand to think—that you, of all men in the world, could have done such a thing—and to Peter, of all people—all people in the world."

He would have liked to explain, defend himself a little—Peter certainly had done his share; but he could not. And he knew he never would.

"But now I'm old enough to understand, it is almost as if——"

"As if what, my girl?"

"I was too old for love."

Her eyes closed. He saw how he had exhausted her. Her lids looked blue. She was not going to open them even to say good-bye. Perhaps soon she'd sleep.

He softly touched her hair. It sickened him to know this, now, was all he really wanted.

The wind whirled at his coat. He grabbed his hat. The roaring night was so dark he could not see a step ahead. The water must be piling up along the wharves. He could not imagine at this moment returning placidly to his mother's house, calmly sitting to supper and perhaps reading aloud to the two women as they sewed in the evening. Although it would make him late to supper, he would go first to the waterfront. See all was shipshape. He thought of the men at sea tonight, and the heave of the deck, snap of sail, the sharp orders, and the *Victrix* plunging like a living thing beneath him. Unconsciously, his stance broadened as though the sidewalk might start to bend beneath him. He took a deep breath. Something had been done. Not much, but something, and yet he felt his spirits lifting and lifting and floating far away on the dark torrents of the night.

❧ 7 ❧

DOROTHY BELINDA GOULD peeked again into the sitting room. Mrs. Inman and Mrs. Frances were still sitting there before the fire, pulling basting threads. Captain Dash weren't to home yet. And the soufflé would be ruined! Mrs. Frances was always ordering bothersome dishes like that.

"Ma'am," she said humbly, looking at Mrs. Inman's beloved face, but supposedly speaking to Mrs. Frances, who was the house-keeper, "shall I dish up now, please?"

"No," Mrs. Inman said. "No. Captain Dash isn't home yet."

"But," Mrs. Frances argued, "I've ordered a soufflé for supper. And they don't keep."

"Captain Dash is the head of this house," Lucy said firmly, "surely the women of it can accommodate themselves to him."

"But he's fifteen minutes late already, Lucy."

The soufflé fell. Not that Linda cared. Mrs. Frances made her a peck of trouble with her fancy receipts. She sat idly in the red rocker, rocked herself, and listened to the howling of the wind. Poor spirits, she thought. Think of all the poor spirits got up out of their graves for a night like this. She shivered slightly, and wished Barbara, the little girl who helped her these-a-days, had not gone back to visit her mother in Lynn tonight. She wished she herself was in Lynn. There was no other town in New England, she believed, quite so full of spirits on Halloween Night as Salem. She got up and looked in her Dutch oven. The soufflé was flat and black. The baked potatoes now were getting sodden. She went again to the sitting room, standing modestly at the door, not interrupting.

Mrs. Frances was complaining that she was faint with hunger, and that Lucy knew it gave her a headache not to eat regularly.

Mrs. Inman flung down the petticoat she was working on. "Oh, Frances, I'm worried! How can you just sit there and talk about your stomach? If you ate less, Frances, it wouldn't get so big — and feel so empty."

"Worried? You mean about Dash? Why, it's only a little past seven. It's only I hate to see good food spoiled."

"But he's *never* late. He hasn't been for *years*. People set their clocks by him. I'm so afraid he went down to the wharf, and it's such a black night. He might have fallen in and . . ."

"Lucy, that's nonsense. Of course, Polly asked him to stay for supper."

"She never has, and she never will."

"There, dear, don't you worry. I'll just ask Mrs. Gould to run over and inquire. No, I don't care a bit if supper's ruined."

"It's the baked potatoes that are gone now, ma'am," Linda put in.

"Oh, there you are. Mrs. Gould, be so good as to put on a shawl and run over to the Mompessons'. Ask if Captain Dash is staying on."

Linda looked at them both with a shy, guilty look. She hadn't the least idea of going. She protested weakly that tonight was Halloween.

"Oh, the boys won't bother you, Mrs. Gould," Mrs. Inman promised. "And it's such a rough night out, I don't think many will be abroad."

It wasn't the boys she was scared of, but she had no idea of telling her mistress.

She did take her shawl from the hook where it hung in the back entry and pinned it about her. Then she stood for a long time with her nose flattened against the kitchen pane staring into the blind night. It was like looking into the eyes of the sightless dead.

Poor cold spirits everywhere.

Over on Charter Street, under slate stones, the dust of founding fathers stirred in their sleep. She wondered if perhaps once more the first Inman was not heaving himself up from his rest, heading for Cat Cove to carry the dust of the first Mompesson pick-a-back through the roaring surf.

Far, far out on curst Gallows Hill, witch and warlock rose shrieking to ride the wind once more.

Now Old Ma'am's house was empty. Nobody was there to see if Tabby Inman made her poppets of wax.

Of course, Mr. Africanus was abroad. He'd tuck his skull under his arm, take that malacca cane King Derby had given him and begin his lonely march for Gallows Hill. His skeleton legs were still clad in the gigantic Hessian boots she had so often cleaned in this very kitchen.

Her blood began to pound, and she prayed God Mr. Africanus might not call upon her tonight. Her ears strained to catch the tapping of a ghostly cane.

The wind lulled, and she thought she heard the pounding of surf. Oh, think of the drowned men, drowned in the cold sea! Now their grasping hands were clutching at the coast of home. And the dead, drowned ships.

Peter Inman. How long had he been dead? It must be nine years now. Well, he ought to be at peace. But once she had thought she heard him cough in the night. And she wondered if he didn't come to see Dash sometimes. She had a feeling Peter came back and haunted Dash. But if he came back to anyone, it was only to Dash. Not to her. And although she may have loved him when he was alive, she would have been scared to death of him now he wasn't.

She wasn't going to be such a fool as to venture out on such a night.

The wind dropped. The beat of the sea came closer, and then she heard a sound just outside the window, feet treading the gravel, and wasn't that the tap of a cane? She jumped back from the window and might have screamed if she had not been so frightened. Waxy, the enormous yellow tom (and lineal descendant of little old Robin), started out of his doze, jumped from his chair and hid behind a keg by the hearth, staring at the door. She saw the knob begin to turn! The knob was turning! Her mouth opened, but no sound came from it. She was petrified. The great headless skeleton of Mr. Africanus. Next moment she'd actually see it.

Dash came in.

"It's so windy out," he said, "somebody must have bolted the front door so it wouldn't blow open. Mrs. Gould, what's the matter with you? You haven't seen a ghost. It's only me."

"Oh, Captain, you gave me such a turn! It is really you and alive and . . . not drowned, sir?"

"Not drowned!" he squeaked back at her. And she put her hands over her face and began to giggle because, just like Mr. Peter, Captain Dash was very witty.

"Why, even Waxy thought you was a ghost, sir. Waxy spit."

"Shouldn't have," said Dash, as he walked with erect, smart, quarterdeck step through the kitchen. She heard him apologizing to the waiting women.

So she unpinned her shawl, took it off and hung it in the back entry, then set to getting the ruined supper on the table.

Chapter Fifteen

S TRANGE TO ARRIVE AT SALEM by steam train, not on a Manning stage. The new depot stood where the old Mill Pond had been. Doctor Hobey remembered the Mill Pond, choked with mahogany, teak, camphor wood, rosewood, and ebony. It was here the merchants had stored it before selling. He stepped into a hack and said, "The best hotel."

A brief clatter up the street and a sign said "Essex House." Billy Gray had built it nigh on fifty years before — smart Billy Gray. He had been the first of the great merchants to leave. The next to buy it and live here . . . confound his failing memory for names! But, of course, he had reason to want to forget. Captain Obrian — Danny Obrian. As he registered and saw the boy taking his modest valise upstairs, he questioned the clerk, but the clerk seemed far more interested in his own fingernails than in his stout elderly guest. Doctor Hobey asked him of certain families — the Derbys, for instance? As far as the young man knew, there was not one of that great name left. Crowninshields? The clerk had a trinket on his watch chain which, opening, disgorged a blunt instrument for cleaning nails, a file, and a tiny spoon for taking wax from ears. He chose the blunt instrument. The old people, he said, still called India Wharf "Crowninshield's." But it was of the family Doctor Hobey wished to hear. Most of them had left before the murder; the rest, soon after.

"Yes, yes, I understand. Of course, they felt the humiliation — very proud men. What of the Inmans?"

The clerk picked up his little file.

"Are they all gone, too?"

"Just one left, I know of — old Captain Inman, up at the old Inman house on Washington Square."

When 'Sephus Hobey had left Salem, the Washington Square house had still been the "new" Inman house. He and Marcy had lived in the old Inman house down at the head of the wharf.

He did not need to ask which Captain Inman still clung to Salem; he knew.

From Canton to Boston he had sailed on an enormous ship, what people these days were calling "clippers." The *Queen of the Sea* had flown the flag of Inman, Poole, and Frost. The navy flag was still cut by a white diagonal, but a red star had been added to represent the Frost interests and a yellow globe for the Poole's — not as clean and simple as the old Inman flag had been. Neither was business these days. Liz had done mighty well, mighty well, indeed. But everything was too complicated nowadays.

He walked down Essex Street, a portly old gentleman, still able to get about with pleasure. What good fortune that he had happened to come to Salem when lilacs were in fullest tide! Oh, spring never came to the tropics. Not even in England, so it seemed to his nostalgia, was spring so beautiful and so brief as in New England. Nowhere in New England were the lilacs as fine as in Salem.

Essex Street looked neat enough, but it certainly wasn't crowded. He noticed a number of shops were shut up. Some were still hung with rusty black, suggesting that when the owner died some years before, no one had ventured to carry on the shop. The old bustle was gone. Now it seemed more like a respectable English provincial town, somnolent, content. Perhaps he preferred it this way than to the pell-mell of its heyday. It was still Salem, he was still 'Sephus Hobey; both had grown old.

Not many young people, and a large proportion of women. The women nowadays seemed respectably, cautiously middle-aged. Yet it was partly the manner of dress — leg-of-mutton sleeves, hair smoothly parted and plastered down, wide decorous skirts. Women had never worn so youthful a style as in the days of his own youth. He had always thought of Salem garlanded with young girls in frail white muslins, tossing their Grecian curls. Dancing sandaled feet — exquisite little faces which turned to tears or laughter as easily as a spring day. Alas, these nymphs were gone now. Either there actually were few young girls left or the present stuffy, staid fashions had obliterated them, or perhaps, Josephus thought, the change is in me.

He came to Washington Square and could not believe his eyes. What he had remembered as saplings were now stately trees. Spring had drawn a green lace veil across them, and beyond was the blue of sky. He wondered to remember the day he had scolded Boots West for letting his goat eat the top off one of these same trees. To his left, serene, unchanging as a sonnet, silent as a mausoleum, stood the Inman house. Not one thing had changed. He took off his hat and mopped his forehead with a silk handkerchief. Bless me — the very gates. He put out a hand to steady himself. The abyss of time opened so suddenly before him, he felt physically dizzy, as though, indeed, he was looking over a precipice. A stout, rambunctious young girl standing between these gateposts. A mop of black curls, bright eyes and glowing cheeks; the torn and dirty dress; the broad square mouth. The mouth opened; out tumbled those ugly words. He could almost see the mud and hats the people of the *Fame* had so long ago thrown at her — almost catch the rhythm of her oaths.

The very same gates — but now he noticed they had been painted so many times the carving was losing its pristine crispness. All about the square stood stately houses. It was hard to remember the ropewalks and tanneries, and folk saying Mrs. Inman was building in a part of town that never would be fashionable. He looked at the Inman house — hard to remember how long it had up its scaffolding, had had to do without Mr. McIntire's cupola, front portico, gates, new stable, or the big columned side porch. "Finished," he said aloud. All the great houses of Salem had been finished long ago. Yet, with this utter completion, the tide of decay inevitably would set in. Nothing was growing now.

As he went to the front door, he noticed the brass name-plate had been polished for so many years the name "Inman" was being rubbed away.

Dogs barked, and after a long time a respectable gray woman and two dogs came to let him in. She peered at him through her spectacles and he gazed back at her through his.

"Why . . . Dorothy Belinda Gould!"

"Doctor Hobey, isn't it? No, is it? Why, Doctor Hobey!"

"Yes. Yes."

"Doctor Hobey, I don't think there's a person left knows that's the name I started out with. My, you've been gone a real long time!"

"And how are you? Can you still dance with a lighted candle on your head?"

She looked shy and guilty, almost as he remembered her.

"No, I guess not." She moved to let him in, and he saw little of the smooth, poetic motions of the young girl were left. She walked as though her feet hurt.

"I'll tell Captain. Can't imagine anyone he'd rather see. You haven't been back once since you left with poor Miss Marcy, have you?"

"No," he said stiffly, "no, I haven't."

Mrs. Gould pursed her lips and shook her head. She knows she shouldn't have mentioned Marcy to me, he thought.

"Captain," she called, opening a door into what had been Mrs. Inman's pretty sitting room, "you can't believe it — guess who's here."

"Whoever is it, Mrs. Gould?" His voice still had a living quality in it. It made no difference what he said or how old he was.

The open door showed Dash had been sitting in a wine-colored dressing-gown, working on papers. He had certainly made himself comfortable in his mother's house at last — a litter of papers, ships' logs and models, books, inventories, curios; another dog, an orange cat on his knee, a gray parrot. He took off his spectacles, and, as he recognized Doctor Hobey, smiled suddenly the brave Inman smile that went from ear to ear. Marcy used to smile like that. The close-cropped gray curls had receded from the square forehead. He was a serene and handsome old fellow. With old age, good quiet living, good food, no worries, there was more color in his face than when he had been a younger man. He actually looked less worn, although, of course, considerably older. He carried himself handsomely, but he was broader, and this made him seem shorter than Hobey had remembered him.

They shook hands, patted each other's shoulders, and said the usual "well wells" and "how long it has been" and the customary lying "you look just the same."

"Step in. Sit, do." His dogs were smelling Hobey's heels with approval. The gray parrot swore. "Where are your things?"

"They call it the 'Essex House' these days. It was Dan Obrian's when I left."

"Mrs. Gould, catch a lad and send for Doctor Hobey's things. You stay here, of course."

"Thank you." Doctor Hobey did not want to face again the supercilious clerk with his fingernails and his sad refrain of departure.

Dash's study was what seamen used to call a "hurrah's nest — everything on top and nothing to hand."

"What are you working on?"

"That will keep. Tell me of yourself."

"Nothing much to tell. By the time I was ready to retire, I had an English wife. So we retired to England — Kent."

They talked a few moments, the stiff, unreal talk of friends who have been too long parted to pick up instantly the threads. Yet both knew it was but a phase they must pass through. The old friendship was still there, but it would take a little time to arouse it into actuality.

"It was when I got on the *Queen of the Sea* at Canton and saw the old Inman house flag (with additions), I knew I had to come to Salem once more. My wife and I had taken a pure pleasure trip to the Far East. I left her visiting friends in Boston. I knew I had to come here."

"You'll find Salem changed."

"I noticed it, walking over."

"Can't say we are starving here, but most of the money is made elsewhere. Let me see . . . was the custom house built before you left?"

"It was started."

"When we had the trade, any old shop was good enough. Soon as trade began to leave us, Government built that colossal afterthought. Governments are always too slow."

Hobey smiled to himself. Dash had never liked governments.

"What do they use it for?"

"Oh, I don't mean we haven't any ships now. And then the new custom house is a great place for retired sea captains, of the right party. They get appointed as weighers, bookkeepers, sealers. 'Bout all they do is sit in the back entry and yarn. There's not much to see on Derby Street these days. It looks a little sad. The back alleys are worse."

"What of them?"

"Oh . . . so many houses shut up or falling down; queer women living alone, doing queer things; lots of widows and spinsters in our back alleys, and they haven't money coming in, of course, from other places. Salem always was something of a woman's town, but the men were always coming back again. Now the able seamen have gone to deeper water; the mechanically minded, inland to the mills and shoe shops. A lot have gone West to new land. Somehow the women got left behind, many of them. And Salem got left behind."

"Salem is still beautiful."

"Yes. Isn't it? But it's naught but the shell of a sea beast cast up on the sand — a beautiful shell. Hold it to your ear and you'll still — and forever — hear the roar of the sea."

Hobey noticed Dash's eyes went to the clock on the mantel. "You'll excuse me? I'm going out. Miss Mompesson expects me."

Doctor Hobey hardly believed his ears, but he managed to ask casually, "And how is Miss Mompesson?"

"Just as well as can be expected. Winters are always a little hard on her. Now spring's here, she'll be picking up fast again. Make yourself at home. I'll be back soon."

Mrs. Gould offered to fetch him tea, but when he suggested she bring a cup for herself and bear him company, she shyly, firmly refused. However, would he care to come to the housekeeper's room and have tea with her there? Obviously, she was no longer a servant, but still far from an equal.

Once this room had been the gun room; now it was fixed over to suit her own taste. 'Sephus Hobey noticed that, like the rest of the house, it seemed a little dusty. He remembered Miranda, complaining that Linda would rather arrange flowers than wash the cellar stairs. He noticed lilacs, apple blossoms, and tulips were bright and fresh throughout the house.

It soon came out that she was the only employee in this large mansion.

"But, of course, we don't use many rooms — just Captain and myself. The servants' ell has been closed for years. I can't even remember when the double parlors were last opened. For heavy cleaning, I hire by the day. But you know two old people don't make much dirt; lots of litter, yes, but not much dirt."

"The stables?"

"Shut up for twelve years, ever since dear Mrs. Inman died; and she died a real nice death, Doctor Hobey. She was laughing hard, and then she began to hiccough and then passed on. Captain never cared much for horses; they made him sneeze."

"And Cousin Frances?"

"You mean the first Mrs. Liz? She's a really clinging lady. You knew that. She's living now in Wrentham with her niece, Mrs. Jeany Saltonstall."

'Sephus wondered. Liz, he knew, had made a fortune. Of Tom he knew nothing, but once both Tom and Dash had owned much Inman stock. Could Liz have crowded out his brothers?

"I heard, as far away as Canton, how well the Inmans had done financially."

"Oh yes. Mr. Liz and his sons, sir — five sons — and folks say every one of them is worth a million. Doctor Hobey, I don't believe it."

"Neither do I. Tom?"

"He and Mrs. Miranda drive over about once a week from Danvers." She screwed up her pale, uninteresting eyes and her voice squeaked, as it always had when she was amused. "Mrs. Miranda runs her fingers over the mantel and tells me to fetch a cloth, she'll do it herself, long as I won't; but Captain and I get along fine. Captain and I just laugh at Mrs. Miranda — behind her back."

"Tom's done well?"

"Oh my, yes. He's a big man in what's called 'industry' these days. Do you remember how Liz would say to him, 'Tom, how's your knitting?' It didn't make Tom mad any. Tom was always real sensible."

"How about Captain Dash?"

"He's got plenty for everything he wants — real comfortable; but of course he has two houses now to keep up."

"This house and Madam Inman's?"

"Oh, sir, the old house at the wharf is naught but a cellar hole and a chimney. Empty houses are apt to burn up, but perhaps you didn't know. When Squire Mompesson died, it seems he wasn't so well-to-do as people thought. He was mostly in real estate, and that's not worth much these days. Miss Polly asked Captain to be her man of business. She hadn't a head for figures. She thinks Captain Inman (folks never call him 'Dash' any more; it would seem funny to call a real elderly gentleman 'Dash,' but I do like to hear you say it)— well, as I was saying, he looks out for her father's property; pays taxes; collects rents and makes repairs. But folks say expenses are higher than profits. Folks say everything she has to spend really comes out of his pocket. Of course, she doesn't know."

"And she still lives in that big house?"

"I'm sure it wouldn't do to move her."

"Why, in Heaven's name, don't they combine their houses — at last?" He paused and blurted out, "Mrs. Gould, why didn't they ever marry?"

"I've pondered, too; but first it was one thing and then another. Captain Inman wouldn't retire, don't you remember? And she was real delicate by the time he did. Captain Inman was too much the gentleman to press his suit hard and too much in love to leave her. Ah, sir, I guess it was written in God's Book not to be, written before either of them was born."

"You mean that aeons ago, God decided that in the last quarter of the last century two children were to be born and love each other all their lives, and live in two big houses in Salem, Massachusetts, and not marry each other — or anybody else?"

"You shouldn't go questioning God's will, sir. Oh, I forgot, you are a clergyman."

"Not for years and years. Frankly, I was well out of it."

"I remember. You began to have doubts or something?"

"Not 'began.' I'd had them for years, but out there in Bombay so many things happened. I'd never been face to face with anything before, but when I was — well, then I found there really was a God and close to me — beside me. Strange . . . Mrs. Gould, I wasn't out of the ministry three years before I began to believe again, not like a natural philosopher; not like a scholar, but — like a child. As I see it, that's the only way."

"What helped you?"

"Marcy."

"There! I wasn't going to ask you about that. Such a disgrace!"

"Yes," he admitted, slowly, "such a disgrace, but it has been lived down many years. Mrs. Gould, you see how easily I can talk about it. It's not anything that happened to me any more — more like a novel I read once. I never was the right man for her, and always knew it. Poor child, she knew it, too. The right man came along at last. There was a scandal, of course. Now it's all right. That's all."

"But you, sir?"

"I married a widow with grown children. She's been a perfect wife for me. Poor Marcy couldn't be, no matter how hard she tried. Well . . . and next? I've written a dozen books on the Far East since you've seen me."

"Indeed? Just like Miss Marcy."

"No. I'm humbler now. I've never written anything half so good, half so living as Marcy."

"Folks still read *It Hardly Ever Pays,* at least 'round here."

"I'm glad to hear it."

"They come look at this house because it was from here Dinah Lee eloped with Captain Hardy. You remember, he couldn't harness a horse — and how we all laughed? And how mad everybody was, especially when they found out it was written by a clergyman's wife? But I never felt Marcy was a clergyman's wife — just Marcy Inman."

"That's really the way I always thought of her, still think of her — just Marcy Inman."

"Mrs. Shean and I were talking about that book only yesterday."

"Mrs. Shean?"

"She who was Flip Dawson."

"The name sounds familiar . . ."

"Miss Polly's Flip? She married our Mr. Shean."

But he could not recall her.

"She used to wear pink dresses — doesn't now, of course; but she's great company for me. They live in the Flanneaus' old house. He has a harness and saddle shop in front. And a real cheery old couple they are. Sometimes they come over and take a dish of tea with me, and if Captain's home, he may join us. Doctor Hobey, I never have — not once — presumed to take tea in his part of the house, but if he wants to join me, why, he can; and when he's there, it seems so like old times, except it used to be Peter that joined us girls."

"He looks more like Peter than I'd have thought possible."

She looked at him as though estimating his credulity.

"It happened very slowly."

"What?"

"Little by little, Captain grew more and more like Peter. It was almost as though Peter's soul came all the way back and lodged itself in him. You remember how calm and easy Peter always was about everything? Now I don't say he led a proper life, for he didn't, but he was always that easy with himself and everybody else. Captain Dash wasn't. You could feel him holding on to himself hard. It was as if he had a devil inside him he couldn't ever digest. But years went along and he got peaceful and easy, too. He's changed more into what Peter would have been if he had lived."

"Those two brothers were more alike underneath than people guessed. In old age the secret springs of human nature are apt to come out."

"Well, I've often wondered. I feel some days it was Captain Dash that died and I'm living here with Mr. Peter. Nothing ever frets him, even a tiny bit — not even Mr. Liz and what he's done with the old firm (and you're right about not much money coming this-a-way from Mr. Liz). It don't fret him ships aren't coming to Salem much any more. He's submissive, too, as an angel, to God's will. I'm referring, Doctor Hobey, to the fact God never did intend for him to marry Miss Mompesson."

She was looking at him through her spectacles, challenging him to deny God's will.

He did not accept her challenge.

~2~

THE GENTLEMEN did not linger over their twice-around-the-world Madeira. Mrs. Gould wished to clear the table and get to bed. It was obvious she had her say-so in the running of the house. The two old men settled in Dash's study, drank their wine, smoked and talked. A stream of oaths and filth came from the parrot.

"You ask how I busy myself? Before all the old captains are gone, I thought somebody ought to get the facts down."

"A book?"

"No, only a record. I'm beginning in 1785, ending 1812."

"Why stop at 1812? You're leaving out a lot of Salem's maritime history."

"No. War of 1812 ended us. I'd thought of stopping 1809 and the Embargo. We didn't realize it at the time, but we never did get back on our feet again. Servant, sir," and he lifted his glass.

"Servant, sir! No trade left?"

"Oh, aye. A trickle. Had a brig in from Sumatra, couple of months ago. A Madagascar vessel in last week." Dash got up and adjusted something that looked like a tea cozy over the parrot's cage. "Now, she'll stop her dirty talk. I call her Mrs. Mullins. She'll go to sleep now. But Salem isn't a practical harbor for anything over four hundred tons. That Inman, Frost, Poole clipper you came home on is about fifteen hundred tons. But——" and he paused a long time. "'Sephus, don't you remember ships three deep along our wharves and still another coming up 'twixt Baker's and the Miseries, and one more reported standing upon the coast, and in every yard a new vessel rising?"

"How could I ever forget?"

Mrs. Mullins uttered one more muffled oath as the old men remembered.

"Salem found out more new routes than all American ports put together. And paid more customs. I'll bet you the ships we built and sailed were the fastest ships in the world — and we could sail closer to the wind."

"I was thinking of the men."

"Lads mostly. Just lads. And they sailed for adventure and to see the world — and the glory (if you will pardon a very old-fashioned word). Money was a side issue. Not true now."

"No."

"Take the Inman, Frost, Poole vessels. They are hell-holes for the crews. Foreign men, mostly. Delivered by crimps. Yankees won't ship on 'em — except as officers. Nowadays a master isn't ashamed to be called 'Bully' So-and-So, or 'Driver' This-and-That."

Doctor Hobey thought of Madam Inman and regretted her name came first in the firm.

He said, "Liz wouldn't have been so ruthless — nor so rich — if he hadn't smashed his face."

"No. If a man looks brutal, he's apt to get that way." Dash sipped his Madeira. "There's lots of scurvy on the new ships. We never had much. And if the food was poor in the forecastle, it was poor in the cabin. We never denied a man a chance to share in profits. There was no flogging. We didn't serve our people 'Belaying Pin Soup' and 'Handspike Hash.' I never heard of a mutiny aboard a Salem vessel until the one Liz started — 'round 1810 or 1811."

Josephus Hobey did not answer for a long time, and in the silence he could hear young Dash Inman saying "my people." It seemed to him a beautiful phrase.

"Captains don't call their men 'my people' any more, do they?"

"No, it's 'the hands' — not even 'my hands' — it's 'the God-damned hands.' And they aren't anxious to take them up through the hawser hole and make officers of them. Of the *Victrix's* first crew, every man I signed became a master except only old Doctor Zack, the cook, and the fellow the sharks got."

"Dash . . . what happened to her?"

"The *Victrix?*"

"Yes."

"She came home to die."

"Ah . . . that's like you. There was always something of the poet in you as well as Peter."

"I never felt the same way about any other ship. She seemed to me like a very intelligent animal. I got to feeling there wasn't a thing she wouldn't do." He thought a moment. "Toward the end, before I retired, I took some real wicked chances with her. She was good to me, but she sometimes raised a little Hell for other masters. I was getting too careless at the end — one reason I was ready to retire; didn't feel I was setting a good example to younger men. But good luck and the *Victrix* took me through a lot." He went to the fireplace, knocked out his pipe, stood for a moment, his head bowed as he cleaned it with his jackknife. "She was cut down for a hide-horn-tallow boat before you left. She got too old for that even. And even cut down, she was mighty cranky, but I suppose she was the greatest ship Salem ever launched, by and large. Well, anyway, she was next a lumber schooner — Nova Scotia to Boston. I guess it was about three years ago word came to me a vessel was breaking up over off Beverly, and she flew the Inman, Poole, and

Frost flag. I went over. She came in on Montserrat beach. Every man was lost. Her lumber was strewn from Plum Island to Nahant. There was a drowned man stuck in her boom nets, all wound up in the figurehead. I told the men to turn it over so we could get him out. I didn't know the name of the schooner. I see you have guessed?"

"Yes."

"Yes . . . it was."

Dash put his hands in his pockets and paced the room. "She lay on her back like a corpse; seemed almost indecent to leave the dead woman, even if she were naught but wood, staring like that. I said, 'Any you boys got a cart?' None had, but they knew a man that had. So I ordered her carted over here. Oh, and one more thing, 'Sephus, while we are on the subject, those fellows wouldn't believe me when I said, 'This is the *Victrix*.' She had been sort of a legend about Salem for years. 'This can't be the *Victrix*,' one of those men said; 'not the ship that went to Japan and broke more records than all the other ships put together, and made more money? Why, this is only a little old tub.' I didn't say a thing, but, 'Sephus, I had to laugh."

❧ 3 ❧

THE NIGHT SHOWER had washed earth, sky, air, incredibly clean. No late May day could have been fairer. The sun came out diffidently at first, to drink up the puddles in the street, and the drops caught in the lilac blossoms. The town was drenched with their wet fragrance, back yards and front yards full of lilacs. It was a heady day, yet ever so little it depressed Doctor Hobey. All this exuberant flowering seemed like a too-youthful hat on a too-ancient head. He should have come to Salem for the last time in dull November, dark December, not in the springtime of the year. But he took off his hat to let the sun drench his bald pate with its false promise of eternal youth.

The short walk down Daniel's Lane to the waterfront sobered him. Once this street had been a great one for sailors' lodgings, master shipwrights, ropemakers, riggers. Now it seemed so dead.

He came out on Derby Street, knowing, dreading, what he would see and only half-believing it could be so. Grass grew along the cobbled street. Grogshops closed — warehouses falling down. He looked out across the harbor. There was not one topsail. Here at old King Derby's Wharf a coal barge was tied up, and some poor woman had tethered her goat there to eat the grass. White's and Orne's Wharf looked no better. He came to Inman's. At the head of it stood the gigantic blacked stone chimney as a gravestone over the cellar hole. Yonder at Crowninshield's Wharf a shabby lumber schooner was unloading, and a proper ship — perhaps the one Dash had said came in recently from Madagascar. The Crowninshields, after their many lawsuits, had the deepest water.

Inman Wharf, he noticed with pride, was in good repair. Here no weeds grew. Here warehouses were neat and painted. The long-legged counting-house gleamed white against the emptiness of sea and sky. Before it hung the Inman house flag, navy cut by a white diagonal. Evidently Dash had not gone along completely with Liz and his reorganization. Everything was in apple-pie order, ready, waiting . . . and waiting . . . and waiting for ships and cargoes that never would come again. At first the good order had pleased him, but the air of anticipation, expectancy, began to sadden him more than the frank abandonment of hope he had noticed at the other wharves.

He walked slowly and began to feel the heat of the hot day. As a consul, he had known that Salem was no longer much of a port, but he had always remembered her with her ships crowding and her warehouses bursting with pepper from Sumatra; palm oil from West Africa; coffee from Arabia; salt from Cadiz; cotton from Bombay; teas and silks from China; cinnamon, cloves, allspice, from the Dutch East Indies; ivory, gum, copal, from Zanzibar; hemp, duck, iron, from the Baltic. So had the wealth of the world poured in, laid at her feet, and the magic of the seven seas had wrapped her in mystery.

Derby Street no longer held dangers for a somewhat cautious old gentleman. In the old days such (and Mr. Africanus as well) had always avoided Derby Street, with its seamen, drunk or sober, frolicking — sluttish girls at upper windows, and sometimes dumping slops into the street below. Surely, hereabouts girls no longer danced with lighted candles on their heads, and the ropewalk men did not march in procession, carrying the cordage to a new ship — the fifes tooting, the drums beating, as they marched; the yokes of red oxen; the long horse-drawn drays; porters yelling and swearing; the sing-song of an auctioneer; the clang of the anchorsmith. All was gone. And in those days, if an old gentleman did not look sharp, he'd get hit by an anchor being hauled from the smithy or trip over masts, bowsprits, blocks, that littered the street. How serene, how peaceful it was!

He sniffed the delicate air. No spice — no coffee nor sandalwood — no tea, not even tar and hewn wood for a shipyard — lilacs still, but the only other familiar scent was of eel grass and harbor water.

He stopped short before the new custom house. Salem's smartest men had already been leaving when it was put up. Dash had called it a "colossal costly governmental afterthought." Above the beautiful doorway and mounting steps a gold eagle leaned forward to scream back at the gulls. Gulls? He remembered the Embargo had frightened him when he had first realized the gulls were lessening, but now they were mostly gone for good. Not enough ships came in to support the thousands of gulls that used to live off this harbor.

The gold eagle leaned forward and screamed at nothingness.

He thought with passion and nostalgia of Salem's lost glory, like the very morning of the world. It was gone now, and, like himself, the men who had sailed those vanished ships were going . . . going — all but gone.

He went into the custom house. To his left was the collector's office. This could hardly be a full-time job these days — some old retired captain, a political appointment, doubtless. No, by Hobey's standards it was an almost young man sitting slouched over a book, his long legs twisted about his chair legs. He glanced up and smiled shyly. He was quite handsome with his mane of heavy hair and fine dark eyes, half-melancholy and half-amused.

"I'm an old Salem man, sir," Doctor Hobey introduced himself. "Just having a look around. I've nothing to declare."

The collector, still smiling, said, a little critically, "Memories? Wouldn't you sit for a moment?"

"Well, yes, thank you. Yes, I will sit just until I get my breath after all those stairs. I've been walking along the wharves. The day's warm, and, as you guessed, it has all stirred memories."

"Here by the window is a little sea breeze, but it doesn't blow in many ships these days."

"Why, thank you. Thank you. My name is Hobey. I happened to be in Boston and came back on the whim."

"Yes, I remember you, Doctor Hobey, and your famous nature rambles, but it was the girls you usually took with you."

"I couldn't manage the girls much, but I could never have managed the boys at all. I'm glad to see that at least one of Salem's young men has not left her."

"Salem suits me well. I like it the way it is, better than when Salem and I were both younger. I like the feeling of ghosts and memories and everything done. Nothing left now but to think about it. Nor am I an especially young man, sir."

"Well, a lot younger than I expected to find about the custom house. I've been told it's a haven now for an odd assortment of retired sea captains."

"So it is. Look in the back entry before you go out. There's little work for them to do, and little to disturb them except the periodic terrors of a presidential election. They spend a good deal of time asleep with their heads back against the wall, waking once in a while to bore each other with their old sea stories and moldy jokes."

In a cross-hall at the end of the main hall he found them, chewing tobacco, leaning against the wall. Each head had a dingy halo where it habitually rested. Here were more sealers, weighers, clerks, assistants, than Salem had need of in her greatest day. What a fantastic collection!

One man let down the front feet of his chair with a bang and peered up at him with eyes bright, bleary, and intensely blue.

"Haven't you got a familiar face?" he asked. He was a huge old man, stout and bald. His face was fiery red. Pinned across his spotted waistcoat was a gold watch chain, the one symbol of his previous prosperity. Obviously, the watch had gone long ago.

"My face is familiar to me, sir," Hobey admitted, "and I did live here once. Josephus Hobey."

With difficulty the old man got out of his chair. He was not only a little spotted; he was downright dirty and smelt strongly of yesterday's liquor.

"You haven't forgotten Danny Obrian?"

"Captain Obrian? As I live!"

"That I am. Well . . . well!"

"There's been a lot of water gone over the dam since last we met, Captain Obrian."

"Yep. And lots of money, too. You may notice some changes."

And yet no change thus far had shocked him more than the metamorphosis of Dan Obrian, "the handsome sailor."

"I was young myself," Dan was saying, "in those good old days, what sailors call 'back in Aunt Gower's day'" — and he went off into what was obviously a many-times-told tale. Hobey hardly listened to his moldy yarn until he noticed he was implying that he had commanded the *Victrix* on her two great voyages to Japan. *He forgets I know. He was Dash's second, and no more.* The tale was ending and the hopeful, bleary eye was cocked at him, asking if he had not earned a drink.

"Where are you living now?" Doctor Hobey asked abruptly, remembering what now was the Essex House in the days of Danny's prosperity — all those screaming gilt eagles and the French mirrors; Italian mantels and statues; the murals in the cupola; the diamonds and plumes on Mrs. Obrian as she stepped out to her carriage.

"It's not much of a place — snug."

"So things have gone right enough with you?"

"Well, you might say so. I struck foul weather 'long in '37, '38, but my wife died before I knew it was a wreck. Me, myself, alone — I'm just as well off without all that stuff."

"And Petra?"

"Ah . . . Petra. She never lived to be twenty, sir; died when her first child was born. You know" — he coughed delicately — "same as her real father." He paused, giving himself and Doctor Hobey a brief moment to recall the little girl. "When I had the money," he said, "I spent it — like a sailor should. You remember all that talk about the gold punchbowl and the crystal chandeliers, and was it Mrs. O's portrait, that sea queen in the cupola? We had fun — Mrs. O. and I. Well, she's gone and that's gone. And I don't regret anything. Federal Government looks out for me — like it ought. I certainly found out a lot of new trade routes. Take that voyage to Japan . . ."

Hobey knew he should offer to take him out for a drink, but he could not bear to. What an amazingly garrulous, boastful old windbag he had become!

As he started to leave, Danny called after him, "What you been up to?"

He told him.

"That's right. And you married Marcy Inman." There was still a roguish twinkle in the bleared blue eye. "And how's Marcy?"

"Very well," he said stiffly, "thank you for inquiring."

"That girl certainly was a handful, but she sobered up and married a clergyman. Well . . . well . . . "

Even after all these years Hobey felt a prick of pain. He wished he might say to Marcy, "I saw your Dan Obrian. He was a dirty, boastful, besotted old liar."

On his way back, he passed Becket's Yard, at least he supposed it was. Dock, burdock, chicory, and witch grass had been growing there for years. Once a last keel had been laid and a last ship launched. The shipwrights' ladders still stood that led to that last deck. She had slipped her ways and been gone, but the ladders remained, stopping abruptly in midair, as though man had thought to build a ladder to Heaven and had become discouraged.

~4~

THE DREAMING DAY grew warmer and still warmer — almost too warm, too still, too silent. At dinner Dash told him Miss Mompesson would be pleased to receive him; if Doctor Hobey wished, he would take him over this afternoon — at four-thirty.

There was a purposefulness about Dash's step. He had none of the air of an old man out for a wander. As always, he looked as if he were going somewhere and knew exactly where that was.

"Oh, by the way, 'Sephus," he said, as they stood together before the Mompesson door, "she can't stand very exciting conversation. I mean things like what happened to Marcy or what our water-fronts look like — nothing to upset her."

An elderly servant woman was letting them in. Doctor Hobey glanced about him. The house seemed utterly unchanged. This had not been true at the Inmans'. He guessed Dash and Mrs.

Gould had got themselves real comfortable. The first thing he heard was the delightful striking of the Iphigenia clock. What a classical era it had been! The old landscape papers in the hall had faded and long been out of style. He doubted if as much as a curtain had been replaced or a new carpet laid for years. It seemed old-fashioned, but still beautiful and romantic.

The woman was telling them that Miss Mompesson would receive them in the garden. The two men went the length of the hall, out the back entrance, across the cobbled court, under the arch, down the steps, and were in the garden.

Here again the first change Hobey noticed was the great growth of the trees, nor was the garden very well kept. Shrubs were unpruned. The slim willow that had wept by Polly's fane was a giant tree, but the little toy pool and the fane were gone.

Polly was lying on a Hindu couch with tables and chairs about her. There was a slight stir over the seating. 'Sephus had almost sat in a bamboo chair with a red bandanna cushion in it, but the servant, aghast, told him that was where Captain always sat. Polly was dressed in the white so fashionable in her youth and wrapped in a white Cashmere shawl. She did not rise to greet them. 'Sephus saw she was not in the least interested in his return in spite of a brief pretense. It was not half as exciting to her as Dash's daily visit. Quickly the two old lovers were off on what the intruder realized must be their daily ritual. Had she had a good night? Yes, a very good night. Was she sure it was not too cool for her here in the garden? Oh no, she loved it. And now that she would be able to be out every day, she would soon grow stronger. These words had been said so many times there was almost no meaning left in them, at least in the words themselves. There was meaning in the saying of them.

Polly's mannerisms seemed little changed, the pretty lift and the toss of the head, the arch of neck or wrist — still the mannerisms, and even the voice, of a young courting girl. Her charm had not broadened, deepened, changed, but withered. Some fate, cruel or otherwise, had preserved her like a fly in glassy amber; made her unaware of the true passage of time. In her half-life she seemed to have aged surprisingly little — a slight puckering of the pink skin, a loosening of the flesh along the jawbone. She was like a rose about to fall, but still almost fresh. And still those beautiful

disturbing eyes, that appealing **downward** turn at the outer corners — stricken eyes, half-melancholy and half-coquettish. Her
figure, wrapped in a shawl, was slight; her hair, snow-white. It
was not parted sensibly in the middle, plastered with pomade and
pulled down over her ears as a woman nowadays wore her hair.
It fluffed and curled about her little head, held by a long-outmoded
Grecian fillet. The change to white is never as startling on a blond
as on a dark-haired woman.

Polly shut herself so completely in her own world, she had little
interest left for Doctor Hobey. He wondered of what that world
consisted — probably bed until noon, a light dinner, and then she
rested until, say, three o'clock, and it was time to dress to receive
the Captain. Her old servant, doubtless exactly as devoted as every
other woman who had ever worked for her, would help her.
Would she wear the amaranthus crêpe and the quilted velvet cape
today? She'd try it on. No, the lavender with the cherry ribbons;
but at last they would settle upon white. So a pleasant hour and a
half might be wasted. And doubtless there was added a touch of
rouge. Dash would never guess. 'Sephus's second wife had often
pointed out such things to him on other women. Then the visit,
for which she lived, but which was, of course, so exhausting she
would surely have to lie down again and soon to bed. So day after
day. Spring came and the lilacs, hot green summer, golden autumn,
white winter, and spring again.

The old servant was cautiously picking her way down the path
with a tray. And suddenly Hobey with shocking clarity remembered Flip, a little pert scalawag in a pink dress. On the tray was
tamarind water and diet bread for Miss Polly. The Captain had
rum, water, sugar, and lemon. So in spite of his grandmother's
complaints that her grandsons drank slops, that's what he was still
drinking.

Carefully Dash measured rum into the glasses for himself and
Doctor Hobey. He cut the lemon and, perhaps as always, Polly
warned him not to cut himself. He answered a little shortly. He
knew what he was about, and she pouted and liked it. She always
had liked it when he scolded her.

Her health had certainly been covered. Next came his. Polly
was asking him about his sciatica. Doctor Hobey doubted if he had
any sciatica. Probably it was something they had cooked up years

before as an appropriate subject for conversation. Next moment Dash was pulling out his watch, blessing himself, and saying time had flown so, apologizing because he had stayed sixty-seven minutes instead of the recommended sixty. Polly started to argue, but gave in because doctor's orders were doctor's orders and must be carried out, as Dash said. Was it Old Doctor West they were still quoting to each other? A short visit every day. Her health. His health. The weather — nothing that would overexcite her. And so home.

The Inman house, he noticed as he entered, was still a living house. Polly's seemed like nothing more than a bunch of wax flowers under glass. Doctor Hobey followed Dash into his study. There waiting for them was another tray, set out by Mrs. Gould. Dash smiled broadly.

"You see, Polly thinks one drink of rum is all I need, but as I get older, I find I prefer two, or even three."

And again he was halving a lemon. There was no one by to say, "Don't cut yourself." Is that why they've never married, thought Josephus. Each is too wedded to his own ways. There was an ease about Dash as he sat thus, surrounded by his own things, doing just as he pleased. Every day he went to that shrine, did as he ought and came home relaxed and satisfied — a worshiper still at Polly Mompesson's shrine. No, that was not the word; "worshiper" was not the word. It was something more of a penitent he had just watched before an ancient shrine. So every day Dash Inman walked to Federal Street at exactly four-thirty and did penance? This was obvious nonsense. There wasn't anything in Dash's life that needed penance.

The parrot used a very low word. A handsome setter was fawning on Dash's knee, begging to be loved.

"Dash," 'Sephus said suddenly, "you know Mrs. Gould put me in Peter's old room. All his books and notebooks of his poetry — it still strikes me as pretty good. I've been thinking a lot about Peter."

There was a long pause. Dash's eyes went to the wall above the fireplace. For the first time Doctor Hobey noticed that he had moved the ill-done old portrait of Peter that had always hung upon the stairway in here with him. His own portrait, Liz's and Tom's, he had left where they were. All had been absurd likenesses, but Dash's eyes lingered on Peter's. It represented Peter to him, even if one ear was higher than the other.

"Peter," he said, and his flexible voice deepened, "was the best human being I've ever known. I don't say he was the wisest. And being good doesn't always mean doing good, but . . ." His setter was pressing herself against him. He fondled her head. "I've known dogs almost as good as Peter Inman, but no other human being. There were some things — there are some things about him no one now alive except only Polly and I know, and it dies with us — the truth about Peter."

He immediately put on his spectacles and picked up the log of the old *Belisarius*. Hobey knew he wished to be alone. A transient guest might upset the nice balance of his calm old age; a wife would have been sure to have. Doctor Hobey excused himself and went to his own room which long ago had been Peter's room.

He sat and thought about this house. It had always been so living a house, and when it had been happy, it was really happy, and so abjectly sad when things were wrong. He supposed he should give Mrs. Inman much credit for the good home that it had been. Perhaps he had always resented her because, although she had a good mind, she was not in the least intellectual — a little shallow? Yes, of course, but it was here in this house young maids were always having giggling fits. The sons and daughters of it had had as much happiness as the human race should expect, and the servants, too — even Mr. Mullins. Far off in Bombay, Calcutta, more recently in damp Kent, he had thought of this house — spring, with the windows open as today — curtains blowing at every window, the scent of lilacs — the sound of voices laughing, an ill-played violin. But through the scent of lilacs came the cold wind off the sea, the smell of salt water, tar spice from the waterfront, calling the young men to their destiny. He had remembered this house in wintertime, snow piled up and up to the sills, candles flickering, chestnuts and apples roasting on the hearth. Then someone would throw upon the fire one of those choice splinters of sandalwood the boys used to bring home — and that, too, recalled the young captains. He remembered the sound of their light, sure feet on these stairs, home from their voyaging, and the heavy tread of porters following with their chests. As he sat and pondered, he half-expected to hear Davy Jones booming from the front yard and Little Joe scratching at the necessary.

He thought of Marcy, and put his head in his hands and wished that he might weep. He had never been as philosophical about her desertion of him as he had made out to her, the world, and Mrs. Gould. Only he and God knew. Only he and God cared.

Once she had been delirious with a tropical fever. The only thing she wanted to eat was a Seckel pear from the old tree in her mother's garden. He'd go out and look at it. In a way, it had always been Marcy's tree. Nobody else had had the industry and appetite to bother with Seckel pears. He'd go out and see if yet it stood.

Neither was this garden well-kept. Whatever stock Dash still had in Inman, Poole, and Frost, it didn't suffice to keep either his or Polly's garden shipshape. He found the gnarled old pear tree in a glory of flowering. Like many humans, it had grown broader with time, but no taller. The long May day was far from ending. Warm still and utterly fair, it lingered, holding scent and memories — holding time like a goblet filled with rare wine. His feet crunched on weedy gravel paths. His hands parted a syringa bush that blocked his way. A mother robin screamed at him out of the nest she was protecting. Nobody had mowed the lawn and probably no one ever would; nobody had replaced the rotting alley boards; nobody had trimmed the box bushes. Some had died to brown sticks. Some went rampant. He was following an all but obliterated path.

Suddenly he saw before him, leaping out of the fragrant box, the wooden figure of a woman. He had never seen the figurehead of the *Victrix* so close before. She was bigger, fiercer, than he had realized. The flying figure flung itself boldly forward, pulling away from whatever roots held her to this humdrum earth. Her eyes were fastened on something she alone saw, something unattainable to man. Clutched in her wooden hands was a fading green wreath, but she would never deign to look down at it. He reached cautiously and touched the wreath. Nothing ever would pry it loose from her. Ah, he thought sadly, she promised something, something that never was to be. You can take her from the sea, fasten her to the sensible earth, but you cannot be fulfilled of her promises.

He stared at her for a long time. Her colors had faded and the paint peeled from her bitter lips.

THE END

Afterword

~~~~~~

I HAVE GIVEN THE *Victrix* the honor of being the first American ship to penetrate Japan's isolation. But the fact is that, after the annexation of Holland by Napoleon, several American vessels were chartered secretly by "Jan Compagnie" or his remains. These left Batavia under American flag and papers — to outwit the British. They came into Nagasaki under the Dutch flag — to outwit the Japanese. So the laurels which should hang upon the bowsprits of the *Franklin,* the *Massachusetts,* and the tragic *Margaret,* I have purloined for the *Victrix.*

To readers who have long loved Salem the connection between the *Margaret* and the *Victrix* may be apparent. Also my indebtedness to William Bentley's diary for such things as the little girl at whom the sailors threw their hats and she swore back at them; the female vagabond who danced in back alleys with a lighted candle on her head; or the blind Negro who eked out his livelihood by remembering things.

There are points in common between the Crowninshields and my Inmans. If there had been no Crowninshields (and their papers at the Essex Institute), there would have been no Inmans.

E. F.